MARTIN STEPHEN OMNIBUS

The Desperate Remedy

The Conscience of the King

sphere

SPHERE

This omnibus edition first published in Great Britain by Sphere in 2009
Martin Stephen Omnibus copyright © Martin Stephen 2009

Previously published separately:
The Desperate Remedy first published in Great Britain by
Little, Brown in 2002
Published by Time Warner Paperbacks in 2002
Copyright © Martin Stephen 2002

The Conscience of the King first published in Great Britain by
Little, Brown in 2003
Published by Time Warner Paperbacks in 2004
Copyright © Martin Stephen 2003

A CIP catalogue record for this book
is available from the British Library.

ISBN 978-0-7515-4162-5

Typeset in Goudy by M Rules
Printed and bound in Great Britain by
Clays Ltd, St Ives plc

Sphere
An imprint of
Little, Brown Book Group
100 Victoria Embankment
London EC4Y 0DY

An Hachette UK Company
www.hachette.co.uk

www.littlebrown.co.uk

The Desperate Remedy

Henry Gresham and The Gunpowder Plot

ACKNOWLEDGEMENTS

I am extremely grateful to Graham Seel for his historical advice, and to Sonia Land, Tara Lawrence, Ursula Mackenzie, Philip Franks and Jenny Stephen.

I would like to thank Cambridge University Library, the Bodleian Library, Oxford, the John Rylands Library, Manchester, and Fitzwilliam College, Cambridge, for research facilities, and the Royal Exchange Theatre, Manchester.

'È necessario a chi dispone una repubblica, ed ordina leggi in quella, prassuppoie tutti gli nomini rei, e che li abbiano sempre a usare la malignità dello animo loro, qualunque volta ne abbiano libera occasione.'

('It is necessary for him who lays out a state and arranges laws for it to presuppose that all men are evil and that they are always going to act according to the wickedness of their spirits whenever they have free scope.')

NICCOLÒ MACHIAVELLI, 1469–1527

Prologue

It was a murderer's moon, with dark, scudding clouds hiding the stars. The soldier moved quickly but silently through ebony night, his stride confident and determined. London was deserted this long after midnight, yet still he was careful, gliding close by the sides of the darkened buildings. He had no fear of the Watch, feeble and infirm as it was, but on his business all complications were best avoided, however minor. Tall, dark and powerful, his mop of red hair was invisible beneath the hat pulled firmly down across his brow.

He arrived at the place, and drew back into an opposite doorway, waiting. He heard the courtier long before he saw his shadow arrive at the door, panting with exertion. The storm lantern was shaking in the courtier's hand. He moved out from the shadow of the doorway and heard the other's indrawn breath of fear, before recognition struck. The courtier might be the finest of servants at Court, bowing and scraping his way up the arse of his masters. He might be lord of all he surveyed below stairs. He was certainly a trusted secretary of one of the most powerful men in England. Yet here, in this place, he was a frightened little man, on his master's orders, in a dark cloak and borrowed boots. He paid for his pleasure and his vanity by this meeting in a dark place.

1

The soldier smelt the familiar stench of fear on the courtier, who scuttled to the door like a frightened rabbit, but he did not show his contempt. He had made a career of hiding behind the bluff manner of a simple man. Deceit was second nature to him. He was even sympathetic to the stinking wretch, enquiring solicitously in a hoarse whisper if he was ready to enter the cellar. A curt, nervous nod was the answer to his pains.

It was a marvellous thing, the soldier's lantern. Its flame had been lit in the man's lodgings, and then locked away behind the ingenious shutters. The flame could breathe, but yet it could not be seen. He opened one of the shutters, and the thin light gleamed on to the lock of the ancient oak door. He drew the key from his purse, and the well-greased tumblers moved solidly and silently back.

The courtier gagged as their feet kicked up the dust of ages. He cursed under his breath as he cannoned into one of the stone pillars that held up the cellar, feeling the fear in the pit of his stomach. He fell back on to a pile of ancient hangings, discarded since Henry VIII's days and left to moulder. More dust rose up and coated their dry tongues. The soldier paused, courteous as ever, his thoughts hidden behind the craggy, pleasing mask of his face.

They reached a pile of faggots and brushwood.

The soldier opened the other shutters on his cloaked lantern. He placed it on the floor. His shadow and the courtier's shadow danced briefly on the ancient walls, elongated, cutting through the mingled smells of fresh wood and decay. He cleared a path through the wood, revealing a stained barrel. Its lid had already been prised open and lay, resting loose, across its top. He took his dagger and flipped the lid to one side. He spoke in a low voice, for all that they were alone.

'Here, you see it?'

There was the tiniest of echoes through the long vaulting. He reached his left hand into the barrel and drew out a handful of the gritty powder within it, holding out his hand to the courtier.

The courtier looked nonplussed.

'It's decayed,' the soldier explained, as if to a child. 'If gunpowder's badly stored, or if it's stored too long, the elements disperse. If they do, it won't explode, but only burn with a fierce fire.' He looked at the cringing figure of the courtier, his face dripping with sweat. 'Fades away. Like a man with too much ale in him,' he added unnecessarily.

The courtier reached out, taking a pinch of powder between shaking finger and thumb. He looked at it, pretending to a knowledge he did not have. He had eagerly claimed to know of gunpowder, to have experience of it, seeing advancement and the favour of his master by his pretence of knowledge.

'Yes,' he muttered, 'I see. In faith, in true faith, I see.'

He looked up into the soldier's face. It was impassive, as ever. Faith, the soldier was thinking, true faith, is something you will never have.

'I shall tell my master so.'

And what is it that you see? the soldier thought. A fine new robe, perhaps, or a jewel to adorn your finger, or even a purse with thirty pieces of silver in it? Or a bucking whore beneath you in your fine bed? Whatever you see, it is not the powder thrust in your face. Nor, in mercy to your miserable little soul, do you see or even dream of the truth. Because if you even wondered at it, your soul would shrivel in the flames of Hell. He kept his thoughts silent, as always. He merely nodded. He flicked the lid back on the powder barrel with the dagger held in his right hand. He looked down at the courtier.

'I must check the other doors. Will you cover the barrel with the wood? I'll leave you the lantern.'

The courtier had no option. As he scrabbled to replace the faggots, the soldier retreated to the nearest archway, resting his body behind it. Let the popinjay put back the wood. Let him experience servitude. What matter if he did it badly? His master was hardly likely to order the cellars searched. Or at least, not yet.

3

He emerged when the scrabbling noises ceased and the courtier's shadow calmed down from its avid dance on the walls. He closed the lantern down to one shutter.

He bade the courtier farewell by the open door of the cellar, hearing him squelch, stumble and mutter his way home through the pitch-black night. He waited until the noise of his going faded into echoes and then died completely. He listened then, in total silence, for a full quarter of an hour. Not a dog howled, not a mouse stirred. There was only the thin whistle of the wind in the eaves. He was safe.

He bent down and silently inserted key into lock. He turned it, securing the house and its cellar behind him, and with the same hand drew down the last shutter on the lantern. He listened in total stillness for a further five minutes or so.

The soldier opened up his clenched left fist. A thin, sharp residue of powder lay within it, stuck to the sweat on his palm. Not decayed powder. Not separated powder. Not powder ruined by damp. Wholesome, fine-ground powder. Powder in prime condition. The best powder. Powder ready to blow to Hell or to Heaven those above it when it was lit.

Guido Fawkes, or Guy Fawkes as he was known in England, made his way silently homeward through the dark streets, allowing a rare, thin smile to cross his lips.

CHAPTER 1

Will Shadwell froze in terror. There was the noise again. Behind him, somewhere in the enveloping and impenetrable dark. He had heard it once before, a tiny crack like a twig breaking and the briefest rustling. Imagination? A cow, a sheep? Some idiot peasant's hog stirring in the field? Or men with knives destined for Will Shadwell's back, creeping up on him through the black silence?

He had trudged on, as the sun had hung like a raw orange ball over the horizon's razor edge, taking an age to set. The sense of danger, the fear, were ever present, tingling his bones. Something was wrong. He knew it.

Hot tears of self-pity welled up in him, burnt his eyes against the cold of the night. He was crouched low in a dry ditch, the dust in his nose and mouth, the debris of a country track already working its way inside his doublet and scratching against his skin. He had never felt more alone or more in terror of the nameless things hidden in the vast sweep of the flat countryside. He was holding back his breath, despite the red-hot iron bars in his chest, the impossible urge to scream and run. He had never meant to be on the road in the middle of the night. It was the horse's fault, that damned animal. He knew nothing of horses, could hardly ride. It had looked as good as any other in the dim light of the early morning, rolled its mad eyes at him like any other horse. He had thrashed it into action, hurling it towards Cambridge and the only man to whom he could turn, the panic driving him on and communicating itself to the animal beneath him. He had to see Henry Gresham. Gresham. The only man he could turn to, the only man who would know what to do with the terrible secret Will Shadwell had stumbled on, the secret he carried only in his head. The only man who might stop this terrible pursuit, take the wolves off his back.

The night spread round him, silent, still. There had been nothing now, no noise, for five minutes or more. Hope flared up in him. He knew every noise in London's mean streets, could interpret every sound. Here in the country the night spoke a different language, every sound of it in his heightened state of terror a possible death threat. Had it been some animal, treading lightly over the ground? Surely no men could be so silent. His breath was starting to come to him normally now, his heart thudding less against his eyes.

The horse had foundered outside Royston. He knew they would come after him, expected someone to notice his sudden run from London. With the horse under him he could at least match pursuit. With its useless carcass dead on the road he had had to branch off to avoid pursuit, on to the side roads and tracks. It had been a mistake, dull-faced peasants eyeing him as the only thing of interest to have passed that way in years, noting his progress and all too willing to tell it to whoever came behind. If only he could have hidden the horse, instead of leaving its lathered hide as a sign to any pursuer.

Dare he move? If there were pursuers still out there they might walk past him in his ditch. They were showing no lantern, lighting no flares, if even they existed. He knew he stank, but if they were there they had no dogs, that much he was certain of. He was lost, of course. The tracks he had taken weaved their way through the

Flatlands, but the stars stayed where they had always been. He reckoned he was upstream of Cambridge, knew if he kept on he would meet the slow, flat river. Gresham would be in bed now in his College rooms, simple and book-furnished for all the man's impossible wealth, a world apart from the magnificence of the house on the Strand and the whore who kept it for him. He would know what to do. Gresham always knew.

He was feeling drowsy, despite the cold that was starting to penetrate the thin, ragged cloak that was all he had time to grab when he fled London. Perhaps he would sleep here in the ditch, wait until morning . . .

He did not hear or even sense the man. He felt his hot breath against his cheek, heard the words cut through the night in his ear, had time to note the almost caressing husky tone.

'Will Shadwell . . . a fine dance you've led us.'

He screamed then, a spasm tearing through his body and hurling him up out of the ditch. He dimly saw three, perhaps four vague shapes where the night was blacker. He twisted away, felt a thorn tear at his boot and into the soft flesh above his ankle. He felt a thud in his back, was knocked forward, and looked down startled at the blade that had appeared through his flesh, just beneath his ribcage. He opened his mouth, and the warm, salty taste of his blood hit him at the same time as the tearing agony of the pain. He felt himself falling, heard rather than felt himself thud into the soft ground. Gagging, gasping, drowning in his own blood, he felt a boot kick him over. The last thing Will Shadwell saw on God's earth was the thin blade driving down towards his eye socket.

'You'll pay me the usual?' sniffed the miller, who seemed to have a permanent cold.

Henry Gresham prodded the dead face with his boot.

'I've told no-one else . . .' the miller added morosely, wiping his nose.

Gresham cut a fine figure by the riverside. Tall, strongly built,

7

there was an inner fire in his eyes and a slight smile that suggested he found the world both ludicrous and amusing.

The body bobbed gently up and down in the tiny ripples that lapped the edge of the millpond.

'I turned 'im over for you,' the miller said, half bowing and putting his head between Gresham and the corpse, demanding attention yet being sycophantic at the same time. The drowned always lay face down, as if turning their heads from the sun for the last time. The body was swollen, white with corruption, but still recognisable.

It was Will Shadwell. A murdered Will Shadwell.

Spy, informer, double-dealer, whoremonger, pimp, thief, gambler, sodomite, drunkard, occasional follower of Satan when the money was good – and one of Gresham's best men. He had possessed no morals, and so could not be suborned by a good cause. He was utterly selfish and ruthless, and therefore a thoroughly known commodity. He was greedy beyond belief, and hence utterly reliable, provided Gresham paid him more than anyone else.

Once, in a Southwark stew, Shadwell had falsely claimed that someone else was paying him more. Gresham had nailed his hand to the table, sinking his dagger through the soft flesh of the palm he was holding out for more money.

'I've given you a good dagger as well as your gold, Master Shadwell,' Gresham had commented mildly, leaving the room with the screaming and impaled man gaping at the blood seeping into the timber. 'Come back to me when it's spent up.'

And because Shadwell was all these things and yet a coward, he had come crawling back to Gresham three weeks later. He did not lie again about how much others were paying him. He appeared to bear no grudge. Violence was nothing in his world. Mastery and power had to be proven. If proven, they were acknowledged, as much a fact of life as lechery or drunkenness. The mark of the dagger was still visible now on the puffy flesh of his right hand. It waved liked a dead weed in the water.

Now he was dead, hunted down, a town creature flushed out of its habitat and hounded to death in the broad sweep of the country-side. Even the water damage could not disguise the tears the brambles and thorn had made in what looked like a pell-mell chase. Something or someone had torn off a boot. He had been skewered from behind, enough to kill him in time. The actual killing blow, the knife thrust, had gone in through the eye socket and upwards, with so much power that it had broken through the top of the skull. It was a classic thrust, requiring pinpoint accuracy.

Gresham nodded distantly to the miller, and again to Mannion, his servant, who was behind them both. He heard the clink of money as Mannion drew a purse from his belt and started carefully to count out coins. The miller slavered over the sight, his eyes fixed on the money and his greed only thinly cloaked by a ragged air of servility.

'Thanks, master,' said the miller, who would have tugged his forelock had there been any hair left on his greasy pate. He gave a curt order to his lad, who started to drag the body out of the water. The miller was turning away to go back to the screaming wife and screaming brood who were warming up for the day in the stone-built mill when suddenly he paused. A thought must have struck him, Gresham realised, an event so rare as to stop him in his tracks. 'Why is it you're the only genl'man who pays to see corpses?' the miller asked, daringly. He sneezed, and a globule of something white shot from his nose and lay on an uncomplaining reed. Gresham turned to look at him.

'Why, a man must keep his finger on the pulse,' he replied, straight-faced, gazing down at an entirely pulse-free corpse. The miller, not surprisingly, failed to get the joke. As a trade millers were universally corrupt and oafish. All within a ten-mile radius of the city were bribed by Gresham to report any bodies in the water to him. Except babies. Gresham did not require to be shown the babies, unless, that was, they were finely dressed. The bodies always ended up in the millstream. At least Shadwell's had not been pounded to a pulp by the great paddle of the millwheel. It was no consolation to Shadwell, who was past caring.

As he went to mount the fine grey mare for the short ride back to Cambridge, Gresham halted, and went back to the corpse. Something had caught the light, glinting fitfully inside a tear in Shadwell's tattered doublet. He motioned to the miller's lad to halt his labours, and bent down to feel inside the sodden, stinking material.

A bead. A single rosary bead, from a string of such beads that sold in their thousands in Europe. A dangerous item for a man or woman to wear openly in Protestant England, where to be a Catholic was all too easily seen as being an enemy of the state. The tear in the doublet looked new enough. Had Shadwell's flailing hand caught at the rosary as he fell to the ground? Well, one thing was sure. Gresham would never find out the truth from Will Shadwell.

A thick mist still clung to the river and its banks, reaching head height in the lower meadows. The dew clung to the ground and the heady smell of wet grass was everywhere. The towers of the great King's Chapel towered above Cambridge in the distance, and the pall of smoke was already beginning to cling to the town from the early-morning fires.

Henry Gresham saw none of it. He was preoccupied with his thoughts.

Why kill Will Shadwell? He and his kind lived in a raw, violent and a brutal world, yet even there the game was usually played by certain rules. Who among the vagabonds and thieves, the beggars and the rogues, the cutpurses and the pimps he called his friends would kill him? An argument over an unpaid bill? Some story of treachery? A whore who had caught the French welcome from him, paying him back as he sweated inside her spread legs? Or some noble Lord who had attended one too many Masses or plotted once too often to restore the true faith to England? Yet for someone as base as Shadwell there was no need for high treachery to explain his death, no need even for low drama. His death could be about nothing more than a debt that had gone on too long, or simply an opportunist robbery in a dark country lane.

It was possible, simple robbery, yet it stuck in Gresham's gullet. Shadwell's killing was a professional's work. Someone had wanted Will Shadwell dead, and had been willing to follow him to Cambridge to see it done. Will had never worked in Cambridge, and had never been there long enough to make an enemy want him dead. That argued for a bigger secret than a debt or the wrong woman bedded. Had he sluiced a rich man's wife or daughter? Or had he latched on to something that the new government in London had decided should remain secret? Or was it the Catholics he had offended, the same Catholics who still carried huge power and influence for all that their faith was unfashionable?

The time was when a self-respecting assassin would never have travelled beyond Deptford. Yet these were troubled times, so early in the reign of King James I. How could they be otherwise? It was Scotland's King who now ruled England, and Scotland was England's oldest enemy. To add spice to the novel situation, the mother of the new King, Mary Queen of Scots, had been put to death on the order of the previous holder of the English crown, Queen Elizabeth, only a few years earlier. Men still alive had signed the death warrant of King James's mother. Henry Gresham had been in that business up to his neck and, in the final count, her neck as well. It was best to hope that King James had not been told of *that* side of his mother's death, for all that there had been no love lost between them.

A bird flew up from under the horse's hooves, with a sudden clatter of wings. Well trained, the mare took stock for a second of the irritating thing, decided it posed no threat and went calmly on its way. Gresham's hand, which had instinctively moved to his sword, relaxed halfway along its travel and returned to his side, his left hand continuing to take loose hold of the reins.

There had been a strange optimism two years ago when the new King had ascended the throne. It was already fraying at the edges,

11

with mutterings in the streets and at Court. His Royal Highness's retinue of Scots Lords were as willing to take any money on offer as they were unwilling to wash, and their rapaciousness was becoming as legendary as their stench. James had offended the Puritans by having a Popish wife, and offended the Papists by declaring them excommunicate and appearing to go against his early promises of tolerance. The majority of the country, who wished nothing more than to be left in peace to procreate and earn a decent living, increasingly went in fear of a Catholic uprising, or a rebellion from the English establishment against the Scottish upstart.

Gresham almost found himself yearning for a return to the days of Good Queen Bess, the arch-bitch. Gresham had learnt the art of survival in part from her. She was an actress of unequalled power, and a ruthless whore who would have murdered her own mother without even a momentary qualm if need dictated it. She was also a Queen who would have wept bitter tears in public afterwards, whipped herself with barbs that, strange to say, seemed to leave no mark and provoked numerous plays as a result, as well as more sonnets than there was paper on which to print them. Queen Elizabeth I may have been so corrupt as to make Beelzebub turn in his grave, but somehow that corruption had never broken through the façade of the Virgin Queen, the pure preserver of the State. It had been true of her chief minister as well. Old Lord Burghley had made enough money to buy the Armada whilst producing an English fleet so decrepit that it might as well have farted as fired at the Spanish. With the Devil's own luck, the wind had farted instead, bringing Burghley the victory his ships could never have done. As one of Gresham's old informers had cheerfully stated, old Burghley may have knifed you in the back, but somehow you always felt it was being done by a gentleman. Burghley's son and successor, the wizened Robert Cecil, had a corrupted body that told all too well the tale of his corrupted soul. The double-dealing, the murders and the struggle for power might still be the same. The sense of style had gone, and there was a rawness to the brutal world of 1605 that had not been seen since Good Queen Bess had herself ascended the throne half a century ago.

Gresham's scalp itched, under his hat. He had a full head of hair, as yet not ravaged by the pox, and it was well washed. It always itched when there was trouble around. He had endured a lifetime of trouble. He neither feared nor welcomed it. It was simply a part of life, like the footpad on the road, the poison in the wine or the first spot that signified the plague. The particularly virulent itching suggested significant trouble. Well, trouble was a normal part of Gresham's life, and had been so for as long as he could remember. What was unusual was his inability to explain his chronic sense of foreboding, his inability to trace the sense of danger to its source.

It was all most irksome, and most inconvenient. Gresham flicked at his reins. The horse picked up a little speed, then deciding its rider's heart was not in it slowed down again to an easy amble. Gresham had lost a good worker in Will Shadwell. Will Shadwell had been Henry Gresham's creature. An attack on Will Shadwell was an attack on Henry Gresham, yet the reason was a mystery. Gresham did not like mysteries. They disturbed him. They cried out in the night to be explained. They threatened his survival. Survival, Henry Gresham had decided long ago, was all one had. Ruthlessness was required to survive. That, and a sense of humour, a dash of loyalty and a measure of courage.

The mystery was still crying out in his brain as he rode into the inner courtyard of Granville College. He had time still to go to his room, change from his riding clothes into suitably sombre doublet and hose and don the long gown of the MA or Master of Arts.

They gathered in the Combination Room, Gresham and the fifteen other Fellows, before going in to High Table. It was panelled, as was the Hall they were about to enter, very much in the new fashion. Gresham loved the depth of the wood, the changing pattern of its rich colour, but a part of him yearned for the ancient stone that lay

13

behind it. The contrast of rough stone with rich hangings draped over it, hard against soft, wild colour against sombre grey, warmth against cold seemed an emblem for life. Contrast, change, the clash of ideas, these were what made Cambridge breathe and live.

'Well met, Sir Henry,' said Alan Sidesmith, the President Gresham had placed in nominal charge of the unruly crowd that went to make up Granville College. 'Was your ride restorative?' Gresham had never seen Alan Sidesmith drunk, nor ever seen him without glass or even tankard in his hand. Alan knew more of Gresham's other business than Gresham had ever told him, but Sidesmith was one of the few men in whom Gresham had complete trust.

'I've a good horse, good health and will soon have a full stomach. And it's summer in Cambridge . . . how could I not be restored?' Gresham replied lightly.

'That would depend, I suppose,' said Sidesmith equally lightly, 'whether a certain miller who sent you a message this morning was wishing to display to you his corn, or whether he had something else in mind.'

Gresham knew better than to be drawn.

'Yes,' he said, as if debating a matter of great significance, 'that would depend, wouldn't it?' He grinned at Sidesmith, who grinned back.

'Now, Sir Henry,' announced Sidesmith in a businesslike tone. 'Those newly knighted such as yourself are best placed to advise me on a tricky question of etiquette. Over *there* . . .' he pointed to a large and prosperous man whose desire to show off expensive clothes had overcome his reluctance to boil alive in the summer heat, '. . . we have a rich London merchant, a Trinity man, who wishes to transfer allegiance for his son to Granville. However, over *there*, we have a new Scottish Lord from Court who claims to have a degree from Europe. Who shall have the seat of honour on my right-hand side – Mr Money In The Bank and a good degree, or My Lord Influence At Court and probably not much else?'

'There is no choice, old friend,' announced Gresham. 'The Scottish Lord already smells to high heaven, whilst the merchant will take a good hour or so to do so despite all he sweats now.'

'Thank you, Sir Henry,' said Sidesmith. 'So helpful, as ever. Perhaps you would care to tell the noble Lord that he has been relegated because he stinks?' He moved off with a smile. The merchant gained the seat of honour on the President's right-hand side, the given reason being that he had his degree from Cambridge.

The great gong struck, and they processed into the Hall. Gresham's money had refounded Granville College, one of the most ancient and derelict in the University, yet he took his place on the High Table in strict order of seniority and the timing of his Fellowship, making him one of the most junior. The students in their gowns shuffled to their feet, benches scraping on the cold floor, as the President and Fellows entered. A student, a thin-faced boy with a face pockmarked from smallpox, came nervously forward, bowed to the President, and recited the long Latin grace. There was a subtle chorus of shuffling and, from somewhere among the depths of the student body, a hurriedly suppressed squeal as an arm was pinched. More bowing, and the business of the meal was allowed to continue.

Gresham's companion sniffed as he sat down.

'Out of sorts, Hugo?' asked Gresham, taking his own linen napkin from his sleeve.

The Fellow in question was a huge man, slobbering rolls of fat hanging over his neck and bulging out his thick arms into rotund sausages of flesh.

'I approve of tradition,' the man replied, grabbing at the warm bread that had already been placed on the platters in front of the Fellows. 'If three tables was good enough for this College in all its history, it's good enough for me.' He was already looking hungrily for the servant to bring in the first trenchers of food, and a glass of wine had already gone into the cavern he called his stomach.

'Ah,' said Gresham, 'but you didn't have the task of telling the eminent citizen of this town that he was good enough only for the second table, or telling that same to a man with an excellent degree who sees some jumped-up favourite of Court dining here on high.' It was an old argument, and Gresham did not offer it to convert, but merely to annoy. It worked. Hugo spluttered and sent dangerously large lumps of bread firing from his mouth across the table.

'It is a *nonsense*! A *nonsense*! I firmly believe . . .' Dinner at High Table was started, and would proceed along its normal path. Gresham had insisted that Granville College have a High Table for Fellows, guests and those with BAs and above, and the remaining tables for those studying for their first degree or those with no degree. He had proposed the abolition of the second, intermediate table to the President.

Alan Sidesmith had smiled.

'It'll cause a rumpus, you know,' he had said, with no sign that it concerned him at all. 'The young men of pleasure we seem to be receiving at this University in such large numbers will dislike a College where they can't buy their way into higher fare, and out of the company of the poor students.' Under the old system, the third table had been reserved for 'people of low condition'.

'What a great pity,' Gresham had replied. 'We'll just have to make do with taking students who wish to learn, instead of those who simply wish to play tennis, get drunk and swagger that they've done their study in Cambridge.'

'Now that would be something new,' Alan had responded, a mischievous twinkle in his eye. 'But I do hope it won't restrain you personally in pursuing those noble aims.'

In fact the young and the rich had flocked to Granville in its new foundation. Its High Table was frequently extended to several tables as it was besieged by the rich and the famous, its simple rule that no man without his Bachelor of Arts could sit there giving it an unexpected prestige. The fact that the rule had been waived only once, for Her Majesty Queen Elizabeth I, had added to rather than taken away from the distinction.

The heady smell of fresh-baked bread and roast meat mingled with the sharper tang of the wine on High Table and the ale and beer cheerily being consumed by the students. Granville College ate a good dinner, the platters loaded with meat and fish and the game pies being offered first to High Table, and then taken down to vanish into the gaping mouths of the students. A senior student was reading aloud from the Bible, one of many monastic traditions the Colleges had absorbed. The difference was that whilst total silence would have greeted the reading in the monastery, here a burble of conversation was allowed to accompany it.

Hugo was denouncing the decline of logic in favour of rhetoric to his other neighbour at table. Gresham turned to the man on his left. A man after Gresham's own heart, he had been fighting for a greater musical element in the Cambridge course.

'How goes the new material?'

Edward smiled at Gresham.

'Slowly, but surely. Master Byrd presents challenges to those who try to do justice to his music.'

'Musical challenges, or other challenges?' Gresham asked innocently. William Byrd was widely believed to be a committed Papist. He had published a book of sacred songs in 1575 which had circulated among Papists and found their way into Gresham's hands, and from thence to the man who ruled over the choir of Granville College.

'Challenges of all types,' answered Edward, with no sign that he wished to relinquish any of them. 'Firstly, it's a matter of debate whether or not the songs should be performed in a chapel at all. Secondly, singing them seems tantamount to declaring an allegiance to Rome. Thirdly, it's the Devil's own job deciding if they need an organ alongside them.'

'So in summary,' Gresham answered, 'their forthcoming presence in our order of service will result in the musical director being excommunicated for singing secular work in God's chamber, burnt alive for being a Papist and beaten by the Chapel organist for doing him out of a job?'

'Sir Henry,' answered Edward with a mock bow of his head, 'how can I challenge the wit and judgement of one so distinguished?'

'Not at all, if you know what's good for you,' said Gresham cheerfully, draining his glass. He was looking forward to the performance. 'But I wonder you bother with that music. There must be easier pieces.'

'When I meet music in which I hear God's hand,' said Edward sombrely, 'I'll risk the judgement of God's emissaries on earth to hear it played.'

There would be another stir when Edward believed he had the music to his standard, and allowed it to be sung. Accusations would fly back and forth, perhaps even the odd pate would be broken. Gresham ran his eye over the Fellowship of Granville College. One Fellow was a sodomite, making a play at every pretty boy who joined the College. Two others were bedding every serving girl who offered herself. Times being hard, there was no shortage of offers of either kind. Another had the pox, and had been seeing a local quack to little effect. Dipping the genitals in a mess of white vinegar was one of the least painful remedies, and the Fellow in question had been coming to dine for weeks smelling like a barrel of wine that had been allowed to go off in the sun. The newest Fellow was involved in a ruinous lawsuit, chasing an inheritance that an older brother would grab, at dreadful cost to the younger sibling. Two of them were Catholics to the core, two of them fierce Puritans. They sat at opposite ends of the table, and a pair of them had nearly come to blows in a recent public debate.

Opposites attract, thought Henry Gresham, and from the clash of opposites comes new ideas. He gazed contentedly, as much as his restless spirit could ever be content, over his High Table and the college he had refounded. He had no children that he knew of. He seemed destined to be barren. In the meantime, the 135 students and Fellows made a contented burbling noise in the Hall Gresham had built. It could hold two hundred with ease, and would do so before too long. His children? Possibly. His Foundation? Certainly.

The meal over, he had two reasons to retire to his rooms. The first was a letter written in his best handwriting, a letter which had been returned to him a few days previously by a man called Tom Barnes. Its style was faultless, and Gresham could only marvel at the sharp logic and intelligence that shone through the written words. There were only two problems with the letter. Firstly, Gresham had never written it, despite what seemed to be his handwriting and signature, and secondly, its content was sufficient to have him hung, drawn and quartered were it ever to reach any member of the Government. There could be many reasons for the existence of such a forgery, and Gresham needed time at least to eliminate from his mind some of the least likely. When that reading was over, he had his copy of the English translation of Machiavelli's *The Prince*, obtained from St Paul's for a King's ransom on his last visit to London. He had read it in the original Italian, of course. He was fascinated to compare the original with the translation. It was not to be.

The knock on the door was loud, insistent. Gresham slipped the letter through the gap in the floorboards beneath his feet, and shouted for the visitor to enter.

The courier stank of horse piss and sweat. He had arrived long after supper, his leathers stained with mud up to his armpits. Cambridge was at its most dank and dark, the Fenland mist swirling round the gates of the Colleges like a miasma of plague, waiting to strike. The feeble flicker of candle from the latticed and barred windows in the inner court hardly dented the blackness. The courier had arrived after nightfall. Every tongue would wag in the morning. Gresham called away 'On His Majesty's business', again. Some would snigger, nod knowingly, and gaze down in their tankards as he strode past to his place at table in the morning.

The Porter ushered the courier into Gresham's rooms. They were

19

on the first stairway, built in the fourteenth century. He was Cecil's man, of course, and exuded a sense of menace. Silently he handed a package to Gresham. The Porter hovered over his shoulder, drunk, inquisitive.

'Time you kept your watch, old Walter,' said Gresham to the grizzled old man. 'Who knows how many fresh young virgins are queuing by your gate to test if men are like wine, better when they're old?'

Old Walter grinned, and clumped down the stairs. Gresham could just as easily have kicked him down the stairs, or snarled at him to mind his own damned business. As it was, Gresham saw nothing but an accident of birth in their different station in life. He treated Walter as he treated all people. God persistently refused to treat all people as equal until they proved otherwise, but that was no reason for Gresham to follow suit. As a by-product, old Walter would continue to tell Gresham everything that went on in the College. As far as most of the Fellows and the students were concerned, old Walter, the drunken sot, was invisible. Gresham had been using his sharp eyes and ears for years.

Gresham did not need to ask who the letter was from. There were only a small number of men in England who had couriers willing to ride through the night. The seal on the letter was far more ornate than the content. Come to London. Immediately. No formal greeting, no 'To that most beloved servant, Sir Henry Gresham . . .' Merely a blunt message. Come. Come now.

Gresham sighed. He sighed again as he turned to his purse, took out a small coin, remembered the courier, and chose a larger one. It was accepted. Without thanks, but with the merest nod of the head.

'Tell him yes. Soon.'

The courier nodded again. It was all that was necessary.

Cambridge was a haven. Its conflicts were explicable, its double- and triple-dealing following a strange local logic. True, its townspeople were low and squat, hating the University that gave them their living. A riot was never far away, which was why the Colleges were built like domestic castles, facing inwards into their courts and quadrangles and with a towered Lodge as their entrance. Yet the sense of power those buildings gave was illusory. The power in London was the power of life and, more frequently, death. The power in England was very simple, for all the puffed-out vainglory of the Cambridge Fellows. England's power was the power of the Court, nowadays the Court of King James I of England, erstwhile King James VI of Scotland.

So now Henry Gresham would have to drag himself out of the parochial world of Cambridge, back to the dark, brutal and blasphemous underworld of London, a world only recently rid of yet another outbreak of the plague.

He was rather looking forward to it.

Jack Wright sat in the darkest corner of the room, pushing the remnants of his meal idly around the edge of the wooden platter. The air in the room was greasy, stale. There were eight of them in all, in a room that would have more easily coped with four or five. The Catherine Wheel in Oxford had been chosen for recruiting the newest conspirators. It was safer than London, and Oxford was less full of Government spies than Cambridge. It was as safe as anywhere for a group of men for whom life would never be safe again. Jack could not stop himself looking nervously at the door every minute or so. He saw in his mind the soldiers bursting through it, the yelled commands, the kiss of iron round his wrists as he was led away. He shook his head, as if to clear it of the image. His nervous glance returned to the door. Part of him was trying to listen to his friend, but he had learnt at times to let the impassioned words of Robert Catesby flow over him, as unmarked as a stone in the river with the clear water washing over it.

John Wright, or Jack as he had been known since his early childhood, had taken his usual seat at the back of the room. He was a stocky figure, his apparent heaviness deceptive. His sword arm was lightning fast, his agility with a blade in his hand legendary. It was a skill he had tried to use much less since God had called to him and he had answered. Would that his mouth had the same skill as his arm. It was not that he lacked thoughts or ideas, but somehow the link between brain and mouth had eluded him all his life. For years he had felt the frustration of hearing the nonsense others talked, seen the strike of wit that won the applause and the adulation, felt the ideas seething in his head but stumbled at the final hurdle of their expression. As a child he had been laughed at and mocked when the few words he could muster had tumbled out and dried up, like an empty barrel with a hole knocked in it. That was where he had learnt his agility, turning to his fists in those days to make sure that his school fellows paid his body the respect they would not give his words.

He had known Catesby casually for years, in the way that all the sons of the oppressed Catholic families banded together and knew each other. They had attended a Mass together, in the small hours of the night when the fewest servants would see and hear and the risk was reduced. The priest had been impassioned, the liturgy powerful beyond faith. Afterwards, Jack Wright had been moved to tears, and Catesby had turned to meet him.

'It's a thing to die for, isn't it, as Our Saviour was willing to die?' he had said, a fierce light in his eyes.

'It is . . .' Jack Wright had started to say, wanted to say that it was more than life, that it was the source of life, a faith and a beauty so poignant yet so tragic . . . but the words had dried up, as they always did, and the red flush of embarrassment crept up on his face as his eyes dropped.

He felt Catesby's hand on his shoulder.

'We don't need words, do we? The words have been written for us. But we know the beauty. We of all people know the terrible beauty. To feel is enough, isn't it?'

Jack Wright looked up. Was it his imagination that a light pulsed from Robert Catesby's eyes? As if a tide of lovingly warm water had been released to sluice through his mind, the tears came to Jack's own eyes. Here was a man who knew, who understood. Here was a man who needed no words. From that moment in a cold chapel was the bond struck between Robert Catesby and Jack Wright.

Catesby's personality shone like a second sun, filling every corner of the tavern's room.

'Men have a *right*, a *right* given by God and by nature to defend their own lives and freedom, a right that no earthly power can take away,' he was arguing passionately, the light of martyrdom in his eyes, thumping the table for effect. 'We Catholics in England are mere *slaves*.' He dwelt on the word, drawing it out in all its shame. '*Lower even than slaves*. We're free men, yet we allow our lives and our freedoms to be removed without law, without reason and without authority. Our very life, our vigour, is being sapped by this passive resistance, this feebleness, this palsy of fear and cowardice that's all we seem able to muster in the face of persecution. We're the laughing stock of Europe: despaired of by our friends, and despised by our enemies as God's lunatics!'

Despite the familiarity, the power of Catesby's personality tugged at Jack Wright's soul. When Catesby talked to you, you felt that you were, for him, the most important person in the world. Catesby could reach into men's souls. His audience stared in rapt silence, almost adoration, as he reviled the King, whipping them up into a frenzy of self-justifying anger against the monarch and Robert Cecil, his Chief Minister. It was a brilliant performance. Jack had seen it many times, yet still it held a measure of magic even for his cynical eyes and ears. For a moment, for all of them, the fear retreated, the gnawing, bitter fear that governed their every step, their every breath.

'And is there hope? *No!*' Catesby spat out the negative, as if it were a red-hot pip from a sour cherry he had just eaten. 'With Robert Cecil pouring poison into the ear of the monarch, turning his eagerness into hate? *There is no hope unless we ourselves create that hope!*'

King James had seemed well-intentioned to the Catholic cause before his accession, and his wife was known to be Catholic. Cecil, the King's Chief Secretary, was widely credited with turning the mind of the King against English papists whilst at the same time toadying up to the Spaniards.

They needed some of Catesby's magic. At the mere thought of the tunnel Wright's flesh began to crawl and a spasm ran through his muscles. It had seemed easy enough. Hire the house, dig through until they were under the House of Lords, plant the powder. Yet before they were six feet into the tunnel they were gagging for air, their sweat turning the loose earth beneath them into greasy, salty mud. There was hardly room to move, the candle guttered and died in the rancid air and terror closed in with the darkness. The arm with the pick or shovel could only move back so far, the picking at the tunnel face tearing the same muscles time after time, reducing them to red-hot strings of pain. Their beards, hair and mouths became encrusted, unwashable, the dirt pitted into the skin. They felt the dust coat the inside of their lungs, their breath foul for hours afterwards, their racking coughs depositing a scummy yellow layer like vomit. They had reached the foundations after a lifetime of effort, half mad with the pain of their bodies, half mad with the thought of the soft, suffocating fall of earth and a hidden, slow and secret death. The ancient stone had seemed to bounce their feeble blows off its surface. They were tired, all of them. In time they would need money, horses, weapons, armour. Now their greatest need was for more brute strength and muscle. The two new conspirators would give them that at least.

Catesby finished his oration with a final flourish, and sat down, draining the tankard to its dregs in one huge gulp. Catesby did everything, from talking to drinking, as if he had half an hour of life left to him, and had to cram a lifetime's experience into a few minutes. He was a meteor in a dark sky. Jack could not help wonder how long that meteor would sustain its light, before it crashed to earth.

'Well spoken, Robin,' Jack said, going up to Catesby and taking his hand. Catesby had slumped down on a stool, as he sometimes did after one of his orations, as if his job was now done and the effort of speaking had drained him of his life force.

Catesby glanced up at his old friend, and smiled. It was a smile of total warmth that lit up Jack Wright's soul.

'I hope it was well spoken. But it's more than words we need now, Jack, much more than words.'

'We have a plan, don't we?'

'We do indeed,' replied Catesby. 'And there'll be those who'll seek to stop that plan before its rightful conclusion. They must be stopped, Jack. Stamped out like vermin . . .'

It was easy in talk to make a death seem nothing more than stamping on an insect. It was different when you forced the steel into the soft flesh, heard the shriek of pain, felt a man's dying breath on your face, saw the light fade from his eyes.

Wright shook the new recruits, Wintour and Grant, by the hand, and made his apologies. Both men were well-dressed, obviously prosperous, but both looked dour, old before their time. Jack hoped their muscles were more vigorous than their manner. The presence of the priest, with all the makings of a Mass, made him nervous. They were hunted men, these priests, hiding from one house to another, facing the rack and their innards ripped out if they were discovered, and bringing the same threat to those who hid them.

He slunk out into the late afternoon, feeling the bite of the wind on his flesh through the loose cloak, hand comforted by resting on the hilt of his sword. It would be more than the bite of wind he would feel if they all played the wrong hand in this particular game of cards.

CHAPTER 2

How could you live and not be excited by London?

It was eternal damnation, a smoke-filled Hell and a cauldron for the plague. And it was deliriously, amazingly and ecstatically exciting. The stench of the shite on the streets and the heavenly smell of a fresh-baked loaf. The waft of the wind bringing the sweet-fresh smell of meadows from outside the city boundaries, and the stink of the open sewer they called the Thames. Everywhere people screaming their wares, a city turned into a multitude of salesmen. A heaving, sweating multi-coloured multitude with their feet in mud and their eyes raised towards the stars. It was a raw, violent and often brutal melting pot, but with all the filth and the putrid vapours of too many people and animals crowded on top of one another came an unequalled excitement. The city had grown in recent years out of all control, the higgle-piggle of streets growing more dense and narrow by the week, spilling out beyond the old walls. Yelling builders and ramshackle scaffolding seemed to clog the routes, fighting with the men, the women and the horses, the sheep and cattle on their way to slaughter, and the open-eyed yokels so busy looking up that they could not see the midden at their feet.

For all the excitement, a nagging question bit at the mind of Henry Gresham. Why was he here? It was not his time to be in London. Yet he had answered the summons, knowing he had no choice.

He had ridden hard. He was a very rich man whose wealth was spent very carefully. One of its objects was horseflesh. Another was Mannion. Mannion, good soldier that he had been, oversaw the stables between Cambridge and London that kept a good horse on permanent standby for Henry Gresham. Mannion also kept an eye on the men who would take Gresham's windblown mount from him, wash it down and give it the love that Gresham, already on his next mount, could not.

He need not have hurried so. Robert Cecil, Viscount Cranborne, soon to be Earl of Salisbury and the youngest man ever to be sworn in as a Privy Councillor, would have waited. As the inheritor of Europe's largest and most efficient network of spies and informers, Cecil spent his life waiting, like a spider at the centre of his web, and watching.

Yet riding as if life depended on it, feeling the rush of wind through his hair, knocking the startled farm traffic aside, the pounding of the horse beneath him on the rough tracks . . . this was life itself, this was oblivion and fulfilment all in the one moment. Cecil could control elements of Gresham's life. No-one could control that wild, rough ride to London.

Previous meetings between Gresham and Robert Cecil's kind had resulted directly or indirectly in Henry Gresham being shot at or lunged at with sharp metal on innumerable occasions, seriously wounded on two occasions and shipwrecked, mercifully only once, on the wild Irish coast. Cecil's instructions had also resulted in Gresham being sentenced to be hung (twice), sentenced to be hung, drawn and quartered (once) and, on another memorable occasion, actually being roped to the rack in the Tower of London.

Yet Gresham kept coming back.

How on earth had he got himself involved in this lunatic world where power was the only morality, and where nothing was as it seemed? It was as if it had been that way for ever, from the moment when as little more than an overgrown boy he had been dragged in to play such a deciding role in the tragedy of Mary Queen of Scots. He had made no conscious choice to become involved. In Gresham's experience, Fate did not consult with humans before deciding the course of their lives, or if they were to have life at all. Falling initially in the way of the Queen's spymaster, old Sir Francis Walsingham, Gresham had increasingly found himself taking his orders from Robert Cecil, the self-appointed heir apparent to Walsingham's vast complex of spies, agents and informers. Gresham and Cecil had loathed each other from the first moment of their meeting. Yet the danger, the excitement and the risk were a heady mixture, and Gresham had carried on, playing the great game until it had seemed that he had pushed his life to the edge and that by then he owed God a death. Then Cecil had summoned him, years ago, wanting him to go on some pitiful and dreary expedition to see informers in Spain. Gresham had refused. Cecil had looked at him, and drawn out of a wallet a piece of writing, carefully copied in a clerk's hand.

'You might care to read this, Master Gresham, before you make any final decision regarding your acceptance of my request.'

Cecil was cool, calm, measured as he always was.

Gresham read it. In a lesser man the colour would have drained from his face and the hand reading the paper shaken. Instead Gresham made himself read it once, twice and a third time, his hand rock steady.

'Yes?' he had said, gazing calmly, matter-of-factly into Cecil's eyes, revealing none of his inner sickness.

Cecil had stolen Walsingham's papers, the complete record of his spy network. Somewhere in those papers had been details of the affair that had blighted Gresham's life, the only thing he had done of which he was ashamed. Cecil had found it out. It was there, written in a neat hand on the paper.

'It would be a pity if this paper were to become known, would it not?' asked Cecil, in a silky voice. 'Known to a wider public, I mean.'

'Why, sir,' Gresham replied, no sign of his fear in his voice, 'the truth will always out. The Bible tells us so, does it not? And what is one man's vanity and reputation against the call of truth?'

'Will it suit you to go to Spain, Master Gresham, as I have asked?' Was there the tiniest hesitation in Cecil's voice, along with the aggression?

It was a deciding moment, Gresham knew. If he conceded the power of Cecil's paper against him now and obeyed, he would never be his own master again. Yet if he resisted, Cecil could provoke his ruin. It was folly to resist, madness. And so because he was who he was, he chose to fight.

'No, my Lord, I cannot go.' *Cannot*, he was careful to say. 'Cannot', not 'will not'. 'I have the strongest personal reasons for requiring to be here in England at the moment. Of course, were the matter more urgent, or were your Lordship's life to depend on it, then I would go at your Lordship's command, without hesitation. I ask to be relieved of this duty, by your gracious mercy.'

By your gracious mercy. That made it Cecil's decision to absolve him from the mission, a favour granted from on high. Yet it also meant that he, Gresham, had not bowed to pressure, had not given in to blackmail.

Gresham carefully took the paper and placed it on the table, among the mass of papers that always surrounded Cecil, midway between them. He had given a form of words that allowed Cecil to save face. Would he take it?

There was a long silence.

Genuine thought, Gresham wondered, or enjoyment of the pain he knew he must be inflicting, for all the calm of the young man before him?

Cecil finally moved, taking the piece of paper carefully with forefinger and thumb, as if it was something faintly distasteful.

'A pity, sir. You would have been an excellent choice. Yet there will be other opportunities, that I do not doubt. Ones you will be

29

more advised to accept, as I choose to exercise my "gracious mercy". As you so gallantly describe it.'

'Your Lordship is indeed most merciful,' replied Gresham, and seeing the expression in Cecil's eyes of the hawk looking down on the mouse, 'most merciful.'

Gresham had not won a victory, that much he knew. The sword was poised, hung over his head, not back in its scabbard. He had merely negotiated an armed truce, and risked being played with by Cecil, as a boy tortures a fly. So Gresham had accepted with enthusiasm several other requests from Cecil, all of them dangerous. As he had done so he had made notes not only of those missions with Cecil, but of his involvement going back years to the days of Walsingham.

The climax had come with the Essex rebellion. Cecil had a habit of triumphing over those apparently better suited than he for survival. For years he had been locked in mortal combat with the dashing and handsome Robert Devereux, second Earl of Essex. Essex had the ancient lineage, the charm and the body that had bowled over every woman at Court, including the Queen. It had done him no good. Cecil's wits, the animal and immoral way in which he fought, had overcome his rival, as they overcame all rivals. The idiotic, ill-fated Essex rebellion had sent Essex to the block, leaving Cecil in total power at Court. Essex's head was still there, picked bare, on London Bridge. There was only one Robert now. Robert Cecil.

The walls of London were ahead of him, and Gresham eased his pace as more and more people appeared on the roadway. He grinned inwardly as he remembered his own decisive part in the Essex rebellion – or, rather, the decisive role he had played in making sure that the so-called rebellion never even spluttered into danger, but fizzled out with hardly more noise than a musket shot. It had made interesting reading, when he had written it down and had it copied, and if Gresham's version had become known he felt it likely that Cecil's thin head might be joining Essex's on a pike. It had been one of his better moments when he had presented a copy, the true account of the Essex rebellion with proof of Cecil's treachery, to Cecil himself. He had trumped it, if it needed doing, by the casual mention of the fact that copies of that and numerous other papers, as well as being lodged in a variety of secret places dotted around England, could also be found in the Papal archive. They were to be held in secret until removed by Gresham himself, their early release authorised only if Gresham were to die. Cecil blanched at that, showing emotion for almost the first time since Gresham had known him. The cellars below the Vatican were one of the very few areas Robert Cecil knew he would never penetrate, and there was a delicious touch of spice in the business by virtue of the fact both men knew that Gresham's access to this unique repository of documents had come through his having done some of Cecil's dirty work in Italy. It was poetic justice.

There was another reason for Gresham's hatred of Cecil, if another was needed. Two years ago Cecil had testified against and betrayed the friendship of the one man Henry Gresham had ever called master. Sir Walter Raleigh was the greatest man Gresham had ever known, a scholar poet, soldier, sailor, courtier and wit. He had saved Gresham's life. When the great wheel of fortune had seemed destined to plunge Raleigh down to the depths, and he had looked to his friends to rescue him from the sucking bog of Court politics, Cecil had betrayed him. Raleigh had been convicted on a trumped-up charge in a court hearing so biased it had shocked Europe. Now Raleigh, larger than life and leader of leaders, was languishing and ague-ridden in the Tower. Raleigh's wife had helped bring up Cecil's ailing child, taking him in alongside her own lusty, bawling brat and seeming to breathe life into his thin frame. This was how Cecil rewarded those who preserved his life blood, by imprisoning them in the Bloody Tower. Gresham could understand a man who betrayed his principles. He could never forgive a man who betrayed his friends.

The towers and roofs of Whitehall Palace were ahead of him

now. Whitehall was Cecil's home, its labyrinthine passages an emblem for the devious and complex mind that dominated the Court more than any other. This was the moment of calm before the storm, the moment before a great venture when time froze and the last chance to turn away beckoned. Gresham's horse had come to a halt. Gently, he urged it forward. In an uncertain world, Gresham knew only two things. He despised Cecil, and whatever task Cecil had for him would bring grief and hardship in its trail. He also knew that he could not refuse the excitement of what Cecil might offer, or run too freely the risk of what he might reveal.

A surly groom took his horse, and Gresham stretched his muscles as he stood on the cobbled courtyard. Gresham was sure it was going to be Catholics this time round. He dreaded Catholics. They were what he did least well. The woman who had brought him up, raised the bastard son of Sir Thomas Gresham, was a Catholic. With her breast milk had come the rosary bouncing off his infant nose. He hated the Catholic business more than any other. The Marlowe business, the Essex rebellion, that tragic creature Mary and most of all his dealings with the Armada had seemed real. His dealings with the Catholics had seemed sad by comparison. Early on in his accidental career he had met a Catholic priest who had seemed to him the nearest thing to a saint on this earth that he would ever know. Months later he had watched that saint hung until near gasping dead, seen his heart cut out of his body and that long-suffering and frail body chopped into four pieces. To Gresham, who was no longer sure that there was a God, the shrieks a man uttered in his death throes were a single language, spoken alike among Roman or Protestant. The mutilation of human flesh in one cause or another seemed just another form of human sacrifice, the practice so widely condemned by Christianity.

Cecil was courteous, as ever. Grey-haired, the rich clothing he wore could only partially hide the deformity in his spine. His desk was littered with papers, and the paintings on the wall showed both his passion for art and his ability to pay for the best.

'Good morning to you, sir,' he had intoned, motioning Gresham to a stool.

The voice was flat, expressionless. The eyes were gimlet-hard, like a rat's. Cecil had a thin, mean figure, and a thin, mean face. His long cloak hid the ludicrously short legs that were such a joke in the marketplaces. There were many who saw a warped body as testimony to a warped mind. How right they were, thought Gresham, who had met many with both afflictions but never anyone who combined them to such effect as Robert Cecil. He moved in a manner that gave least cause to show the wrench in his neck, hidden by an exceptionally large collar on the cloak and an extravagant ruff. He seemed permanently cold, yet he met his network of spies in the largest and coldest room in his Palace. A huge, carved stone fireplace held the most meagre of fires, spluttering to cope with the cheapest of sea coal in the early morning and producing far more smoke than heat.

'How go your affairs in Cambridge?' enquired Cecil solicitously.

'Well, my Lord,' replied Gresham, outwardly deferential and inwardly impatient for the fencing to end. 'The College grows by the month.' Cecil was Chancellor of the University; another power base.

'So good to hear!' mused Cecil with total insincerity, pouring wine into a goblet and pushing it across the table to Gresham. The goblet was gold. It shone forth in this dreary room like sunshine after rain. The wine was cat's piss. Cecil only spent money on things that lasted, like the goblet or fine paintings. On something like the wine, that would be urine in a matter of hours, he spent as little as possible.

Gresham smiled, took the goblet and raised it in a toast. In doing so, he sniffed the wine, and without his smile shifting at all put the goblet down in front of him, its contents untasted. They would remain so throughout the meeting. Even a badly brought-up dose of the pox would have revolted had the liquid in the glass been poured over it.

Cecil's expression did not change, though he certainly noted the rejected goblet. He sat back in his splendid chair, gazing out through the narrow window with its view of the river. His guest sat on a bare, three-legged stool, with one leg shorter than the others. It was all there was to sit on, except the near-throne in which Cecil sat upright.

'We live in wicked times, Sir Henry. Wicked times.' Cecil sighed. There was no goblet or wine for him. In all their meetings Henry Gresham had never seen food or drink pass Cecil's lips.

Well, mused Gresham, you should know, as having created no small measure of that wickedness yourself.

'There are those in our midst who seek to deny the most basic, the most central commandments of Our Lord. Those who seek to do so whilst holding positions of very real power. Wicked men, Sir Henry. Truly evil men. Do you not agree?'

Catholics. It had to be Catholics. Damn, Gresham thought, anything but Catholics.

'You know of Sir Francis Bacon, I believe?' Cecil enquired, responding to Gresham's silence, leaning forward. It was his most beguiling gesture. In leaning forward the collar of his cloak drooped and the ruff dropped slightly, revealing his warped neck. 'Indeed, I think you have dined with him?'

Bacon? Bacon? Gresham's mind, behind its public mask and the half-smile, was in a turmoil. Bacon had been accused of most things, except being a Papist. Bacon's intelligence was matched only by his ambition. He had spent a lifetime trying to get inside the Queen's linen and was now trying to get inside the King's. Gresham hoped it was cleaner than the outside of the monarch. Bacon was just another man of talent trying to compensate for a lack of birth, driven by the same ambition that drove all those who came to Court. What had Bacon to do with the state of the nation?

'He has been to College, my Lord,' Gresham replied light-heartedly. 'He talks well,' he added dismissively. Let Cecil make the running.

'It is not his talk that concerns me, Sir Henry,' replied Cecil. He was sitting back now, ready to launch the blow.

'It is his sodomy.'

Gresham's face did not flicker. His expression did not falter. His pulse missed not a beat. He held down a massive urge to burst out laughing.

'Is it proven, my Lord?' enquired Gresham, his expression serious.

'No,' replied Cecil, looking coldly at Gresham. 'It is not. Yet if it is true, I must have it proven. I believe you to be the man to find such proof.'

Sodomy was a capital offence, certainly. The growing band of Puritans shouted the evils of fornication at an increasing number of street corners, to the hilarity and amusement of the populace. When they denounced the double sin of sodomy, the crowds ceased their laughter and joined in the shouting. Yet more and more the fashionable end of society was turning to experiment, be it with the new weed tobacco, strange concoctions of wine and herbs or the practice of sex. Sodomy was ill-advised. It was hardly the stuff of which the survival of nations was composed.

'I hope, my Lord,' responded Gresham carefully, 'that I have some experience of finding proof. Yet are you not better advised to set one of similar inclination on to this project? Why not set a thief to catch a thief? Am I to believe this is an urgent matter?'

'You might consider my example, Sir Henry. I *believe* very little.' Cecil's eyes bored into Gresham. Gresham did not flinch, the infuriating half-smile still on his lips. 'I *observe* a great deal. I merely use that which I have.'

Touché, thought Gresham. Or if not that, stalemate.

All in all, it left them in their usual state of even balance. Both despised each other, yet had need of what each other had to offer. Each one could destroy the other, but knew the destruction was likely to be mutual. In that room Gresham was in the presence of raw power, pure and simple, and Henry Gresham could not resist the taste and smell of it.

Yet to be set on to determine the destination of Bacon's prick? After a frantic summons to travel without delay and post-haste to London? Bacon was fiercely ambitious. That much was widely known. He was in debt. That was also widely known. And most known of all was the fact that he had one of the best brains in Christendom. He was related to Cecil, but the relationship, complicated by too many embattled women, had not been easy. It was also rumoured that, in common with Kit Marlowe – an earlier tragedy – he thought those 'who liked not boys were fools'. It was all good stuff for gossip in the ordinary and the tavern, but even if Bacon was proven to have buggered every boy in Europe it would hardly set England tottering on its constitutional heels. Essex had been Bacon's patron, of course, before Bacon had turned against him and even helped in his prosecution. Was this Cecil paying back an old debt, slowly destroying the last vestiges of those who had supported his old enemy Essex?

His scalp started to itch unbearably, even though he would swear no flea had made its entry to his head. He refused the overwhelming urge to scratch his itch.

'I will do as you ask, my Lord,' said Gresham calmly. 'It is *my* choice to do so.' Their eyes locked for a brief, fiery clash, and then both went dark. 'Yet I think there are greater issues than one man's buggery, in the present times.'

Cecil mouthed an insincere farewell, failing to rise to show Gresham to the door. There had to be a deeper reason for all this, thought Gresham as he left. At a guess, Bacon had offended Cecil, or was coming to be seen as a threat to Cecil's power in some way. This had to be personal. Would Gresham help destroy the man if it were so? He would see. He had felt no compunction working against Essex and bringing him down, not least of all because he saw Essex as both a threat to the nation and a lifelong enemy of Sir Walter Raleigh. If Bacon seemed a fly not worth the squashing, Gresham would leave him in peace and return an infuriatingly bland report to Cecil.

A servant appeared from nowhere and held open the carved and varnished door. As he passed through Gresham felt a distinct increase in temperature. Was it the room? Or was any room occupied by Robert Cecil colder and darker by virtue of its occupant?

'God's blood!' yelled the informer.

The cheap red wine had spilled out of his mouth and across one of the weeping ulcers that ringed his lips.

If Gresham was disturbed by the blasphemy, he did not show it. He leant casually back in his chair and motioned invitingly to the jug and the man's half-empty tankard. He carefully laid his arm in between some of the more poisonous stains on the table and gazed at the half-drunk informer.

'So *have* you news of Bacon's household?' asked Gresham patiently. Gresham's enquiries after Bacon had coursed out through the underworld of London. This was the latest lead that had emerged from its sewers.

The informer grunted, reached for the jug and poured himself a life-threatening dose of vinegar. He drew back on it, careful this time to make no spillage. He made as if to wipe his lips, remembered in time the damaged flesh thereabouts, and poked out instead a thick red tongue to gather up the residue.

'Yes, I do. Truthfully, I do. The little man has . . . visitors. *Young* visitors.'

The conspiratorial tone he sought to adopt was spoilt somewhat by the vast belch of foul breath that ended his sentence. The explosion of air seemed to rock him back, like a loose-shotted cannon.

Little man? Sir Francis Bacon was not particularly short, though certainly no giant. Those who envied the size and scope of his brain tended to vilify his build, as if the latter reflected the former. It was a common mistake of the time. If it had been true, the pathetic stunted and warped figure of Robert Cecil would not contain the most powerful brain in the country.

'The names of these young visitors?'

The informer's eyes were still glazed with the shock of his own eruption. God forbid he might fart next, thought Gresham. If he did it was likely to have lumps in it.

'Names? Names?' The man took another swig. 'These things have no names. They're sweepings, sweepings. Bastards taken at birth from a whore's bed, or saved from the river.'

The brown and swirling waters of the Thames bore a frequent cargo of new- or still-born children. They were meant to be from the loins of the whores who had matched London's stupendous growth. Gresham cared not to think how many well-born casement windows had seen a private cargo despatched into the waters of Lethe. All new-born appeared alike when swelled by their feast of filthy river water.

'If not names, then witnesses. Who witnesses this nightly progress?'

The informer allowed an expression of alarm to cross his eyes and ravaged face. He took another half-swig, his moderation reflecting a new sense of danger.

'Why, the servants, of course. All the servants.'

'And the Gateman will testify to this? The other servants will testify?'

'Why . . . why . . . they may, of course. Of course, they may.'

Gresham's voice was at its most silky soft. He placed his other arm between a stain that might have been blood and one that was certainly grease, and leant forward.

'Without testimony those visitors are phantoms, just ghosts upon the wind.'

His voice turned from summer sun to the glint of blade in passageway.

'As you, my friend, are so much piss and wind.'

He came to his feet. He was an impressive figure, five foot eight or so and with an easy muscle rippling below the superbly tailored doublet, hose and cloak.

His figure, clothed all in black, loomed over the informer like Death himself. And now the voice became ice, cold beyond belief. It froze the informer, even as it released him. As Gresham spoke, he heard the tinkle of urine falling to the floor from the terrified man, smelt the hot, raw stink of steaming piss.

'You will return here, a fortnight from now. You will bring names, names of young sodomites or names of servants who will testify against their master. Or you will bring nothing. On what you bring you will be judged. Leave. Now.'

Gresham sank back in his chair, a black mood of despair threatening to overwhelm him. The informant, humiliated by his wetting himself and terrified beyond belief, fled, muttering incoherently.

This was going nowhere, Gresham thought. I am facing a man of unbounded intelligence, and all I have to question is fools.

'More work for the laundress.' The gruff voice was Mannion's. Built like a Cathedral, he had stationed himself just outside the door, opening it to let the informer out and himself in.

'More work for the chambermaid,' muttered Gresham, nodding to the steaming yellow pool on the floor beneath the table. He doubted she or the landlord would bother. The floor had seen much worse. There was a virtual history of London drunkenness etched on to the worn boards.

Mannion waited. If his master wished to talk, he would do so. Mannion would listen. Sometimes his master needed to talk and hear no reply. Sometimes he spoke and needed to debate. Mannion would respond, in kind. He would know which it was and, if it seemed proper to do so, would speak.

There was silence, Gresham sipping thoughtfully at his own goblet. As ever he had made sure he had his own wine, not the spew served to the informer. It was the best the inn had to offer, which was not very much. Like much of the City, it was brash, and new and quite raw, and like the City it had a taste of something much older, something sweetly rotten, beneath it.

So there was to be no talking, Mannion reflected. So be it.

'Shame about the candles,' Mannion muttered as they left the room. Gresham had left them burning, most of them not yet half done. The landlord would gratefully snuff them out and use the remaining half, charging Gresham for the whole candle. Gresham did not respond. It was an old joke.

It had been years ago. They had just started campaigning after a dreadful winter. The canvas of the tent had seemed as if it was just drying out, in the rare sun of a Flanders spring. The soldiers had come in silent, angry. Usually an action cleared the blood, exhilarated them. This time the pathetic Spaniard in charge of the troop had not only been concealing the gold they had been sent to rob, but concealing his wife. She was a pretty girl, not yet nineteen years of age. Hidden in a baggage cart, they would probably have left her, heavily pregnant as she was, if they had found her. Even a scream would have caused a laugh and no more. It was early in the campaigning year, they were fat with an idle winter and there were no grudges to pay back as yet. Instead she had climbed out of her hiding place silently, seeking to rush out of the wagon and into the shrubbery surrounding the ambush. The youngest recruit had heard the rustle of clothing behind him and swung round with sword outstretched. His mother had obtained the sword for him. God knew – or so Gresham hoped – how the Toledo steel of a Spanish grandee had found its way into the hands of a woman who had proudly borne six fiercely Protestant sons in an East Anglian farmhouse. The sword was sharp as a razor, despite the youngest son's crude attempts at sharpening it. Its curving arc, powered by all the untrained force of a healthy and terrified eighteen-year-old, had sliced neatly through the stomach of the pregnant woman.

It had also sliced into the unborn boy, so that it was bleeding to death even as it flopped to the ground. It had an audience fitting for such an end in Flanders mud. Its mother saw it bleed to death in front of her, as her frighteningly red hands clawed at her own gut. So did its father and its murderer, and an assorted troop of Protestant and Catholic mercenaries and volunteers.

The young man skewered himself on the sword his mother had given him. He did it badly, of course. He would take days to die as the horrific wound in his belly and bowel suppurated and led to its inevitable conclusion. The problem was, he would scream.

So they came into the tent in varying moods and set about getting as drunk as possible in as short a time as was possible. Henry Gresham was a veteran of two years' standing. Having seen so much, he was later to the bottle than many of the younger ones. He saw the outstretched hand knock the lamp and its oil off the empty barrel and fling its contents against the canvas of the tent. He saw the oil sink into the canvas, inert. He saw the wick, still flaming, sail through the air as if the world had slowed down and God declared a war against time, towards the canvas. He saw the wick hit the canvas, flicker as if ready to die, and then burst out anew on the oil-soaked cloth.

They should not have stored powder in the tent. There was a store for it, only a few hundred yards away. Yet they were veterans, survivors of a war that seemed endless. They knew the perils of powder that had separated through old age, of powder that was damp or badly mixed. They preferred to keep and tend their own, and despite their every precaution the fire reached it.

Henry Gresham never knew what object, flung out by the blast, gouged his leg and thigh to near pulp. He did know the sight of his erstwhile commander, screaming for light with a boiled face and eye sockets permanently burned out. The last thing he remembered was Mannion, reaching out as if to stop him connecting with the ground.

So it was that Henry Gresham commanded candles, not lamps, in his house and in the rooms he hired. A candle, if knocked over, tended to go out. If not, its flame was a slow, friendly kind of fire. Oil simply wished to ignite. He could bear lamps, of course. Indeed, in strange rooms and strange houses where he had no control he hardly even noticed them. Henry Gresham had long ago lost any belief that a human being could control their life. All one could do was to control it where one had power, that being a very small portion of the whole.

'I'll have what's left of those candles snuffed out and in my bag in seconds,' Mannion grumbled. 'You've paid for them, haven't you?' Mannion never ceased to mention the waste of candles. By reminding Gresham, he made the fear normal.

'View it as my gesture of protest against the dominance of night in this world of ours,' Gresham said loftily, and swept out of the room.

'View it as a damn silly waste of money, more like!' muttered Mannion, closing the door behind him.

Mannion also had a sense of humour. By comparison with many other men's sense of humour it was odd in the extreme. What Mannion found funny, and what could not produce even the tiniest stretching of his craggy features, never ceased to fascinate Gresham. Boots, for example, were endlessly funny to Mannion. It was as if he deemed mankind to have been born with feet the aim of which was to trudge through whatever muck God chose to put at ground level. He would accept clogs or the most basic leather footwear as a reasonable recourse against the elements on the part of the dominant species, but in the face of the finery the gentry put on their feet he was reduced to hopeless laughter.

A gentleman would don boots as a matter of necessity. A courtier would like people to believe that his fine shoes would never need to meet muck or mud, unless one was riding, of course. Henry Gresham was a gentleman, fabulously rich and a courtier when he chose. He was also an agent for King James I of England and King James VI of Scotland. So it was that he was planning to walk home from The Mermaid Inn after his rather fruitless conversation. Gentlemen and courtiers rode horses or had carriages. Gentleman courtiers who were spies tended to avoid both, as drawing attention to themselves.

Mannion eyed his own stout leggings, and the supple leather of his master's fine boots.

'Shame about the boots,' he muttered with a grin. Mannion had no fear for the armed gangs who roamed the streets after nightfall. He was highly amused by the prospect of what the walk would do to his master's fine boots.

There was something about London muck that did for fine leather. Too much of Gresham's time was taken up in walking back from shady rendezvous. The worst times were early morning, and late at night. During the day it was not too bad. A veritable army of men scurried to shovel up every human, horse, cattle and dog turd that lay steaming on the streets. There was money to be made from shit, but to make it you had to see it. At night it was invisible, and ever present.

'Remember that dream you told me about once?' said Mannion, as they walked through a street with a particularly narrow over-hang.

Gresham had once had a nightmare where he was leaving one of Bankside's most unsavoury taverns and his way home was lit by endless torches. The dim and flickering light illuminated thousand upon thousand of straining arses, perched over the narrow and overhanging streets and each delivering their message to the street with a hollow thud.

He shook his head, and the image vanished. A grinning Mannion led him down the rickety stairs and through The Mermaid, full as was usual with its theatrical crowd and some of the more daring socialites, tasting a bit of rough and arty for the night. The air was thick and unpleasant, the dancing light revealing the sweat on the fevered brows. Men dealing, men stealing, men intriguing and whores selling. It was a foetid mix, and Gresham could not wait to be out of it.

Gresham's eyes flickered round the room, seeming to see nothing, noting everything. He noted a dour, stooping figure, clearly the worse for drink, sitting alone at a back table. Gresham scrabbled in his memory for the man's name. It would come. They emerged into the black streets. The muscularity of their walk, and the ease with which their hands rested on the swords in their belts, caused the ways to part in front of them. They were the source of menace, not its victims.

'That man, seated in the corner,' Gresham said, 'the one on his own and worse for drink; do you recognise him?'

'Should I?' replied Mannion. 'Shall I go back in and ask?'

'No, not yet at least. I remember him from somewhere. It'll come back.'

As they passed an 'ordinary', light spilled out from the door, and two men fell brawling into the street. There were shrieks and yells, good-natured laughter. Out of the dark a crowd gathered, egging the two on. Gresham and Mannion looked away, preserving their night vision. Inside that same tavern Gresham knew a man could be reading exquisite sonnets to his friends. Shortly after, they were plunged into darkness, the huge overhang of the half-timbered buildings closing over them like a black cloud. It was a residential area. The doors were closed and bolted this late in the night, and only the feeble light of an occasional candle or guttering lamp behind closed shutters showed that some merchant was still up, counting his credit or bemoaning his losses. Or, as a shriek from behind followed by the thuds of two or three blows suggested, a wife was being taught what a man thought was good manners.

It was then that a moment for Heaven came, a moment that summed up for Gresham the magic of London. Shortly behind him two men were fighting, cheered on by a drunken crowd, and a wife was being beaten for doing no more probably than trying to be herself. And then, from a high window, came the breath of Heaven.

Music had always inspired Gresham. It was his greatest regret that he could not find in himself the means to produce what so inspired him from others. *O Jove, From Stately Throne*. That was it. Gresham had met the composer. Farrant? Yes, Richard Farrant, no less. Perhaps it was Farrant, his face ravaged by smallpox, leading the small *ensemble* in the upstairs room, playing and singing beyond all reasonable time, desperately trying to compensate for the ugliness of his own face by the beauty of his music.

The voice of Heaven filtered out through the shutters and on to the dark street, dropping like gentle rain on the heads of Gresham and Mannion. As a man they stopped, raised their faces, and let the beauty fall on their upturned visages like a summer shower.

It was high summer. Even here, in the great city, the sense was in the air. With the warmer evenings fires were lit later and left burning shorter. The smoke that hung over London on a still day like a funeral pall was visibly less. The cattle driven through the streets were fat and full of milk.

The most dangerous thing they met on the journey was a dog, half wild with hunger and trailing a leg damaged in a fight, or in a collision with a cart. It slunk away down an alley.

He had worked himself back into a good humour by the time he and Mannion reached home, his mood generated by what awaited him there. Known simply as the House, the London home built by Gresham's father was situated in the highly fashionable area of the Strand, and with its own landing on to the River it was a prime site. His father had bought it when the monasteries had been dissolved.

The House was well-run. That much was clear. The two well-built men who acknowledged their master as he trudged through the mud to his own doorstep recognised him, but would have recognised an enemy just as clearly, and sounded the alarum. Their pleasure in seeing their master was in no small measure related to the fact that Henry Gresham showed pleasure in seeing them.

'Good evening, Matt, good evening, Will,' he muttered as he passed them by. Mannion grunted at them.

The entrance hall was of marble, brought over at fabulous expense from Italy. The statues and hangings were also Italian. The woman was English.

Jane Carpenter was nearing twenty-three years of age, and was the most beautiful woman in London. She had a face of stunning beauty, cheekbones pushing up round the roundest and darkest pair of eyes in Christendom. Her body lacked the plumpness of many Court ladies, but she had the grace and strength of a young colt, and legs beneath her dress that seemed to cross counties. Yet it was her eyes that commanded attention, extraordinary eyes, with dark lights seeming to flash beneath their surface. Gresham grinned at her as Mannion struggled to pull off his boots, replacing them with soft shoes. She grinned in return. With him she dropped the rather aloof distance she maintained with all people of social standing, the faint tone of terrible boredom.

'Are London's problems solved, my Lord, and can innocent maidens go safely now to our beds?'

'Firstly, I don't solve problems but rather create them, I think. Secondly, I am not nor ever will be "Lord" to anyone. Thirdly, you are not innocent, and fourthly, in your bed no-one is safe.' Feeling rather proud of his grasp of numbers, he reinforced the words, as soon as Mannion had left the room with his boots and cloak, by flinging out an arm, gathering her up and delivering a kiss that shook the fine plaster on the walls.

'Ouch!' she exclaimed truthfully, the hilt of his sword banging into her just under her ribcage. 'Why do men always have to bang at everything?'

'It's in the nature of men to give, and women to receive,' muttered Gresham, nuzzling her hair.

'As gifts go, what men give tends to be rather single-minded and very repetitive,' Jane replied, pushing him away and laughing up at him. 'Must I expect to endure receiving you tonight?'

'If I choose to honour you with my gifts, then yes. Yet as you've always been such an obedient servant, I don't doubt your instant bending . . .' She raised both her eyebrows. '. . . or whatever,' he added lamely, 'to my will.'

She dropped her hands to her sides and looked at him with that rare mixture of exasperation and love.

'Do be quiet, Henry Gresham. And come to your bed.' Your bed? For a brief flicker of a moment, Gresham was taken back to the time when he had first set eyes on this woman. Was it the timbre of her voice that sent him back, or that strange mixture of something brazen with something vulnerable and defenceless?

It had been on one of his first journeys from the calm of his Cambridge College to London, in 1590. He was still hobbling from his wound, and was without the relay of spare horses that Mannion was establishing for him. His horse had thrown a shoe just outside Bishop's Stortford. He had been left to his own devices in a village that did not even boast a poor inn, whilst Mannion saw to the horse and a replacement.

As he sat, picking at the rough grass and throwing it into the dank pond, he became aware that a pair of eyes were gazing solemnly at him from in between some bushes.

He gazed back. The two gazes locked, and held.

A thin, piping voice came from the bushes. 'First one who blinks loses.'

Gresham was so surprised that he blinked.

'There, you've lost. You must pay me a forfeit.'

The accent was thick but the diction clear.

'Well, young madam,' said Gresham as the painfully thin figure of a six- or seven-year-old girl climbed out of the bushes and into full view, 'I've no recollection that I ever agreed to your terms.'

'But you didn't refuse them either, sir, and therefore as a gentleman you're bound to agree with me.'

The logic was somehow faulty, in a way that Gresham could not quite fathom.

'And what if I don't agree?' The girl's eyes seemed to occupy her whole head. They were the darkest blue Gresham had ever seen, with flickering sparkles hidden deep inside them.

The girl shrugged. 'Then I suppose you'll beat me.'

'Do many beat you?'

'All the time. You see, I'm a bastard, and bastards deserve to be

47

beaten.' The little girl said it as if it was a litany she knew off by heart.

'How often are you beaten?'

'All the time. Here, you may see.' The girl dropped her loose tunic over her bony shoulders, down to her waist. Seven or eight red stripes marked her back, with the older blows turning to dull and dark bruises. She turned to look at him, over her shoulder. There was no coyness in her posture or voice, merely a statement of fact.

'They go on further down, but you're a man, so I can't show you my secret places.'

She carefully drew up her stained tunic, and sat on her haunches, looking at him. 'May I have my forfeit now?'

Gresham had often wondered what would have happened then, were it not for the interruption. He suspected he would have given this little vixen a few coins, and shooed her on her way. It was still his time of darkness, not a time when he had a care for any other living creature, being too full of mourning for those he had loved and betrayed.

Yet at the word 'forfeit' there was an outraged yell from one of the hovels overlooking the pond, and an elderly man erupted from the ill-shuttered door.

'You bitch! You brazen whore's whelp! Where've you been, you little whore, when your duty called? I'll teach you your duty . . .'

The girl might have been quick enough to evade the blow, had she not been rapt in her attentions to Gresham. As it was, she was a split second late and caught the blow square on her back.

It was not much of a back, as these things went. It was only seven years old, it had never been properly fed or properly clean. Yet it could bleed like any other back, if a witch-hazel stick whipped across it.

Gresham broke the man's arm. It was easy enough, for a soldier. As he raised it for the second blow on the prostrate little figure beneath him, Gresham sprang up, finding his sword in his hand without consciously willing it there or even knowing it had happened. He brought up the sword arm, with its extra weight of metal, just behind the man's wrist, a split second before he brought down his other arm with terrible force on the outstretched arm 'twixt wrist and elbow. The crack of bone would have shattered ice.

The peasant was bellowing on the ground, his arm smashed. The girl had vanished back into the bushes, nursing a new welt but not, Gresham noted, making a sound. Neighbours were rushing out on to the green to see the cause of the entertainment. In very short order they surrounded the gentleman and demanded reparation not only for the damage done to the man, but for disturbing the peace of the whole village. After all, a sword could only kill one man, and there were ten or more of them there in the space of three or four breaths. There was money in this business, and they knew it, peasants that they were.

Then Mannion loomed over the rise that surrounded the pond, and things became calmer. Things usually did become calmer when Mannion arrived on the scene. The villagers who had been feeling their cudgels with enthusiasm suddenly thought it better to put them behind their backs. A rather more civilised process of negotiation assumed pride of place. The man on the ground howling in his agony – 'William', it would appear by all counts – was a labourer. Well, William would not be labouring for a month or two, that was clear. William was also the nearest thing this village had to a saint, that much was also clear. Taken on his daughter's bastard, he had, that same daughter who had caught God's justice when she died in childbirth with no man to call her proper husband.

Looking at William, Gresham wondered how the bastard girl had ever survived. The midwife must have spirited the poor wean away and presented it back to William when the lump it might have made in the pond would have been too obvious even to the other villagers. Come to think of it, there was a fretful old woman hovering at the back of the gesticulating villagers.

It took precious little money to calm them down. Yet what took all of them aback, including Gresham, was his final question.

'How much for the girl?'

Mannion looked up, startled, at his master, and wondered for a brief moment if he liked fucking children. God knows, enough did. And, Mannion decided almost instantaneously, his master didn't. Yet he too had seen the child sliced out of its mother's belly, and knew that taking on this child might somehow claw back some of the despair from that dreadful day.

And the child could always be handed over to someone else to bring up, when Gresham returned to emotions more proper for a man.

In the final count, the amount paid for the girl was paltry. The expression in William's eyes suggested that his arm was well broken if this was the reward. Gresham had visions of him erupting into the path of every gentleman who rode by, demanding that they break his arm.

She had shown no emotion until the time of their leaving. A mere piece of property, she had been bartered and sold, with no-one thinking to ask her opinion. She vented it, forcibly, when she was seated behind Mannion the servant on his horse, as was only proper.

She screamed and shrieked and pummelled and yelled, causing even Mannion's horse to buck and to rear in protest.

'What is wrong with you, girl!' Gresham exploded.

'You bought me,' the thin, shivering Eve proclaimed through gritted and tear-stained teeth. 'I shall ride on no horse except your own.'

Gresham had killed more men than he cared to count. He had witnessed the person he most loved in Creation die in agony before him, and because of him. He had suffered in a few months more pain than most men underwent in a lifetime. He had a fortune to his name, he cared for no man and he cared for nothing . . . Why, then, thought Gresham, am I riding at a sedate pace and freezing to death, whilst a seven-year-old bastard girl sits behind me in state, wearing my fine cloak?

If he had been able to answer that question, then perhaps he would really have been God.

There was a vestige in him of his own childhood. He too had known what it was to be the bastard.

'Find me a woman to care for this ... minx,' he had said to Mannion as they arrived in London. The girl had been restored to rude good health by a substantial meal. If her eyes had opened any wider on their entry to London they would have consumed her face.

'Find me someone who won't just care for her. Find me some servants who'll love her, as if she were their own.'

And Mannion, as he always did, found what his master wanted.

Jane had fallen in love with the House only slightly less than she had fallen in love with the strange and darkly dressed man who had rescued her from abuse. It had been a dark, dreary and a sad place she had come to, still in mourning for the death of Gresham's father and an heir who seemed determined to neglect it. As a child she had haunted its every nook and cranny, and as she grew older and into womanhood she seemed to light up the building with her love for it. Nominally under the care of the elderly Housekeeper, Jane had grown into that role herself so gently that no-one could point to the exact time when she became the acknowledged mistress of the House.

The House was the best-run house in London. No wine was drunk, no food eaten and no clothing for footmen paid for without Jane being convinced that the expenditure was proper. There was a part of Jane that was the feral cat, a part Gresham knew would never leave her. It accounted in part for her raw sexuality, her enjoyment of the physical act. The servants saw the untamed Jane if they cheated their master, the House or her, and felt it. Gresham had seen her turn on a thieving servant with a cold fury, and a ferocious concentration of anger that was almost tangible. Yet months later she had waited most of the night by that same serving girl's bed when she seemed as if she would die of a fever, and fed her beef tea. That same woman he had seen when a sudden downpour had flooded the hall, her skirts tucked up to her knees, laughing and joking with the servant girls as they all joined to swoosh the filthy water back out into the street. The men servants may have leered at her behind her back, for all Gresham knew. To her face they were strangely protective, their visible respect tinged almost with a certain fearfulness. All the servants spoke in awe of her, grumbling as servants did. Yet it was her food that was the freshest, her room the most clean and her bed linen the most virgin-white. In a way Gresham did not understand, they took an immense pride in her. He knew and accepted almost with complacency that many of them would die for him. It surprised him how many he thought might die for her. Then again, he lived in a world where if the master or the mistress sinned, the servants received an equal or worse punishment. Dying for your master or your mistress was not a choice for the servants of the well-born. It was a condition of service.

Gresham still did not know how the irritating, obnoxious foundling, the by-blow of a hasty assault on a peasant common, had become his mistress.

He had come to the House late one night, obsessed with business. The thin-boned foundling had turned into a strikingly beautiful seventeen-year-old with an imperious will. She had strode about his chamber, showing real anger as she explained the various frauds upon his money that his servants had perpetuated.

'And furthermore, my Lord, there's one even greater crime to which you must answer!'

'And what's that?' said Gresham, wearied beyond belief by decisions that affected all Christendom, not to mention his supposedly immortal soul. How was it to him if a cook was ordering extra chickens?

She stood there, tall and straight as the bolt from an arrow, flashing radiance in the room. 'You, who have every right to claim me as your own, have never looked at me as a woman!'

Well, he had been taken by a fit and had done more than look upon her as a woman that night, to their apparent mutual satisfaction. Yet when he woke, he was more than a man with the edge taken off his carnal hunger by a fine night of lovemaking. More scared than he had been in the face of a Spanish cannon, he realised with an almost sickening fear that he was in love. He knew that he had signed his will away. He had not sought it. He had even tried positively to avoid it, or any other entanglement. It had done him no good.

Yet Jane had steadfastly refused to marry him. He had pleaded with her.

'You seem to have claimed ownership of my body, and doubtless wanted my soul since I first saw you by that cursed pond! I've said I love you, haven't I? Why won't you make a proper woman of yourself, and a proper man of me, by being my wife? Am I fat and stinking of grease? Am I not rich enough for you?'

She had turned away that night, after their lovemaking, peaceful and contented. She let his ranting pass over her, with the inner calm that drove him to even greater fury. She turned round to face him, letting cold air into the bed.

'I've said my thanks with my body. It's all I was gifted with from God. Everything else I have was somebody else's. You've had the only thing I have to give, as I now am. Anything else must wait.'

'Yet you've shown me your secret places. You've let me use those secret places, to my heart's content.'

He remembered the first showing to him of her wounds.

She smiled at him, a radiance that lit up the bed. 'I've shown you the secret places of my body, and willingly so.'

She turned over in the bed, her back towards him. As if from a far continent, her last words came. 'As for the secret places of my soul, for that you will have to wait.'

Gresham knew of no more final goodnight.

And now he was lying in his vast bed in 1605, years on from that first meeting and years on from the night when he had taken her virginity. He was satiated, yet as mystified by this woman he loved as he had been by the side of the pond in that filthy village all those years ago. Perched on the very edge of sleep, the knowable world of Cambridge, the dangerous world of Robert Cecil and the imponderable world of Jane raced round in his head until they blended into a wild half-dream. Cecil was screaming at him, blaming him that his mistress was soon to be elected as Master of King's College. He recoiled in the face of Cecil's spitting anger, yet thinking it would not be the first time a bastard had been involved in the governance of that College.

In his dreams, the bloated face of Will Shadwell rose up from the deep.

'Beware! Beware!' it moaned at him. 'You are in waters too deep for your soul!'

'My soul, poor tattered thing, was lost a long while ago,' whispered Gresham. 'And I have been in waters too deep all my life!'

At that the ghost of Will Shadwell vanished, and Henry Gresham slept in peace. Just before he did so, the name of the man stooped over his tankard in the tavern came to him.

'Wintour. Robert Wintour . . .' What did he know about Robert Wintour? It would come to him. It always did.

CHAPTER 3

Father Garnet was in prison. As prisons went it was pleasant enough. The half-timbered house had been sheltering Jesuits safely for years, its walls peppered with hiding places. The fire burnt cheerfully in the grate, the oak panels mellowed in the evening sun and there was wine at hand. Yet it was still prison.

A curlew sounded in the meadows outside the house, its forlorn, mewing cry echoing the priest's mood. Father Garnet was tired, more tired than he had ever been in his whole life. It was no crisis of faith. When he summoned the image of Our Saviour into his mind the rushing well of tenderness, the biting pain of love were the same as ever, undiminished and unrelenting. Rather, it was simple exhaustion.

How long had he been in England, fighting for the faith that was his life? Fighting for it *with* his life?

He had forgotten how many years, years of being continually shunted from one secret house to another, years of disguise, of whispered Masses in shuttered rooms. The Jesuit priest was a hunted animal in England, yet at least the real animal was given a quick death by the hounds. If the priest was found he would be stripped and trussed to a wooden hurdle, dragged through the streets behind a horse, to be reviled and spat at by the worst sort of scum. Hauled on to a scaffold, he would be dropped and hung until the choking edge of suffocation had plunged him near into unconsciousness, and hurriedly cut down whilst still aware. Rough-handled over to the nearby block, the executioner would then hack off his testicles, to show that he should never have been born, and thrust them before the priest's agonised face. Then the crude blade would strike into the chest, and the heart be torn out, the bleeding, pathetic flesh held up for the baying crowd to see, to the cry, 'Here lies the heart of a traitor!'

Father Garnet's dreams were haunted by the first, coarse feel of that rope around his neck, the gasping panic of strangulation, the sharp, shrieking cut of the metal. Was it weakness to be so scared? Could he pray to be spared this pain, or should he pray to have it inflicted on him, thus becoming a glorious martyr for the Faith? A good man, he prayed for neither. The first was unfair and a coward's way, the second was untrue. He prayed instead simply for the wisdom to understand.

O my God. *Why hast Thou forsaken me?*

Garnet tensed. Horse's hooves sounded outside his window. He looked expectantly at the bell over the fireplace in his room. Were it to ring, tugged frantically by a loyal servant, Garnet would hastily grab his bottle and glass so as to hide his presence, run outside into the passageway and back into the adjoining room. The fireplace there was kept deliberately blackened, ash in the basket, as if used every day. Behind it lay a priest-hole, activated by a hidden lever. Within lay a rosary and a crucifix, scraps of dried-out food and a single, thin and emaciated turd. This was evidence enough that a priest had once lain, eaten and shat therein. The stench of urine, added to every three days by loyal Catholic servants ordered to piss there, gave force to the message.

The real priest-hole lay behind. Two men might crouch in it, but not stand or sit. A thousand men might seek how to enter it, but never find the means of entry unless they were told. Even the fiercest fire built in the first fireplace would not singe the occupants of the second priest-hole, for all the damage it could have done to occupants of the first.

A cheerful call wafted up from the gatehouse, greeting the rider. Father Garnet relaxed again in his chair.

He felt a dread terror as he contemplated that young fool Catesby and his hellish plot. Catesby had told his servant what was planned, then sought to calm the servant's disquiet by sending him to confess to Father Tesimond. The servant, thought Garnet, had a deal more common sense than the master, but then that was usually the way. As for Tesimond, he had received the confession and run straight to Garnet, in turn confessing all to him.

It was a nightmare. Garnet could no more break the secrecy of the confessional than he could sell his soul to the Devil. He could not disclose what Father Tesimond had told him to any person upon earth on pain of the loss of his immortal soul.

It would not just kill the Lords and Government of England, Garnet realised, a single tear forming in his eye and cooling as it found release and trekked down his cheek. It would kill the cause of Catholicism in England for years, perhaps for ever, uniting the country in a frenzy of hatred against the Popish impostors. It was the most awful, the most terrible thing that any young madcap rebel could conceive and carry out. And he, Father Garnet, was bound by the most awful vow of all not to reveal his knowledge. He had to persuade Catesby to give it all up. An emissary to the Pope had to be the answer. Surely if the Pope condemned the plot, even so overweening a vanity as Catesby's would have to recognise its folly?

A sharp cramp cut across his stomach. Too much food and wine, and not nearly enough exercise, he knew. Or an omen of the executioner's knife cutting into his most sensitive flesh in front of the howling crowd . . . He stumbled to his feet, and vomited up most of his day's food into the flames of the fire.

Gresham stood bolt-upright in the rough iron tub, as naked as the day he was born, scrubbing with satisfaction at the few suspicions of dirt left on his reddened flesh. It was before dawn, two guttering candles piercing the gloom, and Mannion stood silent in a corner as the early morning ritual took its course. He held a huge towel over his arm, with the rest of his master's clothing waiting draped over two stools.

It was still a good body, Mannion thought with quiet satisfaction, though God knows why Gresham insisted on spoiling it with water. He knew every one of the wounds that criss-crossed his master's body, could probably name and date the cause of each one. Yet they were superficial, healed. The hips were narrow and muscled, the shoulders broad and strong and the dusting of hair across the manly chest so much more satisfying than the blanket of dead seaweed so many sported there. There was no self-consciousness in Mannion's frank appraisal, any more than there would have been embarrassment in Gresham's receipt of it, had he even realised it was taking place. Mannion knew every inch of that body, had carried it on his shoulders as a child, whooping through the apple orchards. He had thrashed it once, and only once, when its seven-year-old owner had stood up imperiously and demanded that Mannion do its bidding as he was a mere servant. Years later he had washed it when its owner could only whimper, half-conscious, with the searing pain of wounds that seemed never to heal. He had fed it by hand for months, never speaking, holding the sustenance in front of the mouth for hours, sometimes forcing it down the throat when all else failed.

With no obvious signal Mannion stepped forward. Gresham held out his arms, back towards Mannion, to receive the towel he knew would be draped across his shoulders. Without turning, he spoke. 'God, man. Your breath stinks. What on God's earth were you up to last night?'

Gresham stepped out of the tub, turning to grasp the towel round his cold frame.

'My duty, young master,' replied an impassive Mannion.

'And what duty might that be?' enquired Gresham shortly, irritated that his own conversational gambit required him to speak at this time in the morning.

'Why, sir, I'm a man. And the world must be peopled.'

And that, thought Gresham, showed why one should not engage in conversation with the servants.

He allowed Mannion to dress him. He could not remember when Jane had first started to sleep the night with him, regardless of his carnal needs. He knew it was shortly after their first, frantic lovemaking. He had resented the presence in his bed, the last citadel of his private person, when instead of leaving after their coupling she had turned over and lain gently on the far side of the bed, back towards him. Her young and muscled body lay there, its curves as relaxed and bored as a seasoned choirboy's arm swinging the censor. He had willed it to move, and gone to sleep so doing, waking up to find it gone and about its business.

He did not understand how in entering her body he had let her enter his mind.

Jane had never interfered with his silent routine of early morning washing, and Mannion's attendance on it as his body-servant. The relationship between Mannion and Jane was one of life's great secrets as far as Gresham was concerned. After that first day, when she had screamed to be taken off Mannion's horse, he had not discerned so much as a flicker of disagreement between them. In his presence they were formal, even brisk, in their conversations. At times Gresham thought they used a shorthand between each other, a language he could not understand. It never crossed Gresham's mind that what united them was their love of him.

His breakfast was milk warm from the cow, brought from the fields near Islington. The bread was fresh-baked in the House's own ovens, and smelt divine. There was cheese, and strips of bacon burnt to the black as if on a campaign fire, a taste he had never lost. There was a concoction of eggs beaten up with milk and then heated over the fire until it bubbled a gentle yellow, a half-eaten beef pie. Dr Perse in Cambridge had advised him to eat a hearty breakfast above all other meals, and it suited Gresham's constitution. There were many who ate no breakfast at all.

Gresham finished his breakfast. Mannion left the room briefly and returned with one of the kitchen maids, who cleared the wooden table. There was a rustle, and the briefest sense of a fine perfume. Without turning round he sensed that Jane had entered the room. He waved a hand, motioning both to be seated.

Gresham nodded to the small beer and Mannion poured himself a tankard. He drank like a sewer, with a vast, slurping contentment that only just stopped short of the belch he clearly needed to deliver after devouring the whole tankard.

'For God's sake, man, let it go before you explode.' Mannion let loose a torrent of wind that started at his feet and came out finally from his mouth like the blast of the trumpet on Judgement Day. Jane looked at him as he rocked with the force of the expulsion, the tiniest flicker visible at the corner of her mouth. Gresham looked on with distaste, his lip curling.

'You are disgusting!' he said.

'Aye, sir. Disgusting.' Mannion poured himself another tankard and placed it cheerfully in front of him. 'Truly disgusting. But no longer thirsty, for which I thank you.'

It did not occur to Gresham to ask how many other gentlemen of his wealth and standing discussed the most important matters of the day after breakfast with their body-servant and their mistress. As for how many gentlemen were blessed with a body-servant who won both the morning's opening conversational gambits, he preferred not to think. The girl had made it clear from early on that she had a brain to match her body, one source of her capacity to irritate him more than any other person on earth. It was so much simpler to have the body as one container, and the brain in another, and far more convenient for the latter to be contained in a man. He had said so to Jane once. She had considered the proposition thoughtfully, and then hit him with the bedpan.

The upper room in which they sat was one of Gresham's favourites. Dressed with dark oak panelling that had been young in the Wars of the Roses, it had a large window and balcony overlooking the street. Already the hubbub of London was audible despite the lavish expenditure on glass in the window. As with most houses, the introduction of glass had not caused Gresham to remove the old, unwieldy shutters, which were an excellent defence. They had been thrown back as he had entered the room, revealing a watery, smoke-stained dawn.

Gresham gave a brief résumé of where he thought things stood, speaking as if to himself but knowing his silent, attentive audience. He listed the death of Will Shadwell, the meeting with Cecil, the strange task of Bacon. For Jane's sake he went over the story of the informer, the lack of any incriminating evidence on Bacon. They knew his ways, knew that in some way this careful repetition of the facts, this thinking aloud, enabled him to order things in his mind, to speed up thought. The fingers of his left hand began to drum gently on the rough wood of the table. It was a rare gesture for a man who held himself always in fierce physical control.

'I'm uneasy. There's something in the air. Unrest, trouble. I don't know. Yet the feeling is there. As it was before Essex, the same feeling. What gossip is there in the markets and the fine shops, Jane? What are they talking of in St Paul's?'

The old cathedral of St Paul's was the crumbling centre of London. Even though it had lost its steeple to lightning some years before, it still dominated London in its centre. Occupying over twelve acres at the western end of Cheapside, it would have taken Jesus two lifetimes to clear it of its moneylenders. It was here that those caught by the new plant tobacco came to buy, here where every servant in London looked for vacancies on the *siquis* door. It was here that the *gallant* casually threw back his fine cloak to reveal the satin lining, and the younger son skulked in the doorway to hide his ragged doublet. It was here that the scaffold would be erected, the men twitching their last moments in earshot of the sermon being preached from St Paul's Cross. Puritan and Papist, gentleman and cutthroat, fine lady and bawd met, mingled and, not infrequently, came to blows or copulated. The country bumpkins who increasingly flocked to London were drawn to St Paul's and drew with them the lowlife who preyed on their naivety. It was the best centre for gossip in London, exceeded only by the Court itself.

Jane went there nearly every day to visit the booksellers. She had more or less taught herself to read and had devoured the library built up by Gresham's father. The only time she had badgered him for money was to add to the library, to which he had willingly agreed. The House now had one of the finest collections of books in London. As a child she had become almost a talisman among the booksellers, the men vying with each other to attract her to their stalls. They knew her as the foundling of the fabulously wealthy and strangely reclusive Henry Gresham, and latterly his 'niece'. Yet when she made her purchase solemnly every Friday, always from a different stall, she got the best price in London, as well as the best gossip.

'Those who talk of books are full of Jonson's *Sejanus*, of course – it was played some two years ago at the Globe. It's not very good, actually, very loud and long. Martha and I went. Thorp first took it on and entered it in November last, but refused to print it, and Blount's now taken it over. Jonson's friends say it's good to his face but damn it behind his back, and he's very vexed indeed with the world!'

Jane's face lit up as she relayed the tittle-tattle of the booksellers.

'When has Ben Jonson *not* been vexed with the world?' asked Gresham with a laugh, trying to imagine a world where his friend Jonson would be at peace with anything. 'Who wouldn't be vexed, with the ghost of Kit Marlowe grinning up at you from Hell and that clever brat Shakespeare taking the crowds at the Globe? But there must be other gossip?'

'There's always gossip in the places I visit, though none concerning Bacon. Except the normal, that is,' she replied, her brow furrowed in thought.

'So what *is* the normal?' asked Gresham gently.

'The normal is that he's a man of great ambition, a man of law and a man of Parliament, who'll sell his soul to the King for preferment. His fiancée's a shrew, and he prefers the company of young men.' She giggled. 'As, so it's said, does his intended. There's no noise abroad that any of the young men are unwilling.' She looked him straight in the eye. 'It's become fashionable these days to try what's new. A courtier who wishes to be in the light of fashion will say that he needs his women, but that he loves only his young man or his boy.'

'Will they now? How very daring,' mused Gresham. 'Does this gossip talk of sedition, of treason, of plotting?'

'It talks of the King,' said Jane. 'They say the new King screams if he sights cold steel.'

It was rumoured that James's mother, Mary Queen of Scots, had witnessed her Italian lover Rizzio murdered in front of her, in some Godforsaken frozen Scottish palace, while the child that was to become James I was live in her belly. A drawn sword or dagger had ever since sent him into a fit either of madness or of swooning.

'They still talk of Raleigh, of course. Aren't people strange and fickle? The mob used to hate him when Essex was alive, but now they say Raleigh was the first Englishman to be tried and sentenced before the charge was heard.' Raleigh's trial, conducted by the irascible and lickspittle Attorney-General, Sir Edward Coke, had been a farce.

Gresham growled his response. 'Do they talk of how Raleigh was betrayed by the man who protested to be his deepest friend? By the man whose son Raleigh helped to bring up? Do they talk of Cecil so?'

'They talk more of the numbers in the King's service at Whitehall,' said Jane truthfully, 'and how they grow by the day. It's the talk of town that soon every gentleman in the country will be paid a pension to be in His Majesty's Chamber, and every working man in the whole country employed in the King's palaces. The

Scots Lords offend everyone. It's said that they stink, that to sit next to them is to get their fleas, that they've no breeding and that they rut like stags when they're not too drunk to know what they're doing.'

Gresham knew that over a thousand men worked to serve the King in his palace at Whitehall. It was a far cry from the days of Old Bess, for whom each coin she parted with was like a drop of blood.

'The merchants see what the King spends, and worry about their profits and yet more taxes.'

'There's more, though – talk of a Popish plot, now the treaty with Spain is signed. The Catholics are angry. They had high words of promise from the King, and had great hopes of his Catholic wife. It all seems to have turned sour, and the fines are bleeding some of the great families to death, they say.'

'It's not just talk, the first bit,' said Mannion. 'It's true.' He spoke with an air of total finality. 'The girls in the stews hear the pillow talk. The young merchants are full of the Government costing too much and doing too little. And they say the Papists are restless.'

'Well,' said Gresham with heavy irony, 'that has to be it, then. If the girls in the stews say it's true who can deny it?'

Jane carried on, ignoring Gresham. 'Any Papists who heard my Lord Archbishop preach his sermon at St Paul's Cross on Tuesday last will be more than restless. They'll be scared. He damned all Papists to Hell. He said the King would pour out the last drop of blood in his body to defend the Protestant faith.'

So, thought Gresham, there is anger in the country. Three angers, in fact. The anger of the Catholics, the anger of a disappointed people in their profligate King and the increasing anger of the King against the Pope's followers. Yet when had there not been anger in the country? And none of what he had heard explained Will Shadwell's death, or his intuitive sense of unease.

Jane and Mannion were waiting expectantly. He looked at Jane, his expression unfathomable. She wondered what thoughts were hidden by those dark eyes. For all that she believed she knew Gresham better than anyone except Mannion, there were times when she was frightened by her inability to read his mind and his soul. Had she known the image in his mind she would have been saddened and horrified in equal measure.

Gresham was thinking of blood. Its smell and its look. There is no smell like fresh human blood, as there is no smell like rotting human flesh. The first is warm, salty yet strangely thin, the latter so vile as to make a man retch into his boots. Gresham had seen so much blood shed, smelt so much dead flesh. It was so bad at times that even as he looked at Jane, flushed with all the fires of youth and excitement at the joy of living, he saw the blood pumping beneath her fair skin, saw her raped and mutilated by a troop of soldiers as he had seen so many young girls, smelt the rank odour of her death. Gresham saw the skull beneath the skin.

Would there be rebellion so soon again? Had people learnt nothing from the waste, the torment and the agony of the Essex rebellion, so short past? Were fine young men to be butchered on the pikes of mercenaries, their reeking guts to be torn out and shown to their wives? Were the Catholics to launch yet another blood bath in the vain hope that the country would join their rising?

'May I speak?' It was Jane, reluctant to interrupt his reverie.

'Madam,' replied Gresham with a short bow, 'the Four Furies have left for their supper after a hard night riding people down and I am temporarily without my wand of power, or a standing army, so I fear I lack the means to stop you talking.'

Jane waved her hand dismissively, as she would to a rather silly child. 'My Lord, I'm worried that you should become involved between Bacon and Cecil. There's danger in going on to any ground where there's no map. How do we know what argument might exist between the two of them? How can we know that you're not simply being used in some way to gain advantage for Cecil, perhaps at great cost to you?'

'She's right,' said Mannion. 'I'm as good a swimmer as anyone, but even I wouldn't swim certain stretches of the river, where I don't know what the current's doing.'

Gresham thought for a moment. He stood suddenly. Something had sealed in his mind as he listened. He felt a fear and an uncertainty, but now he knew where it sprang from and what he intended to do about it.

'I agree, it almost certainly is dangerous. But I won't know how dangerous until I find out more. Cecil rarely tells the whole truth when he briefs one of his men. He likes to keep his spies in the dark, just as much as he likes to keep everyone else in the dark. Men like him distrust the light.'

He walked over to Jane, pulled her up gently by her wrists and stood gazing at her.

'I see my lawyers this morning.' The vast fortune left to Gresham by his father carried title to thousands of acres of land and numerous properties, and with it continual detail of tenancies and rents. When in London Gresham's lawyer was always desperate to see him, the pile of documents that needed signing stretching from St Paul's to the river.

'After that, I visit Moll Cutpurse this evening. If there's knowledge to be had, Moll will have it. And tomorrow, we see the King.'

Jane gave a squeal of excitement, clapping her hands together.

'Have you no shame, girl, to be so carried away from your wits by an evening of over-bred drunkards and whores cavorting at the expense of the nation?'

'But, sir – I've so little chance to meet either! My life here is quite matronly and respectable. And how can a girl resist drunkenness and envy and pride and greed and gluttony and lechery and sloth and all those other *terrible* things unless she can learn to recognise them? And this is not *ordinary* sin. This is *royal* sin. It's positively my duty as a loyal subject to witness it! Where are we going? What is it His Majesty celebrates?'

Mannion grunted. 'His *Majesty* celebrates a cow farting in a field, as long as he can drink to it.' He took a swig of beer.

Jane appeared perfectly content without a social life in Gresham's absence. Such a life was hers for the asking. Money and fame mattered more than morality in the London of King James I, and the beautiful 'niece' of the wealthy and mysterious Henry Gresham would be a catch for any hostess, and a fine chase for any man in town. She never appeared tempted, but it did not mean that the young woman in her failed to enjoy hugely the opportunities when they arose.

'His Majesty, for once, is being economical. He kills two birds with one stone. The masque is both to welcome the ambassador from the Emperor, one Prince George Lodovic, and to bid farewell to the Spanish Ambassador,' announced Gresham.

Mannion had grabbed a crust which the maid had missed from the table, and was chewing on it with his few remaining teeth. 'They do say as the noble Prince' – no-one could put more loathing into the word *Prince* than Mannion – 'comes with his baggage overstuffed.'

'He brings three Earls,' piped up Jane, eagerly, 'one Baron, twenty-four gentlemen, twelve musketeers and one hundred servants. It's the talk of St Paul's,' she said, with great authority.

'Pigs feeding at the trough!' exclaimed Mannion, stuffing a remnant of Gresham's meal into his cavernous mouth, and spitting out a bit of bacon gristle. Something seemed to have got stuck in what was left of his molars. Gresham's eyes were drawn reluctantly and with extreme distaste to the sight, as Mannion dug for the stuck strand of meat with the enthusiasm of a miner sure he was on to a major seam of pure gold ore.

King James would be displeased at having to break off from his hunting. It was necessary for his health that he should hunt, he had told the Privy Council, and his health was, after all, the health of the nation. He had demanded they help take some of the burden of State affairs off his bending back. Cecil would have rubbed his hands with glee, thought Gresham, at being left to rule over the very fabric of government in the absence of the King. However, there was so much money from Spanish bribes sloshing around the Court that the departure of the Ambassador needs must require the King's return from hunting, and probably provoke the whole Court to go into mourning.

'What's the entertainment?' asked Jane.

'The entertainment will be provided by several fat Aldermen whose health will be put to great strain by the weight of jewels they and their even fatter wives will don for the evening, and a race between most members of the Houses of Lords and Commons to see who can place his face closest to the buttocks of His Royal Highness.' Gresham warmed to his theme. He started to mince round the chamber, bowing to various walls and doors with an inane smile on his face. 'The winner gets a pension, a title and the right to take first shot at Cecil, Earl of Salisbury. The loser has to try and extract an intelligent comment from Her Royal Highness the Queen Anne, but may opt to be hung, drawn and quartered instead, on the grounds that this is a sentence that at least leads to a relatively quick death.'

'My Lord!' said Jane, genuinely shocked. 'You shouldn't speak so about the King and His Queen!' She adopted the cool calm of the enigmatic beauty when at Court, but would talk for hours afterwards when she returned home about who had been wearing what and been seen speaking to whom. Gresham had once taxed her with her love of everything royal, pointing out some of the less savoury features of King James I of All England.

'It's perfectly possible, my Lord,' she had replied primly, 'for the institution to be divine whilst its agents on earth are merely human.'

Gresham looked at the eager sparkle in her eyes, and relented. At least she was not being distant, aloof and dignified, which he hated.

'I'm given to understand that His Majesty has commanded a masque from your good friends Ben Jonson and Inigo Jones, in which the virtues of Faith, Hope and Charity will appear to welcome Prince

Lodovic, and bid farewell to the Spanish Ambassador. We go because Sir Francis Bacon will be a guest – a guest of honour, in fact, reading a pretty speech of welcome from the House of Commons. It's at Whitehall, of course. I remember you told me you had a most commanding book of sermons to read, and so informed the Lord Chamberlain that I'd be going alone . . .'

'Sir!' Jane shrieked in anguish, before the lights dancing behind his eyes told her the truth.

Gresham had obtained details of all Bacon's engagements by bribing his clerk. A word to one of the Gentlemen of the Bedchamber and an invitation to Gresham had been immediately forthcoming. It gave Gresham a grim satisfaction that he had no need to beg an invitation from Cecil. As a major landowner and the patron of what many considered to be Cambridge's leading College, and as a known servant of the Crown for many years past, Gresham had no need of such help.

'Do I do gracious, or do I do alluring?' asked Jane.

'You "do" whatever will preserve and protect *my* honour,' said Gresham, 'which is a far more important thing than *your* female vanity. However, I'll gracefully accept as my due any information you might come across in the course of the evening.'

He had taken Jane with him as his niece to a levée some years earlier and been incensed by her flirting with a young nobleman. He had been about to box her ears when she had poured out to him a torrent of secrets so damaging to the young nobleman's father that twenty full purses would not have bought the information.

'Weren't you ashamed?' he asked, part in horror, part in amazement at the skill with which the little vixen had stripped the fool of his secrets.

'Why?' she had asked, with total sincerity. 'I'm more worried about conceiving a baby than I am about being bedded by one, and anyway I do it for you.' She did, Gresham had realised. This was a woman who far preferred pitting herself against a man in the search for secrets to preparing a fine capon for supper, or supervising the making of the season's preserves. Her *bête noire* was sewing.

Since then he had used her whenever it could be safely done.

Gresham stood up and paced the room. 'Tell me, who goes out with you on your errands to St Paul's?'

'It's usually young Will. He secretly hopes to marry me and he defends my honour . . .'

'No jesting.' The swooping, instant change of mood – like a hawk coming out from behind the sun, Mannion had commented – was upon him, and it froze the air. 'From now onwards you'll take three men with you, two in company, one a way behind. Make one of them Harry.'

Harry had seen service abroad, and been a gunner on one of the ships that had fired so many shots with so very few hits against the vast galleons of the Spanish. He was tough, very strong and totally ruthless.

'As you wish.' Jane curtseyed to Gresham, a troubled look on her face. 'Am I permitted to know why these extra precautions are necessary?'

Because, thought Gresham, *I have let happen what I vowed would never take place. I have fallen in love with you. You are wanton, and then you are saintly, you are strong and hard and then the softest voice I know, you are fierce in one moment and vulnerable in the next, you fight to the bitter end yet you are defenceless. I do not understand you, though I know you in bed, and I know that when I am with you my heart beats faster and my life has an extra colour in its palette. You have become precious to me, and that gives power over me to any person who decides to take you and hold you and hurt you. You could be held and used against me, young miss.*

'Whatever trail it is that Cecil's setting me on it'll carry danger. I can't believe other than that Will Shadwell was on his way to see me in Cambridge, and someone cared enough to kill him. Does that damned bead mean anything? Maybe Will had come across something the Catholics want hidden, or perhaps even Bacon is considering a public return to Rome. I must assume there's a link, even if I don't know what it is.'

'Well,' said Jane, 'Will Shadwell certainly wasn't the type to be coming to Cambridge to sign up for a degree.'

'Cease your nonsense,' said Gresham, caught unawares by her flippancy and the image of Will Shadwell in undergraduate gown and cap. He felt himself starting to sound pompous, and so switched tone, knowing it would annoy her. 'You, mistress, are an additional lure of great value to an enemy. My honour wouldn't permit your being taken and held by an enemy. Were I to be sidetracked by having to extract you from some den of thieves I would lose what little scent I might have followed. It would be most inconvenient.'

Jane stood up. 'Thank you, my Lord. It is good to know.' Her tone would have frozen the River Thames in midsummer. 'A poor thing such as me must never be an *inconvenience*.' She left most of the hinges still on the door.

Gresham grinned at Mannion. 'Call her back, will you, if the stairway's still standing.'

It took her longer than was necessary to reappear.

'I hadn't realised that it was *convenient* for me to appear before you, my Lord. Is it *convenient* that I stand, or would it be more *convenient* for me to kneel at your feet?' No arrow about to be released from the bow quivered with more hidden tension, or stood up straighter and more tall.

My God, thought Gresham, *you would fight God and Lucifer together if they made friends again and joined forces against you!*

Gresham, enjoying his rudeness, pointed a finger at her. 'Will you sit down, you stupid wench, and be silent?'

Jane planted her arms akimbo, looked him full in the face with a fire that beat the burning of Gwent. 'Yes, *sir*, I will sit down, if that be your will. No, *sir*, I am not stupid, nor am I a wench, and no, sir, *I will not be silent!*'

'God's blood!' barked Gresham. 'Am I to be served by an old man who thinks of nothing but beer and young whores, and a

71

young wanton with a voice like a fishwife and a temper to match, who throws a fit every time she is challenged by her master?'

Mannion lacked the education to recognise a rhetorical question, so answered it, thoughtfully. 'Aye, sir. I reckon you are.'

There was a moment of frozen silence, then Gresham, Mannion and Jane burst out into peals of laughter.

Thomas Percy was sulking. It was nothing new.

'I swear the man was using loaded dice. Three sixes in a row, would you believe? I challenged him, but the fool of a landlord came between us and made us go outside.'

Percy was a brilliant swordsman, not perhaps the match of Jack Wright, but nearly so. The difference was that Jack Wright fought to win, with a dark intensity that was as terrifying as his swift movements. Percy enjoyed winging his man, cutting him here and there, taunting him, before moving in for the kill.

'When we got through the crowd, the bastard made a run for it! Coward! Who would believe it?'

'He must have heard of your prowess, cousin. Few men would stand against Thomas Percy with a blade in his hand!' It was Catesby, silky-smooth in voice, sitting at the head of the table where the plotters had dined.

Percy glanced suspiciously at Catesby, looking for mockery. He found none in the bland assurance of Catesby's eyes, and brought out a stained cloth with which he wiped the dripping sweat off his brow. Percy sweated like a pig, or like the inside of glass on a drenching rainy day.

Jack Wright, seated as always at the rear of the room, made one of his rare contributions. He spoke slowly, as if measuring every word: 'What of your peasants and their lawsuit?'

'Animals! Animals!' Percy spluttered into renewed anger, grabbing his tankard and spilling half its contents as he rammed the ale down his throat. Wright glanced at Catesby, the merest hint of a grin on his dour features. Catesby raised an eyebrow. Stirring Percy into anger was so easy that it had almost ceased to be amusing. Men's hair had turned white with fear. Had a lifetime of anger turned Percy's hair so white?

'Am I to let them lie in their hovels all hours of the day and night and pay no rent? How much trust would my Earl of Northumberland have in such a member of his family were I to leave them to stink and rot and pay no rent?'

'Dead men pay no rent . . .' It was Tom Wintour who spoke, Tom who had been in on the conspiracy from the start. A small, dark, wiry man, his restless wit was at odds with the glum pessimism of his elder brother. Robert Wintour had been recruited only recently, following again his younger brother but doing so with markedly little enthusiasm. Well, thought Tom, that was nothing new. He had long ago accepted that of the Wintour brothers he would have to generate the energy for both of them.

'Dead be damned!' Percy was warming to his theme, and never failed to rise to Tom Wintour's wit. 'There was no chance of that! We tickled them a little, that was all. There was a time when men would have taken it as their due, stout men who could take their punishment and not go whining to the law!'

And Percy's men had tickled their wives and daughters, by all accounts, with thirty of the tenants complaining direct to the Earl of Northumberland that his Constable and land agent had attacked them for rent they had already paid.

'And what of it, Robin?' Percy dropped into the familiar name, the one Catesby's friends used. 'Why must I go at my tenants like a dog after a hare? You know why! I need their miserable money! Must I be banker to this conspiracy, as well as its only link to the Court and all else?' Percy flung the question out like a spear, and already the thick sheen of sweat had formed over his whole face. Dark stains were visible under the arms of his shirt, his doublet cast carelessly over a nearby chair, and the same dark stains were on his hose over the cleft of his buttocks, and up his shirt along the line of his back.

Catesby took the angry question with a smile, waving his hand as if to say thank you. Far less of Thomas Percy's money had gone to swell the coffers of the plotters than Percy liked people to think, but he had been asked for, and had given, good coin. If this angry, self-serving torrent of words was the price Catesby had to pay for Percy's money then it was a price he was willing to pay.

'You've done well,' said Catesby placatingly, 'and all of us know it. We're grateful, truly grateful . . .'

The Duck and Drake in the Strand was rapidly becoming one of London's most fashionable taverns, and had long been a favoured ground for the conspirators to meet. It was convenient for Catesby, who had lodgings only a few doors away. Percy subsided into a grumble. It would flare up again soon, Catesby knew. He could write the speech.

Was Thomas Percy not kinsman to the mighty Earl of Northumberland, the patron who had appointed him Constable of Alnwick Castle, the Percy stronghold in Northumberland? Had not the great Catholic Earl entrusted Thomas Percy above all others to act as his emissary to the upstart James VI of Scotland, offering the support of English Catholics to the Scottish King in exchange for simple tolerance of their faith? Had not Percy won the support of the King for the Catholic cause, only to have it wrenched away from him by that Anti-Christ Robert Cecil, the poison in the ear of the new monarch? Had not a month past that same Thomas Percy been made Gentleman Pensioner to King James I, allowing that same Thomas Percy access to the King of All England? Was it not Thomas Percy who had negotiated the rent of the house adjacent to the House of Lords from John Whynniard and Henry Ferrers, the house from whence a tunnel could be dug to undermine the very fabric of England's Government? Catesby's own house in Lambeth was almost opposite, for all the use he had been. It was Percy's power, influence and charm that had closed the deal, Percy would point out, causing Whynniard and the Catholic Ferrers to look the other way.

74

Thomas Percy was a powerful man, thought Catesby, and a useful one, but flawed to his very centre. The anger that seemed to flare continually at the core of his being, anger against his tenants, against the invidious Cecil, against his lot in life, fuelled him but at the same time clouded his judgement. Was he noble-born? Percy's claim to be a member of Northumberland's family was at best tenuous. Yet the real problem was that of all the five original conspirators, Percy was the only one fighting for himself.

Catesby knew he was not fighting for himself. He was fighting for God. From as early as he could remember he had fallen in love with the Mass. The flickering candlelight, the language that resounded to the pit of one's brain, the transcendental union with a spirit higher and greater than that of man – even as a child his soul had risen to the Mass as a flower reaches towards the sun. He had recognised the joy of that faith, but seen the savage surgery it had caused on the body and mind of his father and mother. When he was a mere eight years of age he had seen his father tried in the Star Chamber for housing a Jesuit Father. Robert had known that Father, a foul-smelling man who had smiled all over the young Robert until the evening when he had plunged his hand down the boy's front and fondled his private parts. We do this for Jesus, the Father had said, his thumb and fingers working away. And there is more we can do for Jesus. And for this man my father is facing imprisonment and execution, thought the young Robert. He screamed and punched, even then strong for his age, and bloodied the priest's nose.

The priest had gone soon thereafter, spirited away as they always were. The humiliation, the fierce and burning bitterness, had lasted for years. Catesby had been driven to be the best at everything he had done, driven by the memory of a lost father whose suffering had soured his soul, a father whose suffering was betrayed by those for whom he suffered. Yet the meeting with his Catherine had shown him his true course. He had worshipped her from the first moment they met. When on his wedding night he had joined with her, her

75

giggling turning first to a panting and then to a gasping and then to a scream of pleasure, he had known true salvation. She was the most beautiful, the most lovely, the most heavenly thing that had ever happened to him. Despite his dashing good looks and his charm, it was his virginity that he lost to Catherine on that night. As did so many men, he gave his soul as well to the first woman who opened her legs for him.

He had been lulled by the love of the flesh, human flesh, not the flesh of Christ Our Lord. He had gone as far as to flout the true religion, seduced by his new, human love into denying Divine love. True, he had continued to hide and to host a succession of Jesuit priests, part in honour of his parents, part in honour of many of those priests who truly placed the souls of their parishioners above all worldly concerns. He appeared less and less at Mass, and had his first son Robert baptised as an Anglican, to the scandal of the Catholic community and his father's friends.

'And do I have to settle the score for this as for everything else?'

Percy was being truculent over the bill, and his tone penetrated Catesby's inward pattern of thought.

'No fear of that, Thomas,' said Catesby. 'Here – take it from my purse, and my thanks for your company along with it.' He tossed the smaller of the two purses he carried so that it landed with a solid thump on the trestle. Percy could have picked it up, but he sniffed and turned away, returning to talk at Jack Wright, who nodded every few sentences but said nothing. It was left to Tom Wintour, reliable and ever-restless, to take it, unbar the door and go to find the landlord.

Then his world had collapsed, Catesby remembered, only half deflected by Percy's intrusion. Robert his son, on whom he and his wife doted, died suddenly, to be followed by Catesby's father and then by his lovely, his adorable Catherine herself. He had worn mourning on his body, yet it was his soul that was truly black in shock. It was a punishment from God, retribution for his turning away from the True Faith.

76

They did not realise it, any of the others, but in seeking to destroy the Government of England, the dashing and charismatic Robert Catesby was saying sorry to God and the True Faith.

Percy was droning on still, petulant, like a spoilt child denied a sweetmeat. In a month or two he would probably be dead, as they all would be dead. Yet by their death they would have become martyrs to the Faith, opening the floodgates that would allow Christ to reign again in England. A faint smile played on the face of Robert Catesby as he contemplated the thought. Christ had died so that all of humankind could be saved. What did a few lives matter if by their death England was allowed to live again?

They were in the library of the House, the room where Gresham knew he was most likely to find Jane once her domestic duties were over.

'What new people have you taken on in these past three months?' Gresham asked.

'Two, I think – a kitchen maid and a porter. Why do you ask, sir?'

'Someone must have been watching Will Shadwell. There must be a chance, therefore, that someone is watching his master. The best place to keep watch on a man is from inside his own house . . . Walsingham had a bribed servant in every nobleman's house in London.'

'Sir!' Jane exploded. 'I'd trust every man and woman of them with my life!'

'Jane, they worship you, God knows why – *but there's never any servant on God's earth who's free from sin!* You must learn. I'm truly sorry. It's a hard lesson. *Trust no-one.* Wasn't Judas Jesus's most favoured disciple, and what's a disciple but a servant? In any event, they probably risk too much by trying for someone already in employment. No, the easiest way would be to plant a rotten flower in this garden of rest. What of the two new people?'

'One's a distant cousin of Martha's. She's a lovely girl, about whom I've had to have strong words with your body-servant.' She gazed darkly at Mannion, who shrugged his shoulders as if to ask what a venerable innocent such as he should have to do with a young girl. 'He may pay his dues to your body, my Lord, but he'll keep away from those bodies over which I've charge and care. In any event, she's no spy. She lacks the brains, poor thing, apart from anything else.

'The other's a Northumbrian. He says he's seen service at sea. He comes with an excellent testimonial from my Earl of Northumberland's houses. He's a strong worker. I hired him above the others because he plays the lute.'

Gresham had the extravagant number of five musicians in his permanent employ, who played for him every evening he was in the House. Though Gresham hated public entertaining it was politic for him to drag himself to lay on five or six events a year, the taste and expense of which made them highlights of London's social calendar. For such events his band would be augmented by other musicians. It made for better music if there were such already in the employ of the House, if only through it allowing more of the practice which Gresham knew was essential for any good musician. The Cook played a merry flute, if a little too merry for Gresham's private ear of an evening, but more than good enough for a raucous evening where the finer points of intonation would never be heard by the guests.

'Was he with us when my room was gone through?' The room Gresham used as a study had been carefully searched one night some months ago. Only someone with an intimate knowledge of his papers would have spotted that a search had ever taken place.

'It happened on the first night he was with us,' Jane responded, with a frown.

'Didn't that make you suspicious?'

'Three houses had windows broken that night, on top storeys, including our own. There was a roofwalker about that night, for certain. It never crossed my mind to think that your intruder was anything other than such a man, on the look-out for whatever he might find.'

The houses crowding in on each other in London's streets meant that the roofs of even the finest properties often nearly touched each other. For the brave and the foolhardy, and for many thieves, there were roads across the roofs and into the houses more clearly laid out than the roadways beneath.

Gresham turned to Mannion.

'Bring this new man to me, in a half-hour. Send him to the dressing room, off the back balcony.'

'Do you want me there?' Jane asked.

'I think we're best left to do the business alone,' said Gresham. This time Jane took no offence.

They moved to the rear of the house, facing the river. Gresham's father had built a second great Hall at the back, with one of the finest balconies in London overlooking the Thames. A 'cut' from the main river allowed boats to dock at the House's own jetty. The room they chose to interview the new servant was just off the balcony, small and framed in brick and timber.

There was a clumping up the stairs, and Mannion ushered in the new man. He was tall, well-built and powerful, some thirty-five years old with a mop of reddish hair. There was no change in Gresham's expression as he greeted him.

'Good morning. Welcome to the House. You're pleased with your new post?'

If the man, Sam Fogarty as he had given his name, felt any surprise at this affable expression of interest from his master, he did not show it. He spoke confidently, looking Gresham in the eye. The accent was thick as sewage, but comprehensible.

'I'm well pleased, sir, to be in your Worship's service. It's the envy of London among servingmen to work in such a place.'

Gresham nodded to Mannion, who drew silently closer.

'Tell me, Sam, how long have you worked for my Lord Cecil?'

79

'Cecil, sir?' To his credit, Sam's face hardly blanched. 'I've never worked for Lord Cecil. I came here from the north . . .'

He did not hear the blow coming from Mannion, but merely saw his world explode into stars and an instantaneous moment of blinding pain.

When he came to, minutes later, his feet were tightly trussed with stout cord, and his arms loosely tied behind his back. The top half of his body was extended over the opened trap door, a black hole from which a foul smell blew into the room.

'One push from Mannion,' said Gresham carefully, coming round from behind the table at which he had sat with a goblet of wine in his hand, 'and you'll descend that chute head-first. It's brick-lined. It descends the height of the House, with enough curves in it to break your head to pulp. At the bottom is an old well. It's been spoilt by foul water from the river creeping in. We no longer use it for water. As far as we know there's no exit to the river. Or to anywhere else. Those who survive the descent splash around for as long as they have breath and then drown. We've heard them for a day or more, but they always fall silent. Now tell me, how long have you worked for Lord Cecil?'

Sam's head was aflame, his gut sick with the foul stench of rotting flesh that swept up from the black depths of the trap door.

'I know of no work for Lord Cecil . . .'

Mannion pushed his body an inch or two closer to the drop.

Sam screamed.

'You see,' Gresham responded conversationally, 'I remember faces. I remember being ushered out through the servants' hall of his Lordship's house some two . . . or was it three? . . . years ago. And you were there, Master Sam, with your red mop, holding court to most of the kitchen wenches. I recognised you as you walked through the door. Your voice, as much as your hair and face. You were shouting to the wenches, back then, telling them a bad joke as I recollect . . .'

Gresham grabbed the man's hair and pulled his head back,

looking into his fear-crazed eyes. 'Now tell me, Sam Redmop, for the last time. *How long have you worked for Lord Cecil?*'

'Sir . . . my. Lord . . .' Suddenly, the man's whole body sagged. 'Spare me. Spare me. Four years. No more. Four years only.'

'Break his leg. The left one.'

The body writhed in protest. The crack was sickening as Mannion's club smashed the bone into a clean break. Sam screamed again.

Mannion pulled the body back from the abyss and flung the trap door shut, bolting it securely. He turned then to the writhing and gasping body, cut loose the cord around its legs and with a practised efficiency set splints around the twisted limb.

Sam's body could only flutter now, on the edge of unconsciousness. Gresham yanked his head round, more gently this time.

'We'll pay for a surgeon to look to your wound. You'll walk again, and walk as good as ever you did if you're careful. The pain you'll suffer is your payment for daring to seek to spy on Henry Gresham. No one spies on Henry Gresham. No one enters his household as a spy.

'You'll be held, in a secret place, until you can walk. You'll be given money, enough to get you back to Northumberland, and a little more. After that, it's up to you. Your Lord Cecil will be told that you came to visit the House, and that you suffered an accident in which you were most unfortunately drowned. As far as Cecil is concerned you'll be dead. If he hears of your existence, he'll assume you've deceived him and turned to my service, and he'll kill you. I suggest a new name and a new livelihood. The old one is truly dead.'

Gresham let the head drop, and turned away. He stopped by the door. 'It's not good to seek to betray Henry Gresham. Remember my mercy in sparing your life and sending you on your way.'

He left, closing the door quietly behind him. Two porters entered and carried out the groaning, semi-conscious figure. Mannion growled a sentence of instruction at them. They nodded.

Mannion found Gresham in the Minstrels' Gallery of the Great Hall.

'Is it wise to declare war on Cecil?' he asked bluntly. 'Do you intend to send such a message to him?'

'Old friend, do you think I'm a fool?'

'Sometimes.'

'Well, rest assured. Master Sam believes his death has been announced to Cecil. That makes him truly a dead man if he seeks to return to Cecil's service. As for me, I'll send no message to Lord Cecil. Far better that he should wait and wonder what's happened to his spy, see his man vanish into silence. Let's keep his Lordship guessing, old man. And whilst we're so doing, let's find out what's truly happening out there. And why Lord Cecil wants a spy in my house. He keeps me guessing about Bacon. Now I shall keep him guessing about his spy.'

Mannion pondered this for a moment. 'Who'll tell your mistress that we hired a Judas?'

'I'll tell her. It wasn't her fault. It's only by chance I was able to spot him as what he was. Just as important, will you help me to tell Cook and your mistress why I ordered two rotting sides of beef?'

The trap door over which Sam had been suspended led to no well. It was a service chute, a straight drop to the ground floor where goods delivered from the river could be hoisted up to the top storeys of the House. A shutter at the bottom deprived it of light when closed. Two decaying sides of beef suspended on a shelf feet below the trap door provided the stench of the charnel house that so fixed the minds of those suspended above it.

A short distance away down the Strand, Robert Catesby's party was also breaking up, Thomas Percy still bleating to whoever would listen how hard done by he was.

Catesby marvelled at his own sense of relaxation, seeing and almost tasting the fear on the skin of the others. Even the delay in convening Parliament – it would not assemble now until

November 5th – could be handled. The cursed powder would be subject to its interminable decay. The risk of a chance discovery in the cellar, or drink or pillow talk from one of the conspirators revealing more than was wise, was ever-present and grew with each extra day. Yet they had come this far. They would prepare as well for November 5th as they had for October 3rd. God would protect them.

He began to hum the words from his favourite song of the moment:

> 'Thou art my King, O God . . .'

It had a springy, firm rhythm and a quick tempo, one of Tom Campion's best, he thought.

> 'Through Thee will we
> Overthrow our enemies
> And in Thy Name
> I will tread them down.
> I will tread them down . . .'

Tom Wintour paused as he left the tavern. It had been a week or more since he had had a woman. The whores at The Duck and Drake were of the best kind, aimed at the fashionable clientele of the tavern. Even at this hour a handful were on duty, dressed like Court ladies. Why not, he thought, as his roving eye caught the glance of a particularly fine girl dressed in deep red. Why not? She was one of Moll Cutpurse's girls, he knew, and Moll's girls were the best there were.

CHAPTER 4

Gresham slipped out of the side gate of the House in the early evening. His doublet was worn and stitched in two areas, his hose washed out and his cloak threadbare at the edges. It was more and more difficult for him to act as an unknown in the city, or in Cambridge, but his change into the clothing of a gentleman fallen on hard times was not disguise, but caution. Where he was going, fine clothes were a call to robbery as well as a call to attention, and Gresham wished for neither. His sword hid its fine steel under a plain hilt and a weather-beaten scabbard. Behind him came Mannion, dressed in a rough jerkin.

'We walk,' he announced firmly to his rather sour-looking body-servant. 'You're getting too fat, and you need the exercise.' If Mannion muttered something under his breath, Gresham chose not to hear it.

It would have been far easier by boat, using the House's own vessels, the single bank manned by the vast-chested George, or even the magnificent four-bank of semi-regal splendour. Yet Gresham preferred to walk, despite the filth of the streets and the appalling press of the crowds. A restlessness came over him at times which could only be released by exercise, and in this instance there was the extra dimension of a need to feel in touch with the life and blood of the sprawling and corrupt city. And, of course, it allowed him to be rude to Mannion.

London was at its noisiest. The lawyers flushed out from Westminster were there in force, heading back into the City along the Strand, soberly dressed and bent forward to hear the muttered protestations of their clients. It was a long walk, from the Strand to Fleet Street, entering the City at Ludgate and skirting St Paul's. From Watling Street and Candlewick Street they turned right to cross London Bridge, joining the throng of citizens heading to Southwark for the playhouses.

They passed the stalls of the puppeteers in Fleet Street, each trying to shout above the din of the colliers, the chimney sweeps and the incessant din of the barrel-makers and every other worker who seemed to need a hammer above all other tools. The fresh-water carriers with their yokes and double wooden buckets, the strangely brownish water giving more than a hint of the River, the oyster sellers and the orange sellers all yelled their wares into the summer day.

They crossed London Bridge, its ancient piers supporting the half-timbered shops and residences that made it one of the talking points of Europe. Gresham eyed the pitted and mouldering stone, feeling the bridge shudder beneath his feet, wondering as he always did how much longer it could survive the neglect of its foundations and the thundering torrent of the Thames.

The Dagger in Southwark was Moll's place of business, before the magistrates or her creditors forced a change to another den. A significant portion of London's underworld was gathered there, nursing their sore heads. The assembled mass was one of the most unattractive sights he had ever seen, thought Gresham, a collection of rats and wolves in human form. He gave the merest nod to several with whom he had worked in the past. Gresham was ushered into the inner den of Moll, past three of the burliest men in London, all nursing vast cudgels.

'Hello, Mary Frith,' said Gresham, his face alight with mirth at the figure before him.

At first sight, it was not a woman at all who met their gaze. Dressed in doublet and hose, with hair cut short, Moll Cutpurse looked for all the world like a man, ensconced on a stool, legs set fairly apart and a brimming tankard of ale in her hand. The smoking pipe clenched firmly between her teeth added to the impression of a lad-about-town, determined to enjoy the day and the night as if it were his last. Only on closer examination did the smoothness of her skin and the twin bulges beneath her doublet become apparent.

'Mary Frith! You insolent vagabond, you spittle of Bedlam!' The figure wreathed in smoke put her stool forward on to three legs, where previously it had been resting back on two, and grinned in equal measure at Henry Gresham. 'Mary Frith died years ago, as any true bastard knows full well.'

Henry Gresham, a true bastard, accepted Moll's greeting with a low bow.

'Bastard as I am,' he replied, 'I salute an even greater bitch, be it Mary Frith or Moll Cutpurse!'

'You whoremonger!' she said joyfully, rising up from her stool and moving round the table to greet him. 'You come to me now for news, when you used to come within me! Am I so worn out as no longer to excite your fancy?'

'Madam,' said Gresham, bowing even lower, 'I'm old and weary, starved in my bones, a mere dried-out husk of the man I used to be. I can admire your beauty from afar . . .' he stepped back and looked with admiration at the trim figure hidden beneath the man's clothes, '. . . but, alas, it needs a young man to sire a beauty with so much youth still in her!'

Moll sat down on the table edge, stuck out her feet and took a huge draught of ale. Licking her red lips, she eyed Gresham up and down appreciatively.

'You always were a liar, Henry Gresham, and I like that in a man. You're none of your penny-pinching, arse-grabbing kind of liar. You,' she said as she poked him with the end of her clay pipe, 'you lie like the Devil himself, and take delight in it. For that, I'll even forgive you the bruises! And you always did have a body from Heaven, even if your mind was from Hell.'

Moll was fun enough to deal with and to lie with, but her evil temper was infamous, her mood swings greater than the tide on Dover beach, and she had had men, and women, murdered for a twopenny debt. She was one of the most dangerous people Gresham had ever known. She ran more brothels and stews than anyone except the Bishop of London, offered more watered-down wine and beer to tavern-goers and fenced for half the vagabonds in London. She defied authority, even to the extent of appearing on stage in front of a cheering full house at The Swan to recite bawdy ballads and sing songs that a sailor would blanch at. She had been arrested more times than she had eaten dinners, always bribing herself out of trouble with the seemingly endless money at her disposal.

'Enough of this babbling.' Moll bored very easily. 'You've no more need of poor Moll and her like in the old way, even if I hadn't become a respectable businessman, which I have. And I hear you have someone to keep your bed warm at night, so what is it you intend to rob a maid of instead?'

'I've never robbed you of anything you weren't hot to give, Moll Cutpurse,' said Gresham firmly, 'and for anything else I've taken you've received good coin in exchange. Enough of this babbling, indeed – yours and my own. The business is simple. What do you know that I should know?'

Moll slumped down behind the table, signalled Mannion to take a seat and took another vast gulp from her flagon, motioning irritably for it to be replenished by one of the villains standing guard over the door. He took it in his huge paw, filled it from a nearby barrel and gave it back to her. She looked moodily at Gresham.

'You're the fine one, Henry Gresham, aren't you? The others, they come to me with threats or with flattery, and they come to ask me a question. Where's the purse with seven angels in it stolen from my friend in St Paul's gone to, Moll?' With each question she adopted a different, whining tone. 'Find me a girl, Moll, a nice clean girl. Find me a boy, Moll, a nice clean boy. Oh Moll, my cousin's inherited a pretty penny in plate and keeps it in his house, and it should be mine, Moll, it should be mine . . . I need to throw the dice for high stakes, Moll, or play the cards, and where are the best games to be had, Moll . . . I need a woman who'll do it *this* way, I need a woman who'll do it *that* way, I need a woman who'll do it in ways I haven't imagined . . . so many questions, so many crimes, so many deceivers. Yet you . . . you Devil incarnate . . . *you* ask the one question to which I've to give all the answers.'

Moll got up suddenly, stuck her thumbs in her belt and walked over to the window.

'I know you might as well stick your fine head up a cow's arse as gain any joy from the man Bacon. Neither you, nor the Privy Council nor God in his Heaven will ever prove anything against him that matters a fart.'

It was pointless to ask Moll where her information came from, or which of the many men Gresham had tasked with news of Bacon had reported back to her. There was hardly a major household in London where one or more of the servants was not in her employ, information being as valuable a commodity as gold or women. Gresham knew that on occasions in the past Cecil had used her as an informant – it had been the cause of their first meeting.

'So what else do you know that I should know?'

'Had you come before tonight, I would've had little more to answer. I don't know why you've been set on a goose chase. Maybe there are those who want you set on a far road. But there's something brewing nearer to home, I reckon. Something more in your line of business . . . how much will you pay, for other news, Henry Gresham?'

'A fair price.'

'Then you'd better meet a girl.' Moll gestured to one of the human tree trunks on guard. 'Wake up Nell from her groanings and bring her here – fast!'

A red-cheeked young girl with the look of being fresh up from the country was brought into the room. She had been crying, and there was a livid bruise down most of one side of her face and stains on the extravagant red dress she wore, all crumpled now. She limped, clutching her left hip with every faltering step she took.

'Yes, mistress, what is it, mistress?' the girl said, with fear in her eyes.

'See this man?' said Moll, gesturing to Gresham.

'Yes, ma'am.'

'Well, forget you ever saw him. Before you do, tell him the story of last night. Go on, girl. Do it.'

'It were . . . I was . . . I was downstairs when this man cum in. I know'd him from before, two, mebbe three times. He were quiet, but a swaggerer at the same time, if ye takes my meanin'. We went upstairs, and we did it, and after, as he was coming out of the room and before I was proper dressed or anything, this other man comes out of the other room and knocks into my man, sort of . . . it were an accident, I know for sure, there's no light up there hardly at all and . . .'

'Get on with it, you stupid slut!' growled Moll.

'Well, before you can say a word my man, the one I been with, he has his sword out and he's fightin' this other man. This other man, he run back into my room and I start screamin' an' my man he turns an' clouts me one on the side of the head with the handy bit of his sword an' I goes down screamin' an' he kicks at me to shut me up an' then this other man he trips on his sword . . .' The girl started to blubber and to wail again, dabbing at her eyes. '. . . an' the point of his bloody sword goes in the side o' my arse, it does, real hard and deep, an' it hurts and hurts an' there's a mark there now for life, it be, for life . . .'

'It'll be a short life, that's for sure, girl, if you carry on like that,' said Moll. 'Tell the gentleman here what your man said while he was riding you.'

'Well, sir,' said the tearful Nell, 'he were rough with me, very rough indeed, an' I says, "Now, sir, can you not get as much pleasure by being a little more gentle with a poor girl?" and he says, goin' at it even 'arder, "If I bain't be gentle with that damn'd King and his rotten crew I bain't be gentle with you, girl!"'

Gresham tossed a coin to the girl, which she caught with practised ease, even though he knew it would be taken from her as soon as she left the room. She gave a faint smile to Gresham, and a pleading look towards Moll. She ignored it, motioning the girl to leave.

'That's all?' said Gresham.

'No, not all,' said Moll. 'The man's name is Tom Wintour.'

The name triggered the memory of the miserable-looking man in the tavern. Robert Wintour, Tom Wintour's brother.

'He nearly killed the other man and lost me a good girl for a while, so I was less than well pleased. I had him cornered by three of the lads and taken out round the back, to teach him a lesson, as you do. He caught one of the lads with a dagger he'd hidden on him, and it got serious. He was screaming at my lads something about this not happening to him, he'd God's business to do. It was so bad I came running myself. Before I could get there this Wintour catches one of my men in the neck, dives between the other two and gets clean away. It's bad for business, all round. One of my men might die. There should be no man who beats my ruffians. It's not good for my honour, you understand. The other man he went for on the night has a bad wound and won't walk straight again. And that's bad for custom. Keep it clean, keep it quiet.'

Robert Wintour. Tom Wintour. Wintour of Huddington Court. Gresham remembered now, as it all fell into place. The western Marches were a terrible area for the old religion, defying London to take its Catholicism away from it. He had been sent to enquire into one particularly crusty old Catholic, a Sir John Talbot, heir to the Earldom of Shrewsbury. It was feared he was plotting a rebellion. He was harmless, as it had happened, a fact which had not stopped the Government from locking him up on and off for over twenty years. Gresham had become fascinated by the network of blood relations, marriages and alliances which criss-crossed the great Catholic families of the area, binding them tight together like the finest cloth. Talbot's daughter had married Robert Wintour, Gresham now remembered. Tom Wintour was the younger brother, but the brains of the family. Their house of Huddington Court was rumoured to be riddled with more priest-holes than the Vatican.

'So a swaggerer beats a whore and wounds some men, and damns the King and talks about God's business . . . it's not much, Moll.'

'Not much for you, Henry Gresham, who has his inheritance, and no need to earn a daily crust by the sweat of his brow. Moll here has to work for his living.'

Gresham noted Moll's use of the word 'his' to describe herself. It was a trick she only fell into when she was at her most serious, or her most dangerous.

'Yet there is more,' she carried on. 'Does the name Catesby mean anything to you? Jack Wright? Kit Wright?'

The names echoed somewhere in the channels of Gresham's brain. Catesby . . . a handsome young man on the ill-fated march through London of Essex's supporters, fighting with useless courage as the supporters of the Crown closed in on him . . .

'Minnows that once swam in the great pond of the Earl of Essex?'

'Fools enough to march through the streets of London trying to rouse support for the Prince of Fools, when every girl in town could've told them it would fail!' replied Moll.

'What have these small fry to do with Tom Wintour?'

'A lot to do with Tom Wintour, judging by the number of times they all of them hire a private room a stone's throw away from you in the Strand.'

'And what is to stop a group of friends meeting for a good supper

91

to reminisce over old times and how they nearly overthrew good Queen Bess?' said Gresham, playing Devil's advocate.

'With a priest in the next room to say Mass, and locked doors, and much swearing of oaths? And with young Thomas Percy as thick as a thief with the whole sorry crew?'

The Earl of Northumberland, leader of a significant portion of English Catholics, had recommended himself to Gresham by setting himself up as a firm opponent of Cecil and vilifying the stunted creature, decorously, at every opportunity. As ever, Northumberland's action revealed the capacity of the English Catholics to always back a loser. Thomas Percy Gresham remembered as a runt of a man who claimed more blood links with Northumberland than most thought he was heir to, and who for some inconsiderable reason Northumberland had apparently made steward of Alnwick Castle, the dripping pile of masonry hung on the bleak Northumbrian coast.

'Does Cecil know of this?'

Moll turned to her tankard, discomfited. 'I doubt it. And certainly not from me, if he does. Cecil and I are . . . not dealing with each other, as things stand.'

'Why, Moll,' said Gresham, the half-smile lighting his face, 'what did we do to his Lordship?'

Moll scowled, and then let a half-grin cross her face. 'Why, it was a good song. They loved it at The Swan. Here, it was so good I bought this in the street three hours after I had first sung it.'

Gresham looked at the crudely printed ballad sheet Moll thrust into his hands. He read the words with increasing astonishment and good humour.

'I would believe almost anything of Cecil,' he said, struggling to keep even half a straight face, 'but surely not with a three-legg'd goat *and* a candlestick?'

'Aye, well, we poets must give free rein to our imagination, mustn't we? Careful – that cost all of a penny!' she exclaimed as Gresham pocketed the paper.

'Include it in the bill,' he said lightly.

'There's more,' she said. 'Will Shadwell was a man of yours, wasn't he?'

'He's no man's man now, except the Devil's, I suspect,' said Gresham, interested again. 'What of him?'

'I heard today of his death. He dined here a week before, in the Norfolk room.' Private rooms in the inn were named after the English counties, or so Moll said. Gresham believed they were named after noble lords who had bedded their whores there. 'He dined with Thomas Percy.'

'Did he now.' Gresham's face was stony, impenetrable. Did Thomas Percy have a string of rosary beads around his neck? wondered Gresham.

'Had you considered he might have been on his way with news for you?'

'I'd considered it,' said Gresham.

'Percy got drunk that night. Very drunk. Will was playing drunk, but I swear he was plain cold sober. He was on to something, I'll swear to that too. Will never refused a drink unless he was on to something. Did you know Will was a sentimental old fool?'

'It wasn't my most obvious conclusion, as far as character judgements go.'

'Well, he had a ring, a gold ring, he used to wear round his neck. No-one would know, unless you saw him with his clothes off. He bought it for the first girl he lost his cherry to. She died young – some story or other, I don't recollect the details and who cares? – but he kept the ring about him, always. It was his charm. Never took it off, even in bed.'

'Does this romantic story of young love actually have a point?' said Gresham, rudely.

Moll gazed at him levelly. 'It's always a wonder to me how you've managed to live so long. Yes, it's got a point. The point of a great ruffian in here a couple of nights ago, wearing Will Shadwell's ring on his great hairy finger!'

Gresham was very still for a few moments. 'And this ruffian? His name?'

'Sam Fogarty, or so he said. Great lump of a man with red hair.'

'And a Northumbrian accent as thick as cake?'

Moll looked startled. 'You know him?'

'I think we've met,' said Gresham. It was clear he was going to say no more.

'Well, you great ox,' said Moll, in one of the sudden mood swings that affected her, and turning on Mannion, 'does your master know what bills you run up in my houses?'

Mannion stood up with the lazy ease of a man half his age and delivered a mock bow to Moll. 'I go where my master sends me, Mistress Moll. If I'm to go undetected I can't stand out now, can I, and must blend into the background. Don't the learned say that when in Rome a man must do as the Romans do?'

'By that argument I wonder what you'd do if you found yourself in Sodom,' Moll replied tartly. 'I wonder a man such as you stands for such insolence,' she said, turning to Gresham.

'He has a very small brain,' said Gresham airily, 'which means he thinks with his rod, which is unfortunately much larger. I'll reprimand him, and no doubt he'll weep for his insolence.'

He pulled a purse out from under his cloak and tossed it on the table, where it landed heavily.

'Generous as ever, Sir Henry. Why do you who have so much play these dangerous games? You've no need, surely? Why play Lord Cecil's games?'

'Who's to say it's not Cecil playing my game? I play because I have to,' said Gresham, which was at least true. 'And because of all the things I might die from, I fear boredom more than any other. You above all others know that feeling, old Moll. We're two of a kind.'

She looked at him for a moment. 'That we are – and both likely to die on the gallows or on the rack.'

There was a brief, companionable silence.

'WHAT'S THIS DAMNED POISON THESE OAFS KEEP SERVING ME?'

Without warning she hurled the tankard at the head of the man nearest the door. It smashed against his forehead, leaving a deep cut. A second later a knife flashed out and caught the sleeve of his jerkin as he raised it towards his wounded head, pinning his arm by the cloth to the door.

'*That's* how to fight,' she said with satisfaction, as blood dripped on to the boards from the man's head. 'Quick. Unexpected. Sharp. That's how a man should fight.'

There was no debate about travelling to the Palace of Whitehall for the King's masque. The finery worn by both Gresham and Jane would have died on the streets and suffered a seizure on horseback. Jane's gown was not as diaphanous as the fashion now worn by many of the Court ladies, but was of the deepest emerald green, trimmed with pearls. The necklace she wore had belonged to Lady Gresham, and had at its centre a diamond as perfect as any the King owned. Gresham wore a doublet of black, as was his custom, but of such fine satin that it seemed to breathe with a life of its own, flowing with his body as he moved and accentuating rather than hiding the muscularity of his body. On his finger was the one ring, at its centre the Gresham emerald, another stone to make King James, who was obsessed with jewels, turn as green as the gem with envy.

Four men manned the barge, the edge of each oar tipped in gold. A small house hung on the stern of the barge, with the richest of hangings that could be drawn back to allow a view of the passing river, or closed to give privacy to the occupants of the two gilded seats, almost like thrones in the finery of their embellishment. The larger vessel required eight crew, but Gresham hated the ostentation that would have shown in his use of it for so public an arrival.

A string of vessels was making its way upriver to Whitehall, having to beat against tide and current. The feasting and merry-making had been going on all day, but most guests who were not actually resident at Court would come simply for the climax of the revels, the grand dinner and the masque written by Ben Jonson.

Gresham gazed out over the river, oblivious to the excitement of Jane by his side. A heavy, ornate boat with an inexperienced crew had lurched out of line as an oarsman missed his stroke, and slewed round into a plain wherry, splintering part of its bow. The two boats lay dead in the water, being swept downstream, the boat-man's grapple firmly embedded in the hull of the rich barge. A shouting match was underway between the boatman and the lead-ing servant in the fine barge, the fat alderman in the barge trying to retain his dignity and pretend he was above the demeaning spectacle.

Limitless wine had been available all day at court – Spanish wine, French wine, the sweet white wine so beloved of the King, Alicante, Rhenish, Muscatel, sack, Madeira, fine sherries and even ale and beer – and would continue to flow all night. Every creature that walked, flew or swam God's earth would be skinned, plucked or scraped, roasted, boiled, tossed in oils, pickled or jellied and served up to the throng. Every matter that grew in or on the ground would be harvested, peeled and diced or sliced, placed into pastries or set into jellies, covered in creams and decked with spices, to go along-side the honeyed sweetmeats and the cakes. On the last such event Gresham had attended, a groaning trestle table had given way under the mountain of food, and collapsed with such weight as to break both the legs of the servingman who had placed the last huge side of beef upon it. As darkness came on, torches, lamps and candles would seek to turn the night into day, and the light would glitter on the vast jewels that the men and the women wore to show their wealth and their status. The plate on the King's table would be all gold, and nothing less than silver would grace even the furthest table. Meanwhile in the sweated, smoking kitchens greasy cooks slipped, slithered and yelled for the attention of their underlings and aimed swipes at the kitchen boys with their ladles and heavy spoons. Even by the time they made their landing, Gresham knew that men and women would be spewing in the corners of the court-yards, and sometimes even in the rooms. Increasingly drunken men would piss where they stood, and even some of the women would hardly wait to walk into a shadow before pulling up their skirts and doing likewise, the more brazen shrieking with hilarity at their party as they did so.

Meanwhile, as the torches lit the sweating faces and threw shad-ows into the corners of the beautiful building, as the light glanced off the jewels and the silver and the gold, just beyond the reach of the light, there lay the ordinary men and women of England. Most would be lying on a pallet if they were lucky, on an earth floor with a leaking roof and walls little more than mud. Their meal would have been some portion of a rough-baked loaf, with more sand than flour in it if the miller was up to his trade, some scraps of filthy meat, a fresh-caught fish if Fortune had smiled on them. Their children would be bare-footed, and if the family had a poor animal it would be there in the room with them, its stink just another stench to go with that of the bodies for which soap was a ludicrous luxury.

Contrasts, clashes; the peace of the Church and the violence it caused among men; the beauty of the music echoed by the retching of the drunk and pampered guests; the wildest perfumes alongside the stink of piss. It was all summed up by the person of the King, thought Gresham. The jewels bedecking his body would be worth hundreds of thousand of pounds, never mind those on his wife's flesh, his clothes worth an Emperor's ransom, yet the man himself was unkempt, unwashed and stank to high heaven. What matter the show, if the inside was rotten?

As the four men pulled strongly towards Whitehall and the King's Landing, Gresham asked, not for the first time, how a just God could let such a world exist. The answer was obvious. There was no justice. There was no logic in creation. There was no God.

There was simply survival. The measure of a man was not how he seemed before his maker, but how he seemed before himself. To live long was to succeed; to die young was normal; to die was to cease to exist, and so life was to be lived to the fullest and to the utmost while it was there to be savoured. It was a joke, a joke so vast that no one human could ever properly understand the cosmic scale of its laughter.

He gazed fondly at Jane, her girlish excitement palpable. She had spent the last stages of the voyage excitedly demolishing the dress sense of the other guests as they hove into sight. Immediately they came in earshot she became a haughty and silent presence, stepping daintily from the boat and causing all eyes to turn in her direction.

It did not take him long to find out that he had missed Bacon's speech of welcome – only one of many, Gresham heard, and rather too intellectual and rambling for the taste of most of the early revellers and the Court. Gresham felt a momentary pang of annoyance.

Already casting around and looking for Sir Francis Bacon, his eyes lit on Cecil. He was huddled in a corner with a small *entourage* of cronies. Or perhaps he was standing straight, but just looked huddled. The air seemed to darken around Cecil and his cronies wherever they stood, as they moved through the quadrangle, and become more chill. Cecil's eye caught Gresham's. He raised an eyebrow by the tiniest height, and gave the slightest possible nod of his head, before returning his gaze to his own company.

'Bastard!' muttered Gresham, cheerfully, and sought about him for someone important to torment. Then he remembered Jane, feeling a conscience pang that he must see to her amusement, and was rescued by the sight of Inigo Jones and John Donne with his wife. Jones was a bag of nerves on this night, as his design for the 'machinery' of the masques which Queen Anne loved so much was to receive its first test after the banquet. As for poor Donne, banished from Court for marrying his patron's wife and sent for a time to the Fleet prison, he was allowed back occasionally so the King could pester him into accepting high office in the Church. He could not give up the wife he loved, which stopped him from one area of preferment, and he was at heart a Catholic, which barred him from accepting the preferment offered by the King. Donne was threadbare, but surprisingly cheerful, and the love he showed for his wife was pathetic.

There was a tap on Gresham's shoulder. A servant, plainly dressed, spoke softly in his ear.

'My master requests a brief interview with you, sir. Would you be so kind as to spare a few moments of your time?'

'Your master's name?'

'He would prefer to announce himself.'

Gresham flicked a finger at Jane, muttered a few words in her ear, and left her with Donne who was rewriting the opening of Genesis to suggest how the new King came to be created, to the credit of neither the Holy Book nor King James. He motioned to Mannion, who emerged from out of the shadows where he had ensured a plentiful supply of food and drink.

The servant led them to a small room on the first floor of a nearby quadrangle. He opened it, and invited Gresham to enter. A figure sat in a tall chair, back to the door, in front of a small table and a blazing fire. There were no hangings for a man to hide behind that Gresham could see. He smiled at the servant, who was holding the door half open, bowed down low, and kicked the door back out of the man's hand with all his might. It flew back on its hinges, banging off the wall with a magnificent crash, and rebounding with sufficient force to knock the shocked servant forward on his heels. The figure in the chair started sufficiently to knock over his wine glass, and leapt to his feet, turning in alarm to view the cause of the upheaval.

It was Sir Francis Bacon.

'My apologies, Sir Francis,' said Gresham, albeit with his infuriating careless grin on his face. 'Doors are good places for men to hide behind with a knife, particularly so when one does not know who it is one is being invited to meet.'

That, thought Gresham, will teach you not to give me your name.

Bacon looked as if his heartbeat had returned to merely twice its normal rate by now, and some colour had come back into his cheeks. He nodded to Gresham and invited him to sit down.

'My apologies, sir. I'd forgotten what it is to be a man of action – particularly as it wasn't in that role that I asked to see you.'

There was well-cooked meat on the table, and what looked like a delicate dish of fish. It too was cooked through, unlike much of the food Gresham had seen outside. A fire blazed in the hearth. A man who could command good food, a fire and a private room at one of His Majesty's gatherings was no fool, Gresham thought.

Bacon was a relatively small figure, his most notable feature what his friends described as deep hazel eyes, which his enemies (who outnumbered the friends) described as snake-like. He motioned to his servant, who was muttering words by the door among which could be heard 'oaf', 'ruffian' and even a hint of 'call yourself a gentleman . . .' He was rubbing his hand, which had near been wrenched from the arm when Gresham had hurled the door out of its grip. The servant, with marked unwillingness, brought a bundle tied in tape to Gresham, and surlily plonked it down on the table before him. It was a bundle of books, six in all, identical.

'I call it *The Advancement of Learning*. I've been working on it for many years. In it I ask for the cobwebs to be blown off our vision of learning. I ask that we seek anew to experiment, and to learn from that experimentation, as the only way that true learning will advance.'

'I'm honoured, Sir Francis. But why should I be so honoured, the mere bastard son of a merchant and an occasional supplicant at the altar of learning?'

'I was more inclined to make a present of six copies of my book to the Patron of Granville College, Cambridge, and the man who more than any other is responsible for the rising star of the College.'

Gresham looked at Bacon impassively, inclining his head slightly forward as if Bacon had spoken to him in a foreign language he did not quite understand.

'Forgive me, Sir Henry. I know your wish to be anonymous, and whilst I don't understand it I can be capable of respecting it. Yet I too have my spies – or, rather, I have those in Cambridge who will respect me for my mind, and trust me as such, rather than see me as a lawyer, a Parliamentarian or a candidate for high office. Your secret is safe with me, and with old Thomas here – who is, by the way, the only one of my feckless crew of servants who I'd trust with such a secret.'

A muttered 'young vagabond' could be heard from the doorway. Gresham hoped Mannion would not kick old Thomas to silence him.

Gresham picked on one phrase of Bacon's statement. 'Are you a candidate for high office, Sir Francis?'

'I'm worse, sir. I'm a *failed* candidate for high office. With superb judgement,' he said with heavy irony, 'I backed Essex, who lost, and so I lost the support of the Queen. That was the first disaster. I opposed Cecil, who won, so now I have an enemy in the most powerful man in the land. That was the second disaster. I then prosecuted Essex – who, by the way, ignored all and every piece of the excellent advice I gave him – and in so doing lost the support of any poor fool who had not already left my party. That was the third disaster. I am a mediocre lawyer with an excellent brain, and lawyers don't need a brain. That is the fourth disaster. I am troubled with occasional pangs of morality, and lawyers need that even less, which is the fifth disaster. I am also ruthlessly ambitious, and thereby offend even my few friends, which is the sixth disaster. I am not so much sinking, Henry Gresham, as vanished beyond sight of mortal man!'

Gresham burst out laughing. 'Yet some who appear to sink deepest rise upwards again fastest! You were knighted only two years ago, Sir Francis. Not a disaster, surely?'

'No. Merely a consolation and a leaving prize, earned more by my dear Brother Anthony than by myself.'

'I can only conclude,' Gresham replied, 'that given your own ranking of your good judgement, any regard you have for me is also a doomed misjudgement. Am I then the leading contender for the post of seventh disaster?'

Bacon joined in the laughter. 'Just as those who cook with the Devil need a long spoon, so you'd be as well advised to try and fly without wings as to nail your colours to any part of me. But no, what I want from you, if you're willing to grant it, is simple enough. I wish you to read my book. Then, if you think there's any sense in it at all, I wish you to give five copies to the five people in Cambridge for whose learning and judgement you have the most respect.'

'Just as you say it's not a good thing for a lawyer to have brains or morals, so these commodities aren't always in the most supply at the High Tables of Cambridge or Oxford. You trust me, a bastard and an ex-soldier, to make such a judgement?'

'As for the bastard, the ex-soldier or the many other things I hear you might be, I've no knowledge except what you tell me. Yet I've some feeling for another creature who bears your name.'

'And who might that be, Sir Francis?' enquired Gresham lightly.

'The author of *Machiavelli's Choice*, and also the author of *Sonnets on the Source of Power*.'

To the best of Gresham's knowledge his pamphlet on Machiavelli had been circulated secretly in Cambridge to the tune of only a hundred copies, with no way of tracing the authorship back to Gresham. He had been new on the scene at Cambridge in those days, and wished to test the water of the town before making his commitment to it, to Oxford or even to Wittenburg. Seemingly within days it had been the talk of every High Table, generating considerable excitement and a surprising measure of agreement and approbation. The *Sonnets* had been even more privately circulated, in manuscript and never printed. John Donne had sniffed and said nothing when he read them, so Gresham had known they were good. Bacon was very well informed, or capable of inspired guesswork.

So Bacon knew. So it was done. Leave the past behind. Do not fight what cannot be changed. Gresham rarely spent time making decisions. Life was for living, for deciding, and not for thinking. Showing no shock at Bacon's knowledge, he simply said, 'I'll take the books, Sir Francis, with gratitude, and will do as you wish, provided I like what I read.' He smiled broadly at Bacon. 'If not, I fear I will cast the books as deep as you think your reputation has sunk!'

'Worry not,' said Bacon, 'reputations are shallow, meaningless things, but like all things insubstantial they can rise as easily as they can sink.'

Gresham took another decision. 'Sir Francis, while we're here you might perhaps answer one question that is concerning me at the present time . . .'

Bacon looked up, pleased with the outcome of the exchange, invigorated by the dialogue. 'Of course,' he said.

'Why has my Lord Cecil tasked me with finding damning evidence of unnatural practices on your part?'

The colour drained from Bacon's face, and his mouth snapped open. There was presumably a tongue inside it, but it was finding it the Devil's own work to make a noise. 'He . . . I . . .'

The surly servant bumbled up to the table, looked witheringly at Gresham, and heaved a goblet of wine at his master. Bacon drank deeply, coughed only slightly, and returned to earth.

'As I think I've made clear, I wasn't aware that Cecil had any such designs – and, indeed, can think of no reason why he should do so. I pose no threat to him at present.'

Ruthless? Ambitious? Capable of deceiving? Almost certainly all three, Gresham thought, but somehow not *corrupt*, and, to Gresham at least, not dangerous. Gresham took another decision.

'Sir Francis, I don't know what you do between your sheets, or between the sheets of others, and frankly I don't care, provided you keep out from under my sheets. Tell me, if I were to pursue this chase Cecil has set me on, would I find a truth that would rock

Church and State on its heels, and see you in a court not as a lawyer but as a criminal?'

The eyes of the two men locked together for what seemed a very long time. Bacon spoke first.

'You would find an impending marriage the heat of which wouldn't raise the temperature of a drop of Thames water by a single degree – and might even freeze it. You would find a man for whom talk with women has never been easy. You would find a lonely man, Henry Gresham, more lonely than you might imagine, who surrounds himself with young male servants who cheat him and run him riot and drink and eat him dry, but who fill the air with laughter, excitement and energy. And if some of those young men keep him company at times, then there's no force to it, no violence, and there's comfort for a lonely man and I think something not without a certain value for the young men, if they so choose. I don't mean money, Sir Henry, but something softer. Is that hard for you to understand, with your fine strong girl by your side?'

'No, Sir Francis,' spoke Gresham, softly, his gaze still locked into Bacon's, 'it's easy to understand, for I have been there also, albeit only once.' Bacon's eyebrows rose. Gresham broke the look, and got to his feet.

'You'll hear no more of this from me. I'll tell Cecil you were left in a cornfield as a child by mistake and had an unfortunate meeting with a reaper and a very sharp scythe.' Gresham applied his most serious expression to his face. Bacon, whose hazel eyes had twinkled at the thought of the reaper, assumed an equally serious expression. 'But, Sir Francis, will I get six more of your volumes if I forbear to tell Cecil about the sheep?'

Bacon's laughter followed him out of the room. A man in need of laughter, thought Gresham, and a man starved of it for too often and for too long.

A couple of young nobles had joined the supper party when Gresham returned, of families whose fathers had not gained the pox from their horses, and Jane was at the centre of a crowd of admirers. Her dark eyes sparkled more brilliantly than the jewels that adorned her, the rise of her breasts and the flick of her head to remove a ringlet from out of vision accentuating the raw sensuality she carried almost, but not quite, unconsciously. Beautiful women are so often spoilt, mused Gresham. They know their beauty, they are flattered by it and they use it, as they are made to feel superior by it. But you, my Jane, simply accept your beauty and take no credit for it. You believe in yourself, girl, but not so that others must suffer for your belief. She glanced at Gresham to gain his approval. He grinned at her, pathetically pleased that his opinion mattered to this creature who had him in her thrall.

'What, drunk again, my lady?' he riposted, and she laughed full out loud at the nonsense and the heady excitement of it all, forgetting in the face of him the icy detachment she favoured at Court.

No-one paid any attention to the King, who was following his usual practice of seeming to woo the ladies sat near to him at the same time as veering frequently into appalling rudeness and acid attacks on their kind. The Spanish Ambassador was nowhere to be seen.

Clouds of wet smoke began to drift out over the courtyards and artificial lake created by the workmen, sign that the masque was about to begin. Not all the musicians were drunk, and in the light evening air they made quite a passable noise, Gresham thought. Sufficient wisps of smoke were persuaded on to the lake for at least a suggestion of mystery to be created. A huge gate at the far end of the lake opened silently, and with no visible sign of propulsion the gilded boat drew out from the gate with the flimsily clad figure of Faith in the prow. Large towers rose up from the lake as the ship passed by – Inigo had excelled himself, as every one actually worked – and a choir joined in with the musicians to herald the progress of the boat. It was all rather jolly, thought Gresham to his surprise, as lights sprang up around and on the lake, and he found himself admiring both the ingenuity of his friend and the music, whose composer he did not know.

James, without his Queen, awaited the arrival of the first boat in a gilded palace erected at the other end of the lake. He was drunk, but not embarrassingly so, taking short but frequent sips from his jewel-encrusted goblet. There was spittle on his mouth: some said his tongue was over-large, causing him to dribble.

Inigo Jones had come to stand by Gresham.

'Not bad, eh?' he nudged, and then his face sagged. 'Oh no. Dear Christ, no . . .'

A whoosh of flame came from the barriers between the lake and the bonfires. Something like two dying snakes curled up and flopped over, smoking at the edges. They were the ropes destined to haul back the first boat as it sped towards the King, slowing it down and finally drawing it to a decorous halt by the landing stage under the King's viewing platform where Faith could descend and deliver a beautiful, if over-lengthy, speech to the King. Instead of slowing down it sped on with seemingly ever-increasing speed. Faith began visibly to lose faith, at least in things worldly, lost her lines and began to look round in anguish for someone to do something to stop Faith turning into Despair. This did gain the attention not only of many more of the assembled throng, but also of increasing numbers of the musicians who lost the beat and increasingly played their piece as if its finish was a race where there might be five minutes' difference between first and last.

A peasant girl would have shown more mettle in a crisis, but Lady Broadway had been slapped into playing the role of Faith by her husband, who desperately needed the King's favour. She started to scream and flap her hands, reducing most of the audience to fits of laughter. The boat crunched into the landing stage and she was flung forward through the air, landing tumbling head-first almost into the King's lap, head over heels, her masque dress over her head and showing clearly that my Lady wore no undergarments. The King, who looked fuddled, seemed hardly to notice. There was a cheer from a group of drunken courtiers as Lady Broadway, like her vessel battered but not yet sinking, somehow rose to her feet and tried to deliver a garbled version of her speech.

> 'To thou, Great Guardian of Our Faith,
> Preserver of our country's peace . . .'

Gresham looked down at Jane, who was laughing with such violent physical force that she looked like to burst out of her own dress.

'Well,' said Gresham, 'that was good. I wonder what comes next?'

The remainder of the masque went without interruption, the climax being the delivery of the empty-headed Queen Anne as Charity to her husband. The King clearly believed charity began at home, and left his rostrum almost as soon as his Queen had landed and delivered him an extravagant kiss.

There was a tap on Gresham's wrist. He turned, half expecting to see old Thomas. Instead it was one of the young Scots Lords, half drunk, who through an accent thick as alcohol-soaked ship's timber intimated that His Majesty wished to see Henry Gresham and his niece.

The King was in the Great Hall, rather than the Presence Chamber, a blazing fire sending most of its heat up the chimney and the chill of a foggy summer night beginning to creep into the room.

'Good evening to you, Sir Henry Gresham. I hope you and your . . . niece . . .' his gimlet eyes flickered over Jane, 'have supped and dined well?' He spoke the 'Sir' as if it were 'Sair', the accent thickening the more he spoke.

The words were slurred, but only slightly so. The man had a strange mix of muscularity – no-one who rode to hounds as often as he did could fail to be fit – and the same sense of a warped body that came from Cecil.

Gresham bowed low, to match Jane's deep curtsey.

'Your Majesty, we are humbled and inspired in equal measure by your Highness's generosity and benevolence to your humble subjects. Your Majesty affords us great honour by your hospitality.'

Well, I managed to say 'humble' twice, 'Majesty' twice and Highness once, thought Gresham. *Not bad.*

'I hear you have been of good service to Our State in times past, Sir Henry.'

Ears around the Hall pricked at this. Many of the time-servers were either unconscious of spewing their guts up in their favoured location, or banging at their whores, but the professional power-brokers would neither have drunk too much nor expect to go to bed before His Majesty. There was no sign of Cecil, Gresham noted, but those who reported to him would be sprinkled throughout the Hall.

'What little I have done can never be enough, Your Majesty. Those of us who can offer some small service only regret it is not more.'

Will Shadwell really regrets he could not do more. Like stay alive. Do you know how many die to keep you informed, you Scottish runt?

'Aye,' replied the King, belching delicately into an ornately ruffed sleeve. 'Yet tell me, Sir Henry, why are you alone of my subjects not beating a path to my door requesting favour? We do not see you at court, Henry Gresham. I see no letters from you pleading for advancement.'

The King was rumoured to despise those who did not come to him begging. The endless requests he received – and granted – for largesse were flattering to his soul, confirmation of his power.

Oh God, why I do get into these conversations!

'Sire, it is true I have done work for your State and Kingdom . . .'

Well, everyone's State, if the truth be known – but truth and Kingship ne'er did sit easily side by side.

'. . . which work has been its own reward.'

Well, that was true enough. It had to be, of necessity, for the likes of

Gresham. *The miserable bastards Walsingham, Burghley and Cecil had not paid for so much as a horseshoe.*

'It is also work that has needed little advertisement, and perhaps been best done quietly and discreetly. As for advancement, Fate has been kind to me. I have what I need to be content.'

'Would that the rest of my subjects felt so!' exclaimed James, sipping at the wine in the jewel-encrusted goblet he held in his hand. It was difficult to know if his enthusiasm was genuine or counterfeit. His hand was fine, white, delicate, Gresham noticed.

'May I say more, Your Majesty?'

'Aye,' replied the King, gazing at Gresham from under hooded lids, 'you may indeed, man.' The Scottish accent had become more marked. The Scottish Court was rumoured to be far more informal than the English Court, and James exchanged words with his servants as well as his courtiers at mealtimes.

'It is in the nature of Kingship for the servant to ask of the master. Yet the good servant knows that the master who gives without being asked gives with twice the heart he might otherwise have done.'

And take that up your tight Scottish arse and do with it what you will.

King James I of All England, the first man in history to have had actual sovereignty over the two nations of Scotland and England, gazed speculatively at Gresham. This man is not drunk, thought Gresham, merely liberated by alcohol. Nor is he stupid. No, very far from stupid.

'I go shortly to Oxford. I must not offend by seeming to neglect the great University of Cambridge. Does Granville College have rooms fit for a King?'

'There is no room in the land fit for Your Majesty,' said Gresham, bowing low again.

You creeping little toad. When in Whitehall, do as the sycophants do . . . Yet Gresham was surprised to see a glint of humour in the King's eyes, recognising the ironic flattery for what it was.

'But certain, Your Highness, if such rooms do not exist now they will do so by the time Your Majesty grants us the honour of Your presence.'

'So be it.' The interview was ended, not impolitely. 'I shall visit you, Henry Gresham. You are near to my hunting lodge at Royston, are you not, in Cambridge? I bid you and your beautiful . . . niece God speed and a safe journey home to your fine house on the Strand.'

Gresham let out a long breath as they emerged from the Great Hall.

'What was all that about?' asked a bemused Jane.

'I think he wants you as his mistress, and was just looking to see if you fitted the bill, so to speak,' said Gresham, and received a poke in the ribs for his pains. 'Mind you, looking at you now, it's probably the House he wants, as being more beautiful and certainly more valuable . . .'

'I didn't like the sound of "your fine house on the Strand",' said Jane. 'It's ten to one he wants it for one of his stinking Lords.'

They mounted their barge and set off back to the House. The four men had drunk but were not drunk, Gresham was pleased to see. The river was a dangerous place at best of times, and in pitch dark with a fog it was more dangerous than ever. The torches set all round their boat gave each of the men a halo as the flickering light caught the moisture in the night air.

Jane curled up on to his shoulder, wrapped in a vast boat cloak. He looked fondly down on her dark head, and softly began to sing to her, a song by Tom Campion.

> *'Come you pretty false-eyed wanton*
> *Leave your pretty smiling*
> *Think you to escape me now*
> *With slippery words beguiling . . .'*

She turned her head to look up at him.

'I've no desire to escape, my Lord,' she said solemnly, 'unless you have truly novel plans for the remainder of this night.'

Gresham laughed softly, and then suddenly stopped.

The sound of fierce rowing came to them from somewhere very near on the river, regular, hard splashes in the water, even the sound of men exhaling hard, grunting with effort. Six, possibly eight men, rowing hard in the fog and yet with some skill, and showing no light – there was no missed stroke there, but a hard, regular and practised rhythm. Coming nearer, as far as the fog would allow noise and location to be identified.

Gresham stood and exchanged glances with Mannion. He nodded.

'Douse and arm! Douse and arm!' he hissed to his four men. He turned to Jane. 'Down, down! Into the middle of the boat. Crouch as low as you can, and cover yourself with the cloak.'

Other women would have screamed or asked fool questions. Jane merely nodded, and crouched down low in the boat's centre.

The boat moved gently, rocking in the swell.

Gresham's boat crew were well trained. A rich man's boat at night on the river was fair game to the river pirates, and Gresham's men had often needed to row him into situations where good manners mattered less than sharp blades and a stout heart. The torches at the prow, stern and sides were doused. The men set their oars at the rest position, and scrabbled in the central locker for the crossbows that were kept there, passing one apiece to Mannion and to Gresham. The crossbow was a good, one-shot weapon for the sort of engagement they might face. Once wound there was no need to draw the arm back to fire, merely a trigger to pull and release the short, lethal bolt. The trajectory was flat, ideal for short-range work, release was instant if the weapon was pre-wound, and it could then be discarded for the short boat axe that the lockers also carried. A sword was too long for the close work that fighting on a small deck required, a dagger too short. A heavy, double-sided short axe was ideal, allowing the fighter to carve his way through an enemy and knock aside, with a long knife in his other hand for really close work.

111

The men shipped the oars, silently, only a rustle of cloth and foot on board betraying their presence. The crossbows were well maintained, and wound without the infuriating screech that would have given them away. They drifted in silence, the fog and the darkness blinding them, the only sound the lapping of the water on the boat's hull. Both shores were too far away for what dim light might be showing there to penetrate the mist. If they kept this drifting up for too long they would be swept through, or more like smashed on to, the arches of London Bridge.

The enemy had given themselves away by stopping as soon as the torches had been doused. A nobleman hurrying home would have continued on his way. A large, expertly rowed craft showing no light and coming up from behind, and presumably marking them on their torches, that stopped when they did? It was after one thing: them.

Gresham motioned silently to Mannion to put over the tiller, sending them towards the Southwark bank and away from home. In the dark the other boat would have to move in one direction or another if it was to find its prey. Gresham guessed the other boat would assume he would steer towards the left bank, not towards the darker and more uninhabited right bank.

He guessed wrongly. There was a sudden explosion of water and noise of rowers starting up. A large wooden prow appeared from nowhere out of the mist, smashing into their hull. Perhaps a sudden break in the mist had given their position away. Gresham would never know. A grapnel was flung over and stuck into their hull, and the eight men on the other boat made a mad rush to board.

He exults in this, Jane thought, as the boats crashed together with a splintering blow. The deck lurched up beneath them. Gresham's head was flung back, and he swept up the crossbow with a roar almost of glee. Loosing its bolt, he flung it downwards and hurled himself with maniac force towards the enemy, sword upraised.

The attackers were at a disadvantage in that first moment. The torches had been doused long enough for Gresham's men to gain some night vision. The enemy had made a mistake by hitting them bow-on and not drawing up alongside. The bow of the other boat only allowed two men to stand and jump from their vessel on to the other craft. The crazy movement of both boats affected the attackers, who had to jump, more than it did Gresham's men. The enemy were silhouetted for a brief instant. One of Gresham's men, the youngest, fired high and wildly, but the other three bolts stung home in the flesh and bone of the first two attackers, sending one screaming backwards into the well of his own boat and the other into the river.

Six remaining.

Gresham and Mannion held their fire for the briefest instant. The man who had fallen back into his boat caused the others coming behind to stumble momentarily while they found their feet in the rocking vessel. Gresham shot to the left, Mannion to the right. It was an old routine. One man died instantly, with the bolt through his neck. The other twisted at the last second and the bolt went through his right arm. Weakened, then, but not to be ignored.

Four remaining, with one wounded.

A blow from one of the boarders, who seemed to be wielding a mixture of clubs, swords and daggers, felled the youngest of Gresham's crewmen instantly, yet the unexpected crossbow fire had reversed the odds. A scything blow from Harry, who captained the barge, sent one of the boarders off into the river, another from young Will opened up another's face from left to right, slicing through the left eye and releasing a fountain of blood that appeared black against the white skin of the man's face.

Two left, with one wounded. The fight was over.

Mannion had not left his position in the stern. Gresham had moved down into the well of the boat, behind his men, standing over Jane. He felt rather than saw the slight tugging behind him, the deck moving in a different way beneath his feet. He swung

113

round to see three bedraggled men hauling themselves out of the water from the side opposite the battle. Two of them were stumbling to their feet on the narrow deck, dripping water over the planks. The enemy had been cleverer than Gresham thought, and sent men round to the undefended side of the boat to catch them by surprise. The man with the bolt through his arm took courage when he saw his compatriots, and with a huge bellow lurched upright and hurled himself into Gresham's boat. It leaned viciously, dangerously under his weight.

Six boarders now to five defenders.

Gresham felt the battle lust come upon him. A red haze covered his vision. He lunged at one of the boarders who had not quite made it on to the deck. He twisted away, Gresham's axe landing where his wrists had been an instant before, but still held on. In making his move Gresham exposed himself to the man on his right, whose face suddenly took on the shape of a cross as a crossbow bolt penetrated his head from one side to another. His eyes crossed and an expression of total confusion came across his pock-marked face. 'Oh!' he said quietly, and sank to the deck. The man who Gresham had missed flipped over the hull and on to the deck, jumping to his feet.

Five boarders to five defenders.

Harry looked to have taken a broken arm, but was still swinging gamely with his left hand. Will and the other man were forcing their two remaining boarders back towards the bow. Mannion jumped down to join his master, throwing the crossbow he had reloaded to one side. Gresham made as to pull back for a mighty swing with his axe, saw the man opposite him start to lunge and bent aside, plunging his axe into the back of his head with a sickening thud as he fell past him.

Four attackers to five defenders.

Half turned, he saw a sight from Hell. The boat was bobbing erratically up and down, caught in the waves the battle had generated.

The enemy with the crossbow bolt in his arm was standing over the huddled bundle that was Jane, the boarding axe he had grabbed from the deck raised high above his head, a killing lust in his eyes. Blood from his wounded arm was falling, dripping into Jane's hair.

Slowly, so slowly, the arms went back over the man's head, as slowly, so slowly, Jane appeared to be bowing her head and scuffling about in her skirts. Slowly, so slowly, she flung up her beautiful head, and in her hands was a long, thin dagger of Spanish steel. Like a nun praying for an offering she clutched the dagger in both her hands and in supplication raised it to the man bending over her, thrusting it hard into his groin. His scream of dying agony ripped through the fog, brought even the fighting at the bow to a momentary halt with the animal scream of pure pain. The axe dropped to the deck, and the man toppled backwards, the dagger still inserted in his middle. Jane was clutching at the hilt like a drowning woman, sobbing with her own agony. She seemed unable to let go, and she toppled over with the man, ending lying on top of him in an awful parody of the beast with two backs.

Three attackers to five defenders, all forced now to the bow of the boat, all desperately fighting for their lives against Gresham, Mannion, Will, Jack and the wounded Harry.

In one fluid movement Gresham turned and hurled his axe forward into the forehead of the man in front of him. It clove his head near in half.

The remaining two men looked at their struck companion and dropped their weapons, raising their hands, looking beseechingly into the eyes of Gresham.

'Kill them,' said Gresham.

More screams rang out above the water.

Gresham turned to Jane. Very gently he rolled her off the corpse of the man she had killed, ignoring the frantic sobs that were shaking her whole body. Very gently he prised her fingers from off the hilt of the blood-soaked dagger, the blood already drying and sticking to

115

both their hands. As she let go of the dagger, the man's head lolled back, mouth gaping, revealing his bare neck.

A string of beads, rosary beads, lay on the sweated hair between shoulder and neck.

Gresham placed an arm under her shoulder and picked her up in his arms, carrying her to the rear platform where only a short while earlier they had sat in so much state. The other boat still clung to them, the grapnel holding. It had splintered a V-shape in their side, above the water line, and the boats screeched as if in pain as the broken and exposed wood of both vessels rubbed against each other.

Jane was shivering as well as shaking, great racking sobs heaving through her whole body. He said nothing, as yet. He knew what was to come. Her eyes were wide, startled, endlessly moving in her head. They rested for a brief moment on the man she had killed, his head flung back in the agonised rictus of a shrieking death, the hilt of the dagger still sticking up into the night air like some awful erection.

He held her as she vomited over the side, her meal floating away silently downstream. The vomiting noises continued long after she had emptied her stomach.

'Why?' She turned to him, finally. 'Why?'

He did not answer, merely held her closer as Mannion and the others set about finding where they were and towing the other boat home.

Why, indeed.

Why was he being hunted on the river? Why was life a string of so many squalid little agonies, always ending in death, the smell of fresh blood?

He had the answer to neither question. As for the last question, it had been asked of humankind for all eternity, with no answer that he could believe.

He held Jane in his arms, mourning the death of innocence.

CHAPTER 5

Gresham had lain awake during the night, his whole body tensed with anger. There were few tears left in him, and he shed none that anyone could have seen.

He knew what life was. Two thirds of a woman's children could be swept off from life before they were months old, whilst ague, palsy and the plague could bite into the wealthiest and poorest households alike with no warning. There was only one answer. Live, whilst there was life. Fight the powers that condemned men and women to know the truth of their prison yet have no means of escape. Laugh in the face of the fragility of existence.

Yet the tide of despair had swung down on him, as he had known it would, and engulfed him. The dark of the night flowed into his mind and extinguished all light. The mood came on him rarely, but when it did it threatened all that he was. He felt the pulse beating through his body, felt how frail was a human's hold on life, knew how easily the pressure of that pulse could be let out from its prison by the deftest and gentlest wielding of the knife or dagger. As the blood pounded through his head, causing an agonising pain to throb behind his eyes, the temptation to release the pressure with the sharp cleansing point of metal became almost unbearable. It was as if his blood was prisoner inside his body, screaming and pummelling to get out, as the sailors trapped between decks on the *Maria* had screamed and punched at the unyielding timbers in their frenzy to escape. No more pressure, no more pounding, no more pain. Release. Yet he was a coward, he told himself as he stared sightless into the dark. 'Conscience doth make cowards of us all . . .' That man Shakespeare had it right, damn him.

His own innocence had died long since, and his survival was a matter of pride rather than of necessity. He had known in his heart that a new dawning and a first sight of the night would come to Jane, as it came to all thinking people, and that the black edge of despair would tear at her soul. The knowledge that it would come did not lessen the pain of its arrival. She had killed a man, and such a thing killed a part of the person who did the act. There was no other way. It was the way of life to demand death. So at least he would meet Jane in Hell. Yet he had reluctantly decided before the events of the previous night that any Heaven without Jane might as well be Hell for him.

He had put Jane to bed, and then gone to an old, battered chest that nowadays he rarely had cause to open. Among its contents was a bottle of a reddish fluid. The smell of it hit him as he opened it, and in a second he was back in his cot in the Lowlands, crying for the blessed liquid that would ease his pain and send him back into the numbed, drowsy state that was his only escape from suffering. The physik had been supplied by an ancient orderly. Gresham knew neither its origins nor its contents, but years later he had gone to one of the most secret and successful apothecaries in all London and described the colour, smell and taste of the physik, as well as its effect on a ravaged body and mind. The apothecary had nodded, gone to a back room and emerged with a small vial.

'What you were given was in all probability a much diminished potion than this you see here now,' he had lectured. 'Be warned. What is here is five, ten times the strength of what you had before. Taken in small measure, and only in time of strictest need, it will offer release from pain both of the body and of the mind. Yet be warned. Taken too often, it will imprison the taker whilst appearing to release him.'

So the mixture, whatever it was, was dangerous to know, should only be taken sparingly and if the dangers were ignored would destroy you. Not a bad emblem for his dealings with Cecil, thought Gresham. He forced a minimal dose down Jane's barely resisting throat, and left her. He knew that her drug-induced sleep would fade into a more natural slumber, and that the twin healers of time and sleep would allow her not to forget what had happened, but to accept it and still live on. In time. For the pain in that time he could do little, except help her over the first hurdle.

That done and Jane settled, he posted Martha by her bedside and took himself off to think.

Someone had tried to kill them on the river, that much was clear. Simple robbery? Gresham doubted it. There were easier pickings on the river that night, far easier than a boat manned by six sturdy men. The attacking boat had gone straight for them. It had been well-manned, heavy-built, expensive. This was not an attempted robbery. It was an attempted assassination.

There were too many men, and some women, who might want Henry Gresham dead. There had been a rosary bead on Shadwell's corpse, and Shadwell's final meeting had been with the Catholic Percy. There was a rosary round the neck of the ruffian who had tried to kill Jane. Had Gresham come too close to a new Catholic plot, first through Will Shadwell and then by means of Moll, and made himself their target? Or had he offended Bacon? Did Cecil want him dead, despite the papers that Gresham's death would release? Had someone found out his role in the Essex rebellion, and sought to take revenge in the name of the dead leader? Or had one of the Spaniards flooding the Court after the peace treaty found out about his involvement in the Armada, and decided that to exact vengeance on water would be sweet revenge for the loss of so many Spaniards and so much prestige? The Spaniards were the most

Catholic nation in Europe, with rosary beads enough to fill the Thames. Had King James discovered the role Gresham had played in the execution of his mother, Mary Queen of Scots, so many years ago, an execution which had acted to blood the young Henry Gresham into the world of espionage and intrigue? Mary had been a Catholic . . .

There were simply too many options. Once, hiding in a ditch in Norfolk in pouring rain, a young rabbit had emerged from its burrow on the side of a dried-up stream and gambolled on the bed of the old watercourse, below Gresham. He had welcomed the animal, feeling in it an unspoken companion and noting that his cover must be good if the rabbit had not realised his presence. Then, swollen with the torrential rain, a dyke had burst and a small, rumbling wall of water torn down the old path of the stream. There were four, five, perhaps even six ways up from the bed, and Gresham willed the rabbit to run up one of them to safety. Yet the number of choices seemed to confuse the animal, which was still looking, stopping and starting when the water hit it and tumbled it along in its path, sucking it against one too many boulders. Its broken, twisted body lay there until the crows had plucked half its flesh off through the wet fur. Too many choices confused a man, as they had confused the rabbit. It was not movement that killed, but staying still. Someone was forcing an issue with Gresham. Someone wanted him dead. He must decide who it was.

Concentrate! Will Shadwell's murder had started it all, and a supper with a drunken Thomas Percy. Whatever he had heard there sent him running pell-mell off to Cambridge, and triggered his killing. Percy had command over men, was ruthless and would murder in an instant if he thought it would serve his own ends or ensure his survival. Had Percy ordered Shadwell's murder, regretting what he had told him, and Gresham's murder, fearing what he might find out? Percy was newly and surprisingly appointed to the King's bedchamber. He could have wished to kill Gresham as a

Catholic fearful of the exposure of some plot, or perhaps even on the orders of the King.

Shadwell's ring linked Sam Fogarty to the murder, and because he was Cecil's creature linked it directly to Cecil himself. Yet it could be dangerous to draw too many conclusions from that. Gresham knew at least two nobles who were taking money from both the Spanish Catholics and the Lowland Protestants, and a rogue such as Sam could have two, three or four masters. Sam Fogarty was a Northumbrian. Was he in the pay of the arch-Catholic, the Earl of Northumberland, as well as in Cecil's pay? Or was Sam Fogarty's true master the Catholic faith, and was he a spy in Cecil's household for that faith, as well as a spy for Cecil in Gresham's household? If Fogarty was a religious fanatic then the chances of Gresham getting the truth out of him were slim indeed. Men who were prepared to die on a bonfire for their faith, and who feared the fires of Hell if they betrayed it, often could not be broken even by torture.

If Cecil wanted Gresham dead he would have been better off leaving him in Cambridge, where his only servant was Mannion and where a drunken student could climb into College under cover of dark, never mind an assassin. Yet Cecil had called him to London, to live in the well-guarded House, and where even on the river he was guarded by sturdy and loyal men. Cecil had much to lose by Gresham's death and too many secrets that risked exposure, but how much did he have to lose if the King his master had ordered Gresham's death? Now there would be a conundrum for his Lordship! Ordered to kill Gresham and out of favour if he failed, but very much out of favour if he succeeded and Gresham's papers became public knowledge. Cecil was devious enough to try and satisfy his master and keep Gresham alive by arranging a murder attempt, but ensuring that it failed. Yet if his assailants on the river had been in any way uncommitted to their task, Gresham had seen no sign of it.

One coincidence struck Gresham as too obvious to be dismissed.

Shadwell and Percy had dined in The Dagger. Shortly afterwards, Shadwell had been murdered. And where had Gresham chosen to go almost as soon as he could after seeing Cecil? To The Dagger, to meet the most notorious purveyor of information in London. Shortly afterwards, someone had tried to murder him. Visits to The Dagger were clearly very unhealthy propositions at present, and not only because of the quality of the ale. If Thomas Percy was behind the murder of Shadwell, Gresham's visit to The Dagger must have sounded every alarum bell in the man's head. What if Percy believed Shadwell had left a message for Gresham, writing down secretly whatever it was as insurance in case he never reached Gresham? What if Shadwell had told Moll whatever it was he had learnt, knowing it was only a matter of time before she met Gresham? It was time Moll left town, even if only as a precaution. She and The Dagger were too close to this fire for it not to burn her sooner or later, and he had too much affection and need for Moll to want to see her share Shadwell's fate.

Gresham roused Mannion, who slept on an old army mattress by Gresham's bedroom door. Hastily he scribbled a note by the flickering light of the candle.

'Here, take this to The Dagger, to Moll. Don't leave before you see it in her hands. Go armed, and wake three men to go with you.'

It was two o'clock, with not even the bakers nor the milkmaids stirring, but Mannion did not question his orders. He gave a simple nod, and left. If Moll Cutpurse had any sense she would be gone from London by dawn, or hidden in some rat-infested warren in the City where even the King or a Catholic God could not find her. She would know when to emerge. Her kind always did. Would whoever the murderer was have gone for her already? He doubted it. A killing on the river, shrouded in fog, was one thing. It would take longer to flush Moll out of her den, cunning vixen that she was, and longer even than that to mount an assault on The Dagger, with Moll's private army of ruffians around her.

He was no nearer an answer, though if Moll took his advice he might at least have stopped another murder.

Should he have kept one of his attackers alive? In terms of Gresham's code of conduct the answer was clearly no. Life was the cheapest of all commodities. There was a simple rule for such piracy, as there was for the footpads who preyed in gangs on many roads: kill, or be killed. From the moment that prow had appeared out of the fog every person on board both boats, except poor Jane, knew that no quarter would be given. He killed only those who sought to kill him. It was life and the nature of death. In terms of information, would preserving one have helped? Probably not, he mused. Of course one of them could have been persuaded to talk. Any man could be persuaded to talk, given time. Yet torture could easily make men talk not the truth, but what they thought their interrogator wanted to hear. Under torture truth became less important than the release from pain. Gresham doubted any of the men even knew who their employer was. The boat would have been picked up from an anonymous wharf, the leader of the men recruited by a nameless nonentity in a back room in some ordinary or cheap tavern, and the leader then left to recruit his crew. Whoever had planned this attack was no amateur.

The key was a series of names, the names provided by Moll: Thomas Percy had in some way to be the key, and his name led to the others: Tom Wintour, Robert Catesby, Kit and Jack Wright. They were all Catholics, all members of the ill-fated Essex rebellion. Something one of them knew had caused someone, possibly one of them, to mount one murder and try another. What was the cause on which they were meeting? What did they know that had to be kept at all costs from Henry Gresham?

He needed a way in to that group. He needed a lever, a way of prising open the door to this group and letting his ears and eyes into their dealings. He waited in silence, allowing the candle to gutter and die, until the first flush of dawn streaked the sky and he heard Mannion return.

'She's not a woman that likes to be woken up, master, that's for sure!' Mannion seemed undisturbed by being awakened in the small hours, and sent halfway across London with no breakfast.

'If she takes my warning she won't be going back to bed tonight. She's at the root of all this, or at least The Dagger is . . .' Gresham explained briefly his thinking and the conclusions it had led him to.

'This pack of Catholics is the key, the names she gave us. I must find out what they know. Every cutpurse and vagabond, every spy and traitor, every whoremonger we know – I want them all on the trail of these names. I want to know when they launder their linen and where they throw the piss from their chamber pots . . . and work through those few we know we can trust. We mustn't be linked to these enquiries. *And we must move fast!*'

Mannion nodded. This vast trawling for information looked as if it might be the biggest they had undertaken, but its principles and its urgency were not new. Yet despite that urgency, he did not move immediately.

'Master?' Mannion was unusually hesitant. Gresham turned to him, expectantly. Mannion spoke slowly, as if he had given the matter much thought.

'She's young. She's strong. She's more than in love. She's given herself to you. She'll survive anything. Except your despair.'

Gresham thought for a moment.

Must I forever hide, he thought for a brief moment. Then the moment passed.

'Thank you,' he said, simply. The two men, divided by age and by breeding, locked eyes with each other. Words and thoughts for which no language had been invented passed between them in an instant. It was all that was needed.

Gresham became brisk, businesslike. He gazed at Mannion thoughtfully, and spoke with a light-heartedness he did not feel.

'I've no doubt you'll have been bragging about the twenty men you killed on the river?'

For once, Mannion did not respond with a grin. 'Too serious for that, master. I've been in fights enough, you know as well as I. But it was a close-run thing last night, too close. Someone wants us dead, and they don't mind who else they kill in doing it. It was different, seeing her involved.'

'Who wants us dead? Who is it this time?'

Mannion did let a grin light his face, then. 'Why, there's no shortage, is there? It's a fine job you've done of offending just about everybody, in this country and half of Europe, and you not halfway through your natural life as yet.'

'Be serious, old man. You must have your thoughts, as I've mine.'

'I don't think,' said Mannion firmly. 'I just do. That's what I'm best at. I leave the thinking to you.'

'But you have a nose on you, don't you? Who do you smell in all this? Percy and his Catholic brood? The King? Cecil? Spaniards?' Gresham issued the names as if he was punching the air with them.

'My nose tell me this one stinks to high heaven. And there's only one person I know who stinks that much. Cecil. He's in it somewhere, I'll warrant.'

'If Cecil's the one who wants me dead, he must think he can bear exposure from the papers I have lodged in Rome. Does that bring any of our recent visitors to mind?'

'Tom Barnes?' responded Mannion.

Tom Barnes was a devious, sideways-looking rat of a man, servant to one of the greatest villains in London, Tom Phelippes. Phelippes was a forger, code-breaker and general villain to the Government, who had tried one intrigue too far against his masters, and was now residing in less than comfort in the Tower of London. He had been betrayed by his servant Barnes, who had a disturbing habit of turning up on his master's business at midnight and banging on the downstairs shutters of the house he was visiting, instead of the door. Gresham had received just such a visit shortly before his departure to Cambridge, and shortly before Barnes had betrayed his master. Barnes had brought with him, and demanded a pretty price for, one letter in particular which he had stolen from his master's desk. That same letter was still under the boards in Gresham's Cambridge rooms. Gresham had been about to take the matter up with Phelippes himself when the man had suddenly been removed to the Tower.

'Well now,' mused Gresham, 'I think Mr Barnes and his papers are suddenly explained to me, in a way that was not clear before.'

'Are we going to the Tower?' asked Mannion.

'Yes,' said Gresham simply. 'We must.'

'Can we have breakfast first?' asked Mannion.

The Tower of London stood guard grimly over the eastern section of the City walls, where they joined with the Thames. They went by boat, the only sensible way to travel such a distance. Gresham had four armed men come with him. He had not won a pitched battle on the river to be wiped out in some street skirmish. Rather than using one of the House's own vessels, with no Harry fit to take command, Mannion stood by the House's jetty and cried, 'Eastward Ho!' Knowing Gresham's mind, he dismissed several boats, vying for the rich trade of the great houses on the Strand, until one with a young head came in sight.

'Do you land, or do you shoot the arches?' enquired the young man, grinning at his passengers. The hundreds, thousands of men who plied their trade on the river were as filthy with their mouths as they were with their clothes and bodies. This one looked almost healthy. Most people landed before the bridge, picking the boat up again if needs be after it had leapt through the narrow stone arches of London Bridge.

'We go the *fast* way,' said Gresham firmly. Young as he was, the boatman was both strong and skilled. There were feet on either side of them as they shot through one of the narrow arches of London Bridge, the speed and the danger as exhilarating to Gresham as it always was.

They smelt the Tower before they saw it. A permanent dispute existed between the Lord Mayor and the Lieutenant of the Tower over the City's draining of the town ditch into the Tower ditch. The dispute had been raised to a new level when the City had opened the sluices that let all the sewage from the Minories into the town ditch and so into the Tower ditch. The stink was vile, and even the hardened inhabitants of the Tower were gagging for sweet water. He left the four men to await his return by the postern gate, and took Mannion in with him.

He remembered the first time he had gone to see Raleigh after his farcical, trumped-up trial. Here was the man who had taken on the might of Spain and defeated it, a man with the mind of a scholar, the tongue of a poet and the heart of a lion. A lesser person would have been in tears, and Gresham knew that Raleigh had already tried to take his life. Yet there was no sign of that in the man sitting quietly at his writing desk in the Bloody Tower where he was lodged, still dressed in Court finery. He had raised an eyebrow as Gresham had entered the room.

'Well, my friend, how goes the world with you?'

'I'd thought rather to ask the question of you,' Gresham had replied.

'With me? Why, as you can see, all is well. The thickest walls in England protect me from my enemies . . .' he motioned to the environs of the Tower around them, 'and I have my wife and son at my side.'

He called out and Bess, the early cause of his troubles with Queen Elizabeth, came into the low-ceilinged room, wiping her hands. She was pale and hollow-eyed, but her face lit up as she saw and greeted Gresham. Bess Raleigh had mothered many more men than her own son, and saw Gresham as a favoured, albeit wayward, stepson.

'My Lord,' said Gresham, 'how can this be?'

Raleigh gave a dry, gentle laugh.

'How can it be that I'm accused of being a traitor in league with Spain after having spent all my life fighting that country? How can it be that I'm convicted in a trial where the only evidence is retracted and I'm never allowed to confront my accuser? How can it be that one of my oldest allies and friends seems to be my chief accuser, the man whose sickly child my own dear wife helped to nurture and feed?'

Bess smiled at the mention of the boy she had treated as her own. Cecil's sickly son had been welcomed into the warmth of Bess Raleigh's household and brought up alongside her own bawling bundle of extreme good health.

'Why, my friend, the answer is simple. I'm a mortal being, and I live in the world God has created. And I have pride.'

He was not standing, Gresham realised, because he could not stand. The strain upon him, recent illness and his attempt on his own life had left him too weak to stand. The body had come near to being broken. The spirit, Gresham realised with an upsurge in his heart, was very much alive.

Raleigh's pride and arrogance had made him many enemies, but the wits at Court were saying that he was now the only man whose guilty verdict at trial had proved him innocent in the eyes of the great mass of people. The numbers queuing up in the hope of seeing him, on the narrow walk by the Bloody Tower that fronted the river, had swelled, until it seemed that every person of note in London was lining up hoping to see the great man, the last of the Elizabethans. The Bloody Tower itself still smelt of the new building work and fresh timber brought in to accommodate such a distinguished prisoner. A prison, thought Gresham, needs no bars.

Two years now into his imprisonment, Raleigh welcomed Gresham warmly. Mannion he clapt on the shoulder, thrusting a bottle and a fine silver drinking goblet into his hand.

'Here, you great Goliath, take this out on to the river walk and shout out that you're the great Sir Walter Raleigh!'

Mannion grinned and left, closing the door behind him.

'And as for you,' he continued, turning to Gresham, 'drink this.' Raleigh offered a beaker to Gresham.

'Water?' asked Gresham.

'Drink it and see.'

Gresham took a reluctant sip, tasting the fluid on his lips and mouth. There was a slightly brackish, unpleasant tang to it, but it seemed wholesome enough.

'Don't worry!' roared Raleigh in laughter, seeing the expression of distaste on Gresham's face. 'It won't kill you, or at least it hasn't killed me this week past. It's nectar, young fellow Do you know what it is?'

'Is that a question in rhetoric, or one I'm expected to answer?' said Gresham dryly.

'That fine fluid you're guzzling was once sea water. Sea water, mind! The water that taunts mariners on their longest voyages, those mariners who're dying of thirst but yet can't partake of the water that surrounds them. Imagine what it could mean for exploration not to have to take casks of water aboard, to take your very drinking water from the sea itself . . .'

'Is your concern the health of the mariners, or the extra looted Spanish treasure you could cram on board in place of the water casks?' asked Gresham innocently.

'Both!' roared Raleigh, rocking back on his heels with an explosion of mirth. 'It's my ability to combine the practical and the spiritual that marks me out as a great seaman!'

'It's my ability to agree with my master that makes me such a good servant,' replied Gresham. 'Even if it means lying like the Devil.'

Raleigh was in the best of moods, his huge energy refusing to be constrained. As well as writing a *History of the World* he had a chemistry laboratory in a room a short way off from the Bloody Tower, where he had concocted the brackish water from a sample of sea water.

'Time,' he told Gresham, 'time is what I need. The process for the distillation is not right yet – it works only one in five, six times – and the machinery is too cumbersome and yet too fragile

129

ever to set to sea. No point in having fresh water only until the first blow lays the ship on its side. And time, time is what my Lord Cecil and His Majesty the King have given me in plenty!'

'Time is what someone is trying to take away from me . . .' Gresham revealed to Raleigh what he knew, and what his fears were.

A sombre expression fell over Raleigh's face.

'You're right, there are too many names,' he said. 'And Sir Walter Raleigh is hardly the person to ask for advice in evading an enemy's clutches,' he said ruefully. 'One thing's clear, you need to get inside this Papist crew. But that'll take time. The man Fogarty – Sam, was it? – will be of no use to you. He's either Cecil's man, in which case he'll be more frightened of Cecil than you, or a Catholic, in which case he'll be more frightened of Northumberland or God. Tom Phelippes, now, he might be an answer. You say this man Barnes, this servant of his, brought you letters? Incriminating letters? Then Phelippes is your man. Try not to kill him, will you? It does seem to be getting something of a habit with you.'

'Is he a friend of yours?' asked Gresham, startled.

'Not a friend, but a new face, and one with some interesting tales to tell. The social circle within the Tower may be very select, but it's also somewhat restricted. Prison's worst punishment isn't loss of liberty. It's the onset of boredom. Phelippes had the look of someone who might liven up more than one evening's dinner.'

'On that basis I'll try and take off only bits that aren't life-threatening. Remember it as just another sacrifice I make for my lord and master.'

'Take care, Henry Gresham.' Raleigh was suddenly serious. 'They have me in their clutches. One free spirit is enough for them. Take care not to give them, or your Maker, another one into their power.'

This time Gresham did not make straight for the gates when he had finished with Raleigh. The guards were as slack as ever, and a small bribe allowed Gresham and Mannion into the room occupied by Thomas Phelippes. Getting out of the Tower was always much harder than getting in, but for prisoners in the Tower with their own money life was akin to that in a reasonable inn with a fractious and bad-tempered landlord. The door to Phelippes' room – or was it a cell? – was unlocked, the turnkey needing only to unlock the door that blocked the end of the dank corridor.

Phelippes' accommodation was not the best, Gresham noted. The famous prisoners in the Tower, including Walter Raleigh and his accuser and friend Lord Cobham, were kept in lodgings that had some style, and could use the Warden's garden. Phelippes was incarcerated in one of the poorer towers. The window in his cell was high in the wall and heavily barred, and there was no view out on to the garden area that the best class of prisoners could use and the next best class at least gaze out on. There seemed to be little furniture in the room.

Thomas Phelippes was a small, physically unprepossessing figure with a stoop and a pockmarked face. His origins were obscure, and he had been despised by the Court for his lack of breeding, but he had risen to be one of Walsingham's espionage chiefs by virtue of his intelligence, his ability with languages and most of all his ability to create and penetrate the most obscure ciphers.

'Good morning, Tom,' said Gresham, as cheerfully as the setting allowed. He of all people had no reason to feel cheerful in the confines of the Tower, given the various humiliations and pains he had had inflicted on his person whilst within its boundaries. Yet even without his own memories it was a dreadful place. It stank from its own ditch, and the central block of the White Tower, dating back to King William, was as blunt and as cruel a statement of power as Gresham had witnessed, a building with no concessions to form or beauty and a record of cruelty within its walls second to none. The outer walls, though representing a huge span of English history, were similarly uncompromising. The Tower was a fortress, pure and simple, a blunt instrument in the wielding of total power.

It was an evil place, a place where even music would be sucked into the darkness and silenced as so many souls had screamed soundlessly within its space.

Phelippes had risen to his feet when Gresham and Mannion entered, his features lightening for a brief instant. Then his face fell back into a worried frown, though his pleasure at his visit was still clear. Gresham noted, but did not comment on, the frown.

'Henry Gresham, by God! And that walking tree trunk of a manservant who always hangs about you! How are you, sirrah? How goes the real world about its business?'

When Walsingham had died, the empire of espionage he had built up had slowly decayed without the power at its centre. Tom Phelippes had been left in the comfortable position of Collector of Subsidy, with easy bribes at hand and a comfortable house that gave him the chance to witness all those who set sail to France, and report on them to Cecil, his new master. He lived in apparent amity with Arthur Gregory, a Dorset man whose greatest ability was to open sealed letters and reseal them without the final recipient being any the wiser, and that disreputable little runt of a spy by the name of Tom Barnes. It had all seemed very happy, until of a sudden Phelippes had been whisked off to the Tower, apparently at Cecil's command, and left there.

'The world changes little, Tom,' said Gresham easily, 'and the people in it are as corrupt as ever.'

'Well, then,' laughed Phelippes, 'things don't change at all.'

He busied himself with the contents of the basket Mannion had brought with them – the best the kitchen of the House could provide, with three bottles of very speakable wine from its cellar, the best laid on top. Gresham noted the hunger with which Phelippes attacked the food.

Phelippes finished his mouthful, took a swig of wine from the cheap wooden beaker on the bare table and looked at Gresham.

'Others would talk. Ask questions. You just wait. And bring me food and wine. Why?'

'Why wait? Or why bring you food and wine?' Gresham asked. He eased himself forward on the three-legged stool on which he sat, one of the few pieces of furniture in the cell. 'I wait because you're a crafty old fox who'll tell me what you wish to tell me when you wish to tell me, and not before. I bring you food and wine because it costs me little, and because that crafty old fox helped me once in the past, and, who knows, may help me again now.'

'And what help do you need, Sir Henry, with your fine fortune, your fine house and your fine lady? What use can a crafty old fox be, if he's been locked in his lair and looks likely never to leave?'

Gresham spoke softly, without self-pity, as if relating a simple matter of fact: 'They are trying to kill me, Tom.'

A sudden silence descended in the dark, damp room. Was there just too little surprise on Phelippes' face?

'Not for my fine house, I think, nor my fortune, not even for my fine lady. I don't know why, and I don't know who. And you will know that for us, knowledge is all.'

'Aye, I know well enough,' replied Tom, his first hunger assuaged and the lure of the wine taking over. 'Or at least, I used to know. They've tried to kill you before, and will no doubt do so again. And one day, Sir Henry Gresham, they'll succeed, as they will with all of us.'

'Why, Tom,' exclaimed Gresham cheerfully, 'if they don't succeed, God or the Devil certainly will. But before that I'd like to think I'll give them a run for their money.'

'How many have died so far?' asked Phelippes glumly, looking at Gresham with eyes that had not lost their shrewd cutting edge.

'On my side, just the one. Poor Will Shadwell. Remember Will – the plague in human form, with more illnesses than a trugging house, but loyal in his own way, and worthy of a better death than drinking too much river water. As for the others, hired men, on the river, at night. They won't be the last, on present form.'

'I remember Will Shadwell. He would have died happy if he

133

drank himself to death, but not on water. So what can this poor prisoner do for you?'

'First, tell me how you come to be here in this pit. I thought things were going well for you, before this business. Why has the wheel of fortune cast you down so readily?'

'I became idle, too comfortable. I relaxed – the one thing *you* have never done. I'd wind of a Papist storm brewing abroad. Too many comings and goings, from the wrong sort of people. I wrote to that damned villain Hugh Owen, calling myself Vincent, pledging myself to whatever cause he was espousing, hoping he'd reveal himself to me, and write back with something I could show to Cecil. There was no reply.'

Phelippes took another swig of wine. The bottle was already half gone.

'So I replied to my letter myself.'

'You wrote to that traitor Owen abroad . . . and then replied to your own letter yourself?' asked an incredulous Gresham.

A wide grin split Phelippes' ravaged face. 'Why not?' He spread his arms wide. 'A man must live, after all. Cecil wouldn't know a proper spy if one came at him and bit his arse. I put the reply in my best cipher, and called myself Benson. Benson wrote a good letter, hinting at many dark plots against Crown and Country. So I sold his letters to Cecil.'

There was an explosive laugh from Mannion, and an equal snort from Gresham.

'So you forged a letter to Owen, forged his replies and sold them to Cecil? A most economic use of material, Tom. Didn't the Lord Cecil smell a rat?'

'A rat? He smelt nothing except the sweet smell of conspiracy, and loved every second of it. And then that fucking bastard, that . . . *slave* Tom Barnes stole a copy of a letter in Vincent's hand and a letter in Benson's hand – Cecil had only seen Benson's hand, you understand – and showed them to Cecil. I hadn't bothered to use a different hand. It wasn't at all part of the plan for Cecil to see

Vincent's letters. How was I to know Cecil would see samples of both handwritings, which were, of course, identical?'

'Whereupon his Lordship became . . . cross?' mused Gresham.

'Cross! He pissed his fine linen and sent for me straightaway, pissed all over me and with a fair dose of shite as well and sent me here, the warped devil that he is. He's no sense of humour, that man. After all I've done for him and his scurvy State!'

'Is he more cross with you by the minute? Your quality of accommodation is hardly the best the Tower can offer.'

'No, that's not Cecil. I do believe he's forgotten I'm here. It's that walking fart Waad – Sir William Waad to you – that walking fart with *lumps* in it. You know his Fartship is now Lieutenant of the Tower, sworn in only days ago. I could do some swearing. Raleigh and some of the important prisoners put him in a terrible mood when he inspected his new fiefdom. He's too scared to touch them, except with words, but I'm easy meat. I was moved two days ago.'

Phelippes settled back on his stool.

'Enough of me. I accept your charity with good grace, yet there must be a price. Speak. What is it you want of me?'

Gresham gazed calmly at Phelippes. They had known each other for years, and if not friends had at least been comrades in the dark, shadowy world of spies and double-dealing intrigue.

'An explanation, Tom, just an explanation.'

A film of sweat was on Phelippes' brow. It was a warm day, but the cell was dank and chill despite the heat of late summer.

'An explanation? Explanation of what?'

'Of why when your servant Tom Barnes stole letters to show to Cecil, letters you most certainly did not wish Cecil to see, he found a packet of letters which most definitely were for Cecil, one of which appeared to be in the hand of one Henry Gresham. Letters written by you, forging my handwriting and appearing in every regard to come from me. Why, you old devil, you'd even used the same paper as I use myself! Well, Tom Barnes decided to show that packet to me, instead of obeying your orders and delivering it to

135

Cecil. He knew I paid well. You write a fine hand, Tom, particularly so when you seek to make it my hand.'

'I know nothing of . . .' spluttered Phelippes, real fear showing now in his eyes.

'They are interesting, these letters I seem to have written, Tom. I didn't know I was a Catholic, though my plea to the Pope to support an invasion of England to throw King James off his throne is as powerful a piece of writing as I've never put pen to.'

Not only was the letter a superb forgery. It would have discredited Gresham for ever in the eyes of the masses, showing him a mere lackey of the Spaniards and an enemy of England. With that reputation Cecil's chance of ducking whatever furore the letters in the Papal archive created would have been vastly increased. Who would believe accusations written by a traitor? And, thought Gresham, it was even cleverer than that. The very provenance of the letters giving the dirt on Cecil – letters lodged in the Papal archive – would in itself suggest that Gresham was in league with the Papacy, and therefore a traitor.

'Why, Tom?' asked Gresham, gently. 'Why help to spread false tales about me?'

'I . . .'

A dagger had appeared in Gresham's hand, and Mannion had moved to be in front of the iron-bound door.

'I'll kill you, Tom Phelippes, if I have to. You do know that, don't you?' said Gresham conversationally, the fine point of the dagger resting gently on top of the table's rough planking, held vertically there by the tip of Gresham's finger.

'I know it,' said Phelippes, whose face had gone a deathly colour, the pockmarks standing out lividly on the flesh of his face, 'yet if he who gave me the orders to forge your writing kills me for telling, as he surely will, why should I not choose an easy death now?'

'Because you can never know for certain that he will kill you, or find out what you told me, but you know you are surely dead by my hand if you don't tell me.' The level gaze of Gresham's eyes held and locked Phelippes' vision. He started to blink rapidly, like as rabbit caught in the light of a flaring torch. He shook his head, a tone of defiance beginning to underpin his fear.

'You can't kill me here, Henry Gresham!' he announced. 'I've no knife, I'm searched for weapons. Only you are with me. They'll accuse you of my murder as surely as Herod was accused of the slaughter of the innocents.'

'Perhaps they would, Tom, if I were to kill you with my knife,' mused Gresham. 'But you see, you've already drunk your death in that wine I so kindly supplied, and which you were so kind to drink in such quantity. My good friend Dr Simon Forman assures me of the potency of the mixture. You've drunk your death, Thomas Phelippes – unless, that is, I care to let you drink this antidote I happen to have in my purse, within the hour.'

Gresham withdrew a thin, stoppered bottle from his purse, containing a clear fluid. Phelippes' eyes followed it, as they would a vision from Heaven or Hell. Simon Forman was rumoured to have concocted more poisons than the Borgias.

'So do you want your next drink, Tom Phelippes? Or will you have done and be content with your last drink? Your last drink ever, that is . . .'

'You wouldn't do this to me!' spluttered Phelippes.

'I wouldn't *have* done it to you, before you betrayed me. Those letters you forged in my hand are my arrest, my trial and my hanging, drawing and quartering on the block, Tom Phelippes, as you full well know. Your death would seem a fair exchange. Enough of this chatter. Do you talk, or do I leave you to die?'

'I talk. The antidote . . .'

'Comes when you've finished speaking. First the letters. Why?'

'Because Cecil commanded – why else do you think? And because he paid. You know the loyalties in our game. To money and to preservation. Friendship comes a long way third.'

'Your honesty does you credit. A pity it didn't come earlier. Here, you may drink from the one bottle.' Gresham tossed the glass towards him. Phelippes grasped at it convulsively, ripped the stopper out and crammed the fluid down his throat. 'It takes two bottles to stop the work of the poison. The second is there when you finish. These names. Tell me what you know. All that you know.'

Gresham tossed a piece of paper to Phelippes. On it were the names given him by Moll Cutpurse.

Tom Wintour, Robert Catesby, Kit and Jack Wright and Thomas Percy.

Phelippes looked up, startled, his professionalism temporarily overcoming his fear. 'Catholics, one and all. A set of brothers. All related, by birth or by marriage. Catesby and the Wrights were held in the Tower together in '96.'

'Tell me about each one.'

'Why, do you think I've a clerk to hand?' Gresham held the glass bottle over the flagged stone floor. 'This has to come from my head, you know! Peace, peace, I'll try.'

Phelippes rocked back and closed his eyes.

'Catesby . . . old Catholic family, handsome devil of a man. Good swordsman too, by all accounts. Caught up with Essex, wasn't he? You would know better than I . . .' He gazed slyly at Gresham, who returned his look unmoved. 'Wife died, so I believe; thick with the priests. House in Lambeth, or used to have one there. Also lodgings in the Strand . . . A hothead, powerful, many friends. One to watch, definitely, one to watch . . .

'The Wright brothers . . . Catholics to the core, good swordsmen both . . . reckoned some of the best in the country. Up to their necks with Essex and his song and dance, with their friend Catesby. Travellers to Europe, both of them, up to no good. It was me who tipped off Walsingham about them . . .

'Tom Wintour . . . Wintours of Huddington Court, sitting on a fortune with the saltpans at Droitwich — God knows what they have to rebel about with their money. Another known Catholic, younger brother. Restless, fiery, witty, fond of the women and the wine . . . another traveller, up to no good I would guess . . .

'Percy ... now there's a man of piss and wind. Does Northumberland's dirty work for him, went to negotiate with good King James for Northumberland, angry, vainglorious ... King seems to like him ... hates Cecil ... nettles in his arse and an ambition that burns him dry. Wild, wild, to be steered clear of ... master of no-one yet servant to none in his heart as well ... For God's sake, man, *will you give me that bottle!*'

'Eventually,' said Gresham calmly. 'One more thing. You're a professional traitor, Tom, aren't you? So who's my lever into opening the lid of this affair?' Gresham's eyes could have pierced through the timbers on a ship's side as they looked at Phelippes. 'Who can be bribed into betraying their friends from this group? Who is there of your kind amidst these men?'

Phelippes looked longingly at the bottle. Gresham made no move.

'Tresham,' he croaked. 'Francis Tresham. I know he's not on your list, but he's been in bed all his life with those who are. He's a thieving, violent, angry little runt, and if his friends and relatives are up to mischief you can bet Francis Tresham won't be far away.'

'More,' said Gresham. 'I want more.'

'Big Catholic family.' The sweat was now running in small beads across the cavities on Phelippes' face. 'Father a patriarch, big builder, big spender. Had to bail the boy out endless times. Had to bribe him out of here, the Tower, after the Essex rebellion. Young Tresham's lucky still to have his head. He's a wild one, out of control – *for God's sake give me that bottle!*'

'Here.' He tossed the second bottle to Phelippes, who fell upon it and managed nearly to swallow the bottle as well as its contents.

'Don't betray me again, Tom,' said Gresham as he took his leave of the miserable cell and its occupant. 'In an hour or so you'll start to feel ill, and then your body will seek to expel the poison you fed it, by venting your bowels and your stomach. It'll be forcible, and it'll hurt, I'm pleased to say. A lot. You'll be able to take no food for three, four days, perhaps even a week, and your gut will hurt all that time as if it had been fed molten lead. But you'll recover, unless you catch the plague in the meantime. And by the way, the other wine is pure.'

It took them an interminable time to move through the various gates that let them out to the Thames, twice as long as it had taken them to enter.

'You've not used poison before, master,' said Mannion. There was no accusation in his carefully guarded tone.

'I haven't this time,' said Gresham.

But I was sorely tempted. Forman gave me the bottle of poison that is here still in my purse. I was ready to pour the wine into the goblets we brought in the basket, and slip the poison in by sleight of hand. I wanted him to die, to suffer for what he had done. And I don't know why I stopped in time.

'There was no poison?' asked Mannion incredulously. Gresham's act had clearly convinced him.

'No poison in the wine. The last bottle contained a potion that Forman assures me will give Thomas Phelippes a gut-ache that he'll remember for the rest of his misbegotten life.'

Mannion started to laugh, his hilarity causing his whole body to shake so that he had to grasp one of the rotting wooden stakes by the jetty.

'In dosing him I did no more than my civic duty. A change gives as much peace as a rest, and those who tend Phelippes will soon have a new stench as a change from that of the ditch!'

Gresham laughed alongside Mannion. In his laughter was a sense of release. Without conscious thought on his behalf, he now knew who his enemy was.

Jane had awoken when they returned to the House. Traces of the drug were still in her. She was sitting in a back room overlooking the river, thin and drawn, with a blanket over her shoulders despite the summer's day.

Gresham was brusque with her. 'I think I know why someone tried to murder us on the river last night.'

She turned to look at him, the fire in her eyes dead.

'Wake up,' he said to her, more gently. 'Wake up, or give in. You never let that stinking village kill your spirit. You never let me kill your spirit. Now choose. Are you going to let a ruffian who wanted your life take it from you, even though you killed him?'

Something like a tiny flicker of fire, as if from a grate where the embers had been left overnight, came into her gaze.

'It was . . .' She was about to collapse into sobs again, Gresham could see. He spoke, sharply, unkindly.

'It was indeed. It happened. You can't change that. Either let it destroy you, or conquer it. There's no halfway house.'

Instead of shouting at herself she did what Gresham had hoped, and shouted at him.

'How can you stand there so calmly? How can you let the blood wash off your hands so easily? How can you forget? These were men last night, not animals. We were so happy, and then from nowhere . . . this *awfulness* came and hit us and I . . . I had to . . .'

'You had to kill!' He was shouting now. 'Do you hear? You had to kill! Do you think you alone of God's creatures have a special existence? Do you think in this Godforsaken world God would come back to give you a special exemption from reality. Wake up, woman!' He moved close to her, kneeling down to breathe in her ear. 'And never tell me that I forget. You don't have that right. I remember, all of the times, all of them. *And I do not forget.* I learn to hide the memories.'

He knew then he had won, and he knew then why he loved her for her courage, for her independence and for her strength. She sat for a moment head bowed, then looked up at him. There was no extra line on her face, no extra wrinkle or grey hair, yet she had aged in a way that no physical mark would ever show. She would never be the same again, but she would be stronger, more able to survive. What she had lost to gain that victory he did not know. It was the price for survival.

'I'm sorry,' she said, with a slight sniffle still in her voice that made her pathetic, still vulnerable. 'I was rapt in my own grief. It's as you say. Do you remember it, on that horse all those years ago, me with your cloak over my village filth?'

'Remember what?' Gresham was confused.

'What you said then. I don't think you knew much about little girls. You spoke to me very solemnly, as you might your bride taking her home in splendour on their wedding day. You said, "Your life starts here. We wipe out the history of every day as we live it, and if we're brave we can start it all over again with every new day. This is your new day." I thought you were mad, and very, very handsome and dashing. No-one had ever spoken to me like that before.'

'Was I really that pompous?' If the truth be known, he did remember it.

'And still are. But I'll forgive you. I'll try very hard to make it a new day. But you must be kind to me. There'll be times when it's hard, and when I'll need loving, and not shouting at, to keep me from falling into the abyss.'

In the imperceptible way that it is with people, something in them had meshed again, and moved forward with an unspoken, unseen power.

'So why was I turned into a murderess last night?'

There was a flippant edge to her voice, as well as a dark undertone. Gresham sensed that the use of the word 'murderess' was deliberate, part of her feeling her way to an acceptance of what had taken place. He did not challenge her description of herself. Let her feel her own way to her own form of salvation. There was no simple rule.

He told about the forged letter that Tom Barnes had brought to him.

'Why didn't you tell me about the letter?'

'I wanted to tell you when I had an answer, not just the question.'

'Is that wise? To share the information with me as it comes isn't to admit weakness, it's simply to recognise that two minds can sometimes do more than one.'

'On that basis,' said Gresham, 'I should share all my information with Mary the maid, Martha the Housekeeper and Harry the boatman. Oh, and there's young Will, Cook of course, and . . .'

She cut him short. 'The difference is that none of them have a mind like mine. And they may love you in their fashion, but I love you in mine. And mine is stronger.'

That shut him up, for a moment. She carried on.

'The forging of the letter was a long-term plan, anyway. Who tried to kill us? What triggered . . . last night?'

'I think I know now. I've been confused, ever since Will Shadwell's murder. At one time I had Percy killing Shadwell, and organising the business on the river in case Shadwell had left a message for me. Then I thought even the King might be involved, or Bacon, or even the Spaniards. But I was wrong.'

'So who is it?'

'Cecil. It has to be Cecil who tried to kill us. I think Cecil was trying to outflank me anyway, probably before all this started. He knew I had papers that would damn him. He must have hated my having that hold over him, wracked his brains to get himself out of the trap. Letters apparently in my handwriting pleading for a Catholic overthrow of England was an idea of brilliance. It not only makes me a wholly unreliable witness, but it makes my papers coming from the Papal archive an admission of guilt.'

'All you've said is that Cecil wanted to be able to counter what you had that threatened him. Why did he suddenly decide to have us killed?'

'Will Shadwell, I'm sure. He's at the heart of it. Will must have heard something that sent the poor fool scurrying to me, and the evidence is that he was murdered by one of *Cecil's* men, not by Percy or anyone else. I've been too clever for my own good. I invented all sorts of reasons why Sam Fogarty could have been working for Northumberland, or perhaps for Rome and the

Catholic cause. The only two things we know for certain are that Fogarty works for Cecil, and he was involved in Shadwell's murder closely enough to have taken Will's ring. That links it back to Cecil.'

As Gresham had hoped, the chance of explaining why her horror had happened gripped Jane, drew her mind out from the depths of her depression, forced it to work.

'But Cecil didn't try to kill you after Will Shadwell. He called you back to London and sent you off after Bacon.'

'Cecil must have feared something Shadwell knew enough to have him killed. Then he must have wondered if Shadwell had got the news to me. Whatever it was, it must have been of such great importance that I couldn't be allowed to know it and to live. Cecil wouldn't want to alarm me unnecessarily in case I knew nothing, so he must have called me back to London on a wild-goose chase after Bacon to sound me out. I didn't give him any cause for suspicion when we met because I knew nothing then that linked Will's death to him. Truth is always the best defence. Cecil read me right that day. I didn't suspect him of Shadwell's murder, or of anything other than being the slimy rat I know he is. So Cecil must have felt really pleased with himself, and sent me off after a red herring in the hope it'd keep me out of trouble and off the scent of whatever it is he wants to hide from me.'

'Then why did he then suddenly want to kill you?'

'It has to be my trip to see Moll. Cecil must have thought I'd gone to pick up a message from The Dagger. It was stupid of me to go so openly. There must have been endless numbers of Cecil's spies in that place, seeing me walk through and reporting back. Shadwell met Percy in The Dagger, and Moll puts out that she knows everything, even if she doesn't. What was to stop Shadwell leaving papers for me back at The Dagger, as insurance in case something happened to him? It's what I would have done. Poor Cecil. He must have congratulated himself that he's stopped the trail and sent me off on a wild-goose chase, and then I turn up bold as brass at The Dagger. He must have had a seizure. I sent Mannion to warn Moll. She'll go into hiding. Cecil is bound to be after her, to find out what she did know.'

'And I suppose once he'd commissioned one set of letters to prove you a traitor, he felt he could simply commission another to cover for your death. One other thing points to him,' said Jane. 'The boat that attacked us, it was new, well-found, expensive. The men on it . . . may have been thugs, but they were trained, after a fashion, and many of them. All that signals money, resources, the power to gather a crew and a boat at short notice. There are few people in London outside of Cecil who could call on resources to that level. But why the rosary beads?'

'Who knows? Even Cecil can't have that many thugs at his disposal. The man whose beads Shadwell broke could have been the same man you killed on the boat.'

'Do you really believe that?' said Jane. 'Or are you trying to make me feel better? I didn't kill a man, you're trying to tell me. I simply executed Will Shadwell's murderer?'

She was too clever by half, thought Gresham, too astute for his tricks even in the immediate aftermath of her grief.

'It's possible. Or it's Cecil setting a false trail, suggesting Catholics are behind the murders, putting up a smoke screen behind which he can hide. Rosary beads are cheap enough, after all.'

'We may have got closer to *what* happened,' said Jane, 'but we still don't know *why*.'

'True,' replied Gresham. 'Well, Tom Phelippes may have given us our key into these Papists. Francis Tresham, he said. A pleasant piece of work by all counts, but I'd back Phelippes to know a traitor any day. He looks at one in the glass every morning, so he should know.'

Jane rose. Her gait was tired, the movement an effort. 'I'm going to bathe and to change, and shout at a few servants to stop them sympathising with me and treating me like a sick woman.' The

House knew what had happened on the river, of course. Gresham doubted if his own boat crew had stopped telling the story even now downstairs in the kitchen. It was a good story. Let them tell it. It bred a pride in his servants and it made sure that the crossbows in the boat would be well oiled. 'But just one thing more. You've warned Moll. Yet won't Cecil be suspicious of Tom Phelippes, if you walk up to him as you walked up to Moll? Won't you have signed Tom Phelippes's death warrant, as you nearly signed Moll's?'

'Will I?' said Gresham carelessly. 'Well, now, there's a thought.'

'Is that all you care?' said Jane.

'Yes,' said Gresham, 'it probably is. He betrayed me. And it'll be interesting to see if someone tries to take his life, won't it? If they do, it will prove Cecil's involvement. No-one else has the key to let an assassin into the Tower, do they?'

Raleigh hated most of all the time when the bell tolled and the Tower was emptied of all its visitors. In the day he could lose himself in the bustle of the King's prison, in his laboratory and in his writing. At night too he could turn, in the silence, to his books. Yet in the late afternoon, when the people hurried to leave the Tower, then it came upon him that he could not leave, that he was truly a prisoner.

He had freedom to walk in the inner ward, though a warder would trail him quietly if he did so. The image of Robert Cecil haunted his mind. Cecil's power had destroyed Essex, and was now set to destroy Raleigh himself. In a strange way, it was probably not personal at all, Raleigh mused. He believed that Cecil had been, probably still was, genuinely fond of him. Affection had never stopped Robert Cecil ordering a man's death. Why would he do it?

Because Raleigh had the two things that Cecil most dreaded in a rival; the capacity to hold a crowd, to be a popular leader, and the capacity on occasion to act on principle, and not simply through self-interest. Cecil would never make a crowd eat out of his hand, and he had always feared those who could cut direct through to the hearts and minds of the common people. Nor could he predict which way a man might jump if ever he stepped off the predictable path of self-interest, and on to the more dangerous road of principle, and Cecil hated those whose moves he could not predict. It needed only the tiniest push to separate Raleigh's head from his body, he knew. He had become a threat to Robert Cecil, a potential rival for the heart and mind of the King and the heart and mind of the people. Already with no charge to answer he was locked inside the strongest prison in the land. One slip, and Cecil would have him in his shirt on Tower Green, ready to kiss an axe in place of Bess.

Henry Gresham was a man's man as well, thought Raleigh, a born leader and someone men would die for. Yes, and women too. He too had caught Raleigh's habit of not only having principles, but occasionally letting them command his actions. Was that why Gresham now seemed to be Cecil's target? Perhaps in part, but it could not be the whole answer. It was Raleigh's potential to sit in Cecil's chair by the side of the King that made Cecil want him dead, and Gresham would never aspire to sit next to any throne, though he might condescend to underpin it. Was the long battle between Gresham and Cecil finally coming to an end, in Cecil's favour as it would have to be? Anger at the power the man Cecil was able to wield fought with black despair at his powerlessness to make things change.

He turned towards the Tower which lodged Phelippes, expecting to find the door locked for a less privileged prisoner. It was ajar, he saw, to his surprise. He quickened his pace. As he reached the ancient, heavy wood and iron door he heard a crash as of an object being hurled across a room.

He had no sword or weapon, but the old warhorse needed no second notice. He pushed through the door, ran to the cell, crashed through that half-open door. A tableau met his eyes, as if cast in wax.

A tall, powerfully built man in a rough jerkin with a hood pulled over his head was standing in the middle of the small room, a dagger in his hand. Tom Phelippes, his eyes wide-staring in terror, was hunched behind the trestle he had grabbed and was using as a shield, on his knees, his face pleading. Such scant furniture as the room offered was thrown around the room. Raleigh guessed the attacker had come in silently, perhaps behind Phelippes, whose animal instinct had alerted him in some way. He must have hurled the stool at his attacker, and then grabbed the trestle as his only defence.

'Halt!' Raleigh's roar of command had cut across the decks of Spanish galleons, brought drunken crews to order and quelled mutiny. In that small room it had the force of a cannon blast. Yet Raleigh was unarmed.

The attacker swung round, face half-hidden by the hood. There was silence, a triangle of people – Raleigh by the door, Phelippes crouched on his knees in the far corner, the attacker in the middle. Slowly, carefully, never taking his eyes off those of the attacker, Raleigh raised both his hands in front of him, and moved, one gentle pace at a time, to clear the way to the door. He could take the man on, but the dagger put the odds firmly in the attacker's favour. Yet if he tried to kill Phelippes and beat off Raleigh then he might be overcome, the dagger won from him and used against him. Raleigh moved aside two more paces. The path to the door for the attacker was clear. Raleigh nodded towards it, raising an eyebrow quizzically. Leave, it said, with your job undone but your body intact. Or stay, and fight two men, and run the risk of killing the Tower's most famous prisoner. The attacker returned Raleigh's gaze, glanced briefly towards Phelippes. Was there a hint of a smile on the half-hidden, unshaven face? The attacker drew himself up to his full height, gave a short, almost formal bow to Raleigh, and backed out towards the door. He was out through in an instant, the soft pad of his feet vanishing up the passageway. There was no shout of alarm, Raleigh noted, even though the warder trailing Raleigh could not help but be outside the tower.

'Well, well,' said Raleigh, stooping to help Phelippes to his feet.

The man was gibbering with fear. 'I had thought it was my misfortune to be tried and killed in public, but it appears we guests of His Majesty have more to fear from a private reckoning . . .'

'Can I get you out of here?' Gresham asked. He had obeyed Raleigh's summons to come to the Tower. 'You know it can be done, has been done . . .'

'No, I think not,' said Raleigh. 'I'm not at risk from a vagabond murderer. Even Cecil wouldn't dare have me murdered here, though I don't doubt even now he's thinking how to achieve the same end within what passes for the law. No, this was all about our friend Tom. He had one chance at Phelippes, and if it had been done silently and quickly it would have been a three-day wonder. He daren't try it again, and I'm safe enough.'

'But that's not why you refuse to escape?' queried Gresham.

'No, I suppose not. You know me too well. If I escape, where do I go? To Spain, and prove that I was a traitor all along? All I do by running is prove my accusers were right. My battle is here. As you have reason to know, I'm not a man who runs away from battles.'

'Yet you're suggesting that I should do just that?'

'Not run away, no. Hide, yes. Go to Cambridge and lie low there, perhaps? It's such a small place you'd be bound to hear of any outsiders coming to the town who might pose a threat. Go abroad? You've enough hiding places there, haven't you? Cecil is all-powerful. He wants you dead, for what you might know, just as he wants me dead for what I might become. You can swear until Doomsday that you know nothing and he won't believe you. My advice is to take a leaf out of that girl Moll's book. Lie low, go away.'

'I accept half the advice,' said Gresham. 'Hide and lie low, yes. But not in Cambridge, nor in Europe. Here, in London, in Cecil's back yard, where I can still do my work, turn the tables on him. I have my battles, like you. Like you, I don't run away. I stay and fight.'

CHAPTER 6

Robert Catesby was riding through the gently rolling, lush-green pastures of Worcestershire. He had made good time on his journey to meet Ambrose Rookwood and enlist him into the conspiracy. He had cultivated the friendship of Rookwood for years, waiting for just such a moment. He needed Rookwood's wealth, and the horses that wealth would buy. No-one understood his genius, he mused. There was no-one else who could have had the vision he had, conceived of the plot and welded so many different individuals to it. Well, history would know.

They had abandoned the tunnel. It had come near to killing them, not their victims. It had to be God's will that just as the tunnel had proved impossible the lease on a house with cellars directly under the House of Lords had become available. It was stacked now with powder, hidden under piles of faggots and firewood. With one blasting roar of flame that would light up London and burn for years he would destroy all semblance of government in Britain. Into that vacuum of power he would ride with three hundred men. Horsed, armed and ready, they would first of all sweep up the Princess Elizabeth from her thinly guarded home at Coombe Abbey and offer her as the heir apparent. The same three hundred men, swelled by then with other Catholic supporters, would race through the Midlands and along the Welsh borders where Catholic support was at its strongest, gathering strength all the time. Meanwhile the 1,500 Spanish troops idling at Dover would throw off their pretended stupor and race in turn to Rochester. With no army to oppose them, they would sit astride the Thames and starve London into submission if it failed to support the uprising. Fawkes had promised it would be so, returning from Europe with secret assurances. Catesby and every Catholic who could ride a horse would by that time be streaming in their thousands to the gates of London, whilst Sir William Stanley would be bringing his English Regiment over from Europe, land them at Southampton to underpin the new regime, regardless of Spain's support. Again, Fawkes had confirmed that all they were waiting for was the excuse to move. With Percy acting as intermediary to the Earl of Northumberland, and the threat of all his power sweeping down from the north seemingly assured, God had to be on their side.

Robert Catesby would change the world. He smiled to himself as he urged his horse onwards.

The countryside he rode through was dressed in shades of green, with the increasingly darker and richer colours showing the first heaviness of autumn. The thick woodlands on the tops of the gentle hills contrasted in their untamed wildness with the neat rows of the tilled land in the valleys and the strips of pasture. Seen from the inside of a healthy young body, astride a fine horse and with a thick cloak to hand to keep out the chill of evening when it came, it was truly God's green and pleasant land. One could almost forget the rising tide of persecution that was first of all choking and then surely killing off the great families of England, who for years had asked nothing but peace to worship God in the one and true way of the Faith.

Catesby reined in, and gazed out over the pastoral landscape, with a few wisps of smoke showing the whereabouts of peasant cottages, and a fine stone manor on the hillside exuding calm and authority over the scattered holdings. He imagined his own men pounding through and over the harvest-bare fields, the glinting helmets of the Spanish troops catching the sun as they struck fear and trembling into the hearts of the ignorant peasants in the fields.

If the grand vision was simple, and the grand players in place, it was the detail, as ever, that caused the problems. The men had kept their mouths shut, Catesby knew, but there was talk among the women, and of course among the servants. It could hardly be otherwise. The stockpiling they had already done, under the guidance of John Grant and Robert Wintour, could hardly have gone unnoticed by the womenfolk. The stables were fuller by the minute. There would have to be more horses, more weapons. Most of all, he was desperately short of money, and in particular money for horses.

Well, Catesby had an answer to all those problems, he thought as he rode on his way to Huddington Court, the home of Robert Wintour. You could not defeat gossip, but you could block it by spreading other stories and simply overloading the capacity of the tongues to wag. As for money and horses, there were three names he was prepared to risk as new conspirators now there was so little time left to go for them to get it wrong – Ambrose Rookwood, Sir Everard Digby and Francis Tresham. Three young and moneyed men were about to be persuaded to give God, and Robert Catesby, some of their wealth.

His horse shied as some loose stones dislodged by its passage rattled down the steep embankment upon which he rode. It was a nervous creature, but strong and powerful, and he instinctively leant forward to soothe its nervousness.

Horses were the key. Catesby had timed his visit carefully. Ambrose Rookwood had one of the finest stables of any man in England, and his love of horses was legendary, as was his love of fine clothes. That same love of fine horses meant he would never stay with the women and the others on the recent pilgrimage some forty of them had taken to Winifred's Well at Holt. He would ride on ahead, stopping over at Huddington on the way to his own ancestral home at Coldham Hall. It was a woman's thing, this pilgrimage, thought Catesby, but Rookwood's love of his wife had sent him on it and his desire to drive a good horse hard meant that he would ride ahead on its return. That in turn meant that Catesby would see him without the presence of Elizabeth, his wife. Rookwood was a dandy and a showman, but he listened to his wife, who had a great deal more sense than he did. The last thing Catesby wanted was pillow talk the night after he had enlisted Rookwood.

He rode into the courtyard and handed his horse over to the groom who came rushing up to him. Other men might take their mount to the stables themselves, and see it in its stall, fed and rubbed down. Catesby saw no reason why he should do what a servant could do just as well. He had more important fish to fry, as the small, dark and elegant figure of Rookwood did him the honour of coming down the steps, almost dancing with joy, and caught him in a warm embrace, as if it were his house and not Robert Wintour's.

Yes, thought Catesby, as they went arm in arm into the house. You have two things I stand most in need of. You have horses and you have wealth.

Catesby felt a growing excitement as he agreed to a warming cup of wine, even before taking his boots and riding cloak off. The dour Robert Wintour had appeared, radiating as much warmth as if Catesby were Anti-Christ come to visit. Rookwood was chattering on about a new Hungarian riding coat he had just acquired, with its velvet lining. You have a fine fortune and a fine wife, Catesby thought, and enough brats scampering about your home to fill a farmyard. Your days are filled with your fine horses, your fine wife, your fine sons, your hawks and your hounds.

Rookwood brushed aside the servant hovering to take Catesby to his room, as if it was he and not Robert Wintour who was master of Huddington, and strode up the stairs himself in his eagerness to show his friend where he would be resting his head.

Catesby followed his friend up the stairs to his chamber. Once

Catesby had held a loving wife, had the fine son and the fine house warmed with love and happiness, before they were cruelly dragged away from him. Rookwood's family faced destruction and execution from the involvement Catesby brought, the friend with the viper in his pack.

That, thought Catesby, is their problem, not mine. Life dealt cruel blows. Why should Rookwood, Digby or any other body on earth have the happiness that Catesby had been denied? If there was a hint of pleasure in Catesby's damnation of his friend and all that his friend loved and cared for it was a very private emotion, one he chose not to let see the light of day.

Gresham had gone to the cellar where Cecil's spy, Sam Fogarty, was being held until he had strength enough to be carted out of London. The man had cried out in fear as Gresham had entered.

They had been ordered to kill Shadwell, he had said. He did not have to say whose orders these were. He was Cecil's man. They had cornered him finally on the outskirts of Cambridge, stalked him through the night, hurled the body into the river. No, he did not know why the death had been ordered. Why should he and the others be told? Their business was to kill, not to ask why.

By the time he had finished, the man was speaking almost confidently, believing he was useful to Gresham. Gresham looked calmly down at him.

'This is for Will Shadwell,' he said. In one swift movement he lunged with the dagger in his hand, penetrating the eye exactly in the centre of the pupil and driving upwards until the splintering sound of bone told him he had carved through the soft brain to the skull. It was the blow that had killed Will Shadwell. As the man fell he flung his arms out, hands facing up to the ceiling as if in supplication. They were still trembling. Gresham pulled the dagger away, and stood up.

Jane had woken in the night, as he had known she would. He had held her as the truth had returned, bringing on wracking sobs, imagining it to be like holding a woman through the pangs of birth. Yet it was not a child that had been born from her, but knowledge. Later, at night, they had made love, gently, in the way that she had taught him for the times when the edge was gone from their violent, urgent need for each other's bodies. It had seemed as if his whole body had poured its passion and its intensity into that one focal moment of release, met by her soft cry. For a few seconds after that moment, even sometimes for a few minutes, Gresham felt at peace, the demons inside him stilled. So it was with Jane, he suspected. A new demon was in her, a shared demon. How it would fit with the others inside her head, the restless spirits whose nature he could only guess at, only Jane would know. There would be no more tears for others to see, Gresham knew. She had killed a man. She would learn, like him, to cry inside her head .

He needed to hide, to take cover, to go to ground. Yet at the same time he needed London and the access it gave to his network of spies.

He woke with his mind clear. Breakfast over, he spoke with Jane and Mannion, his tone clipped and definite.

'Raleigh was right. We have to lie low, to hide ourselves until we can find out what all this is about. We're moving, to Alsatia,' he announced. 'Or rather, I am moving. Jane, you can stay here. If you do, you'll be well protected, as protected as money and men can make you. Even then, we can't guarantee there won't be an assault on the House, or more likely a fire to drive you out and into the arms of whoever wants purchase against me. In Alsatia we'll be on our own. Safer, for a while, until our identity leaks out. Yet more in danger, from those we'll be surrounded by. Not to mention plague and pestilence.'

He looked at her, noting her chin jut out just that little bit further as he spoke, sensing as much as seeing the head tilt upwards.

'I come with you, my Lord, if you'll have me.'

'So be it.'

Alsatia lay between Whitefriars and Carmelite Street. No

constable or night watchman ever troubled the narrow streets of Alsatia, no law enforcement agency ever lightened its paths. It was a haven for any criminal escaping the hue and cry. Authority in Alsatia lay in a man's brute force and cunning. A force of order, but never law, was more or less enforced by whatever criminal warlord had dominance at any given time, but mastery could change hands three or four times in a year as rival groups and gangs fought their silent and bitter wars out of sight of any judge or jury. Unlike other areas such as Southwark, where the brothels and gambling dens could flourish until the law took notice of them, Alsatia offered little or no entertainment, merely a kennel where wild dogs could hide and lick their wounds, if they were not first killed by their own kind also in hiding. It ranked with the brick kilns of Islington and the Savoy, its distinction being that of all the human cesspits in London Alsatia was the most foul and the most extreme, talked about with bated breath by the good citizens of London, and with the reddest flush of embarrassment if ever mentioned by a woman.

'But first I have another shorter journey. To my Lord Cecil.'

There was a gasp of breath from Jane. Mannion looked glum, and sucked at his tooth with the hole in it. Whenever Gresham took a decision Mannion thought was ill-advised, a piece of flesh or bread always seemed magically to reappear in that tooth.

'Surely not!' said Jane, emboldened by shock and fear. 'He must be behind all this! What madness is it to walk into his parlour!'

'It *is* madness, which is why he won't consider it, because it's something he would never do himself. That's why he's not his father's son. Oh, he'll plot and scheme and poison and murder, but he's cautious, always cautious. He thinks all men are lesser versions of himself. He's at his weakest when dealing with someone totally unlike him, someone who's never thought like him in all his life.'

Gresham took Mannion and four men with him to see Cecil. Unusually, he rode the cumbersome great coach that his father had ordered. It was a monstrous machine, and made every rut and

canyon in the roadway seem three times
fit only for old men tottering their way fr
fine ladies too fat or too well-bred to
Gresham hated it. Yet it had solid wall
very cumbersome nature turning it in
under attack.

It was fitting that a man with imp
palace. Gresham barged his way through to the
With the King returned from Oxford, and happily killing as many
wild animals as he could find in Royston, Gresham knew Cecil
would be sitting at the centre of his web. A crowd of hopefuls were
waiting kicking their heels, desperate for an audience.

Gresham approached the Clerk sitting like a little God at his
desk.

'The King's Chief Secretary is far too busy to see those who
come without prior arrangement,' announced the Clerk, sniffing
through an elongated nose whilst looking down it at Gresham. 'If
you insist I will take details of your petition,' he added in a tone
that made it clear the petition was doomed never to meet his
Lordship's eyes. A host of other eyes focused on Gresham, from the
threadbare old man with a tattered bundle of papers clutched in his
hand to the *gallant* in fine silk and satin but with a haunted look in
his restless eyes. The place stank of fear, of despair and of lost
hopes.

Gresham leant over and whispered something in the Clerk's ear.
His eyebrows rose until they were entangled in his hair. The Chief
Clerk to the King's Chief Secretary scuttled off to knock hesitantly
on the guarded door. He emerged a short while later, looking even
more flustered, and bowed to Gresham, ushering him in. Mannion
remained outside, impassive.

Cecil was alone. It was possible that he might have had a hurriedly dismissed floozy with him, more likely one of the wild Irish
harpers whose music he had so taken to. The expensive hangings
could have concealed any numbers of doors. How could a man

...liness in his soul have so much love of fine art and ...t Gresham. Yet somehow Gresham doubted Cecil ...ith anyone. Cecil simply liked to keep people waiting, ...d on the anxiety and desperation of those parked outside ...or, almost as if the power to deny them his presence con...ed the very power that he held.

The setting was different from the room where Cecil met his spies. It was opulent, with the hangings alone worth a small fortune. It was vast, the mullioned windows letting in bars of strong sunlight that glowed on the richly polished table in the centre of the room. Cecil sat in a huge, ornately carved chair at the head of the table. The usual mass of papers was spread before him. Why so many papers, thought Gresham, for a man with the most ruthless memory he had ever known? Ten perfectly carved matching oak chairs were ranged each side of the table, with a single, simpler chair at the end of the table. Ordered around the room were twenty or so other chairs, each worth a yeoman's ransom. The message was clear. This was a room that dwarfed the individual. It spoke of meetings of powerful men, of decisions taken by rulers.

It was also a room where clearly the petitioner was meant to sit at the end of the table with a vast lump of gleaming wood between him and the Chief Secretary. Gresham, who was never good at obeying orders spoken or unspoken, simply stepped round and marched up the side of the table.

Was there a flicker of fear in Cecil's gimlet eyes? It was difficult to say, the damned table was so long and Cecil so far away from the door.

Gresham walked the length of the table, remembering to drag his feet a little. He stopped by the side of Cecil, pulled out an adjacent chair and casually seated himself, as if drawing up a chair to his oldest friend. As he did so he pulled his sword scabbard aside with just a touch more force than was strictly necessary.

'Do sit down,' Cecil said softly, making a vague motion with his hand, long after Gresham had done so. There was no sign of anger that the man he had tried to kill was here, alive, seated in front of him.

'Thank you, my Lord,' said Gresham, gracefully.

There was a silence. It stretched into an uncomfortably long time. Gresham sat calmly, a quizzical smile on his face, his eyes never leaving Cecil's impenetrable black gaze.

Cecil broke first. 'You did ask to see me, I believe?'

'Did I?' said Gresham, in a surprised tone. 'My apologies, my Lord. A number of your servants have attempted to *make contact* with me, and so I assumed the invitation was yours. I wondered perhaps if you wished news of Sir Walter Raleigh, your Lordship's old friend?'

'My servants?' said Cecil, apparently equally surprised, and ignoring the gibe about Raleigh. He knew Gresham's relationship with the most distinguished prisoner in the Tower. 'You surprise me, Sir Henry. I was not aware of sending any servants to speak with you.'

No, thought Gresham, *you just sent a group of ruffians to murder me. I suppose you could call them your servants.*

'That is certainly true, my Lord,' replied Gresham, 'as the servants in question did not have the holding of speech with me as their first priority.'

'I am surprised, therefore, that these speechless creatures were able to identify themselves as my servants. Are you sure in your surmise? I would be angered indeed if there were those seeking to impersonate servants of His Majesty the King's Chief Secretary.'

Mistake, Gresham thought. *Your first mistake. You should not need to use your rank to boost your credibility.*

'I would not worry overmuch, my Lord.'

'And why should that be, sir?' enquired Cecil, raising one thin eyebrow and feigning boredom despite the patronising impertinence of Gresham's tone.

'The scoundrels in question were an unhealthy lot. Indeed, I believe all but two of them died of a sudden, one is near to death and another broke a limb.'

Let Cecil think one of the murderers lived on. All the bodies could not have been washed up yet, and even Cecil could not keep a count of every body in the Thames.

'How very unfortunate,' mused Cecil.

'Not at all, my Lord,' replied Gresham. 'Rather I view it now as God's justice on any soul impertinent enough to pretend to be in your Lordship's employ. Thanks be to God.'

'Well, well,' said Cecil, flatly. 'This has been most interesting. Most interesting.' His tone suggested it had been as interesting as an examination of his master's scrotum. 'But do tell me, *as you are here*, how things go with the investigation of . . . Sir Francis Bacon.'

Gresham leant forward, suddenly, conspiratorially. Even the icy control of Cecil could not stop him from a sudden, sharp movement back in his seat.

'I have it on the firmest evidence,' said Gresham with total sincerity, 'that he is the Fiend incarnate.'

'How so?' said Cecil, revealing more interest than he intended.

'It is said that he possesses the Philosopher's Stone, the alchemist's secret, the magic stone that turns all it touches to gold. There is one problem, and one problem alone.'

Cecil's avarice overcame his intelligence. 'Problem?' he said, his eyebrows knitted together in concentration. 'What problem?'

'In its present refinement Sir Francis's stone will turn to gold only the turds of members of the true aristocracy. He has tried it on all manner of substances, and on all manner of turds, but it will only work with those produced from men of the highest breeding.'

Gresham stared hard at Cecil. Cecil's family was of low birth, brought to ascendancy by the mind and not the breeding of Cecil's father, old Lord Burghley.

'This is a problem indeed, my Lord, because as my Lord knows better than I, there are many *cheap and imitation Lords* about the place nowadays, my Lord, Lords who claim, my Lord, high birth and breeding but who are only lately come into their Lordships, my Lord, and have no more breeding than a turd. My Lord.'

If ever hate could burn a hole in a man's eye sockets there is smoke in your eyes now, thought Gresham.

'Clearly,' Gresham continued, relaxing against the hard back of the chair, 'this matter is of equal importance to the enquiry into Sir Francis Bacon's sodomite tendencies, a matter which I know carries the highest importance to the welfare of the nation. Indeed, one part of the anatomy seems to turn up wherever one looks in the case of Sir Francis. I shall enlarge the scope of my enquiries to cover both areas, so to speak.'

Cecil was stock-still, as if frozen. Gresham could see the tick, tick of the pulse in his neck. It was double Gresham's pulse.

I think you do not have a very great sense of humour, Chief Secretary to the King, particularly where the butt of the humour is yourself.

'On less serious matters, I must report, my Lord, that I have been experiencing minor difficulties in the conduct of my investigation.'

Cecil's eyes had gone on a brief journey to Hell, noted the suffering that could be inflicted on a human body, and returned to the land of the living with renewed enthusiasm, particularly as they looked at Gresham.

'Do tell me,' he said, in a voice of coach wheels on gravel.

'I suspect the wicked *Sir Francis* has detected my enquiries.'

Let's play you at your own game, thought Gresham, *bluff and double bluff. Let Sir Francis be my code for Robert Cecil. Let's see your mind race to break that code.*

'*Sir Francis* has set men to spy upon me and scoundrels to murder me. I believe he has also forged letters in my hand, purporting to show me as a Papist.'

'Good heavens!' said Cecil softly. 'Such wickedness!'

'I know, my Lord,' said Gresham, shaking his head in sadness, 'such wickedness is almost beyond the imagining of men of good conscience such as you and me. However, I am reassured in my heart. You see, I have weapons against such villainy.'

161

'You do?' enquired Cecil, his voice caressing Gresham.

'I do, my Lord. You see,' he leant forward to whisper the information near to Cecil's ear, 'I have letters from *Sir Francis* to the Infanta of Spain offering his support to her claim to succeed Her Majesty the Queen upon Her Majesty's most untimely death – whilst at the same time he was expressing his total loyal service to His Majesty King James when His Majesty was King of Scotland! Can you imagine such infamous double-dealing from a servant of the Crown! And what is more, these letters have *Sir Francis's* very own personal seal on them, the seal he never lets off his hand. They are potent proof, beyond the wit of even the best forger.'

'And how,' said Cecil in a voice that was almost also a whisper, 'did you acquire these letters?'

'I murdered the messenger that was taking them to Spain, as he sought to board a ship in Dover,' said Gresham flatly. 'You will understand, I am sure, my Lord. We servants of the King have sometimes to take drastic action to preserve the peace. They are good letters, remember. The hand and the style are unmistakable, and, as I said, they are sealed with . . . *Sir Francis's* seal. His special signet. I believe he uses it still.'

Gresham did not glance at the signet ring on Cecil's finger, the ring containing his personal seal. Nor did Cecil.

'Yet *Sir Francis* could still do you great harm, Sir Henry. The Papist threat is ever with us. You would do well not to be implicated.'

It had taken very little time for Cecil to pick up the code.

'That is true, my Lord. But were you ever familiar with the work of that great rogue, Kit Marlowe? The lines are from his *Doctor Faustus*. I believe it is Mephistopheles who speaks them. "It is great consolation to the damned to have companions in distress." If *Sir Francis* succeeds in implicating me, I know of course I would have your Lordship's support in any charges brought against me. Your Lordship has always supported his friends.'

Take that in Raleigh's name, and for his sake!

162

'Not to mention the support of several Bishops in the House of Lords who know my fervent Anglicanism. Even were that mighty support to fail, I would at least have the comfort of knowing that I would drag my accuser down to Hell alongside of me.'

'So many secrets, Sir Henry. So many secrets,' mused Cecil. His eyes swivelled back from the window where they had rested their gaze, and fixed on Gresham. There was no change in the tone of his voice, or the posture of his body. 'Tell me, does *Sir Francis* know that you once sodomised a young man in the Low Countries, and that the young man in question was executed in a most gruesome manner when you refused to acknowledge your crime? I am sure that your . . . niece knows what happened. I understand you are very close to her. And that servant of yours . . . and the students in the fine College you have endowed in Cambridge, and its Fellows. It is in the nature of academics to be forgiving, of course, and they and students never gossip or laugh at a man . . . how could they, when their studies bring them so close to God? No, I am sure those who have cause to love you will find forgiveness in their hearts, should this thing become known . . .'

The sinking feeling, as if given a sudden blow to the stomach. He had known it would come. This was what had been in the papers Cecil had stolen from Walsingham, in the paper that Cecil had produced in order to blackmail him into going on that stupid mission overseas so long ago. He had steeled himself for it, knew that Cecil would not be able to resist playing his final card. It was a victory over Cecil, after all. It was Cecil declaring his hand, when he, Gresham, had cards in hiding still. Victory; yet it hurt still like the pains of Hell.

No-one looking at Gresham's neck would have seen the tick of his pulse increase. There was no film of sweat on his brow. Knowing that the human eye could sense the tiniest tightening of muscle – it was the sense that had kept him alive on several occasions – he forced his muscles to relax, kept himself draped nonchalantly over his chair.

163

'You are kind in your concern for my past, my Lord, and for my future. As it is, I told Sir Francis Bacon of the incident to which you refer.'

The tiniest, tiniest flicker of a muscle in Cecil's eye . . . Always start a lie with a truth . . .

'And my niece and servant know everything I know and everything I have been . . .'

Which if I have knocked you off your guard you will not realise does not include everything I have done . . . Now. Now was the time. Now he signed his death warrant, or arranged a little longer life for himself, for Jane and for Mannion . . .

'Yet you are correct, my Lord. I know my secrets are safe with such as your Lordship, yet it would cause me grief if some were to know of what you speak. There is a further matter.'

It was vital that Gresham injected the right blend of bitterness, near-shame and worry into his voice if he was to be believed.

'I am . . . ill, my Lord.'

'You are?' said Cecil, coming to life, and with a gleam of hope in his voice. 'I am saddened to hear it.'

For only the briefest moment Gresham was tempted to confess to the plague, if only to see how fast Cecil could run.

'It is . . . a growth, my Lord, here in my side.' It was actually a penny loaf, strapped to his side whilst still warm from the kitchens, but producing a suitable lump just under his ribcage, bulging under his satin doublet. Thank God Cecil did not keep hounds in his hall. They would have sniffed at the doublet and in all probability tried to drag the bread from under his shirt.

'I am told it is serious. It would have been most interesting to pursue *Sir Francis*, to enact revenge for his assaults on my person, but unless I obtain total rest I am assured that I will do to myself what *Sir Francis's* men tried to do to me. I am leaving London, my Lord, with those closest to me. It will be difficult for *Sir Francis* to find me out. I am practised in hiding. Should I be pursued or harried any more I have made arrangements for the letters I mentioned to be delivered to someone who hates him, and who will guarantee sight of them to the King.'

That would set Cecil thinking. The list of men with good cause to hate him would stretch three times round Whitehall and still reach all the way to the Tower. And they did say the King liked younger men, men with straight bodies and golden hair . . .

'I wish you a full and speedy recovery, Sir Henry. You are master of your own affairs. But if indeed you propose to "vanish", as you put it, I am sure *Sir Francis* would not over-exert himself in finding you. He will feel, I am sure, that his point has been made. Men such as he hate meddlers, do they not?'

'It would appear that men such as *Sir Francis Bacon* do not just hate meddlers, my Lord. It would appear they try to murder them.' Gresham drew a deep breath. 'Which leads on to my final question, my Lord.

'Why was Will Shadwell killed?'

Gresham put the ragged edge on his voice, forced the sweat to coat his forehead. A man required to control too much, a man for whom serious illness and the ordeal of a growth being hacked from his side was pushing him over the edge, a man desperate to clear his affairs in the knowledge that he might not be of this earth for too much longer – all these Gresham tried to cram into his question.

'Shadwell?' said Cecil. 'Shadwell? I do not think I . . .'

'My Lord!' Gresham interrupted him, made his breathing heavy, short, let his hand creep to his side as to contain pain. 'Enough of this play-acting! It was a game I played once. I am not the person I hope to be at this time. I lack patience. Time is not my friend. Will Shadwell was murdered, on your orders. The murderer has sworn this is so. Will Shadwell was my man. Foul thing he may have been, but he was bound to me as my servant. He who kills my servant stains my honour. I have redeemed that honour by killing the man who killed Shadwell. Can we for this once speak plain? *Why did my man have to die?*'

There was a long, long silence. Would the fencing cease? Would he ever get a straight statement from Cecil? Cecil moved his gaze away from Gresham, the eyes seeming almost sightless, resting somewhere beyond even this room. What is passing through his mind? thought Gresham. What certainties, what agonies of decision? What happens inside the mind of such a man as Robert Cecil?

'Imagine a land,' said Cecil, getting to his feet, 'a troubled land. A very troubled land.' His voice was soft, whispering almost, a tone Gresham had never heard. Cecil walked slowly, almost limping, to a portrait hanging on the wall opposite the window. He is in pain, thought Gresham. He finds it hard to walk. He hides this pain, but now for a moment he has forgotten to hide. The portrait was of a young woman. The old Queen, Queen Elizabeth, Gresham saw.

'Imagine a land,' said Cecil, looking up at the portrait, 'that deludes itself into a sense of its greatness. A poor land with powerful neighbours, threatened always from without and from within. A land with no obvious ruler to take over. Let us imagine that a ruler is found, at last. An experienced ruler, a ruler who has survived in a colder and even bleaker land, a ruler who offers some hope of peace and stability. Such a ruler is a treasure, to be guarded and preserved. Yet all things come at a price. In this imaginary land this imaginary ruler is . . . troubled by women. His upbringing has not left him at peace with women. He prefers the company of men. And it is rumoured, in the vile way that such rumours will grow, the company of boys.'

'And Will Shadwell?' Gresham's voice had also dropped almost to a whisper.

'Scum. The scum who for countless ages have greased and oiled the wheels of power with their rank sweat, and their blood. And let us imagine that one of these scum, a perverted, evil creature, a creature who lies with women and yet who lies with boys and men, believes he has found a boy . . . hurt by this ruler. Found him, lain with him, and now wants money to silence him.'

Cecil moved back to the table, and sat down, heavily. His

hooded eyes looked at Gresham, with the nearest thing to passion in them Gresham had seen in him.

'A Minister to a King may be threatened, and he may fence, parry and lunge, may battle with his wits against his enemies. But a King, a King is different. No man, be he scum or be he noble, can challenge a King. No man who threatens a King can live. The King's health is the nation's health. Whatever threatens that health must itself die.'

Gresham spoke softly. 'There is no threat to a King from me. Nor ever has been.' He paused. 'There would have been no threat even had Will spoken with me. Will never spoke. He had no time. And you were worried about a note, or some secret letter from Will to me? Was that why my rooms were ransacked in the House?'

Cecil was silent. Both men took the silence as meaning yes.

'Well now, there's an irony would have appealed to Will. You see, I know my men. I know those who work for me. *And I know that Will Shadwell could neither read nor write to save his life.*'

He stood up, remembering to make it look painful, and left without ceremony given or received. Cecil was standing by the window, motionless, as the great door closed.

He had told the truth about Will Shadwell to Cecil, at any rate. If Cecil had bothered to check, instead of simply ordering Shadwell and Gresham murdered, he would have found Shadwell could neither read nor write. As for Cecil's tale, it could be true, or it could be another lie. Thomas Percy was a newly appointed Gentleman of the Bedchamber, better able than most to supply details of who entered the King's inner chamber. Cecil probably did think he was protecting the realm from its enemies by all he did, that he was the saviour of the nation.

Mannion was waiting for him. The crowd of hopefuls had not diminished.

'Now for Alsatia?' enquired Mannion, expressionless.

'Now for Alsatia,' confirmed Gresham, remembering to limp slightly as if in pain from the load strapped to his belly until they were well away from Cecil's lair, and sure they were not being followed.

There was no Watch to call out the hour in Alsatia. No constable or serjeant-at-arms entered Alsatia to serve his warrant. There were no walls around Alsatia, yet its boundaries excluded friends of the state just as the iron walls of the Tower excluded its enemies. If London was a fine ship, Alsatia was its bilges, the lowest sump where all that was foul-smelling gathered and stank. Gresham's spies, his scum, came to the various meeting places in ones and twos, draped and cloaked not against the cold but against discovery and recognition. No-one walked straight in Alsatia. All skulked along in the shade of the leaning, stinking buildings, all sought to walk in shadow.

The House lay shuttered, many of the servants sent home to the country to help with the harvest. The dust gathered in Gresham's rooms at Granville College, his place on High Table empty.

Gresham had set up camp on the first floor of a foul-looking three-storey house with mildew rotting the outer timbers. Inside it was a different story. Stout new doors blocked the way into the first-floor rooms, which were newly floored. The shutters of seasoned timber had had paint loosely splashed on them to make them look old, but underneath the mess were also clearly new.

'You've had these rooms prepared?' asked Jane. She looked thinner, and there was still a slightly haunted look to her eyes, but her spirit was returning.

'Of course,' said Gresham, genuinely startled. 'This isn't the first time I've had to vanish.'

The pile of books in the corner was one antidote to boredom. Disguise was the other. Mannion adorned himself in the rough jerkin and cowl of the stonemason, tools strapped to his belt. Gresham wrapped himself in a poorer version of Mannion's costume, setting himself up as apprentice to the older man. Jane they put in a filthy smock. She could be a common-law wife, a whore or even a sister to Gresham. In Alsatia no-one cared, and in the wider streets of London no-one had time to notice.

Slowly, excruciatingly slowly, the information dribbled in, often as tattered and piecemeal as those who brought it. It was three weeks of boredom, of trudging through the filthy streets, of keeping two eyes in the back of their heads, of disturbed nights when a scream or a howl sent Gresham and Mannion grasping for their swords. Three weeks before a real picture began to emerge. Most of it came from servants, of course. There was no house where the servants did not know more than their Lord and mistress about what was going on.

Sharpy Sam was one of Gresham's most valuable sources. An elderly, grandfatherly figure, he was a wandering tinker who would sell you an occasional pot or pan and sharpen your knives, or sing you the latest ballad over supper, and was tolerated by the authorities in his illegal wandering life simply because he was useful. Many an unsuspecting scullery maid had taken pity on Sharpy Sam and invited him for a morsel of food and a warm by the fire, to find herself left a short while later with a memory of pleasure and a bastard in her belly.

Gresham knew Sam's annual progress. The Midlands and the west in high summer, London in late autumn and the south coast for the winter months. He had sent one of his own men, a young, lusty recruit with a love of horseflesh and women, to ride hard after Sam and brief him with the same names Moll had given him. Catesby. Kit Wright. Jack Wright. Tom Wintour. Thomas Percy. And Francis Tresham, of course. Even before Sam presented himself to talk to Gresham there was news enough, so much news indeed that Gresham marvelled at even Cecil's not finding it out. The men had been meeting regularly. They were all Catholics, all linked by blood or by marriage, and frequently by both. Then, out of the blue, a greasy John at one of the taverns in the Strand reported another name. Guido or Guy Fawkes, an armourer and mercenary.

The name and his profession clinched it for Gresham.

Why did a group of Catholics, many of whom had a history of rebellion only a few years earlier with the ill-fated Essex, want to meet with a soldier and armourer? Such men knew about weapons, armour and powder. The presence of one of Northumberland's relatives and henchmen had to be crucial. So did the servant gossip of great stocks of weaponry and horses over and above any conceivable need being laid in.

A group of dissident men in regular conclave. A professional soldier. A potential leader drawn from one of the oldest aristocratic families in the kingdom. Weapons and war supplies being bought in.

It had to be an uprising.

With the Spanish troops quartered in Dover? Possibly. Was Northumberland involved? He was the only Catholic with the breeding and the standing to act as Protector if King James was done away with. If Gresham were in Northumberland's rich shoes, he would not bother with the Spanish troops in Dover, except as perhaps a distant threat to divert Cecil's attention. Rather he would turn not only to all the young English Catholic men blooding themselves and defining their manhood in the European wars, but to all the disaffected soldiers in Europe who might smell easy meat in knocking a new Scottish King off an English throne. After all, had not a Catholic ambassador described James in the hearing of his court as 'a scabbard without a sword'? Europe was more scared of Queen Bess than they were of James. Scottish Kings were brought up to defend themselves by a knife in the back, not a cavalry-charge to the front. There was nothing approaching an army in England, and the only man left to build and lead a fleet was Sir Walter Raleigh, languishing in the Tower on a trumped-up charge of treason.

Gresham paced up and down the small room, spilling his thoughts to Jane and Mannion.

'It must be an uprising!' he exclaimed. 'These men aren't

170

courtiers, men who wish to rule! They're gentry, foolish idealists, men who think because they've held a sword and fought off a drunken ploughboy in a market-town brawl that they're soldiers. I don't believe the Earl of Northumberland could stir himself to be King if he was asked by Jesus himself! No, their plot must be to kidnap the King. He makes it easy. The man's besotted with hunting. Where easier to grab a monarch than in a forest where his men are bound to be split up? Take him, hold him in some stronghold with two or three hundred well-armed men. Move your mercenaries and your missionaries over from the Lowlands before a navy or an army can be mustered. The King's a coward. Show him some cold steel, prick him a little, make him sign what you will. Make him call a Parliament, make him promise God on earth to the people. Ride him in state back to London . . . they will have to kill Cecil, of course . . .'

Gresham's mind was racing ahead, as it always did, plotting the moves he himself would have undertaken in order to turn the uprising into a new government.

'Would it work?' The question was Mannion's.

'It could be *made* to work. I must meet these men, this Catesby and this Tresham above all. Then I will know.'

Then, almost at the end of September, Sharpy Sam had sent a message to the House for Gresham to meet him, in a Deptford tavern a stone's throw away from where Kit Marlowe's murder was meant to have taken place.

Sam was a Devon man with a deep burr in his voice. Like most of his kind he was a pirate at heart, but for some reason had turned from the sea twenty years past to take up his wandering trade.

'They were on a pilgrimage,' he had told Gresham over their third flagon of ale. He spoke slowly, measuring every word as if it had a value. 'Would you believe it? As bold as brass they were, some forty of them, paradin' through the marches as if they owned the land, priests in tow. Not as some of them looked like priests, as I remember,' he said disapprovingly. He took a pull of his ale, rolling the taste around his tongue before swallowing it. 'I made for Huddington, thinkin' I'd let them come to me instead of my chasin' all over the countryside, and got myself taken indoors. There's no doubt the servants and womenfolk are all a-twitter – more horses in the stable than the Duke of Parma, more swords than the Armada. They says it's for the young folk to go an' fight with the Archduke. Archpiss, if you ask me. More like that lot want the Archduke over here, rapin', lootin' and pillagin'.' The phrase obviously rang a bell with Sharpy, who repeated it, rolling it around his mouth like the ale. 'Rapin', lootin' and pillagin'.'

'Disgraceful,' said Gresham, 'all this rapin', lootin' and pillagin'.' There was a sniff that could have been a splutter from Jane, but which turned into a loudly blown nose. She was parked behind Gresham, dirt all over her face, and training herself to look longingly at the beer the men were drinking. 'Noisy girl, isn't she?' enquired Sharpy. 'Nice tits, though,' he added approvingly, and grinned at her. If Sharpy realised that Gresham had suddenly acquired an inability to put a 'g' on the end of his words, he did not show it.

'Well, there's two bits of news as might interest you. The first is that man Catesby. Handsome bugger, fancies himself. Pure luck, as it happens. I was down at Huddington – that cook they 'ave, she's special in the kitchen and special up against an apple tree – when this Catesby rides in to see his friend, Rookwood. He'd come ahead, seein' as he likes fine horseflesh, and likes to ride them hard. Lovely boy, Rookwood. Dressed like a paint shop. Talk is among his servants, Catesby gets going with Rookwood, he comes over all miserable, spends the night on his knees in a tiny room there, one candle. He's mumblin' a prayer, and they tries to listen. Can't hear much, except somethin' about "God's vengeance" and a "great enterprise" and "preserve my family". That put the fear of God into the servants' hall, I can tell you. Well, anyhow, next mornin' Rookwood takes a great mass o' money out of his chest and gives it to this Catesby. Catesby's up to somethin', that's sure.

An' it's somethin' that needs a ton of money, that's sure as well. I bin there with Essex and his bunch, I were there with Babington and *his* bunch, I seen it and I smelt it before. It's rebellion, I tell you, the stupid buggers. Some people don't deserve to be born with heads on their bodies. Should be taken off at birth, to save the hangman the trouble later on!'

'There was other news, Sharpy?'

'Right enough. Another tankard of this would be welcome . . . thanks. That boy Tresham you asked after? News is, his father's dead. Not before time, by the sound of it. Pompous old bugger, they says as know. Left a ton of debt, but young Francis got a pretty penny still. Not before time. They say as how he's up to his young neck in debt. 'E's a bastard, that one. Tried to do in a pregnant girl, fiddled his father out of land.'

'I don't think I'm going to like this Francis Tresham,' said Jane.

'I think you'd better pray to God you never meet him!' answered Gresham.

The house in Alsatia was starting to feel like home, Gresham thought ruefully as they finally made it back there from Deptford. It was not the house that depressed him, he knew, as he mounted the stairs and slumped down on a chair, the black mood mounting in him.

Mannion went downstairs, to bring them wine.

'Does it matter, this uprising?' Jane had tuned in to his mood, was trying to tease the melancholy out of him without seeming to do so. 'All Kings and Queens are rotten,' she said calmly, in a sweeping generalisation that Gresham noted as disposing of humanity's favoured form of government for several thousand years past. 'Look at our King. His legs can't hold up his body, his tongue's too big for his mouth so he slobbers like a baby and his clothes are as ragged as the jewels he places on them are bright. He stinks and he's lousy. He learnt his statecraft in a small nation that's only learned to survive by alliance with France and by murdering its rulers, and so he negotiates a treaty with Spain instead of realising that we're victors over Spain and a great power now in our own right. His wife has no brains and his favourites no balls . . . excuse my language . . . are we worse off if he's knocked off his throne?'

'You know Machiavelli? The books I gave you?'

'I've read them, yes.'

'And?' enquired Gresham.

'He's like most men. He thinks he's talking about everyone but he's actually only talking about himself. He's arrogant, so he spoils a good idea by claiming too much for it.'

Gresham thought for a moment. 'Machiavelli was captured and tortured when his Prince failed to be ruthless and strong. We don't need leaders who are good, or beautiful, or kind, or generous. We need leaders who're effective. Most of all we need peace. Stability.'

'You sound like Cecil, if what you told me about your little chat with him was true. How can you say that, who was brought up to war? You, who've lived your whole life as if it were a war? You, who of all people I know seem to exult in a fight?'

'Because I know for what I fight.'

'And what might that be?'

He sat in silence for a moment, reflective.

'I fight to survive. It's all I can do. It's all I know. You, me, Cecil, we think we're in control, but really we're all actors in a play written by a madman, a play with no meaning and no sense. I know we can't win that fight, I know death is more powerful than any of us – but at least if I fight to survive I haven't given in. That way, death at least takes me on my terms. None of us can make the sun stand still. Yet we can make it run.'

'Is that why you fight Cecil?'

'I'm fighting him firstly because if I don't, I die. We've a truce at present, while he thinks I'm ill, but what he tried once he could well try again. The more I can find out about what he doesn't want me to know, the better armed I am against him.'

'Yet you could destroy him.' Jane said it as a simple matter of fact.

'I could destroy Cecil, I think, rather than merely keep him at bay. I *choose* not to. This isn't just about his life, or my life. For all his evil and his double-dealing, for all that he sums up everything I hold in contempt in a man's lust for power and wealth, his very evil helps hold the country together. It is as Machiavelli says. A man doesn't have to be pure to be a good ruler. He merely has to rule, and if in so doing he consigns his soul to Hell, then that's the price he pays for his worldly power. I fight Cecil only when he fights me, and when he ceases to rule well and with power. If there's an uprising planned and he can't see what's brewing, then I'll fight his ignorance only.'

'Is that all?' asked Jane. 'Would you fight for me?'

'I'd do more than fight for you,' he said simply. 'I'd die for you.' It was a simple statement of fact, uttered with no sense of drama. 'But I fight for someone else as well.'

'I'd rather hoped I was the only one . . .' said Jane, who to her obvious irritation had managed to get something in her eye that was making it water.

'I fight for John Plowman, thin-wrapped in the bitter cold, pissing in the field in which he works and coming home with his hands bitten and scarred by the very plough that feeds him and his family and his Lord. For Meg Milkmaid, who's there waiting for John Plowman as he comes home. He may growl at her, or he may kiss her, or he may have her against her will, but that's in the way of things, that's how we were made, that's how we were meant to be. I know there are few freedoms in their lives – no freedom from hunger, from pain, from illness or from a corrupt and vengeful master. Yet they've some choice, and they make some choices. There's a freedom in the air they breathe, in the sight of cold blue light on a frosty morning, in the first leap of a fish in Spring. There's something good in their children, ragged-arsed though they be, some good in the work they do.'

'Well,' said Jane, pragmatically, 'this particular Meg Milkmaid remembers something a little different from her upbringing in this wonderful countryside you talk so lovingly of.'

'At least you were there for me to find you. You hadn't been trampled under a warhorse's hooves, stuck as a bleeding trophy on the end of a pike and ridden through the lanes with soldiers whooping for joy.'

He turned on Jane, not seeing her, but seeing instead the horrors that haunted him still at night.

'I've seen such things . . . such things as make me despair of God or Heaven. You remember Marlowe? "Why this is hell, nor am I out of it . . ." Well, I've seen no God, not here on earth, but I've heard God in music and in words, seen something of a God in the sunset or in a light-filled stone chapel in Cambridge as a song rises to Heaven. Yet I too think we live in Hell, and like Marlowe I despair of God, and from that despair comes my anger. And what have we, when all is left? John and Meg, living a life of hard toil, lit only by their need, their lust to survive, to see things through, to feed and clothe themselves and pass on that bare sustenance to their children. There's dignity enough in their mere survival, in their struggle to have and to hold a little human happiness to themselves in their short time here. They have enough to cope with, without we inflict rebellion and war on them. They need our help to survive. What difference to Meg and John and their growing horde if it's a James, an Elizabeth, a Henry or a Richard on the throne? What means it to them if it's a Plantagenet, a Tudor or a Stuart? What matter, as long as the soldiers stay in their barracks and their whorehouses, the enemy dare not invade and their Lord stands in some fear of London if he takes too many liberties with his tenants?

'We gentry, we nobles, we fight for the glitter, Jane. We fight for our power, our jewels and our wealth. Most of all we fight to gain power, because in wielding that power we give some meaning to our pathetic, flimsy little lives, before they are snuffed out by illness, by bad luck or simply by time.

'*We fight for the wrong things*. We shouldn't fight for our own power, our own lusts. We should fight to preserve a life for those who have no power except their power to survive. We should fight for those who have no power to fight for themselves.'

There was a silence.

'My knight in shining armour,' said Jane, part teasing and part heart-torn, 'mounted on his pure white charger. Hasn't your charger gained a little dirt during the fight? How many men have you killed, Henry Gresham? How many of them do you remember, when you lie awake at night, thinking that no-one knows, or when you dream, and mumble restless names in your sleep? Do you really know what you fight? And is it so John and Meg can have peace in their mud hut of a home?'

There was a strangely flat tone in Gresham's response. 'So John and Meg can be left with some vestige of choice for their own lives. So they can survive too, with a shred of their dignity left to them as well.'

'He's right, mistress.'

They both jumped. Neither had heard Mannion enter the room. For one so large he could move like a cat when he chose.

'You take your pleasures where you can. You fight when you must. It's not about winning. It's about survival.' He handed them both a chalice of wine. 'See that there? Drink it. Enjoy it. It won't taste at all when you're dead meat. Nothing tastes when you're dead. So the whole game is to stay alive. Just that. There's no living at all for the dead.'

Jane levelled a dark look at Mannion, and then at Gresham. 'So by the men's philosophy, if you've to kill a whole nation to stay alive yourself then it's justified? What about Meg and John and their brats then?'

'It don't come to that, hardly ever,' said Mannion easily, sitting down and slurping from the tankard of ale he had brought for himself. 'Only Kings think that the whole country dies if they die, and so kill all their folk in the name of their reigning! No, and that's why they need men like Sir Henry here, to work for them and do their dirty work. It's what he does. He puts them right. His job is to see that only enough men die. Bastards like that Essex, bastards like this Catesby, they reckon their glory is in how many people they take with them. Forget how many Sir Henry's killed. Ask how many he's saved.'

'Women think differently,' mused Jane. The fire was crackling in the grate, and throwing shards of red and yellow light over their faces as they sat in an unconscious circle, framed by darkness. 'We carry a future in our wombs. We don't see life as stopping with ourselves. Rather we see ourselves as the means of carrying it on.'

There was an awkward pause, as the childless Gresham looked into the burning heart of the fire.

'Well,' he said finally, 'one of us here is redeemed. With the number of bastards you've fathered, old man, we must have a future. Though God help us in it if the bastards take after their misbegotten father.'

It was an old joke, and as with many such it was not the sense of it that drew them together, but simply that it had been spoken at all.

Jane spoke at last, after a long pause. 'You realise the danger if you infiltrate this group of Papists? Cecil will kill you if he finds you're active. The Papists will kill you if they find you're in on whatever their stupid secret is. The Government will kill you first and ask questions later if there's even a hint you're implicated in the plot. You're already tainted with being one of Raleigh's few remaining allies.'

'I always liked being popular,' replied Gresham calmly.

'I'm serious,' said Jane. 'If you walk into this plot, if you somehow get hold of this man Phelippes put you on to, it'll be a gate that slams shut behind you. There'll be no going back, and no knowing what lies in front of you.'

'Humans were designed to go forward, not look back,' Gresham said. 'That's why our eyes are in the front of our head.'

'So is this man going to be your gateway in? This Tresham?'

'Francis Tresham is the man. I feel it. He's our way in, our only way in.'

Gresham curbed the impatience that was threatening to tear him apart. His informants told him that Catesby was still off on his travels. Whatever it was that Catesby planned, he would need to be at the centre of things in London to organise the final planning and co-ordinate his uprising, even if the main action was subsequently to take place in a Hertfordshire forest where His Highness hunted the stag. They had some time, he told himself, though how much only God and Catesby knew.

Then the news came in. Francis Tresham had been seen in London.

All that remained now was to kidnap Tresham.

Syon House, London home of the Earl of Percy, was on alert. The Earl, often a quiet and studious man, was in one of his tempers. Henry Percy, ninth Earl of Northumberland, noted the hesitancy in the step of the servant who came in answer to his furious ringing of the bell. Increasingly deaf, and slow in his ways, Henry Percy had shown from his earliest days an ability to conjure up a temper out of nothing. They used to call him the Wizard Earl, though not because of his ability to conjure up a rage. Rather it was their ignorance, their seeing black magic in his simple experiments and refusing to accept that knowledge could be advanced by such means without recourse to God or the Devil. Raleigh had been an ally, and his reward had been a farcical trial for treason and a judgement that left him rotting in the Tower. Others of the so-called 'School of Night' had died scandalous deaths, like Kit Marlowe, or simply faded away. Now only he was left. His power in the north – that dreadful land of rain, mist and pickpockets – was unchallenged, even reinforced by the accession to the English throne of a Scottish King. True, neither King James VI of Scotland nor King James I of England could stop the reivers and the incessant border raids, and no-one ever would. Yet at least the Earl of Northumberland knew that he would not have to be the vanguard against an invading Scottish army in the lifetime of the present

King. No, the threat to him no longer came from the north. It came from London. Yet precisely from where in London it came was more difficult to answer. From the carcass of James I, leader of the nation the Percys had been in bitter conflict with for centuries? Or from the twisted body of Robert Cecil?

Percy shuffled across the room. There were no rushes nor fine carpet on the stone flags of the floor, and the fire in the vast hearth was unlit despite the chill the stonework inflicted. He had inherited Syon House from his wife Dorothy, who held the leasehold on it. He was well rid of her, and in keeping the house and losing the woman he had kept the better part of the bargain. Autumn would have come early to the north, as if the harsh countryside resented the warmth of summer and could not wait to return to the cold. The noise of the grey sea crashing against rock the colour of the castle walls was one of his most vivid memories of the north.

He stood by an open window, letting the taste of London wash against his face and skin. His so-called relative, the young Thomas Percy, would be busy telling the City how he had the confidence and the assurances of the ninth Earl of Northumberland, his relative and patron. So much to the good. Young Thomas would learn as many had before him why the senior branch of the Percys had survived the savagery of the north and all the politics of London could bring to bear, and why there had always been a third person present at their meetings. A flicker of something that might have been the start of a savage smile lifted the corner of the Earl's mouth. He would learn, would Thomas Percy, as would all enemies of the Percy clan and the Catholic faith. They thought him easily led, as if he could not see through their pathetic flattery. They joked about his inability to keep a secret, not realising how carefully he had cultivated that image. Well, Robert Cecil, jumped-up Earl of Salisbury, would find soon enough whether Henry Percy, ninth Earl of Northumberland, could keep a secret, a secret that when revealed would destroy Robert Cecil for ever.

CHAPTER 7

'I still don't think I like the sound of this man Francis Tresham,' said Jane, working through the pile of papers on which Gresham had scribbled notes and records of interviews.

Mannion's proposal for securing the undivided attention of Francis Tresham was simple. Waylay him in a street, knock him on the head and drag him off to Alsatia. Even in London's anarchic streets it struck Gresham that this direct action might draw unnecessary attention to those involved. Jane had the simplest and best idea. Send Tresham a note in his lodgings, a note promising that he would hear something to his advantage if he came to their address in Alsatia, with a time scrawled on it.

'Spiders don't go chasing flies,' said Jane. 'Flies come to spiders.'

Jane had read her man correctly. A sensible young man, newly come into his inheritance, would not have risked the trip into Alsatia on what might have been a wild-goose chase. But Francis Tresham was not sensible, not once during his whole life.

'So he comes here, knocks on the door – and then we knock him over?' suggested Mannion hopefully.

'He'll be on his own, if we tell him to,' said Gresham. 'If he's come this far, we're hardly going to need to drag him in through the door unconscious, are we? Do you only have four ways of responding to anything?'

'As many as that?' enquired Jane innocently.

'Eat it, drink it, bed it or hit it. Has it ever entered your mind to *think* about something?'

'No,' said Mannion, 'takes too much time.' He gathered up the breakfast dishes. 'And whatever it is I do, it's kept me alive all these years.' He clumped down the stairs, clearly feeling himself fully justified.

Tresham's servant gloried in the name William Vavasour. He looked down his nose at the hefty bribe Mannion put with the note to his master, but did not refuse it. Tresham's greed triumphed over any discretion he might have had, and he turned up on cue at the door of the ill-favoured house as night was falling. A huge rat was feeding off something that might once have been flesh. It looked haughtily up at Tresham, and scuttled off only when it had delayed long enough to show who held the real command. The grumpy and ill-looking couple Gresham had installed on the ground floor of the house let Tresham in, and the man motioned with his head for him to go upstairs. As he did so, the door clanged shut behind him, and Tresham turned to see the doorway blocked out by the figure of Mannion.

'Upstairs . . .' Mannion breathed at him, and he fled up the thin wooden treads like a bolting rabbit.

Gresham sat at the table. The shutters had been closed, and the room was full of lamps. He was dressed in black, with a small, neat white ruff the only contrast on his dress. Several of the Gresham jewels sparkled on his fingers and his clothes. There was a chilling stillness to him. He flicked a hand, inviting Tresham to be seated.

Tresham was a wiry, unkempt figure in his late thirties, Gresham knew. He would have guessed him some years short of that, his boyish face showing few wrinkles. At first glance he was quite handsome, but the effect was reduced by a set of thin lips and eyes that flickered all the time like a snake's tongue. His shirt was filthy, the doublet over it richly slashed and pointed but crumpled and dirty. He wore muddy riding boots over a fine hose that would not have shamed an audience at court.

'Who are you? What do you want?' Tresham barked out the words, his hand fingering the fine sword hanging by his waist.

'I'm your avenging angel,' said Gresham mildly, 'and I can send you to Heaven or to Hell. What I want is to decide which one it will be.'

'You have no hold over me, you . . .'

Gresham cut Tresham short with one simple motion, holding up the palm of his hand.

'Francis Tresham, born 1567, first child and only son of Sir Thomas Tresham of Rushton and Muriel Throckmorton of Coughton. Educated at St John's College and Gloucester Hall.

'First arrested in June 1591. You altered a Privy Council warrant, didn't you? Instead of some Godforsaken tailor who owed you money you substituted the name of a troublesome tenant. Then you beat him up and his pregnant daughter.'

'That's not true! The man was a rogue, he . . .'

'Shut up,' said Gresham, quietly, and for some reason Francis Tresham did so.

'Bailed out by your father this time, and countless times thereafter. Married Anne Tufton of Hothfield, and soon one of the wild band who gathers in Essex House giving promises as rashly as they spend money they do not have. Arrested again in 1596 for possible involvement in a Catholic conspiracy, and arrested in 1601 for involvement in the Essex uprising. Bribed out of the Tower, to the near ruin of his father. The father who is now dead, of course. The loving father who spent thousands of pounds on rescuing his son, despite the fact that the son in question, allowed to live in the manor of Hoxton, tried to cheat his father out of lands he owned there . . .'

Tresham had sat with head bowed. Suddenly he placed both his hands under the table and heaved it up at Gresham, following it with a mad rush, his sword half out of his scabbard. It had worked for him in countless taverns and brawls.

He could not remember properly what happened next. The strange, dark man was suddenly not behind the table, but standing to one side. Tresham felt a huge blow to the side of his head, and then a searing, roaring pain. The dark man's toe connected with vicious power between his legs, the flat of his foot sending him flying through the air. He flew into the wall, cracking his head on a timber, and blackness descended.

'I knew you'd have to hit him,' said Mannion contentedly, dragging up the prostrate figure and propping him upright against the wall. 'Shall I tie him up?'

'No,' said Gresham. 'Let him try again, if he needs to. He must know who his new master is. He won't learn tied up.'

When Tresham came round he was aflame with pain. The most beautiful girl he had ever seen was sponging the blood off what felt like a large hole in his head. He felt sick with the agony in his groin.

The girl spoke calmly, as she took the sponge away. 'I think I'll not try to ease the pain down there,' she said. 'Look at me.'

He did so. Her eyes were the most startling dark pools he had ever seen, burning with an intensity he had only seen before on the coldest and clearest star-lit night.

'Take my advice. Don't fight him. Here, or elsewhere. He'll win, and you'll die. Listen, do what he says, and you might live.'

She placed the bloodied cloth in a rough wooden bucket, and moved out of the light. Was he in Heaven, or in Hell? And was this stunning creature an angel or a devil?

'What do you want?' asked Tresham, muzzily.

'Shall we start again?' It was the same figure, dressed in black, seated behind the same table that had been returned to exactly the same place. Yet this time there was a silver jug and two goblets on the table, and a delicious smell of fruity wine. The wild thought crossed Tresham's mind that the man had known he would hurl the table back, had not placed the wine on it until the first, annoying little trial of strength was over and they could get down to business. A different type of fear began to flood through his veins, a fear so sharp that it started to soften the physical pain and make it less important.

'Guido or Guy Fawkes. Robert, or Robin as he is sometimes called, Catesby. Thomas Percy. Thomas Wintour. Robert Wintour. John Grant. Kit Wright. John Wright. Robert Keyes.'

Suddenly the pain returned.

'Do you want to come and sit at the table? To take some wine with me? You're not bound.'

The confidence, the sheer arrogance of the man. As far as Tresham could see there was only the woman in the room, seated in a corner. They had not even taken his sword or dagger away. An overwhelming sense of defeat came to Tresham. He crawled to his feet, sucking in his breath as the blood flowed through his broken head and sent needles into his brain and groin.

'What do you want? Who are you?'

Tresham knew the questions were sounding like an increasingly pathetic litany.

'I want you.' Gresham spoke as if it were the simplest thing in the world. 'I know that something evil is being planned by a group of men who number you among their friends. I believe you either know of it, or are in a position to find out. And I know that you face ruin and prosecution already, because you've been in trouble too many times, and you'll be associated with whatever these your friends are up to regardless of whether or not you're involved. You're a very lonely man, Francis Tresham.'

He paused for a moment.

'And you're a fool. You've chased every fashion and innovation the world could offer, without thought, without sensitivity and without feeling. You've lived your life as if life itself was created only for you, and for your enjoyment.'

Tresham looked up, startled.

'Granted, you seem to love your wife as much as you love anyone except yourself, but even that's not much. I believe you're one of nature's traitors. A spy. A double agent . . .'

'My father was a pompous old fool.' There was defiance, a cruel arrogance in Tresham's eyes. As well as a capacity for a very quick recovery. 'He spent thousands on vainglorious buildings. What matter if some of that money was diverted to my vainglory? At least I was a living thing, not a thing of cold brick and stone! For him I feel no guilt.'

'I'm sure you don't,' said Gresham. 'But now you'll turn traitor for me.'

'And why should I do that?'

'For self-interest, as you've done everything in your life. Because if I know that your friends are about to behave most dangerously, so will others know, and you're too selfish to wish to be dragged down with them. Because I'll give you a great deal of money. And because I'll kill you if you don't.'

'How much money?'

Gresham told him. His eyes opened wide.

'Can you prove to me you have that much money?'

Gresham tossed a purse on to the table. It shivered under the weight. Tresham pulled it open, let the gold coins run through his fingers. Gresham felt rather than heard Jane's disapproval from behind him.

'Do you have to give good money to such a . . . *stench* of a man?' Jane had asked. She had never quite got used to, and never quite brought herself to believe, how much Gresham was worth. He saw money as a tool. She saw it as security.

Tresham's mind had been focussed by the gold. Perhaps here there was real profit, as well as mere survival.

'If my . . . friends are as indiscreet as you say, what if their ship breaks up and they're cast on the shore while I'm still inside it?'

'If needs be, you'll be spirited out of the Tower and sent off to France.'

186

'You can do that?' Disbelief mingled with wonder caught Tresham's voice. The sheer weight of gold had shocked him.

'Yes. Enough bargaining. How much do you already know of what your friends are planning?'

There are moments in life when huge crossroads come to bear in one time and in one place, not just on the life of one human, but on the life of countless thousands. A decision taken one way, and history spins instantly down one road, making that road seem the inevitable, the only choice. Yet there are countless other roads, and but for one decision, one moment frozen in time, the inevitable might never have happened. Without realisation, without seeing a tiny fraction of all the roads that might have been, in a filthy hovel, Francis Tresham chose his road, and in so doing chose the road for countless other souls. There was no priest there to sanctify or bless the act, no ritual to clothe and comfort the deed, no scribe ready to record a laundered version for later generations. There was only a man dressed in black with a neat white ruff and piercing eyes.

Tresham sat back, reached forward for wine as if daring Gresham to deny him.

'I know Robin Catesby has some idea to remove the Government and to bring in Catholic rule to England. He and the others have been talking for years. We've all been talking. Yet we've done nothing. Until now. Those names you mentioned. They've been meeting, all of them, more even than normal. There's talk, gossip. Whatever this plan is, it has the women all a-twitter, and the priests looking like a woman had been elected Pope. I know no details. Catesby's sworn me to secrecy. He told me it was safer if I knew nothing that could be tortured out of me, but that my time would come. He told me that he must keep me warm for the fire that would break out later. I think he's nervous of me.'

'You mean your friends don't think you're trustworthy?'

Tresham shrugged, carelessly.

An interesting young man, Gresham thought. Not without

courage – the trick with the table would have worked with someone of less experience and speed. The crack on the head and the kick to the prospects of the next Tresham heir must still be causing him considerable pain, as would the shock of realising that his secret was in the hands of a potential enemy, yet he had recovered quickly, was thinking on his feet. He was offering no emotional pleading, no excuses. He was scum, thought Gresham. Will Shadwell with money and some breeding. An adventurer, a wanton.

'How do I know you'll pay me the rest?'

'I will,' said Gresham. 'It's as certain that I'll pay you if you spy for me as it's certain I'll kill you if you don't. Anyway, in the gospel, even Judas was paid.'

How would he take that hit?

Tresham blinked, but recovered. 'Without Judas, Christ might have lived. And if that had been true, we would have been deprived of all the bishops and prelates the world has ever seen. How could we have lived deprived of such comfort? Perhaps even Judas was sent from Heaven.'

Witty, too, thought Gresham, in a clumsy sort of way. His victim was speaking again.

'Who are you? For whom or for what do you work? Are you one of Cecil's men?'

'Be careful,' said Jane from her corner, 'unless you want the other side of your head broken, and more besides!'

'No,' said Gresham, 'I'm not one of Cecil's men. I'm someone who sees a torrent of blood falling on the heads of innocent and guilty alike. I can't stop that blood. I can, perhaps, limit it.'

'How can I know that? You're asking me to trust my life to you, without even a name I can call out should I die doing your will.'

'Then best make sure you don't die. And best make sure not to betray me. It's not good for those who seek to do so.'

'That I do believe. What do you want from me, if I'm asked to join whatever is planned? Just to betray my friends? Or to kill someone?' Neither prospect seemed to alarm Francis Tresham.

'Your friends have betrayed themselves already. I suspect they're like you, dead men merely waiting the fall of the executioner's axe. As for the rest of it, I want information.' Gresham felt like adding that whatever he asked for and received, its aim would be to get as few killed as possible. That might make it less attractive for Tresham. He kept silent.

'There's something I've not told you,' Tresham said, reaching another decision. He had adapted to the new circumstances with ferocious speed, thought Gresham. 'I'm bidden to dinner with Robin Catesby next week. At William Patrick's ordinary, The Irish Boy, on the Strand.'

'Who else goes?'

Tresham reeled off some names. One of them was Ben Jonson, the playwright, another the Catholic peer Lord Mordaunt.

'There'll be another guest. Myself.'

'How so? Do you want me to ask for another invitation?'

'No. How I get there is my concern. All that's required of you is to give no sign of recognition at the dinner. This Catesby,' said Gresham, 'describe him to me.'

Mannion escorted Tresham back to his lodgings, following a few paces behind. Francis Tresham had suddenly become a very valuable commodity. Gresham stayed with his other valuable commodity.

'I was right,' said Jane, 'I didn't like him at all.' He had leered at Jane as he left. 'I'd hate to be a woman in his power.'

Gresham needed to meet Catesby face to face. The man described by the informers and the man described by Francis Tresham was a larger-than-life figure, a maniac preacher with the capacity to lift people off their seats and brand them to his cause. Yet Gresham had known such people who were pure charlatans, whose bravado vanished at the first hint of reality. Was Catesby such a person, weaving a huge web of intrigue to feed a massive pride, a vessel of much noise and no substance? Or did he have the power to mount an uprising, to knock settled government off its perch and into the raging seas of rebellion and unrest?

Gresham had to see this Catesby, had to meet him, had to taste the flavour of the man in the flesh.

So it was that there was an extra guest at dinner in The Irish Boy.

Robert Catesby waited outside Harrowden, his horse restless, shaking its head and pawing the ground. It was as if the animal picked up the unease of its master. Tom Bates looked questioningly at his master, to ask if he wished Bates to take the horse walking round the yard. Catesby shook his head.

Everard Digby was taking an unconscionably long time to say farewell to his wife and children, he thought. It was not as if they were riding to the ends of the world. It was only some fifteen miles from Harrowden to Gayhurst. They had all gathered at Harrowden, both the Vaux women, the new Lord Vaux, the other women and the priests and all the other band of wittering folk. They thought him hot-headed and rash, but he had the sense to realise how dangerous these gatherings were so soon after the pilgrimage to Flintshire had wound its very public way through the marches.

Digby – Sir Everard Digby – had also been one of the company at Harrowden, which was why Catesby had invited himself to attend. Yet the moment to get Digby on his own, to broach the plot and the vital part Digby had to play in it, never seemed to present itself. In desperation, Catesby had hinted at how much the party would enjoy a stay at Gayhurst, Digby's home, after the dilapidated state of Harrowden. When the ever-innocent Digby had agreed with his usual enthusiasm, it had been easy for Catesby to suggest that the two old friends might ride on ahead, to check that all was ready to receive the new guests at Gayhurst, or Gothurst as it was sometimes known.

Catesby saw all people through the mirror of his own soul. He had seen for years how the power and the charm he could direct on to his fellow men and women would eat away at their reserve and caution, however hard they tried to resist it, and make them as clay in his hands. For most of his life luring people into the web of his personality had been a game, a pleasure to put alongside hunting, gambling and, latterly, bedding a pretty woman.

Yet he felt uneasy over his final recruits. Francis Tresham was a wild and an angry thing, a man with no real belief that Catesby could anchor on to. Yet Catesby had always known that Tresham would also acquire a great deal of wealth on the death of his father, something which all along had made him an attractive proposition. Well, he would clinch it in London and then at Clerkenwell. The need for money was too pressing to allow for any delay, and once sworn in Tresham, like all the others, would have too much to lose by betrayal.

Everard Digby was a different proposition. Catesby needed him not only for his money, but for his personality as well. One of Digby's attractions was his innocence. Another was his staunch Protestant background. He had been converted by the priest Gerard, who not only behaved and dressed like a gentleman but, thought Catesby, actually believed he was one. Father Gerard had caught Digby somehow when he was ill, and used his panic to show him the true path. Amusingly, he had converted Mary, Digby's wife, entirely separately, with neither of the pair knowing of the other's conversion. It was typical of Gerard to keep the news from them and enjoy their consternation at the discovery.

It was that radiant innocence, that wholesomeness that Catesby needed. Everard was not only known at Court. He was feted as one of its rising stars. He looked like a God, and he rode a horse as if he had been sewn to it in the womb. He was an excellent swordsman and, by all accounts, a brilliant musician, though the latter was something Catesby had never acquired the taste for. Someone had to invest Coombe Abbey and take away the Princess Elizabeth. If it was a rat-arsed Tom Wintour, John Grant with a face that looked like it had come from Hell or a drunken Thomas Percy who broke in to Coombe House to take the Princess Elizabeth, the servants would as like fight to the death as do the decent thing and

191

surrender before anyone got hurt, reckoning they were dead already. The Princess Elizabeth was only a girl after all, and too much fear could cause God knew what complications with her. Didn't girls who thought their virtue was threatened throw themselves off high walls? Any girl with half her wits about her seeing Wintour, Grant or Percy coming towards her would know she was going to get more than a handshake. Yet if Digby was the attacker there might well be no fight at all. He was a Court favourite, a knight and one of the new King's Gentlemen Pensioners, known as a family man through and through, and with a visage that could calm a raging bull. Princess Elizabeth was no use to Catesby or to Catholicism skewered on a blade or cast down into a ditch. Why, Digby's charm might even keep the truth away from her about what had happened to her mother and father for some crucial hours. All the more likely if Digby himself did not know the truth – or at least, not the whole truth.

Why should Digby throw away a beautiful wife, a beautiful family and some of the best prospects in the country to join a wild plot? Catesby smiled to himself as Digby came pelting down the steps to his waiting horse, full of apologies and orders to his men. Beneath the sweet innocence the world saw in Sir Everard Digby, Catesby saw a mulish determination and stubbornness where it came to religion.

They set off along the deserted road, Tom Bates riding behind and carefully out of earshot. For a while they let the horses have their heads. It was as if they could not wait to shed the inactivity of the night in the stables, the pounding of their hooves driving the stable dust out of their bones and the remnants of the night out of their riders' bodies.

'Digby, old friend, will you do something to please me?'

They had reined in by the side of a brook that was almost a trickle, but which in a month would be roaring like a mini-torrent.

'I'd give my life to please you, Robin. You know that.'

'Will you swear an oath of secrecy to me? An oath that on all that's holy, and on all that you hold holy, you'll never reveal what I say to any living soul on earth?'

The ever-present smile on the youthful face of Everard Digby had gone now. There was still the flush of outrageous good health to his face, a face that had been full of happiness and contentment at his fine mount, the fine October morning and the excitement of riding with his friend. A frown of uncertainty caused little-used lines to crinkle in his face.

'I do so swear. You have my word as a gentleman. But why . . .'

'I've asked you to swear a simple corporal oath, old friend. The others, the others who're sworn to secrecy, they've had to swear and seal the oath with the blessed sacrament. It's a measure of the faith I have in you, you who've always been special to me, that I need no more than your word as a gentleman. Here . . .' Catesby produced his dagger from his belt. A fine silver inlay, its hilt formed the sign of the Cross, 'swear, here on this dagger. Swear you'll be secret. Swear you'll be silent.'

They made a strange tableau that fine October morning, two finely horsed gentlemen etched against the skyline, the luxury of their lives a mystery to any peasant who might have seen them, imagining some joke or jest to be passing between them as they rested their horses by water.

'I swear,' said Digby, nervous now, but laying hand on the hilt. How cold it felt.

The pair moved on, the ever-present Bates behind them.

'Do you believe in me? Do you believe that I see things others don't see, understand things others don't understand? Do you?'

'Why, yes, of course . . .' Digby was nervous, unsettled. 'You know I've always looked up to you above all others, Robin. Wasn't I one of the first to recognise and tell you that you were special?'

Catesby put out a hand and stopped Digby's horse. It snorted, pushing its head up and down, irritated to be halted.

'Digby, I'm God's messenger. I have known it for years. God is working through me. Do you understand? Do you believe in me?'

He had stopped so the sun was directly behind him, and perhaps the threatening summer shower and the humidity was responsible for the faint aura that seemed to glow round Catesby's head and shoulders.

Everard Digby felt the hot tears scorch his eyelids, and a mixture of embarrassment, fear and awe caused him to stumble in his words.

'I . . . I do believe in you, Robin. You've always been so certain, always known best . . . yes, perhaps it is God I hear speaking through your mouth . . . I . . . I . . .' The hot tears broke their confine and flooded down his face.

'Sssh,' said Catesby, taking his hand and laying it gently across Digby's mouth, as if he were a kind father soothing a baby. 'And listen to me. We plan to destroy the King and his minions. We've powder stacked beneath the Lords, primed and ready. On the day when Parliament is opened, when the King and his heir, when Cecil and his crew, when all those who've oppressed the True Faith are gathered under the one roof, we'll light a fire that won't be extinguished until God's rule is again dominant in England. We'll blow them all to Hell. Even as the blast is happening we'll seize the Princess Elizabeth, and ride through the Midlands and west, raising thousands to add to the three hundred we've assembled. Percy will bring his men down from the north, the Spanish troops in Dover will throw off their idleness and march to Rochester, strangling the Thames and London's life blood. From the south will come the Catholics of Europe . . .'

It is doubtful if Digby heard beyond the first half of Catesby's words. The colour drained from his face. His hands clutched at the horse's reins so hard as to make the animal jump and slither in protest. It was not the movement of his horse that made him put a hand on his pommel, but the sudden wave of sickness and fear that came over him. He stumbled into words.

'This is . . . strange beyond belief. It's a terrible thing, a terrible thing. You ask for my support . . .'

'I *demand* your support.' Catesby leant over to his friend, driving hard with his voice as his chin jutted forward and his voice rose. 'This is no fancy, no boy's play. This is God's work, I know it, a blast that will echo up to Heaven and down to Hell! There can be no-one on the sidelines in this. You're in, or you're a coward. Are you a coward?'

Digby was too young and too spoilt to see that he was being goaded by the accusation of cowardice, goaded into not thinking.

'I'm no coward!' The cry was drawn out of him, as if from a drowning man at the bottom of a deep well. Catesby gave him no time to relent.

'You'll join us then? You'll risk your life for your faith? The faith you've so newly found? Or will you give it up as easily as it came to you? Are you a Christian, or do you simply worship at the altar of ease and comfort, saying the words but denying the duty of faith? Is your belief real, or is it false coin?'

A small tear formed in Everard Digby's right eye, and rolled gently down his cheek. The wind whittled away at it, making it tremble as it hung on his flesh.

'Must I join, Robin? Must I do this?'

'If you're a Christian, you must. If you're a coward, do nothing, except remain secret. Let the men risk all for justice and for their faith, while the children stay at home.'

If the barbs hit home there was no reaction on Digby's face, as round, as innocent and as woebegone as a boy who has been told that Christmas will not happen after all. It was a face that would have melted the heart of a devil, but not the devil sent to accompany Sir Everard Digby on his lonely road to damnation, the devil who went by the name of Catesby.

'I'm no coward, nor no boy. If I must join, I will join your hellish plan, God help me and my loved ones.' There was a pathetic dignity in his tone.

But you have not yet said that you *will* join, Catesby thought. And I need you. I need your wealth, I need your horses, and I need your chivalry and your access to the Court so that the Princess

Elizabeth will come sweetly and there will be no second blood bath. They rode on in silence. Catesby's skill lay in knowing when to talk, but also in when to stay silent.

'What of our friends, Robin? What of the Catholic Lords? Are they to be blown to perdition, as well as our enemies? How could God forgive such a crime?'

'Rest assured, it's taken care of. Those who're worth saving will be preserved, without knowing how or why they were saved. We've thought long on this, and we need you.'

'What of the priests? What do they say? How can a priest sanctify murder?'

'The priests know. They've approved the matter,' Catesby lied. Perhaps a priest knew under the secret of the confessional, but that was not to approve the act, merely to recognise that nothing could break that secret and the bond it established between a man, his priest and his God. How could he head off the young fool going to Father Garnet to confess? Garnet would not reveal the confession directly, but he could take steps in Europe to deny Catesby the help on which his rebellion would depend.

'When we reach your home, I'll show you the texts that make what we do a necessary evil. The Scriptures have always allowed acts of violence against the heathen – were the innocents on the walls of Jericho to be spared before the anger of the Lord? Were the Philistines to be allowed to triumph over God's people and his armies? Didn't the Pope sanctify the death of that whore Elizabeth when she declared herself against God's people?'

Catesby leant over again, and reined in his friend's horse. Gayhurst was visible in the distance, a wisp of smoke and nestling buildings.

'You know what threats we face. Do you want your children to inherit from their father? Do you wish our cause to be ruined, our people cast into penury, our faith trampled into the dust and mud? Then do nothing. Or rise up against the tide of fortune, and fight. *Fight like a man.*'

Sir Everard Digby gazed out on to the home of his wife and his children, the scene of his idyllic marriage and a life as near perfect, in his opinion, as the age could offer. There in the brick and stone of Gayhurst was a future to bring redemption to Hell, a smile on the face of the universe. Was he to risk it all in one fateful throw? Was it his duty? Was it his lot to suffer now, having been blessed so much in his early life?

He turned to his friend.

'You say the priests know of this? They've agreed to it? You'll show me these passages?'

I have you now, exulted Catesby. I have you, and your fine horses, your money and your manners. I have you.

'I will, Everard. Upon my life and upon my soul, I will.'

He set his face into a hard frown, as befitted a man set on serious business, hiding his exultation. Was there a particular pleasure in wrenching a man away from his beautiful wife and fine sons, in placing that wife and her brood in the way of risk and total loss? Digby had been too happy, thought Catesby. No mortal deserved that happiness, it was not the way of the world. Pain, suffering and sacrifice, those were the way of the world. Pain, suffering and sacrifice that all the world had to experience before they could gain entrance to God's kingdom. He was doing Everard Digby a favour by plunging him into Hell on earth. It would guarantee him his place in Heaven.

Ben Jonson's Court was The Mermaid tavern, his Presence Chamber its tap room and his courtiers a huge and adoring crowd of actors and writers, and an equal crowd of would-be actors and writers. However, The Mermaid was far too public a place for a man to be seen who was not meant to be in London at all. The next best bet was Jonson's lodgings.

Jonson had money, now that his liaison with Inigo Jones was producing a torrent of Court income. Gresham doubted that his friend's incomings would ever exceed his outgoings. His lodgings were in a back street a long way away from any fashionable area, but gratifyingly near Alsatia. It was not early in the morning when Gresham, in a workman's uniform, arrived at Jonson's chamber door. He had brought Mannion with him, feeling threat in the very air he breathed. Jane he had brought partly because of the feeling that she was only safe when with him, and partly through the realisation that it was folly to leave a young and beautiful woman on her own in Alsatia. She was also becoming very bored, a sulphurous cloud of tedium hanging over her in the tiny environs of their bolt hole.

The landlord knew Gresham, and let him in with a grin. Jonson had been too drunk to bolt the door when he had fallen into his bed. He lay fully clothed, his snores shaking dust off the ashes of the dead fire. Gresham crept up to him from behind, placed a dagger gently against his throat and hissed loudly in his ear, 'Pay me the money you owe me now, or die!'

Jonson leapt up as if a charge of powder had been set off beneath him, and landed back on the bed, feeling the steel against his throat, eyes as staring wide as a dead fish, unable to see his assailant. He started to gargle, white froth coming from his mouth.

Jane spoke. 'Or he might let you off if you give him a mention in your next play. Ugh! Do you *ever* wash a shirt?'

Jonson's whole body subsided back on to the bed, hearing the familiar voice, as if the life had drained out of it. Jane was wandering round the room, which looked as if an exceedingly dirty garrison of troops had been stationed in it for months. She picked up various bits of linen, wrinkling her nose as she threw them into a pile.

Jonson rolled over on the bed. 'You bastard!' he grunted at Gresham.

'True. But at least *my* poetry's good,' responded Gresham with a grin.

'"Calumnies are answered best with silence",' responded Jonson. When he quoted from his own works he always stuck his chest out.

'*Please* don't quote from your own work, Ben,' asked Gresham. 'Only someone of exceptional arrogance would even remember what they had written, never mind spout it to an unsuspecting public at every opportunity.'

'I am exceptional in everything I do,' grunted Jonson, rubbing his head and heaving himself upright.

'Exceptional as a sycophant, I believe. What were those lines you wrote to celebrate Robert Cecil's sudden uplifting to be Earl of Salisbury? Do I remember . . .

> *"What need hast thou of me, or of my Muse*
> *Whose actions do themselves so celebrate?"'*

'Aye, well,' Jonson responded, pulling on a pair of boots, 'a man has to live.'

'"I do honour the very flea of his dog"?' asked Gresham, quoting from *Every Man In His Humour*.

'Please don't quote from my works, Sir Henry,' said Jonson solemnly. 'I find it degrades the beauty of my lines.'

Jane was an avid playgoer, and Gresham had become converted during his time with Kit Marlowe. They had known Jonson for years. He traced his roots back to Scotland, and had done so when it was not fashionable to be so linked, and was a Catholic, when it had never been fashionable. He was also an entirely self-taught classical scholar of awesome knowledge, a brawler who had killed a man, a poet of huge genius and a boor, a man of great intuition who at times showed the sensitivity of a stone privy in the Tower. Ben Jonson's body could be and had been caged. His spirit was uncontainable. That at least he shared with Walter Raleigh.

Without expression, Jane picked up the overflowing yellow chamber pot from beside the bed, opened the shuttered window and hurled out the contents into the street below. A fierce yell and a squeal suggested it had found a target. Jonson stopped rubbing his head and feasted his eyes on Jane's trim figure, a beatific smile on his lips. He recovered quickly from shocks. His life had produced enough of them for him to have had to learn quickly.

'Avert your gaze, old lecher, and listen to me. You dine with Lord Mordaunt and Robert Catesby soon enough, I hear?'

Jonson struck a dramatic pose on the bed, the effect somewhat ruined by a button popping off as he raised both his arms. He launched into verse:

> '"*Come, my Celia, let us prove,*
> *While we can, the sport of love!*"'

'My name's Jane,' replied the object of his attention, poking with her foot at the remnants of what could have been last week's meal on the floor. 'As for your kind proposition, "all the adulteries of art/They strike mine eyes, but not my heart".'

'Spoken beautifully!' exclaimed Jonson, gallantly. 'Almost as well as I could do it myself!'

'Lord Mordaunt? Catesby?' interjected Gresham.

'You're well informed, as ever. What of them?'

He got up clumsily from the bed and walked over to a low, rough-carved table with some bottles on it. Jane stood before it and glowered at him. He veered in mid-course, changing direction to the jug and ewer with something like fresh water in them. He bent over it, motioning to Gresham, who came and poured the contents slowly over his head. He stood up and shook his wet mane like a dog coming out of the river.

'I'm growing thin. I stand in need of a good dinner,' Gresham said, replacing the empty ewer. 'I will be your Scottish cousin who's arrived from the north, in the hope of rich pickings in this city which has newly learned to love a Scotsman so much. Under the circumstances, young Catesby will be delighted to add an extra place to the table, so your kinsman can taste the delights of life with the nobility.'

'Hmmph!' grunted Jonson. 'I trust you've a good Scots accent?'

He looked enquiringly at Jane, and when she stepped aside went to the table and poured two beakers of cheap sack. He offered one to Gresham, who declined it, sipped appreciatively at his own life-saver and offered Gresham's to Mannion. 'You're invisible, I see . . .' It was the phrase he used when Gresham did not wish to be recognised. 'Why this sudden interest in my friends?'

'Is Robert – Robin – Catesby a friend of yours?'

Jonson sat down heavily on a stool. He tossed some written sheets to Jane with an inquisitorial raised eyebrow. She caught them, nodded and settled in a corner to read the scribblings that were Jonson's next play.

'It's most unfair and unusual that someone so beautiful should have intelligence as well,' grumbled Jonson, changing the subject. '"Blind Fortune still/Bestows her gifts on such as cannot use them."'

'Is Catesby that beautiful?' asked Gresham, pretending not to notice.

'Not him, you fool. Her. That angel who has mistakenly taken to living with an old satyr such as yourself. Perhaps she's hoping to reform you. Beautiful women like to reform lost men,' he added hopefully, watching her as she became instantly lost and totally absorbed in the manuscript.

'I thought it was her honesty you most liked?' There had been a massive row between Jonson and Jane when she had last criticised a piece of his writing. He had called her a lying slut and broken a perfectly good stool by hurling it against a wall, following which Gresham had broken his head. He had rewritten the piece though, Gresham had noticed. 'But you haven't answered my question. Is Catesby a friend of yours?'

'I know him. Everyone of my faith knows him. A friend? Hardly. I refuse to acknowledge the sun shines out of his arse, which is a prerequisite of anyone wanting friendship with him. Young Catesby sometimes has difficulty distinguishing between worshipping our Saviour, and his being our Saviour. He's not a good . . . influence, I think, on our younger people. But he has a good table. And I'm a good guest.' He gazed sadly down at the remnants of liquid in the now-empty beaker. 'They'll all be Catholics there. Are you after Catholics? Will your presence at our table bring harm to our faith?'

Gresham thought for a moment. If he was to expose a plot to kidnap the King, harm would come to the plotters. But to Catholicism? More harm would come if the plot were allowed to go ahead than if it were destroyed.

'To your faith, no. To some people of your faith, in all probability, yes. To you, too, Ben, if you plan to be in rebellion against the State, as well as against every person of culture and taste . . .'

The bantering tone did not hide the seriousness of Gresham's answer.

There was a bellow of laughter. 'Me? A rebel! God help me! Don't you think trouble enough comes looking for me, without me sending out invitations for more of it to come visiting?'

Ben Jonson had a mouth as big as his capacity for drink, and a wild reputation, but Gresham had never known him betray a secret. Or, at least, never betray one of Gresham's secrets. Gresham had rescued Jonson from the bailiffs and debtors' prison. The old secrets between them stood custodian over the new ones. Jane gave instructions for the bulging bag of washing to be sent off by servant to the laundress at the House. His manuscript she took away with her. The boredom of Alsatia was due to be lessened at least a little.

'There's risk in this dinner,' said Mannion flatly on their return. He was right. For all its huge size, London was a small town where those at the top of its society were concerned. The other guests seemed unlikely enough on the surface to recognise Gresham for who he was, but disguise would be prudent, and Gresham worked on two principles. Either one altered the original hardly at all, or one went for something outrageously different. He opted for the latter.

'Hold still, will you!' said a cross Jane as she applied the last of the dye to his hair and beard. It had been turned from the darkest black to something reddish, if not verging on positive ginger. A salve applied to his face, neck and hands (and, on Jane's insistence and in the face of his firm opposition, to the whole of the rest of his body) turned his skin dark, almost like that of a Moor. He had not trimmed his beard since they moved out of the House, with the result that it now straggled and looked, as Mannion said, 'Like a badly blown cornfield.' From his extensive wardrobe Gresham had chosen a suit of clothes that a country bumpkin might have been offered by the worst country tailor as being the height of fashion in London. The whole dreadful mess was topped off by a vast bonnet that clashed with his hair and beard and his suit of clothes, and a large eyepatch.

'For the first time in my life, I fear death,' he said to Jane as she finished the last patting on of paste to his beard.

He saw her face fall, and immediately regretted his teasing of her.

'Why so? If you feel that way, you must . . .'

He raised his hand to stop her. 'Can you imagine what my tailor will say if I go to my coffin dressed like this?' he asked, aghast. The swinging blow to his head was arrested only just in time as she realised it might disturb the newly applied colour.

Dressed like a country bumpkin, and a Scots one at that, Gresham was near besieged by every criminal on duty in London, who saw him coming and could not believe their luck. After he had been pestered with offers of women, card games, bowling alleys and dice halls where only yesterday a fortune had been made to rival Lord Salisbury's, couplings of such power achieved to rival Samson's, and various places where both had been achieved simultaneously, it was a relief to arrive at William Patrick's ordinary. Jonson always arrived at dinner as early as possible, to maximise the amount of time spent troughing at someone else's expense. He met Gresham, held back a brief explosion of apoplexy with commendable restraint, and brought him in to the company.

It was a lively affair. The Irish Boy served excellent food, with wine that was certainly drinkable. Gresham, who had a nose for these things, noticed that Catesby did not stint himself either with the room he had taken or the food and wine served. The room was fresh-painted and had clean rushes strewn on the floor, with hangings of some expense on the walls. A large window let some of the noise of the Strand through, as the cracks in the floorboards and door let some of the noise of the thriving, bustling ordinary up to assail their ears, but not enough to impede conversation.

'It's guid tae meet yae al, guid, guid . . .' Gresham, who had decided to be called Alexander Selkirk, slurred his words and let them tail off incoherently, a man middlingly drunk but also bemused with new sights and sounds.

He need hardly have bothered. Catesby barely glanced at him before he was dismissed. Jonson was the man, the star brought in to show how well-connected Catesby was, and all eyes were on him. A major playwright, a talking point at Court who was also a Catholic: Ben Jonson was a superb social catch.

'Well met, sir, well met.' It was Tom Wintour, shaking hands with the company, clapping those he knew well on the back. So this was the man for whose sake a whore's bottom would be sore for weeks to come, thought Gresham.

'Here, this is Selkirk, Alex Selkirk, a cousin of mine from Scotland . . . Cousin Alex, meet Tom Wintour . . .' Jonson was barely remembering to introduce Gresham. There was a crowd of people, there was good food, there was wine, and Jonson was expanding with almost every minute that passed by. Tom Wintour had come with Catesby. He was a short, stocky figure, with a round face and a cannon-fire way of speech. He was quick, agile, keeping his wit under control but showing a pushy argumentativeness that Gresham imagined could be explosive in more confined or tense situations.

'Have you brought a lot of your friends with you down from the north?' asked Tom Wintour with outward innocence. The reference to King James's horde of hangers-on drawing a guffaw from another member of the company.

'No, no,' replied Gresham, 'but I may hope tae do so if the pickin's are reet guid enough!'

A man to be watched, thought Gresham, someone with the power of the hothead but also the determination and intelligence to be a dangerous enemy. He had the body of a fighter too, Gresham noted, for all that he lacked height.

'My, and you must tell me who your tailor is, Mr Selkirk!' It was Tresham. He had given no flicker of recognition. 'Clothes like that will make a stir anywhere you go!' Another guffaw from the company, except Lord Mordaunt, who thought himself too refined to laugh. Tresham seemed to delight in wearing clothes that had clearly cost good money, but which were crumpled as if tossed carelessly aside at the end of the day. He played his part well, making several scurrilous jokes about the Scots that would have perplexed the real person Gresham was pretending to be, yet got home to other town guests.

Jonson talked endlessly, largely about himself, but he did so with such power, force and good humour that there was a dance in the eyes of all those who listened. The appalling rule of the Lord Chancellor and his power over the plays, the sheer vagabond criminality of all printers and the complete lack of any resemblance to a civilised race of theatre managers and actors, the wonder of Latin, the plan for the next masque, the plan for the next play, the belief that a grateful city should afford its greatest living playwright a theatre of his own, the dreadful affair between Sir Robert Dudley and the mistress he wished to marry . . . fuelled by greater and greater quantities of alcohol, Jonson's genius and his buffoonery climbed towards the stars in harness.

And what of Catesby? Was this a man full of piss and wind, or a man capable of kidnapping a King? As Gresham observed him it seemed as if the room became darker and darker, the sense of an evil presence almost unbearable. As even Jonson grew tired, and the stories thinner and more unbelievable, so quietly, with hardly a ripple, Robert Catesby began to dominate the conversation, the room and all the people within it.

'We're all victims to the printers!' Jonson was almost shouting now. 'They buy the work, they print the work, they bind the work and they sell the work – and, if they so please, they put another man's name on the cover! And they get the profit, whilst the poor man who produces the work, whose brain sweats it out over weeks and months – he gets the leavings after the cursed printer has done! Why, these men are nothing more than vultures!'

Catesby broke in. The very quietness of his voice commanded attention.

'Why,' he said to a perspiring Jonson, 'you revile the printers, yet they're as the lice upon your body. They lie still and wait for you to come to them. They backbite and they infect, yet you've no remedy. They feed off you, yet you stop them not. If they grow fat on your blood, isn't it your fault? Throw off your old clothes, man. Scrub your skin. Take the louse between your thumb and finger . . .' he picked up a nut from the table, 'and crack it . . . thus!' The nut shattered over the table. 'Blood for blood; take back your blood, man, or cease your complaining.' It was said gently, conversationally, yet it had the menace of steel slithering out of a smooth scabbard.

There was a pause, and conversation resumed along with the bringing of two fine, freshly baked pies. Later, another of the guests, Lord Mordaunt, raised an obscure theological point, on whether to equivocate or withhold the truth was the same as to tell a lie. Catesby fixed Mordaunt with his eyes and led him down a theological line that had the man tangled in his own arguments as badly as a young ostler caught in the reins of a train of horses.

Catesby knew his Bible, Gresham had to give him that. Textual evidence dropped from him like other men oozed sweat. Gresham had mimed becoming progressively more drunk as the evening wore. He decided to speak.

'I dinnae like the Bible.' That brought a hush, as Gresham knew it would. He had spoken in his thick Scots accent, as a drunk would when suddenly brought back to awareness for an instant. 'There's tae much blood, tae much killin'. Tae many of ma friends have deed . . .' Gresham started to sob, in the maudlin way that drunks did when they had uttered a profound alcoholic truth.

Catesby did not even look at him as he replied. 'Too much killing, Mr Selkirk? No, surely not. There can be no life without death. Christ wasn't our Saviour until he died in agony.'

'But ma poor wifie! Ma lovely Agnes! An innocent wee lass, taken awa' before she had time to say her prayers . . .' Was Gresham pushing it too far, would the reference to the dead and innocent wife draw forth a response? It did, but not of the type Gresham expected. Catesby smashed his tankard down on the table with such force that three wooden platters jumped off and rolled along the floor. No-one moved to stop them.

'Innocent? Innocent! We're alive now because we feed on the dead flesh of animals, *innocent* animals! Like the lamb in the Old Testament, the innocent must be sacrificed so the higher order may triumph. Their squealing over their death does them no credit. Rather they should praise those who sacrifice them, praise those who make something meaningful come from their paltry death. Did Joshua ask for the innocent to leave the walls of Jericho? When the walls fell, do you imagine the soldiers asked who was innocent and who was guilty before they raped and pillaged in the name of God? Innocence is not a virtue. It is a handicap.'

On that note the party ended. Gresham had met many men in his life, some good, some bad, most merely human with all the frailty and weakness humanity brought along as their natural baggage. Pure goodness he had met, surprisingly, far more often than pure evil. Indeed the number in that latter group he could count on the fingers of one hand.

Tonight, Gresham knew he was in the presence of evil. It was in the eyes. It was always in the eyes. Catesby's had a fierce, fixed gleam, an inner light that did not come and go with the moment, with the rising fumes of wine to the head, the excitement of sex or even the lust of battle. The intensity of that madman's gleam did not waver or flicker. Yet it was so gentle, a flash of yellow deep in the pupils, deep and intense burning, that it was almost buried in the proud and handsome tilt of the chin. Gresham had seen that light in the eyes of a judge, in the eyes of a hangman. It was the evil of a man who could not conceive he could be wrong, but whose self-belief could only be satisfied, like a dread hunger, by feeding it with the belief of others. All men, and all beliefs, were simply fuel for Robert Catesby's vanity. In the handsome, dashing figure of Robert Catesby, for a brief and terrible moment, Henry Gresham saw the pride of Lucifer, walking on earth.

'Normal men suspend their feelings,' said Jane, trying to wash as much as possible of the dye off his body, and trying to understand what Gresham, still shaken, had told her. 'When they kill, or when they rape and mutilate, they lock away their feelings behind a great iron door, only opening it when the business is done. Because they didn't feel it when it happened, they tell themselves it never happened. This man, it seems, has no door to shut. Perhaps it was ripped off its hinges when his wife died?'

'Or perhaps it was never truly there.' Gresham shivered and not only with the cold. 'Here, your hands are cold. Let me take over.'

'When I've finished the bits you can't reach. Be still.'

'Why do I doubt so much? Do you doubt? Everything?'

She had hardly ever seen him like this, reverting almost to a child-like questioning and simplicity, the veneer of cynical amusement and wit broken through and shattered. It was not that his body was naked before her. For a brief moment, it was his mind. She was careful not to interrupt the measured sweep of her hand, or reveal her feelings in her voice.

'Sometimes I doubt. Who isn't prey to doubt?'

'Catesby. Catesby isn't prey to doubt. He takes the fear, the worry, the doubt we humans have and he forces it out, drives it from him somehow in a way he doesn't and I don't understand. And then he turns it into something evil, a fire that draws other people to it like a moth to a candle, and burns them up before they've realised what's happening. Or perhaps makes them so they don't care, makes them so they want to be destroyed.'

They made love in the tiny bed, little more than a mattress cast on the floor, and Gresham felt the warmth creep back into his soul.

Well, his question was answered. Not so much piss and wind, Master Robert Catesby. More an avenging, fallen angel, willing to unleash the winds of Hell on earth.

CHAPTER 8

It was dark outside, the first wind of winter dashing against the houses, and bringing with it a fine rain that first put a layer of watery, tiny jewels on a woollen cloak, and then soaked it through.

'I saw him as if for the first time last night,' said Francis Tresham. He was sitting at the table with which he had tried to knock the brains out of Henry Gresham only a few days previously, sipping morosely at the fine wine Gresham had placed in his hand. 'He's a vulture, isn't he? I suppose I've been under his spell most of my life. I think it was your being there that let me take a step back almost, to see him as he really is. He doesn't care about God, does he? Or perhaps he thinks he *is* God? Either way, I realised last night, for all his talk, who Robin Catesby does care about. Himself.'

Which is perhaps why you would recognise it more easily than others, thought Gresham, as it describes the pair of you equally well. Gresham's hair and beard had returned to their normal black intensity, apart from an occasional flash of orange when the light caught it from a certain angle.

'I could ask Jonson who you are,' said Tresham. He frequently changed the tack of a conversation, without warning. It followed the restless, ever-changing direction of his eyes, as if anything he

210

gazed at for more than a few seconds became too hot for them to rest on. Perhaps it was a trick to catch the listener unawares, perhaps it was just his nature.

'You could ask,' said Gresham calmly. He knew Jonson was safe. If Tresham did not know that fact, he would find out easily enough without need of words from Henry Gresham.

'Tell me again what it is you offer me.'

'When we've amassed enough information to deal with this plotting, you'll receive travel documents to France, a thousand pounds in your purse and secret passage to a ship, out of the way of your friends or Cecil, whichever one is most hot to kill you.'

'How can you do that?'

Because, young man, I have had a plan waiting these years past to release Sir Walter Raleigh and get him to sanctuary in Europe, a plan he has refused to use, believing it would be taken as confession of his guilt were he so to escape.

'I can do it. That's all you need to know. You'll be taken to the south coast and there put on a boat, and delivered to France. The thousand pounds is in addition to any money you can raise yourself. You'll want to tidy your affairs, won't you, and leave as much as possible to your wife and family? You'll be given another name, and papers in that name that will pass any muster.'

'What about my family?'

'That's up to you. They can come later, when the hue and cry's died down, or you can leave them. You can tell me later.'

If Tresham had decided whether he would desert his family or not, he was not going to let Gresham see it.

'I think I'm to be inducted on Monday. I'm bid to another dinner, at Lord Stourton's, in Clerkenwell. The invitation came from Robin. Stourton's my kinsman.'

'I know,' said Gresham, whose mind by now carried an encyclopaedic list of the inter-relations between England's Catholic families. 'So is Lord Monteagle. It's no secret.'

'It's strange the invitation comes from Catesby, not from my

211

relative. It makes me think there's a reason other than the pleasure of my company for my being invited.'

'Then you must go.'

'What freedom do I have?'

'Freedom to do what?'

'Can I speak as myself, or do I have to speak from a script that you've written?'

'There are only two conditions. Firstly, you must speak as keeps you on the inside of whatever is happening. If by staying there you can bring it to an end, then so much the better – *but you must under no circumstances be so dismissive that you're excluded*. You're no use to me in ignorance. The second is that you must report back to me immediately, and tell me everything that took place.'

'Here?'

'Usually, yes. On Monday, no. There's an inn, the sign of The Mermaid, at Clerkenwell. Ask to be shown to the room taken by Mr Cecil.' Tresham's eyes widened. 'Mr *Robin* Cecil. I'll meet you there.'

'Can he be trusted?' The question was Jane's. She had read Jonson's manuscript, liked it, and was now descending into restless boredom again. It was going to be called *Volpone, Or The Fox*, his play. It had made her yearn to go to the playhouse again.

'We'll find out soon enough. While we're under this threat I don't want you out of my sight.'

'I know,' she said simply. 'But if we're found out then I'll be the least of your troubles. I can be secret, too, you know. When it really matters.'

A number of those Tresham had been at school with, and some of his adult friends, were now dead. Several had died of the plague, one thrown from a horse, others of illnesses that seemed to have no name and no cure. Another had been knifed in a brawl, and spoken gaily to Tresham as the life blood had ebbed from him. The death of his father had shattered him more than his so-called friends knew. Enemy that he had been, his father had offered a strange security and comfort. Sir Thomas Tresham had been an anchor point in his life. And now even that great certainty was gone.

He had felt so brave, when he was young. Now all he felt was fear.

Clerkenwell lay outside the City walls. Until recently a village to the north of the City, bounded by the Fleet on one side and Charterhouse on the other, the relentless march of London had swallowed it up, its residents claiming that the country winds blowing over it from Islington kept the plague at bay.

Stourton had married Frances, Tresham's sister, and though there was a twenty-year age gap between them he had become close friends with Catesby. Lady Frances Stourton had a permanently world-weary look to her, and conducted all her business distractedly, as if something terribly important was happening elsewhere.

'Francis, you're very welcome here, as ever.' She used the same tone of tired affection, as ever. She was in mourning, of course, and Lord Stourton all commiseration at the loss of his father-in-law. At the same time, he seemed distracted, removed from his usual self. Catesby was no different, seeking first to charm Frances and then turning his attention on to Stourton. Yet dinner was ended early, and Catesby asked leave to hold a few words with Tresham. Tresham felt his heart tighten.

Winter was drawing in, and a steady fire in the new hearth lapped at the edges of the cold. The room was square, with latticed glass looking out over the garden. The panelling was light, almost irritatingly so, being so new as to not have darkened or weathered properly. Family portraits glowered at Tresham. They were a proud crew, the Stourtons.

Catesby looked at Tresham, and felt, not for the first time, the stirrings of unease. For long simply a plaything, a stringed instrument on whose neck Catesby could play whatever tune he pleased, Francis Tresham would always be a risk. A risk of a different kind, Thomas Percy, had failed to deliver the rent money due on the

Westminster house whose cellar hid such a terrible secret. Fawkes had had to be sent to pay Henry Ferrers and Whynniard what they were owed, masquerading as 'John Johnson', Percy's servant. Just as pressingly, Fawkes was insisting on the money needed to hire the ship from Greenwich that would take him abroad after the explosion. Fawkes had been hired for his skill with powder. It was not expected that he would remain on after the explosion, but nor had Catesby expected him to be quite so pressing with the money for his escape route. That great baby Everard Digby had provided some coin, but Tresham was now heir to a rent roll of £3,000 a year. Tresham was rich, was from one of the great Catholic families, wasn't he? Then it was time for him to be called on.

Francis Tresham could feel the blood leaving his face and hands as Catesby told him the bare bones of his plan. Rarely had he heard anything so mad. Could a man's heart stop and he still live on? How could he report this to the man in dark clothes? He drew a deep breath. He recognised the tactic from lesser conversations. Catesby had first of all delivered the shock, and now was winding up into full justification, a passionate torrent of words starting to flow from him, in contrast to the almost jerky rhythms with which he had described his plan to take most of England's nobility to Hell. Tresham stood up, held up his hand.

'Stop this, cousin, stop this. Will you be silent?' No-one told Robert Catesby to be silent. A flicker of yellow covered Catesby's eyes, and vanished as quickly. 'Are you mad? Would you damn us all?' Tresham started to pace the room, unconsciously wringing his hands together as if to squeeze the correct words out of them.

'This isn't damnation – it's salvation,' Catesby answered, urgent to make a speech.

'Forgive me. I hadn't realised God had taken a simple little word out of "Thou shalt *not* murder". How can it not be damnation to kill so many, guilty and innocent alike? Why, to kill some of our greatest friends? Of a sudden you have a monopoly on Divine judgement, do you, cousin?'

'I don't, but those who do have sanctified and approved the plan. You've heard Father Garnet speak of how a smaller evil is permissible in the pursuit of a greater good. Of how if the innocent in an evil city are besieged then they must take their chance with the rest? I can show you the texts that . . .'

'Faith! Damn your stupid texts! And damn the stupid priests who read them! Hold off that, will you? I'm no scholar of theology. Yet if you really do believe that the Bible sanctifies such an act, let Francis Tresham for the first time take on the robes of a saint. The Bible be damned. *I* tell you this act is an act of madness, as well as an act of murder! It'll kill us all!'

'Are you then willing to be the only Catholic in England too much of a coward to take up the cause? Are you willing . . .'

'Hold off again!' Tresham had never before interrupted Catesby, never mind doing it twice in quick succession. Few had, when he was in full force, or seeking to get there. A force of nature, his father had once described him, not entirely approvingly as he had seen every servant girl go weak at the knees in his presence. 'You can forget the old cowardice trick. It's been used once before, and it doesn't work. Remember poor Tom in the orchard?'

Years ago at Harrowden three of them had planned a raid on a neighbour's orchard, seeking the sweet apples that were his pride and joy. When they had seen the neighbour working in a far corner of the orchard the other two, one of whom was Tresham, had argued for strategic retreat. Catesby had roundly accused them of being cowards, at which the other boy, Tom, had leapt the wall and crept towards the trees. His howls as the neighbour had laid a springy branch with far more force than was necessary across his buttocks had kept Catesby and Tresham company as they huddled on the other side of the wall. 'I hear Tom speaking to me,' an angry Tresham had whispered harshly to Catesby, 'telling me how much pleasure he takes in being a hero!'

Back in the present, Tresham was too angry to be diverted from his point. 'This isn't about cowardice. Have you thought, man, that the nation will be appalled to think such an act could be undertaken in the name of religion – a religion that preaches peace to one's neighbour! Every act of repression, every crippling penalty, will be justified by reference to this act of evil. Common folk will rise up against us! More than common folk! Every decent person in the kingdom will want our blood in revenge! This won't save Catholicism! It'll ruin it for ever! Are you mad?'

If any of Tresham's passion was penetrating Catesby's self-belief, it was not clear to Tresham.

'It must needs be done,' he said, calmly. 'It's the necessity for all Catholics. We're forced to dangerous measures. We've no choice.'

'And what support will you get? Where are your troops, your invading armies? Do you think Spain has signed a treaty so we can go to war again?'

'The Spanish troops in Dover will march to Rochester and strangle London at the neck of the Thames. Percy's hordes from the north will march, and Catholics from Europe will flock to our support!'

'And on whose word will these mighty offers march? Has the King of Spain told you in person that his troops will be at your beck and call? Has mighty Percy told you his peasants will march in winter to uphold your glorious act, those peasants he hasn't seen for most of his life! Have the commanders in Europe given you their word in writing they'll make that perilous voyage to put out a fire in London that'll never cease burning! You're mad, cousin, mad!'

Catesby seemed unmoved. There was a strange light in his eyes, an almost unnatural calm in his manner. 'Fawkes is a soldier, a man of tried and tested mettle. He's been in Europe. He brings us word from the most high sources that the Spanish troops will act in our favour. He also brings word that Sir William Stanley will bring the English Regiment over to aid us. As for the Earl of Northumberland, he speaks through Thomas Percy, in whom his actions show complete trust.'

'Fiddle-faddle! This Guy Fawkes, who is he? I guarantee you he's as close to the King of Spain as my nose is to my arse! Stanley is a clapped-out old man looking for a pardon and a safe return home, and God help us all if Percy's on your side. Why, that sweating idiot would betray his own mother for a farthing and a pint of piss!'

'Calm down, cousin. Here, take a drink.' Tresham noted for the first time the jug of wine placed in advance in the room, and the exquisite goblets, new like everything else in the house. 'This is new to you. To others of us, those who've lived with it a long time, the shock isn't so great. Give it time. Give *us*, your friends of long standing, some of that time. Surely we're owed that much.'

'But what of our friends? Of Montague? Mordaunt? Of my relatives? Monteagle? Stourton? You can't kill every Catholic noble in all England!'

Tresham's heart was racing, his whole body pounding. He sat down heavily, drank deeply.

'We can try and warn some of them,' said Catesby. 'In dangerous times all men face grave dangers.'

'Money. I'll give you money.'

Catesby got to his feet, ready to embrace Tresham.

'No, not money to further this idiocy. Money to go away.' Catesby frowned. 'At least let this Parliament sit itself out, let's see what it does, what acts it passes. Who knows if the rumours are nothing but noise? Take a hundred pounds, take more. Take yourself and your hot-headed friends off to the Spanish Netherlands. Take time to think, and watch.'

'And leave thirty or more barrels of powder sitting under the Lords' chamber? Risk removing it, being discovered? To be hung, drawn and quartered on a public scaffold for *not* having blown our enemies to Hell? Surely not, cousin, surely not.'

Catesby was chiding him, as he might a child who had made a wrong translation.

'So, are you on our side, or a traitor to it?'

The irony of being called a traitor by a man who was about to blow up England's Government was not lost on Tresham. The heart of him wanted to cut and run, to leave the whole damned business behind him. Yet his head told him it was of no use. He had been so close to these men that he would be swept up and hung when news of it leaked out, as it surely would. This meeting with Catesby had sealed his fate, he realised. If they could condemn Walter Raleigh, what chance had he? Besides, he thought as caution tugged at the heels of his flying imagination, his only way out might be his interrogator, the gentleman with the piercing eyes and beautiful . . . whore? Consort? Even wife? From now on, whatever he did, he would be seen as one of the conspirators. He looked into Catesby's eyes, and realised that he had never truly known him. If he denied the conspiracy he could not even be certain that Catesby would not kill him. His calm was more terrifying than his anger would ever have been.

'You've made me a part of your confounded plot. I supped with you last week, and now I'm dined here. Laying a trail, are you, one even the stupidest hound could follow? I've known you all my life. If your plot fails, do you think any of us will escape? You've hooked me to your line, cousin, without me even knowing there was metal in the water.'

'So are you on our side, or a traitor to it?' Catesby's tone was mild, but relentless.

'I'm a coward in your cause, Robin. Nothing but a bad cause can make me a coward.'

It was starting to get dark when he flung out of Lord Stourton's house and struggled through the streets of Clerkenwell. The summer's dust and two-foot-deep iron ruts had been replaced with clinging mud and filth that threatened to go over the top of even long boots, or suck them off the feet that wore them. He found the sign of The Mermaid and doing as he had been bidden asked for the room kept by Mr Robin Cecil. The innkeeper, a surly figure, called out a tap boy and sent him to guide Tresham. He left him outside a first-floor room. Tresham knocked. There was silence. He looked around him. The wooden balcony which ran round the three sides of the inn, facing inwards into the yard, was empty. The inn seemed near deserted. Those who had colonised Clerkenwell had enough money to keep a full table at home, without need of the inn. He knocked again. Silence. He tried the door. It was open. The room inside was bare, cold. No lights, no sign of anyone having been there in days. Leaving the door swinging on its hinges, he went down the rickety steps, and out into the increasingly gloomy late afternoon.

'Your news?'

He jumped and had his sword half out of the scabbard before he recognised the figure in black.

'Not here, surely?' Tresham stuttered. Something like a grin flickered across the face of his interrogator. He led Tresham to another room on the other side of the yard. Inside there were the remnants of a meal, a good meal as far as Tresham could see. And the woman, together with the huge man Tresham had seen before. Without a word the ox of a servant began to clear, assisted by the woman. There was an extraordinary relationship between the three of them. Master, servant and whore? Man, wife and servant? Friends? Co-conspirators themselves in some plot he could only imagine? There was an ease between them that dismissed hierarchy, an intuitive understanding so at times they hardly needed to speak to each other to understand.

Tresham sat down on a stool, took the offered wine.

'I know what it is they plan.'

Without a word being spoken Tresham heard the other two draw near.

'Speak,' the dark man said.

Tresham took a deep breath. 'My cousin has stacked thirty-six barrels of prime gunpowder beneath the Lords' Chamber at Westminster. It's in a cellar, hired by Thomas Percy, hidden under firewood. They plan to blow up Parliament, at the State opening, killing the King, the Prince, Lords, Commons and all. Three weeks. Three weeks from now. November the fifth.'

There was a gasp from Jane, and even from the normally stalwart Mannion. Gresham sat like stone in his chair.

'Is this . . . serious? Will they do this thing?' he asked, after a long pause.

'It's serious. They'll do it.' Tresham was warming to his theme, feeling strangely more at home with this man and his woman and his servant than he had with his brother-in-law and with Catesby. 'The powder's there, placed by a man they brought over from Europe on Stanley's recommendation, one Guido or Guy Fawkes. My cousin Percy's a Gentleman of the Bedchamber. The house is hired in his name, with this Fawkes masquerading as his servant. John or Jack Johnson, I think they call him. They mean to do it. The plan is to kidnap the Princess Elizabeth from Coombe House, and put her on the throne.'

'They're mad!' Gresham spoke almost in a whisper.

'I said as much, but to no avail. There's no reason in my cousin.'

'Who else is involved?'

'Those you know of. Some others you don't know. Is it necessary I give their names?'

'I doubt very much that I'm the one who will do them the greatest harm.'

'Over and above the ones you know? Ambrose Rookwood. Everard Digby. Tom Bates, Catesby's servant. That's all I know.'

'No nobility?' Gresham asked, with sudden interest. 'Who is to be the Protector if this succeeds? Who's driving it? What about Northumberland?'

'He was mentioned through Thomas Percy. Apparently Tom has given Robin his word that Northumberland's hordes will come streaming down once the Parliament is blown to Hell and backwards. Yet it could be bombast, from that man of all men. None others of true quality were mentioned by Robin. For God's sake, man, Stourton's married to one of my sisters, as is Monteagle! These are my *family*!'

Family has never meant very much to you before, thought Gresham.

'May I speak?' It was Jane. Gresham nodded.

'What good will come of it? Why can they think your religion will be helped by this . . . this slaughter?'

In a tired voice Tresham explained the Spanish troops, the English Regiment and again the hoped-for involvement of the Earl of Northumberland.

Gresham got up and paced the room. His tension was clear.

'It makes no sense. Northumberland hardly knows his northern lands, never mind commanding enough loyalty from his minions up there to let them come down and put their heads on a block.'

'It don't always need blue blood to shed plenty of the red kind. Commoners can kill as well.' Mannion spoke, and Gresham swung round to him.

'But commoners need a leader. Even the Peasants had Wat Tyler,' responded Gresham.

'Is Catesby such a leader?' It was Jane who spoke the words. They hung in the air.

'Could it be so? That Robin sees himself hailed as Protector? Surely no . . .' Tresham was aghast, unwilling to be convinced of what his heart told him.

'Lucifer thought he could defeat God and be hailed in Heaven,' said Jane. 'Why should his works on earth have any less pride to them?'

It was pure accident that brought Catesby into direct contact with Viscount Montagu. He had been walking through the Savoy, on his way back to the Strand, when he turned a corner to find himself face to face with the young Catholic Lord. A brave young man, Montagu had spent five days in the Fleet prison as his reward for speaking out in Parliament against the acts of recusancy. Just the sort of man to make Francis Tresham snivel in pity at the thought of his death, thought Catesby. Did they not realise, he and his kind, that if Christ had to die to save the world then a few men dying to save Christ was no price at all to pay?

Catesby could not afford to ignore Montagu. He had been seen and recognised. The great Catholic families of England not only knew each other; they had frequently been brought up with each other.

'Good morning, my Lord,' he said, bowing low. 'Are you well?' It was verging on the impertinent to speak so directly to one so well born, but Catesby was increasingly fed by a fire of risk. If Montagu was offended, he did not show it, asking after Catesby's health in turn with every show of sincerity.

'Is it the Parliament that brings your Lordship to town?' enquired Catesby. Montagu's home was in Sussex. He offered to Catesby the fact that he was visiting his aunt, and hoped to gain the King's permission to be absent from Parliament. He did not need to specify his reasons to Catesby. Both knew that the devout young man would baulk at being present if any more laws against Catholics were passed, and might land himself in prison for an even longer term if he spoke his mind.

'I'm sure your Lordship takes no pleasure to be there,' offered Catesby sympathetically. Well, if Montagu was already chasing the King for leave of absence, there was nothing Catesby needed to do more, except offer Montagu's likely absence as his doing to Tresham and the others.

A storm was brewing, Catesby knew. His plot had been based on the Catholic family of England, the blood links between them that formed a mutual bond of huge strength, despite their bickering. Yet families protected their own. The death of some members of that family – leading members, the nobility who had held sway for years – was proving a sticking point. Catesby needed to stiffen their resolve, in this most crucial of all times.

He knew that Fawkes, the Wright brothers and Tom Wintour and a servant were due to meet that day at The Bell in Daventry. He had sent his own servant, Tom Bates, to keep an eye on them. It was time to start drawing them all to London now. Whatever the risk, they had to meet with each other more and more. Only with them under his eye would he be assured that they would keep to his path. He had seen dissent in plots before, seen how disunity tore a plan of action apart. He was their leader. Only with him would they haul together on the one line, bring the strength they needed to the great project.

'I need a Bishop, and a College of Theologians.'

'What's a theologian?' asked Mannion, unhelpfully. He had been let off the leash for half a day, and had returned to the house in Alsatia looking smugly self-satisfied. Gresham and Jane had pointedly not asked him what he had been up to. Despite the length of their time in the bolt hole, Gresham had seen no sign that they were being watched. His scalp had not itched. He wished he could give Jane the same freedom, albeit she would not choose the same destination as Mannion. Perhaps another disguise and a trip to the playhouse was an answer.

'Why would they help?' asked Jane.

It was late evening, and the house should have been in bed. It was Gresham who kept them up, feeling forced to take pen and paper, and to try and sketch out the problems that lay before him.

'Why, I'd listen to what the Bishops said, and know that the opposite answer was the right one. Or I'd listen to the theologians argue, and become so angry that I'd choose a path, even if only to silence them and their ramblings.'

'Will it help to speak the problem out again?'

'Perhaps. Who knows? It's all a question of what we do now. I believe the story of this powder. It's fanciful, even farcical, too much so to be an invention. No, the powder is there, right enough. Why it's there, and what to do about it, that's much harder.'

'Surely we know why it's there?'

'We know why Catesby and the others think it's there. We know how they intend to use it a bare few weeks from now. But such a monstrous evil . . . I can't believe there isn't blue blood at the heart of this, somewhere.'

'Well, you have three Catholic Lords in Cecil's pocket – Suffolk,

223

Northampton and Worcester. Between them they run over half of the country.'

'That's the problem. What've they to gain by a plot to overthrow the King and his Chief Secretary? They're well in bed with both of them, sitting very prettily on top of their own particular dung heap. They'd be mad to rock the boat, never mind blow it to pieces.'

'Northumberland then?'

'Possibly, but if so, only at a distance. The old Earl is no archplotter. He prefers his study and his experiments, and brooding in silence on how harshly the world has treated him. He's deaf, you know. Deaf people live in fear, fear of things going on that they don't know about. Northumberland is more frightened than most. He knows his family history. He knows no-one in London trusts a Percy. If he's in this, then he's pulling strings, like a puppeteer.'

'Surely all this is irrelevant? What they plan is obscene. It's an evil to end all evils. It must be stopped. Can't you simply swallow your pride, go to Cecil and reveal everything you know?'

'Cecil wants me dead, remember? I daren't go to him, not without threatening one other person I care for greatly.'

'Raleigh? Surely Sir Walter would never be involved in something such as this?'

'Sir Walter involved? Never in a thousand lifetimes! Raleigh has never had to hide his powder, and I would have been the first to know if this was his hatching. But Raleigh's life hangs by a thread, and Cecil needs only the flimsiest of excuses to cut that thread. One hint of a plot and Raleigh is dead. Raleigh doesn't need to be involved in reality. All Cecil needs to pin the plot on to Raleigh is the slenderest of leads. You see, Raleigh is a real threat to Cecil. While he rots in the Tower, and the people line the riverbank to cheer him on his daily walk on the walls and a King who has had him condemned can't run the risk of executing him – now there's a threat not just to a King, but to the Chief Secretary who betrayed his friend! Popularity, Jane. Popularity. Raleigh has become *popular*.'

Gresham was on his feet now, pacing the room.

'It's the one thing Cecil can never have, the one thing he fears! Cecil has intellect in plenty. He has wealth, he has power and he has cunning, and he's cautious beyond belief. Yet the one thing that threatens him is a popular uprising. He's no feel for the common man, no, nor any love for them. He can sit in his palace and scheme and manipulate and plot and plan, but he can't reach out like Sir Walter can reach out and make people's hearts sing and their spirits rise just by the sight of him. So he fears Raleigh above all others, my poor captain in his captive tower, and he fears that Raleigh might win over the King. Raleigh's the symbol of the popularity Cecil will never have, and a power he'll never have, the power to move people's hearts and minds. Cecil knows it's a power that could be used to knock him off his perch, so he fears it as well as envies it.'

'But what's the link between this and this powder plot?' asked Jane, genuinely bemused.

'What if Cecil knows something is brewing? The details can't be clear to him. No man like him would knowingly leave a ton of powder beneath his seat of power. But say he's caught the rumours, and sees in this plot a way to prove Raleigh a traitor at last? Say he bides his time and then seizes as many of the plotters as he can find. How many under torture wouldn't confess to Raleigh's being the ringleader? It would explain so much. Why Cecil is desperate to keep me out of the way, why he feared me so and set me off on a false trail. I've made no secret of my allegiance to Sir Walter. For God's sake, I visit the man in his prison openly! There are few men who could unstitch a plot to make Raleigh appear a traitor, and few who would want to do so as much as I. I'm one such. Perhaps the only such.'

'Did it kill Will Shadwell?' asked Jane.

'Of course,' said Gresham. 'Percy must have blurted something out to Shadwell when he was drunk. I wonder if Will took the story to Cecil first of all? That would be a fine joke. Cecil watching this lovely little plot bubbling away, his marvellous excuse to get rid of Raleigh once and for all, and along comes Will Shadwell ready to spoil it all with an early disclosure. I flattered myself thinking Will Shadwell was running with a story to me. I bet he was running *away* from Sam Fogarty and his crew; he must have picked up he was being followed, and seen me as the only person who could protect him against Cecil.'

Jane was looking perplexed. 'But I still don't see why you can't just go to Cecil? Expose the plot and you stop a slaughter . . .'

'And I give Cecil myself as well as Raleigh, served up nice and hot on a plate! Think what happens if I appear in front of Cecil with the details of this fantastical plot. One of Raleigh's fiercest supporters, and a spymaster to boot? I'm clapped into jail the minute I open my mouth, and instead of saving my master I become an agent for his death! How easy to have me not as the *discoverer* of the plot, but as one of its *leaders*? There's a forged letter to prove me a Catholic. What was done once can be done again! I've supped with the plotters, haven't I? And I have a direct link to Raleigh. They can have me backwards and forwards between the plotters and the Tower quicker than a pair of oars in the flood tide. They can rack me until I say what they wish, never even need to bring me out in open court. Look at Raleigh's trial – his chief accuser was never even presented!'

'You would never testify against Raleigh!' exclaimed Jane.

'I would never *willingly* or knowingly testify against him, while I was in possession of my own senses. But courage and fortitude have nothing to do with torture, Jane. Christ himself on the Cross denied his father. It's not just their bodies men lose on the rack. It's their minds. Anyone can be broken, in time.'

'So you can't speak out, and you can't remain silent. Aren't there others you could reveal the details to?'

'That must be the answer. Young Tresham's a complicating factor. He's to be stopped from cutting and running, by the way. He's impulsive by nature. Before too long he'll weigh the odds –

God knows, I would if I struck a deal where I could be arrested and taken to the Tower as a traitor if my mad cousin spoke one word to the wrong people – and work out that it might be better for him just to vanish off to France on his own.'

'So who do you tell, and how?'

'There're enough pompous fools in the employ of the Crown who'd leap at the chance to discover a plot, but the mere discovery isn't enough. If the powder is simply found, it could still be proven as Raleigh's as much as anyone else's. No, however it's done, it has to be by some route or other that keeps it within the Catholics, identifies the whole awful business as driven by religion.'

'Well,' said Jane, 'you'd better get that pen and paper ready. How many Catholic sympathisers do we know?'

Someone was crying, not too far away in the house. The noise could be heard even above the noise of a great house being shut up and closed down, a keening wail that seemed to have no start and no ending. It would be one of the servants, Tresham thought. He was still not recovered from his madcap ride from London to Northamptonshire. Many of the servants had worked their whole lives for the Tresham family. They were wailing, as servants always did, yet little they knew how much better for them it would be to be dispersed before the avenging angels of Cecil descended on the house crying treason. He had done with Rushton, whatever happened. Already the house felt as if it belonged to someone else.

Tresham believed he could still stop the plot. If that was the case, Rushton could be opened up again easily enough. The death of so many Catholic nobles was the key, he was sure. It might not work as an argument for postponement on Catesby, but it could work on the others. He had laboured the point with his dark angel. The man showed so little resemblance to Alexander Selkirk, the semi-drunk Scot who had accompanied Jonson, that Tresham had to pinch himself to know they were one and the same. 'Selkirk' had not disagreed with him, but gazed levelly into his eyes and said resignedly,

'You must try, as best you can. It's best you don't know of the other plan to destroy this plot before it happens. You'll be all the more surprised when you do hear of it. Remember when you're challenged to stick with the truth.' Tresham had pondered on that, not really understanding, and pleaded to be allowed to ride north and close up his home, bringing his family down to London.

'Why should you wish that?' the man had asked.

'I leave this country for a while, whatever happens. I need to put my affairs in order, gather my money and bring my family together so that when I vanish they can help and support each other. I must also consider being arrested.'

'Why so?'

Tresham had had the same thoughts as Gresham. 'One loose word from any one of the plotters and they could be betrayed. I'm implicated now, regardless. If I'm arrested I can plead that I tried to stop the plot – which is quite true – and stayed with Catesby simply to act from the inside to further act against it. If I move my family to London it will confirm my innocence. A man who fears the fire doesn't move nearer the furnace.'

'No,' said Gresham, 'but a man who wants to light it most certainly does.'

You are, thought Gresham, very optimistic indeed about your likely fate if this plot is discovered. Live in hope, though. It does no harm.

'A lesser brain than yours,' he continued, 'might think to strip his house and gather his wealth, then return to London and vanish quietly before anyone knew what was happening.'

Was this man a mind-reader? Just such thoughts had been gaining increasing strength in Tresham's mind.

'Such thoughts wouldn't merit serious attention, from a sensible man, for two reasons. Firstly, a man who vanishes is still alive, and can still be found. Secondly, there is a watch on you at all times. It's an experienced watch, by people who make their living out of it, and would as soon as kill you as keep tail on you. We'll decide when you leave, together. Let this be our own private little conspiracy.'

So it had ended, and Tresham taken the mad ride to Rushton. Dust was rising everywhere, as hangings were taken down and the few precious carpets taken up, clothes and bed linen assaulted to rid them of dust before being packed tight into the chests that littered the halls and stairways. What few fires there were blew smoke throughout the house, as doors were banged open and shut to the carts and horses waiting outside.

There was one final thing to be done, apart from face the anger and incomprehension of his mother, wife and sisters. The family papers, so carefully tended and preserved by his father, had been sealed three times over, and placed in the house where no unfriendly eyes would ever gaze on them. It felt like a burial.

Tresham headed for White Webbs, the Enfield home of Anne Vaux. He knew that Father Garnet would be there, together with Catesby, Fawkes and Tom Wintour. Catesby had assured him that Anne knew nothing of the detail of the plot, yet he felt a deep unease. White Webbs had become the gathering centre for the conspirators. It was riddled with priest-holes, and conveniently close to London. He could not believe Anne Vaux would agree to mass slaughter in Parliament. Yet he could not see how she would not know, given the iron hand of control she and the other Catholic women exercised over the Faith in England. Father Garnet was a garrulous fool, and to be trusted as much as any Jesuit, yet how had he supported this murderous plan? Catesby was insistent that Garnet knew about the plot and endorsed it.

Tresham felt a deep, inner exhaustion as he entered the familiar doors, doors that once had been comforting to him. Catesby, Fawkes and Tom Wintour were there, with Robert Keyes. He had not liked Fawkes on their one previous meeting, feeling in him a contempt for the civilians with whom he was temporarily involved. His dislike had increased now he realised that this was the man who had planted the powder, and the man who was prepared to light the fuse to it. To Hell with the Lords in Parliament, who probably deserved to go there anyway. The powder could blow up whoever it pleased, but there was a terrible danger of Francis Tresham being caught in the blast.

From the start Tresham sensed a difference in Catesby. They were seated together in a room of dark oak panelling, bare of portraits but with mullioned windows overlooking the tended garden. By it a kitchen maid was poking at a mass of green in the kitchen garden, seeking the best plants to take back inside to Cook. Tresham looked enviously down on her bent back, noting her complete absorption in her task. Could his life ever be that simple?

'We're bound to blow up several of our own kind. Not just common people – the people whose leadership we depend on! Are we Catholics, or are we cannibals, feeding off our own kind?' Tresham was pushing at the point.

There was a sardonic grin on Fawkes's face. He rarely spoke, and when he did it was with a strange tang of Yorkshire and Spain in his accent.

'People die in wars,' he said now. 'Innocent people, as well as guilty people and soldiers.'

'For too long,' said Catesby, 'we've seen our battle as being about ideas and faith. Those things aren't what we fight *with*. They're what we fight *for*. And fight we must. Do you think those who might die in the Lords would think their lives ill-lost if by their death we bring God's rule back into England?'

'They won't be able to tell us, will they?' grunted Tresham. 'They'll be dead.'

'Some, not all. Many won't come, because they know they'll have to pass legislation against our kind. Others we can warn.'

They ran through the list. It was far too long. There was young Thomas Howard, recently appointed Earl of Arundel and restored to that ancient title. How could the young Lord Vaux be allowed into the massacre, given what the Vaux women had done for the Faith over the years? Tresham argued, as he had to, for his two brothers-in-law, Monteagle and Stourton. Then there was Lord Montagu . . . why, Catesby had dined with two of them hardly a week past. Had he taken their supper whilst looking at them and knowing he was signing their death warrants? . . . Tresham had an unexpected ally in Robert Keyes, when he spoke in defence of Lord Mordaunt. Keyes was Tresham's age, a large man with a flowing red beard, but a generous soul, for all that he was a poor man. He had been one of the first to join the conspiracy. Perhaps it was the pair of them speaking out in favour of Mordaunt that provoked Catesby to show his fangs.

'Mordaunt!' he sneered. 'Why, I wouldn't tell that man a secret for a room full of jewels! It's precisely because of men such as him that we can't tell all and sundry what's to happen. They'd destroy us as readily as if we marched to tell the King ourselves.'

'But the young Arundel,' said Tresham. 'Surely if we kill such as him we're killing our hope for the future?'

'Why, then, stop him from coming by other means. Isn't there a man here who could give the boy a wound that'll keep him in bed for a week or two?'

A splutter of conversation broke out around the table. Catesby let it run.

'Hold!' he announced firmly, after fully quarter of an hour of pointless debate with no conclusion. 'I myself have warned Montagu.' He glared round the table, daring any there present to deny him his right. 'One or two of the others, possibly, I might tell hours before, if I so decide. You will leave it with me.'

There was total silence around the table.

'This is no petty squabble,' he carried on, in a low voice that carried as if it had been sharpened. 'This is the battle for the soul of England. Didn't Christ die to redeem us all? Wasn't Christ innocent of all evil? Didn't his mother, and his father, have long hours to mourn his death? Sometimes the innocent must perish with the guilty, sooner than lose the battle.'

They arranged to meet again on October 23rd, at The Irish Boy.

A wider gathering was planned for the day after at The Mitre tavern in Bread Street, between Cheapside and the river, though not for the conspirators. Catesby was cheerful enough to muster a smile when he told his devilish company not to meet him there. He was due to meet ambassadors for the archdukes. He had spread the word that he and Charles Percy, Thomas Percy's brother, were forming a troop to go and fight in Europe, partly to lure away any Government spies in the taverns, partly to reassure Anne Vaux and Father Garnet. For those who did not probe too deeply, the expedition was good enough cover for their purchase of horses and weapons.

From Bread Street, mused Francis Tresham, you could see both the Tower of London, its White Tower with its four new pepper-pot cupolas, and St Paul's, still without its steeple after a lightning blast in Elizabeth's reign. Prime executions spots, the Tower and St Paul's. He felt a clawing in his stomach, and wondered if the crowds would be gathering in one of those spots to see his disembowelment before November 5th.

It had to be stopped, this madness. It had to cease.

CHAPTER 9

The miners were thin, wiry creatures with an aversion to washing their backs and muscles made of corded steel. If they were to avoid discovery, it was essential that their work was done at break-neck speed, and in silence. The men could be housed easily enough, shutters kept tight and a single candle the only light. Food and drink were brought in after midnight, with those bringing it carting the waste away at the same time, usually choosing to dump it in the river where it was sluiced away. The men had been well briefed. Any curiosity they might have had was torn out of them by the sheer physical pressure of the work. The armed guards placed there to ensure that none of the bumpkins went sightseeing had an easy job.

'Silence!' Their overseer barked a whispered command and the men froze, those still in the tunnel slinking back. A rattle of hooves and wheels outside had stopped. There was a shouted command, the cart started up again. The men relaxed, the remainder climbing their way out through the hole in the floor, dripping sweat on to the newly sanded boards.

The men worked naked in the tunnel, though a few made a rough pouch for their testicles, to protect them from cuts, or placed a sweatband round their head. By their standards it was not difficult work, the main opening having been cut, but the scenes underground still looked like a vision of Hell. The feeble yellow light flickered over the naked bodies, glinting off the sweat that caked them, and seeming to emphasise the dark patches where muck and earth had become embedded in the miners' flesh. The air was foetid, stinking of sweat, piss and decay, and the light cast huge shadows on the rough wall as the miners hewed away at the subsoil and rock. The shadow dancers seemed like huge mythical creatures, beating punishment into an unyielding earth to the tune of the picks' out-of-tempo clink and thud. The job would soon be done, the miners sent back home richer but none the wiser.

Above the ground, London went about its normal business. The bankers and moneylenders bowed low and opened the doors of their fine timbered houses in Goldsmiths' Row, whilst yards away, hidden from sight and mind, the rat-infested rookeries held families of eight or ten souls, crammed into the one room. The prosperous shop owners took their over-dressed wives to sit on the benches by St Paul's and to hear the sermon, watching all the time to see which Privy Council member and which wife of which famous Lord was sitting in the privileged north gallery of the Cathedral wall. Meantime hungry-eyed men waited for the gawping sailors and country bumpkins come to see the great Cathedral, knowing that a false dash at a purse would mean the gallows only a few yards away from where the word of God was being preached. God was a strange master in this greatest of all cities. A wretch was being whipped through the street at the tail of a cart, for having denied God, whilst the moneylenders thronged the aisles of London's Cathedral. The bright-painted two- and four-oar wherries cried out for trade on the riverbank, peaking as the time came for the afternoon performances in the playhouses across the river in Southwark. Sitting on one of their plush-covered cushions was a young girl, dressed as if for Court. She ran her hands through the water, the same water on which swans were floating a short way away. She had been told not to, but the pattern of the water and the sensuality of its cold across her hand were too great to resist. Later, she sucked her hand without thinking, watching as they neared their landing jetty and gazing in wonder at so many fine ships on the river. In seven days she would be dead, the incessant bleeding to which her surgeons submitted her sapping her body's resistance to the flux which raged through her thin, under-developed body. It is London, and in the playhouse Hotspur is about to proclaim:

> 'O gentlemen! The time of life is short;
> To spend that time basely were too long.'

When the play is finished, many of the same audience who listened to Shakespeare's poetry will stay on and pay to watch wild dogs tear a bear to pieces, the bear being tied to a stake.

'The one who worries me most,' said Gresham, 'is Monteagle.'

'Why more so than the others?' asked Jane. They had filled pages of paper with their scrawlings, gathering together all they could reach on the Catholic Lords.

'He hunts with the hounds and runs with the hare, I think,' said Gresham. 'If you were to pick someone more likely to be in this foul business, it must be him. His family are Catholic through and through. He's connected to the Howards and the Stanleys, through his mother. He fought with Essex in Ireland, even mounted a madcap rescue of him. He was at the siege in Essex House, and managed a pardon somehow. Tom Wintour acts as his secretary. He's married to Tresham's sister Elizabeth. He must have dined with every Catholic sympathiser in the country this past year or so . . .' Gresham's hand swept over the papers where they ha̶̶ ̶ to record the whisperings and reports of the spies the̶ '

'And, to cap it all, he's a bosom friend of Catesb̶ he declares in public that when Catesby goe̶ out in his life. Good God. If someone s̶a̶'

'Sir Henry,' said Jane, fluttering her eyelashes, 'when you leave my presence the sun goes out of my day, the moon goes out of my night and the liquid goes out from my . . .'

'Shut up!' said Gresham. 'You're a disgrace to your sex.'

'Surely Monteagle must be a conspirator, then?' said Jane, unabashed. 'Isn't he a prime contender for your blue blood, waiting behind the scenes and pulling all the strings? Catesby might have his own good reasons for not letting Tresham know Monteagle is involved. If you ask me, it's Tresham's money Catesby needs more than anything else. If Catesby had really wanted Tresham in he'd have recruited him much earlier. If he's suspicious of Tresham, wouldn't he hide Monteagle's involvement from him?'

'It works as a theory, but only to a degree. Why hold back on Monteagle, when he's told Tresham that the Earl of Northumberland is involved through Thomas Percy? Northumberland's a far bigger fish than Monteagle. And then there's the other side . . . look at all this. Monteagle gets given a massive fine after the Essex business – but there's no sign it was ever paid. Then look what happens. No sooner is he let out of jail and a new King on the throne than he gets his estates in Essex restored, and his right to sit in the House of Lords. Suddenly, everyone wants to know Lord Monteagle. James asks the French King to let his brother out of jail, he's made the Lord Commissioner who pro- rogues Parliament, wins a nice job in Queen Anne's court, gets his name on the charter when Prince Henry gets made Duke of York. My, my! Our Lord Monteagle is very popular all of a sudden, don't you think?'

'Everyone knows James favours those in the Essex rebellion,' said Jane, 'not just you.'

'I'm one of the few who knows James helped organise it,' said Gresham, 'however much others might suspect it. But there's more in it than that. This man's had good fortune positively poured all over him.'

'Good spy,' said Mannion.

He had seated himself on a stool, gazing out on the narrow, foetid street as night closed in. He had given the appearance of not listening, but it was always a mistake to assume that Mannion was not listening.

'Explain,' said Gresham.

'Monteagle. He'd make a good spy. He's an insider with the Papists, isn't he? An insider by birth, what's more, something you can't just buy. So if I'm Cecil, what do I do? Pay off his fine, or even simpler, write it off, provided he keeps me informed about what's happening with the Papists. That fine would've ruined Monteagle, ruined anybody. *I'd* be a bloody good spy with that fine hanging over me. Fits all round. Cecil hates common people. He'd far rather work with one of Monteagle's kind, all velvet-arsed and coach and horses.'

'That would explain why Catesby hasn't trusted Monteagle with the plot!' said Gresham. 'What a fool I am! Mannion – you're a genius. Of course Catesby must wonder why Monteagle wasn't ruined by an £8,000 fine! Of course he must look at all this preferment, and reach his own conclusions!'

'Well now,' said Mannion, 'I'm a genius now, am I? That's not a description I've had from you before. It's the tobacco, I believe, it grows the brain.'

'Grows the vomit, more like,' muttered Jane, who had banished Mannion from smoking his reeking pipe anywhere inside, but could not banish the smell of burnt sewage he carried on his clothes, his breath, his beard and seemingly his very skin.

'Monteagle has to be the man,' said Gresham, as if relieved of a great weight. 'He must already be one of Cecil's informers. If he's told of the plot, he'll have to run like a rabbit to Cecil. That fine won't be suspended for very long if one of Cecil's supposedly best inside men with the Papists doesn't know about something like this until too late. It'd be death for Monteagle.'

'So how are you going to tell Lord Monteagle?' said Jane. She was out of sorts, her playful mood suddenly changed, sulking. 'Get

me to dress up as a milkmaid and walk up to him in the street . . .
"Forgive me, my Lord, but do you know that your Papist friends
have put a ton of powder under the House of Lords and are planning to blow you to Heaven or to Hell when it's opened by the
King?" Or write to him with a list of names? "*Item*: one raving
idiot, named Robert Catesby. Talks a lot. Thinks he's God. *Item*: a
second raving idiot, named Thomas Percy. White hair, sweats a lot.
Item: various other conspirators, assorted. *Item*: one stack of gunpowder, fuse inserted . . . "'

'You're rarely boring,' said Gresham. 'Infuriating, yes, but boring,
no. You're in danger of becoming *really* boring. Will I write him a
letter, yes. Do I need your help with it, yes I most certainly do. And
if it's the wrong letter, then hundreds of people might die unnecessarily and a civil war decimate this country.'

Jane's mood changed instantly. 'I'm sorry,' she said. 'It's an explanation, not an excuse, but I've found these past few weeks here
some of the worst weeks in my life – or, at least, my life after I met
you. I'll try.'

'Thank you,' said Gresham. The women he had known before
Jane were strange, inward, mysterious creatures. Jane had that quality of mystery, of being a book with most of the pages still withheld
from his eyes and understanding. Yet in her also there was a simplicity. He would not need to secure her apology with gifts, with
cooing words, or be blackmailed later by her because she had given
in to him. She had said. It was done. It was also a change of mood
that would test the patience of a saint.

'So what form must this letter take?'

'It must seem to come from a Catholic, to stop this business
spreading out to affect Raleigh or any other innocents for that
matter. Bad enough if it's seen as the Pope's business, but better that
than it becomes all England's. It can't be seen to come from any one
man, or woman for that matter, because it must make them mount
a general search for powder, not a single search for one man.'

'You're missing the important thing,' said Jane.

'Which is?'

'*The letter must seem to come from a plotter*. One of their own. An insider. They must hear the letter's been delivered and read. They must know one of their own has written it. Only that way will they not know which way to turn. They'll feel betrayed. Their insecurity will make them break, and flee for cover.'

'You realise,' said Gresham, 'that if I do that I throw suspicion on to Tresham? He's the last to join, the least committed. Monteagle's his brother-in-law. He's the one with the most to gain, as far as they can see, from the plot fizzling out. Won't they kill him?'

'He has to take his chance, doesn't he, as we all do?' There was no venom in Jane's voice. She had been on the river that night, she had read Machiavelli. She knew now that power and survival were not easy bedfellows with any simple morality. And she had taken a strong dislike to Tresham. 'Anyway, it's not that simple. Rookwood and Digby have even more to lose than Tresham. Anyone who knows Percy seems to understand why people associate treason with the family. And Tresham won't know about the letter. He'll be genuinely surprised. And if he feels the pressure building up too much, we ship him abroad. In fact, why don't we do it now? We've no further need of him.'

Gresham shook his head as if to clear it of debris. He was not thinking tonight. He knew the plot. The date was decided by Parliament, not Catesby, so he could not argue that he needed Tresham in with the plotters. Indeed, if Tresham fled it might work up an even greater panic among the plotters, force them to cancel their plans even more readily.

Yet that could wait. The important thing was the letter.

It took them two days. Firstly, the text had to be worked on and devised, a task that burnt the candles down to the base of the candlesticks. Then Mannion had to be sent, in disguise, to St Paul's to buy clean, fresh paper. One seller had a consignment fresh delivered from the Spanish Netherlands. It amused Mannion to think of the letter written on Papist paper, so he purchased it. The letter itself was written by Jane. When she had been learning to write, Gresham had come across scraps of paper in various hands, all of which he learned were Jane's cast-offs. From very early on she had shown the natural forger's instinct. She had an inventory of writing styles she could call up from memory, as Gresham had a library of accents he could use at will. The hand she chose was clear, flowing, large. It was the old-fashioned hand of a lawyer who had drawn up a draft will for Sir Thomas Gresham, years ago. In a house where paper was never thrown away, Jane had come upon it and practised her writing on its back, deciding to copy the hand on the reverse side halfway through.

When they drew back from the table it was with almost total exhaustion. The letter lay before them, a rectangle of new paper with the clear lines marching across the page. There was a word scratched out on the first line. Jane in her tiredness had written in 'your' too early and made to throw the paper away, but Gresham had stopped her. In some way the scratched-out word made the letter look authentic, as if written in some haste. The text read:

'My Lord, the love I have for some of your friends breeds in me a care for your preservation. Therefore I advise you, as you care for your life, to think of some excuse to be absent from this Parliament. God and man have come together to punish the wickedness of our times. Do not dismiss what is written here, but take yourself off to the country where you may await events in safety. Even though it appears no trouble threatens I tell you this Parliament shall receive a terrible blow, and yet they shall not see who hurts them. Do not condemn this warning. It can do you no harm, and it may do you some good. The danger is passed once you burn this letter, and I hope God will give you the grace to make good use of it. I commend you to His holy protection.'

It was perfect, thought Gresham. It would hand Monteagle a God-given opportunity to do a service to the State which would see him set up for life. If Cecil and the King had any sense they would check and clear the cellars in ample time, and another plot would have been dismembered before it could do harm.

'Will it do?' said Jane anxiously, rubbing at her aching wrist.

Yes, thought Gresham, it will do. It has the certainty of a man convinced he is right, and just the right element of lip-smacking at the thought of evil being punished. It flatters Monteagle by singling him out. Is 'a terrible blow' explicit enough? Not for a man wanting to warn the Government, but explicit enough for a man simply wanting to warn off Monteagle. Would it work when it was shown to the King, as it had to be? Yes, thought Gresham. It would appeal to King James's sense of his own cleverness. It was a riddle a child could solve, but which a King would think had required Divine intelligence to work out. If it got to the King, and to Cecil.

If it did, and it was believed, there would be no explosion, no tangle of twisted limbs, stone and beams at Westminster, no smell of fresh blood on the morning air, no weeping and mourning, no terrifying purges and counter-purges, no executions and trials. A Catholic Lord would have exposed a plot by Catholic madmen well in time for it to be defused, literally and figuratively. In doing so the essential loyalty of the Catholics of England would have been proven, Catholic families would rally round to condemn the planned act of madness and many who would otherwise die would live on, to do with their lives as they wished.

If it failed to reach Cecil and the King, if its message was not deciphered, then that was another story.

'It's magnificent. When I tire of you, you can work as a lawyer's clerk, and make eyes at all the handsome men of law.'

The eyes that glared back at him looked as if they would put to best use a barrel of powder under Gresham. She was not to be teased out of her worry.

'This is no joke!'

'What's no joke is that the job's only half done,' said Gresham. 'What if Monteagle is the man behind the plot? What if he's the puppeteer? I don't believe it, but I can't discount it. If he is, he'll read it and burn it. He might not even tell the other plotters. We must make sure as well it's placed in his hand. What if Tom Wintour as his secretary opens it, and decides to mount a witch-hunt and still keep the plot alive?'

'Is nothing ever simple, in this world in which you live?' asked Jane.

'Tom Ward,' said Mannion. 'He's your answer. He runs Monteagle's house for him.'

Lord Monteagle was dining at his house in Hoxton, north of London. It was originally a Tresham house, and it had come to him when he had married Tresham's daughter. Tom Ward had just seen his master in to supper, and was checking to see that the main courses – salt beef and mustard, a leg of mutton stuffed with garlic, a capon boiled with leeks and a pike in a rich sauce – were ready to serve. It was unusual to eat so well at seven o' clock in the evening, but Lord Monteagle had been at Court, and asked for a fine supper to be served in place of the dinner he had missed. Ward felt a tugging at his sleeve.

'There's a genl'man outside says he has a most urgent message for you, sir, 'bout your sister.'

Then why the Devil can't the man come inside and give it, cursed Ward. Yet a lifetime of being a Catholic, of never knowing when he might have to hide his faith, of a religion conducted in secret, made an assignation in a dark street just another fact of life, and no rarity. He went out into the street, lit only by the light spilling over from the still unshuttered windows of the house. A man in a long riding cloak, with hood drawn about his head, was waiting in the shadows. He stepped forward, not enough to reveal his face, and proffered Ward a letter.

'This is from Robert Catesby to your master. It's a matter of life and death – true life and death, your own, your master's and those of your faith. Your master must see it *now*, read it *now*. If there's delay in this, you'll have more blood on your hands than Pontius Pilate!'

The figure turned and moved away, leaving a stunned Ward holding the letter in his hand.

He went back into the house, his mind made up. His master fawned over Catesby, and if this letter was from him then there was no reason for Ward to deny it his master, nor reason to think its origins were suspect. Ward knew, as all the Catholic servants knew, there was a stir about, wild talk everywhere. All the more reason to get the letter to his master.

Monteagle was in good form. His table was groaning with the best of food and wine, his company gathered around him, his future secure. What man would not be happy who only a few years before had been banished from London, and now found himself done honour in Parliament and made a favourite of the King? The wheel of fortune had indeed turned in his favour, from his being cast down to his heading for the topmost heights.

Ward leant over and whispered in his ear.

'What? What?' he asked, irritated at the interruption. Ward was still trying to keep his voice low. Monteagle was near to bellowing back at him. 'A letter? What letter? Oh, away with you, man, give it to me here.'

He took the letter without looking to see if there was a decipherable seal on the wax, and broke it open with a grin to the others that bespoke a man so burdened with office that he could not keep importunate messengers away even at a time when all decent men were in their house and home. His eyes were blurring with the smoke that had blown back from the fire, and he only dimly saw the large, almost child-like handwriting, beginning, 'My Lord, the love I have for some of your friends . . .' Oh God, he thought, another begging letter for money or preferment. What it was to have influence in the Court! There was food on his fingers, and in any event it was impolite to read letters in company at table.

'Here, Tom, read it out, will you? My eyes are furred with this damned smoke. Whoever swept that chimney deserves a thrashing, not my good coin!' It would be amusing for his family and friends to hear the type of letter famous men such as he received.

Ward stepped up, took the letter, and squeezed his eyes as if to help him concentrate. He was not a fluent reader. Nor, he was thinking, am I an actor in the playhouse, to be set up in front of all the company to give a public reading. He stumbled as he tried to come to terms with the unfamiliar handwriting.

'My Lord, the love I have for some of your . . . friends breeds in me a care for your . . .'

'Enough, enough!' cried Monteagle, laughing and making the company laugh. 'We don't have all evening, Tom. Here, you, you can read. Take it and enlighten us.'

Bad enough to be asked to stand up and perform, thought Tom Ward, but worse to be humiliated by having the task removed. He gritted his teeth. Another footman, unusually able to read, took the letter nervously and began to speak it out.

'My Lord, the . . . love I have for some of your . . . friends breeds in me a care for your preservation. Therefore I advise you, as you care for your life, to think of some excuse to be absent from this Parliament.'

The laughter and the small talk faded into silence.

'God and man have come together to punish the wickedness of our times. Do not . . . dismiss what is written here, but take yourself off to the country where you may await events in safety. Even though it appears no trouble threatens I tell you this . . . Parliament shall receive a terrible blow, and yet they shall not see who hurts them.'

There was total silence now, the noise of clattering pans in the kitchen coming through into the room. The faces of Monteagle's family and guests were upturned and glistening in the light of the candles, looking towards the footman. The servant looked down at Monteagle, seeking his permission to carry on or to stop, his throat dry, his heart pounding through his head. Monteagle gazed like a stone ahead of him, eyes fixed on something invisible on the wall. The servant waited, then carried on.

'Do not condemn this warning. It can do you no harm, and it may do you some good. The . . . danger is passed once you burn this letter, and I hope God will give you the grace to make good use of it. I . . . commend you to His holy protection.'

There was total silence.

'Is this some joke?' Monteagle demanded of the company. 'Some idiotic *pasquil* to stop me from my duty?' There was no-one who felt able to answer. The silence lengthened.

'Saddle my horse,' said Monteagle, quietly. 'I ride to Whitehall. Now.'

Without a further word, he swept out of the room. Behind him his company for supper looked and waited for who would say the first word. It was a long time in coming.

Gresham watched from the alleyway a short distance up from Monteagle's house. He heard the yelling and the stirring in the stables, saw the lights move back and forth in the darkened yard, heard the rasping sound of rough bolts being drawn back on stable doors. With a spurt of mud Lord Monteagle and two other horse-men sped out of the house, and down the street in the direction of Whitehall.

The cold had taken all feeling out of Gresham's feet, and his hands were little better. The old serjeant who had coached him in the Netherlands would be chiding him now, were he alive. 'Yer have to keep the blood flowing inside yer limbs if yer want to stay alive,' he would have said, 'and stop someone shedding it outside yer body!'

Well, the business was under way. It had a power and a force of its own. Gresham saw history like a great river, with estuaries beyond number flowing in intricate patterns away from the main course and then, after interminable rambling, back in again. He did not have the arrogance to think that he could stem that river, unlike many men. He knew that at times he had placed a dam across one of the estuaries, blocked the course it would otherwise have run. So the water would not take the course it would otherwise have done. Perhaps it would go where he willed it to go. Yet water, and rivers, had minds of their own. No man could determine Fortune. All one could do was try.

Gresham did not see Tom Ward retire to his own small chamber, produce a pen and paper and write a hasty note, which he then sealed with a copy of his master's seal. The various marriages between the Ward and the Wright families had cemented a relationship which had gone back decades. God only knew what the letter Ward had given to his master meant for Kit and Jack Wright, but if there was devilment afoot Tom Ward guessed they would be in it to the hilt. The man who had given him the letter had mentioned Catesby. Well, Tom Ward knew Catesby was at White Webbs, most likely with one or both of the Wright brothers, from what he had heard. Ward scribbled down the barest details of the letter and its disclosure, and sealed what he had written. Within minutes of his master's riding forth, one of the strongest riders in Monteagle's employment was similarly pounding through the mud, this time on Ward's orders to head for Enfield. Within hours Catesby would know of the letter.

It was a shaken and dishevelled Monteagle who loudly demanded entry to the Chief Secretary's private apartments at Whitehall. Yet he was not as dishevelled as on a previous appearance, not far from this very spot. To his shame and chagrin he had fallen into the Thames and nearly drowned during the Essex rebellion, being dragged out looking little better than a corpse. Even now as he was rowed up the Thames the cry would come across the river from an anonymous wherry, 'I thought that's one as preferred to swim the river!', followed by a guffaw of laughter.

These were not the rooms to which he had been taken, several years before, in fear of his life. His reception there had been as icy-cold in tone as he had expected, but very different in content. Cecil had recruited him as an informer with the clinical certainty of a surgeon sawing off a leg. What choice did he have? The deal allowed him to retain his religion and its observance, and acquire the state he thought had been lost for ever. In return he only had to keep Cecil informed – and as Cecil had said, that information was more likely to preserve both the peace of the nation and peace for Catholics than it was to disrupt. Well, if ever he was to prove that true it was now.

The door swung open into the brightly lit room. A supper such as he had just left was about to be served on a sumptuously carved table. At its head sat Robert Cecil, Earl of Salisbury, Chief Secretary to King James I. It was not the sight of Cecil that took Monteagle aback. It was his guests. Edward Somerset, Earl of Worcester. Henry Howard, Earl of Northampton. Thomas Howard, Earl of Suffolk. Four of the most powerful men in all England, and three of them known as either Catholic or Catholic sympathisers.

The irony of it would have struck Monteagle less forcibly had he noticed the letter on the table between the four noble Lords, a letter written on paper from the Spanish Netherlands, in a broad, large and almost child-like hand. Cecil had turned it over, face down, smoothly as Monteagle had burst into the room. It read:

'My Lord, were you and my Lords of Northampton, Suffolk and Worcester to meet for supper on Saturday evening at your palace in Whitehall you will find a message come to you there that will preserve your souls as good food preserves the flesh, and do much to preserve the nation and your self.'

'Will it work?' Jane had asked.

'Who knows?' said Gresham. Jane's hand was stained with ink, crooked with the time she had spent crouched over the paper. He leant over and placed his hand over her own. His hand was cold, hers warm. 'The presence of the three great Catholic Lords when the letter's delivered will serve two purposes, if it can be engineered. It'll force Cecil into action even if he's biding his time to implicate Raleigh in some way. It'll clear the Catholic Lords of any involvement.'

'If I was Cecil,' said Jane, 'I'd think some madman wanted all four of us together to assassinate us.'

'You'd need an uprising to do that, and an army to go with it. The request's for them to gather in the heart of Cecil's stronghold, not for him to come unarmed to a field in Islington at midnight. No, there are two key words in it for Cecil – "souls" will tell him it's to do with Catholics. I'm sure he doesn't know details of the plot, but if all London is buzzing with rumours that there's a plot of some sort he must have heard something, and he'd be madder than he is to ignore anything linked to those rumours. And we've mentioned *his* "preservation". There's nothing closer to his heart than that. It might work. We're not lost if it doesn't. The presence of the Catholic Lords is a bonus, not the main prize. The main prize is to get that powder removed and the plotters dispersed.'

Monteagle knew nothing of this. He had steeled himself to present before the Chief Secretary, and now found himself facing a court consisting not just of one but four of the people in the strongest position to influence his life, career and prospects.

The slippery element in Monteagle that had let him survive as long as he had came to his rescue. He bowed low to all four men. Collecting himself, he asked if it were possible for him to have a private word with his Lordship, with no disrespect, of course, intended to the other three noble Lords.

Cecil glanced at the other three, nodded briefly to them, and motioned Monteagle over to a side room. The servants had laid the wine there, before bringing it in to the supper, and one of them scuttled out as if branded as Cecil swept into the room.

Give me your damned message, Cecil was tempted to say, so that I can at least know where I stand in a business that is becoming too complicated for its own good. But, of course, he said nothing, merely enquiring politely about Lord Monteagle's health.

Lord Monteagle's health, he mused, would not stand many more rides such as he had clearly just made. He was having trouble catching his breath, the mud was caked up his waist and sweat dripping down his cheeks on to his beard. Monteagle was pouring out the story, offering Cecil the letter finally, after he had given a highly embossed version of its contents.

A slight shudder passed through Cecil as he saw the hand on Monteagle's letter, matching that on the paper turned over on his table.

'Thank you, my Lord,' said Cecil carefully, refolding the letter. 'It is good that you have brought this to my attention, whatever the consequences might be.' He nodded to Monteagle, ushering him out and back into the main chamber. The three Lords waited like gargoyles on a Cathedral wall, only their flickering eyes betraying their tension.

Without a word, Cecil handed the letter to Northampton. Northampton's ferocious ambition was widely known at Court, being born out of so many years in the wilderness during Elizabeth's reign. As a convert will cram a lifetime of passion into whatever years remain him, so Northampton was determined to make the best of what time remained to him by the political fireside. The letter was passed round to the other two, who read it in silence. Unknown to Monteagle, Northampton glanced down at the earlier letter, lying in the centre of the table, eyebrows raised. No, Cecil's eyes signalled, let that remain between us, not between ourselves and this young Lord.

'Government receives many such letters, my Lord Monteagle, as you may well know,' said Cecil finally, breaking the long silence.

Monteagle was visibly deflating in front of the harsh glare of power. His shoulders slumped. Had he made a complete fool of himself?

'Yet I have had word for some months past of scheming abroad, scheming, I fear, from those of your faith. We will show this to His Majesty, expose it to his wisdom and invite his view. Plots are as fruit, my Lord. They need time to ripen.'

Show it to His Majesty? Tonight? Tomorrow? Had he done the right thing to ride through the night and interrupt this supper? Or would his letter be placed in a pile of submissions or petitions, to be dealt with in due time and in due order?

'His Majesty . . .' stumbled Monteagle.

'Is in Royston,' answered Cecil, calmly, 'hunting. He remains there until the thirtieth, when he stays at Ware, returning to London and Whitehall the next day. There is no invisible blow waiting in the forest, I am sure,' said Cecil condescendingly, turning to the other three Lords. He was rewarded by thin smiles from them.

'We are grateful to you for your care in this matter, my Lord. Be assured, it will not harm your credit with His Majesty. You may return to your supper with a·heart and mind at rest.'

He was being dismissed. He bowed low and backed out, even as servants began to bring in the delayed meal to the chamber. It was a perplexed young Lord who rode more slowly than he had come through the dark streets, to a supper by now hopelessly spoilt.

'You didn't need to put me so close,' said Mannion, rubbing his hands by the fire. 'With the noise he made you'd have thought it was an army coming to Whitehall, not just three men.'

Gresham had stationed Mannion by the main gate of Whitehall, to check that Monteagle had gone where it was intended he go.

'What do we do now?' asked Jane.

Gresham gazed at her for a moment, then moving so quickly that she could not react he grasped her round the waist, pulled her towards him and placed a long and lingering kiss on her full lips.

'I'm not a meal to be picked up off the table when it pleases!' she exclaimed, pulling away. She had returned the kiss, though, he noticed.

'Don your serving-girl clothes!' cried Gresham. 'We go to the playhouse!'

'Can we afford to? What if we're seen?'

'After all this time in this hovel, I think we can't afford not to. We'll dress as servants and stand at the back of the Pit. And after that, we're back to the House and civilisation, I think.'

'Are we out of danger, then?'

'I'll limp back into town as if a growth has been carved out of my side and I'm only recently recovered. Wherever I go people will look at me and feel ill, though I shall of course keep to my bed for weeks on end. An invalid will present no threat to Cecil. And anyway, the plot is out – what has Cecil to fear from me?'

Robert Catesby had spent the morning trying to ease the worries of Anne Vaux at White Webbs. It did not matter if he succeeded in demolishing her fears. All that mattered was that he allayed them. Hardly a week to go, and then he could throw off this continual need to hide behind fabrication and deceit. A week from now, and the world would know the truth.

The letter arrived at midday, brought to table by Tom Bates. The messenger, a simple serving lad, had become hopelessly lost, as a result of riding through the night, and had nearly killed his mount. Catesby read the hasty scribble, expressionless, and carefully folded it before slipping it into the large pocket sewn into his breeches. He finished his meal quietly, allowing Anne to chatter about the fate of various neighbours' experiences of childbirth and children in general. He rose from the table, thanked Anne politely and nodded to the others round the table. Tom Wintour needed no hint or secret signals to rise shortly afterwards, and join him. Not long after, the Wright brothers followed suit.

'We appear to have a slight problem,' said Catesby dryly, handing the note to Wintour, and on to the Wrights. The colour rose in Wintour's face as he read it. 'We owe a debt to your kinsman, Tom Ward, I think,' added Catesby, as first Kit and then Jack Wright took the letter. Both the Wrights had been in on the plot from its earliest days, and neither Kit nor Jack Wright would utter three words where none would do. Two strong, taciturn men, they grunted as the import of the letter sank in, and looked to Catesby.

'We're discovered!' For a brief moment, the hatred that drove Wintour to contemplate an act of mass murder showed clearly on his face. Stupidly, he turned to look over his shoulder, as if even then the troops of the King would be trampling across the lawns of Enfield to arrest them both.

'Peace, cousin,' said Catesby. 'We're safe as yet. Think. Think what it means.'

'It means Cecil and the King know about our plot!' Wintour's face was grotesque, distorted with the mix of anger and fear that coloured it dark red.

'It means no such thing!' Catesby's words were like a slap across Wintour's face. 'True, the letter sounds a warning over Parliament, but they'll look for an army to be the agent of harm, not one man in a cellar!'

'We're not named. Not any of us.' It was Kit Wright, who often spoke both for himself and for his brother.

In his haste to warn Catesby and the Wrights, Tom Ward had written only that Monteagle's letter had advised him not to attend Parliament and had warned him of a strike against Parliament. Would Catesby's relative calm have been shattered if Ward had told him of the phrase 'terrible blow', and the letter's emphasis on the invisibility of that blow? He was never to know, never to see the letter and destined only to hear about it from a frightened servant relying on memory. That particular estuary received no dam, and its water trickled along unhindered down the path Fate had set.

'We'll know soon enough if we're discovered. Do you think if any of us are suspected Cecil and the King will leave us to go about our business? Fawkes can keep a watch on the cellar. If there's any interest in it, then we'll know we're truly discovered, and plan accordingly. But before that, look at what this letter must mean.'

Wintour looked blankly at him.

'A traitor, Tom, a traitor! One of us must have written that letter. We've a snake in our little garden.'

The redness had begun to recede from Wintour's face, but it came back with a flood. 'Tresham! That bastard Tresham!' he roared.

'Possibly – but be cautious. Digby and Rookwood have more to lose than most of us, and wives who may fear they will lose their husbands and their livelihoods. Perhaps one of the other women . . . a priest who's heard too much in confession . . . a servant who's overheard his master . . . perhaps even your brother.'

'Robert! Never in a thousand years! He may be nervous, but if he isn't loyal then the Pope's not God's appointed.'

'We've to consider everyone, haven't we?' It was as if Catesby was discussing a game of cards.

'You'll call Tresham here? Now?' Wintour's face made it clear that Francis Tresham would be walking into his death when he came to White Webbs.

'Call him, yes. But not now. We're due to meet at Temple Bar on Wednesday. Tom, we must keep silent about this letter at least for a while. We must! You know the others. We can't let them think it's all over yet. Let's wait and see if a hue and cry starts. There were no names in the letter, were there? It will take time to examine, time in which we'll know if we're being followed or watched. Let's tell the others on Wednesday, and watch Tresham as a man has never been watched. Then let's decide.'

Wintour's face made it clear what his decision already was. As far as Tom Wintour was concerned, Francis Tresham was a dead man. The four conspirators ordered a bottle of wine. Catesby doubted there was more to discuss, yet there would be support in the wine and in the companionship of its drinking.

Francis Tresham, unaware of the plot being hatched on his life, and blissfully unaware of the Monteagle letter, lay in his rooms at Lincoln's Inn Walk. There was a knock on the door. He leapt as if for his life, grabbing the sword that lay by the bed. His servant, the learned but dilatory Vavasour, was out buying wine. There was another knock on the door, loud and urgent. Tresham held his sword poised, and wrenched it open. Something hit him, and he was suddenly on the floor with a ringing head, his sword held in the left hand of his visitor. It was the ox of a servant, Selkirk's servant.

'My master sends you the first down payment.' He tossed a package towards Tresham. 'And I wouldn't open doors suddenly, with a sword in your hand, if I were you.'

It was a passport, a travel warrant from the Government. It permitted him to travel abroad for two years, with horses, servants and other necessaries.

'The money, and the details of the ship, come when he's finished with you. Don't run out on him, will you? I'd hate to ruin that fine doublet you're wearing.'

'Why so long?' Gresham's scalp itched so that he longed to tear the skin off his head, his head was pounding as it had not done so since the river. 'Why is nothing happening?'

Gresham had revelled in the return to the House, and Jane had gone straight to her beloved library as if it were an old friend brought back from the grave. Yet as his impatience grew it was seeming more and more like a prison, more and more like the rooms in Alsatia.

There was the tedium of keeping up the pretence to cope with. The paste that kept his skin sickly-white needed to be re-applied twice a day, and Jane had to use a thin linen cloth rather than her hands, in case they too turned white. No lump in his side was necessary, the theoretical growth having been theoretically cut out, but it was necessary to keep a supply of fresh pig's blood to stain his shirts with, the amount decreasing every day very slightly, as well as suitably gory 'dressings' to be sent out with the servants. Gresham trusted the servants in the House more than he had let Jane know, but all it needed was for one to comment in the market or on the street about Gresham's miraculous recovery for unwanted attention to be directed on to him.

Yet the real worry was the lack of action on Cecil's part. It was as if the letter had never been received. The careful watch Gresham had placed on the cellar and house Percy had rented, as soon as Tresham had told him of it, had reported no untoward action or even interest in the place. The story of a plot being hatched in France was still current on the streets and gaining ground, but there was no hint to it of something closer to home, and no hint of gunpowder or mass murder or regicide. Tresham had been summoned to meet the conspirators again, but there was no sense of any special reason behind the summons. Sending the travel documents had been a gamble. They had cost him a small fortune, but as Jane had commented, quality never came cheap. In this instance, it was not quality he had paid for, but authenticity. The corrupt clerk who had charge of such matters had slipped the paper for signing into a heap so high that his master had yearned for it to come to an end with the intensity of a schoolboy wishing the end of school. Gresham needed his mole in the plotters' burrow to report. Had they noted men following them, questions being asked of the servants? Was the pressure on them to disband? Had the news of the letter reached them, through the servant, Ward, who was so close to the brothers Kit and Jack Wright, as Gresham had planned?

Gresham knew that impatience was his greatest weakness, yet the pressure of not knowing what was happening, coupled with the fear that nothing was happening, was near to destroying any peace of mind he might have. He called for music, and settled himself to listen as the lute dropped jewelled notes in the way of the long walk of the strings and the nasal urgency of the wind instruments. It helped, but not enough. In public he was still bed-bound for most of the day, so it was on his bed that he lay back and tried to let the music soak into his veins, as the musicians assiduously played for him.

It was dangerous for so many to gather at one time in London, but Catesby deemed it necessary. They had planned it long ago, for a week before the explosion. To cancel it now would cause panic. The presence of the others would lull Tresham into a false sense of security. He would hardly expect a gathering in London to be kept if his comrades knew the plot had been exposed, reasoned Catesby.

The taciturn Fawkes was there, inscrutable as ever. Rookwood had come down to receive his instructions, and to be fortified by Catesby if necessary. Tom Wintour was there, trying to hide the murderous gleam in his eye, whilst Thomas Percy, wild-eyed and stained from travel, had finally broken from his rent-gathering in the north to make it to London.

Tresham looked nervous, tense, almost distracted. Catesby raised an eyebrow, and Tom Wintour's hand stiffened towards the dagger in his belt. Rookwood had been given the task of buying dinner, not sensing the patronising ease with which Catesby treated him at one and the same time as friend and servant.

'Is all well?' Rookwood enquired nervously. Wintour flicked a glance at Catesby. These well-born, idle rich were food for Court and fine lace and fancy manners, he thought, but no good when push came to shove. The rich had time for a conscience. Men such as Wintour had time for action. That was the difference. Wintour cursed the day they hatched a plot which needed the money of such as Ambrose Rookwood.

'All's well indeed,' said Catesby reassuringly. The wine Rookwood had provided and drunk of so liberally had not calmed him, but if anything made him more nervous. 'We're not discovered.

The King hasn't hurried back from his hunting. None of us have felt ourselves watched, have we?' Heads were shaken in the negative, around the table. 'Stout hearts and courage are what we need now.'

No response from Tresham, who was turning continually to look out on the street, as if hoping for someone to walk by and rescue him.

'None of our number would betray us!' said Wintour, in far too loud a voice. Tresham started, but whether through guilt or simply the explosive noise of Wintour's interjection was difficult to say.

'What say you, cousin?' said Catesby to Tresham. 'You're strangely silent.'

'I'm sorry,' said Tresham. 'I've things on my mind. I shouldn't trouble you with them.'

Catesby and Wintour exchanged glances.

'I must have some of your money, cousin,' said Catesby easily. 'You know how pressing the need is.'

'Are you still set on this? Can't we at least delay until we know what legislation Parliament will pass?'

'You know the answer. As I know you won't betray us.'

There was a decided flicker across Tresham's face, a sheen of sweat across it. This was too public a place to kill him, thought Catesby. It would panic Rookwood, and draw attention to them. Not here. Not now.

'If you still have reservations, cousin, now isn't the time to discuss them. White Webbs, Friday, two days from now. Come and dine with us there. And, I pray you, bring some of your gold with you. My purse has been deep, but it's drawn dry. Until Friday then. I hope you'll come ready for a reckoning!' laughed Catesby.

CHAPTER 10

Though Gresham did not know it, the mood of William Parker, Lord Monteagle, was as destructive and tense as his own. He had waited for news every hour since his abrupt dismissal from Whitehall, yet none had come. The King was due back from hunting today, he knew. He could restrain his impatience no longer. Hurrying to Whitehall, he at least suffered no delay in being shown in to Cecil's presence. Indeed, barriers seemed to melt at his name. Gratified at the sudden power he seemed able to wield, he bowed in a rather cursory manner to Cecil, forgetting for a moment who was Lord and who was master.

'My Lord Monteagle!' said Cecil, an icy warmth in his voice. 'You must think I had forgotten you and your recent good service. Nothing could be further from the truth. These are weighty matters, matters we have let ripen on the vine.'

'You will tell the King, my Lord? Today?'

A flicker of annoyance crossed Cecil's face. 'In time, my good Lord, all in good time. Trust me, my Lord, as a friend, as well as an elder.' Cecil's tone softened, became almost caressing as his gimlet eyes fixed on the young man with his strong, straight body. 'You are beholden to me for a very large sum of money still outstanding against your name, are you not? You are beholden to me for restoring you and your family's standing and fortune, are you not? You have received those very great gifts in exchange merely for a little information, have you not? You may trust my judgement in these great matters of state, as I trust your judgement in lesser matters.'

Damn you, thought Monteagle. I am not your friend. I am your slave. As he left, his bow was deep and low.

'The men we sent out, they're still reporting, some of them.' Mannion stood by Gresham's side. 'They say these Papists are back in London, mostly. Gathering together for some devilry, I guess. Do you want to see three of them? Percy's booked dinner for three at The Mitre, in Bread Street. It's a haunt of theirs. Bold as brass. Our men say there's no sign of anyone else watching them.'

Why not? Gresham agonised. Why were these men gathering in London, instead of fleeing for their lives? Why was every Catholic sympathiser in London not being hounded down?

Could Gresham risk being an onlooker at this devils' supper? He was driven to it by his own demon, the frustration tearing at him as a real growth in his side would have done. Even the basic questions that were grist to his survival seemed irrelevant. Should he change his complexion from its deathly white? What disguise should he wear? Should he slip out of a side door of the House, or go as if to an appointment with his surgeon?

Why hadn't this powder plot folded in on itself? Had Monteagle been so unconvincing in his presentation of the letter?

Had he even presented the letter at all?

Robert Cecil knew little about warfare. It seemed to him that it excited men of a certain type, that it was costly beyond belief and that its results were unpredictable. It also seemed that an army large enough to fight a war was necessary to accompany the King on one of his hunting expeditions. The already astronomical expenses of the Royal household rose by the minute, and Cecil sighed as the endless train of horses and carts and assorted wagons brought back His Royal Highness King James I from his pleasures.

He waited until the afternoon following. Friday was an unlucky day in common belief, but also the first of the month, symbolic perhaps of a new start. King James was in his Gallery at Whitehall, alone.

Cecil approached, bowed, and offered the Monteagle letter, without comment. James raised an eyebrow, took it and read it. He looked up at Cecil, who made no comment again. He read it a second time, taking more care.

'It was delivered at night, sire, to my Lord Monteagle. He brought it straight here, to me.' And it was undated, thank God, thought Cecil. Would James be angered at the length of time it had taken to bring this letter to his attention?

'Clearly, my liege,' said Cecil, 'whoever wrote this is a fool.'

'In which case,' said the King, 'it were as well not to receive it likewise as a fool.'

Intelligence and experience, thought Cecil, his heart racing behind his composed exterior. Never forget this man has survived by his wits as King of the Scots. Never forget that conspiracies are second nature to him. Never forget there is no-one as wise as a fool.

Where were the others? thought Tresham as he entered White Webbs. He was shown to a room he had never entered before, and before he knew it the door had slammed behind him and he was facing Robert Catesby. Tom Wintour stood behind him. He drew both bolts on the door.

It all hinged on one sentence, Tresham was to realise later. If Catesby had said to him, in that terrifyingly calm voice of his, 'Why have you betrayed us?' Tresham's face would have broken down into a confession of guilt. He had betrayed the plotters to 'Selkirk', as well as betraying his marriage vows, his religion and, for all he knew, the God he had never properly worshipped.

But Catesby did not ask why Tresham had betrayed his friends.

Instead, he chose to ask, 'Tell me, cousin, why did you send the letter?'

The letter? What letter? The last letter Tresham had sent had been a peremptory demand for unpaid rent from one of his newly acquired tenants. Genuine confusion crossed his face.

'What letter? I've sent no letter!'

The instant vehemence of his response caused Catesby to pause. Even Wintour, poised behind him, shuffled uncertainly. Catesby spoke again.

'Don't pretend ignorance. Who else would send a letter to Lord Monteagle – *your brother-in-law* – warning him not to attend Parliament if he wished to preserve his life?'

'Now you mention it, I'd gladly have sent such a letter, if I'd only thought of it! You know what I think. We won't build our faith by this act, we'll destroy people's faith in it. I confess I'd thought of writing a warning, not to Monteagle, to one of the King's secretaries, but I never sent any such letter. Do you hear me? *I never sent a letter!*'

Sincerity strikes its own note. Sincerity uttered with a man holding a drawn dagger at your back strikes an even deeper note. It was picked up by Catesby and Wintour.

'If not you, who else?' It was Wintour this time, almost hissing in his intensity.

'How would I know? And can the condemned man at least sit down? It's not much of a last request!'

Tresham's genuine exhaustion, physical and mental, came to his aid. His tiredness was clearly no counterfeit.

If I can keep saying what I know to be true, I might yet walk out of here alive, thought Tresham. That would be an irony, for a man who was a congenital liar.

Gresham was exhausted, though mentally rather than physically. The strain of having to act the invalid in front of every servant, the strain of waiting, had all taken its toll. Standing to wash that morning he had felt himself shivering, something he had never done unless he had a fever. Mannion had said nothing, but Gresham noted the fire had been stacked higher than normal when he went to eat his breakfast.

Mannion had arranged the next meeting with Tresham in a stew, or brothel.

'It makes sense,' he had remonstrated. 'There's more control over who comes into a whorehouse than there ever is in a tavern. It's across the river, so we can get you over in a covered boat from our own jetty.'

In the meantime, Mannion had surpassed himself at The Mitre. Pretending to be searching out a room for his master and finding out which room Percy had booked, he had taken the adjacent one for an hour earlier. By the time Percy occupied his room the servants would have finished bringing the food and have left them to their bottles. Even better, an iron hook from which a lamp had hung had worked loose from the rough plaster of the dividing wall in Percy's room, and been fixed anew an inch or so up, leaving a hole. It had taken Mannion a split second with his dagger to drive through the hole and leave a clear mark on the wall of the adjacent room. It was the work of a few seconds to enlarge the hole so that one man could look through. Yet he worked with the utmost care at it, as the tap boy left their room. The plaster was old and rotten, and too much pressure would not open an eye hole, all but invisible in the other room, but rather tear out a great gaping hole.

Reluctantly Gresham had allowed Jane's importunings, and taken her with him, heavily hooded. At the inn it was just another well-bred lady coming to an assignation with a gentleman. They extinguished the lights in their room as they heard Percy and his guests enter. Mannion was first to look through. He had the descriptions of the others from Tresham and from the agents he had sent out.

'That's Percy,' Mannion whispered, 'the tall one with the white hair and beard. They say he sweats all the time. The other big one, red beard and hair, he must be Fawkes. The third one . . . he might be Grant, Robert Grant . . .'

Gresham took over from Mannion, peering through the tiny hole to the well-lit room beyond. How normal they look, he thought as the men started their meal. How much easier things would be if those determined to bring mass destruction to nations somehow looked different from their fellow men.

Tresham realised that his life had hung in the balance at White Webbs, but it took time for the shock to hit him. He had swaggered his way through the meeting, but gone into a near collapse afterwards when he had realised what had so nearly happened to him.

The smell of bodies and stale sweat in the room they used suggested it had only recently been used for a different purpose. They had come by separate routes, the most devious way possible, Gresham in a closed boat over the river to Southwark. Tresham had not been followed, Mannion was prepared to swear.

'Tell me what happened.' Gresham spoke calmly, sensing the rising terror in his spy.

Slowly, with much prompting, Tresham told his story. There had been a letter, to Lord Monteagle. It had caused Wintour to panic, but left Catesby strangely calm. The plotters had not been named. No action seemed to have been taken. The powder was secure. They were meeting tomorrow again, a group of them, to discuss the situation.

'And I'm the prime suspect,' he confessed. 'If they'd asked me a different question there might have been a different ending. Catesby . . . I don't know about Robin. I think he believes me when I say I've written no letter. Tom Wintour, now there's a different story.'

Gresham thought for a moment. 'Are you prepared to be arrested for your part in this plot? Taken to the Tower?'

Tresham gaped at him. Even Mannion started and showed surprise.

'Arrested? Taken to the Tower? Is the world gone mad, and am I the only sane person left? If either happens then I'm a dead man! I might as well throw myself off the boat home and into the Thames.'

'An understandable conclusion,' said Gresham, 'but not necessarily true. Think on it. If you're arrested peacefully and can claim to have used your best endeavours to stop the plot, that'll give them pause to think. You're a late recruit. Persuade them of that, and they'll leave you 'til last. With any luck you'll escape torture. It has to be sanctioned by the King, and that'll take time.'

'Escape torture if I'm lucky! Hell's fire, man, what do you think I am?'

'Someone who might prove very lucky in his friends. I said imprisoned in the Tower, not die in the Tower. Do you realise that when the news of this plot breaks you'll be a hunted man all your life? Well, our two interests come together. I need you to report to me for as long as possible, and that carries the risk that you'll be caught up in the exposure before you can get away. You need a new life – and you'll only get that if the world thinks you're dead.'

'And you can arrange that?' said Tresham incredulously.

'Did you realise that you've been receiving treatment for a complaint for some years past, from my good friend Dr Simon Forman?'

'Forman? That quack! I'm no woman wanting to miscarry quietly or to poison her husband, nor no idiot paying a fortune for a false horoscope.'

'Leave ranting to your friend Catesby. Forman is a better doctor than many who claim more training in that science. Now listen . . .'

Raleigh had told him on his last visit that he must drop the escape plan. He would never use it. His wife had pleaded with him. He had looked at her in that special way, the way he used for no-one else, and had stroked her head gently. 'A man does not run away,' he had said. 'A man lives by his honour, and if then he needs to die for his honour, then that too is part of the bargain.' What more fitting than that a plan that had been refused because it was not an honourable course of action should be used for a man who had lost all claim to honour?

It could be done, Gresham knew. Simon Forman could produce almost any symptoms to order. A urinary strangulation, he had favoured. Easy to fake with potions, easy to act. Forman could also produce substances that would slow the heartbeat down almost to nothing, make the body appear cold. The tricky part was getting the corpse diagnosed as dead, and into the coffin. Weeping women helped, flinging themselves on the corpse and keeping the doctors from a lengthy examination. They let the women in if the prisoner was seriously ill, knowing a man received better care from his family.

What would Cecil's reaction be when this plot was exposed? If it was done quickly and quietly, if the credit could be given to Cecil, who knows? He might save Gresham all the fuss and pretence and have Tresham declared dead in the Tower. If, that is, his gratitude to Gresham outweighed his hatred. Well, time would tell. With good fortune they would have these madmen cured of their plot and dispersed before Francis Tresham found himself a prisoner.

'Why not let him get himself arrested and then just leave him to die in the Tower?' Jane had asked sourly.

'Because I don't particularly want him implicating me in this business, and there's always the risk that he's seen and knows enough to find out that Alexander Selkirk is actually Sir Henry Gresham. But more important, I made an agreement with him. In exchange for his services I agreed his survival, as well as his wealth.'

'With scum? With people who make a rat look civilised?' said Jane.

'His personality is one thing. An agreement is another. It's a matter of honour. It wouldn't matter if the agreement was with Satan. Agreements must be honoured.'

If the truth be known he was more worried about the letter. Francis Tresham should have been able to be up and gone by now, the plot vanishing like smoke in the air. So the letter had been received and reported. Yet no action had sprung from those facts. What had happened? Had his letter been simply too vague to ring the right alarum bells? Had the King dismissed it? Had Cecil dismissed it as a forgery, a ploy to distract attention away from a more real threat, such as a foreign invasion?

Back at the House the itching in his scalp was unbearable. He called for water and a basin, dipped his head and scrubbed at his hair with the beautifully scented French soap. The first and the second buckets, drawn as he had insisted from the sweet water of the House's own well, had been brought by servants. The third was brought by Jane.

'Are we washing out the stains of the world?' she enquired, pouring the contents on a head still half full of suds. Her fingers massaged his scalp, moving slowly and firmly through the tangled hair, easing the froth down and into the basin. A reddish tinge was still occasionally visible amidst the white suds.

'I must go to Cecil,' he said quietly.

There was no gasp of breath, no exclamation, only a slight faltering in the pressure of her fingers on his scalp, before the smooth, fluid motion recommenced.

'The letter's failed,' he said. 'I'd thought to spare bloodshed by naming no names, thought to spare Raleigh, thought to be honourable to Tresham, thought to disperse a plot before it could act. Well, I've failed.' He sat back, feeling the cold droplets of water course down his neck and back before Jane placed the towel on his head. 'One man has visited the cellar, our watcher swears, a man answering Fawkes's description. No man else. That cellar must be identified, emptied. Without the powder there's no plot.'

'How will you do it? Empty it yourself?'

'And have them fill it up again? Or be arrested as chief plotter? No thank you! I'll simply tell Cecil that on my sickbed I received notice that a certain cellar below the House of Lords is crammed full of gunpowder. I'll make it impossible for him not to search it. And you, Jane, will make sure it's searched, should I not return.

Searched and exposed. With the powder gone there's no powder plot.'

'And Raleigh?'

'He once told me that honour was the difference between a man and an animal. Is it more honourable to preserve my old master against a harm that might not come to him, or to preserve the nation from another blood bath that certainly will come unless I can stop it? I must take a gamble with the man I'd least willingly put at risk. How long have we been meddling with this plot? In all that time we've found not a whisper, not a syllable that could link it to Raleigh. Oh, I know, they can fabricate what evidence they wish, but I've been thinking.'

At times it felt as if he had been doing nothing else, lying awake for most of the night, the thoughts churning through his head.

'Raleigh has had one trial where there was no true evidence, and what there was consisted of lies. It was unpopular, hugely unpopular. I think it surprised Cecil, shocked him even, as only a threat to his own power would shock him. There's no real evidence to link Raleigh to any of this. I have to gamble Cecil won't risk another false trial with false evidence so soon after the last.'

'You're a stupid man, Henry Gresham.'

'Why so? Am I putting Raleigh at too much risk?'

'No, it's not Raleigh. It's you. You're never content, are you?' She knelt at his feet, wiping the shreds of soap off his shirt and hose. 'You say that survival is all a man can hope for, yet you put your own strange form of honour far beyond mere survival. You say you can influence nothing, yet you seek all the time to exert just such an influence. You think yourself ruthless, and you are ruthless with those who let you down or stand in your way, yet you'll risk your own life in the name of honour.'

He drew her hands gently off him, and stood up. 'Today, I ceased to be ill. Life is for living, isn't it? And when I see Cecil tonight, I'll at least know I'm alive, in every pore of my body, even until that life's extinguished. And after, I doubt my corpse will care.'

'No,' said Jane, 'but my living body will care. And the mind it contains.'

They looked at each other in silence.

The letter is confirmed,' said Catesby. It was Sunday, November 3rd. It was the last planned meeting of the conspirators, or such as could be mustered in one place. The news of the letter had shattered the peace of mind of those who had heard, as if there had not been tension enough already.

'Are we lost, then? Do I ride to Dunchurch?' It was Everard Digby, ever the dandy, leaning nonchalantly on the table in a doublet double-slashed in yellow and purple. In the morning he was due to ride to Dunchurch, where a 'hunting party' was to gather at The Red Lion. This party was a crucial element in Catesby's plotting. It was from here that Digby would move to Coombe House, a mere eight miles away, and capture the Princess Elizabeth, and this gathering was to be the base of the three hundred horsemen Catesby believed he could muster.

'I urge delay.' It was Tresham who spoke, causing an uneasy stir and a poisonous glance from Tom Wintour. 'Here, see these.' There was a slap as the package containing his travel papers landed on the trestle. 'I'll pay for some of the same, for all of you. Let's wait out this Parliament, see what comes to pass both with the law and the letter, take ourselves to France for some month or two. We can come to no harm in France, and we preserve ourselves to act when we think fit, when there's no cloud of suspicion over us.'

'Your cloud of suspicion will easily be dispelled with a cloud of smoke, smoke shot through with fire! Is it conscience that makes you speak, or fear?' Tom Wintour spat the words out.

Tresham rose to his feet, as did Wintour. Tresham felt a hand on his shoulder, pushing him back down on to his stool.

'Peace? If we fight ourselves how can we fight others! You ride, as we planned!' It was Thomas Percy, his vehemence startling the others. 'Yet we're cautious as well. We've two days to wait, and to watch. We've a ship moored on the Thames, ready and waiting our presence. We can be there as quickly as it takes to hail a wherry, and drop down the river before any hue and cry can catch us. You, Guido, you can keep an eye on the powder, report back any mischief there. Granted, we can't be rash. But nor should we waste years of planning before we have to.'

A heated discussion followed, but Tresham could see that Percy's passion had won the day.

Percy knew he had dominance. Yet it seemed he wished to cap it all:

'I've the means to test whether we're discovered. I'll use it.'

'What means?' It was Digby.

'The Earl of Northumberland's a member of the Privy Council, isn't he?' said Percy. 'I'll go to see him, at Syon House, tomorrow, on the excuse of needing a loan.' He barked out a laugh. 'It's not a new thing for me to do. If the letter's caused any serious problems, I must hear it. They'll detain me, for certain.'

'You'll take that risk?' Catesby seemed genuinely moved.

'It's a lesser risk than many we've taken,' said Percy, 'and yes, I'll take it.'

There was actual applause round the table. Yes, thought Percy, smiling through clenched teeth at his easy victory. I shall go to see my Lord the Earl of Northumberland at Syon House, and make sure that every servant at Syon House sees and hears me there, and that we talk in the Hall alone, out of earshot of all others. And then I shall go to my nephew Josceline Percy, in the employ of my Lord the Earl of Northumberland, and similarly make it known that I have been there. And then, he thought with a warm glow of vicious satisfaction in his heart, then see if my Lord the Earl of Northumberland can escape being implicated in what is to happen. Then, having steadied the plotters and unbeknown to them signed the death warrant of his kinsman, he left them. He had business, he said, to attend to in town.

Had Percy and Catesby worked it all out before the meeting?

thought Tresham. There was no way of knowing. If only they had taken his bait and gone, now, there and then.

It was dark as Gresham rode to Whitehall, the lantern Mannion bore before him giving out a pitiful light as it swung back and forth with the rhythm of the horse. Cecil must be getting tired of late-night interruptions, thought Gresham, though at nine o'clock he must at least by now have finished his supper. Prime fillet of baby, perhaps, with a snake's venom sauce. He felt a strange inner calm, as he always did immediately before an action of great risk.

In Walsingham's day the spies and agents had used a small, private door, just off one of the jetties that served the Palace. Its use had lapsed, with Cecil preferring to work with ambassadors and the gentry abroad who came in through the front door, rather than the lowlife Walsingham acquired in such large (and effective) numbers. Gresham called out to Mannion, and reined in as the glow of Whitehall appeared before him, the flaring torches still lighting the main drive to its gate. Some inner voice spoke to him, and he dismounted, handing the reins to Mannion, asking him quietly to wait where they stood. A tavern with some sign of life still in it was nearby. Normally Mannion would have jumped at the chance. This evening, he seemed uneasy.

'Don't you need me there, with you?'

'He'd never grant you admittance. And I might need to leave in a hurry.' Mannion nodded, reluctant, undecided but as always obedient.

Instead of the main path, Gresham broke off to the left, by the river. The vast expense of the Royal Household did not spread to employing enough gardeners, Gresham noticed in the dim light that spun off from the Palace. A handful of weeds, drooping from the winter but still virulent, were invading the edge of the path.

A gate barred his way, with two guards standing by it. They were cold, stamping their feet, and they let Gresham through with only a cursory question. He was finely dressed, and not for the first time

Gresham realised how much stress his age placed on dress and outward appearance. He gave his name as 'Sir Alexander Selkirk', with a grin of memory. The path kinked round out of sight of the guards, and there was the side gate. It was unguarded. He approached it, noting the signs of neglect, the wild grass lapping the bottom of the door. He looked round. A household of thousands was here each going about their particular business, but none looking out at this particular spot at this particular time. He tried the door. It was locked. He had not thought of entering secretly before that moment, but the slight give on the door put the idea into his head. His inner voice, that very calm commentator who seemed to live in his brain and talk to him only at moments of high drama, whispered to try the door again.

The frame on the outside was covered in mildew, probably the result of the proximity of the river. Gresham took his dagger and poked it into the wood. It sank in a great way, meeting almost no resistance from the spongy, rotted timber. He looked round again. Nothing. There were a series of narrow, unlit windows running off on either side of the door. Storehouses, if Gresham remembered correctly. Iron bars had been placed over them, too small for even a monkey to climb through. He examined the nearest window. The mortar was crumbling, the workmanship old, and shoddy. He picked at the base of the nearest bar with his dagger, and a chunk of mortar fell away, revealing the red, rusting base of the bar. A few minutes' more work and it was completely exposed. He eased it from its setting, leaving a neat, round hole in the better-textured mortar at the top where the bar had lain. The bar was heavy, perhaps a finger's thickness. He eased it into the gap between the door and its frame. The door's timbers were still relatively sound, but the rotten frame allowed him to push the bar, half an inch, then a whole inch in. Gently he forced the bar back. He could feel it bending, just as he could visualise the screws on the inside of the doorframe coming loose from the wet timber, the screws that held the iron box into which the lock fitted. He stopped, reinserting the bar into the even larger gap that now existed, and forced it away from his hand. There was a gentle tearing noise, and the door gave, shrieking on its rusted hinges. He slipped inside, pushing the door to. There were bolts top and bottom, he noticed, the topmost bolt seated in what looked like firm timber. They had not been pushed in.

He knew his way up the stairs, which had a layer of dust on them with only a few footmarks. He stumbled in the almost complete blackness, feeling his way with a hand on the walls. The chamber where Cecil met spies was at the top of the stairs, with three corridors branching off it. One led up to the main and State apartments, one was the access route that Gresham had used and the other he had never trodden. In addition there was a door in the panelling, leading to not so much a secret as rather a private passageway, part above ground and part tunnel, to Westminster.

Torches burnt in the passage, throwing a garish light on the unadorned walls. This was a business area of the Palace, shorn of frippery. Gresham advanced to the door, expecting to feel silence and emptiness at this hour of night, and that he would need to go up a floor to the State rooms where, no doubt, Cecil was still ensconced.

He froze as he heard low voices from within the chamber, inaudible and no more than a dull rumble. There was a scraping as of stools being pushed back. Gresham dipped back into the doorway from where he had emerged, wrapping its shadow round him. The door ahead of him opened. A blaze of light splashed out into the corridor. Cecil himself emerged, gave a brief glance along the corridor, and stood aside. Two figures followed him, glanced themselves up and down the corridor, and moved over to the door in the panelling, opening it and vanishing.

The figures were unmistakable. Gresham had seen them only the night before. Both were so tall as to have to duck under the lintel of the door as they entered the private passageway.

Guy Fawkes. Thomas Percy.

Gresham leant back, his head resting on the cool brickwork in darkness, controlling his breathing.

Guy Fawkes and Thomas Percy. Discoursing in the room the King's Chief Secretary used for his spies and agents. Discoursing with that same Chief Minister. Two of the leading agents in this powder plot.

And allies of Robert Cecil.

CHAPTER 11

'Fool! Fool! What a complete fool I've been!' Gresham's anger was uncontainable. It surged through the House, seeming to shake the very walls, threatening to tear him and all it came into contact with apart. The candles had been out, and hurriedly relit. They guttered, smoking from where there had been no time to trim the wicks.

'Do be quiet, will you?' Jane seemed angered by his anger. 'It's not foolishness I hear, it's self-pity! If you're a fool then we're all fools! Who could've dreamt of the King's Chief Minister wishing to blow up the King and Parliament?' She was scared. The rampaging thing that was Gresham was like a wild creature. She felt her world falling apart, torn by forces beyond her control.

The accusation of self-pity stung him like a slap across the face, because it was correct.

'That's where we've all been fools. How could I not have seen it? He doesn't want to blow up Parliament. *He wants the credit for discovering the plot to blow up the King and Parliament!* Can't you see? He's been in control of this from the start. The only people who benefit from this are the King and his chief henchman.

'It all makes sense now,' he continued. 'Unpopularity – I said that was the key. The King's increasingly unpopular, and Cecil's never been popular. The Raleigh business gives them a permanent thorn in their side, which they can't remove, and the Treaty with Spain's laughed at. Everyone knows the Court's awash with Spanish pensions and bribes. When this so-called plot is exposed, at the last minute, Cecil will go down in history as the saviour of the nation and the Protestant faith, and James receive a huge backlash of sympathy. They'll ride on the back of this for years to come. It's all too easy for them.'

'But I'm still not clear,' said Jane, her brow furrowed in thought. 'Did Cecil start the plot off?'

'I doubt it. Catesby probably gave it to him on a plate. A God-given hothead, on whom Cecil placed a saddle without him even realising he was being ridden. Catesby must have walked straight into the arms of one of their agents overseas when they were looking for someone to deal with the powder.'

'And Fawkes?'

Gresham started to rampage among the vast pile of papers he had hurled on to the table when he returned. They were the reports of the spies and informers they had engaged at the start of this business, page after page of painstaking notes.

'The agent he walked into, of course. Either turned years ago, or suborned latterly. Look at his record! Born to a fine Protestant family, sells up his inheritance to go and fight in the Netherlands. All right, when he gets there he chooses to fight for Spain. So? Who has the money and the gold in the Netherlands? Who's paying a pension to nearly every one of James's courtiers at this very moment? The Spaniards. To Catesby and Wintour he's been a soldier of conscience. What if he's only ever been a soldier of convenience? A mercenary, fighting for the side that gives him most and pretending a religion to win promotion? Whilst taking a fat purse from Cecil to spy on the Spaniards, his employers, in the meantime!'

'So Catesby walked unbeknowingly into a trap set by Cecil?'

'Catesby triggered a series of thoughts in Cecil's mind, more like. The idiot goes blundering through Europe, looking for someone to blow up the Houses of Parliament, and latches on to one of Cecil's double agents. What a stroke of luck for Cecil – he has a real, a genuine conspirator to make the plot look real, and all the while he's paying the man with his hand on the fuse. It can't go wrong for him, provided he keeps a sufficient distance. No wonder he wanted me somewhere else.'

'What about Percy?' asked Jane.

Gresham threshed around among the papers again.

'Just look at *his* record. As wild as they come. Where is it . . .' he pounced on a piece of paper, '. . . *thirty-four charges* of dishonesty proven against him by Northumberland's tenants. He's nothing more than a bully boy, and then all of a sudden he marries a woman and converts to Catholicism – what a miraculous conversion! I'll bet anything you care to put down that was when he was grabbed to spy on the Catholics. What a bargain – he could tell them about the grand Earl of Northumberland, as well as the lesser kind. If you think about it, a Percy must have seemed like God's gift. Being a traitor is poured into them at birth, and what better guard against a northern rising than to have one of Northumberland's kinsmen on the inside!'

'I . . . I just can't take this in,' said Jane. 'Is *everyone* in the spy or a double agent in this world? Is there no-one . . . *normal?*'

'Oh, yes,' said Gresham, 'there're plenty of normal people. They die young.'

'Well,' said Mannion. 'That's all fine and well. A bit of philosophy always helps at a bad time, as I'm first to admit. But now that's over, can we decide what we're going to do?'

'What indeed,' said Gresham.

He looked almost devilish, his face receiving the light flung up from the lamps on the table. Jane felt a shiver of fear run through her body. How well did she know this man?

'I'm sorry,' she said, 'forgive me for being a stupid woman.' She glared at Gresham. Wisely, he said nothing. 'But how do Fawkes and Percy get out of this? The plot has to be discovered for James and Cecil to get the benefit, but if it's discovered it's death for Fawkes and Percy.'

'Fawkes just makes sure nothing does actually blow up, and then he's off on the nearest ship on the Thames. New identity, new life and a great deal richer than ever he was before. As for Percy . . . how do you think a knighthood and some fat manors would do him? The brave discoverer of the infamous Gunpowder Plot! The man who risked life and limb to ensure that every man involved in this blasphemous endeavour was brought to justice. Or he could simply take a fat purse and a different name . . . but I doubt it, somehow.'

'So what do we do now? Expose Cecil's involvement? Or just let the plotters walk into Cecil's trap, and pretend we never knew?'

'There you have it. It's Machiavelli's choice, isn't it?'

'Machiavelli died some years ago. We're still alive, in case you hadn't noticed. So, for that matter, are the plotters, King James and Robert Cecil,' said Jane acidly. 'I think we can keep Machiavelli out of it. After all, he played the wrong game and ended up being tortured and put out to grass, didn't he?'

'But the basic quandary he posed lives on, as it lived before he was born and as it will live on whilst humans seek and abuse power.' Gresham was lecturing her, unconsciously adopting the pose of a Fellow of his College talking to a young student. 'You see, Machiavelli said that truth wasn't necessarily worth very much, if it meant thousands of people dying. Good rulers put the welfare of their people above such minor things as truth and morality.'

'You're not a ruler,' said Jane, practically.

'No, but I could bring down Cecil and King James, I think.'

'Do you have evidence?'

'I could gain it easily enough. Men like Fawkes and Percy were paid to be traitors to their kind once. Pay them enough and they'll turn on Cecil as easily as they turned on their supposed friends.'

'So what will you do?' asked Jane, the anxiety cracking her voice.

'What will I do?' mused Gresham. The fire had smoked badly on being re-lit. In their panic to reawaken the household some wet timber had been placed on it. Now it had caught, and the cheery red flicker of the flames reflected in Gresham's eyes.

'What will I do?' he repeated. He turned towards Jane, with a thin, broad smile on his face. 'I shall be Machiavelli.'

The instructions to Fawkes had been clear. The frightened messenger was the same ambitious little rabbit Fawkes had showed the powder to an age ago. Fawkes was Cecil's safety catch, his half-cock on the pistol. Fawkes had to remain on guard until the last possible moment before the discovery of the powder, in case one of the other plotters decided to take matters into their own hands and light the fuse. Also, Cecil could not appear to know too much. A search party could not simply go directly to the cellar and find the powder. There had to be two searches, the first of the whole area. It would be told simply to observe and to report, to take no precipitate action that might trigger off the plotters. As such there would be no risk to Fawkes, particularly if the barrels were well buried under the faggots and firewood. If questioned he could claim quite truthfully to be servant to Thomas Percy, the tenant of the house. Who would distrust the servant to someone so recently appointed a Gentleman of the Bedchamber?

Suffolk would do to lead the search party. And Suffolk would be told to arrest no-one, to take no action that might start a panic, thought Cecil. He would summon that fool Monteagle to go with Suffolk in the first search party. Let Monteagle report that the pile of brushwood really was very large for the size of house above it, so they could go back to it later. It would all add credibility.

The second search, the one that would go back to the cellar, would take place at one o'clock in the morning.

'One o'clock!' whispered the frightened rabbit, though there was no-one nearby to hear or to see. 'The time is most important! My

Lord says you may leave after midnight, but not before! If a hothead such as Catesby were to hear the plot exposed he could still seek to blow up the building and so provoke rebellion.'

My Lord may go and fuck himself, thought Fawkes, if he has enough red blood in him to fuck anything, which I doubt. An hour was cutting it too fine, but he did not doubt that my Lord would have a watcher in the vicinity. Cecil was right, of course. With a gaping hole where Parliament had been the rumours could fly, and who knows what might catch seed in the confusion.

The rabbit scuttled out of the cheap lodgings, and did not notice the figure in expensive doublet, hose and short cloak detach himself, after a decent interval, from the wall and tuck in behind him on his route back to Whitehall. The figure could not fail to notice that two other men, in rough jerkins and with pockmarked faces, were also following the courtier, ahead. Typical of his type, the courtier stuck his chin in the air and barged his way through the common people, a testy 'Make way! Make way!' issuing from his lips. Suddenly he came upon two working men who, instead of moving aside in the busy, narrow street, put shoulder together to shoulder. He cannoned into them. Did one flick his heels to help him down into the mud? It was difficult to see, but certainly one of the men caught him a heavy blow on the head with his foot as he walked past the figure he had just helped knock over. Almost instantly, the two other men came up to the prostrate figure, and knelt down as if to offer help. There was a momentary flash of steel, so fast that no-one watching could be certain they had seen it, and the two men stood up and moved on, becoming lost immediately in the crowd.

The courtier's throat was cut, his life-blood ebbing away into the mud and staining the fashionable yellow starch of his ruff. Cecil had closed off one possible leakage of information in advance of the final act of his great play. The courtier gaped up at the figure in doublet and hose, gasping, terror in his eyes.

'They . . . they have stabbed me!' he croaked, unnecessarily.

'On your master Cecil's orders, be sure. If you wish a surgeon,' said Henry Gresham, bending down and whispering into the courtier's ear, 'you must first tell me what you said to Master Fawkes.'

The search party had seemed as inept as the rabbit had promised. Lurking outside, Fawkes had given his name as Johnson and told the leader he was Thomas Percy's servant and this Thomas Percy's rented house. The senior Lord in all his finery had seemed to be in a hurry to be anywhere except where he was, and the other young popinjay had tried to ask more questions but been hauled away by the other.

At eleven o'clock he took a simple lantern and materials to make the fire and light the fuse. The rabbit had been insistent that these were left by the powder, as if to suggest that everything was ready to ignite it at a moment's notice. He dressed carefully for the cold night, the spurs jangling as he walked for the last time to the cellar and opened the ancient door. Keyes had given him a watch, to time the fuse, as he thought. He had little realised that it would time Fawkes's escape. He sat on the stool he had lugged down into the cellar, not lighting the lantern, just letting the darkness and the silence enfold him. The dust, the ancient smell of decay, had become almost a comfort to him. So much danger in these barrels, so much threat, yet so much silence and peace here, underground. A broad grin lit his face in the dark as he thought on his master, Cecil. He wished he could see the expression on Cecil's face when the surprise was delivered. A pity he would be long gone.

He dimly heard the church bells strike midnight, and rose stiffly to his feet. He needed no light to walk to the door, the path learnt off by heart. He stopped, suddenly. A noise? From outside? He waited. Silence. A dog, or the wind. Nevertheless, he was careful in drawing back the door. Silence. He poked his head round the door for one final inspection. There was the tiniest flicker of light . . .

A roaring yell, and the full weight of the door was flung against his unsuspecting body, hurling him back into the cellar. He was down, and three, four, five men were on top of him . . .

'Leave off!' he screamed. 'I am under the orders of . . .' A sixth sense made him close his mouth. Something had gone wrong, horribly wrong. Yet these men – King's men, he saw by the uniform – were clearly not going to kill him or it would have been done by now. My Lord Cecil could not bear to have his part in this exposed . . . No, while he was alive he had power. This must, must be a mistake. He could surely stave off the truth until Cecil found a way of releasing him . . .

As the bound figure of Fawkes was bundled away by his men, Sir Thomas Knyvett mopped his brow, despite the cold of the night.

'A dreadful business, Sir Henry, dreadful business. You note the man was booted and spurred for flight? Cloak and hat and all! Had you not come in all haste with the message to commence our search early I fear he would have escaped! A dreadful business, dreadful . . .'

'It was, Sir Thomas, a pleasure to be of service to you, to my Lord the Earl of Salisbury and to His Majesty the King,' replied Sir Henry Gresham.

Kit Wright could not sleep. He envied any man who could do so, on this night of all nights. He was uneasy at being parted from his brother. As children the others had always joked that they hunted in pairs, and without his brother he felt strangely incomplete. Essentially a pious and a decent man, Wright prayed with his bare knees against the splintered boards for half the night. He failed to find his usual consolation. The same deep anger was there still in his soul for the seeming death of the religion he loved in the country he loved, the anger that Catesby had seen and tapped into. Until now that anger had killed any qualms of conscience he might have, but now, with the terrible thing so near, he could not rid his mind of screaming, the screaming of those buried under the rubble of Fawkes's powder.

He gave up sleep, dressed, and lay on his cot, fully clothed. There was a noise, surely? He got up, and opened the shutter. His heart stopped. A tide of torchlight was coming up the Strand, twenty, thirty, maybe even forty men. For him! For him! They must be coming for him! He turned and grabbed a cloak, buckling his sword as he flung open the door of his room. Even in his haste, he was not the first. The landlord, ludicrous in long nightshirt with offensive stains round its middle, had already unlocked the door and was standing, barefoot, gaping at the outside. Wright pushed past him, and halted as a dazed and half-dressed Lord Monteagle thrust past him, to be hailed from horseback by a finely dressed noble. 'My Lord! My Lord!' the noble was saying, as Monteagle's servants tried to put him in contact with his horse in the increasing melee of people. 'We must call up Northumberland! Now! With haste!'

There could be only one reason for every noble's house on the Strand to be being woken up this long after midnight. The plot had been discovered. How long did he have? Keeping as close to the sides of the houses as he could, Wright ran to Wintour's lodging, at The Duck and Drake. Breathlessly he gasped out the news. Wintour, as ever, kept control, pulling his clothes on as he spoke.

'Go to Essex House,' he commanded. 'Listen; they'll have the true story there, if they have it anywhere. If it's as we fear, go to Percy's lodging. Tell him to leave, now. It's his name on the cellar lease. He'll be the first warrant they issue – *and find out if Fawkes is taken!*'

'He's a calm one, my Lord!' The first questions were being asked of John Johnson, the man found in the cellar. 'He tells us nothing except his name, and that he's a servant of Thomas Percy. I didn't expect to see such calm in one so evil.'

Why had that fool Knyvett gone so early? Why?

He was here now, bustling in his own importance.

'Your messenger came most timely, my Lord.'

Messenger?

'He did?' replied Cecil.

'Sir Henry Gresham made fine speed to inform me of the change in plan.'

A great darkness opened up in front of the Chief Secretary.

One by one the plotters were roused, and, bleary-eyed, headed for the stables where their horses kicked and rose, sensing their owners' nervousness. From over London, they drove their mounts furiously, heading north, following the route Catesby, Bates and Jack Wright had taken the day before, the route to The Red Lion at Dunchurch. It was there they had planned to meet, to rally the band of armed, mounted Catholics who would sweep through the West Country raising a fire of rebellion as red as that burning at Westminster. Fear made them flee, some homing instinct sending them to where they had planned to go all along. No-one raised the alarm with Francis Tresham, and not only because he was a newcomer. The further away he was, the more belief in his guilt spread like a cloud of smoke among the plotters.

Meet at Dunchurch. It was the only security they had left.

If there were legends to be told about this affair, thought Ambrose Rookwood, his ride would be the greatest legend of all. He had left London last, except for Tom Wintour. He had supplied the horses for the others, but kept the best for himself. Thirty miles in two hours, on one horse! His head was aflame with the power and the exhaustion of it. His every limb ached, and he could hardly distinguish between his own sweat and lather and that of his present horse. He had overtaken Robert Keyes just beyond Highgate, then Percy and Kit Wright. Catesby, John Wright and Bates he saw on the horizon just beyond Brickhill.

They reined in. Catesby looked calm, but his eyes noted the state of Rookwood and Keyes.

'Well, Ambrose, your horses have done you proud to stand the pace! But why so fast?'

Rookwood had no other words. He blurted out, 'We're discovered! Fawkes is taken . . .'

Catesby. Bates. Jack Wright. Kit Wright. Keyes. Percy. Rookwood. The seven men stood in silence, the loudest noise the breathing of the horses, its steam stretching out in the cold air. The six scarves the men wore fluttered gently in the morning breeze. They were fine work. Rookwood had provided them. The weaving contained representations not only of the cross, but of items used in the Mass. Tom Bates had none, of course. He was a servant.

Silence. It was broken first by Jack Wright. His reaction was to start to curse, slowly at first, but with a rising voice of fear. The others looked, instinctively, to Catesby.

'Hold your noise, Jack!' Catesby's voice was like a whiplash.

'All is lost only when we all lose heart! There's chaos in London, isn't there? Confusion? Signal enough for all good Catholics to rise up on our side. We have horses, we have armour, we have weapons, don't we? We have men gathered at Dunchurch, don't we? All we need is stout hearts!'

Despite themselves, the men felt the warmth of his magic work its way back into the freezing bones. They rode, the Devil behind them and the Devil in front. Percy and Jack Wright tore at their cloaks, hurled them off into the hedgerow, as if by that small loss of weight they could drive their horses even faster.

Catesby yelled something back at them, in a delirium of speed and pounding hooves. They grinned insanely back through the blinding sweat and muscles that ached as if it was the men's feet driving them forward.

The furore outside seemed to bend the timbers of the house. Francis Tresham waited for the door to be flung inwards, to feel the hands round his throat, the blows to his body and head or even the stinging slash or probe of a blade. He waited. Why had they not come for him?

*

'Are you wishing to go the way of Lord Walsingham?' Mannion asked Gresham, glumly. Walsingham, Elizabeth's spymaster, had nearly bankrupted himself keeping a web of agents up and running. Gresham had placed one, two men on each of the plotters, one to watch, one to report wherever possible. The cost was appalling.

What was Tom Wintour playing at? The plotters were running now, running as he had hoped they would do when the letter was delivered to Monteagle. Gresham had nearly followed Catesby out of London, but to follow a man on those lonely, deserted roads without being discovered was almost impossible, and Gresham's instinct was to stay in London at least for a while to keep track of the anarchy he had unleashed. He had tracked Tom Wintour, choosing him instead of Thomas Percy because Wintour was the closest of all the conspirators to Catesby and, Gresham suspected, the born leader among them.

Gresham had witnessed Wintour issuing instructions, and then expected him to run for the stables where he kept his gelding. Instead Wintour had headed purposefully towards Westminster itself, the seat of the crime. Was it him escaping discovery by sheer bravado? Had he so much faith in Guy Fawkes resisting interrogation?

He saw Wintour stop and listen to a group of excited men in the street, and then followed him as he headed down King Street. There a crude barrier had been erected across the road, and a soldier barred his way. Wintour showed immense control, his shrugging manner, his easy craning of his head to look down the street perfectly those of the idle man caught up in a flood of gossip, speculation and interest.

Or was his gazing down the street simply the act of the vacuous onlooker? What *was* it that he so clearly wished to gain sight of? Whatever it was, he was unwilling to give it up. He walked round almost the whole perimeter of the Palace of Westminster, but there was a pattern to his ramblings, Gresham noticed, always returning to the one spot.

Whynniard's house. The phrase came back to Gresham from something Tresham had said. The plotters had started by hiring a house in the precincts of the Palace of Westminster, a house owned by John Whynniard. They had started a tunnel from there, Tresham had said, but given up the idea as beyond their physical and technical skills. That was when the cellar under the Lords had become vacant, allowing them to ditch the unfinished tunnel.

There it was. Whynniard's house. Gresham had been sufficiently interested when Tresham had mentioned the house to walk past it himself, and keep a watcher on it for a week. It was shuttered, empty. Yet now the empty house seemed to be the common denominator in Tom Wintour's appallingly dangerous trek round Westminster, even though the cordon thrown round Westminster meant he was unable to get closer than a stone's throw to it.

A soldier was starting to look suspiciously at Wintour. He had stopped for the third time in the same spot, the one nearest the house. Without seeming to notice, Wintour began to melt towards the back of the crowd, breaking off from it and heading in the direction of the livery stables when Gresham knew he kept his horse. The house, thought Gresham, might repay some attention. But now his most urgent aim was to keep up with Tom Wintour. Had the plotters dispersed? Or had they run to some assembly point, from where they would try to rouse the nation? The game was still being played, and Gresham guessed the next rounds would be decided out of London.

'You will leave us!' Cecil spoke with a fierce intensity, hating the dullness of the guards as they looked fearfully back at him. They were below ground level, the dismal, dark room set into the very foundations of the White Tower. He knew what the guards were thinking. Leave Robert Cecil, Earl of Salisbury, alone with this blackguard, this Devil on earth, this Guy Fawkes . . . fear of what would happen to them if the Chief Secretary was attacked fought for a brief moment with fear of the Chief Secretary. Fear of Cecil won. They backed away, bowing. Cecil closed the door. The bottom of it grated on the filthy floor.

Fawkes was huddled on the floor, rubbing his shoulder where the guards had hurled him to the ground. His head was badly gashed where he had been thrown down, the blood half-dried, fresh seeping through the caked residue. The cell was lit by the flames of a rough torch hung in an iron bracket. Even by its light the wetness on the walls glistened and sparkled on the five-hundred-year-old stone.

'Why did you betray me?' Fawkes's voice was rough, but steady enough. Cecil was caught off guard. It should not be Fawkes, the prisoner, opening this conversation.

'I did not betray you!' hissed Cecil through clenched teeth. The cold was penetrating even through the thickness of his rich cloak. 'You were betrayed by the fool who brought the orders for the search forward by an hour.'

'My Lord, we had a bargain.' There was fear in Fawkes's voice, but also resolution, and a tone Cecil could not quite track down.

'The terms and conditions appear to have changed very significantly!' he snapped.

'You'll have to have me testify, my Lord,' said Fawkes. The blow to his head must have disorientated him. He spoke in starts, as if suffering from momentary losses of concentration. 'I think it wouldn't be in your Lordship's interest to have me testify the truth.'

Fawkes's body was shaking now with the cold, Cecil noted with satisfaction.

'Many better than you have died in this Tower, without word and without testimony,' said Cecil, looking with loathing at Fawkes. 'Many have screamed for weeks in this Tower before they welcomed the sweet release of death. Have a care what you threaten.'

'No,' said Fawkes, 'have a care what *you* threaten.' His teeth were chattering now. 'If someone knows enough of your plans to bring the time of the search forward an hour, then someone knows enough of your perfidy to place you, my Lord the Earl of Salisbury, in this Tower, to die or to scream for your death alongside me. You need me, you need me to give a confession that will confirm your version of events, to name your other conspirators. If I stand firm, my Lord, many can challenge your honour's actions. None can prove them false.'

How grating was that accent of Yorkshire, how ludicrous the Spanish lilt laid over it.

'As you seem so much in control,' Cecil said as his eyes flicked over the manacles that chained Fawkes's feet to the wall, 'you will certainly be able to tell me what you wish me to do.'

Fawkes was shivering heavily now, his arms clasped round himself in a feeble attempt to keep warm.

'Move me to a secret chamber, a chamber with warmth and food. Many who have been tortured here have never been heard. Now may one be tortured who never was. Put out that I was steadfast, then that I was put to the torture. Write me a confession, what you will. I'll testify to your plot, as you'll have me do.'

'And then?'

'And then I shall die, weakened so far by the unspeakable pain you put me to that my constitution gave in. Here, in this Tower. Out of sight. And you will get me to France.'

There was something of desperation in Fawkes's voice. As well there might be. Cecil's mind was racing.

A live, testifying Fawkes would be an asset, if he testified correctly. The Keeper of the Tower, Waad, had incriminated Mary Queen of Scots. Hiding the nature of what was happening to Guy Fawkes was a mere biting-on compared to the meals that man had eaten. As for France, it was a long journey from London to Dover and across the Channel. A long and dangerous journey.

'Guards!' Cecil shouted. 'This man is no good to us dead with cold. Take him to a chamber with fire in it – warming fire, not the torturer's brazier! And keep his legs in chains!' he said viciously, as he left to discuss matters with Sir William Waad.

Robert Wintour had been having supper with Catesby's mother. Catesby had determined to tell his mother the truth before riding on to Dunchurch, but as he sat on his sweating horse outside his home he felt for the first time a chill wind blow through the heat of his self-belief. He could not face his mother, not now. He sent Tom Bates to summon Wintour to a field outside the house. Robert Wintour had always been a baleful recruit at best, unlike his fire-brand younger brother. Now he was totally downcast.

'We should surely throw ourselves on the King's mercy,' he said, 'and with God's grace some mercy might be shown.'

Catesby hardly bothered to answer.

'There will be no mercy. We must ride on to Dunchurch, to meet with the company. Only then can we decide.' He did not give a single backward glance to the house under whose roof his mother fretted.

There were over a hundred people gathered in and around The Red Lion. Brothers, cousins, relations, younger sons of Catholic families, all had gathered. Catesby had hoped for more, at least a hundred and fifty. Yet even now it might be enough. A babble of voices greeted Catesby's arrival. His heart began to beat faster, as it always did when he stood in front of a crowd. The blood began to speed through his veins. He held his hand up to command silence.

There was silence.

Briefly, quickly, he told them of the plot, that the powder had been discovered, but that London was aflame with rumour and suspicion.

'Are we sheep or cattle, to troop gently to our slaughter? Or are we men, men with a faith to be fought for? We have horses, we have guns, we have powder. If we ride now, ride for our freedom and our Faith, hundreds will join us from the west, the west where the Faith has always lived and flourished. We must strike now, strike while confusion reigns. Are we men of faith, or are we cowards?'

He was shouting now, standing up in his stirrups.

There was silence. They looked at him in the feeble light of a few torches. Then one, then a second, then a third turned away from the light, edging their horses off into the darkness. There was a pause, then a fourth, a fifth and then a stream. A muttered, muted babble of conversation rose between those left. Just as it seemed the departures were ended, another two or three would turn and move away, like rows of infantry having remorseless gap after gap blown in their line by withering cannon fire as they waited for a charge.

Robert Catesby had failed. For the first time in his life, he had spread the cloak of his character, the fire of his personality, out to a group, and seen it fall on stony ground. Soon, there were hardly forty left in the square outside the inn, making it seem almost deserted.

The fire cooled in Catesby, leaving a solid, hard dark nugget of cold in its place. He would die now, he knew. Perhaps he had always known. In a strange way the realisation took a dread weight off him. He was certain now, certain in a different way. He owed himself a good death. Himself, and the others he had brought along for all these months and years. They would want, would need to die with him, he knew.

He smiled, disconcerting even more those nearest to him. He allowed the runt of his rebellion, the rebellion that never happened and never would happen, to eat and rest a while. The sulky landlord and servants were desperate to be rid of them, desperate to avoid the taint they knew their association would provide. Even now they were remembering the detail they would so willingly give to the King's men and the Sheriff's men when they arrived, as they most assuredly would arrive.

And then, shortly after eleven o'clock at night, they began the ride. It should have been told of in some ancient saga, become a story to read out by the fireside on late, cold winter's nights, to frighten the young children. It was a ride of despair and desperation, of harsh and stupid courage. It was helpless and hopeless, madness in human form, a ride of the Valkyrie where only the horses had hope and their riders were dead men already.

From Dunchurch to Warwick Castle; the stables there raided, ten fresh horses taken to relieve the mounts of those who had ridden from London. Robert Wintour wringing his hands – 'It will make an uproar in the country!' – Ambrose Rookwood disdainful, his supply of fine horseflesh inexhaustible. On, on to John Grant's house at Norbrook, to pick up the powder, shot and muskets hoarded there. Through Snitterfield, across the treacherous ford of the Alne, on to Alcester. Through Arrow, then out along the Worcester Road, and then on the back roads and by-ways to Huddington. Two o'clock on Wednesday afternoon. Fifteen terror-driven, bone-crunching, muscle-wrenching hours. Sleep. Mass at three o'clock on the Thursday morning, then down to dress in armour, to pick arms and take ammunition from the long tables loaded with weaponry, the remainder hurled into carts. Six o'clock on a bleak morning, bodies crying out in agony at seating again on a saddle. To Hanbury, across Bentley Heath to Hewell Grange, Lord Windsor's house. The house empty, glum villagers standing by as they broke in, taking armour, more weapons, powder and money from a trunk containing over £1,000. Burcot. Lickey End. Catshill. Clent. Hagley. The names reeled off like so much flotsam passing a watcher by a riverbank, the names blurring into one another, increasingly meaningless. Sullen people, watchers, onlookers. 'We fight for the Faith!' No response. Occasional yells, muttered reply, 'We live for King James!' Onwards. Stourbridge. Heavy rain, drenching men, animals and powder, the ford racing, dangerous for fit men, perhaps lethal for tired men and horses. Holbeache House, the home of Stephen Littleton. Enough. They were exhausted. Sixteen hours to travel twenty-five miles. Rookwood had galloped thirty miles in two hours, earlier, on the one horse. Catesby had made over ten miles an hour, on his ride out from London. They were slowing, had stopped.

They must have rest.

They were pathetically fewer now. Servants had deserted, snapping off the road and away from the cavalcade when an opportunity arose. They had boxed in the party at front and back, but there were not enough of them to guard the sides and length as well.

Catesby had withdrawn into himself, even Percy seemed to be quiet. Only Tom Wintour, who had joined them late, had energy, walking, talking, organising a defence. They needed more men, if they were to fight off the likely assault on Holbeache and live to ride again. An outrider had reported a party, probably the Sheriff of Worcestershire, trailing them. Not one Catholic had joined their progress, which had leached men like a sandbag leaching out in the rain. John Talbot lived ten miles distant, at Pepperhill. He was Robert Wintour's father-in-law. Would Robert go to ask for men and support? 'How may I go, when he'll guard my wife when I am dead?' Tom Wintour looked with contempt at his brother. Without a word, he put his aching body on his horse again, and rode out to John Talbot's house, seeking the help he knew in his heart would not be offered.

Gresham rode harder even than he had ridden on that day from Cambridge to London. They had spirited Tresham out of his lodgings, placed him in a safe house. Dunchurch, he had said, repeating it as if it were a litany. They must go to Dunchurch. It is where they planned to gather, under cover of a hunting party, to raise the country up in rebellion. They will go to Dunchurch.

Gresham arrived at The Red Lion as the rump of the party was leaving on its mad, foolish dash across the country.

'Where are they heading?' he had hissed to an ostler, trying to thrust coin into the man's hand.

'To Hell and beyond, as far as I cares!' the man had replied, thrusting the money aside and running back into the inn, distrust visible in his every gesture.

Catesby's crew had rested, taken food. Gresham had no time. With an inward groan he remounted. At least following was not difficult, despite the driving rain. Servants and other riders peeled off from the party at regular intervals, to much shouting and yelling. At the start their leaders tried to give chase, but soon exhaustion crept in, and they simply tried to box in the cavalcade with their own horses. Still the leakage from the party continued, still the numbers, dimly visible sometimes, audible always, diminished. They were slowing down all the time, like a drowning man whose flapping at the water becomes more and more feeble as his strength leaves him.

Gresham had never felt more tired. He was soaked through, shivering violently with the cold, his teeth chattering so that he could hardly bite on the hard-baked meat he had flung into his saddlebag as he had left London. Yet he had to keep on guard. The servants and gentlemen who had escaped Catesby's party flew past him on the road, drawing their swords if they had them and fearing he was a pursuer. One had even taken a scything blow at Gresham's head with his sword as he had passed, Gresham blocking it only at the last second with a clang of steel. Finally, just as his horse was about to expire beneath him, the tattered, pathetic remnant of the party had come to rest at Holbeache. They could enter the house, with its warmth, its fires and its food. Gresham was examining the lay-out of the courtyard and steps up into the main house, wracked with icy cold, when his passport into Holbeache emerged from inside. The courtyard gate opened, revealing another horse and rider. The horse was a thoroughbred, a beautiful animal, but its rider was clearly a fleeing servant, whose riding experience was limited to sitting on the back of a cart on its way to market. The man was bouncing violently up and down on the back of the horse, clearly terrified. Gresham forced his own mount out into the road-way with perfect timing, taking his foot out of the stirrup and giving the rider a hefty boot as he was at the top of his bounce and halfway out of his saddle already. He fell with a yelp, escaping being dragged along only because his feet had never properly found the stirrups of his own horse.

Gresham took the rough jerkin and trews from the stunned man and sent him, half naked, bouncing along the road on his own exhausted mount. Liberally covering his disguise in mud, he walked into the house, or rather stumbled and gasped into it.

'A bite of bread and ten minutes by a fire, I beg of you?' He did not have to feign exhaustion. 'I've ridden from Dunchurch, but my master, he took off without me just outside the house. Help me, please. I've no master, no home and like to have no head when all this comes out . . .' The harassed woman he had spoken to had hardly listened, glancing all the time nervously over his shoulder, pushing him in the direction of the kitchen.

He was inside. The kitchen was a babble of noise. Servants shared their master's fate, and there was real terror in their ranks. Old campaigning instincts took over. Gresham grabbed a fistful of greasy, half-warm meat from a stone table and a mug of small beer that appeared somehow out of the chaos, and crammed both down his throat. The plotters were together in the Hall upstairs, he heard. They would not be leaving now, he thought, with night coming on. They were blown, exhausted. There was enough of the real Henry Gresham left to light a tiny smile in the corner of his mouth. He was inside the lions' den. It was about time he decided what use to make of his achievement.

Thomas Percy looked at the sodden crowd of his fellow plotters and cursed the luck that had exposed Fawkes. Clearly, Cecil's plan had misfired. Or had Cecil betrayed them? He doubted it. If Cecil had wanted both of them out of the way Percy would not have been let to go with the others to end up in this dreadful hole of a house. Percy caught the tail of his fear, which was starting to fly up and away like a kite out of control, and brought it back down to earth again with an effort. He had to assume that his job remained what it had always been, to kill Catesby and as many of the other conspirators as possible. Cecil had always feared Catesby, recognising in him the capacity to lift and sway an audience. He had been willing to use him, the perfect unwitting foil for a plot that would bring Cecil nothing but credit, but yet he had always feared his power to incite. Cecil had been too much scarred by the ability of Sir Walter Raleigh at his trial to win hearts and minds by the power of his words and the attraction of his figure. He did not want Robert Catesby standing at the Bar, weaving the same spells with his audience that he had woven with the conspirators. Catesby had to die decently early, and that was Percy's role.

He had considered killing him on their journey, but no chance that did not threaten his own life had presented itself. The life of Thomas Percy was a very important thing, and soon to become even more important. Once Catesby had been disposed of, and the other plotters either killed or handed over to authority – Cecil had wanted some two or three at most, no more, if possible – then Percy would return in triumph to London bringing Catesby's body slung over a horse. He had thought on that, and thought that it would look best stripped to its shirt, as it would have been for an execution. He had reminded himself that he must drape the body over a horse as soon as possible after Catesby's death, before it froze in death and stuck out on either side like a bar across the saddle. In the midst of that triumph, he and Cecil would discuss the details he would give about the treachery of the ninth Earl of Northumberland, how the evil Earl had unwittingly placed in the hands of his kinsman the details of the treachery and the revolution he planned – his kinsman, who having handed the fate of the ninth Earl over to Cecil would, of course, become the tenth Earl of Northumberland. Had he not always claimed, even to the ninth Earl himself, that his branch of the family was older than that represented by the ninth Earl? Well, now he would prove it.

The powder they had taken from Hewell Grange had been loaded into an open cart. The drenching rain had soaked it. Their plan now was to rest for as long as it took to get their breath back, and then dash into Wales to gather support and await news of the landings and the Spanish troops that Percy had lied about to

Catesby. There never were any plans for invasion, and never any knowledge of any part of the plot by the ninth Earl – a delicious irony which Percy intended to savour when he became the tenth Earl.

Yet they might have to make a stand at Holbeache. The Sheriff of Worcestershire was on their trail. A servant who was probably running away had run into the Sheriff's party, over a hundred men, and gone back to Catesby as the lesser evil. Catesby and Wintour were convinced they could beat off the Sheriff's party, who would be untrained men in the face of a determined, well-armed opposition fighting defensively and for their lives. It was a classic situation – thirty men defending who were fighting to keep their lives, a hundred or so attacking who could only lose them.

'The powder from Hewell Grange is soaked through. If this place is put to siege, we might have need of it.' Percy spoke gruffly, in the old-soldier manner he had adopted from the outset with the conspirators.

'What do you suggest – warm it with a match?' It was Digby, a pale imitation of himself.

'Almost. It's wet enough to make spreading it out before the hearth safe enough. If Tom manages to bring back some extra people, the more dry powder we can show them the more likely they are to think we've a chance.'

He was surprised they agreed to it, but it was exhaustion speaking through their actions, and despair. Any action seemed to put back the tide of hopelessness.

They spread the powder out on to the stone hearth, moving the rushes aside first. The fire was well established, the wood seasoned and long since past spitting. Catesby, Rookwood and Grant took seats at the long trestle table to one side of the fire, hastily drawing up plans for the defence of the house. Henry Morgan, one of the few from the Dunchurch 'hunting party' who had stayed with them, joined them, as did Percy, for a while. Robert Wintour was huddled in a corner.

'I had a dream last night.' His sepulchral tones startled the men by the table, all of whom looked up.

'I saw church steeples bent awry, and sad, terrible faces inside the churches, looking out. Faces of despair.' Was he talking to himself, or to them? It could have been either. The men turned back, one by one, to their crude plans for defence. The problem was that few of them knew the house, and the owner was out of it with Tom Wintour.

Percy stood up, announcing he was going to piss. As he went to the door, it opened in his face, and the frightened figure of a servant came into the Hall, a huge pile of fresh logs held in front of him, half covering even his face. Percy pushed him aside, causing him to stumble and drop the top two or three logs. The servant mumbled apologies, as scared as the rest of the Holbeache servants, placed the remnant of his load on the floor and scrabbled to pick up the lost logs. A few of the conspirators glanced his way, disinterested, and looked away. Very carefully the servant made his way to the side of the hearth. He stopped as he saw the powder laid out, carefully moving round the black earth piled on the floor. He bent to lay his logs on top of the others on the side of the hearth, but the top log seemed to leap out from the pile of its own accord and fell into the fire. It crashed into the flames, dislodging embers that flew almost gently through the air and landed red among the black of the powder. The servant, who could see what was coming, flung the rest of his logs forward and dashed for the protection offered by the side of the jutting stone fireplace.

There was a blinding flash, and a sucking roar. For a brief instant Holbeache was turned into Hell. From a scene of almost peaceful domesticity the Hall was reduced to smouldering ruin. Panelling had caught fire, and those upright in the room were rushing to smother the small flames. The peculiar, acrid stench of powder mingled with the stench of burnt flesh and smouldering wood. John Grant was sitting on the ground, making small keening noises, rocking backwards and forwards, his hands clutched to his eyes.

They were burnt out, even blacker than the surrounding skin in his crisped, baked face, his hair, eyebrows and beard half gone and scorched. The man Morgan still had some sight, but was badly burnt. Catesby and Rookwood were badly scorched, both in obvious severe pain.

The two Wright brothers had been dozing in a corner, now jerked into wakefulness by the blast of fire. Percy rushed back into the room. Robert Wintour had escaped the worst of the searing heat, huddled in his corner. He was standing now, staring wild-eyed at the devastation. He stuck his arm out, a shivering finger pointing at Catesby and the others.

'The faces! The faces!' he said. 'The faces in my dream! These are the faces!' He waited, as if for an answer. His hand dropped to his side. He raised his eyes, locked them on to the pain-filled vision of Catesby. 'Well,' he said, in a low voice of total hatred, 'you have your blast now, cousin!' He turned and left.

There had been exhaustion, some despair and fear in the room before, but also some bravado. Now there was nothing. It was as if they realised it was over. It had to be God's judgement. Those who had intended to blow up their enemies by powder had themselves been blown up. The link was too clear, too obvious.

Catesby was recovered enough to speak. The fire had caught the one side of his face, pulling up his lip so that it seemed he had a permanent snarl. Robert Catesby. Jack Wright. Kit Wright. John Grant, writhing on the floor, hands fluttering at the wet bandage round his destroyed eyes. Ambrose Rookwood, moaning as the cold of the bandages touched his burnt flesh. Thomas Percy. With the exception of Rookwood and Wintour, the men stood at the end of the affair almost as they had stood from its outset.

'We are too few to fight.' Thomas Percy spoke the obvious.

'Then we must die fighting.' It was Catesby. No-one raised his voice against him.

Tom Wintour stopped as he entered the hall, his face draining of all blood in shock. He ran to Catesby, looking in horror at his ravaged and twisted face. If only he had brought good news! There was no help coming. Sir John Talbot had not even let them inside his house, but shouted them off as he might a carrier of the plague. A fleeing servant had told them of the explosion, and Stephen Littleton, the owner of Holbeache, had slipped away from his side. Everard Digby had gone. Tom Bates, the ever-faithful servant, was also missing.

'Where is my brother?' It was Tom Wintour, his eyes roaming the room.

'Gone.' It was Kit Wright. 'With all the others.' Robert Wintour had waited this long in his life to take a decision of his own.

Henry Gresham had picked himself up from the side of the fireplace, where the blast had thrown him. He was bruised badly enough, but nothing was broken. The heat had singed the back of his head, in between the collar of his jerkin and his bonnet.

He had intended only to eavesdrop on the plotters. The smell of the powder had hit him even through the door. In an instant he was back in the Netherlands, and it was as if the pain that had been his constant companion then for months came back to hit him also. Picking up the logs strewn outside the door and going in had been a terrible thing for him to do. When he had met Percy his heart had stopped, but Percy was not the type to recognise a lowly servant.

He had wanted to be sick as he had contemplated the fire, the powder and the need to fling his log into the midst of the fire. Yet the irony, the awful, dreadful irony, of firing these men up with powder, the sheer justice of it, had driven him. Loose powder does not explode, he knew, but burns off in an instant, developing a searing heat and light.

Those who know an explosion is about to take place can profit in the seconds immediately following. With no mental shock to add to the physical, Gresham was able to pick himself up in the immediate aftermath, scuttling through the door before anyone thought to ask of the servant who had caused the blow. He doubted any realised even that it had been the servant, so great was their confusion. What a pity Percy had chosen that moment to leave. Gresham was surprised by how little damage the fire had done. He could not judge at that moment the damage it had done to the spirit, as well as the bodies, of the plotters.

Gresham knew that the Sheriff of Worcestershire was hastening to lay siege to the plotters. The servant whose clothes he had taken had babbled of little else. Percy had to die at Holbeache, that much Gresham now knew. The question was how.

Thomas Percy was much taken at that moment by the other side of the question. How to preserve his life? He had believed they could beat off the Sheriff's men easily enough, with a pistol ball in the back for Catesby in the dying moments of the fight, or on their flight into Wales. That damned explosion had killed no-one, but merely increased the odds for their attackers and made the plotters vow to fight to the death. Well, so be it, mused Percy. There was risk in all things. He was playing for an earldom. He would wait for the siege, kill Catesby and then prove his credentials by firing a ball into one of the others – Tom Wintour by preference – and shouting that he was an agent of the King's. Far better than an agent of Robert Cecil for these country bumpkins.

The call to arms came some time before eleven o'clock. They propped the blinded Grant up in a corner, still moaning. Rookwood declared his intention to fight, though God knew if he could see enough to hit anyone, thought Percy. At the windows, they could see that it was more than a hundred men gathering outside. Torches lit those out of range, whilst movements in the shadow showed men running up under cover of the darkness to hide close to the walls, there presumably to make an assault through the main gate into the yard. Suddenly, a flickering light showed them more. Someone had lit a fire, almost under them. They were being smoked out. Damn! If they had more men they could have mounted a guard on the outer perimeter.

Catesby turned his head stiffly, and looked at Wintour. The

latter nodded, the briefest of gestures. Grabbing their weapons, they moved out and down into the yard.

Torches had been thrown over to give light, and lay guttering on the cobbles. It was too late. Enemy men were already in the yard. As Wintour burst out of the door shots rang out, most ill-aimed and wildly high. One caught Wintour, shattering his shoulder. He shrieked, a weird, unearthly noise, fired a wild round from his pistol and hurled it to the ground, dragging his sword up to defend himself as men with pikes started to circle warily round him.

Catesby had come down the stairs hanging on the arm of Percy. Jack and Kit Wright leapt out through the door and more shots rang out. Both dropped to the ground. As if by accident it was Catesby's body that swung round and forward as they came out of the door, moments later. One shot banged viciously into the night air, but the others had fired at Wintour and the Wrights, and were clumsily reloading. It looked as if Catesby and Percy were standing back to back, but Catesby had swooned as they hit the night air and was only half-conscious.

Gresham was standing by the side of the courtyard. He had floored one of the first soldiers to creep up over the wall into the yard with one blow from the stock of the hunting rifle he had taken from the house. The helmet was too large to fit, the leather jerkin hanging off his frame. Other men flooded into the yard. Gresham saw Tom Wintour rush out and spin round in response to a fusillade of shots. Then the Wright brothers were dropped like gamebirds. Rookwood was clearly wounded, as was Morgan, stumbling around with the injured Wintour. There was a pause in the firing, partly through the need to reload, partly through the growing realisation that this pathetic band posed no threat.

A trooper had run to Gresham's side, his eyes full of the glazed fear that Gresham had been so familiar with in Flanders. His musket was unfired, waving wildly in the air. Gresham decided he might as well act to stop the boy shooting him.

'Soldier!' he snapped. 'Come to it, man! Give me your name!'

'John . . . John Streete, sir,' mumbled the boy, regaining a grip on his musket.

Wintour yelled, for Catesby, Gresham thought, and the soldiers turned towards him. Catesby emerged in the doorway, hanging off Percy. As if in slow motion, Gresham saw Percy place his pistol against Catesby's side, saw the flash and the body of Catesby stiffen and slump, mouth agape. As if in one single smooth movement Gresham brought up his gun, aimed and fired, the crack of the rifle almost simultaneous with that of Percy's pistol. Percy's mouth was also agape, he was about to shout out and cast Catesby's body to the ground. The bullet caught him and he jerked violently backwards, his inert body almost bouncing on to the cobbles.

Gresham turned to John Streete, standing gaping by his side. He pulled the boy's musket arm towards him, yanked the trigger and caught the gun as it recoiled, firing into the air.

'There, boy,' said Gresham. 'Two birds with one shot. Go on, claim the credit.'

Gresham turned, and saw Catesby crawling back into the house. The pack of soldiers were advancing on Rookwood, Wintour and Morgan. Wintour made a mad dash forward. His sword was knocked out of his hand, and a soldier, crazed with fear, was about to plunge his pike into the wounded man's midriff. There was a barked command.

'Hold. Hold! Some of these are better kept alive for His Majesty!'

Catesby had crawled just inside the door. He was holding his gold crucifix, sobbing with pain and exhaustion. He half turned as Gresham clattered through the door.

'Selkirk!' he moaned, in frightened recognition. Then the light went from his eyes. He slumped to the ground, dead. Gresham heard the noise of advancing men. Quickly, he tore a picture of the Virgin Mary off the wall where it adorned the entrance to Holbeache House, and wrapped Catesby's still warm fingers around it. As the first of the other soldiers burst in through the door, Gresham retreated into the shadows.

The soldiers were out of control. They were stripping the corpses of everything they bore. Even Kit Wright's boots had been taken, and the silk stockings he wore under them. Percy's body, half naked, lay on the cobbles, mouth open, eyes staring. A soldier who had missed the best of the plunder gave it a vicious kick as he passed by. His head lolled back with the blow, slack, empty.

Gresham gazed back at the lights, the shouting and the smashing noises as the house was torn apart. He turned, and without a word he started the ride back to London.

CHAPTER 12

'B e careful,' said Jane. 'He fooled you once.'

'Fooled me?' said Gresham. 'I prefer to think he left me asking the wrong questions for a short period of time.'

Gresham was putting the final touches to his dress. It would be his fourth visit to Cecil. He felt more in command of this one than he had with several others.

Gresham arrived, without appointment. It was a different clerk from the last time, a biddable, pleasant-mannered figure, clearly rushed off his feet and worried. The usual crush of humanity was stinking the place out, shouting its case to be the only person with a real need to see the King's Chief Secretary.

'I shall take your request to the Earl, Sir Henry,' he replied to Gresham, 'but he is monstrously busy, I fear to say . . .'

'I do understand. Tell him Sir Henry Gresham wishes to see him, and that it concerns matters of high treason.'

The clerk's eyes opened wide, and he waddled off. He was clearly surprised on his return, and bowed low.

'Sir Henry! The Earl will see you immediately. Please follow me.'

Cecil was crouched at the head of the table. A litter of papers filled its top half. Among them, Gresham noted, was an unsigned letter in a familiar hand. It was already known as the Monteagle Letter. Gresham had heard of its new name with a wry grin.

'Sir Henry.' Cecil's voice was flat, expressionless.

'My Lord.'

'I see you are recovered. Please accept my congratulations.'

'I was never ill. It was merely a ruse designed to divert your Lordship's unwelcome attentions away from me, while I discovered what you so clearly wished to keep from me,' Gresham answered, in a brisk tone.

'Indeed?' Cecil raised an eyebrow, maintaining his icy control. 'And did you discover this great secret?'

'Yes, my Lord, I did,' said Gresham.

'Which was?' asked Cecil, not entirely able now to keep the tension out of his voice.

'Guy or Guido Fawkes, otherwise known as the servant John Johnson, was a double agent, supposedly working with Catholic forces in Europe for some years, but in practice working for you. Robert Catesby, the true leader of the Gunpowder Plot or whatever you will choose to call it, either stumbled into him, or was directed his way by another of your agents, when Catesby and a group of Catholic hotheads needed someone who could lay a slow train of powder. You knew about the Gunpowder Plot from the start. You used Fawkes as one of your inside men for the whole duration of the plot, allowing it to ripen so that you could discover it amidst the greatest public attention and so win a lasting popularity for you, and for the King. I believe – though I have no evidence for it – that you let it blossom also in the hope that it would reveal a leading noble as one of its leaders, perhaps one you saw as posing a threat to yourself. Did you hope to implicate Raleigh? Or was it simply Northumberland? In any event, you encouraged another of your double agents, Thomas Percy, to become involved and to work again on the inside of the plot on your behalf. Fawkes, I suspect, was to be bribed with money and a free passage out, perhaps even to go back to Europe as a hero and remain on the inside of the

Catholic rebels over there. Percy was to be bribed, perhaps even with the Earldom itself.'

'And how do you know all this . . . fantasy? This . . . invention?' Cecil's eyes had never seemed more dangerous, his hunched body more ready to pounce.

'I have had my own man on the inside of this plot. I wrote that letter you have on your desk, to splinter and disperse the plot before harm was done. I brought Knyvett out an hour early, so that Fawkes could be found. It was I who caused the powder to ignite at Holbeache House. Oh, and by the way, I shot Thomas Percy.'

'You dared to challenge my will?' Cecil was roaring now, the first time Gresham had ever seen him lose his control.

'Challenge your will? Are you God, as well as Secretary to His anointed?'

'You have no evidence of this. No evidence at all.' Cecil's voice had dropped, his body fallen back into the chair.

'I have a story that men will believe, because it fits so many facts and fits the hatred and suspicion they have of you. I have the drafts of that letter you have in front of you – and a devil of a time it took, I can tell you – in the same hand and in a manner that progresses so convincingly that all will believe the authorship. And I have a plotter. Francis Tresham, to be exact, kept where you will not find him.' Gresham doubted that last comment, personally. If Cecil pulled out all his resources he could find anything, even a clean spot on the King's body. 'And several signed accounts by Tresham, undeniably in his hand, and witnessed, hidden also where you will not find them.'

'What is it that you want from me?' hissed Cecil.

'A chair would be pleasant,' said Gresham, with a polite smile. He was still standing. Angrily, Cecil motioned him to sit, never once taking his eyes off him.

'Do you hate me, Henry Gresham?'

It was an odd question, coming from the source it did, but Gresham paused to answer it.

'Yes, most certainly. More so than perhaps any man alive or dead.'

'Then you wish to destroy me?'

'Oh, no!' Gresham's laugh so startled Cecil that he fell back a little, and blinked owlishly. 'You see, only a person whose soul stinks like the foulest sewer could run a country such as this. A murderer, a torturer, an abuser, a liar, a cheat and a lost soul before God. These are necessary in a ruler. Some people have to die, of course, some have to meet the rack and some have their guts sawn out in front of crowds to make peace happen. Some, it is true, have these things happen to them who do not deserve them, or who are unlucky, or who happen to be in the wrong place at the wrong time, but all things come at a price. Peace and stability carry a higher price than many. And they carry the highest price of all for the ruler, the leader of that midden we call politics and human life. They carry the price of a lost soul, and eternity spent in Hell. Yes, I hate you, Robert Cecil, Earl of Salisbury. Because I hate you, I am happy for your soul to be the price of peace in this country. I would like to kill you, to see you suffer and writhe in front of me as you have seen so many others. But I must make Machiavelli's choice, and go for the greater good at the expense of some of the lesser pleasures.'

The silence extended for a minute, perhaps more.

'So what it is that you want from me?'

'Nothing.'

'Nothing?'

'Well, nothing really. I wanted to have the pleasure of your knowing what I knew, that your attempts to gag and mislead me had failed, as well as your pathetic attempts to blackmail me. I suppose I ought to have your oath that you will take no steps to harm me, or those closest to me. No strange deaths in alleyways, or long decaying illnesses from poison.'

'Is not the Papal archive enough?' asked Cecil, his hatred of Gresham beginning to infect his voice.

'I thought it might be, but you proved me wrong. And it's not

307

just the Papal archive where I keep papers, believe me. But you see, there is something strange about you, rotten and corrupt as you are. I have never known you go back on an oath you have sworn. Quite extraordinary. But this oath will be special. You will swear it on the life of your son.'

'On the life of my son . . . but I . . .' Cecil was almost speechless, grabbing for words.

'You had better pray for a long and peaceful life for me, my woman and my servant. Because if we die, in any way that might lead back to you in any way, your son will die.'

'You would not . . .'

'Yes, I would. You cannot lock a child away from life. Unless you can hide it away completely you cannot lock it away from the reality of death. Look at me, Robert Cecil. And then tell me if you think I lie.'

Unwillingly, Cecil found himself looking straight at Gresham.

'You have sought to bring your full power against me. You have failed. You will swear to do everything in your power to ensure that no harm of any kind comes to Henry Gresham and those nearest and dearest to him. And if you break your oath, your son will die.'

There was no lie in Henry Gresham's eyes. There was a look that told of all the innocent children those eyes had seen slaughtered, the women raped, the babies with their throats slashed. There was a look that told of the plotter Kit Wright, fighting for his religion, leading a mad, hopeless and courageous charge into the yard at Holbeache. Kit Wright, the stolid, dependable Kit Wright, the man who thought quite genuinely that if one believed in something then one had to be prepared to fight and to die for it. Kit Wright, who could in many respects have been Mannion, if Mannion had chosen to give his total loyalty to Catholicism instead of to Gresham. Brave and foolish Kit Wright, lying in the filth of the courtyard, with a rough soldier frantically yanking at the silk stockings on his dead legs for booty.

Yes, thought Robert Cecil, my son will die at this man's hands if

I break my oath. The hatred gleaming in his eyes, with every word dragged out of him as if by red-hot pincers, Robert Cecil swore his oath.

'Well, that was good,' said Gresham lightly. 'Every good boy deserves favour, and so I'll give you something else for your pains, and as a gesture of my goodwill. I wouldn't have you deposed, Chief Secretary. It amuses me to have that in my power, but it's a power I won't exercise. Someone less evil might come along to run the country, and perhaps if you were deposed you might have time to take a part of your soul out of the Hell it so richly deserves.'

'Cease this jesting!' said Cecil. 'Have you not had your satisfaction?'

'This isn't jesting,' said Gresham, 'and if there's any satisfaction in the air, it will be your own. You hold Guy Fawkes, don't you, in the Tower at this very moment?'

Cecil did not answer. He knew Gresham knew the truth.

'Wondering what to do with him, no doubt. What jolly talk there must have been between you both, when he was brought in by Knyvett's men. Has Guy Fawkes ever mentioned to you his relationship with the ninth Earl of Northumberland?'

'His *relationship*?'

'Yes. You thought Fawkes was your man, didn't you? It never crossed your mind that he was someone else's. Before he started to receive money from you he'd been employed by Northumberland. From the outset, in fact. It was Northumberland who spotted him as a young man, sent him over to Europe and paid to settle his wife – Maria, I think she's called – and their son Thomas, in his absence. You see, Fawkes never was a soldier of fortune. He always was a soldier of conscience. When you came along with your offer for him to turn spy, Northumberland encouraged him to say yes. Northumberland always despised you, never trusted you. It amused him to have one of your spies in his pay.

'And then Catesby came along. Northumberland knew the plot was a disaster, knew it would turn the country against Catholics.

And he knew exactly why you were urging Fawkes to go along with it. So he planned a little surprise all his own.'

'Are you seeking to tell me that this Guy Fawkes was in the pay of Northumberland?' said Cecil.

He was a clever man, thought Gresham, you had to admit. He had never actually admitted to any involvement in the plot, or that he had employed Guy Fawkes. Even the oath he had sworn had not been an admission of guilt.

'*Is* in the pay of Northumberland.'

'And what was my Lord of Northumberland's aim in all this?' To his credit, Cecil recovered quickly. Gresham could almost see the machinery of his brain grappling with this latest problem.

'Very simple, really,' said Gresham. 'He was going to let you expose the plot, take all the glory and revel in it. He was going to wait until you put on trial whatever few pathetic plotters you had managed to keep alive.

'And then he was going to blow up the House of Lords.'

Cecil's face went as white as a full moon.

'Oh, don't worry,' said Gresham cheerfully, 'he wouldn't have killed anyone. Or at least no-one important, just a few servants. He'd have blown the mine when the House was empty. And because of where it was, it wouldn't have been the whole House of Lords. Probably just one wall or so of it.'

'The mine?' Cecil could hardly force the words out.

'Remember? They tried to dig a tunnel under the House of Lords, before they found and hired the cellar. It came to grief against the foundations; they simply couldn't drive through them. You thought they'd abandoned it, didn't you? Well, the plotters did, but Fawkes didn't. Northumberland brought some miners down from the north-west. They were kept in isolation for a week, never told what they were doing, and sent home with a fat purse. Probably dead by now, if Northumberland has any sense. They widened the tunnel, secured it. Didn't have to dig all the way through the foundations, just part way in. Enough to bring a wall down.

'They packed it with barrels of powder. Fawkes used some of the good powder from your cellar. You'll find the stuff in the cellar is all decayed, more or less. The rest they bought in. If the powder held out, they were going to blow up the mine on the day you had your first show trial. Robert Cecil, Earl of Salisbury, and the hero of the Gunpowder Plot! Except the Catholics fooled him, kept another mine hidden from him and blew a wall out of an empty House of Lords just to prove how little Robert Cecil was actually in command on the very day he was bragging just how wonderful he was.

'You'd have been a laughing stock, forced into immediate resignation. The King would survive, the laughter rebounding on him and blowing a hole out of his authority. If I was them I'd have had pamphlets printed, pointing out that the Catholics could have blown up the whole farce with the people inside it if they'd wished, making it clear they had the power to provoke a rebellion, but had chosen not to use it. James would almost certainly have had to call in Northumberland as his Secretary after that, to make peace with the Catholics. Beautiful, isn't it? Let you make all the running, let you blow yourself up to maximum height and then prick your balloon with a gentle little explosion where the only physical casualties are a few bits of stone, and the only other casualty is one of the Papists' most bitter enemies: you.

'It's still there, of course. I mean the mine, and the powder. I set my servant guard over it when we found it, but called him off when I came here, just in case you sent someone and he got arrested as a conspirator. We wouldn't want old Mannion to find himself being nabbed like Guy Fawkes, would we? So I suppose Northumberland could have sent someone down there right now to blow it up, since you appear to want to implicate him in the Gunpowder Plot.'

Gresham stood up easily. He looked out of the high window in the direction of Westminster, as if for a cloud of smoke.

'I'd get someone down there pretty quickly, if I were you. Someone to secure it, take the powder away. Someone you can trust not to talk. We wouldn't want London knowing there was a plot you knew nothing about, would we?'

Gresham made as if to leave.

'Oh, by the way,' he said, 'there is just one other thing. I'll make Francis Tresham give himself up, so you can have your full set of conspirators. But I want no torture, and I want a fake death to get him out of the Tower and out of England. He won't trouble you again, I guarantee. Are we agreed – on that oath you swore? Tresham has just become both near and dear to me.'

Cecil nodded, a curt, hard nod. Gresham nodded ironically back, and left the room, almost casual in his manner. As he reached the nearest wall out of sight of Whitehall, he leant back against it, and breathed for what seemed like the first time in an hour.

Why had Gresham remembered Tresham's talk of the tunnel Fawkes and the others had tried to dig from the house they had rented, the tunnel they had given up on when the cellar under the House of Lords became available? Perhaps it was simple curiosity, perhaps it was the realisation that a secret tunnel leading up to the walls of the House of Lords was an open invitation for the future, a hostage to fortune and a loose end that simply needed to be tied up. Perhaps most of all it was Wintour's staying on in London, for far longer than was reasonable, and Wintour's obsessive attempts to reach the street in which the house was situated. Had he been trying to hide in the tunnel? Or had he hoped to re-open it himself, ironically wishing to stage the same embarrassment for Cecil as Northumberland had planned all along?

It had been easier than Gresham had thought to gain access to the house from where the plotters had started. A desultory guard was on duty now the first excitements were over, easily bluffed into allowing Gresham and Mannion entry by the obvious wealth of Gresham's clothing and his casual use of Cecil's name and title. Gresham had half expected to find nothing, or at best the caved-in remnant showing what happened when amateurs tried to play at being miners. They had found the shaft under the floor, despite the care of the miners in re-laying the boards their work had scuffed and splintered.

Mannion had been voluble in his insistence that Gresham should not enter. Gresham had ignored him, stripping down to his shirt and crawling through the surprisingly spacious tunnel. This was no work of amateurs, he realised, noting the simple yet effective pattern of timber framing that held up the roof of the tunnel. At its end a positive chamber had been hollowed out, the powder stacked neatly in the seven- or eight-foot-deep hole that had been made in the old foundations, rumoured to be some eleven or twelve feet thick in total. Nothing had been left to chance. Lanterns, tinder, flint and fuse had been stored there, awaiting whoever came to blow the mine. There were two pointers to the originators. A napkin or towel was stuck behind one of the barrels, pinned between it and its neighbour, as might have happened if it had become trapped as a man manoeuvred the one barrel into place by the side of the other. It was simple stuff, of the sort that would be put at table to wipe a guest's hands. Embroidered into the top corner was the Percy crest. Gresham knew that Northumbrian miners worked naked in the tunnels, sometimes discarding even a loincloth, but wrapped a piece of towelling round their brow to wipe the stinging sweat off before it reached their eyes. They must have given the miners napkins from Syon House to take the place of the towelling. Gresham had worked with the moles in the Netherlands, which was why he looked carefully on the ancient stone of the foundations. Those who cut through stone like to leave a mark on it. Eventually he found it, scratched on to a stone, perhaps with the edge of a pickaxe. 'AK for God and HP'. HP. Henry Percy. Perhaps the ninth Earl had deliberately recruited Catholics to work his mine, and perhaps even given whoever had supervised them a hint of what it was all about.

Gresham had guessed at much of it, of course, but Cecil had not denied it. He had known Fawkes had to be a triple agent as soon as he had seen the completed mine. It was Fawkes who supervised the mine early on, Fawkes who put the powder in the cellar and kept watch on it. The activity needed to finish the mine would never have escaped him.

Mr Fawkes, thought Gresham, was about to have an interesting exchange with Cecil.

They had come upon him at midnight, dragged him out of his sleep and from his comfortable chamber and down into the bowels of the White Tower. What had gone wrong? His grim-faced gaolers would not speak in answer to his entreaties. He knew they showed prisoners the rack, the mere sight of the obscene contraption enough often to break men. His hope died as they strapped him to the machine, still without a word being spoken.

The pain was the most terrible thing that had ever happened to Guy Fawkes. There were no words for the appalling agony that drenched through every fibre of his being, the pain that defied all experience, the pain that made his scream simply a tiny little thing heard far away on the winds of his destruction. They did not take him from the rack when finally he lost consciousness. They threw filthy water over his tortured, strung-out frame, and waited for part of him to emerge from the dark. When he did so he could hardly think. In losing its absolute top, searing edge, the pain had almost worsened, spreading out in equal measure to every limb and every extremity of that limb. It had broken his body, that he knew. He would never walk properly again, stand up like a man. It had broken his spirit too, that he knew.

The face of Cecil loomed over him, devilish in the torchlight.

'You did not tell me about Lord Percy,' he said. 'That was a pity.'

He turned to the gaoler.

'Rack him. And then rack him again. Yet keep him alive. He must walk or be carried on to the scaffold.'

The screams followed Cecil as he swung out of the chamber.

Cecil and Guy Fawkes met only once thereafter, alone. Fawkes had been tossed like a rag doll on to the rough cot in his cell.

Courteously, Cecil had asked one of the gaolers to straighten out his limbs as they lay on the bed, contemplating his fingernails as Fawkes screamed and sobbed as each limb was gently rearranged. Cecil waited. Patience was something he had always had plenty of. When there was something resembling a light of intelligence in Fawkes's eyes, he spoke.

'You are a dead man, of course. You must realise that?'

Something that might have been a nod came from Fawkes.

'So the issue is not whether you die, but how. We could arrange for you to be kissed by the rack again . . .' A shudder passed through Fawkes's frame. 'Or, of course, we could arrange for a clean break at your execution.'

Those sentenced to be hung, drawn and quartered were first of all hung, and then had their entrails dug out before being chopped into pieces. If the prisoner made a suitable confession and prepared to die in a manner that pleased the crowd and the executioner, he was let to hang until he was either dead or wholly unconscious, and only then cut down and dismembered. Other prisoners would be cut down almost immediately the halter had tightened around their neck, and left to experience the full pleasure of the executioner's crude surgery.

'Now,' said Cecil, almost gently, 'let us consider. Is it the rack, or a slice through the tongue to render you speechless and a long death on the scaffold? Or no more meetings with the rack and a quick death? Well, it will mean a trial, of course. And we could always try to speak out there, couldn't we? And an execution, too, where we might wish to speak more than the people should hear. But it would be good, very good for Guy Fawkes to go to his death and say nothing. What talk can there be of conspiracy if the man who was set to blow the powder says nothing of it? Oh, they will talk and conjecture, for a thousand years for all I know. But with you silent, my friend, they can never know, can they? No, my friend, much as it grieves me, we are in a bargaining situation. You have something I need – your silence. I have the power to grant you an easy death, little though you deserve it.'

Fawkes stirred on his cot. A croak emerged from his mouth. Cecil gazed carefully at the prostrate figure, checking that no knife or weapon was lurking on his person, and bent down close to listen.

'Ah, my Lord of Northumberland? You are still loyal to him, are you? A very praiseworthy thing in a servant.' He bent down again, to listen to the muted whisperings. He stood up, a colder and darker tone in his voice. 'Agreed. I swear on my oath that Henry Percy, ninth Earl of Northumberland, will not be brought to execution by any power or inaction on my part. Strangely enough, as another has recently pointed out, I have never broken my sworn oath.

'Yet I wonder if your concern for the ninth Earl might not be linked to his support of your wife and child? Yes, I know of it. And of them, though a devil of a time it has taken me to find them. So I will swear another oath, swear that they will both die, most horribly and at most great length, should you break your oath of silence.'

Why take the risk? thought Cecil, as he swept from the room, leaving the broken figure behind him.

Gresham would have told him. Gresham would have said that he was a man whose whole life had been based on control, on having the strings of the puppets in his hands. Then a figure, Henry Gresham, had come along and shown that those same strings, the strings Cecil thought he held, were in fact held by another man, a man who had taken control completely away from Cecil's hands. Could Robert Cecil, by force of will and by imposition of pain, bend this man Guy Fawkes to obey him, to take the secrets he held to his grave? Cecil needed to know he could do this thing. If he could then his power was undiminished. He was like the mighty Mark Antony, whose power failed him only in the face of the one man, Octavius Caesar. He would block Gresham from his mind. Yet hidden from Cecil's own sight, he and Gresham knew that the secret of Cecil's survival lay in one man alone, and that was not the man who would go to his death on the scaffold with the other plotters.

*

There had been a brief flurry when at the trial Fawkes had pleaded 'Not Guilty'. Cecil's heart had started to beat louder, but he had kept his outward calm and merely looked at the broken man in the dock. Fawkes had mumbled – he could hardly speak – that he had not understood some of the charges, and the crisis had passed. In fact, Cecil mused, it had probably been not so much a potential rebellion against Cecil, but more an attempt to protect some of the Catholic priests implicated in the plot, and Father Henry Garnet in particular. It was to no avail. Garnet would die, in agony, as was right.

It had been a bitterly cold morning when the first four had been dragged through the streets. The sentence had been for the traitors to be hauled at the tail of a horse, heads dragging on the ground. Amusing though the humiliation was, interpreted in its simplest form it meant the prisoner was likely to drown in the filth of the streets, or have his head banged so much as to make the executioner redundant. The crowd must not be deprived of their sport, so the prisoners were placed on a wicker hurdle for the first part of their ordeal. Would Jane wait and watch for him in a nearby house as he was dragged through the streets? wondered Gresham. He hoped not. You were best seen as already dead at this stage in the proceedings, and no dignity was to be acquired from any part of what went on.

Everard Digby's wife and children had managed to find a spot on the roadside. One of their little boys had cried out 'Tata! Tata!' as their father was dragged past, the baying crowds silent for a moment, the clods of earth ceasing their hurtling towards the traitor. Did the little boy notice the spit staining his father's shirt and body? wondered Gresham. Tom Bates's wife had dashed out to him on the street as well. He had apparently told her where some money was stashed, practical to the last.

Poor Digby, innocent baby that he was. He had played the romantic fool at his trial, and he spoke at length, and to very little purpose, on the scaffold. It had not helped him. He had been cut down almost as soon as he had hung, and carved up fully conscious. Immediately after the crowd had gone its way, the rumour had started that when the executioner had held up the bloody lump of flesh that was Digby's heart, with the cry 'Here lies the heart of a traitor!', Digby had cried out in his death pangs, 'You lie!' Well, Gresham reflected, someone might have heard those words. All he had heard was Digby's final agonised screams. Old Robert Wintour and John Grant had died decently enough, Tom Bates needing to make a speech.

The second batch of executions contained Fawkes. Tom Wintour, now recovered enough to die, Ambrose Rookwood and Robert Keyes went along with him. Keyes cheated the hangman at the last, hurling himself off the scaffold and breaking his neck the minute the halter was around it. Fawkes was last to go. He mumbled a few words – 'forgiveness' and 'the King' was all Gresham could hear, near as he was. The pathetic figure had to be helped on to the scaffold. His neck broke cleanly as he was hung. Strange, thought Gresham, that the crowd were denied the full bloody rites of this perceived ringleader. Stranger still that he had made it to execution, knowing what he knew. Or was it the real Fawkes? For all Gresham knew, some village idiot had been acquired in the place of the man who had died on the rack. He hardly cared. All he did know was that Cecil would never allow Guy Fawkes to live.

Mannion had come with him on both occasions. 'Nothing like a good execution!' he had stated with enthusiasm, and even now he was comparing the eight deaths with others he had seen, for all the world like a man comparing plays or sonnets. He munched on a mutton pie as the conspirators were put to death, one by one. Jane had not come. 'I've excitement enough in my life,' she had said, 'without needing to smear my eyes with blood.' Gresham had found her crying, the night in between the executions.

'Why are you crying?' he had whispered to her, reaching out in the night.

'For the women,' she had sobbed, 'and for the children. For the innocents, left behind with no inheritance, their lives ruined by these *stupid* men. These men who care only for their great cause, and leave behind them weeping the only true great cause a man can have.'

Gresham could have said how those damned were only a tiny proportion of those who would have suffered if rebellion had broken out, if the plot had not been smashed and exposed. Yet was it so? Would more, or fewer, men have died, women been widowed and children been orphaned if Gresham had kept out of the whole affair? Cecil had it under control, did he not? Fawkes would have lived on, Percy been ennobled, a few plotters executed.

So what had Henry Gresham done, except send Guy Fawkes to the rack and Thomas Percy to his grave?

Gresham lay awake, the occasional ripple of a sob still passing through the beautiful body lying next to him. Was it Machiavelli's choice that he had made, to keep a corrupt ruler in his place? Or was it simple vanity?

EPILOGUE

It was a cold wind blowing across the marshes. The small boat that would take them out to meet the tiny pinnace was rocking in the water, the slap-slap of its hull loud in the night. Gresham wondered if there were troops at that moment searching the south-coast port where he had let it be known that the embarkation would take place. He doubted it, but it would be a good test of Cecil's word.

The priest, Father Garnet, had been arrested. He had tried to defend himself at his trial, but he had no defence. What did a court of King James care for the secrecy of the confessional? If he knew of treason and a plot to murder the King, his duty as a subject was to report it, never mind whether he heard it in a wooden box with incense all around him. He was a dead man from the moment they laid hands on him, and Garnet knew it as well as the court.

Francis Tresham slipped out of the fisherman's hut in which he had been waiting. Gresham and his men had needed to check the area, to exchange the password with the two sailors in the small boat. He could smell the fear on Tresham, as well as the drink with which he had been filling himself for days. Spiriting him out of the Tower, supposedly dead, had been ease itself with Cecil's word behind the conspiracy.

'Here,' he said, thrusting a parcel at Tresham and forcing himself not to speak in a whisper. 'Money, and your papers. You are now Matthew Brunninge. Your passage to Spain is booked. Congratulations. Like Jesus, you've risen from the dead.'

'Will he live happily ever after?' asked Jane, snuggling up to him as they watched the boat move gently out through the creek.

'I doubt it,' said Gresham. 'But then again, who can say who'll live happily ever after?'

'Sir Henry,' said Jane, stepping away from him, 'I think it's time I became your wife.'

For once, Gresham let his shock show on his face. What the Devil had this woman? To talk of *marriage*? On a windswept Norfolk coast, surrounded by potential enemies and busily involved in spiriting away a traitor and sworn enemy of the Crown, not to mention someone who had supposedly died of a urinary infection in the Tower!

'God help us!' exploded Gresham. 'I . . .'

'You see,' said Jane, ignoring him completely, 'it's one thing for me to be your whore. It is another thing for our son to be born a bastard.'

Dramatis Personae

Francis Bacon, 1st Baron Verulam and Viscount St Alban (1561–1626), failed to establish himself at Court under Queen Elizabeth I, probably because Lord Burghley saw him as a rival to his son, Robert Cecil. His career blossomed after the death of Robert Cecil in 1612, but he fell from grace in 1621 when he was convicted of bribery, briefly imprisoned in The Tower and then allowed to retire in disgrace.

Robert Cecil, 1st Earl of Salisbury (1563–1612), was the creator of Hatfield House, and died 'much troubled in mind and body' after a long and painful illness.

Moll Cutpurse (c. 1570–1650), known also as Mary Frith and Mary Markham, was the daughter of a shoemaker, and died of dropsy in Fleet Street. She is the basis for the play *The Roaring Girl* (c. 1607) by Middleton and Decker, and appears as a character in *Amends for Ladies* (1612) by Nathan Field. She was prosecuted in 1605 for appearing in man's attire at The Fortune Theatre, uttering lascivious speeches and singing bawdy songs whilst playing the lute. Among her many achievements, she robbed General Fairfax of gold during the Civil War, shot him in the arm, was pursued and arrested and sentenced to be hung. She bribed her way out of this at a reported cost of £2,000.

John Donne (1572–1631) is recognised as the leading light of the Metaphysical school of poetry. Finally ordained in 1615, he became Dean of St Paul's in 1621.

Dr Simon Forman (1552–1611) was a notorious self-taught physician and astrologer who among other things predicted the day of his own death. Linked to Sir Walter Raleigh's 'School of Night' and a famous poisoning case featuring the Countess of Essex, his 'play books' contain the first eye-witness accounts of some of Shakespeare's plays in performance.

Inigo Jones (1573–1652) was a designer and architect whose partnership with Ben Jonson in the presentation of Court masques was to last from 1605 until 1631. Jones played a major part in introducing the proscenium arch to English theatre, and was responsible for the original layout of the piazza in Covent Garden.

Ben Jonson (1572–1637) was the leading playwright of his day after Shakespeare, and wrote a fulsome prologue to the published version of Shakespeare's plays. His partnership with Inigo Jones in presenting masques for the Court of King James I was long-standing and successful. As a Catholic and someone who had dined with members of the Gunpowder Plot conspiracy, he was questioned following the plot, but not accused.

William Parker, 4th Lord Monteagle (d. 1622), died peacefully and prosperously in his bed.

Henry Percy, 9th Earl of Northumberland (1564–1632), was imprisoned after the Gunpowder Plot and not released until 1621.

Thomas Phelippes was a key figure in Walsingham's spy empire for Queen Elizabeth I, specialising in 'deciphering', code breaking and formulation and forgery. He was reputedly able to break ciphers in five languages and was instrumental in the conviction and execution of Mary Queen of Scots. He fell out with Robert Cecil when Cecil inherited the remnants of Walsingham's empire.

Sir Walter Raleigh (c. 1554–1618) spent thirteen years imprisoned in The Tower, before being released to go on one last ill-fated expedition. He was executed by King James I, largely on the urging of the Spanish Ambassador, in 1618. His eldest son, Wat, was killed in 1618 in an heroic engagement against the Spanish-held village of St Thome in the 'Indies'.

The Conscience of the King

Henry Gresham and The Shakespeare Conspiracy

For Jenny

ACKNOWLEDGEMENTS

I am extremely grateful to Sonia Land, Ursula Mackenzie and Tara Lawrence for the faith they have placed in Henry Gresham, and in me. Thanks to Lawrence James, Philip Franks, Val McDermid, Jenni Murray, Simon Russell Beale, Graham Seel and Len Rix for all their help and advice, and for Jenny, Neill, Simon and Henry for putting up with me and Henry Gresham. I am grateful to Dr Andrew Stephen for advice on matters medical. I also owe a great deal to Cambridge University Library, the Bodleian Library, Oxford, the John Rylands Library, the University of Manchester, Chetham's Library, Manchester, and Fitzwilliam College, Cambridge. For access to the rarer parts of King's College Chapel, Cambridge, I am indebted to the Provost and Fellows of King's, the Domus Bursar and Mr John Boulter.

AUTHOR'S NOTE

Historical notes on the characters mentioned in this work of fiction can be found at the end of the book.

Sir Francis Walsingham created what was arguably the largest and most sophisticated espionage network in all of Europe for Queen Elizabeth I, funded largely out of his own pocket. He recruited a number of poets and dramatists to act as couriers or spies, most notably Christopher Marlowe and Anthony Munday. Walsingham's spies frequently used aliases: Anthony Munday, for example, used the name George Grimes. 'William Hall' is mentioned several times as an agent, but nothing is known about him except his name and that many of the people he is known to have been involved with were acquaintances of William Shakespeare. Thomas Thorpe published an edition of Shakespeare's sonnets in 1609 in which he states that 'Mr W.H.' is the 'only begetter of these ensuing sonnets'. The word which follows 'Mr W.H.', with an extended space, is 'All'.

'A significant feature of Shakespeare's life history … is that virtually all the records that would have referred to him have mysteriously vanished … The suspicion is that someone or some agency, backed by the resources of Government, has at some early period 'weeded' the archives and suppressed documents with any bearing on William Shakespeare …'

John Mitchell, *Who Wrote Shakespeare?*

'The mystery of William Shakespeare is thus exacerbated. If the Stratford Shakespeare *was* the great playwright, how did no one in his home town appear to know? No one writes about him or speaks of him as a dramatist, his tomb honours him merely as a grain dealer, and his epitaph reads simply 'gent'. Why is there no indication of his learning? There is no record of his education, he apparently buys no books, nor does he leave any in his will … Why does he leave no writings? There are no letters, diaries or mere jottings that survive … What of his poems, plays or manuscripts? None have surfaced, nor are they ever mentioned in Elizabethan Stratford … He only signs his name to documents drawn up by others …'

Graham Phillips and Martin Keatman,
The Shakespeare Conspiracy

'Shaksper as a person seems to have left no literary impression on anyone … In his will Shaksper left detailed instructions … but he mentioned no manuscripts, no books owned or borrowed, no rights to published plays or poems … Geniuses such as Mozart or Michelangelo arouse great feelings during their lives and at their deaths. The man from Stratford aroused none. An inferior playwright Francis Beaumont, who also died in 1616, was buried at Westminster Abbey, but no such public honour was accorded William of Stratford until 1740'

Kevin Gilvary, '*Twelfth Night*', '*A Midsummer Night's Dream*'
and the 'Earl of Oxford'

PROLOGUE

30th May, 1593
Deptford, South London

'A great reckoning in a little room . . .'
SHAKESPEARE, *As You Like It*

'Time for you to die.' Poley's voice was quiet, menacing.

The river by Deptford was stained a dark red-brown. The slaughterhouses were at work. They cut channels in the hard floors to take the blood of the slaughtered animals and feed it out to the waiting Thames. The river was foul enough anyway, carrying all London's sludge with it, and on killing days the blood, shit and piss of the terrified beasts stained it an even deeper brown. The noise of the animals, sensing their own death and the death of their kind, was terrible, shrieks and roars that could have come from the mouth of Hell. However deep they dug the channels, the blood seemed to splash against the timbers of the walls and rot them quicker than the wettest winter.

'I will decide when it is time.' Marlowe flung himself on the window seat. Christopher Marlowe. Kit Marlowe. The greatest, the first and the finest dramatist in England. His extravagantly slashed black velvet doublet was stained, elbows rubbed to a matt sheen where they had rested on tables in so many taverns.

'You no longer decide things. We do. You lost the power to

decide anything when you became unsafe.' Poley spoke as calmly as ever, but with the slightest edge to his voice. 'You had a bargain. You did as you were told and you kept silent. As all of us do. But you had to speak out, didn't you? You had to make a noise, draw attention to yourself.' There was hatred in Poley's eyes, in his voice. A hatred of weakness. A hatred of men who let their emotions take control.

'Sweet Jesus!' said Marlowe, grinning stupidly. 'Is even the great Master Poley showing signs of strain?' But to die in Deptford, he thought to himself. The heroes and villains he had created in his plays had bestrode heaven and hell, and all that lay between. The poet who had given them life was to die in London's arse-end.

'It's time.' The control in Poley's voice was more frightening than any anger. 'It's time *now*.'

He was right. The agreement was that Marlowe would die in a dispute over the bill for the meal they had shared. The meal had been eaten. It was time for the reckoning.

Marlowe jumped up steadily enough. Poley remained seated, watching him, outwardly calm, as emotional as drawn steel. Frizer and Skeres, the hired help, edged back, nervous, eyes flicking between Marlowe and Poley, waiting for orders. Marlowe looked at them and let a thin sneer curl his upper lip. He started to strip off, first the doublet, then the lace collar he had always preferred over the ruff. The poor clothes lay on the table waiting for him, the jerkin stained and stinking of sweat.

They had supposed they would find a young sailor to kill for the body that a simple local Justice would accept as being that of Christopher Marlowe. Bodies of all sorts were cheap in Deptford, and souls even cheaper. Then providence had intervened. They had decided to hang a mad Puritan, the writer of the infamous Marprelate tracts, four miles up the road at St Thomas-a-Watering only yesterday evening. John Penry was a year older than Marlowe and, ironically, also a Cambridge man. Some money to a sexton who cared little where a hanged man was

2

buried had emptied the cheap coffin, and a ruff in place of Marlowe's lace collar would hide the rope marks well enough. It was better than the sailor. They would have had to have got him drunk, which would have been easy, and then separate him from his friends, which would have been harder. True, no one would miss another dead seaman. But they would miss someone already dead even less, and a body whose fingers had the dark stains of ink on them and were untroubled by hauling ropes for a living was an unexpected bonus.

The act of putting on the filthy clothes sobered Marlowe. The purse was heavy, and he half waited for an attack from Poley and the two other men. It did not come. They would try to kill him, of course, despite their agreement and the bond struck with Henry Gresham. Poley had not lived and prospered as long as he had in England's dark underworld by being stupid. He wouldn't risk doing it in the house. There would be one or two men waiting on Deptford Strand, Marlowe thought, or, even better, one of the sailors on board the brig Poley knew he was to sail on with the tide. Well, sweet Robin Poley was in for some shocks of his own.

Marlowe nodded to the men. Poley stepped out of the door, and returned a minute or so later.

'It's clear,' was all he said. The less Poley spoke, the more dangerous he was.

Marlowe felt stupid in his stained workingman's clothes. He wanted to make a grand exit, like one of the characters in his plays, or speak an epilogue to his own life. What were the lines he had written for Faustus?

> *Cut is the branch that might have grown full straight,*
> *And burned is Apollo's laurel bough*

Instead, all he could think of was a line from the same play:

> *Why, this is Hell, nor am I out of it*

The three watchers saw nothing of Marlowe's inner turmoil. One moment he was standing by the low wooden door, silent, unmoving, the next he was gone into the deepening light of the evening. It was the last any of them would see of him. In a few moments they would start the ruckus that would lead to the supposed death of Christopher Marlowe, and poor John Penry's body, already suitably mutilated, would be laid out and buried in an unmarked grave in Marlowe's name.

1

May, 1612
The Globe Theatre, Bankside, London

'Murder most foul'
SHAKESPEARE, *Hamlet*

The blue of the sky was almost painful to the eyes. The thin pall of smoke hanging over Bankside was pungent, the smell of unseasoned wood, the sap bubbling and boiling and snapping at the nose, mingling with the heavier, earthier stench of sea coal. The smoke had given up trying to dampen the warmth of the sun, roasting the men and women still for the most part dressed in heavy, winterish woollens that exuded the thick, musty smell of a long winter.

Five hundred years ago, the Norman conquerors had set down the forbidding bulk of the Tower of London to control men's bodies and the mass of St Paul's Cathedral to control their minds. Both still squatted over London's citizens, a raw glare of power. Yet now there was a new power afoot, uncontrolled, anarchic, threatening. The theatre had come to London.

They came to the play in their thousands. Shipwrights and sailors from St Dunstan's; weavers and cobblers from St Giles Cripplegate; the silk weavers from Allhallows Honey Lane. From the fine, high-timbered merchant's houses to the acrid stench of the hatmakers' workshop, through the narrow streets where the shrieks and cries of the vendors seemed to overwhelm the ears, they flocked over London Bridge or called out from the landing stages – '*Westward Ho!*' '*Eastward Ho!*' – to be ferried across the Thames. The boats buzzed and flicked around the jetties like flies to horse dung.

The flag flew above The Globe theatre, its sides high to wind and weather. It was a packed house. The timbers cracked and spat like an old man roused from slumber by his family.

'Like an old woman, isn't she?' John Hemminge was one of the founders of the company. 'All the paint and gilt in the world can't cover up her cracks!'

The Actor listened and smiled despite his sickness. He loved The Globe. He had been there on that famous night eleven years ago when the players had taken down the timbers of The Theatre plank by plank and seen them off in a string of wagons and then boats across the river to build The Globe. The Lord Chamberlain's Men, the finest troupe of actors in the realm, had not owned the land on which The Theatre sat, but they had ownership of its timbers. The bastard Alleyn, who owned the site, had threatened to foreclose on them. So they had taken what was their own and moved it piece by piece over the river to make their new home: The Globe.

'Don't watch too long, old friend.' Hemminge spoke softly to the Actor. 'Watch too long and you might start to think we have any real importance.'

Thousands flocked to see them play. They had kings and admirals as their patrons. They stood in the sunshine of public adoration and fame. Yet, thought the Actor, the players were little more than piss and shit in the eyes of the power brokers. At best they were seen as popinjays with no breeding. At worst they were considered seditious, riotous drunkards. Those in power detested most of all their capacity to arouse deep emotions in their audiences. What had a noble lord said recently of them? 'Of no more worth than a common beggar.'

The newer, younger members of the company groaned and grumbled, affecting a distaste for the cramped and crammed hordes filling the playhouse. 'Oh God!' one of them murmured as he wafted by, scented handkerchief held to costumed lips, 'so very many of the poorer sort! This is so *vulgar*.'

Hemminge exploded, rounding on the new recruit. 'And what's *vulgar* about good people wanting to see us perform? Stick your vulgarity up your arse! This *vulgarity* is what we exist for. *Two and a half thousand people* out there, two and a half thousand people who've paid to see us perform! D'you hear, young 'un? There's fewer people at a king's funeral!'

The handkerchief wondered whether to have a tantrum, remembered who he was talking to and bowed instead. He felt the excitement. The Actor could see it in the boy's face and in his body as he walked away. They all did.

'We've spoilt them, haven't we, these young fops?' John Hemminge grabbed a cheap stool, a long-forgotten prop from a play, and sat opposite the Actor. 'Let them forget their meat and drink, forget where they really come from. They've had it on a plate; never had to fight, as we did.'

Too many indoor performances, the older ones said, either at Court or in the new theatre at Blackfriars.

'What about this new play?' asked Hemminge after a moment's pause, patting the pocket specially put into his doublet to hold his pipe. 'This lost manuscript. By Marlowe.'

The Actor felt the band of pain tighten across his brow. 'Steer clear of it, John,' he said. 'Well clear of it. Marlowe was trouble when he was alive, and people like him are trouble when they're dead. God knows what he knew. If he's put half of it into this damned play no one appears to have seen, I dread to think what the consequences will be. The last thing this company needs is the government down their throats after a riot. Can you imagine? They say this mysterious manuscript has the King as a sodomite and his favourite as Satan.'

7

'Strange, isn't it?' mused Hemminge, contentedly drawing the foul smoke down into his lungs and making a small 'o' of his mouth as he gently exhaled it, 'how Marlowe could be so prescient as to write a play about a sodomite king and an anti-Christ favourite? With Queen Elizabeth still on the throne when he died and six years – was it six? – to go before good King James took over? Remarkable.' The smoke rose slowly until the air, agitated by the vast crowd, caught and dispersed it. The two men's eyes locked for a moment. 'They do say it's very, very powerful. A masterpiece, they say, those few as are meant to have seen it. Better than anything anyone else has done . . .' A thin smile crossed Hemminge's face as he mused, outwardly at peace with the world and his pipe.

The sweeping tide of nausea came on the Actor again, as if his lips and nose had been sealed. The thin, bitter vomit rose in his throat, burning as it cascaded on to his tongue. Thank God he had not thrown up, in front of them all.

'Are you . . . well?' asked John, always sensitive despite his bluster, always his friend.

'No,' the Actor said simply, 'not well. Not well at all.' Neither in body nor in mind, he added silently. Not for some months now. He paused, swallowed, felt the beads of sweat break out across his forehead. 'It's this same sickness, the one I told you about before. It doesn't go away.'

'Can you play?'

'There's no option. I have to.'

'Perhaps not. I think one of your parts turned up an hour ago, pleading for work. Old Ben Thomas, remember him? We sacked him for drunkenness – two years ago, was it? A bit player, but good enough when he works at it. Well, he's out there, sober for once, and he knows the play.' John Hemminge looked down at the Actor, more worried than he tried to show. 'Take a rest. You look as if you need it. And Ben certainly needs the work.'

'Will you ask him? And thank you,' the Actor replied.

'Yes, of course,' said John, throwing the words back over his shoulder as he strode purposefully away. 'Provided *you* pay him!'

Hemminge went off to the back room where the actors were gathering, and where Old Ben had gone to scrounge whatever food, coin and drink his old companions might give him. The parts were easy, undemanding, thought the Actor. Rather demeaning, actually. What they revealed was that the Actor was not really a very good actor at all. Well, he had made Ben's day at least.

The boy came round, pasting up details of the plot backstage along with a list of scenes and who was required in each one.

From where he sat the Actor could see out into the Pit and the galleries. The merchants, the doctors, the lawyers and the incessant flood of foreign visitors crammed the galleries, their ladies giggling as they tried to keep decorum while forcing their way up the narrow stairs to the seats. The vendors were moving among the crowd, cheerfully breaking the law by selling their nuts, apples, ginger-bread, pears and bottled ale. It was the noise and smell he would always remember. Two thousand and more bodies crammed together: the sweating excitement; the rustle of silks and taffetas from the ladies in the galleries; the shouts of the vendors; the cracking of the nut shells and the clink of glass on glass; the conversations in roars and the conversations in secret whispers; the raw smell of dock tobacco mingling with the stale smell of beer and the tang of garlic. The half hour before a performance to a packed house was better than being drunk, better than sex – it was all life's excitement rolled up into one ball and flung in the face of time. Caught up in it, the Actor even forgot the pain in his gut.

The tension in the air now was palpable. One of the younger players looked as if he were about to be sick. Stage-fright, the Actor thought, and understandable. Where else since Roman times had a man been able to speak in the voice of a poet to thousands of souls gathered before him? It was the power of the gods, the power of kings.

The Actor realised Henry Condell was sitting by him. He had

9

not heard him come, realised it must have been a result of Hemminge tipping his other old friend off that there was something wrong. He and Condell gazed for a moment on the seething mass of humanity waiting to hear their play. Old friends do not always need to speak in order to communicate.

'A bad business, the other night.' It was Henry who broke the silence.

'Bad for us,' the Actor answered, 'and even worse for Tom.' Tom was the porter at The Globe, given his bed and keep there in order to guard it overnight and in the few hours when it was not occupied. He had been found by his young apprentice, his throat slit, two nights previously.

'Why steal two manuscripts only? Why not take the whole lot?' Henry spoke in a musing tone.

Two manuscripts had been found missing from the store where they kept the precious paper. The real text of a play was the most valuable thing a company held, after its costumes. They had paid Tom to protect both.

'Why indeed?' the Actor responded as his heart jolted. He knew why. And not even one of his oldest friends could be allowed to share in the secret. He had brought death to old Tom. Was he to murder his oldest friends as well by telling them a truth they did not need to know?

'And then all this fuss about Marlowe's lost play . . . When ever has there been such fuss about manuscripts?' Henry looked into the Actor's eyes. There was no response.

The trumpet blew for the last time. As much of a hush as ever fell over an audience at The Globe dropped down on them. They opened.

'Who's there?'

'Nay, answer me. Stand and unfold yourself!'

Hamlet was still one of the great attractions, old as it was. And even greater with Burbage in the lead. The audience were moved in a moment from an English summer to the freezing battlements of

Elsinore, moved by words alone. Two frightened men on guard, terrified by a ghost. It shut the crowd up like a finger snap. They were off and away.

The Actor had fallen asleep for a while, something he noted he often did after the sickness came upon him, and woke with a start. In the play-within-the-play Old Hamlet, played by Ben in place of the Actor, was about to have poison poured in his ear. Lucianus, the poisoner, flourished the bottle with much evil gesturing and grimaces. Strange, the Actor thought, it was a different bottle. His usual prop was a nasty green thing, its colour screaming something wicked. This time Lucianus had an expensive blue bottle, rather elegant in fact. He poured the poison into Old Hamlet's ear.

The Actor had always hated this part. Whatever he did, the fluid in the bottle was cold, and he could never persuade the others to leave the bottle empty and mime it. It had become something of a joke within the company. When the cold water hit his inner ear he always jerked convulsively with the shock. It was no bad thing, of course. As the stuff was meant to kill him he would have to jerk up and down anyway.

'Ben's going overboard on this one, isn't he?' Condell had drifted back to the Actor's side. Old Hamlet was throwing huge spasms, hurling himself around on the bed with gasps and muffled shrieks of heart-breaking proportions.

What a pity, thought the Actor. All that effort from Ben for no reward. The play was broken up in chaos just after the moment of the poisoning, the real King rising in guilt and anger and storming out. With Hamlet mouthing off and the King just about to ruin the party, no one would have time to look at an old actor going way over the top in a death scene no one was interested in anyway. Ben was wasting his energies, even to the white froth he had managed to make come from his lips.

Something was wrong.

The Actor could sense it, even on the sidelines. The actors on stage had picked up a signal, the tremor that goes round live performers when things start to go wrong. Horatio's eyes were flickering backwards and forwards, Hamlet ill at ease and muffing some of his lines. The King, Claudius, had risen to his feet in uncontrollable anger. The whole assembly – courtiers, actors – should have splintered from the stage in apparent chaos.

Old Ben's body was still on the stage.

'Bloody hell!' said Condell. 'Sodding bloody buggering fucking hell! *Why doesn't he get up and go?*'

You never left a body on the stage. It was the golden rule. It spoilt it if the audience saw a character they had just been told was dead suddenly get up and walk off before the next scene. It wasn't as if they could draw a curtain over the stage. Yet this was different. The audience knew that the body in the play-within-the-play was an actor's, had not really died. He was expected to run off with his tail between his legs, realising the actors had caused offence. Yet Ben lay there, stiff, unmoving.

They were seconds away from the audience realising something had gone tragically wrong. Ben lay flat out on the bed, eyes agape and mouth open, a thin line of dribble from his lips over his chin.

'I do believe,' said Condell, in a tone of hushed disbelief, 'that the stupid old bastard has gone and died on us.'

The Actor turned to Condell. He had only half-heard. 'It's all over,' he said sadly.

The great Burbage, playing Hamlet, had gone glassy-eyed and had lost the plot completely. The line should have been: '*O good Horatio, I'll take the Ghost's word for a thousand pound!*' Instead, Burbage started to gabble complete nonsense, '*For thou dost know, O Damon dear . . .*'

'Damon? *Damon!* Who the fuck's Damon when he's at home?' Condell was incandescent.

> *This realm dismantled was*
> *Of Jove himself; and now reigns here*
> *A very, very . . .*

There was an appalling pause . . .

'*Paiock!*'

'Oh sweet Jesus!' moaned Condell, wringing his hair. 'What's he doing?'

'He's regressed,' said the Actor. 'Don't you remember? He's mangling lines from that monstrous load of old garbage we did years ago – *Gorboduck*, wasn't it? – and it was bad enough then.'

On stage, Horatio turned to Hamlet, a look of total scorn on his face. '*You might have rhymed . . .*' he said tersely.

Horatio saved the day, with no help at all from Hamlet. He motioned firmly to one of the actors off stage and together they draped Old Ben over their shoulders. Never explain. Never apologise. If you make it look as if you meant it, the audience will believe you. It was a basic rule.

They dumped the body by the Actor's feet. He gazed into the staring eyes of Old Ben and a pain like an icicle in his chest clutched his heart. Vaguely he was aware of Hamlet's voice: '*O good Horatio, I'll take the Ghost's word for a thousand pound . . .*'

Burbage had got it together again. They were back on track. It hardly seemed to matter to the Actor. Old Ben was dead, clearly. Condell bent down to feel in his neck for a pulse, for form's sake. There was nothing.

The Actor smelled something. His hand shot out, stopping Condell just as his bony fingers were to touch the corpse's flesh.

'Hold it! Don't touch him!'

The smell, that metallic, vinegary stench with an acidic burn to it. He had researched poisons, knew their reality. This was not water that had been poured into Old Ben's ear. Someone had substituted the green bottle with its harmless contents for a sophisticated and expensive poison, the ingredients known to only two or three men in London at most. Someone, carefully and methodically, had sought to murder the actor taking the part of the Player King. Only at the last minute had a different man taken on the role for that one performance. Ben's death was no accident.

Which meant that someone had tried to murder the Actor. Or to be more precise, actor, poet and playwright. Shakespeare. William Shakespeare, the author of this very play, *Hamlet*. William Shakespeare, the actor who had always taken the role of the Player King, the actor who should have been playing it this afternoon except for a last-minute change because he felt sick.

The sickness came upon him again, wave after wave, and did not go away. Cecil, he thought to himself, I must tell Cecil. It had gone too far, gone on far too long.

One moment he was there. The next moment he had gone. In his tension and sickness he failed to take note of the small, cloaked and hooded figure, following him with burning eyes and a strange, high-prancing step.

2

May, 1612
The Merchant's House,
Trumpington, near Cambridge

'There was given me a thorn in the flesh, the messenger of
Satan to buffet me.'

THE KING JAMES BIBLE

Henry Gresham sat in the great high-backed chair, looking out
through the tall mullioned window over the East Anglian
meadows. For a few moments he was at peace, the sardonic smile
gone from his face, features relaxed, the book lying almost unnoticed in his lap. The smells of early summer wafted across the Great
Hall, grass and turned earth mingling with the faint smell of smoke
from garden fires.

He felt extraordinarily calm. He had risen early that morning,
noting the still-warm other half of the bed. For years Jane, now his
wife, had always managed by some alchemy to rise before he did,
and grant him the space to re-enter the world in private.

In private, that is, except for the figure of Mannion. If the one
certainty in Gresham's life was that Jane's slim, warm body would be
gone from his bed when he awoke, the other was that Mannion,
that immense hulk of a man, would drift in silently to the room
almost as soon as Gresham's feet touched the floor, towel in hand,

ready to guide his master to the adjoining room where the bath had already been filled. This morning he had rejected the ritual, putting on instead a rough country jerkin and trews over his clean linen, stuffing a simple cap on his head and walking out past the startled servants wiping the sleep from their eyes as they came to terms with their own world. He had strode out of the house, lungs taking in great gasps of the still, chill morning air. Mannion, with a wistful eye back at the house and breakfast, had followed him in silence. He knew where Gresham would be going. It had to be Excalibur's pool.

Gresham had called it that when he bought the house. If ever there was a pool from which an enchanted hand might bring Excalibur, this was it; a bend in the river channelled out by the years into almost the size of a small lake, the water deep in history, cool and pure.

Mannion sniffed as Gresham stripped off and prepared to dive into the pool. Gresham heard it, as he was meant to. He turned to his body-servant, grinning, stark naked in the still-cold morning air.

'This is a magical place! An enchanted place! Can't you feel it, old man?'

'Funny how you can miss these things,' Mannion replied in a tone that did not imply any great respect for magic or enchantment. 'I thought it was just cold and damp.'

'Have you no imagination?' Gresham half shouted as he prepared to dive in to the darkness of the pool, thin strands of early morning mist still clinging to its luminous surface.

'No,' said Mannion, at least able to close that one up without further discussion. 'And if I did have, you can be sure neither of us'd be standing here catching our deaths this morning!'

Gresham pulled back, aborting his dive, interested.

'And how do you reckon that?'

'Because it's your so-called imagination that's got you into most of the scrapes that my lack of it has helped pull you out of. Now are you going to dive in, or are we both going to die of your imagination?'

16

Not for the first time, Gresham reflected that it was usually a bad thing to engage the servants in conversation before breakfast. He gasped as the cold river water bit benignly into his flesh. Mannion was waiting with the towel as he climbed out, dripping, on to the grassy bank. Mannion noted with approval, as he always did, the firmness of Gresham's body, the muscle under just the right layer of flesh. In the cold, patches of Gresham's skin, all down his right side, had turned just the slightest shade paler than the rest of his flesh. If Mannion remembered holding Gresham in his arms for weeks on end, or Gresham his screaming for release from his agony when the powder had burned all that side of his body, then neither said anything. They did not need words in order to communicate.

They walked back in companionable silence to The Merchant's House. Medieval in its origins, it had once been little more than a Great Hall with a kitchen attached. Extended and added to over two hundred years, Gresham could feel the heat of the house extend towards him like outstretched arms. He found it difficult to explain its magic, but he knew it was centred in the Great Hall. Once, in a different age, whole families and their retainers had lived, squabbled and loved in this Hall, with only the kitchens, store houses and rooms for the master and mistress separated off. Now, with its tapestries and fantastic gilded and beamed roof, the Great Hall was simply the largest room at the centre of a complex of corridors, levels and parlours, a positive industry of a house, the noises of which Gresham could perpetually hear faintly in the background. Summer was truly in the air, and there was a sense of reawakening in all the subdued sounds around him, a stirring of limbs aching from the winter. Yet the Great Hall seemed almost impervious to this tumult. In its time it had seen and hosted all that human life could offer. It was called The Merchant's House, but Gresham guessed some rich merchant had bought it from the nobility who had first built it and then fallen on hard times, or perhaps even fallen on the executioner's block. No merchant would have built that Hall. Its confidence was the confidence of a blood-line, not of earned money.

His children had come in through the door at the other end of the Hall, talking quietly to each other. The room gleamed, rich with the shine and smell of polish. Gresham felt an irritation, and half rose to banish them from the formal room of the great house, the room that was his to be alone in whenever and howsoever he required it. This was an adult room, not a nursery. Then he fell back, unseen, as he caught the words of their conversation.

'Sssh!' It was Walter, six this year and the older of the two, who happened to be making the most noise. 'If they hear us they'll make us leave!'

'Why will they make us leave?' That was the small, piping voice of Anna, rising five. Learning to speak extraordinarily early, she had always done so with perfect clarity.

'Because adults do that sort of thing.'

'Then are adults not very clever?'

'I . . . I . . . I don't know!' said an exasperated Walter. 'Let's get on with the game.'

Gresham relaxed back into his chair, grinning, still hidden from his two children. Now there was the subject of his next academic work, he thought. Man, the dominant species, brought to a grinding halt by the seventh rib asking a sensible question. And what was Man's answer? 'I don't know! Let's get on with the game!' How many men had Gresham known who treated the deadly serious business of life as simply a game? The only difference between Gresham and other men was that he had learned long ago that there was no answer, that life was indeed a game and survival its only victory.

The game in this instance, or so it appeared, consisted of skipping the length of the vast table centred in the Hall and placing something a few feet past its end, itself only a few feet from the back of Gresham's chair. Feeling increasingly like a naughty child himself, Gresham looked round to catch sight of what his daughter had laid on the floor.

Good God. It was a bum roll. Or two bum rolls, to be precise. These were the padded half-hoops that a woman wore resting on her bottom to exaggerate the size of her hips and the narrowness of her waist, and to put a barrier between the flesh and the steel wires that extended her skirt out to the ludicrous lengths required by Court fashion. There would be hell to pay when their loss was discovered.

The game quickly became clear. Walter and Anna each had a packed leather ball. Underneath the table was a narrow tunnel formed by the extravagantly backed oak chairs tucked under it. Bowling the ball under the entire length of the table so that it emerged to rest in the centre of one of the bum rolls acquired top points. Bowling the ball so that it hit the end of the bum roll meant no points. A few points were scored for clearing the table but not reaching the embrace of the bum roll.

The temptation was too much.

'Can I play?' asked Gresham, standing up.

Children were meant to doff their caps to their father after his breakfast, ask him to pray for them and invite his formal blessing. Formal. Restrained. Fathers did not romp with their children on the floor.

But it was a good game, and he did want to play.

His two children, ludicrously small now that he was upright, jumped back as he spoke but calmed immediately as they recognised their father.

'Do you . . . do you . . . do you mind us being here, Father?'

It was Walter, the brave little soldier standing in front of his officer, always unsure of what erratic authority would decree yet wanting so much to get it right.

'Of course I do!' said Gresham firmly. 'You've disturbed my peace and quiet and you've no right to be here.'

Interesting, he thought, most children's faces would have fallen at that. His children were too young to control all their muscles. Both flickered, and blinked, but their control at what must have seemed disaster in their tiny lives was remarkable. Both stood straight before him. Unwilling to demand more of their courage, he spoke again.

'But then again, this looks a good game, and the least you can do if you've disturbed me is let me play it too.'

They smiled then, shy little smiles. Trust and fear, thought Gresham, and some affection. Three of the ingredients that make a fine commander. Am I treating my children like soldiers under my command?

If he was, one soldier kept a lawyer in the barracks.

'Your arms are bigger than ours,' said Gresham's daughter. 'You must have a forfeit!'

Where had she learned to speak like that at her tender age? Those huge, dark eyes; the thin, wiry little body; the intensity and the control in the voice. In a moment Gresham was rushed back to his first meeting with her mother, Jane. A bastard girl in a godforsaken village, beaten to perdition by a vicious stepfather, demanding that the gentleman pay a forfeit because he had blinked before she did.

He blinked now, and saw his daughter before him again. Yet as it had always been with her mother, he felt a strange, defenceless feeling overwhelm him. She was very like Jane.

He became businesslike. Fathers should be formal, precise and definite with their children. In a very short space of time it was agreed that he should have a five-point handicap on a match of six throws. He had argued for three points, his children for ten, and they had compromised at five. His children forgot who he was as he totally threw away the first ball, hitting the leg of the third chair along.

'Damn!' he said, engrossed, then looked round with a guilty start. Walter and Anna pretended they had not heard him. Walter landed his neatly within the circumference of the bum roll and Anna lodged her ball just outside of it.

When Lady Jane Gresham entered the Hall, with Mannion beside her, it was to find her husband, Sir Henry Gresham, kneeling on the floor in peasant's jerkin and trews, beating it with his fists and yelling in mock horror that he had lost to devilry and witchcraft. Walter and Anna were dancing round him, alternately shrieking, 'We won! We won!' and trying to hug him to say thank you for the fact that he could be so silly.

Jane had seen Gresham kill a man by cleaving his head in half with a boat axe, an exultant grin on his face as his teeth drew back over his lips. He had consigned men to torture, had himself been strapped to the rack. She knew he could be without pity or remorse for those who threatened him, or her. And here he was, treating his children as if they were the most fragile alabaster.

The children saw their mother and rushed towards her, all decorum forgotten. In a trice they were wrapped round her.

'Mummy, Mummy, Father came and we thought he was angry but he played with us and we won . . .'

Jane was dressed plainly, to manage the house and her children rather than to impress at Court. Nonetheless, every lady painting and corseting at Court would have given their souls to look as she did. The body was straight as an arrow, the complexion clear, the legs as long as heaven and the breasts the reward for having made the journey. Her head was chiselled and her face extraordinary. Its classical beauty was simplicity itself, yet it flickered and changed and flashed a different reality every second. The eyes. It was always the eyes with her, almost black but with a strange sparkle to them and the same primeval depth as the pool that Henry Gresham had dived into this morning.

'Good morning, my lord,' said Jane, managing to manifest total control, exasperation and a mild, irritated affection all at the same time. 'I thought I had only two children in my care. Now it seems I have three.'

Gresham stood up. 'Madam,' he announced, standing to his full height, 'I must make formal complaint regarding your motherhood.'

The two children disengaged from their mother and stood back, alarmed.

'Sir Henry!' replied Jane, sweeping to her full dignity, 'I am appalled. How may I have failed in my sacred duty to your heirs?'

'You have failed, my lady,' replied Gresham in the most sonorous tones he could muster, 'in that you have had the temerity to bring into this world two young striplings,' he glowered at his children with such severity that they fell back, 'who have managed to beat me fair and square at bowling!'

With that, he flung out his arms and his children ran in glee to their embrace.

'Take these young hounds outside,' Gresham said to Mannion after a moment, gazing swiftly at Jane who nodded imperceptibly, 'and give them some exercise, so they learn to leave their father undisturbed and, of course, to let him win.'

Mannion, like a vast and ragged hen, gathered the two chickens under his arms and led them off, chattering happily. He would walk them for an hour or more through the woods, as he had done with Gresham when he was a child, pointing out to them the different notes of the birds and the names of the wild flowers. They would know how the other birds fell silent when a hawk was in the wood, spot the patches of water where the fish were to be found in the river and learn which leaf to rub on a nettle sting.

'They're good children,' Gresham said when they were alone.

'Well, I'm glad,' said Jane. 'It'd be a little difficult to put them back from whence they came if you didn't like them.' They talked for a while, the tittle-tattle of houses and servants. There was no mention of the sadness that joined them, the memory of the baby who had been born dead. The baby who had broken the fragile cycle of Jane's fertility. There would be no more children born to Sir Henry and Lady Gresham.

Was he finally calming down, this husband of hers? Jane wondered. With a king secure on his throne, a brilliant heir to the Crown and the Catholics vanquished, would he cease to be Henry

Gresham the soldier and spy she had always known? Would he increasingly be taken over by the College he had refounded, and become Sir Henry Gresham the gentleman and the academic? A part of her soul yearned for it to be so. The other, stronger part told her the truth. Yet for a moment she allowed herself to gaze on Gresham, slightly dishevelled, seemingly at peace with himself.

It did not, could not last. It was late in the afternoon, the rooks and the men in the fields starting to head home, when they heard the sound of a tired horse, and a beating at their door.

Cecil's messenger. Robert Cecil, First Earl of Salisbury. Lord Treasurer and Chief Secretary to His Royal Highness King James I of England and Scotland. Cecil hated Gresham with the malice of acid on steel. It was a feeling returned with interest by Gresham. Yet each needed the other, a poisoned symbiosis that grappled both to its breast. Cecil's messengers had summoned Gresham countless times, always the harbinger of potential death and destruction, always the guarantor of trouble, and always, for some reason, coming just before or after nightfall.

'Perhaps,' said Jane caustically, cynicism the first cover she could find for her growing fear, 'he lies waiting outside for the last two or three hours of daylight, so as to make an entrance?'

Cecil was dying, they both knew. Those who had seen him said he stank and was rotting from within, his thin limbs no longer able to support him and racking him with pain. Jane had not expected this last summons. The fact of its coming from a man so nearly dead chilled her to her bones, made this last call from Gresham's old enemy the most terrifying of them all.

The messenger's name was Nicholas Heaton. Gresham took care to know these things. He was muddied enough, almost as big as Mannion, sweat-stained and stinking from his ride. His hair was thinning on top, though he tried to cover it with long, lank strands plastered down over the bald patch on his pate. As if to compensate for the lack of hair on his head, he wore a huge, florid moustache that extended in two luxuriant curls beyond the side of his face. It would have been ludicrous were it not for the almost palpable sense of threat the man emanated.

Heaton managed the merest nod of a bow to Gresham.

'My master is dying. He requests that you might spare time from your academic pursuits to visit him on his way to Bath. He has urgent need of speech with you.'

A man soon to be out of a job might be expected to show more respect. Gresham had too much self-respect of his own to allow Heaton's insubordination to get beneath his skin, yet he was intrigued.

'And after his death, what fate befalls you, Master Heaton?'

'My master has arranged for me to transfer my service. To the King.' There was pride in his voice, and arrogance.

'I'm delighted for the both of you,' said Gresham with an unctuous sincerity that only a liar could muster. Suddenly his tone cut the air as a razor through soft flesh: 'Take care. Those who rise to greater heights have far further to fall.' Only much later was Gresham to realise the appalling irony of his words. 'As for your present and still-living master, I'll come. I've always come, haven't I? Tell him so. Where do we meet?'

'He's left Theobalds to go to Bath. Some of his physicians believe there'll be a relief from his pain there, in the waters. The pain is constant, and agonising. You should be warned, Sir Henry. My master is not as he was.'

'Well, that's good news at least,' said Gresham briskly. 'He couldn't be any worse, and perhaps he's improved.'

They did not offer Master Nicholas Heaton lodging, and he did not ask.

'Will you ride tonight?' Jane asked, seeing the nervous energy beginning to flow through Gresham.

'It might be wise. If Cecil's as ill as his messenger says he is—'

'Please. We know what this summons means. Cecil's never invited you into anything other than mortal danger. Tonight, stay with me. Let's remember who we are.'

Gresham half turned towards the door. Mannion was standing there, blocking it. No words were spoken.

Gresham drew himself up to his full height, arms akimbo.

'Am I the lord and master of this house? Do I have authority over my wife and my servants?'

Jane dropped her eyes, her shoulders sagging slightly. Her normal spirit seemed to have been sucked out of her by the messenger and all that he stood for. She could cope with Gresham. Sometimes it was his life that overwhelmed her. She gave a slight curtsey, an almost involuntary reversion to a childish state. His heart went out to her in a fierce bite of love. So strong. So vulnerable.

'You know that I'm yours,' she replied softly.

Good God, thought Gresham, what must it have cost her fiery spirit to say that? A pang of guilt hit him like a blow to the stomach. Who was he to march like a peacock over those whose only fault was to give him their love? None of it showed on his face. Impassive, he turned to Mannion, who had folded his arms and was stood before the door like Leviathan. 'And you?'

'Yes to the first. You're lord and master of this house. And you've certainly got authority over one of the other two, though I'm damned if I know which one . . .'

'Do you defy me?' Gresham stuck his chin in the air, glaring at Mannion.

'Only when it matters,' he replied.

'And you?' Gresham turned to Jane.

'I just want you to spend the night with me.'

None of the haughtiness, the icy distance she could muster with a king and the frightening authority she could exert over the servants, was there now. He loved her, he thought, more than he had ever thought he could love anyone.

Gresham looked from one to the other, Jane now looking directly into his eyes. He grinned.

'We ride at dawn for Bath. I sleep the night here. *I* have decided.'

25

Mannion refrained from winking at Jane. Of course he had decided. Yet not without a little help from his friends.

They were holding hands as they left the room, Mannion noticed. Babies. Babies. And the two people for whom he would cheerfully lay down his life.

3

May, 1612
Bath

'Are all thy conquests, glories, triumphs, spoils,
Shrunk to this little measure?'
SHAKESPEARE, *Julius Caesar*

The sun was hidden behind a grey haze as he mounted his horse at dawn. The mist that had been but thin wisps yesterday was now a blanket, waist high, converting the flat landscape to a world of ghosts.

Was this the last summons to Cecil that Gresham would ever answer? In farewell to his ancient enemy, Gresham rode as never before. The hooves of his horse hit the ground with such force that it was like a hammer to his spine, the mud and earth they flung away from their impact flying up with the force of cannon balls. The wind tugged at his hat and as the leaping, shaking, shattering world ran by his watering eyes he urged the horse on, faster and faster. It was as if his mount knew that summer had come, and felt its strong legs stretch to three times their length, the fine muscle tightening like steel and releasing again with every movement of the insane gallop. For some wild minutes man and horse were as one, invincible, immortal in their speed and shared madness.

It had to end, of course. Gresham was not a man to take pleasure in riding a fine horse to the ground. He allowed the beast to slow down, praised it for its strength and beauty, timing it superbly so that before too long his once fiery mount was ambling along like any farmer's hack. He waited for Mannion, cursing under his breath, to catch up, and grinned at him. Mannion stayed on a horse and with a good seat, but no one in the kingdom could catch a well-mounted Henry Gresham with the devil in him.

Gresham was wealthy enough to have his own horses stabled at stages along the road to London from Cambridge. Each horse was ridden like the one before, so that when Gresham reached London the fine leather of his boots was in tatters, every muscle ached as if a hot iron had been passed over them and he was near dead with exhaustion. He slept for three hours. There were none of his own horses between London and Bath. Rather than trust to those he might find to hire or purchase along the way he took a string of his own animals, knowing that from there on his pace would have to be more seemly. He spurned the coaches that increasingly clogged the muddied roads and brought London traffic to a halt. He was not that old, not yet.

The waters of Bath had been used, so they said, in Roman times and ever after to cure the elderly and the infirm. Some of the Romans seemed never to have left, judging by the presence of the elderly and infirm. The old Abbey dwarfed the town, almost as if by squatting over it its dead hulk took life away from the miserable place. There was an air of decay everywhere. Gresham was used to the stink of towns, but this stench had the tinge of rotting flesh in it. They brushed bugs from their sweating faces as they rode. Even this early in summer, everything in Bath was fly-blown.

Mannion had taken a drumstick from one of the birds they had been served at the last inn and was now devouring it, on horseback. 'Do you want to know what I think? he asked now, a small

28

piece of dessicated meat shooting from his mouth past Gresham's left ear as he spoke.

'You mean you *can* think? I'm not sure I want to go anywhere near your mind if your physical actions in any way reflect its contents. But,' Gresham sighed, 'I expect you'll tell me anyway.'

'In the past he wanted to use you, and didn't mind if you died in the process. Now he's dying, he'll want to use you *provided* you get killed in the process. He'll want to take you along with him to hell. You're the only one who's ever got the best of him.'

Gresham did not challenge the conclusion. Instead, he looked at the population of Bath. 'Do people ever walk in Bath?' he asked, looking round. 'Or do they only hobble, or be carried by servants?'

He was surprised at the address he had been given by Nicholas Heaton. It was grand enough for a successful provincial lawyer but too poor by half for the King's Chief Secretary. He said as much as his knock on the door was answered by an obsequious servant dressed in Cecil's livery.

'I wonder at my lord of Salisbury taking such lodgings. Aren't they beneath his usual style?'

'My lord has great pain in any movement. It's necessary for him to be as near to the baths as possible.'

They waited in a dingy room. Its panelling had been brightly painted quite recently, in the current fashion, but the job had been badly done and paint was flaking off already. The hangings had faded almost completely into drab greyness, and only a few vague figures could be discerned among the overwhelming pattern of dust that was all that held them together. The glass in the windows was of poor quality and had a sickly yellow tinge. Everything was coated with filth, and the smell of damp in the room made it stink like something unwashed. Another servant brought in wine. He was fresh-faced, little more than a boy, with eyes wide open to the wonder of the world and his luck in being servant to such a great man. '

'Thank you,' said Gresham, whose life had been saved on more than one occasion by a servant who had noticed that Gresham called him by name and treated him as a human being. 'Your name is . . .?'

The servant halted, on his way out of the room, surprised to be addressed. 'Me, sir? I'm Arthur, sir . . .' Arthur gazed at Gresham in total awe, unaware that his mouth was hanging open. 'Sir . . . sir, forgive me, I . . .' Arthur was clearly bursting to say something.

'Spit it out, lad,' said Mannion.

Arthur saw a tall, muscled figure dressed from top to toe in black except for a white collar worked with breathtaking and exquisite skill. The clothes breathed money, despite being almost ostentatious in their lack of ostentation. The body they covered seemed as if it were a coiled spring, ready at any moment to break out. Yet it was the face that Arthur could not take his eyes from, a face of arrogance, of immense strength, of flickering humour yet strange vulnerability – a face that seemed to have all the humours of the world in its angularity.

'Sir . . . sir . . .' Arthur was stuttering. 'What I wanted to know, know more than anything else was . . . did you meet Guy Fawkes, as they say you did?'

Gresham looked Arthur straight in the eye. 'Yes, Arthur, I did meet Guy Fawkes. As they say I did.'

Yes, thought Gresham, I did meet Guy Fawkes, a rather decent and honourable man in many respects, certainly more honourable than many of those who hounded him to his death. And I was responsible for stopping his escape, springing a trap upon him and delivering him to a death no animal should endure, administered by your master, Robert Cecil. And by failing to tell the truth about Guy Fawkes, quite deliberately, I helped keep your master in power and a dribbling Scottish homosexual as king. All in all, I did a brilliant job.

'And, sir,' said Arthur, so intent and intense that he forgot to splutter, 'was he as they say? Was he the devil incarnate?'

'Yes, Arthur,' said Gresham solemnly. He felt the mischief in his soul bubble and start to rise. 'He was the devil incarnate. And I tell you what very few other people know, a secret you must vow at all costs to keep to yourself. Do you vow, on your soul and all that you hold holy?'

'I do, sir, I do, I do . . .' Arthur was transformed by a paroxysm of yearning.

'When he was examined, it was proven that he had a cloven foot!'

There was a moment of extraordinary silence.

'Sir!' said Arthur, standing to attention, real tears in his eyes. 'I shall never tell a soul! And . . . thank you!' He rushed from the room.

'Well,' said Mannion, 'that'll be round the servant's hall in five minutes flat. Still, at least you made him leave the jug.' Mannion helped himself. Cecil's wine had always been cat's piss, served in golden goblets, a strange emblem for the man. Mannion would have drunk real cat's piss quite cheerfully if it had been proven to be alcoholic.

There was a noise of carriages outside, in surprisingly short time, and much shouting and apparent confusion. The Earl of Salisbury had made haste back from the baths. He was bustled in to the room in a chair carried by four men, another man by his side.

There was a moment of stunned silence. Cecil was shrouded in blankets, a thin, emaciated version of his former self, shrunken, wizened and dried out. The skin on his face was drawn tight over his skull like a death's head, only the hard, dark eyes recognisably the same as ever. One hand protruded slightly from the blankets, shaking uncontrollably. This was a wreck of a man, thought Gresham, a pitiful caricature of what had once been. A stench of something foul and rotten came from within the blankets. There was scant dignity in death, and what little that there was had been taken away from Robert Cecil. And what good to you is it now, thought Gresham, that you are the First Earl of Salisbury, that you have held power beyond the desire of monarchs? You have no power over this ignominy, this humiliation that leaves the vision of a demented cripple as your memorial.

'Good day, Sir Henry,' said Cecil. The voice was thin, wavering, but still recognisably the same. It reeked with the same insincerity. 'As ever, it is a pleasure to see you.'

'My Lord Salisbury,' said Gresham urbanely. 'And Sir Edward Coke.' He nodded to the figure beside Cecil. 'Not only the normal pleasure, but a pleasure almost doubled.'

Cecil's companion was a surprise. After Cecil himself, Sir Edward Coke was the man Henry Gresham most loathed above all others. Old now – he must be sixty – Coke exuded a youthful energy, a magnetism that all near him felt. Setting himself up as England's leading legal expert, and of ferocious, icy intelligence and application, Coke had been chief prosecutor at the trial of Sir Walter Raleigh. A charade, the trial had turned Raleigh from one of the most hated men in England into a folk hero, by virtue of its palpable unfairness and the dignity with which Raleigh had defended himself. Denying Raleigh any legal representation, Coke had not even allowed him to call his chief accuser as a witness, and had made a mockery out of justice. Every reason for hating lawyers, and for hating men with no principles except their own vainglory, was summed up for Henry Gresham in the figure of Sir Edward Coke. And now both he and Cecil were facing him.

'Have you both had a pleasant day?' asked Gresham solicitously. Cecil was dying in agony. Coke's idea of a pleasant day was finding yet more reason to hate papists, sodomites and his own daughter, not to mention anyone the King needed convicting at short notice. In Gresham's experience, being nice to such people caused them more agonies than anything else.

'I am lowered into the baths, Sir Henry,' said Cecil in a parody of his former voice, but still with a practical, factual tone to it.

32

'They do it in a strange contraption of a chair they have built specially for me. The ropes snag on occasion, which is not pleasant. My numerous physicians tell me it is important I go no deeper than waist height.'

'Indeed, my lord,' replied Gresham easily. 'I must attempt to be present the next time they hoist you over the watery void, and see if I can cut the rope—'

'My lord. Is this . . . impertinence necessary?' Coke spoke with chilling calm.

Cecil turned to Sir Edward Coke with an effort that cost him dear. The lawyer held Cecil's gaze, then only reluctantly dropped his eyes. A tall, forbidding man with a long, oval face, Coke was ill at ease, unhappy and uncertain with this fencing between the two men. He lusted for control, for power, and hated any situation where power seemed to be ceded to others. Coke had become too used to being both judge and jury, Gresham thought.

Cecil produced something that might almost have been a chuckle, with a strange, dry rattle to it.

'Ah, Sir Henry! So droll, as ever. How much I have enjoyed your sense of humour over the years I have known you.'

'Yes,' said Gresham, 'much as the body enjoys the dagger that enters it, or the hare enjoys the hounds.'

'I wonder if it is not time . . .' Coke's voice was gravelly, sharp, though not pitched at the roar he used in court against those he had decided to condemn. They said he was charming to prisoners in interrogation, turning into a frothing fiend when later he had them in the dock. Cecil held up his hand, the blanket dropping away. Coke swallowed his words, waiting. Gresham looked in horror at Cecil's arm. The skin was discoloured, the flesh almost all wasted away. His lips drawn back over rotten teeth, the gums retreating as if the outgoing tide on a beach, it was clear that even the gesture of holding up a hand for silence had caused Cecil acute pain.

'You think, perhaps, Sir Edward, that if I do not make haste to stop this small talk then I may be dead before we can reach an outcome?'

Coke's self control was enough to resist the sally. 'Of course, such were not my thoughts, my lord.' Outwardly servile, the phrase 'of course' made Coke's comment shiver on the edge of impertinence.

'But you would be wrong to deny it!' Something of the old spirit came back into Cecil's voice. 'You would be right to urge me to make haste, Sir Edward. I command all England, but even I cannot command death.'

No, thought Gresham, though you have commanded enough men to their deaths.

Cecil turned to Gresham, in obvious pain at the exertion. 'Sir Edward is here because he will live on after me. He is a man of power . . .' Coke drew back, and gave a short bow towards Cecil. His face and posture gave nothing away. 'His power will be necessary to see a certain business through. It is this business that will need your help.'

Now it comes, thought Gresham. The muscles in his face did not move, the colour neither rose nor fell in his skin, the pulse in his neck remained constant. Those outward tricks he knew. Yet inside it was as if a slow-burning fire had burst into full riot of flame.

'Sir Edward, you will please leave us for a short while. And, Sir Henry, perhaps that great ox of a man you carry with you might leave as well.'

Gresham nodded at Mannion, and he slipped out of the room, moving quietly and silently in a manner that belied his bulk. Coke was less happy. He drew himself to his full height, chin jutting forward, hand posed on the hilt of his sword.

'Is this wise, my lord?' The thinly veiled arrogance in Coke's voice was like the flick of a whip across Cecil's words. Yet Cecil's authority held, just.

'We agreed that I would approach Sir Henry with a certain

proposal. I wish to do so, in these my last few days on this earth, in private. You will lose no information that you need to know. And you will gratify the whims of an old man to whom you have some cause to be grateful.'

Coke stood for a moment, as if wondering whether to challenge Cecil. Finally he gave a curt nod to Gresham, ruder than no bow at all, and clattered towards the door. He was wearing a sword, probably for no other reason than to show off to the citizens of Bath. Yet he was clearly no swordsman, and like all men who did not understand the weapon they wore he had no knack of controlling it when he moved suddenly. The scabbard swung as Coke wheeled round, and as he reached the door the sword and scabbard jammed across the entrance, bringing him to a sudden halt. The leather of his belt was too strong to tear, but Coke's boots skittered out from under him and he fell forwards to scrabble on the floor. His sword landed at his feet, the hilt towards Gresham.

'I accept your surrender, Sir Edward,' Gresham murmured, 'though I am accustomed to rather more of a fight beforehand . . .'

Coke's eyes blazed pure hatred. He still favoured the huge ornate ruffs that had been fashionable in Queen Elizabeth's time, and his fall had skewed one side of it so that it hung by his ear, ludicrous. He flung himself to his feet, picked up his sword and thrust it back into his scabbard, and left, slamming the door behind him. Dust shot from the hangings and danced in the putrid light that came through the windows.

'Well, Sir Henry,' said Cecil, voice almost back to its old strength, 'you have a quite extraordinary capacity to make men hate you.'

'Thank you, my lord. We share that at least. To be hated by certain people is a privilege. And is there any man who Sir Edward likes except himself?'

Cecil started what might have been a laugh but turned instantly into a cough, a tearing, searing cough that seemed to pour acid from the depths of his belly to his lungs and out through his thin lips. Gresham moved to help him, but he was waved feebly away until the fit ceased.

'Ring the bell, for the servant. He has medicine . . .' For a moment Gresham thought Cecil was going to die there and then. He rang the bell and the servant who had been waiting outside the door entered quickly. From a pocket in the side of the chair he brought a stoppered bottle, and forced some of it down his master's lips. It settled Cecil. At the merest nod, the servant left.

'I will be ready to speak in a few moments,' Cecil gasped, and paused. God knows what this is costing him, thought Gresham. He is shortening his life by every sentence he speaks.

'You are aware of my lord the King's affections towards young men?' Cecil's voice was clear again.

'The whole country could hardly be unaware of them.'

'And do you know Viscount Rochester?'

'My lord, I am in Court on occasion. Who does not know of Robert Carr, Viscount Rochester? I believe also that the good lord was given some property belonging to a friend of mine.' Carr had a special place in Gresham's catalogue of sinners. King James had taken away Raleigh's beloved estate at Sherborne to give to his lover, on whom it was wasted.

Robert Carr, a lowlands Scot with the body of an angel and the brain of a sheep, had been King James's favourite for several years, dominating his company and, it was said, his bed. With Cecil's impending death there would be no barrier to Carr becoming the sole source of favour at Court.

'I understand Viscount Rochester was recently made a privy councillor?' Gresham said, as if it were a point of no real consequence. It was known that Cecil had bitterly opposed the appointment. As his illness had grown, so Cecil's power over the King had been slipping. King James had a morbid fear of death, and the smell of death was all over Cecil.

Cecil ignored the jibe. Gresham knew him too well to believe that he had not noticed it.

'I will be blunt with you. It appears that letters exist between my lord the King and Robert Carr – or Viscount Rochester, as he now is – that are of a compromising nature.'

'How so?' Gresham's interest quickened.

Cecil coughed again and Gresham waited for the spasm to pass.

'I have not seen these letters. I am given to believe they are . . . specific . . . perhaps even . . . highly coloured . . . concerning relationships between men. The physical nature of relationships between men. And between two men in particular.'

'Ah,' said Gresham. There was silence for a few moments. 'I take it that in effect these are love letters between the King of England and his male lover. *Specific* love letters.' Cecil said nothing. 'And,' Gresham continued, 'that were these letters to become public it would not help the status of the monarchy?'

Cecil's eyes turned up towards Gresham. There was more in them than the pain of a terminal illness.

'*Help?* It would destroy all I have worked for in these years of trial! The Church would condemn the King instantly. The Puritans in Parliament would call out the hunt of the self-righteous upon him. The saner element in Parliament would look at the uncontrolled expenditure they are increasingly asked to fund and call foul on a sodomite king. And England would laugh at its monarch! Do you hear me? *The country would laugh at its monarch.* Monarchy can withstand many things – corruption, abuse of power, immorality. Ridicule it finds hardest to survive.'

Cecil had feared ridicule more than anything else in his life. A cripple, the runt of the litter yet brought up as a great man's heir, he had more to fear than many in an age which mocked deformity. Gresham thought for a moment. He settled on a poor stool, one of four by the scarred and battered table in the room.

'There must be more,' Gresham said. 'No monarch has been laughed out of power. The executioner's axe cuts short laughter alongside life.'

This time it was Cecil's time to pause.

'Yes, there is more. The King increasingly withdraws from political life, seeking only to hunt obsessively and spend time with his young men, Robert Carr in particular. Yet this is not the time of Queen Elizabeth, when the only alternative to her was rule by Spain or Civil War.'

'Prince Henry?' Gresham interrupted.

'Yes. Prince Henry.' Cecil's voice was so dry and wasted that Gresham had to lean forward to hear it, like a rustle of dead leaves on the earth. 'We have a brilliant young prince, an heir to the throne who promises more than any other in living memory. A statesman, a man of faith, a man of intelligence and skill – and still only a child! O dear God in heaven! Had I had such material to work with! What a world we might have made!'

The intensity in the whispered voice was all the more frightening because of its fragility, the impression of a man clinging on by willpower alone.

'Well, it is not to be. But there are those, not least of all the Prince himself, who see the way things are going with King James in charge, and who seek a change now, before the monarchy rots beyond redemption. These letters could be just the cause they need – not to kill the King or rise up in rebellion but to force him to step aside for his eldest son and heir.'

'"Had I had such material to work with." My lord Cecil,' said Gresham, 'if the disclosure of these letters would bring about such events, why should you or I oppose them? You yourself have praised the heir. Why not King Henry IX? Why should he not take over?'

'*Because they must not learn how to depose a king and replace him with another!* Do you not see? Parliament, the Puritans, the country . . . once they are given the right to choose a king, they will never lose it.'

'Would it be such a bad thing?' mused Gresham.

'*It would be a terrible thing!*' hissed Cecil. 'Politics can never look at the man. It must always look at the principle. They rid themselves of a king they do not like, justifying it on the basis that the heir is different. Then what follows? What if the heir turns rotten? If he dies? If he offends one of the great noble families, who then turn to one of their own nominees? Then turn to the next best, or the most promising, and do so time and time again. This way is madness. It must not be allowed to happen!'

'And do you think these letters could depose a king?'

'I think a king can depose a king, if the king is a sensual fool whose instinct for survival lessens with every month that goes by. King James is indolent, and confident. It is a dangerous, dangerous mixture. The letters could be the push that topples him over the edge of his own making. *I do not know what will come to pass!* I would know, if God had only allowed me to live, and I had been able to advise and perhaps even influence the outcome for the better. Now others must do it for me.'

'What role does Sir Edward Coke play in all this?'

'It was reported to him that the letters had been stolen, from Sir Thomas Overbury. I suspect Overbury sees Coke as powerful enough to take action, lawyer enough to relish the intrigue and self-serving enough to realise how much credit the safe recovery – and destruction – of the letters would bring him with the old King. In any event, Overbury will work with Coke to regain the letters, which is more than that most impossible of men will do with any other.'

Sir Thomas Overbury was Robert Carr's dark angel. They were inseparable. Intelligent, ruthless, determined and arrogant almost beyond belief, Overbury was seen by many as Carr's manager, providing him with the intelligence he himself lacked. If any incriminating letters existed, Overbury would want their power and be most aware of what the loss of it would mean.

'However, these letters are not all. You are a playgoer, I believe, Sir Henry?'

'I frequent the playhouses when I am in town, yes.'

'Two manuscripts were stolen recently from The Globe

theatre. Both were plays, both written by the man they call Shakespeare. You know Master Shakespeare.' It was a statement, not a question.

The air thickened between the two men. There was a long pause. Finally Gresham spoke.

'I know him, though I knew him first by another name. William Hall, was he not? Or at least that was the name he used when he travelled abroad on state business and claimed his thirty pieces of silver.'

'You overestimate Hall's part in your friend Raleigh's downfall. As does Raleigh himself.'

'I doubt it,' Gresham replied. 'But what I do accept as truth is that Mr William Hall – whose company of players, I seem to recall, suddenly became The King's Men and the most favoured actors in the land very shortly after Sir Walter Raleigh's conviction and imprisonment – has hung up his spying boots and become Master William Shakespeare. Actor, poet and play-maker, no less. He's done very well since Raleigh was imprisoned on a false charge. Very well indeed. Was that the reward you chose for him? To make his disorderly crew The King's Men? And, yes, I know his plays. They are very good, unfortunately. Outstanding, even, better perhaps than any others. Surprisingly so for those of us who knew him when he was doing a different job.'

'You will know what price is placed on these manuscripts, and what security surrounds them.'

There was an insatiable demand for plays for the theatre as companies were putting on sixteen or seventeen shows a season. Any company with a hit on its hands kept the manuscript as secure as a prized daughter's maidenhead. It did not stop rival companies from putting shorthand writers in the audience to scribble down the text of a hit, or bribing leading actors in a company to dictate a verbatim account of their parts – and what they could remember of other people's parts. To lose a manuscript was to give your play to your rivals. Apart from reasons of security, the expense of copying out whole texts meant that full versions of a play often only existed in at most three copies. Actors were given their own lines and cues on separate sheets for rehearsal and learning, and these were counted out and counted in as if the paper they were written on was twenty-four-carat gold.

'Difficult for the players if a manuscript is stolen,' mused Gresham, 'but hardly life-threatening for the King, I would have thought?'

'Life-threatening for the porter who was murdered to gain the manuscripts,' croaked Cecil. 'Yet the players are The King's Men, are they not? They see this theft as an insult to the King himself – or so they say, in asking for his help. But the importance is that our information suggests the same person who stole the manuscripts may also have stolen the letters. A Cambridge bookseller, we think – another reason to call on you and your local knowledge. Identify the man who stole the manuscripts and we believe you will identify the man who stole the letters.'

'So what is my role in all of this?' asked Gresham, frantically working to process the information he had received.

'Sir Edward Coke is a lawyer, not a spy or a diplomat. Whoever has these letters needs to be found, then killed or bought off. Coke would kill readily enough, but he only knows how to do so by means of the law. He lacks the skill to find a secret package, and lacks the experience of dealing with its owner once found. Skills you have in plenty, Sir Henry. And you, of course, know Cambridge very well.'

Gresham's use of his father's wealth to refound Granville College in Cambridge was widely known.

'I am to mind Sir Edward? One of the people I despise most on earth?'

'You have worked with me plenty of times. In comparison, your hatred of Sir Edward is mere flash-frying, while mine has lingered long in the oven.'

'And why should I help?'

'Firstly, because for all your oft-expressed selfishness and lack of faith in anything, you know that peace, continuity and stability are the most important things for this country. These letters threaten all three. Secondly, because Sir Edward needs watching. He is a man of overweening self-importance and ambition. In his heart he does not believe in the absolute power of the king, but in the absolute power of the law – the law as defined and exercised by himself, of course. As things stand, he wishes to find these letters and destroy them. It would take little for him to use them instead to destroy the King. I think you would not wish your enemy to have such power.'

'So I am to find some letters that could blow the present King into hell, but do so while allowing a man I hate above all others to think that it is he who has found the letters. Then I am to watch him, and if needs be kill one of the country's leading lawyers in order to allow a sodomite king uninterrupted access to his pleasures for the remainder of his natural life. And at the same time I am to find stolen manuscripts of plays written by a man who betrayed the one man I truly love.'

'An admirable summary, Sir Henry,' muttered Cecil. 'You miss the final point, however. And by so doing, preserve peace and the reputation of the monarchy.'

'And do you trust me to do all this?'

'I trust you to do the right thing for all the wrong reasons. I trust you to take this whole sorry mess on board because it has the raw smell of danger, and for no other reason. I trust you to think it through after you have taken the decision, and to discuss it with your beauty of a wife and your clod of a servant, and then through the red haze of your excitement see some sense to it. And I trust you to survive, Henry Gresham. For that is your code, is it not? Survival as the prime virtue? For as long, that is, as God decides to spare you an illness such as mine.'

The raw hatred of Gresham, and of his own plight, that burned out of Cecil's eyes would have heated an ocean to beyond boiling.

Gresham took the decision that Cecil had known he would.

'I'll assist Sir Edward. It will be amusing to see how long he can cope with help from someone he loathes.'

'Sir Edward loathes everybody. And he would work with Satan if he thought Satan would help him win his case.'

'Well,' said Gresham lightly, 'you'll soon have the edge on us all. You'll be able to ask Satan yourself, face to face.'

'At least I believe in God, Sir Henry,' grated Cecil. 'At least I may intercede with Him. You, who have no belief, will surely go to hell.'

'If there is a God, He and not you will decide that. As for death, I prefer Master Shakespeare's vision of an "undiscovered country". Perhaps I'll be able to present the record of my life to an unbiased judge when I die. Perhaps, and God forbid, I'll meet the reincarnation of Sir Edward Coke. Perhaps I'll sense nothing except sweet oblivion. You're right, I've no certainty. I echo a line from *Hamlet*: "The readiness is all." There, you see, I do know Master Shakespeare's work.' He paused for a moment. 'I'm ready for whatever I meet, Robert Cecil. Are you?'

For a long moment Gresham thought he had killed Cecil. His head had slumped forward, his breathing had become inaudible. Just as Gresham was about to test to see if there was a pulse in Cecil's neck, Cecil raised his head.

'"The readiness is all"? We are ready in our different ways, I think, and I am certainly ready for what I will meet after death.' Cecil's voice seemed increasingly to be coming from a pile of stinking blankets and not a human being.

Gresham rose to his feet. 'I'll arrange to meet Sir Edward in London,' he said lightly. 'Goodbye, my lord. We shan't meet again, I fear. I could pretend regret. You'd see it as a lie. I wish you well on the journey you're about to take.'

'There is only one certainty, Henry Gresham. It is that you will take that same journey, sooner or later.'

'That's why I wished you well,' said Gresham as he left the room. 'And I intend, my lord, to make it later.'

43

He did not turn round to take a last look at Robert Cecil, First Earl of Salisbury. He wondered, as he slammed the door, whether the dust from the hangings would settle on Cecil, and how long it would be before someone thought to brush it off.

4

May, 1612
Sir Francis Bacon's Residence, London

'No man can serve two masters . . . Ye cannot serve God and Mammon.'

THE KING JAMES BIBLE

Sir Francis Bacon and Bishop Lancelot Andrewes sat on opposite sides of the fire, outwardly companionable enough. Sir Francis, author of some of the greatest works of natural science ever written; Bishop Andrewes, prime component in the greatest translation of the Holy Bible ever published. The two men had waved the servants away, and brought two chairs closer to the blazing hearth. It was summer, but the old stone of the building kept the chill that was so welcome on a hot day but which could bite into the bones at night.

There was a wariness between the two men, something admitted by Bacon.

'We're old friends, my lord Bishop,' said Bacon, gazing into the fire, his hand loosely clasping the goblet of wine. 'Yet it shouldn't be so.'

A thin smile crossed the face of Lancelot Andrewes, Bishop of Ely.

'And why shouldn't the King's Solicitor General and his Bishop of Ely be the best friends in the world?' Andrewes replied lightly. 'We've known each other for many years now. You certainly need someone to safeguard your soul, and at times I need someone to tell me about the way of the real world. We face a common threat, after all. We're both deemed by others to be men of wit. And we've both been disappointed, I think . . .'

It had been a year since King James had made another, weaker man Archbishop of Canterbury, when all the world and its priests thought Andrewes was the only candidate. As for Bacon, his life-long battle for preferment seemed to have stalled on the rock of Sir Edward Coke, apparently the lawyer more trusted by King James.

'All of which is true,' said Bacon, not turning to look at his companion. 'But the real reason's elsewhere. You see . . .' And now he turned to look Andrewes full in the face. 'You, for all your ambition, are a man of morals. I, for all my ambition, have none.'

'All men have morals,' replied Andrewes mildly, his eyes amused despite himself.

'Perhaps. But mine appear to have been lost by the wayside at an early age. It doesn't make me an evil man, you understand.' Bacon spoke as if lecturing a child. 'Indeed, the fact that I've placed self-interest above morality, and made it my substitute, means I'm actually very predictable. Far more so than many who've been bitten by the illness of religion. For example, I'm quite likely to spare someone because they amuse me, rather than kill them because they have a different religion.'

'There's a difference between religion and faith,' answered Andrewes. 'Religion is the institution man erects around faith, and because it comes from man it must be fallible. Faith is what we're given from God. It's pure.'

'Well preached!' said Bacon, without malice. Andrewes was renowned as the best preacher in the country. His sermons were a potent blend of intelligence and wit, but the driving force that drove his congregation to tears was the combination of humanity and sincerity. 'But we really do need to move off spiritual matters and on to Mammon. Or Cecil, to be precise. You've heard he's about to die?'

Andrewes crossed himself instinctively. 'How certain are you?'

'As certain as one can be in these matters.'

'And are you pleased?' Andrewes spoke with no hint of accusation.

'Yes, I think so. He's blocked me all these years, been the main reason for my lack of preferment despite our family links. His death will certainly open up new opportunities for me. But that's not why we needed to meet. Cecil sent a summons out from Bath yesterday.'

'A summons? To whom?'

'To Sir Henry Gresham.'

There was silence.

Andrewes spoke first, hesitantly. 'And what do you think was the purpose of this . . . summons?'

'I can only guess that it's the business that joins us. As far as Cecil's concerned, it's perhaps the greatest loose end in his life. Started by his father, watched over by him but never ended. Now threatening to blow up in the face of the country he thinks he's ruled for all these years past, damaging – perhaps even destroying – the stability he thinks is the inheritance he's left to the future. Gresham is the obvious man to bring it all to an end.'

'Is Gresham as dangerous a man as his reputation allows?'

'In some respects, my old friend,' said Bacon, sipping his wine thoughtfully, 'he's very like you. He has more wit and intelligence than he knows how to handle, a brain as powerful as any I've ever known and as sardonic a sense of humour. He's as restless as you. In the room he occupies, time seems to go just a little faster, as it does in any church where you preach. Oh, and at times he's crippled by a sense of duty. Far too much of this dreadful morality; just like you.'

'And the differences, assuming I accept your rather wild description as holding any truth at all as far as I'm concerned?'

47

'Well now, there's the problem,' mused Bacon. 'Gresham's fabulously rich, so he needs bow his knee to no man, and he's utterly ruthless, sometimes even cruel. He really doesn't care about his own life. He's probably the best fighter – and I do mean fighter, not just swordsman – in the country. He and Cecil loathe each other with a venom I've rarely seen anywhere else, yet they seem to have an understanding between them that no outsider comprehends. If Cecil sets him on the trail of the truth, the odds are more than even that he'll find at least some of it.'

'Are the consequences for us and the others as bad as we've persuaded ourselves they are?' asked Andrewes.

'They vary for each of us, I think,' said Bacon. 'For you and me, there's the fact of us having been involved in a deceit, telling the great public a lie for so long. It's not good for lawyers or for clergymen to be seen as deceivers. Then there's what it is we've been doing. Given the ferment in my Parliament and your Church, we're not clever to be seen as active in that particular field. In your case, the risk is greater. There are things the man responsible for the greatest edition of the Holy Bible ever written can't be seen to be involved with. As you've been so involved. Finally, for both of us, there's the humiliation of the real truth. More so in my case than yours.'

'And for the King?'

'The same. With the complication of these letters. A great complication, I fear. And the madman who has them now.'

The silence hung heavy.

'I won't have him killed.' Andrewes' tone was peremptory.

'Who?' said Bacon, startled out of his reverie for a moment.

'Shakespeare. I won't have him killed.'

'Yet if he's stopped, much of the danger goes away,' Bacon stated factually. The part of his mind that from his earliest days had been distanced from him, an eavesdropper perched over his ear listening and reporting, wondered how this sight would look to an outsider. The Solicitor General and the Bishop of Ely quietly discussing the merits of murdering a man.

'As you've said, I have my morals.'

'I take the point. Yet there must be a chance that Gresham will kill him. There's no love lost between them. Gresham won't be constricted by your morality,' said Bacon.

'I've no control over Gresham,' replied Andrewes, aware of how thin the theological and moral ground was over which he skated.

'Well,' said Bacon, a sigh accompanying his words, 'the job may be done for us, without our lifting a finger. It seems they're queuing up to do away with Master Shakespeare.'

5

Late May, 1612
The Anchor Inn, Bank Street, London

'The evil that men do lives after them,
The good is oft interred with their bones.'

SHAKESPEARE, *Julius Caesar*

The disease was affecting him now, Marlowe knew. He was starting to lose feeling in his hands and feet, could not always sense the hardness of the ground under him as his feet landed and so had the prancing, high-stepping gait of the pox sufferer. The doctor had said the growths would come eventually – hard little carbuncles on his flesh that first blackened and then fell out, leaving a gaping hole behind them. They would be active around his penis, the doctor had said. He would piss like a watering can. The cures could stave off the end, but that it would end in death was inevitable. So little time. So much revenge.

The Anchor Inn was by the Clink Prison and there was little to choose between the clientele of both places. They were all lost souls. The river pirates used the Anchor as their base, as did several highwaymen. A warren of passageways allowed escape down to the river. This was a sump, a noisome gathering place where many of the conversations were in grunts, where men came to become seriously drunk in the shortest possible time and where nameless deals were struck in dark corners. Occasionally a flash of light from one of those darkest corners would reveal a jewel or a necklace being covertly shown, before being stuffed back into the stinking cloth in which it was wrapped. The women here were old before their time, cackling hags at twenty-five years. Marlowe had no pity for them. It was one of their kind that had launched the acid of the pox into his body and into his mind.

He had paid one of the boys to keep filling his tankard. A thin, small-faced creature with a great lump and a bruise on the side of his head, he seemed incapable of moving forward, favouring instead a crab-like sideways walk, his chin permanently held down into his puny chest as if to avoid a blow from any of the roaring mob that frequented the inn. His face was quite beautiful, Marlowe noted, if you cut through the grime and the swelling, the big green eyes and the high cheekbones set off surprisingly well by a mop of auburn hair. His innocence was pathetic. Well, innocence did not last, thought Kit Marlowe.

As his hand caressed the letters he remembered his failure. The porter they paid to guard The Globe theatre had been old, and sleeping off his drink. It had been easy to slit his throat while he slept – who would have thought the old man had so much blood in him? – and pleasurable to watch as he writhed and twisted down the slippery road to hell, trying vainly to scream his fear as the air whistled out through the bloody slice in his air passage. Marlowe had broken into the room as easily as he had slit the throat of the porter, leafed frantically through the hundreds of papers. These were fair copies! Not the original manuscripts he craved! Only one scabby piece worth stealing, and that in the writing of a man long dead!

Marlowe took his grief, as he had learned to do over the years, and folded it over and over until it was a small package. Then he dropped it in the furnace of his hatred and watched it catch light and burn, renewing its strength.

With hindsight, his failure to kill Shakespeare had saved him.

The man he had known as William Hall must know where the papers are, must have lied to Marlowe's spy when he said in his cups that they were stored at The Globe. His revenge would have been wonderfully byzantine, but the devil must be guarding him so that Shakespeare was still living. He would talk, again. And this time Marlowe would make sure it was the truth.

In the meantime, there were other debts to be paid. It would be too simple to kill Henry Gresham. Gresham must suffer, as Marlowe had suffered over the years. There was a most enjoyable way of achieving that end, he thought, as a grin seemed to tear his scarred face even further.

6

Late May, 1612
The Merchant's House,
Trumpington, near Cambridge

'O cunning enemy, that, to catch a saint,
With saints doth bait thy hook . . .'

SHAKESPEARE, *Measure for Measure*

'It stinks!' said Mannion. 'As usual, he hasn't told you half of it,
and the half he hasn't told you is what'll get you killed.'

They were in the library. Gresham had had it built on when he
had first bought The Merchant's House, with long windows set
almost from ceiling to floor and a gallery. It was less splendid than
the library at his London home, known simply as The House, but
somehow it felt more like home. He loved the smoke-free sky of
East Anglia and the glorious cacophony of light in its sunsets and
sunrise. He loved the mist over the meadows in the morning, and
the thrusting turrets of King's College Chapel, forcing themselves
to dominate the Fenland on the ride from Trumpington to
Cambridge. He loved his relationship with Granville College of the
University of Cambridge. His college. His contribution to history.
His only contribution until the arrival of Walter and Anna, his
children after a lifetime when he had thought himself barren.

'Of course it stinks. Do you think I'm fool enough to believe that

what Robert Cecil chooses to tell me is even half the truth?'
Gresham was pacing the room. In front of him were Mannion and
Jane, his council of war.

Gresham had been a bastard son. He had never known his
mother. The whispers had been there as long as he could remember. The fabulously wealthy but elderly banker widowed, his only
child dead. The enforced guardianship of Lady Mary Keys, sister
of Lady Jane Grey and victim of an imprudent marriage. There
was no one left now to confirm or deny Sir Thomas Gresham's
secret, the name of Henry Gresham's mother. At least the distant,
cold figure of his father had taken the boy in, clothed and fed
him, let him roam like a wild young puppy through the house. He
was left to drag himself up in its entrails, adopted in a strange
father and son relationship by Mannion, himself a boy just turned
man. Mannion had been the only servant Gresham's father had
trusted near him in his final days. Gresham had been a non-
person, a boy with no real status, a servant yet not a servant,
gentry yet not gentry. A bastard, but with noble blood. He had
inherited the fabulous Gresham wealth when he was nine years
old. The servants who had been there remembered the thin, wire-
straight boy with round eyes gazing steadily into those of the
ancient lawyer, eyes that did not flicker as the nine-year-old was
told he was now one of the richest men in the country. Henry
Gresham had learned very young how to withdraw into himself.
He had first learned how to fight when, on his rambling through
the night streets of London, street urchins had sensed the smell of
money and set upon him. He had learned at times of crisis to
force all other thoughts from his head, to develop a concentration
of almost unnatural power and ferocity. He was showing it now,
pacing like a wild beast up and down the room, almost unaware of
the others in it.

'What do we actually know?' he asked, punching out the words.

It was Jane who answered. She could not keep the tension out of
her voice, nor, to her regret, the fear. She knew fear was weakness,

prayed that her weakness might not in some way reduce his respect for her.

'We know that whenever Cecil's entered our lives in the past, your life's been put at risk. The man's like some evil daemon, a harbinger of death, pain and suffering. He asked you to get involved in two things: these letters and the manuscripts.'

The tiny part of Gresham's brain that was always distanced from him, watching, waiting, picked up the tension and the fear in Jane's voice. A sharp pang cut across his heart. Fool! How easy for him to turn his agony of worry into the exquisite release of action. How terrible for her, condemned by the way men and women lived to be the passive recipient of his actions. His step did not falter. His eyes did not flicker. He would act, and speak to that fear. Later.

'Let's start with the incriminating letters. Would James be fool enough to write in explicit terms to his lover?' Gresham was acting as devil's advocate.

'Yes,' said Jane firmly. 'The ladies at Court say he kisses this Robert Carr full on the lips in public. They also say he fingers his codpiece as he walks along with him. Quite openly. That's not just a man taking his pleasure. It's someone who wants to fling what he's doing in people's faces, or who's simply forgotten to be discreet. Either way, it's hardly more of a risk writing letters. It's like when he fingers his codpiece, only he's getting pleasure from his pen.'

'Did you say his pen?' asked Mannion, confused.

'Yes,' said Jane with a look that would have frozen hell. 'Pen.'

'Ah . . .' said Gresham thoughtfully. 'Well, let's concede that King James could be so . . . blown away by passion as to put his experiences into writing.' He grinned at Jane, which annoyed her. As this had been his aim, he carried on with renewed vigour.

'But how damaging would such letters be?'

'Very damaging,' said Jane. She was in her stride now, given a role, certain of herself. She knew she was Gresham's eyes and ears, knew his total trust of her judgement. 'The Puritans get louder and louder as the Court gets more and more openly sinful. The Puritans are increasingly powerful in Parliament, and James needs Parliament to approve the money to fund his goings-on.' Jane listened to all the Court gossip and reported back to Gresham. Just as importantly, she listened to the gossip among the booksellers at St Paul's, with whom she had long been a favourite and was almost a mascot. 'The Puritans are looking to Prince Henry to bring a new age of goodness and purity to Court. I suppose they could always try to speed things up and get James to abdicate.'

'So where does that leave us?'

'The manuscripts.' Jane was away now, allowing her mind free rein. 'The stolen play scripts. They have to be more important than Cecil's owning up to, however damaging these letters might be. That's how Cecil's mind has always worked. Always give a dog a bone, and hide the butcher's shop from him.'

'You know how crucial these manuscripts are to the players.' Gresham was unconvinced. 'It's not unreasonable for The King's Men to put in a plea to the King's Chief Secretary to get them back, particularly if the thief is linked to the letters. Yet their value only holds good for other players or rival companies – and the actors might get drunk and brawl but they've never killed each other before for a stolen manuscript. What's so important about these plays? I know there's a power in the theatres Cecil's scared of, something he can't control for once, something that could challenge his law and order.'

'We don't know,' said Jane. 'But Cecil did, and that's what matters. There has to be something we're not being told. They're always is with Cecil.'

'There's something else that bothers me. Why steal only two manuscripts? If you're going to go as far as to murder an old man for them, you may as well take the whole lot.'

'Perhaps the thief was disturbed,' said Jane. 'You can't base anything substantial on the number of plays they took.'

Gresham stopped his pacing and sat down abruptly. The library had a view out on to the river and its peaceful, meandering summer mood, a band of blue winding its quiet way through the green of the pastures. 'And Shakespeare is a traitor. As well as a genius.'

'Are you sure?'

'Shakespeare was as rough as they come when he first arrived in town, and ready for anything. He was a natural recruit for Cecil. The players get everywhere, into Court and into the taverns. They travel the country – Europe even. And they drink and womanise too much and'll do anything for ready cash. Many took different names when they were paid. Shakespeare was always William Hall. Some Stratford link, I think. Raleigh believes it was Shakespeare – in the days when he was William Hall – who hit lucky and betrayed him in the Bye Plot. I've no proof, but straight afterwards Shakespeare's crew were made into The King's Men, and Shakespeare bailed out of the game. Raleigh's sworn to kill Hall, or Shakespeare. By his own hand. He was most insistent it should be by his own hand.'

'Was?'

Gresham turned to his wife, his hand resting lovingly in her hair for a brief moment, running it through his fingers. 'I was on my way to do it myself. Raleigh stopped me. I've his order to kill the man if Raleigh dies in the Tower. If he's ever released, Raleigh will do it as his first act.'

'That much hatred … .' mused Jane, considering the brave, tragic, foolhardy figure of Raleigh, his heart being eaten out every day by hatreds from his lurid past. Raleigh frightened her, not for what he was but for what he was allowing himself to become.

'That much betrayal. Raleigh'd helped the man get a place with the actors in the first place.'

'The theatre's always been trouble, hasn't it?' said Jane.

'It's a new art form,' said Gresham, 'come screaming and yelling into the world. Come to London to be born. Sometimes I think it was conceived by God, like poetry and music. Cecil thinks it was conceived by Satan. He could never see its beauty. Only its power.' Gresham's own sonnets had been published anonymously to wide acclaim.

57

'What's an art form?' asked Mannion, finger in mouth and digging in his tooth for something dead.

'It's when you paint a bottle of wine instead of drinking it,' said Gresham.

'Doesn't sound much fun to me,' said Mannion, adding, with gross illogicality, 'I like the theatre.'

'The Puritans think it's Satan's doing,' said Jane. 'They frighten me, much more than Catholics ever have.'

'We took away the Puritans' natural enemy when the Gunpowder Plot blew the Catholics into limbo,' said Gresham. 'They've no one to hate now, except people who like cakes and ale, and the theatre. Or anyone who has fun!'

'The last time I was at the bookstalls,' said Jane, 'I saw a man with one of those stupid black hats they wear come and let loose a tirade against a bookseller who had play texts on his shelves. It was frightening. His eyes were rolling and half the time all you could see was the whites. He was shrieking, and there was white stuff round his mouth. The bookseller kept having to clean the man's spit off his precious covers. He was scared. So was I. I thought the man was going to do a clearing out of the Temple, and scatter all the books.'

'Men who think God's on their side often have trouble realising they're not God.'

'There's one other bit of stage gossip,' said Jane.

'Yes?' said Gresham, part intrigued and part wanting no more complications.

'They say there's a lost play by Marlowe that surfaced recently. *The Fall of Lucifer.* Apparently it's too dangerous to perform, so wild and heretical that it could shake governments. No one's seen it, though there's lots of talk.'

A strange, unfathomable expression flitted across Gresham's face at the mention of Marlowe's name. Jane carried on. 'If this lost play is so dangerous, and the sort of thing that causes a riot, could it have been this manuscript that the murderer was looking for? On

Cecil's orders? You know how frightened he is of the theatre and its power over the common people.'

'So you think Cecil's real wish might be for me to find this lost play? Hide from me what it is? It's tempting, but it doesn't really work. If whoever murdered to steal these two manuscripts was in Cecil's pay, Cecil doesn't need me to hunt them out. I can't see a link between the letters and these two stolen manuscripts, never mind a play written by a dead man that no one's seen.'

A young serving lad must have pinched a maid laden with bedding as they walked past the door. An outraged but part-pleased shriek was muffled in to silence as the pair realised their master and mistress lay behind the door.

'What do we know about Shakespeare?' asked Gresham. 'What's the gossip about him?'

'No one really seems to know him. He keeps a very low profile in town, and they say that back in Stratford, where he spends most of his time now – he owns half the town, apparently – they think of him as a grain dealer and hardly anyone knows about his plays! He's stopped writing, they say, and wants to sell his share in the company.'

'Well,' said Gresham, 'I suppose I'd better renew my acquaintance with him, as the new man he is rather than the person I knew. I see Sir Edward Coke in London four days from now and I'm not feeling as if I'm going there knowing much more than I did when I left Cecil.'

'I'd be happier steering clear of this Sir Edward Poke,' interrupted Mannion.

'Sir Edward Coke,' said Gresham patiently. Mannion had taken an instant dislike to the man.

'Whatever,' said Mannion dismissively. 'He's trouble. I've got a nose for these things.'

'Be thankful your nose can't smell your own breath, old man,' said Gresham. 'As for Coke, you know I'm no friend of his.'

'No. But you ain't had to fight him before. Not direct. And I bet Sir Edward Joke can stop being funny right quick.'

'Coke . . .' Gresham started to say limply, and then gave up. He turned to Jane.

'Be careful,' said Jane in a sombre voice, before he could speak. Why waste her words? Henry Gresham could act almost all things except being careful. 'You've a weakness. This is the man who gave Raleigh a show trial, who preaches the law and then suspends justice when a king wants a man condemned. You hate him before you know him. Your hatred could blind you.'

'Well, we know more about Coke than we do about Shakespeare.' Gresham was pacing the room again, head down, hardly seeing the others.

'Top lawyer,' said Jane, 'but . . .'

'Go on?' said Gresham.

'The legal booksellers say that he trades on that reputation, and sometimes gives outrageous judgements which no one else dares challenge because of his reputation with the other lawyers.'

'What about the clash with Bacon?' Gresham asked. Sir Francis Bacon had brushed across Gresham's life as an academic author but never as a political opponent. There were very many who disliked Bacon intensely. Gresham had always found him human, amusing and able. He had a brain the size of a Spanish galleon, but much nimbler and faster. Of course he had no morality at all, except to his own self interest, but had freely confessed as much to Gresham with an engaging wit and honesty that somehow robbed his amorality of its venom.

'You know more than I do,' said Jane. Bacon was homosexual, tied to a wealth-generating but loveless marriage.

'I know he's locked into bitter battle with Coke over who'll be the next Attorney General. The popular bet has to be Coke. He's got himself the image of a legal god, he's done James's dirty work for him in court time after time and Bacon can be his own worst enemy.'

Jane prepared to reply, then noticed Mannion looking with excessive interest out of the window. Alice was the newest and youngest of the servants recruited to The Merchant's House, sent to work in the kitchens. A rather bewitching, fair-haired girl, she had been ordered into the kitchen garden to beg herbs for the cook from the gardener. Did she know how her hips swung as she walked into the garden, basket clutched before her? Or was it mere innocence?

'Do I have to warn you again?' Jane's voice was low and so threatening that it stopped even Gresham in his tracks. Fascinated, he watched a rare insight into the hidden relationship between two of the four most important people in his life. 'That girl is in my charge. I talked to her mother, I gave my word she would be looked after. *You will not touch her.*'

Mannion looked direct into her eyes.

'She's simple,' said Jane. 'She doesn't appear so. You might be forgiven for thinking her normal. And she's very beautiful. Her mother was in despair because no one would take her into service and all the men wanted to take her into bed. I said I'd help her. And if she finds her John the Ostler, who'll love her because she's the most beautiful thing he's ever seen, and who'll forgive her a simple mind, then so be it. That will be her choice, and his. But I'll not have her spoiled by a careless and powerful man, in breach of my word to her mother.'

'Well then, mistress,' said Mannion, grinning at her. *Grinning at her?* Gresham was part amused, part outraged. Would he have dared grin at Jane in such circumstances? 'You're lucky to have me on your side, aren't you? There's only one real man who could put her in harm in this place, and only one real man as could protect her. And I'm both.' He ambled over to Jane, as if to put his cup down on the table at which she sat. 'You see, I'm happy to go for the willing. I've never gone for the weak.'

'I know,' said Jane.

'You want her wed to John the Ostler?'

'He needs to love someone other than a horse, and her simple nature won't stop her being a good wife to him.'

'Leave it to me,' said Mannion.

And they both smiled.

'Excuse me!' said Gresham, 'and hello. Is there any possibility of my being allowed back into this conversation?'

It was rare for Jane to flush, but she did so. It was left to Mannion to resurrect the conversation.

'We were talkin' about Sir Edward Bloke, weren't we?' asked Mannion innocently.

'Sir Edward *Coke*, you blunt-wit ignorant peasant!' shouted Gresham, his patience at an end.

There was so much he did not know, the clinical part of Gresham's brain was telling him. Well, inaction would find nothing out. That sense of total concentration that Jane and Mannion knew so well came over his whole body.

'London. All of us. To meet Sir Edward. And to visit the theatre.'

7

26th May, 1612
Sir Edward Coke's Home, London

'The first thing we do, let's kill all the lawyers.'
SHAKESPEARE, *Henry VI*, Part 2

Sir Edward Coke had let it be known that he rose at three o'clock every morning in order to extend his working day. It was an easy story to circulate and, thought Gresham, easy to maintain once it was established, without actually having to get out of bed.

They set out at noon. It was only a relatively short walk from The House, with its favoured position on The Strand, to Chancery Lane. Gresham and Mannion could have taken a boat, ridden or taken the vast coach that Gresham's father had had built when those cumbersome contrivances had been fashionable. Today Gresham felt the need to walk, to get back in touch with London's ebb and flow, feel its pulse.

It had been dry for weeks and within seconds a thin layer of dust covered Gresham's boots. The clouds hanging loose in the sky threatened rain, had done so for days. At least they were spared the sucking, clinging mud, but not the steaming piles of horse shit littering the road or the stained yellow and brown earth where night soil had been thrown carelessly into the street. The smell of grass still blew in from the green fields visible past the houses on the northern side of The Strand, to mingle with the stench of the river and the open sewer that occasionally the street was allowed to become. Then there was the endless, richest smell of all: the smell of humanity. The perfumes and scents worn by the wealthy men and occasional lady; the nosegays of sweet orange or apple designed to ward off evil vapours; the sudden, intrusive, raw stench of sweat from the carters or porters carrying huge loads on their bending backs; the stale, warm, sickly sweet smell of the men and women who could neither afford clean linen nor to have what linen they owned washed every day.

The nearer they came to the old City walls, the closer together the houses grew, the more cramped and crammed the streets. The steep-pitched roofs almost touched their opposite neighbours. When it rained an avalanche of water poured from the roofs on to a few yards of street below, digging a trench with sheer force of water. You could sink deeper than your knees into the mud of a London street, and leave your boots in the sucking mire when your friends dragged you out. The noise was incessant. The cries of the street traders were everywhere, raucous, yelling, insistent.

Coke may or may not have stinted on his sleep but he certainly did not stint on the furnishings he allowed himself. Mannion had been left in an ante room with a sniffing and disapproving clerk. Coke's study was vast, with crimson taffeta curtains and a turkey foot carpet laid over polished boards. The wall hangings on three walls were particularly fine. Coke must have had them commissioned. One showed Solomon giving judgement, another Moses damning the Jews for their worship of a golden idol, with a smoking mountain in the background. Very judicious. At a guess, Sir Edward Coke wanted to be Solomon and thought he might be Moses. It was only a short step for him to believe that he was God.

'Good morning, Sir Henry.' Coke spoke as if to a rather poor and badly behaved Ward of Court. He gave Gresham the merest glance and continued to inscribe a careful signature on the document in front of him. 'I am, as you see, most busy, most busy indeed . . .' The table at which Coke sat was littered with papers and bound volumes. He had not risen as Gresham entered, an act of extraordinary rudeness. Gresham adopted a solicitous expression and sat down on one of the ornately backed and armed chairs on the other side of the table, without being asked. From the slight stiffening of Coke's body Gresham knew he sensed the return discourtesy. *Touché*. One all. Gresham's eye was caught by not one but two fine portraits of Sir Edward, posing magisterially, adorning the wall over the vast fireplace, and a third showing him with what Gresham assumed was his first wife and vast brood of children.

'It's a pleasure to come and meet you, Sir Edward,' said Gresham in his most understanding and sympathetic voice. 'Unlike your busy self, I've nothing at all to do with my time.' Coke did not look up. He was too much in control for that. But he had, Gresham noticed, managed to ruin one of the letters by the jerk his hand had given in response to Gresham's remark. He had done it just as he was forming the 'o' in his name, so that one missive was now apparently signed 'Ed. Cqke'. Gresham carried on. 'It's also always a pleasure to meet someone so exalted who is yet so . . . humble, so . . . well-mannered and lacking in vanity.'

Coke put down his quill, measured, making sure Gresham knew he was not hurrying. This was not a man to be underestimated, Gresham reminded himself. Coke had survived and flourished too long in the bitter, adversarial world of the law for that.

'You should know, Sir Henry, that the Earl of Salisbury is dead. He died yesterday at Marlborough.' Coke spoke solemnly, playing the part.

Cecil dead?

'Oh, good,' said Gresham, that same infuriating bland smile on his face. 'I'm so glad.'

That did get through to Coke. He had too much self control to rise from his chair but his colour roared up the scale towards red and Gresham saw his scrawny Adam's apple bobbing up and down several times as he swallowed. The skin was leathery, wrinkled, that of an old man.

'You are . . . *glad*?' asked Coke, voice barely under control, rasping as if from a dry throat.

'Delighted,' said Gresham.

This man was an amateur! thought Gresham. He almost found himself missing Cecil. At least Cecil would never have let his true emotions show under such simple goading.

'How typical, Sir Henry, that you should go for a *theatrical* effect rather than deal with a serious matter with any degree of substance.' Coke put a special measure of loathing into the word 'theatrical'. Was he a Puritan? Gresham wondered. Or just someone who hated the thought of people letting their hair down and enjoying themselves.

Coke paused, and sipped from a king's ransom of a glass goblet. 'Quite frankly, Sir Henry, I was never able to see why the Earl wished you to become involved in this business.'

Coke's overwhelming sense of his own value and significance would never let him see why he could not be trusted with all and everything. Sharing a job was to Sir Edward Coke as much of an anathema as sharing a prosecution.

'No, Sir Edward, you would not be able to see why the Earl wished me to become involved in this business. I suspect my late Lord of the Flies recognised your weakness, which is that you think you know so much. Such people are a risk to themselves. They need to be placed with those who are willing to admit their ignorance.'

'You claim to know too little?' asked Coke, flat-voiced, his lawyer's brain leaping like a ferret at a rabbit's throat. He was almost visibly working to categorise and pin-point the nature of his opponent.

'I claim to have been *told* too little by my lord Cecil, and to recognise all the dangers to myself that lie therein. But then again, I'm more than used to working to Cecil's half-orders. You, I think, are a novice.'

'You are so little concerned for your own life that you would risk it, by your own admission, for you know not what?' asked Coke, his fish-eyes giving nothing away this time.

'Good, Sir Edward, very good,' replied Gresham. 'Our language is starting to reverse. Your questions are becoming shorter and shorter, my answers longer and longer. If this carries on I shall start to reveal more and more about who I am to your lawyer's brain. Is this always how you trap witnesses?'

'I do not trap witnesses.' There was acid in Coke's voice. Gresham said nothing. The silence between the two men lengthened. It was Coke who broke first. 'I care more for the law, and for justice, than you can ever imagine,' he said.

'How can you know what I imagine?' asked Gresham.

'Do not play with words with me!'

'Isn't that what lawyers do?'

'How can such as you presume to be a man of law?'

'I don't presume. I have too much self respect,' Gresham replied self-deprecatingly.

Cut. Thrust. Parry. Cut. Thrust. Parry. Gresham was starting to enjoy himself. Coke was energised now, the power almost visibly flowing through his ageing body. He spoke with scorn, hurling his words at Gresham.

'Self respect for yourself! Self! It is all you know, all you can speak of! The law speaks of respect for all people and their rights. Your self respect is little more than glorified selfishness!'

'True,' said Gresham. The best way of disarming an opponent was always to recognise when he spoke the truth. 'Yet my adoption of selfish survival as my creed is a response to those such as you who plead the law and justice as your creed, using it as a cloak for your greed and vanity.'

'A feeble defence!' grated Coke.

'Honesty is no defence against corruption, and never has been. Honesty merely makes men weak.'

'The honesty of the law is its strength!' said Coke, as if stating a truth that could not be denied.

'It would be, if it were honest.'

'A feeble plea!' said Coke, voice full of scorn.

'True again,' said Gresham. 'As feeble and as frail as the humans you tear to pieces in your courts. Yet the difference is that you claim to be honest to all people while seeking power and wealth through your sycophancy. I know only how to be true to myself.'

That seemed to halt Coke in his assault. Had there once been a decent man buried among that arrogance, and had Gresham somehow reminded him of the betrayal of his soul?

'So what is it that you live for, Sir Henry?' asked Coke, part scornful, part in fear.

'*For my honour*, Sir Edward.' Gresham said it simply, with a dignity that undercut the crowing of Coke's legal brain. 'So that when death comes to me, I will be able to say that for all the stupidity of this life, at least while I lived I made things happen. To say that I survived. To say that I kept my honour, my self respect and my pride.'

Coke was trying to answer, Gresham could see. Half-formed words seemed to launch up into his throat and work the muscles there, but somehow died before they reached his mouth. Finally his words emerged.

'So you will die happy, Sir Henry?' Coke tried to put a world of sarcasm into his words but somehow the sting was lost.

'No man dies happy. I hope to die at peace with my honour, Sir Edward. You? You pretend to serve the law yet serve yourself. I hope you die with honour. I suspect you will die merely with possessions.'

There was a long pause.

'It doesn't matter, really, does it?' said Gresham, his voice almost kind. 'You see, we only need to work with each other.'

68

'*Can* you work with me on this matter?' Coke's voice had regained its composure. The previous conversation had been inconvenient. It had provoked thoughts of the wrong kind, therefore it had been dismissed. Not forgotten, but placed somewhere in a file where it could be coldly remembered without impacting on present day reality. Good, thought Gresham, very good. Not as good as Robert Cecil, not yet, but getting there.

'I can work with Satan if I have to,' said Gresham. 'After all, I came near to doing so when I worked with Robert Cecil. As I was saying, shall we get down to business?'

The two men looked at each other. Again, Coke broke first. He glanced away, down to his long-forgotten papers.

'Then, as you said, we should get down to business. These letters that were stolen. Cecil had spies.' Coke raised an eyebrow in Gresham's direction. 'Spies other than yourself. They reported that a Cambridge bookseller had been involved in the theft. Rumour, you understand, only rumour, based on one single instance where a man who *might* have claimed to be a Cambridge bookseller *might* have tried to sell letters to one of Cecil's agents which *might* have been the ones we are seeking to find. That was one reason why the Earl thought of you to help us out, with your knowledge of Cambridge.'

'Does this bookseller have a name?'

'It is here, somewhere . . .' Coke rummaged among his papers. 'Ah, yes! "Cornelius Wagner". How very elaborate . . .'

A sudden, vague chill took Gresham's heart. Cornelius Wagner. There was no bookseller called Cornelius Wagner in Cambridge. Gresham knew them all. Yet he also knew of a Cornelius, and of a Wagner. Where had he heard the name?

'I had hoped to meet you with Sir Thomas Overbury,' Coke said, 'but it appears he must have been delayed . . .'

There was a ruckus outside the door then, shouting and a heavy thud. The door impacted inwards with a sharp crack and the servant whose head had appeared round the door earlier was flung into the room by what was clearly a hearty kick from the man standing in the doorway. The servant's head was bloodied from a cut that ran across his forehead. He was crying with a mixture of shame and anger, his hand wiping away tears and blood until they mingled and ran down his wrist to stain his shirt with a pink wetness.

'Sir!' The servant tried to speak. 'I am so sorry, I . . .' Coke raised a hand to silence him. The boy rose clumsily to his feet, a tear ripping half the leg of his hose. He bowed his head.

'You may go now,' said Coke, gazing at the figure in the doorway.

'Insolent pig!' said Sir Thomas Overbury as the servant scuttled past him, hand raised to ward off further blows.

As a consequence of his close relationship with James I, the vast majority of the King's correspondence was passed on to Robert Carr, unopened, for him to deal with. Carr, whose brain was small as if to compensate for his magnificent body, passed it on unopened to his oldest friend, Sir Thomas Overbury, who then dictated the answers. Overbury had brains enough for both of them. A tall, handsome figure capable of biting wit, his power as the *eminence noir* behind the King's favourite had added to his natural vanity and arrogance, until he was frequently described as insufferable by even the mildest men at Court. The King tolerated him because he was in love with Carr, but in truth, he both distrusted and disliked Overbury. Queen Anna, otherwise a feather-brained and overblown lapsed beauty, hated Overbury with unequalled venom. In a rare display of power, Queen Anna had forced Overbury to flee to Paris the year before. He had been allowed to return simply because without him Robert Carr had floundered under the duties imposed on him by the King. It was a very tender and fragile truce.

Overbury advanced into the room. He ignored Gresham completely. 'Your servant is insolent, Sir Edward,' said Overbury, peeling off his fine-fitting gloves and flinging them carelessly upon the table. 'He presumed to question the time of my arrival. I've been deep in matters of state. I disciplined him, as you saw. It were better, of course, to come from his master.'

Well, well, well, thought Gresham. This one is very special. He looked with amusement to Sir Edward Coke.

It must have been Overbury who supplied details of the theft of the compromising letters to Coke. Why else was he here? The loss of these letters must be truly embarrassing. For all that he had made a show of his entry, and been deliberately late to make a point, the fact remained that Overbury *was* here, and at Coke's bidding. Rescuing the letters would therefore give Coke huge credit in Overbury's eyes and, in all probability, the eyes of Robert Carr and King James himself. It would also give Coke a huge moral advantage in his dealings with the King should he choose to act as saviour, and, the cynic in Gresham noted, an equally huge opportunity for blackmail.

Were the letters in King James's own hand? wondered Gresham. If they were, and Coke recovered them, he held the whip-hand over James. If they were in Carr's hand they could be more easily dismissed as forgeries. Either way, Carr could lose huge favour with the King if he was responsible for the permanent loss of such damaging letters. If Carr's reputation was at stake, then Overbury would be involved.

Yet how on earth was Sir Edward Coke, a man of no small vanity himself, going to rein in his tongue in the face of this wholly offensive, reeking apology of a man? This is going to be more fun that it first seemed, thought Gresham.

Overbury sat down without invitation and knocked a few papers aside to show his superiority. His gaze wandering round the room, he finally allowed it to fall on Gresham.

'Gresham,' he said flatly, with a raised lip, an expression of total scorn and without so much as the merest nod of his head. It was extraordinarily ill-mannered. Duels had been fought and lives lost on the basis of lesser insults. Good manners were not simply outward courtesy. They were the measure of the respect in which a man was held.

Overbury swivelled his eyes round the room once more, then brought them back to rest on Gresham. Just at that moment Gresham's pupils seemed to enlarge. It was as if Gresham's gaze had decided Overbury was of no importance and looked through him in search of something of significance. Along with the eyes that did not seem to see him, Overbury was aware of the queer, sardonic half-smile on Gresham's face. It was as if he was being mocked and ignored at the same time.

'Gresham!' Overbury's venom reinforced the insult. 'Why do we need a . . . *spy* to help us in this matter?' Overbury spoke to Coke. His tone was scornful, dismissive.

Gresham did the one thing Overbury found it hardest to cope with. He ignored him completely. His eyes turned from the window at which he had been gazing, through Overbury without registering his presence and on to Coke's own eyes.

'As I was saying, shall we get down to business?' Gresham asked of Coke, outwardly thoroughly relaxed.

Overbury's mouth dropped. 'Cease your petty games, Gresham!' he announced, 'or I'll have to break your pate as I broke the servant's!'

Do I let it take its course now, or do I back down? This man would never bend, thought Gresham. So let it take its course.

Gresham waited politely for Overbury to finish, then carried on as if Overbury's words had never been spoken. So strong was the impression given by Gresham that there was only he and Coke in the room that Overbury almost had to shake himself to confirm he was actually there.

'Cecil was of the opinion that these incriminating and embarrassing letters must have been stolen from Carr or Overbury. If we're to do business, we really do need to stop playing games. I'm assuming that the letters were stolen from Overbury.' Gresham's tone made for no recognition whatsoever that Overbury was in the room with them. 'Overbury's clever enough to know how potentially explosive and destructive such letters would be. He's treacherous enough to keep them for future use against either his friend Carr or the King. He's arrogant enough and fool enough to lose them, and hated enough for any of his servants to risk stealing them if they thought that by doing so they could harm their master.'

There was a moment's silence while the enormity of what Gresham had said sank into Overbury's mind. He exploded. He leaped to his feet with a roar.

'You cur! You dog! You whore's whelp!' His sword was half out of its scabbard and he was rushing to fall upon Gresham . . .

. . . and suddenly he was flying through the air, landing to the sound of a sickening crunch followed by the sharpest stab of pain and then blissful unconsciousness.

The pain was the first thing he remembered as he came to, the sharp, red-hot pain and the bubbling noise as air tried to pass to and fro between the blood from his nose and mouth. Dimly he heard a voice. It was Gresham.

'. . . so all in all there's little likely to result from our investigating the point at which the letters were taken. Whoever did it will cover their tracks. Equally, whoever took them will want to make either political or financial advantage out of them. They'll have to make themselves known. This Cambridge bookseller might do just that. Cecil's spies will have prided themselves on the fact they found this man out as having some involvement. It's more likely he made sure they knew what was going on. It has to be this bookseller. Here's where we'll have our chance to retrieve the letters. The real question is whether we do it on his terms, or invent terms of our own.'

Sir Edward Coke was frozen to his chair, eyes passing rapidly between Gresham speaking fluently and clearly to him and the tumbled heap of Overbury lying on the floor. It was not so much the fact that Sir Thomas Overbury had been knocked out and bloodied while launching an assault on Gresham. It was the sheer clinical speed with which it had been accomplished that had silenced Sir Edward, and provoked real fear in him for the first time he could remember in many years. He had almost forgotten the taste of fear. Things had happened in a blur of movement. Overbury, goaded, had embarked on a mad rush towards Gresham. Gresham had hardly seemed to move, merely sway to one side. The momentum of Overbury's forward rush was such that it carried him onto Gresham's outstretched foot, tumbling him over and forward across the floor to crash into the far wall, head and nose first. In a blur of movement, Gresham had resumed his seat almost before Overbury had ceased moving – surely it could not have been so? – and carried on talking to Coke as though nothing had happened. The servants had rushed through the door. Gresham had ignored them. Even the one with the broken head who might just have been smiling as he saw the mess that was Overbury on the floor. Coke had motioned them away.

They both became aware that Overbury was stirring back into a painful consciousness in the corner.

'You must interview Overbury's and Carr's servants to find out as much as you can about how the letters went missing. I will interview Master Shakespeare. It's almost certainly a waste of time. Yet it has to be done.'

Coke spoke sharply. 'The manuscripts are secondary. Plays are not our concern. Letters are.' Coke was showing that phenomenal capacity to take unpleasant facts and sideline them, lock them away so that they did not interfere with his management of the moment's business. Yet was the tone just a little too urgent in dismissing these plays? Gresham immediately racked them up to a higher priority.

Sir Edward Coke glared balefully at Gresham. He had thought Gresham an irritant and an inconvenience when Cecil had insisted on informing him of the missing letters and manuscript, but necessary if the one thing that Cecil and Coke needed to happen was to take place. He had agreed to Gresham's involvement because he had believed that Gresham was being used as livebait. Now the bait had revealed himself to be an extraordinarily dangerous figure. A dreadful fear crossed Coke's heart. Was he using Gresham? Or was Gresham using him?

'Do I have your attention, Sir Edward?' Gresham's tone was solicitous. Coke had done something he had spent a lifetime training himself not to do, drifted away from a conversation. Cursing inwardly, he dragged himself back. 'We must understand one thing, Sir Edward.'

'And what exactly is that "one thing"?' asked Coke, his voice almost a hiss.

'I don't for a minute believe that I've been told the whole truth. But as Robert Cecil might have found time to tell you before he died, I usually do find the truth eventually.'

'What do you believe?' snapped Coke.

'I believe I've been told some of the truth. I believe in these letters, and I believe both they and some play scripts have been stolen. I believe both items have the capacity to get someone important into deep trouble. I believe there is a hidden agenda which means you need me to flush out the thief because you can't or daren't do it yourself.'

This was so close to the truth that even Coke could not stop a tiny tremor from crossing his face.

'Quite,' said Gresham, noting the tremor. 'I repeat: I do usually find the truth. You and Cecil believed I was an arrow that you could shoot in the direction you wanted. Your arrow has become a hawk, a lethal weapon with a mind of its own.'

Coke had always hated hawks. The total, unflinching, single-mindedness of their eyes, their utter focus on the prey, their inability to be distracted or diverted both undermined and angered him in a way he did not understand and could not therefore control.

Overbury groaned, rubbed his face and threw up as he felt and saw the blood on his hand. He tried to get to his feet, but fell on all fours.

'But don't worry too much,' Gresham said to Coke, almost sympathetically. 'Hawks get killed too. Who knows? Perhaps this is when my luck will run out.'

Coke tried not to show on his face just how very much he hoped that Gresham's luck would truly run out.

'By the way, Sir Edward,' Gresham said as he rose to leave, 'there's a foul stench in this room.' By the merest movement of his head he seemed to gesture towards Overbury. 'A stench of something rotten. Perhaps one of your hounds is so old or ill that it can't stop itself from breaking wind.'

There were no hounds in the room. Coke viewed them as unhygienic and anarchic.

'Such animals are dangerous. For all that they're useful, they can infect their masters with their own corruption.' Gresham flicked a speck of dust off the arm of his glorious velvet and silk doublet. 'If for pity's sake you can't have them put down, then you're well advised to keep them at a distance.'

Two sets of eyes directed glares of undiluted hatred at Sir Henry Gresham as he left the room.

Overbury dragged himself to the table. 'I . . .' he began to bluster.

'Will you be silent for once?' hissed Coke. And, for once, Sir Thomas Overbury remained silent. 'Gresham is dangerous. Above all, he's dangerous. You saw how dangerous. God knows why you seek to taunt and antagonise everyone you meet.'

Overbury flushed, and lowered his bloodied head. 'Why do we need Gresham?' he mumbled through bloodied lips. 'If he is so . . . dangerous, why welcome this viper to our bosom?'

Do you ever listen, Sir Thomas Overbury? thought Coke. Have you ever listened in your life?

'We need Gresham,' Coke explained patiently, as if to a child, 'because the Cambridge bookseller is Christopher Marlowe. Kit Marlowe. Diseased, syphilitic. Returned from the grave with homicidal mania for all those who wanted him dead, and for all those who conspired in his exile.'

Sir Thomas Overbury vomited over the table, the thin yellow spume staining a multitude of papers on Coke's desk. It seemed to make him feel better. He sat up, ready to speak through his battered lips. Coke decided to get in before he did so. The acid, sweet smell of the vomit filled his nostrils.

'Marlowe simply wants to destroy: the King, the monarchy, you, me. He came back into the country with enough information from his past to do very, very serious damage. He stole those damned letters – from you, Sir Thomas! – so now he has even more powder in his gun. And he has the manuscripts. He wants to see his damned play—'

'*The Fall of Lucifer*,' croaked Sir Thomas. For some reason he had remembered that.

'Yes,' said Sir Edward, looking at his own fallen and bloodied Lucifer, '*The Fall of Lucifer*. He wants to see his damned play performed, and is convinced it will provoke a revolution.'

'Nonsense!' said Sir Thomas, learning how to speak again and fingering his lips. 'Plays don't provoke rebellion!'

'No?' said Coke, stung to a response. 'And when my good, and very dead, Lord Essex mounted his rebellion, didn't he inspire it by commanding a performance of *Richard II* by that upstart crow Shakespeare? The rebellion failed. The provocation worked very well.'

'Oh God!' said Overbury, 'I'm sick at heart.' He sank down in his seat.

'I think, Sir Thomas,' said Coke, 'that you're sick everywhere. We need Gresham because *we can't find Marlowe*. Cecil believed that if we set Gresham on to Marlowe, Marlowe will rush at him like an old man at a whore.'

Overbury raised his head again. 'And kill him?' His tone was almost lascivious.

'Possibly,' said Coke. Good God! he thought. Overbury was now tracing patterns on the wood of the table with the yellow fluid of his own vomit. 'But more likely draw him out and be killed himself. Safely killed, with no direct government involvement.'

'So we hope that Marlowe goes at Gresham like an old man at a second, young wife?'

Coke had recently married again, to a young girl who was leading him a merry dance. Suddenly Coke knew why so many people wanted to kill Sir Thomas Overbury. I will ignore this, he thought. That foul fiend Gresham has shown me the way. *Ignore him.*

Overbury's finger paused in the middle of an intricate pattern. Most of the patterns had arrow-point heads, Coke noted. Overbury lifted his head once more. The effect was spoiled by the blood that smeared his whole face and had dried into his beard. Yet it was not spoiled for Overbury. For he had not just been bloodied and beaten by an opponent. It had never happened. It had been wiped out of his mind. Perhaps he even had the power to force his mind to cut off the signals of pain. All the old arrogance returned, his beating dismissed. It was a pity Gresham was not there. He would have noted the short-term effect of hitting someone and pointed it out to Mannion. Mannion believed in things that could be eaten, drunk and slept with. In addition, he believed anything that did not work properly, particularly human beings, responded to a careful, cautious and judicious thumping.

'Who can guarantee that any man will kill another? Gresham? Scum. A spy. A double-dealer.'

'How easily could he have killed you, Sir Thomas?' said Coke in words of ice.

For another moment at least, Sir Thomas Overbury was silent. God help them all, thought Coke. They had released an uncontrollable force of nature on to the hunt for Kit Marlowe. They had placed all their money on one bet, that these two very different forces of nature would neutralise each other. Gresham would find Marlowe and kill him. Then a source would be closed off, permanently. Or Marlowe would find Gresham and kill him. Then the only person who could find the truth would be dead, and the only dangerous person who knew the truth would have revealed himself, and so made it easier for him to be murdered.

It had to be the right policy. Yet why did Gresham's presence in it fill him with such dread?

8

26th May, 1612
The Globe Theatre, Bankside

'. . . within this wooden O . . .'
SHAKESPEARE, *Henry V*

Rain had fallen, perhaps only for a few minutes, while Gresham and Mannion had been inside Coke's house. Slight though it had been, it had calmed the dust and placed little diamonds of light on the crazy, leaning rooftops.

Mannion looked enquiringly at Gresham, who had halted and was gazing abstractedly up at the sky. Then, to Mannion's surprise, he turned on his heels and started to walk. In the wrong direction. Mannion swung his eyes around instinctively. No one was watching them, or no one doing so obviously. No sudden interest in the fine gentleman and his purse walking down the street, no nods between two or three men with one setting off to bump into Gresham while another cut his purse from his belt. Reassured, Mannion set off after his master.

They were going to The Globe, the round 'o' of a building with its centre open to the elements. It was late afternoon when they reached their destination, that afternoon's performance finished, the crowd long gone and evening already starting to set in.

'What are we doing here?' muttered Mannion. He could see the reason for their long walk if there was a play to see, but no reason at all to visit an empty shell of a building.

'Looking,' said Gresham absent-mindedly. 'Just looking.' A theatre was naturally easy to defend, he was thinking. Entrances were kept down to a minimum so that everyone who went through one had to pay, and the high, outside walls of the building had little need for windows.

It was that time of day when no lantern was strictly needed to guide the way, but its warmth would still have glowed in the failing light. Gresham went to one of the narrow ground level entrances. The wood was thick but scarred and dry, leached with age. Gresham tried the iron handle, rattled the door. The great white curtain wall of the theatre was cross-hatched with the squares of its timber beams, standing out more and more as the gloom deepened. There was give between the latch and its lock, enough for a crow-bar to wrench it open, but it was secure against anything except a direct and brutal assault. It was quiet now, especially after the noise and yelling bustle of the great city on the other side of the river, and Gresham waited while the echoes of iron on iron could be heard to ricochet around the vast empty space of The Globe. Nothing moved. No one stirred.

Gresham looked enquiringly at Mannion.

'Someone killed the porter here not so long ago?' Mannion asked. 'Glad they've tightened up their security.' He spat thoughtfully into the damp earth at his feet, looking carefully to see that his spittle was clear. Satisfied, he hitched his belt up round his tunic and waited for Gresham to decide what to do next.

They started to walk round the girth of The Globe. Others would have looked for a lantern, for servants to guard them. There was a casual ease to Gresham's walk, his hand carelessly on the hilt of his sword, and clear menace in the bulk of Mannion. An onlooker would have sensed why these men needed no extra guard.

The theatre seemed deserted, silent. Like all great buildings that come alive when thousands throng into them, there was an almost death-like concentration to its stillness when empty, a sense of artificiality and yet of a great beast sleeping. Why did some buildings have a sense of history being made in them, thought Gresham, while others, outwardly more important, seem bland and inert?

They reached full circle. No sign of a new porter. Was he safely locked away inside, too terrified by recent events to explore the noise by the door? What had happened on the night of the murder? Had a door been left unlocked, by accident or on purpose? Had the porter been called to the door or had he known the person who had summoned him? Had it been someone already inside the theatre who had turned on the old man?

Too many questions, sighed Gresham. There always were too many questions. He had learned to stop the rampaging flow of his mind, haul himself back, restrict his questioning to one answer at a time. Well, there were no answers at The Globe, not yet. Except perhaps one. The King's Men were clearly not expecting a second break-in at their theatre or security would have been positively hanging off the walls. There was no shortage of ruffians and ex-soldiers to stand guard for those who had enough coin to pay them. Was that an answer in itself? Did it mean that those who ran the company had some reason to know that there would be no repetition of the break-in?

'Boat?' asked Mannion hopefully. It was their quickest way home, and Mannion hated walking nearly as much as he hated washing. There was not an ounce of excess fat on his great frame but how he kept himself as fit as a twenty-year-old was a mystery to Gresham, who had never seen him voluntarily work up a sweat.

'Boat,' agreed Gresham, his mind still wrestling with what he had seen and the realisation of just how much he did not know.

Behind them, the white mass of The Globe dominated the skyline, enigmatic, silent and empty.

9

25th June, 1612
Granville College, Cambridge

'The middle of humanity thou never knewest, but the extremity of both ends.'

SHAKESPEARE, *Timon of Athens*

In winter it was cold and damp in Cambridge. The chill winds blew in from Siberia. The low mists that breathed out from the river in the early morning gave a sense of mystery to everything they touched, as the snow gave a sense of magic. At night, with a clear sky, the moon picked out the stone and buttresses of the colleges with cold clarity, bathing them in white light. With snow on them they became monuments of stunning beauty.

In summer, even on the brightest day, the air was often thick and heavy, as if infected by the Fens. The flies were everywhere, even staying on meat as it was speared by the eater's knife and lifted to his or her mouth. The river flowed like a dark sludge, stinking, its water seeming to thicken as it slapped against the hulls of the boats plying their trade, staining the painted wood. When the air and the smell became particularly thick Gresham had seen people freeze in their tracks in the muddied street when a man sneezed. The plague looked over Cambridge's shoulder at all times, the sneeze one of its first symptoms.

Gresham was back in his rooms at Granville College, the rooms in the medieval court he had claimed from the first days when his wealth had started to reinvigorate and refound the college. The shelves were country carpentry, rough-hewn but solid and not bending beneath the weight of books and papers Gresham had loaded on them over the years. Gresham doubted his guest for the evening had noted the books. He doubted he could read.

Candlelight usually hid a multitude of sins. In LongLankin's case it exposed them. The gentle light of the wicks flickered across LongLankin's face, revealing it for the battleground it was. Two or three huge boils disfigured his face, crusted volcanoes, enough to throw long shadows across it when the light glanced in a certain direction. The few teeth in his face reinforced the black, gaping holes where the others had been, emphasising the empty space rather than compensating for it.

'I dunno,' he said, 'I just dunno.' He swilled the remnants of his small ale round the tankard Gresham had filled for him. LongLankin never drank wine. Maybe he thought it might make him middle class.

'Let's try again,' said Gresham. '*Remember*. What did this book-seller look like?'

'I told yer. I were drunk. I was rubbished. I wouldn't 'ave recognised me own mother if she'd shoved her tit in me mouth.'

'LongLankin,' said Gresham with evident distaste, 'please: spare me the details of your weaning.' No one ever called him 'Long' or 'Lankin'. For some reason, he was LongLankin. One word. Indivisible. And he was very drunk, with the memory of an alcoholic colander.

'Look,' said LongLankin, 'It's as easy as this.' He spoke with the certainty of someone who has completed the drunk's progress. Sober. Mellowed and softened. Drunk. Very drunk. Trashed. Unconscious. Awake and in agony. Nearly mellowed and softened again. 'He were . . . a man. Shrunk. Warped. Dwarfed.'

'LongLankin,' said Gresham with a patience he did not feel. 'That doesn't help me find him. To be frank, Cambridge isn't agog with news of shrunken dwarves claiming to be booksellers—'

'Plays!' LongLankin had remembered something. It was a new experience, and he was clearly pleased with it. A smile appeared on the linked crevasses of his face. One of the boils on his neck, Gresham noticed, had a single tuft of thick hair sticking out of it.

'Plays?'

'He said he . . . said he did things with plays.'

'What did he do with plays?' asked Gresham, intrigued, his boredom forgotten.

'Said . . . said . . .' LongLankin's memory was fading again, like a candle guttering out its last few moment of light. 'Said he wanted the students to put one on, like. Y'know, like they do.'

Gresham knew. There had been riots lasting two days last year when the John's men, coming to see a Trinity comedy, had been locked out for shortage of seats. The John's men had tried to break into the college, and the Trinity men had taken to hurling the heaviest objects they could find from the rooftops and gatehouse. Plays were hot material in Cambridge.

It was no good. LongLankin could tell him no more, and all he had confirmed was the existence of a man masquerading as bookseller, and the link to the theatre. Gresham bundled the semi-comatose man out of the room, and sat back in the high-backed oak chair. It was at a moment such as this that he savoured his loneliness. It was a huge luxury, another privilege of his vast wealth. Most of the other Fellows would board three or four students in their rooms, the Fellow taking the main bed, the students on truckle beds.

So there was a man who called himself a bookseller, appearing suddenly in Cambridge. Yet the few people this man had introduced himself to had heard nothing about stolen letters from the King to his lover. Plays. It was all he had talked about.

Plays. Theatre. Was this about politics? Or was it about plays? The only certain thing was that it would be about power. It was always about power. Gresham needed to regain his feel for the theatre. He and his family would go to the play.

10

July, 1612
The Globe Theatre, Bankside

'King: "What do you call the play?"
Hamlet: "The Mousetrap."'

SHAKESPEARE, *Hamlet*

Summer was the best and the worst of times for the players. The best was when the weather allowed the old theatres to be packed to the hilt, with a roof open to the heavens. The worst was the plague, which could close the theatres and take the actors from roaring profit to catastrophic loss and god forsaken tours of the sticks. So far in 1612 their luck had held.

Going to the play was a ritual in the Gresham household, and huge fun. Soon they would consider bringing the children, but as things stood it was an outing for Gresham and Jane only. And, of course, the servants. Mannion considered it his divine right to accompany his master and mistress everywhere they went. Gresham also paid for some of the more senior servants to go with them, as well as some of the young ones. In return, the servants had to row the great eight-oared boat that was the pride of The House to deliver themselves and the couple from The House's own jetty across the bustling river to within a few hundred yards of The Globe.

'So which idle varlets do we take to the play today?' asked Gresham, squaring his bonnet and straightening the sleeve of his doublet.

'Well,' said Jane, ticking them off on her fingers, 'there's Harry, of course, as boat captain. And I think we ought to reward the younger Harry, the one who joined us two years ago. He's put himself out to be pleasant, and he works like a horse. Then there's Jack in the stables—'

'Can any one of them *row*?' interrupted Gresham.

'Well,' said Jane, smiling sweetly, 'we'll all of us know the answer to that very shortly.' Jane commanded intense loyalty from the servants, despite an occasional fierce temper and on very rare occasions an ability to revert to her peasant upbringing and adopt a very forthright and robust style of conversation with a servant thought to have pocketed the occasional item, or bought two chickens but magically only delivered one to Cook. At such moments a dread hush descended over The House and people walked on tip-toe.

There were a few low clouds scudding across the blue and a brisk wind lifted their faces as they came out of the Water Gate and advanced down the stone jetty. The lapping of the water was music to them, alongside the creaking of the wood and the shouts vaguely heard from the river. Coming up to midday, the river was at its busiest. Every type of boat, from the gilded splendour of a king's barge down to the tiny, rotting tub with only one oar carrying what looked like a beggar erratically cross-stream, was scurrying up and down the length of London's main street. With a brisk wind, those that had it put up sail, the stark white of a brand new set contrasting with the faded and yellowing canvas of the commercial traffic. Ropes snapped across the wooden pile of the masts, sails cracked in and out as the wind blustered, and everywhere was the lap of the tiny wavelets on the wooden hulls.

Their boat was for eight oarsmen, four to each side, with room at the prow and stern for easily that many passengers. Gresham and Jane took their seats at the stern, covered by a sumptuous awning. Jane had never favoured the pearly white complexion of the court lady and Gresham loved the subtle tinge of bronze her perfect skin always carried. She seemed impervious to sunlight, her upbringing having given her an immunity denied to other Court ladies. Gresham had questioned the need for the awning, designed to keep the sun off a lady's skin as much as to keep off the rain.

'Surely you don't need that great waste of money flapping over your head?' he had asked.

'My lord!' she had exclaimed. 'What would the world be coming to if Court ladies only demanded what they strictly needed?'

The motley collection of servants grinned at them in delight as they climbed on board, doffing their caps, not hiding their excitement and pleasure. What better day could it be? They served the handsomest man and the most beautiful lady in London, and were viewed with awe by other great men's servants because of their master's dark reputation. They had good food in their bellies and good cloth on their backs. They were to ride in style on the best boat on the Thames. The sun was shining, there was a snap in the air and they were off to the playhouse. It was good to be alive on that fine July morning.

'Well,' said Gresham, standing and looking down at his men as they pushed off, 'can you sorry-looking collection of apologies for men find the strength to hold an oar? Or have we wined and dined you and kept you in such luxury that with one pull you'll be moaning that you can do no more?'

The response was eight oars hitting the water in unison, and a massive surge out into the river that would have had Gresham off his feet had he not known exactly what was coming.

'Feeble!' he said mightily, gazing down on them with the half-smile that his face fell into in repose. 'Well, keep trying. At this rate we might make it for the third act.'

Gresham sat down again and raised an eyebrow at Jane, who was gazing out across the river with fascinated concentration. Mannion, behind them, had a firm grasp of the tiller.

The river here was fast-moving, muddy brown even in summer and with a blue sky. Unlike the Fleet river, which was little more than a stinking ditch of sewage, there was a semblance of health if one did not look too closely into the brown water. Yet only the crassest of fools would drink from it. Neither Jane nor Gresham had ever washed in it.

The flag was flying bravely from the thatched roof of The Globe, a many-sided brick and timber construction dominating the skyline. They landed the boat at a private jetty whose owner guaranteed secure berthing, and whose collection of thugs (most of them his own children) would have frightened off Attila the Hun and all his hordes had they come a-thieving.

The men held the boat while first of all Jane and then Gresham crossed on to the shore. Gresham looked down on the head of the younger Harry.

'Ready for the play, then, Harry?' Gresham took care to know all his servants by name. It was, he thought, one of the basic gestures of respect to the people with whom one lived and on whom one depended.

'That right I am, sir!' grinned Harry, tousled hair ruffed up by the brisk wind.

The roads leading to The Globe were narrow, and the vast coaches that some of the audience insisted on using could block whole streets, as had happened today. Gresham, Jane and his men marched through the throng and on to the gate that they and some of the more select of the audience used to gain access to their seats. The doorkeeper nodded them through. Gresham was well known. More and more mutton dressed as lamb going to the old theatres, thought Gresham, with each year that went by, despite divine visitations from the likes of whoever was in the coach. Further sign that the richer and better bred went to the indoor theatres, leaving the old ampitheatres such as The Globe for riff-raff. Oh, there was quality enough still, if one looked. The lawyers and MPs who had always supported The Globe were still there, but fewer, and there were more young men in cheap shoe buckles and rosettes, with extravagant embroidered waistcoats in appalling taste and bursting their seams because of cheap thread almost as soon as they were worn.

'Sir Thomas! How delightful to see you again!' Gresham spoke easily as the figure of Overbury clambered up the narrow stairs to the first tier. Overbury started, and turned around. His face was a mess, Gresham noted happily, a riot of black and blue bruising around his mouth and nose, ascending to a massive black eye. Overbury's lip curled as best it could.

'The bastard and his whore!' he sneered at Gresham, daring him to fight, hand on his sword.

It was beginning again, thought Jane. Her stomach turned cold. The hatred. The violence. Men pitted against men. At least in the village that had spawned her you could predict the relationships, awful though they might be. Here, in the world of a Court lady, bitter hatred could be revealed in a glance from those who knelt together at the communion rail, vicious enmity enflamed by a chance meeting at the theatre.

'Why, Sir Thomas,' said Gresham, 'there's no need to refer to yourself in those terms. We all know you've no breeding and that your mother was a whore. But those of us who frequent high society know that the best sort are always liars.'

Sir Thomas made to draw his sword. Something in Gresham's easy smile, and the men who moved to his side, stopped him. He gazed at Gresham, scorn enough in his voice to blister paint.

'You will pay for that. Not here. Not now. But in some other place.'

He turned, and with his servant brushed aside the bodies crowding up the stairs as they strode purposefully down them.

They took their seats, their servants in front of them. Gresham watched the audience, as much a show as the play itself. For many of the young blades the theatre was somewhere not to watch but to be seen. Preening and pandering, they were so tightly corseted they could not bend, and their vast collars or ruffs seized their heads and necks as if in a vice. Their hats rose like steeples into the sky, marking them out. Forced by the clutch of starch and lace to gaze down stiffly on everyone they saw, they could only look at a person by swinging their whole body round to face them. The apprentice boys were out in force in the Pit, brawling, scuffling and swearing to impress the schoolboys who would pay twice over for their place, once by their precious penny and another by the thrashing they would endure, bent over the block, as a result of their truancy.

The tier was full, unusually so, apart from the benches Gresham's money had reserved. Gresham was relaxed, happy. The momentary stain of Overbury's presence had rippled but not dented his composure. It seemed to have upset Jane more, but now she was gazing happily around her, nodding to an acquaintance, sharing as they all did in the excitement of so many people gathered in one such small place, feeding off the raw human energy the sheer intensity of contact generated.

There was what the players would call a fanfare of trumpets and what Gresham would call an unholy blast of noise. It was the traditional start to a play.

The audience called it *Beatrice and Benedick*, after the hero and heroine who were deeply in love but whose bickering and witty battling for position had caused audiences to howl with laughter and cry with sympathy for years. It was one of the plays that had made Shakespeare's name, a play loved by both the Court ladies and the groundlings in the Pit. The actors called it *Much Ado About Nothing*.

The play was beginning. A duke-like figure, gorgeously costumed, was speaking to two girls. The boy actors playing the girls were breathtakingly convincing.

'I learn in this letter that Don Pedro of Arragon comes this night to
    Messina . . .'
'How many gentlemen have you lost in this action?'

The first gallery usually housed the men of substance. There were
other, more private boxes in the tiers, but the first gallery was a
favoured and expensive spot. Gresham's mind had already engaged
with the play, the extraordinary way in which a few words from a
painted actor could take two or three thousand souls instantly into
a strange court in a foreign land, and make them believe they were
there. A distant, detached part of his mind noted that among the
wealthy audience who patronised the tier were an unusually large
number of heavy, thick-set men. Which other gentry had brought
their servants to the play? he wondered idly, without sufficient
interest to look around and trace the man.

'I pray you, is Signior Mountanto returned from the wars or no?'
'He hath done good service, lady, in these wars.'
'He is most in the company of the right noble Claudio.'
'I will hold friends with you, lady.'

The house was restless. Sometimes in a play the noise would
lower itself to a gentle hum, the nuts be consumed early on. Those
selling their produce or their bodies in the Pit would be drawn into
the play themselves. At other times the house spun and buzzed
like an angry wasps' nest, the actors clinging on to every word and
holding on for their lives. For no apparent reason, this was such a
day.

'Good Signior Leonato, are you come to meet your trouble?'
'I wonder that you will still be talking, Signior Benedick. Nobody
    marks you . . .'

Something extraordinary happened. Three rather beautiful, pure amber lines of liquid arched from the very top gallery and splashed gently on to the crowd below. Confused, thinking it raining on a sunny day, men and women looked up, open-mouthed, and caught the liquid on their upturned faces and in their lips.

It was piss. Human piss. An appalling, humiliating, unbelievable insult to the honour of those soiled in the mess. Three louts had stood on the edge of the top gallery and pissed on the groundlings in the Pit.

There was an almost soundless roar as those desecrated in the Pit caught sight of the men who had dared to do this. As a single, heaving mass, the men among them, and a few of the commoner women, made for the stairs to confront their attackers.

Oh God, thought Gresham, as realisation of the truth banged down inside his mind like portcullis after portcullis smashing down on stone. There was chaos in the Pit, uproar as those dirtied by the act were ignited by it in a riotous desire for revenge. Panic spread through the two and half thousand souls in the audience, the play forgotten, reality smashing through the play's carefully wrought fantasy. Those not set on revenge rose to their feet, drew their loved ones to them, looked around in confusion.

Under cover of this total chaos, unseen by the audience blinded by fear, Gresham noted with horror the fourteen or fifteen men dressed as servants rise to their feet as one, reach inside their tunics and rough jerkins and draw out hardened wooden cudgels or wickedly edged cheap knives. Their target was clear.

Gresham.

Jane.

For a single, terrible, bleak moment, Henry Gresham gazed full into the face of his own death. In less than a second the appalled realisation of what he had done thudded into his brain. Lulled into false security. Seduced into relaxation by pleasure, like the man knifed at climax by his lover. His servants, his eight men, were here to enjoy. They were not armed. He started to draw his weapon out from the scabbard, as if in slow motion. It would be there fully two or three steps ahead of the man fixedly charging at him, club already upraised. He would, he could kill that man. *But what of the horde of others that followed him?*

He was too much of a fighter to take his eye off the man who would either be killed or who would kill him: the first in the mad rush of his attackers, the one with the brute strength to have hurled himself to the forefront of the charge on Gresham. Yet part of him disengaged from his main self, almost as if it floated above him.

Something extraordinary was happening.

His men were standing on their seats, drawing weapons from their tunics and jerkins. There was panic in their eyes, fear, confusion. The look of soldiers. The glint of metal. Boat axes! A heavy, short wooden shaft. A glinting, razor-sharp cutting and chopping edge on one side, a vicious sharp point on the other.

Mannion. Shouting orders at them. Not shrieking, nor yelling. Shouting – clearly, firmly, almost calmly. Mannion, who had risen to his feet a split-second before the attackers, a crucial, life-saving split second, to warn their men of danger. Mannion, who, for no reason he nor any other human would ever know, had quietly ordered the boat crew, as he usually did, to take the boat axes out of the locker, and a knife or two if they wished.

Just in case.

Gresham used his other arm to fling Jane viciously to the ground. Never taking his eyes off his attacker, he waited until the man had drawn back his cudgel for the blow that would have smashed in Gresham's skull. At that precise moment he flicked the blade of his sword across the man's face. He caught one eye, missed the second by a hair's breadth. The shock was terrible. Even though Gresham's flick had not caught a single muscle controlling his arms, the man's hand suddenly flexed open as his eye exploded and the club flew out of its grasp. Caught by his own momentum, lunging forward, Gresham stepped up on to the bench as his assailant, his face a bloody mess, flopped by him to crash senseless to the floor.

Someone screamed. Jane. Some primeval communication made

him look not at her sprawled body on the floor but to his left. He had chosen the right assailant. The man rushing at him from the right had been the nearest, the most dangerous. Yet the man rushing down on him from the left had been only a second behind. Gresham's brain had mathematically computed the threat and turned instinctively to the right as the greater risk. It left him with no time to deal with the man charging in from the left.

The man had a short, flat forehead and thick, bushy eyebrows. For a moment Gresham's sword felt as if it weighed several tons, as if the act of dragging it round to meet his second assailant would take a whole lifetime.

Would his sword have met the man from the left before his cudgel or his knife met Gresham's flesh? He was never to know.

Suddenly, unexpectedly, a hole opened up in the forehead of the second attacker. A flicker of light, and a boat axe was embedded there, between the bushy eyebrows.

As of a moment the light of life was expunged from the man's eyes. His sightless, mindless body flung past Gresham as had the other man's. Mannion had flung the axe. Mannion, hauling a second boat axe from his jerkin even as he yelled encouragement to Gresham's men.

One or two seconds, that was all it seemed. One or two seconds for the first of the attackers to be halted by Gresham, the second to be killed by Mannion. One or two seconds to cause the mass of men to falter, shocked at the sudden loss of two of their fellows. One or two seconds enough for Gresham's men to hurl themselves to their feet and gather round their master.

The attackers wavered. For another second it looked as if they might halt, turn and run, but their momentum as much as anything else carried them forward. They broke on the curtain wall of Gresham's servants, the strong keep of Gresham and Mannion, a double line before the prone body of Jane.

There was a sickening thud as body met body, club met flesh and muscle and sinew fought against muscle and sinew. The men grunted as they landed their blows, grunted as they took a blow and felt the pain searing up their limbs.

One of Gresham's men was lifted half off his feet by a blow from a cudgel, flung back into the benching. Another man, scarred face, missing teeth, broke through a gap and lunged at Gresham. Off balance, Gresham lunged back, using the extra length of his blade, knowing that a swordsman against a club had only one chance. His sword pierced the man's shoulder. He screamed and fell, hand clutching the wound. Gresham's blade was stuck, in flesh or ensnared in the rough woollen cloth. With a final sobbing heave he yanked it clear.

They had to reach the back wall of the theatre. They had to position themselves so that they were only dealing with an enemy coming at them from the front. Thank God Jane was wearing a skirt more like a countrywoman's, without the huge hoops and farthingales a more vain person would have chosen.

The three men who had pissed on the Pit had vanished, the surge of men and women hunting for them dissipated in the long haul up the stairs and the fruitless search of the top gallery. There was chaos, men and women looking fearfully up at the roar of battle coming from the first tier. They were streaming out of the theatre as fast as the cramped exits and their legs would allow.

Three attackers had come leaping at four of Gresham's men.

'Get to the back wall!' Gresham yelled, his voice cutting through the shouts and screams. Clambering, clambering all the while for that damned wall. Thrusting as the pack closed in. Feeling their hot breath, the stink of garlic from one, the dreadful stench of rotting teeth from another. Keeping that grip on Jane's wrist. The grunts, sharp, spasmodic explosions of breath from both sets of men. Muttered curses, shouts, a scream as a blow landed. Feeling with his feet the broken benches beneath him. Only able to risk the quickest of glances backwards.

Young Harry had tripped over a bench and exposed himself to a blow from a swinging club. It hit his ribs, blowing the breath out of him. Just as his assailant was about to land a final blow on his pate, Harry turned aside, dodged. The club intended for his head smashed on to a bench. Splinters flew, the bench cracked near in half.

A rough, hard surface bit into Gresham's back. The wall! Now they could point outwards, a sharp-tipped semi-circle daring someone to break it. Jane suddenly dropped down behind a broken bench. Wounded? No, thank God. Sensible. Gresham was dimly aware of something lightly flitting past his face, a thud following on a short moment later. A fly? A bird? He had no time to ponder it. Was this Overbury's doing? Revenge for his humiliation? So where was he?

Some of the attackers were losing heart. This length of battle was not what they had been paid for. Yet by now the theatre was almost empty. The thugs decided to make a last throw of it.

They had guts, he would give them that, thought Gresham. That, or they were being extraordinarily well paid for their thuggery. The attackers hurled themselves at the line of Gresham's men. With Jane secure behind the upturned bench, Gresham leaped forward, sword in hand.

Two of Gresham's men went down, but several of their assailants grunted, screamed or dropped like stones. Gresham's line swayed, seemed to buckle but then flexed out again. Knocked back, the man who was the leader of their attackers turned and swore at the rest for being cowards, and then leaped forward, flinging himself at the line with immense courage from the height of a bench. Whatever else he may have been, he was no coward.

He was a thin, wiry figure, with a goatee beard and small, close-set eyes. As well as a club, he brandished a long knife. Screaming, he leaped forward with his club arm upraised.

Suddenly, his hand was no longer attached to his arm. The severed body part, with the club still clenched in it, dropped to the floor while a jet of bright red blood shot from the stump. The man looked on in disbelief at his own hand falling to the ground. The blow Gresham had delivered with his sword was almost impossible.

Bone needs an axe to slice through it, not a sword blade. A sharp edge helped, of course, but the real trick was a flick of the wrists – it could only be done two-handed – at the point of impact that delivered all the strength not just of the swordsman's arm but of his whole body. There was a sickening thud as Mannion delivered what must have been a death blow, breaking soft brain tissue as well as bone.

The attackers looked at the severed hand, the smashed head of their leader, the stump of his arm. Without a word, to a man they turned and ran. They were disciplined, still, after a fashion. There was a scream from one of them, and they turned to pick up their own. Eight or nine were grievously wounded, but still able to walk or be supported. Two of them dead? Three? Gresham reckoned it could not be less. Four with their leader. Two of the attackers, one heavy built, the other a light weight, made to grab their leader, legs stuck ungainly over a bench. Gresham's men growled, moved forward.

'Hold!' said Gresham. It was a croak, no more. His throat was dry beyond belief. It was enough. His own men held back. 'Take him,' said Gresham to the mob. His sword pointed at them, menacing, all-powerful.

The two men looked at him. His authority was complete. They darted in, grabbing the body, the bloodied head bumping pathetically as it dragged over the bench and floor. Gresham's men did not move. The heavy-set man flung the body of his leader over his shoulder. The stump of the arm was still losing blood, a thin stream now, almost in droplets. The pale, pathetic thing that had once been a human hand lay on the planks, still.

Gresham reached back to grasp Jane's wrist.

It was not there.

Then he heard a scream. Jane. Jane's voice. 'THERE!' it said.

He turned, and his heart froze in his ribs. Jane, his beautiful girl, the thing he loved more than life itself, was smeared in blood, huge blotches of blood on her face and arms and the bodice of her dress.

Where was she wounded? Where was she wounded?

Then he realised that the blood was not hers but the blood of the man whose hand he had severed, flailing over her like an obscene shower. Her eyes were wide open, and the hand Gresham had grasped so tightly was pointed over his shoulder, behind him. A part of his brain found time to notice the rough, red marks all round her slim wrist, where he had manhandled her and held on with such force.

He turned, feeling as he did so that his every movement had been slowed down ten or twenty times, noting Mannion's mouth open ever so slowly in warning, suddenly inhabiting a world of total silence. There, almost on the other side of the theatre, was a warped figure in a black cloak, the hood thrown back to reveal a whitened and shrunken pate with a wig ludicrously hanging off to one side. He held a crossbow in his hand, the bolt resting in its groove and notched, the string cocked. Slowly, ever more slowly, Gresham saw the fumbling hands, hands behaving as if they could not feel the wood and iron, raise the crossbow and hold it rock steady.

He must have watched the whole fight. Organised it. Hidden the crossbow earlier. His insurance.

The finger tightened on the release. There was a twang. The figure threw the crossbow away. It tumbled to the floor, and the figure scurried out of The Globe.

A scream of agony tore its way from Gresham's heart to his throat, but he heard nothing. He saw the bolt leave the weapon, and with agonising, awful slowness compared to the speed of the bolt turned again to thrust Jane to the ground and himself in front of her. But his hand found nothing on which it could push. Jane had dropped to the ground with a lightning reaction. With nothing to block his momentum, Gresham knew his body would coincide exactly with where Jane's body would have been, with exactly where the bolt was heading. With the very last of his strength he sought to twist in mid-air, to at least present his arm and rib cage to the bolt rather than his exposed back.

100

He was like a man doing a back-flip over a high bar, feet just off the ground, head flung back, chest arched upwards, when the bolt struck.

It pierced his doublet as if the satin was thin air, and ran across his rib-cage with such precision that the line of its passage was not marked with red swathe over the whole flesh but simply with reddened areas where the upwards thrust of his ribs had felt its passage. The bolt thwacked into the rear wall with massive force, embedding a third of its length into the soft timbers. Pinioned, Gresham hung by his doublet for a moment, suspended, face up to the sky. Light, sound, colour and heat returned to his life as by the click of fingers.

Mannion, in the last second of his mad rush towards his master, crashed over the broken bench and tumbled on to his back.

'God's blood!' said Gresham, drawing his head up to look at the bolt that suspended him from the theatre wall.

A quiver of something that might have been release ran through Mannion's body. Picking himself up, but making no attempt to remove the pin that hung his master from the rear wall, he announced casually, but in a loud voice, 'I've told you what happens to people who hang around the theatre.'

The smooth silk of Gresham's fine doublet, any more than the linen of his shirt, offered no resistance to the steel of the crossbow bolt. Gresham dropped unceremoniously to the floor, in a tangle with both Mannion and the blood-stained Jane.

Suddenly Mannion's comment was the best joke ever made by anyone in the history of the world. Young Harry, a great wound on the side of his head already beginning to dry and blacken, started it with a thin, almost insane giggle. It spread through the other men, to Mannion, to Gresham and to Jane, so that they rocked and sobbed with laughter, making the very floor shake.

Their laughter did not last long. For many the pain was too keen to be overlaid by relief. One man was unconscious, another still only half conscious. Three others were coated in their own blood, groggy, confused, nursing wounds that made walking difficult. At least one had a broken arm. Others would find, in a few minutes, as the red heat of battle dissipated in their blood, that they had broken a finger or even a rib. Those that could stumbled to their feet, the wounded ones pathetically trying to smooth their dress while new red blood seeped through the blackened mess.

'Not bad,' said Mannion matter-of-factly, 'for beginners. Not bad at all.'

They stiffened with pride. Proud of what they had done. Proud of what they had prevented. Proud of their master, who had out-guessed their enemy from the start, who had thrust himself forward at perilous danger, who had risked his life first and in some strange way not commanded but rather asked them to risk their lives second, if that was their choice. And, if the truth be known, proud of their mistress. No screaming, no pouting, no fainting. A mistress who had become in a moment a soldier, one of them, obeying orders. Who could look at her and deny that she was a woman? Yet who could see her courage and deny that she was in every vital respect a man?

'Thank you,' said Gresham. They nodded. It was all that was needed. The talking had been done by their weapons, their bodies and their courage. 'We need to get young Harry home to some clean water and a bandage,' he said easily. 'And we needs remember that there could still yet be an enemy out there for us.'

That sobered them, the thought of the men they had fended off regrouping, waiting for them in the narrow streets outside.

The world had heard about the disturbance. There was excitement in the streets, women huddled in corners looking up quickly as they passed, pointing, gossiping. They put Harry in the centre of their group, with Jane, who saw no shame in helping to hold him up. The crowds, chattering, watching, curious, parted before them as they marched, heads held high, alert, towards the boatyard. They reached it without incident, followed by a crown of street urchins. Even they were silent for the most part, gripped by the stern, dark figure of Gresham and the startlingly blooded figure of Jane, who had only been able to clean off a portion of the mess in the theatre.

'D'ye want a man or two to help you back over the river?' asked the surly owner of the boatyard, moved to interest for once.

'Do we need help?' asked Gresham. His men stiffened, looked offended. 'No, thank you. We don't need help.'

The wife of the owner rushed out, a dumpy little woman with three chins and rosy cheeks. She carried a jug of clean water and a surprisingly clean cloth. She was all flustered.

'My dear . . . mistress . . . I just wondered if you might want to . . . I mean, I don't know what's happened, but . . .'

Jane gazed down silently on the head of the woman, who was becoming increasingly sure she had made a dreadful mistake with the great lady. Fancy calling her 'my dear'! Why, what was she . . .

Jane put her hands on the woman's shoulders. Surprised, the woman lifted her head. Jane planted a kiss firmly on her forehead.

'You're the kindest thing I've seen all day,' Jane said.

'Oh, my lady!' said the woman, blushing from her roots, overwhelmed. 'Do keep the jug and the cloth . . .' At that she rushed off back into the timber-framed house she occupied with her husband. A few moments later, Jane's face and hands at least were clean.

'Can you helm a boat as well as fight off an enemy?' Gresham asked Jane.

'I'd build the bloody boat myself if it got me home and into a bath!' she muttered, gathering up her skirts and grabbing the tiller, a huge tract of her mind still numb, anaesthetised by shock.

Only three of the men were fit to row. Mannion and Gresham looked at each other. Gresham pulled off his doublet. There was a film of blood on his shirt where the crossbow bolt had grazed his ribs and the collar he wore was torn. Mannion took up the place by his side, replacing young Harry and the other most seriously hurt man. The men grinned, amused by their master taking on their role.

Gresham turned to Mannion. 'Old man, whatever you do – don't breathe over me!' Mannion belched contentedly and settled to his oar. 'Now row!'

And they moved out of the wharf, limping in comparison with the speed they had made when they left the jetty at The House only a few short hours ago. They were clearly a grand boat, of the sort to attract attention anyway. The presence of someone who was clearly a gentleman at an oar, wounded men at the back of the boat and, most of all, a glorious beauty manning the helm, got them more attention on the crowded river than the Armada had when it first entered the Channel. There were whistles, hoots and then cheers from professionals running the ferries back and forth, which in turn attracted the attention of all the other traffic on the river. Before long, they had an admiring escort of small and some quite large boats, intrigued, following them to wherever they were going.

Someone from The House must have spotted them, and spotted that this was not a normal return. Figures began to gather on the jetty. More and more joined them, until it seemed that every occupant of the warren that was The House was gathering to welcome its lord and its mistress. A hush fell on the assembled crowd of servants, from the might of the steward to the lowliest of the kitchen boys, when they saw their mistress's bloodstained clothes, and wounded men in the bay of the boat. They counted the numbers. Had everyone come back? Then young Harry raised his head and managed a grin, and one of the other wounded waved a greeting. There was an almost explosive roar of relief as the gathered crowd realised that all their team had returned, and that even the wounded were walking. A huge rolling cheer rocked the jetty.

There seemed to be hundreds of hands reaching out to grab the prow of the boat and ground it. Jane, her lips pursed in concentration, was determined to make no mistake. The boat kissed the jetty as lightly and as delicately as a mother kisses her firstborn. She's about to burst into tears, thought Gresham. That first quiver. It's there. She's had enough. He rose to his feet, rocking the boat.

'Next time,' he said loudly, matter-of-factly, 'steer a little finer, will you? Otherwise, that was *quite* good. For a woman.'

She looked at him and stiffened. The tremor vanished. Three weeks of words passed between them in an instant. Gratitude. Annoyance. Anger. Amusement. Understanding. Fear. Pride. Worry. Total exhaustion. Gresham went to her, took her hand. He looked over to what must by now be every resident of The House except, he dearly hoped, the gateman.

God, he was tired, he thought. As ever, there was the physical tiredness. But it was the mental exhaustion, the throbbing pain in his head, that was by far the worst. Yet he had to say something, didn't he? The whole house had gathered to welcome their master and mistress home. They would remember this for generations, tell each other stories into the small hours of the morning as the filched candles in the servants' hall guttered and died. He glanced at Jane. She nodded, imperceptibly. How not to sound pompous and vainglorious? How not to patronise these men and women, who had fought for him and shown every willingness to die for him. How to say the impossible?

'Thank you for your concern,' said Gresham, bloodstained, a thin line across his chest and on his arm where a glancing blow from a club had scathed his skin. Not for a moment did he realise what an extraordinarily violent, dark and powerful figure he cut.

The boat was bobbing under him, uneasy in the short, choppy waters of the jetty. He kept his feet easily.

'We went to the theatre, and a group of men liked us even less than the play. There were . . . how many of them were there, young Harry?' asked Gresham theatrically, looking at the bloodied figure still slumped on the deck.

'Fifty!' came the clear reply, to a cheer from the others in the boat.

'So we defended ourselves against a hundred men,' said Gresham seamlessly, to a roar of laughter from his assembled servants. 'And, of course, The House won.'

There was an uproar from the assembly. The reality of blood, and pain, and man's vicious inhumanity to man, excused by jokes and bravado. Unbidden, lines came into his head. Shakespeare. *King Leir*.

> As flies to wanton boys are we to the gods.
> They kill us for their sport.

He helped Jane out of the boat, and politely shook off the offers of help as he put both feet firmly back on dry land. They clapped them both as they alighted from the boat. Gresham turned, embarrassed, to his men in the boat, the ones who had done the real men's work. They were clapping him too. *They* were clapping *him*? Sweet Jesus, was there no justice in this world? He should be clapping them.

Jane was delivered into the hands of numerous women, with a clucking and fussing of vast proportion, and vanished up the jetty. For once, Gresham noted, she succumbed to it willingly. This was a woman who really wanted her hot bath. Young Harry was delivered into the arms of an equal number of women, though rather younger than those who had flocked to Jane, Gresham noted. Well, he was guaranteed a good night, one way or the other. The other wounded were ushered up the jetty, the hubbub of conversation diminishing with their progress.

Two men took the boat back to the boathouse, bobbing their heads as they passed Gresham, a thousand questions in their minds which would never pass their lips. There was still a fair crowd left gathered on the jetty, gazing in awe at Gresham and Mannion. Gresham wanted to dismiss them, to walk back to The House with

Mannion as he had walked with him after so many battles, fights and feuds.

Then, all of sudden, he saw what neither he nor Jane had noticed before. The nurse had brought out little Walter and Anna to watch the return of their parents. They had stood at the back, and not even Jane's huge sensitivity to the presence of her children had alerted her before she was whisked off. What on earth happened to children when they saw their parents come back bloodstained from a battle? Surely it was too early in their poor, innocent lives for them to realise that their parents, and the whole damned world, were mortal? And why the hell wasn't their mother here to sort this dreadful finale out? Women knew about these things! Men were . . . men were there to do the fighting, not the explaining!

His son and his tiny daughter were standing either side of their nurse, hands in her hands. Both tiny figures gazed at Gresham with eyes as round as full moons.

'Well,' said Gresham, eyes locking on those of his children. It was, of course, entirely in his imagination that the other servants drew back to let him speak to the children, 'the truth is, some nasty men . . .' He felt, rather than saw, a flicker rumble through Mannion's body as he tried to stop the laughter inside him. 'Some nasty men . . . decided to be . . . not nice to me and to . . . Mummy.' Was Mannion about to spontaneously self-combust with hilarity? Or was it Gresham's imagination? 'Then some nice men . . .' If he didn't stop this now, Mannion would certainly die. 'Oh, bugger it!' said Gresham to his children. 'Some bastards tried to kill your mother and me. We won. They lost.'

There was a huge cheer from the servants.

'And I was wounded a bit, but not badly.'

Gresham's children were still looking at him as if he was the eighth wonder of the world.

'And the truth is, I'm really tired, and I wouldn't mind a helping hand from you both to get me back to the house and into a warm bed.'

The children ran to him instantly.

'It's all right, Father,' said Walter. 'We knew you needed to swear.'

'Are you really not hurt?' piped up little Anna.

'Look, little one,' said Gresham, picking her up and cradling her. He pointed to his chest. 'A scratch. No more than you do when you fall over a stony path. Less, probably.' He put her back down on the ground, hiding his pain as he did so.

Walter was trying to push his father's hand so far upwards to support him that it threatened to imbalance Gresham. Anna was content to hold his hand lightly, taking care to match her step with his so that she did not jar his arm. At the same time, she did not let go of Mannion, who was holding her other hand with a gentleness that belied his size.

'Jesus Christ!' said Gresham as they both collapsed inside the first doorway that offered itself after the children had been detached from them. 'Can we go to bed?'

'No!' said Mannion, firmly. 'At least, not before we've washed and cleansed that wound across your chest.' Body-servants had, after all, a duty to the body of their master.

11

July, 1612
The House, The Strand, London

'To unmask falsehood, and bring truth to light'
SHAKESPEARE, *The Rape of Lucrece*

The shock had set in for Jane, as it always did, when it was no longer necessary for her to cope, to keep a good face in front of others.

She had tried to take up some needlework. It was a task she hated above all others, but a strange sense of duty drove her to try, believing it to be a proper accomplishment for a lady. She stabbed and hacked at the poor backing cloth, her stitching for all the world like the work of a mad doctor on an open wound. She sucked in her lips, muttering as the needle went where it wished. This morning her normally erratic results were self-evidently unspeakably bad.

Gresham watched her in silence. How extraordinary that a woman's body, the same size more or less as a man's, could achieve so much more. That slim body, perhaps a half inch shorter than his own, needing all the organs his body needed, had managed to grow and nurture two children, house, home and feed them within the confines of one flesh for nine months apiece. If so great a portion of her body was given over to childbirth, wondered Gresham, how about the mind of a woman? Was the child to her mind in its life as it had been to her body in pregnancy? Would her love for him persist, or would it drain away silently into the love of her children? Men loved themselves, thought Gresham. So much so that many failed to see when love in others had died.

Jane spoke, eventually, as he had known she would. 'That was . . . appalling,' she said, with a catch to her voice. She was white-faced, and the fingers of her left hand were trembling very slightly, Gresham noticed. It made the stitching even worse. 'To go to the play, and to be set upon by a bunch of murdering oafs . . . Is there nowhere safe?' She was clean, sweet-smelling and outrageously beautiful. In the privacy of the room, her black hair was loosely gathered above the nape of her neck, like a sweeping, swooping coil of ebony. The remnants of breakfast had been cleared, and she and Mannion were grouped round the table with Gresham.

They looked expectantly at Gresham. He had been distant all morning, not hostile but rather withdrawn. They knew the mood of old. His mind had gone deep, weighing up what was known and what was not known, trying to draw the map of where they were and where they should be. He got up and started to pace the room.

'Safe? It's not a word I can recognise. Not when the plague or an ague could rip any one of us out of life and into oblivion at the flip of a coin. At least in the theatre there was an enemy you could see, an enemy you could fight.'

'An enemy you could fight!' said Jane. 'An enemy gathered in your business! All I can do is run, not fight. All I can do is receive the hatred of the enemies you make.'

There was no answer Gresham could utter that would deny the truth of what she said. He stopped pacing for a moment and looked at her. 'I'm sorry,' he said. 'Truly sorry.'

'So am I,' she said, holding his eyes. 'Sorry for what happened. And sorry if I seem to blame you for the evil of others. And I never said thank you. For saving my life.'

110

The emotions that flickered across Gresham's brow were too complex for words, but she saw them all the same, and understood. Gresham's tone became businesslike.

'The man with the crossbow has to be this Cambridge bookseller Coke was so concerned about. The description fits too well. What's new is that he wants to kill us as well as sell some papers – and no, I don't know why. He could be working independently, or with Overbury. I humiliated Overbury. He was there at the theatre. Though he took no part in the fight.' Gresham was pacing again. 'For once it's not *why* that bothers me. It's *how*! There are a thousand ways to kill a man if that's what you really want. Slip a servant in and drop some poison into the man's wine . . .'

'That couldn't happen now. We take too much care over who we hire as servants,' Jane said. Years earlier Cecil had slipped a spy into Gresham's house.

'It's *less* likely to happen now,' corrected Gresham. 'The minute you allow yourself to think it's impossible you're placing yourself at risk. Bribing a servant would still be the easy option for this book-seller, or for Overbury. Or there's a knife in your back while walking down a dark street, or a crossbow bolt from a deserted alley. Poison, knife, arrow, gun – if you want to kill someone, why do it in front of two thousand spectators at the theatre, for God's sake?'

'Go on,' said Jane. There was clearly more.

'And why try to kill you as well?' he said to her, swinging round to face her. 'You're hardly going to carry on the investigation after my death, are you? For all Overbury knows, you're as feather-brained as the rest of the women at Court.'

Jane forgot her depression for a moment and a smile tugged at the corners of her mouth. She mock-fluttered her eyelashes and swooned. 'My lord, as a Court lady I do not need a brain. What I need is—'

'But think seriously on it,' Gresham interrupted quickly. 'The theatre. That's what's worried me all along. It runs through this in a way we haven't got hold of. Right from the start it's not just been

111

a set of letters from two male lovers, it's been manuscripts of *plays*. This bookseller . . . he tells LongLankin he wants the students to put on a *play*. A man gets murdered because someone wants the manuscripts of two *plays*. They try to murder us in a *theatre*.'

'Bloody expensive way to go about it,' said Mannion. 'And risky. Never know what might happen with that many people around. And not exactly secret either.'

'Why does the theatre run through all this like a thick vein? We just don't know!' The tension came through in Gresham's voice, the way he still walked up and down the room.

'Well,' said Mannion carefully, putting down his tankard. 'Mebbe we do.'

Gresham and Jane looked at him, startled.

'Come on, old man. Don't keep us in suspense.'

'I've been thinking,' said Mannion.

'That must have hurt,' said Gresham with compassion. 'Have another drink to get over the pain, and mind you don't do it again.'

'Ssssh!' said Jane, irritated at his banter and intrigued. Mannion did have a brain. It was simply not the organ he found most use for. He also had, when he cared to use it, an outstanding memory for faces and people, as well as a capacity to make instant and lasting judgements.

'I reckon as how that bastard with the crossbow wasn't any bookseller, not leastways any one as I've ever seen. I think that bookseller was Christopher bloody Marlowe.'

There was a stunned silence.

'But Kit Marlowe died in 1602 . . .' said Gresham, his mind spinning.

'We was *told* he died in 1602,' said Mannion. 'But then again, *we* told everyone he died in 1593, when we bloody well knew he hadn't. If he died once when it was convenient for him, but didn't really die, why shouldn't he do the whole trick again without our help?'

'Now I remember!' said Gresham, clapping his hand to his head. 'Cornelius Wagner!'

'Who's he when he's at home?' said Mannion.

'It's the name Cecil's spies gave to the "Cambridge bookseller".
Coke told me when we met. Cornelius Wagner. Cornelius and
Wagner are two characters in Marlowe's play, *Doctor Faustus*.
Wagner is Faustus's servant. It all adds up . . .' Gresham's mind was
racing. 'Are you certain it was Marlowe?'

'I spent time with him, didn't I? It was me who got him over to
France,' Mannion replied.

'You faked Marlowe's death? Got him over to France? Alive?
And now he wants to kill you? I don't know this story at all,' said
Jane. She felt the great tidal wave of intrigue, of double- and treble-
dealing, of plots, of deception, tugging at her, the tidal wave in
which her husband had chosen to swim for most of his life. Or was
it a whirlpool, sucking them to their deaths? Together with
Gresham, Jane had been swept away by the magnificent verse of
Marlowe's *Tamburlaine*, chilled by *Doctor Faustus*, horrified by *The
Jew of Malta* and *Edward II*. 'Tell me.'

Gresham laughed. 'Did we get him over to France? Yes. Did we
fake his death? No. That was Marlowe's idea.' He nodded towards
Mannion, who pulled his tankard towards him and continued the
tale.

'Marlowe'd got himself into trouble. Well, to be truthful, he was
never out of it. 'Cept this time it was real trouble. He was a spy, for
old Walsingham, spying on the Catholics. Leastways, meant to be
spying on the Catholics, but with a nose for trouble that meant he
ended up spying on everybody, including some very inconvenient
people. Like the Queen, f'example. When Walsingham died he
started to work for Cecil.

'Always getting drunk, he were, always fighting, always shooting
his mouth off. Bad thing, for a spy, that. Started to shoot his mouth
off about Cecil being left-handed, so to speak.' Mannion used the
slang term for describing a homosexual. 'And loads of other stuff no
one could understand. Cecil's father, old Lord Burleigh, decided he
were a risk too far and got him summoned to the Privy Council.

After that, he'd have bin referred to the Tower, and probably died of some mysterious illness short after . . .'

'He never was a very good spy,' said Gresham. 'Too fiery, too intelligent, too much wanting to be the centre of attention.'

'Anyways, we gets to hear of it too, before Marlowe even. Sir Henry here, well, Marlowe's a bit of a hero for him, literary speaking.'

'I thought the man was a genius,' said Gresham simply. 'A pain in the neck, right enough, but a genius for all that. Burleigh and Cecil wanted him dead and even then I was pleased to do anything I could to put a stop to Cecil's plans. I thought in exchange I might get some real dirt on Burleigh, and on Cecil. And I really did want to stop them killing the man who had written *Doctor Faustus* and *Tamburlaine*. Think of it as my early patronage of the arts.'

'So what happened?' asked Jane.

'I warned him that if he went to the Privy Council hearing he'd never walk out of it alive or a free man. I arranged to spirit him over to France,' said Gresham, 'but that wasn't good enough for Marlowe. He had to fake his own death first, with the biggest crowd of villains in the country. We got to hear of that too late to stop it, but we reckoned those particular villains would take his money, do what he'd arranged and then kill him anyway. That way they could claim a second payment from the government. Mannion managed to tail him on to the brig we'd hired to get him over the Channel.'

Gresham looked to Mannion.

'As it was, two of the crew on the brig over to France tried to murder Marlowe in his sleep.'

'What did you do?' said Jane.

'I killed 'em,' said Mannion simply, slurping at his small beer. 'Anyways, I got him over to France. We know he took himself off to Spain after that – separate story. We heard he'd died or been killed in 1602. He always were a stupid bugger, excusing my language, mistress. It were no surprise to hear someone had topped him.'

'Are you sure it was him at The Globe yesterday?' said Gresham.

'Yes, I reckon. He's changed a lot. Shrunken, sort of. Lost his hair. So it took me time to spot him. But that's who it is. Marlowe. Back from the grave. Reckon he's got a dose of the pox. Did you see him with that crossbow?'

'I saw him fire it,' said Gresham.

'I saw him put his hand on the release,' said Mannion. 'I mean, he rested the bow on the woodwork, wedged it into his arm and then he put his hand on the release with his other hand, as if he couldn't really feel it. That's what they do with a bad dose of the pox. They can't feel much in their hands or their feet. I know about these things.'

How Mannion had avoided a dose of the pox was a quite remarkable story of there being no natural justice in life. There was no doubt that his extra-curricular lifestyle brought him into contact with many who had not been so lucky.

'Well, well,' said Gresham. 'My old friend Kit Marlowe.'

'Why should he want revenge on you?' asked Jane, bemused. 'You helped him get away, didn't you?'

'I think I know,' said Gresham. 'Hold on here while I fetch something.'

Gresham left them in the breakfast parlour and moved through the corridors with a greeting, by name, to the servants who bobbed, curtseyed or doffed their caps to him. He went to his private study, at the centre of The House and guarded by its stoutest door. Lifting the extravagance of carpet that lay on the floor, he revealed the planking. He gave a sharp tap on the end of a join, indistinguishable from the others. The plank-end jumped up, and settled down a half inch or so higher than its neighbour. Gresham lifted it, revealing that it was hinged at its other end. The cavity exposed as the plank swung back had a dullish sheen to it. Gunmetal. There was a metal box beneath the floor, with its own lock. Gresham swung back the heavy door with a key from his golden keyring. No money lay there, as might be expected in a rich man's house, a rich man who had gone to the expense of constructing a special metal box hidden beneath the floor of the most secure room in his property. Nor were there deeds of land, or sureties, or any of the paperwork beloved of the lawyers. Rather, there were letters. Letters and papers. Of no apparent significance or value to the idle viewer. Gresham smiled inwardly as his eyes lit on some of the papers. Monarchies, kings and queens were compromised by those innocent-looking documents.

Men have to tell their secrets, to prove that they are men. Great men merely have to know great secrets, and tell no one.

Gresham found the two letters he had come for and closed his private store. Would it survive a fire? he thought. For a while, perhaps. It was gunmetal, after all. More likely, the survival of it and its contents would depend on him or one of his very few trusted servants making the gunmetal box their only priority in the case of a fire. Nothing was certain, Gresham thought, except death. The readiness is all. You cannot predict. You can only prepare.

He brought the two letters back into the room. Mannion had replenished his tankard, Gresham noted.

'Two letters,' he said to Jane, 'three months apart. Both from Marlowe. June and August 1602. Someone had just tried to kill him, he said. I hadn't saved him at all, he said. I'd set the whole thing up on Cecil's orders, so Cecil wouldn't be embarrassed by the revelations Marlowe would have made at any trial.'

'They weren't planning any trial!' said Mannion with a guffaw.

'No, but Marlowe'd obviously imagined one, with himself playing the heroic role. He'd have been meant to go to France, but went to Spain instead and sold himself as a spy to them. Worked with them for years, as I understand it. Then he fell out with them, and blamed me and Cecil for poisoning the Spanish against him.'

'Had you?' said Jane.

'God help us, no,' said Gresham. 'To be frank, I'd more or less forgotten about him until these letters came. He'd have been better off dying in The Tower, he said. There, you can read it. He was in poverty. He'd never had the recognition he deserved . . . and more. And, of course, the accusation that it was Cecil and I who'd tried to have him killed.'

'Had you?' asked Jane again.

'I hadn't, of course not,' said Gresham, shrugging his shoulders. 'There was no need, no reason. He was just history as far as I was concerned. I suppose I hoped he'd write things abroad, under another name, set up theatres in Europe . . . I remember feeling quite shocked when we heard he had actually been killed, after he'd written to me. It was in September, I think. I also found something out later that convinced me Cecil had done it.'

'What was that?' asked an intrigued Jane.

'For a long while I don't think Cecil knew Marlowe was alive. He took over Walsingham's spy service but he never ran it properly. Preferred to work through ambassadors, official people. Well, the letters make it clear someone tried to murder Marlowe in 1602, in Spain. I think it was Cecil. I think that's when Cecil found out Marlowe was alive, and who he was working for. It must have been the biggest shock of his life.'

'Why the biggest?' said Jane. 'We know he had quite a few shocks in his life, even before 1605.' She could not help smiling at the memory of the Gunpowder Plot, and the exact nature of the shock administered by Gresham to Cecil.

'Because in 1602, when it was clear Elizabeth was dying, when everyone thought Robert Cecil had chosen King James I as the new King of England, and when Robert Cecil himself was writing away to James and declaring himself his most loyal servant, all the while the bloody man was plotting with the Spanish to get the Spanish Infanta on the throne in place of James! He was riding both horses, wasn't he?

'Well, Cecil is fearful of the Queen finding out he's been writing to James in Scotland, and fearful of her *and* James finding out he's been trying to ride two horses and back Spain as well. Then, lo and behold, what does he discover? That Marlowe's been an agent for the Spanish for years! Marlowe, who hates him! Marlowe, who's privy to all the Spanish secrets – might even have seen some of his cursed letters. He must have ordered Marlowe knocked off as soon as he heard. Obviously Marlowe got away, if it was him you saw this afternoon . . .' Gresham glanced at Mannion, who nodded.

'Are you sure Cecil was riding both horses? Backing the King and the Infanta?' asked Jane. 'It's absolutely explosive if it's true. Elizabeth could have had him killed for it, and James could never have let him run the country for him.'

'Oh, I'm sure, right enough,' said Gresham with the grin of a devil on his face. 'You see, I've got two of his letters to the Spanish! I've held them as a bargaining counter for years. It's one of the main reasons Cecil didn't have me killed long ago.'

Jane's head was reeling. 'Are you telling me you could have proved Cecil a traitor since 1602? And I know you could have done it again in 1605 with the Gunpowder Plot? If you hated the man so much, why didn't you topple him?'

'You know why,' said Gresham. 'Power is a filthy business. It dirties all those who wield it. There's no room for a good man in government. We've had peace for years now, haven't we, over the land of this country at least? No babies killed, no villages razed to the ground, no women raped, no harvesting of all the best young men to die stupidly in battles no one understands. If the price we pay for that peace, that stability, is to have the anti-Christ on the throne, I'll take it. Cecil's evil, the fact he had no morals, the fact he would assassinate without thinking to keep the peace – we need someone like that as our ruler. And if he damned himself in the process, why should I care?'

'So you're saying Marlowe got away some'ow, and buggered off somewhere to lie low? When he knew people was trying to kill him?' said Mannion.

'Must have done. The Americas, perhaps? Or Russia? That's where I'd have gone. Wherever it was, it must have turned his brain. Not that it ever needed much turning. And now, all of a

118

sudden, he turns up in England again,' said Gresham, 'and I bet I could dictate the letter he sends to Cecil. "I'm going to get my revenge on you at last," he says, "and on that arch-villain Gresham who helped you ruin my life."'

'Oh dear God!' said Jane. 'I see it now . . . it's so simple.'

'Isn't it?' said Gresham.

Mannion, whose face was screwed up like a cow's, was clearly not finding it simple at all. Gresham carried on.

'Cecil sets me, his best agent, on to finding Marlowe, carefully not telling me it is Marlowe, of course, just to add a bit of spice to it. So I'm moving about with the highest possible profile, more or less guaranteeing that Marlowe's going to come screaming out of a side alley and try to kill me. If I kill Marlowe, which is the best option of all, then what a joke for Cecil from his grave. He's got his oldest and bitterest enemy to preserve his reputation, pure and unsullied, for all of history. That would appeal to Cecil's sense of humour. And if Marlowe kills me – the second best option – what a joke as well! Cecil's oldest enemy follows him to the grave with a helping hand from Cecil, and the killer is the person whose escape I arranged twenty years ago partly to spite him! Poetic justice and the wheel come full circle, isn't it, if Marlowe kills me?'

'Are you sure Cecil's *first* aim wasn't to get you killed by Marlowe? We only survived by luck. If you hadn't been pre-pared . . . What an evil man,' said Jane. 'What a horrible mind.'

'Brilliant mind,' said Gresham in appreciation. 'Almost as good as mine.'

'Well,' said Jane, ' at least we know why everyone's talking about a lost play by Marlowe. He must have written his masterpiece in all those years of exile.'

'And now one of his aims is to get it performed,' said Gresham. 'He's obviously been peddling it in the disguise of this bookseller.'

'But not got it performed yet,' said Jane.

'Any decent company's going to get itself laughed out of court if it claims a play's by Marlowe without concrete evidence. It'd take time and money to get one of the respectable companies to put it on. I doubt Marlowe's got a great deal of either.'

'It's almost pathetic,' said Jane, 'if he is trying to get the students to put it on. It's almost like a homecoming. Or beginning all over again.'

One of the greatest playrights of all time reduced to having students put on his play? There was little sympathy for Marlowe in Gresham's heart. That commodity had been used up long ago.

'So where do the buggers' letters come in?' asked Mannion, direct as ever.

'Do you have an answer?' asked Gresham.

'How about this?' replied Mannion. He got up and put his mug down on the table. It was half full. It was almost unheard of for Mannion to put down a mug with drink still in it. 'You're Marlowe. You've got dirt on Cecil and you want to cause as much 'avoc as possible in as short a time as possible. Who do you go to?'

'The King?' suggested Jane.

'No!' said Mannion scornfully. 'Think on't, mistress! How does Marlowe get to the King? Goes up to 'is man on the door, does 'e? "Excuse me, Mr Gatekeeper. I'm a sodomite ex-spy and playright who died in 1593 and who's been working for the Spanish ever since. Oh, and by the way, I died in 1602 as well. Anyway, I'm here and I've got the dirt on the King's right-hand man. So let me in, will you, to talk direct to His Majesty?"'

'Put like that,' said Jane, 'it doesn't sound that easy.'

'Marlowe's a spy, isn't he?' Mannion was pacing up and down now, his brain engaged. Did he realise how like his master he looked? 'He knows about real power. So who's the real power in England?'

'Carr. Robert Carr. The King's lover,' said Gresham, happy to feed Mannion, fascinated by what he was seeing.

'No, master! Not Carr! Carr's just the beautiful body! Who's the brain? Who's still trawling taverns and going to stews where gentlemen shouldn't be seen? Who's accessible to a runt like Marlowe?'

'Overbury,' breathed Gresham. 'Sir Thomas Overbury.' Someone had just opened a window in the darkness of his knowledge. 'It's about comfort. It's all about comfort.'

'What do you mean?' asked Jane, perplexed now.

'The King's tired, losing himself more and more in hunting and wine and beautiful young men, selling out to comfort.'

'There's men as can't take power,' said Mannion, speaking to Jane. 'We've seen 'em often enough in the wars. Men who get tired of decisions. First it's the wine. Takes the place of thinkin', blocks it all out. Then, if that don't work, beggin' your pardon, there's women.'

'But it's a young man in King James's life!' said Jane, unabashed.

'Yes,' said Gresham, 'and a brainless one at that! All James wants is comfort and freedom from strain, and all his lover wants is the same! Robert Carr can't make a decision to save his life, other than what doublet to wear – and I bet that takes all morning and most of the afternoon. So that's where Carr's friend comes into his own. Overbury. Sir Thomas Overbury. Able. Intelligent. Wanting nothing more than to take the King's decisions on his behalf. Wanting nothing more than his share of power.

'The King's lover, more perplexed and far less able to deal with matters of state than his master, breathes a sigh of relief when his friend offers to help. Overbury. Brash. Arrogant. Receiving at third-hand unopened papers of state. It is Sir Thomas Overbury who now wields part of the power that Cecil once held. Yet Overbury has no protection of office. Ordinary men still have access to him. As did Kit Marlowe.' Gresham was speaking quickly now, as if to preserve his view in words before it slipped from his grasp.

'Marlowe goes for Overbury. Tells him he can destroy Cecil. Overbury's flattered. What power! Takes him in. Pays for him to be lodged out of harm's way. Talks to him. And then, one evening,

Overbury lets slip the existence of these letters. Too much drink, probably, fed him by Marlowe. Brags to Marlowe that Marlowe isn't the only one who has power over people.'

'"They could be your insurance policy, these letters!" Marlowe says to Overbury. "They could be your pension!"' It was Mannion now, picking up the baton. '"Think on it. Your friend Carr will lose his looks one day. There are enough pretty men in the Court, aren't there? And the King hates you. And his Queen. Let *me* have a look at these letters. I'm a spy, ain't I? I know about these things." So Overbury brings these letters along, to show off. Lets Marlowe hold them. Tells Marlowe where he keeps them. Puts them back somewhere Marlowe knows about.'

'So the next thing that happens,' Gresham said, 'is that the letters disappear. Marlowe's also gone. And Overbury's set up to be the biggest fool in the country. Carr will lose faith in him if it becomes known he's the reason the letters are in the hands of an enemy. James will kill him, or kick his creature Carr out, which'll be just as bad. So how does Overbury cover himself?'

'He reports the letters are stolen,' said Jane, realisation dawning on her face, 'but stolen from Carr, not from himself. And he reports it to Sir Edward Coke, the legal bastion of the kingdom. Knowing full well that Coke will run to Cecil, of course. Suddenly it's somebody else's problem. He's covered himself brilliantly. But . . . why would Cecil care so much about Marlowe? He was dying, knew he was dying,' she continued. 'It seems an immense amount of effort to go to to get someone killed, when you won't be there to be disgraced. Why would Cecil bother.'

'*Reputation!*' said Gresham. 'More than anything else, he wanted his reputation not only to live on after him but to grow. Marlowe's the threat to that. I'm the other, knowing what I know. So set the two against each other. That way he can guarantee one threat at least's removed.'

'So Cecil wasn't really interested in getting the letters back?' said Jane. 'All he really wanted was for you to kill Marlowe and preserve his reputation as an honest broker and a loyal servant?' Something in her soul rebelled at the thought of Gresham being used merely as an unpaid assassin.

'Oh, I think Cecil would rather the letters were destroyed than not. He wouldn't wish more instability for the King he'd made his life's work out of. But they were just the lure to get me into the arena, draw me in. My getting the letters was always the secondary aim. The first was to force Marlowe to reveal himself to me, and for me to kill him.'

'Or for Marlowe to kill you. Why didn't Cecil tell you it was Marlowe? Why use this Cambridge bookseller thing?'

'Do you think I'd have taken on the job if I'd known straight away the real reason was to save Cecil's reputation for posterity, instead of the King's? I'd have laughed in Cecil's face.'

'Where do these plays come in?' added Jane. 'The manuscripts by Shakespeare? We can explain everything else, but not them.'

'God knows,' said Gresham, 'but haven't we solved enough problems in one sitting? Marlowe wants to stir up as much trouble as possible, and get some play of his performed. Probably reveal himself, like a genie out of the bottle, on its first showing. Look at me, everyone. The late, the great Kit Marlowe – alive and well! What a show-stopper that'd be . . . And anyway, that's not what bothers me . . .' He had to stop and think for a moment before completing his sentence '. . . what bothers me is you.'

'Me? What've I done wrong?' asked Jane, rather plaintive.

'Nothing. You've done nothing wrong. Cecil gambled that Marlowe would risk showing himself if it meant killing me. But haven't you spotted the really terrible thing?'

Jane looked nonplussed. Gresham stared at her. He had to tell her. For all the hurt, for all the pain, he had to tell her. If she was to protect herself she had to know.

'He didn't try to kill me. He tried to kill you, Jane.'

'But I don't—'

'I saw his eyes in the theatre,' said Gresham. 'They were looking at you, not me. The second bolt was aimed at you. And that first bolt, the one I felt go by me earlier. It hit the wall just where you'd been a second before. I was six or eight feet away.'

'*What have I done to deserve this?*' she cried out. 'I've never set out to hurt or destroy anyone *in my life*.'

'He's a sick man, Jane. Sick in his mind as well as his body. He was always unstable. Now he's fired up with years of festering revenge, and the pox. I think he's decided the best way to hurt me isn't to kill me, not yet at least. It's to kill my happiness. To kill you.'

The silence seemed to stretch on for an eternity. She had fought against the thought that she and Gresham were equal targets for whichever madman was hunting them down. The realisation that she was the target, the way of inflicting the most pain on those she loved, threatened to clutch at and cut the parts of her mind that moored her to sanity. *Where was the justice in this world?*

'Not here, not on this earth with us,' said Gresham. Jane had not realised she had spoken out loud.

'So what hope is there?' She turned her face, despairingly, towards his.

'The hope in our own strength,' he said intensely. 'Justice lies with how strong we are. Safety lies in how strong we are. Survival lies in how strong we are.'

'I feel very weak,' she said.

'We all feel weak sometimes,' said Gresham. 'The strong are those who fight the feelings and carry on living.'

'I'll try,' she said, feeling like a lost little girl.

'I know you will,' said Gresham simply.

'Are you sure?' It was a very small voice that Jane spoke in.

'That you're my happiness? Absolutely. That it's you he wants to kill, to hurt me? No, not absolutely. But it'd be wise to assume it, until we can prove otherwise. We both know you're my weak spot. You and me, we're both at war with Marlowe, and Overbury for all I know. You know what it means. We're under siege.'

Oh God, not again, thought Jane. No leaving any house without an armed escort, no going out at all unless it was totally unavoidable . . .

Mannion chose not to help Gresham, but to answer a different question. His mind had been working on it, clearly.

'That bastard Overbury wasn't behind the lot trying to do us in in the theatre.'

'Why not?' It was Jane who answered. 'He has reason enough to hate your master, and it's surely too much of a coincidence that he was there on the afternoon when it all happened.'

'He were surprised when he met us. You could see it in his eyes. And he only had a couple of men at best with·him, and neither of those armed. He could have made a real difference in the fight, with a sword, but he cleared off. Are you telling me a bastard like that wouldn't want to watch and gloat if he'd gone to all that trouble?'

Gresham thought for a moment. 'You could be right,' he said, 'but it makes no difference if it's one man or two we've to guard against.'

He was pacing the room again, hand running unconsciously through the black mop of his hair. 'It's the mystery I want solved. The mystery isn't Sir Thomas Overbury or Sir Edward Coke, or even Christopher Marlowe. It's Shakespeare and these confounded manuscripts. We need to meet with Master Shakespeare. Urgently. All three of us.'

'I'm flattered,' said Jane, seeking to hide the pain in her mind and the awful, threatening waves of paralysing fear. 'But why do you need me?'

'Firstly, to stop me killing him on sight. Secondly, to stop me being too rude to him, and thirdly, because you're a trained hand in dealing with drunken writers.' Keep it flippant, make light of pain. Ben Jonson, now masque-writer-in-chief to the King, had been a friend of Gresham and Jane's for years. Only the three people in the room and Jonson himself knew that Jane read Jonson's manuscripts in draft. He howled, swore and hurled things around the room when she made criticisms, and called her every name under the sun and several from below the moon. But he always made changes, Gresham noticed. In fact, he reckoned Jane had written nearly a quarter of Jonson's *Volpone, or The Fox*.

'It's a pity we can't call Ben in on this. He's a great pal of Master William's, or so he says.' It was Mannion. Jonson was touring Europe as tutor to Sir Walter Raleigh's son, one of Gresham's better ideas for a pairing.

'Well, yes,' said Jane, 'but there's a lot of jealousy as well. He's always trying to put Shakespeare down. Come to think of it, Ben's actually put me off meeting Shakespeare once or twice.'

'I think I must meet this genius,' said Gresham. 'Or rather, meet him again, with his new name. We'll need to be careful. He'll know I'm one of Raleigh's party, and if he thinks I'm after him he'll run. Mannion, send our people off to see if he's still in London. He was there at the play, doing a bit part, I saw him. Maybe he's scuttled back to Stratford, like they say he's doing more and more now. Find out where he is, but do it quietly. And fix a time – a time very soon – for me to meet him with my mistress.'

12

September, 1612
Granville College and King's College,
Cambridge

'No place, indeed, should murder santuarise.'

SHAKESPEARE, *Hamlet*

The trail had gone cold.

It had happened before, often, in Gresham's life, but of all eventualities it was the one that left him most restless and ill at ease. He craved action. The combination of tension and inaction made him like a pent-up hound that turned to chew its own flesh in frustration. Shakespeare had apparently fled town immediately after the riot in The Globe. The men hired by Mannion had scoured London and then Stratford for a trace of him, but had found nothing. At least there had been no more attacks on Gresham or his family. That fact did nothing to relieve the tedium of living their lives under permanent guard.

At least the evening ahead might offer some excitement. Was Gresham becoming a creature of the night? he wondered as he put on his academic dress for the evening meal. Work started at dawn and finished at sunset for students as well as for farm labourers. The main meal of the day at Granville College was therefore at noon. Candles and lamps were expensive, servants need to be abed early if they were to be up before the dawn to light the fires, and students needed at all costs to be discouraged from treating night as day. It all argued for the main meal to be in the full and free glare of God's sunlight. Yet Gresham had instituted, and paid for, three feasts a year, to be held in the evening in the Hall his money had built.

Why go to the extra expense? It was not something Gresham could explain easily. The light flickering off the walls and the portraits hung against the panelling, its yellow contrasting with the roaring red of the huge fire blazing in the magnificent fireplace halfway along the left-hand wall, was magical to him. That light gave the evening dinners the air of a happy conspiracy, the flowing food and drink easing conversation and loosening inhibitions. He revelled in the sense of holding back nature, flinging a challenge of light and warmth and noise into the face of the all-encompassing darkness and silence of the night.

The Fellows all met in the Combination Room before the meal, the noise of the students gathering in the Hall filtering through even the thick oaken door. The room was a new development, the common rooms of the colleges hitherto being largely the local taverns. Alan Sidesmith, the ageless President of the college, stood and greeted the Fellows and their guests as they arrived. Gresham had never seen Alan without a drink in his hand, yet had never seen him drunk. Sidesmith had a guest of his own tonight.

'Be on your best behaviour, Sir Henry!' he warned Gresham with a twinkle in his eye. 'No less a person than the Bishop of Ely has asked to come to tonight's dinner.'

'Asked?' said Gresham.

'Indeed,' replied Sidesmith. 'He was preaching at Great St Mary's some weeks ago, and I went to listen, as one does. We were admiring the new tower. If I remember, his words were that if the college would see fit to invite him, he would see fit to accept. Oh, and by the way, he asked explicitly if you would be dining.'

The instinct for survival had placed tiny trip wires in Gresham's mind, trip wires that rang a jangle of bells inside his head when they were disturbed. Suddenly the noise was deafening, audible only to Gresham. One of the greatest theologians Cambridge had ever produced and the ex-Master of Pembroke Hall was entitled to invite himself for a dinner, wasn't he? And Gresham's dark reputation might be an added lure for a stately prelate, might it not? Whether or not he would appreciate the company of Gresham's guest was another matter. Bishop Lancelot Andrewes and Sir Edward Coke as bosom friends? Gresham rather doubted it. Yet such strange meetings were at the heart of college life – the clash of ideologies, the spur of debate and the strange conjoinings of people united only by their intelligence.

It had amused Gresham to invite Coke as his guest. It gave Gresham an edge, forced Coke to conform to the rituals of being an invitee. It was also time they met on home ground. Coke was a Trinity man, and Gresham guessed that curiosity about the torrent of novelty that was Granville College would override suspicion on Coke's part. He also guessed that under the carapace that hid Coke's real feelings from the world lay the fierce, burning fascination with university felt by all men who had left it.

'Are your rooms to your satisfaction?' enquired Gresham solicitously as Coke sidled in to the Combination Room. Coke never walked, Gresham had noted. He either paraded or sidled. The rooms in question had been built to receive James I on his visit to Granville College.

'Quite satisfactory, thank you, Sir Henry,' replied Coke drily. His eyes flickered over Gresham's face, forever seeking advantage, weakness, a loophole. 'Fit for a king, even. ' A sense of humour, noted Gresham. A very *limited* sense of humour, dry almost to despair, but a sense of humour nonetheless and therefore very interesting. Was Coke offering an olive branch? More likely it was poison ivy. Gresham motioned Coke aside and into one of the bay windows that flanked the room, unaware of the natural courtesy with which he treated one of his bitterest enemies.

'Let's make this a university night, if you agree. But there is business. It can be disposed of quickly, if you're willing,' said Gresham.

It was as if he were on holiday, Gresham thought, sensing the lightness in his own soul. The college did this to him. Its backbiting and its petty rivalries followed known and even agreed rules. The backbiting and petty rivalries of Court knew no rules, nor any limit on the damage they might cause. By comparison life in a Cambridge college was heaven on earth to the hell of the Court.

That hooded look came over Coke's eyes, and he could not resist glancing over his shoulder, but he nodded. You would be no spy, thought Gresham. That look over your shoulder tells any interested party that you are worried about what we are going to discuss. It screams guilt to the careful watcher.

'Firstly, I know it's Marlowe who has possession of these papers.'

A tic started in Coke's left eye.

'He's already tried to kill me in the theatre incident you know about.'

Coke's face went red. Interesting. Most men went white when shocked with sudden news. Was the red the red of anger? Did Coke become angry when shocked, seeing everything as a personal attack?

'I've a host of men out searching for him, here and in London. He'll be found, eventually, though he's gone to ground.'

'How long before Marlowe is found?' Coke's voice was grating, sharp. He did not challenge the identification of Marlowe. It was as if his mind ticked an issue off, like a clerk with a list of household goods up for sale. Once ticked, however threatening or revelatory, it was gone, merely a piece of information.

So you knew, thought Gresham, who this Cambridge bookseller was, as did Cecil. Yet you did not think it important to tell me.

Coke's eyes were dark pinpricks. Gresham decided to answer his question.

'Tonight. Three months on. Who knows? Patience is crucial to this game we play, Sir Edward. Without it, the tension eats us up from within, burns our soul. And another concern who's gone to ground is Shakespeare. Vanished from London and from Stratford.'

'Shakespeare was always the lesser concern,' said Coke, a little too hurriedly. 'Could Marlowe have killed him?' Coke was uncertain, hiding it beneath a face that might now have been carved out of plaster. Clinical. That was the word. He was driven by huge self-esteem and vast pride, but at the point of contact with his conscious mind all that emotion, all that energy, became focused into something as hard and cold as steel. His own ambition. Does this man have the capacity to love another human being? thought Gresham.

'Marlowe's made one very theatrical attempt to kill him already. Equally, with that knowledge in mind, Shakespeare may have simply gone into hiding.'

The real cause of Old Ben's death had been known to very few people. One of them had been willing to talk to Gresham for a purse that could have doubled as ballast for a big ship by its weight.

'Your answer on Overbury?' Gresham asked. He had written to Coke detailing the bare outline of the attack, and been unequivocal in his demand. Find out if Overbury was behind the attack on Gresham and Jane.

Coke sighed. It was a theatrical gesture, but for the briefest of moments, his age – he was sixty – showed through the veneer of his face.

'As best as I can judge, Overbury knew nothing of the attack on you. He is an impossible man.' There was venom in Coke's voice. 'The only certainty about him is his arrogance. I base my conclusion on the vehemence with which he expressed the wish that you and your kin had been slaughtered, while denying setting up the assault. If it had been his idea, he would have bragged about it.'

Coke had the capacity to be glaringly honest when he so chose. It was an excellent ploy, thought Gresham. The brief moments of sincerity served to validate the months of lies.

'We must join the assembly,' said Gresham. 'Before we do, tell me about the atmosphere in Court. Is the King troubled by the loss of these letters? Indeed, does he know the letters are lost?'

'The King? I have told him. After much agonising on my part. It seemed best,' said Coke.

Best? thought Gresham. The theft of the letters shows Carr and Overbury to be fools, it tells the King that Robert Cecil trusted Coke above all others and makes it clear that Coke is a man of discretion, not one to blab secrets to the whole world. *Best*, therefore, for Sir Edward Coke. 'He is troubled, certainly,' Coke carried on smoothly. 'The letters are, by the way, in his own hand, so I believe.' And therefore infinitely more damning and damaging. What prompted men to put things in writing? Or women, for that matter? It had killed Mary, Queen of Scots, and could have done the same for Elizabeth. 'Yet His Majesty . . . seems more fickle by the moment.'

Fickle? Drunk, more likely, and settling in to an ever-increasing lassitude. Nor had he appointed a successor to Cecil, though it was believed to be only a matter of time before the job went to the beautiful Robert Carr. Which meant, of course, that the real power would be in the hands of Sir Thomas Overbury.

'We'll stay in touch,' said Gresham lightly. 'Now let me introduce you to the feuding clan I call my Fellowship . . .'

Whatever else the joint invitation to Coke and Andrewes had done it had certainly set the other Fellows alight. Granville College was entertaining the greatest theologian in the land, the man who many said had done far more than translate much of the Old Testament in the new King James Bible, and also dining the man held to be the greatest lawyer of the age. It was a coup.

They filed into the Hall, Alan Sidesmith leading with Andrewes by his side, the Fellows in pairs either with their guests or with each other. There was a rustle and scraping back of benches as the students, over a hundred now the college was expanding so rapidly, stood up and fell silent. It was early evening, and the golden light of the sun slanted through the high windows and gleamed off wood and silver. The candles and lamps were not yet lit, and would not be so for another hour or more. There were two high tables, to meet the number of guests. Unusually, there was no distinction among the lesser tables. Other colleges allowed money and influence to buy a place at high table, and had separate tables for pensioners, the students who paid for their education. The poor scholars, the sizars, held a third category of table, if they were lucky enough to be fed at all instead of serving their fellow students to pay their way. Gresham had pioneered a simple rule. Only those with a Cambridge or Oxford degree could sit at high table. So in Gresham's college on the night of a feast, sizars and pensioners sat together and ate the same food. He paid for outsiders to come and wait at table on these nights. Let the poor students be served for once or thrice a year. Their brains were no worse than their richer peers so let their stomachs be treated as the same. Gresham had appointed a new cook, the best in Cambridge, before he had appointed a new president. It was the main reason for the college's huge popularity.

There had been two exceptions to the rule that only those with a Cambridge or Oxford degree sat at high table: Queen Elizabeth I and King James I.

The gong was struck and a senior student rose to read the long Latin grace. At a normal dinner his peers would have tried to pinch him, or fallen into a spasm of coughing. On a feast night they let him be. The student had a deep bass voice. The sonority of the Latin grace rolled around the great Hall and up into its beautiful rafters, increasing the raw power of the language. The grace ended. The feast began.

For all that Gresham's money had saved Granville College from total collapse, his place on the Fellowship had started at the bottom. Now he was quite advanced, in the top third even of the Fellows gathered. Traditionally, a Fellow's guest sat on his right, the President's guest at his right at the top of the table. At Andrewes' request, Gresham and the President had exchanged guests. Sir

Edward Coke sat by the side of Alan Sidesmith, surrounded by an adoring audience of sycophantic law Fellows. Andrewes sat to the right of Gresham, three or four seats from the top of the table. He let the theologians who surrounded Andrewes have their fill of him.

It was not until the candles had been lit and the flames were dancing over the faces of the guests that Gresham and Andrewes turned to each other, each confident that they had paid their social dues to those sitting within earshot. Andrewes had been witty, Gresham noted, in telling stories of how the forty-six members of the panel drawn together to write the King James Bible had undertaken their duties in very different ways, but not a note of malice had crept into his conversation.

'Well, Sir Henry,' said Andrewes at last, 'can you confirm the rumours I hear, and tell me whether or not it is in fact the anti-Christ by whose side I sit tonight?' There was a sparkle in his eyes, alongside a strange darkness, and a lightness of touch in his tone.

Gresham replied equally lightly. There was no offence in Andrewes' tone, and none taken. 'Before I answer, my lord Bishop, perhaps I could ask if I am indeed sitting next to the Saviour Himself, a man so pure as to be canonised before the formality of his death?'

Andrewes laughed out loud, a rich, gurgling noise of such deep humanity and happiness that it caught Gresham unawares.

'Why, Sir Henry,' said Andrewes, wiping his face with the linen napkin supplied to him. 'If I'm as far from the description you've heard of me, then I must guess you're as far from the description I've heard of you! Is it possible we're both mere mortals, with all the sins and all the strengths associated with that kind?'

'On the other hand,' said Gresham idly, 'it's probably more fun playing at being Christ and anti-Christ. Now there's a dialogue to light up a high table.'

'If lighting up a high table is your pleasure, then so it would be.'

There were few men who could hold their gaze with Henry Gresham. Andrewes was succeeding, with no sign of flinching. 'But it would only be play, wouldn't it? Like so much of the talk at these evenings, splendid though they are. We're both too intelligent to believe that we're God or Satan. I fear we'll hear neither of them speak tonight. Only alcohol, and good food . . . and a fearsome headache for too many of us when dawn breaks!'

'My lord Bishop,' Gresham responded, 'if we're not here to play – with words, with our illusions, with our own self-importance – then why do we dine at high table?'

'Perhaps,' said Andrewes, 'to enquire after the truth?'

'Well,' said Gresham, 'that would be a rare thing in a Cambridge college, wouldn't it?'

'True,' said Andrewes, 'but I understand you're a man who sets precedents, rather than believing he should slavishly follow them.'

There was a moment's silence before Gresham answered. 'So, my lord Bishop,' he replied, 'would you care to set a precedent and tell the truth here tonight?'

'I'll do more than that,' responded the Bishop of Ely, 'I'll tell you a secret. Or rather, part of a secret. After all, there could be no safer place, here among all these people.'

Now you would have made a spy, thought Gresham, in a way that Coke never would. As the evening wore on the triple spell of good wine, good food and good company had worked their magic, loosening the tongues and heightening the sensitivities. Nowhere in the world were there more people talking and fewer people listening than at a Cambridge feast, except perhaps in a court of law. The deal to insert the serpent into Eden could have been concluded tonight, and no one would have heard.

'My lord,' said Gresham, a rare intensity in his tone. 'Tell me what you will, but I can guarantee you no secrecy in return. Be careful before you confide in such as me.'

'Ah,' replied Andrewes, lifting the goblet to his mouth but merely brushing his lips with the wine, 'but, you see, I come prepared. I've done my homework, Sir Henry. I've asked people their opinion of you.'

'And who have you asked, my lord Bishop?' asked Gresham, intrigued at the inner calm of the man.

'Not the courtiers, the politicians and the prelates, that's for sure. For them you're a strange and fearful creature, to be trusted as much as Beelzebub, a man rumoured to have had a strange hold over Robert Cecil, and even the King. A dark, explosive force, they see you as. A man who has killed, and who has ordered others to be killed. A man with a remarkable capacity to survive. And, of course, a man to be envied above all others. Vast wealth, a stunningly beautiful wife, fine heirs, a good brain and a good body . . . My, my, Sir Henry, how you do provoke the sin of envy in others.'

'Thank you, my lord, for telling me who you've *not* asked. My question, if I may be so bold and impertinent as to repeat it, is who you did ask.'

'Your servants, Sir Henry,' replied Andrewes, taking a clear drink of his wine at last. Gresham stiffened. Andrewes noted it – a good spy indeed! – and put out his hand as if to calm him. 'Don't worry. They haven't let you down. The opposite, in fact. I always go to the servants when I want to find the quality of a man or a woman. Your servants are particularly good at telling those who question them nothing. Details of your whereabouts and your movements? Details of your security arrangements? The layout of your houses? I doubt most of them would give up those secrets even under torture. But, you see, a servant doesn't feel bound by any vow of secrecy when it comes to telling how proud they are to serve their master, or their mistress. And even if they don't say it, they make it clear in the language their bodies speak whether or not they would die for you.'

Gresham, embarrassed, interjected, 'All men give up their secrets under torture, if the torturer is skilled in his trade. All too often servants are not given the choice of whether or not to die for their master.' Why was this man in danger of forcing him onto the back foot?

'Well,' said Andrewes, 'your servants trust you, and your mistress. They do rather more, actually. They love you both. But forgive me for being an old cynic, if you will. I rate the trust on a higher level than the love.'

The hubbub around them was increasing. There was a sheen of sweat over most of the faces, and fingers were being pointed and tables thumped as points were made.

'You were summoned by Robert Cecil, I believe, for a very last meeting?' Andrewes continued. 'I also believe that at that meeting the loss of certain papers was discussed, and a rather unholy alliance forged between you and your declared enemy, Sir Edward Coke, for the retrieval of those papers.'

Good God! thought Gresham. Had Cecil posted a broadsheet around London detailing their meeting? And, what was it to do with an East Anglian bishop, a master of sixteen languages? Gresham revealed nothing of his inner turmoil. Instead, he consciously relaxed every muscle in his body.

'I thought men of God were committed to the ultimate truth, my lord. I didn't realise how skilled they were at fiction. You have no proof of your version of events.'

That hit home for some reason. Tiny muscles contracted along Andrewes' face and neck. Tension. A shock. Gresham filed it away.

'Well,' said Andrewes, recovering quickly, 'let's stick to truth. Very many of those papers you've been set after have no relevance to me.'

'And no capacity to harm you?' Gresham asked.

'Neither relevance, nor harm,' said Andrewes. 'Politics I despise. I'll do what I have to with courts and with kings. They exist, as does a final hill on a long and wearisome journey, or the need to pay the shopkeeper before acquiring the food. They exist, and as such need to be met. But they're not existence. Existence is about the soul. The spirit. That which places us above the animals. There's little to be learned about that in courts, or in converse with kings.'

'So what is it that you fear in these papers that I might have been set on to find?'

'You know Sir Francis Bacon, I believe?'

Another change of course, another shock for Gresham. He showed none of it either in his body or his voice.

'We've met.'

'Sir Francis and your guest tonight, Sir Edward Coke, are locked in battle for royal favour and for the legal dominance of England. You appear to be in alliance with Sir Edward.'

Appearances can be deceptive, thought Gresham, without intending to speak it. Andrewes continued.

'Not unreasonably, Sir Francis opposed my coming here tonight. Gently, of course. Unlike you, he doesn't deal in force.' Ouch, thought Gresham. A hit, a palpable hit. 'He thought no purpose would be served by my confiding in you. He even thought it could be tantamount to suicide for us both. He said that you answered to your own masters, and that they were different masters to those I serve, and to those he served. Not better, nor worse. Just different. Are they that different, Sir Henry?'

'How can I know,' answered Gresham simply, 'until I know you, and Sir Francis, and who your masters are, far better than I do now?'

'A fair point,' Andrewes sighed. 'So let me tell you my half truth. The papers you most need to find are between a monarch and his . . . friend.'

'And do you condemn such friendships? You, a bishop of the Church of England?'

That stopped Andrewes in his tracks, Gresham was pleased to note.

'That depends,' Andrewes replied at length.

'Are bishops allowed to depend?'

'Probably not,' said the Bishop of Ely, 'but this one is contrary. At least in being so he is true to the habits of a lifetime, if not to the doctrine of the Church.'

'Contrary? But God's will is clear. It is definite. At least, it's so in the eyes and ears and heart of every bishop I've ever talked to.'

'Perhaps this bishop is aware of the difference between being God's representative on earth and being God himself!' snapped Andrewes. 'As for my condemnation, I condemn lust. I find it far harder to condemn love.'

'The difference?' asked Gresham, intrigued.

'Lust? It satisfies the needs of our bodies. Love? It satisfies the needs of our souls. The body dies, and shrinks through appalling and sickening putrefaction after death. It is fallible and rotten. The soul lives on.'

'So if a man finds solace for his soul in a relationship with another man, and the bodily relationship is merely a passage to that meeting of souls, then he is free from sin?'

Why was the silence between these two men so separate from the noise which surrounded them? How had they managed to create their own private globe of communication amid so much letting down of barriers?

'I . . . I . . .' For once in his life, Bishop Lancelot Andrewes was lost for words. Sir Henry Gresham spoke for him.

'You've offered secrets to me. Now let me really surprise you. Let me offer a secret, a hugely damaging secret, to you. I offer it in the full knowledge that you can give me no vow of secrecy in return.'

Now the shock was on Andrewes' face. Of all things, this was not what he had expected. The burning intensity in Gresham's face and voice was frightening. Such intensity did not convince or heal. It burned an inexorable mark into the recipient.

'I once loved a man. And, yes, for one night, and one night only, that love ceased to become spiritual and became physical. And later that same young man was charged *with my sin*. I was the leader. I was the instigator. I was the master. I pleaded to be the victim. And as they . . . executed him, I sobbed out loud to be the one who was blamed. And as—'

Even Gresham was forced to pause.

'And as they did . . . unspeakable things to him on the way to his death . . .'

Was it true? Were there tears in the eyes of Sir Henry Gresham, that famous dark force against whom there was no resistance?

'He cursed me for the suffering I had brought upon his poor body and his poor soul. And so he died, in hatred of me. So tell me, Bishop Lancelot Andrewes, *is there forgiveness in the Church of England for men like me?*'

'No,' said the Bishop simply. 'No forgiveness. Not from the Church. But from another poor mortal such as me, yes. Forgiveness. And pain for your pain. And, if you would believe me, understanding. And one more thing. The screams a dying man gives out in his agony are not the truth. I do not hold that Christ in his agony believed that his Father had forsaken him. Yet he asked if this was so. If you remember the dying moments of your friend, you remember him as his enemies wanted him to become. Remember him rather as the man you loved. As he, I believe, will be remembering you, in his new place of rest.'

There was no absolution that could cleanse Gresham's soul, no alchemy to heal his wound. He had thrown his bitterness and his story at the Bishop as a weapon, to unseat the man and see whether the calm he radiated was genuine or merely a front. In return, for the first time in twenty years, something had crossed the air between them that touched Gresham. For the first time, something approaching a sense of peace started to seep in to that most damaged part of Gresham's brain.

'Well,' said Gresham, snapping back to life and his normal sense, 'you have my secret. Are you still willing to tell me yours?'

'More than I ever was,' Andrewes responded, his face retaining a smile of intense compassion, 'but I'm still bound by secrecy. I can – no, I will – only tell you half a tale.'

'It will like be more meaningful than many that are being exchanged around us.' With a faint nod Gresham pointed to the man opposite, who, in gales of laughter, was telling the story of the student whose illicit emptying of his piss-pot always seemed to hit the same servant, and the servant's novel revenge.

'If you find these letters, you will have a choice,' said Andrewes. 'You can hand them over to Sir Edward, who will use them to promote himself with the King. You could hand them to Sir Francis Bacon, who will do likewise. I suppose you could hand them back to Sir Thomas Overbury, were it not for the fact that he would lose them again to the next flatterer who came his way. You could even try to use them yourself, for your own advantage. Or you could hand them to me.'

'To you, my lord Bishop? You said you had no interest in politics?'

'Precisely. That's why I would destroy them. Their revelation serves no purpose other than to unsettle the state. Their use is only for personal ambition. They were better never to have been written. Once written, they are better burned.'

'Why could I not burn them, if I find them?'

'Because your reputation is such that no one would believe you'd done so. Me they will believe.'

'Forgive me, my lord,' said Gresham, 'but you've no cause to love the King. He gave Canterbury to that pliant fool Abbot when you were the obvious choice. We have a king who's said in public that he doesn't give a turd for religion. How do I know – in the mythical state where I have these letters – that you wouldn't use them for your revenge?'

'You don't know,' said Lancelot Andrewes. 'You'd have to trust me. As I've trusted you by this request. You see, Sir Francis Bacon, with whom I am involved in this for other reasons, doesn't know that I've made this request. He thinks I'm seeing you on a different matter.'

'Is there a different matter?' asked Gresham.

'Yes,' said Andrewes. 'With these letters are other . . . papers. I won't tell you of their nature. I will tell you that they hold great potential to damage me, and Sir Francis Bacon. You know Bacon's hand? Here's an example of mine . . .' Andrewes reached into his purse and brought out a folded half sheet of paper. It held notes for an old sermon, Gresham saw, in a clear, flowing style. 'You'll recognise any papers that concern Bacon and myself. They'll be in our respective hands. I ask you simply to destroy them, immediately. Not even give them to me, or to Bacon. Destroy them.'

'And you will trust me to my word, when you've just told me that the world won't do so?'

'I will trust *you*, Sir Henry Gresham. I've no power over whether you trust me.'

Love letters again? thought Gresham. Did Andrewes, this most saintly of men, have a past to regret? Had he and Bacon even been in dalliance? Bacon made no secret of his fondness for young men. He filled his household with them, and allowed them to milk his estate for all it was worth, to the vicious amusement of Court circles.

'You may trust me, my lord Bishop,' said Gresham levelly, looking full into Andrewes' eyes.

'Yes,' said Andrewes, 'I think I may.'

Gresham was not drunk, but he knew his head would show that he had drunk the next morning. He eased off his gown in his college rooms, sensing his loneliness. Jane was safely tucked up in The Merchant's House, well-guarded. Mannion had seen Gresham into college, then signed himself off for a night roistering in Cambridge. Even he believed Gresham safe behind the locked gates of college.

He reacted to the noise almost before he consciously heard it, a sixth sense forcing him to swing round and grab his sword silently from its sheath. The third floorboard up on the staircase had been deliberately rough-sawn so that it squeaked when trodden on. It had squeaked now, after midnight, when all of college should be in bed and no one walking up the staircase that led only to Gresham's room.

He had not closed the outer door to his rooms, and the inner door was simply on its latch, not bolted nor barred. There was a sound of heavy breathing from outside, a rustle of clothing and then a click as the latch lifted and the door opened slowly.

Gresham waited until it was half open, and then kicked it back on itself as hard as he was able. The door shot back, met flesh and bone, and whoever it was creeping up on Gresham was flung back down the stairs with a wail of pain, protest and shock. Gresham ran out of the room, to see what mess, living or dead, waited for him.

It was LongLankin. A tumbled, head-over-heels and half-conscious LongLankin. But judging by the language, definitely alive.

'What d'yer fuckin' do dat for, yer pox-blasted twat!' he mumbled reproachfully, feeling gently for his loose teeth and a nose that looked broken. He drank the ale that Gresham had found for him with a shaking hand.

'What did you go creeping around college for in the dead of night?' asked Gresham malevolently, with a total lack of contrition.

'To find you, o' course. To tell you 'bout that man, that book-seller.'

'The bookseller?' Gresham felt a shock go through his system.

'Yeah, 'im with the play. E's in town tonight. E's got a room down a back street.'

It appeared LongLankin had been making his way home after a night of intellectual enquiry, and taken a turn down a back alley to relieve himself. Standing to do the job he had noted a light on in the downstairs room, its window curtained over. He had wondered if it was a whore setting up business on her own, and had gone to peer through the thin gap in the curtains. There he had seen the strange figure of the so-called bookseller, and come running to tell Gresham.

'How did you get into college?' asked Gresham. Doors were bolted and barred, a porter on duty.

'Never you mind,' said LongLankin truculently. Well, Gresham did mind, and tomorrow there would be a review of security. Moving as fast as the man would allow him, Gresham asked for a clear set of instructions for finding the house and then bundled LongLankin out to the porter's lodge with some money for his pains. He had with him a dark cloak with hood, his sword and dagger, and a lantern, its shutters closed for the moment so that no light escaped from it. Nodding to the startled porter, paid extra so as not to question Gresham's comings or goings, Gresham turned left out of the gatehouse, passing St John's on his right, turning again past the darkened bulk of Trinity College, dominated by its Clock Tower and the Great Gatehouse, heading towards the old Trumpington Gate.

It was a bad night for stalking, with a cloudless sky and the fullest possible moon. This was poor housing now, earth-floored and stinking. The house was there right enough, the light still burning in the room as LongLankin had described.

Was it wise to be out here on his own, when men had already been mustered to kill him, in a street of hovels where the proceeds of his cloak alone would feed a family for a month? How sure was he of LongLankin? What if the man, a vagabond and a vagrant, had been set up to lure Gresham out from behind his stone walls and the protection of his men? Gresham had rushed off on LongLankin's word with hardly a thought. The chill of the night and the funereal, harsh white light of the moon were giving him second thoughts. He grinned sharply to himself. Was he more frightened of nameless men waiting to ambush him in the dark, or the reaction of Jane and Mannion to his foolhardy casting of caution to the winds? He had been careful for too long! He felt the pulse of excitement again in his veins, and picked up his pace, still moving silently through the deserted, moonlit street.

A noise from the end of the alley. Gresham pressed himself back into the wall of the mean house he was standing by. The building had shifted at some time in the past, as if a giant had pushed it forward, so the already steep overhang of the roof was doubled, creating a pool of darkness from the moon's glare.

It was only one man. He was heavily built, lumbering rather than walking, making noise enough for an army. He stopped at the door of Marlowe's house and knocked, a peculiar tap-tap-tap that was obviously a code. The light moved from the curtained room and spilled out under the cheap, warped wood of the doorway. It opened to reveal a short, hooded figure.

Marlowe.

Something tightened across Gresham's heart as he saw the figure he had last seen firing a crossbow bolt at Jane. Hold back! Clamp down on the emotion, use head, not heart. Revenge would come. A greater need now was information.

Marlowe muttered something at the man. All these years on, and still that same odd, high-pitched voice. As Gresham watched he managed to reduce the lantern's outpouring to a mere sliver of light, and handed it to the man, motioning him to start off. Marlowe was dressed for the night, boots and heavy, black cloak. He used that same high-prancing step.

At this late hour in the dark, close streets, anything live scuttled and scurried rather than walked, unless it was the drunk singing softly as he staggered solemnly round and round in a circle, thinking all the while he was headed home. Gresham kept his distance, moving crab-like from house to house as he followed the two men. They were moving to the centre of town, Gresham saw, past Bene't Church and on to King's.

The chapel was even more magnificent bathed in the stark moonlight. It rose over Cambridge like a blessing, soaring yet monolithic, so simple yet so infinitely complex.

King's College Chapel? Why was Marlowe headed there? It was long past midnight – there were no services. The strange couple made their way to the west end and its door. Locked, surely, at this time of night? If they had a key then Gresham had no hope of following them inside, presuming Marlowe would lock the door behind him. No. No key. The door simply opened and swallowed the two men, closing softly behind them. So someone had been bribed to keep the door open. Cheaper and far less risky than letting a stranger have a key.

Gresham flitted over the ground to the door. He could hear nothing through its thick, ironed oak. Gently, ever so gently, he lifted the huge handle. It was smooth, easy: grease. The mechanism had been greased beforehand. He could smell it.

He paused for a second, the great door ready to swing open. His senses were screaming signals to his brain. Did a man ever feel so alive as when he risked his life on one throw of the dice? In battle, perhaps, or in the moment of sexual relief. If he went in it was to face two men who knew where they were going and what they were doing. He was far from any help or assistance. If he died here, it would be unseen and unexplained, a mystery to keep the high table talking and the taverns full for six months or so, and then to be forgotten, just another of the strange legends of Cambridge. The spy who was found dead in King's College Chapel. Was he to be like Marlowe, an enigma whose death history would argue over for ever?

He took three, careful, deep breaths. With infinite gentleness and in one single fluid movement he entered the chapel. Its walls were not walls at all, but windows, bursting out in colour in the daylight, now an eerie patchwork in the intensity of the moon. The windows rose to the intricate, soaring passion of the fan vaulting, visible now only as the merest variation in light and shade in the blackness of the roof. A rare cloud passed over the face of the moon, and a blanket of total darkness swept up the chapel like a threatening high tide. Gresham stood just inside the door. So gently had he slipped into the building that the air had hardly moved around him. He stood, poised, waiting, in total silence, listening. Waiting for the blow, the sudden indrawn hiss and snap of breath so many men took before a sudden action.

Nothing. Silence. Wait. Yes, there it was. The tiniest scrabbling noise, soft in itself and coming as if through a door or other barrier. There, in the corner. The narrow doorway that led up to the roof through one of the corner turrets. He eased across the stone floor, sword in hand, just another silent shadow. The doorway up into the turret was ajar. The slightest of sounds made it clear that Marlowe and his hired help were scrabbling up the narrow, circular staircase. One of them must have kicked a piece of loose rubble. It skittered down the stone steps, each noise as it landed as loud as a gong in the prevailing darkness and silence. The noise startled Marlowe and his companion. They halted. Silence. A brief whispered conversation and they started off again, both panting and heaving with effort. Unfit, thought Gresham. Dying, in Marlowe's case, from a rot within. Dying for the third time.

Gresham eased himself on to the first of the steps. They were smooth, cold. The soft leather of his fine shoes kissed the stone and made no noise. There were long, thin, slit windows up the side of the tower, more like those built for archers in a castle than those built for a church. Gresham's night vision was perfect now, and the harsh moonlight shafting in from the thin windows was just enough to allow him to discern the pattern of the steps. No tricks here, Gresham thought grimly. In some of the places he had fought the builders had put in a straight run of ten or twelve steps of uniform size and then put in a step with two or three extra inches of height or depth. The effect on attackers hurtling up them was catastrophic, catching them out and sending them tumbling time after time.

He was coming to the first exit now, the one that would lead off into the gap between the top of the magnificent fan vaulting that formed the ceiling of the chapel and its lead and timber roof. The small door led to a stone corridor that ran the whole side length of the chapel. It had windows, and pools of moonlight interspersed with black holes of dark. To the right was a passage up on to the top of the vaulting. For all its fine and delicate tracery, hanging suspended as if floating, the magnificent, unprecedented fan vaulting was built of the heaviest stone, each of the central corbels that seemed to draw the delicate strips of stone together weighing over a ton. A man could easily walk along the centre of the vaulting, which rose up in a quarter circle from both sides, without a tremor. In effect, the two halves of the stone roof met in the middle, leaned against each other and supported their vast weight, passing it down to the buttresses on the side walls.

Light! Not the petrified light of the moon but a lantern, flickering a third of the way along the side of the vault. Marlowe was muttering, cursing. His man was reaching clumsily into the area behind where the great roof beams nestled snugly on to the outer wall. Behind each beam was a cavity, perhaps a foot or eighteen inches deep, a perfect masonry box without a lid. The man grunted and brought out a package which looked for all the world like an oiled, canvas satchel.

The papers. The papers which seemed to have haunted him and so many others for so long. It had to be them.

What a magnificent place to hide documents. The space between the roof and the vaulting was dry as tinder, ventilated by the wind that drove through the end windows. There would be no mould or decay, though God knows there was enough dust. Each of the vast, arching roof beams formed in effect an alcove, several in number. Who would think to look behind the timbers, reach down and fumble for a package in the hidden cavities that lay there?

Marlowe and his man were less than halfway along the roof space. Their lantern stood at a tilt on the curving stone of the vaulting. Silently, Gresham reached out for the random, rusty nails embedded in the great timbers. He prayed for no clink of metal, hung his darkened lantern over the largest and sturdiest nail. Then, in one swift movement, he flicked open all four shutters of the lantern with a twist of the wheel that operated the mechanism and stepped behind the nearest beam, his back to the door that led out again into the tower.

The shock was dramatic. The extra light speared through the darkness at the end of the chamber. Marlowe gave a sharp cry and whirled round, losing his footing and falling with a curse to the floor. His man said nothing, but let out an animal grunt and came charging, instinctively aggressive, towards the source of the light. He dragged from his belt a cudgel, a club of hardened wood that some men would have found too heavy to lift, never mind swing. In confined spaces it was a good weapon. Gresham had seen one snap the fine blade of a sword in half, before being driven down to crack wide open the swordsman's skull. Marlowe looked up, saw the man and his satchel charging down the length of the vaulting, and tried to cry out to stop him. It was no use. Marlowe was part-winded. Even if his strangled noise had been heard, the brute of a man had the wind behind him and would not be stopped. As he reached the lantern, looking wildly round him, Gresham rose like an avenging nemesis out of the side wall and grabbed the strap of the satchel. The man's headlong rush was stopped sharp by the pressure of the canvas around his neck. His feet skittered out from under him, and as he hit the floor Gresham gave a savage, downward jerk of his arms. The hulk made a noise between a gurgle and a cry, and lay silent. His mouth lay open, and Gresham saw that the man had no tongue. That was why his noises had been so animal. Had he killed him with the blow? No. He was still breathing. Damn!

Gresham sensed rather than saw or heard the movement from further up the roof and instinctively swung back behind the beam. There was a flicker of silver and the knife – an Italian throwing knife, Gresham had time to note – swished by like liquid metal to embed itself, quivering slightly, into the next beam along.

Marlowe was standing now, fumbling for a second knife, eyes blazing hatred. It was not clear if he recognised Gresham. Without stopping to think, Gresham reached up to the rear beam, dragged the still-trembling knife from deep in the old wood and hurled it back to its owner.

It was a bad throw, taken in too much haste. Instead of heading for the centre of the rib cage, it veered to the right. Marlowe was holding the second knife now, hand and arm upraised, ready to throw. His own returned knife sank into his wrist, just below the hand. Marlowe was flung backwards, the second knife flying out of his grasp and landing with a clang on the centre of the vaulting, from where it rolled down to the side. His scream was more animal than human, a tearing, wrenching noise that opened the doors of hell. He crashed to the ground, looking in appalled horror at his own knife embedded in his arm, the blood starting to seep down to soak invisibly into his black cloak. With a last, croaking cry, he passed out.

Or had he?

There was red in Gresham's eyes. The overwhelming, overriding urge to survive had him in its wildest grip. He must kill the brute with no tongue. He must kill Marlowe. *Now*, while both were defenceless. *Now*, before they could rise up on either side of him.

He had his sword raised over the throat of the brute nearest him, choosing him first.

Then he stopped.

Fool! Was he an animal to be dominated by a blood lust? He needed Marlowe alive, needed him to tell him the truth, needed that truth to plot Gresham's own survival through the tangled paths of Coke, Bacon, Overbury, Andrewes, King James and the ghost of Robert Cecil.

With all his force Gresham kicked the huge man in the stomach. He hardly moved. Satisfied, Gresham ripped the man's tunic further apart at the neck along the stitching and dragged it half down over his unresisting body, pinioning his arms to his side. Then, for good measure, he took the flapping arms of the tunic and tied them across the man's back in a fierce knot, making an impromptu straitjacket.

Eyes on Marlowe's prone figure, he crept forward. His every sense was on sword edge. There was no need to test Marlowe's unconsciousness. The knife through his arm would have him screaming if he were conscious. Noting distastefully the blood that lay around the body – it would not be a fair gift to Jane to pick up a dose of the clap from this man's bodily fluid and pass it on to her – he picked up Marlowe's booted foot, noting the stench of the man as he did so, and dragged him, head bouncing off the floor, to join his servant. He took a leather studded belt off the servant and used it to bind Marlowe's feet together. That left Marlowe with one arm free. He would not be using the other to unpick any belt or rope, not with his own knife embedded in it. Time! Time! This was all taking far too long! He would have to bind Marlowe with his own doublet, then hope to carry him unseen through the streets. The other servant had better be imprisoned too, which meant Mannion and others coming back up here, all before dawn. Time! Why was there never enough time?

Time stopped. Motion stopped. The world froze.

A noise.

A noise of hasty breath and a footfall. Faint. Very faint. A flickering shadow of a noise, as of the softest of feet making the quietest possible haste along the corridor alongside the vaulting.

He *had* no more time.

Was the man on the roof, waiting? Or was the noise him fleeing the violence below? It made sense to have him on the roof at the start. Send someone in ahead – someone to unlock the door even – to scout out the ground. Mount to the roof, wait there in silence. Hang the tiniest of lights from the parapet – no one to notice it at that time of night – to show the coast was clear. Whoever it was may have left his post to greet Marlowe when he saw him scuttling across the green. That would explain why the watcher had not seen Gresham, following on and skirting the edge, a minute or two later.

So was he on the roof? Or waiting in the corridor outside? Damn! With enough lanterns lit to guide an armada, Gresham had lost his night vision. If he doused both the lanterns now the listener would have the advantage. There was no alternative. He chopped the light, then crouched back against the wall, having first placed Marlowe's lamp across the entry a man would have to walk over if he entered the vault.

151

Silence. Not even a breath of wind. Harsh moonlight cutting through the end window. Even the upward side of the vaulting was beautiful, though only a handful of men would ever see it.

Gresham rose to his feet and moved carefully out into the corridor, then up a few flights of the tower's circular staircase and on to the roof. Inch by inch, he crept upwards. His sword he extended at full length ahead of him. Anyone lunging down would be pierced before they could reach him. The coward's way, an old sergeant had laughed at him in the Lowland Wars. Three weeks later the man was dead, killed storming a tower. Not the coward's way. The survivor's way.

The door was open at the top. Gresham could see an arch of the night sky outlined at the stair's head. Quandary. Was there room behind it for a man to hide, to plunge the door into his face as he had done with LongLankin? He moved up on to the last step. The slightest breath of night air touched his face. He had not noticed his thin sheen of sweat. He took two or three deep, silent breaths. Then, gathering himself up into a ball of muscle, he hurled himself through the opening. As he landed over the threshhold, out in the open now, his foot caught in the clumsy wooden duckboards that ran alongside the roof. He fell, still gripping his sword, with an almighty clatter.

He rolled forward, freed his sword. Silence. Nothing. He lifted his eyes to the line of the roof.

Nothing.

The thin rooftop passageway in which he lay was faced to his left with ornate stonework, shoulder high, the parapet wall of King's College Chapel. To his right, the roof rose steeply to its ridge. The moonlight showed there was no one in sight. Yet the further along the channel the eye went, the more the shadows merged into each other.

Where would Gresham have hidden?

Suddenly he knew the answer. It was a terrible risk. He knew what he would have to do to find his enemy. It would hinge on a moment of balance, a reaction a split-second early.

But life was risk. It was not the fear that mattered. All people felt fear. It was the ability to conquer it.

The roof ladder, laid flat on the roof itself, was a clumsy thing, roughly fashioned out of unseasoned timber, leading up to the ridge. Its partner would lie on the other side. To crawl up it or to stand on its bottom rung and walk up? He stood.

The ladder was rock firm, surprisingly so. As he walked up the roof, ever so carefully, measuring each step, his sword arm upraised, his other arm flung out preposterously for balance, he sensed rather than saw how high he was. Something dropped in the pit of his stomach as he imagined his height above ground. With each careful step he took, the ridge line of the roof dropped one notch towards him. Agonisingly slowly, the top line of the roof came to his head height. Next step and his eyes were above it. Next step and his shoulders . . .

The man had lain himself flat on the other side of the roof, by the side of the ladder. As Gresham's head appeared shadowed against the moonlit sky, the man leaned slightly down on his left shoulder and slashed his sword arm from the right side of his body through the area occupied by Gresham's head and neck.

He had acted too early! One more step up the ladder and the whole bulk of Gresham's upper body would have been there to meet the blow. As it was, a normal man would have flung his head back as the flicker of a blade headed for his eyes, thereby probably unbalancing himself and falling backwards off the roof. Instead Gresham leaned forward and parried the blow with his own sword, inches from his cheek. He held the other's blade, slammed his wrist down to a rasp of steel and waited for the hilt to engage with the hilt of the other sword. A fierce, vicious twist. The other's sword flew through the air, over the ornate stonework. It must have fallen on earth. There was no noise. The man was spreadeagled below Gresham now, struggling for a knife, a hand clutching the timber of the roof ladder. Pitilessly, Gresham brought his blade back, selected his spot and plunged it through the neck of his assailant.

Kill or be killed. This man was no innocent. He had made his choice, taken his chance. And he had lost. A spasm passed through the prone body, the hand gripped even tighter to the ladder for a moment, and then let go. His body slid down the smooth surface of the roof, tumbling into the narrow passageway at its foot.

Gresham looked around. A ghostly mist, some fifteen or twenty feet high, shrouded Cambridge, the moonlight picking out its every curl and fold. Housetops and church spires poked out from the enchanted smoke, glinting with moisture. The throbbing in his head began, the throbbing he knew would develop into an agonising pain, the pain he knew came with the killing and the fear.

He walked down the opposite roof ladder. To his surprise, he found the man still alive. Dying, certainly, blood pouring uncontrollably from his neck, but still living. With an agonised last pulsing of muscles, the man turned his head towards Gresham, the blood thickening and spurting as it streamed from the wound.

Gresham stopped, as if struck by a blow.

It was Heaton. Nicholas Heaton. Cecil's messenger. The man who had been so confident of serving the King. And who was dying, covered in blood, an accomplice to Marlowe, *wearing the livery of the King!*

'What does your master have to do with this man Marlowe?' hissed Gresham, hauling Heaton up to face level, dagger pressed against his chest. Heaton's eyes were glazed, blinking. With a superhuman heave Gresham hoisted him on top of the ornamental stonework that fringed the wall, hanging him over it, facing the terrible drop to the ground. His thick blood fell before him, showing the way, leaking from his torn neck.

'Will you tell me now?'

But Nicholas Heaton was dead, carrying whatever secrets he held with him. There was much here for Gresham to think on.

Minutes later, and with a final heave, Gresham pushed at the body. It slid, about to fall to the ground, but hung for a second by the tunic, ludicrously, off a cone of carved stone. Then, with a

154

ripping and tearing of cloth, it slid over the edge. What was it he had said to Heaton all that time ago, at their last meeting?

Take care. Those who rise to greater heights have far further to fall.

Marlowe had gone. The servant still lay there, comatose. The belt, severed with stabbing rasps of a knife that Gresham must have missed, lay at his feet.

Well, if Marlowe was in league with King James, killing him might have been a murder too far, until Gresham could ascertain the nature of their link. Much more here to provoke thought.

Clutching his satchel, Gresham finally left the chapel. One servant would be found pulped on the ground the next morning. The other would probably still be in the roof. Did King James hold enough power to keep what had happened secret? Or would Cambridge be buzzing tomorrow with strange murders and men falling off college roofs?

Gresham, the pain growing in his head, decided he didn't care either way. He had a satchel to open.

13

September, 1612
The Merchant's House, Trumpington

'There is no fear in love; but perfect love casteth out fear.'

THE KING JAMES BIBLE

'How could you leave the college with no guard? On your own?' Jane was incandescent. He had never seen fury like it. To her, a vision of him slumped like a broken doll at the foot of the college, the sheer madness of his going out to meet Marlowe, felt like a betrayal of their love. 'Do you think your wife and children want to live without you? Are we so little to you that you can throw basic caution to the wind? How would you have spoken to me if I'd run off into the night with your children, on the word of a drunken informer, because in the final count excitement mattered more to me than my love!'

She was right. That made him even more angry. Mannion was no help. He had said nothing about Gresham rushing off into the night, but he looked mournful and reproachful, like a vast cow that had not been milked or a dog whose owner had suddenly ceased to walk or feed it.

The letters, the damned, cursed letters, had been there in Marlowe's satchel, in lascivious detail, the hand presumably that of the King himself.

'Well? Will you give the letters to your Bishop, as he asked?' said Jane. Was her anger subsiding, or did she merely have it under her control?

'Probably. Possibly. I'll think on it.' He was trying to show his hurt at her failure to understand why he had had to go out into the darkness and confront Marlowe. *So often there was only the one chance!*

Why are men such *children*? thought Jane. If a child's tantrum is ignored it loses its power. So she would ignore his tantrum. With a massive effort she reined in her anger.

'Are the other papers useful?' He had shown them to her so she was in a position to make her own judgement. By asking him for his thoughts she placed herself below him. Well, God had made the first mistake in creating women second. Who was she to deny God? Except that by a subtle use of her second place she might still lead this damned fool of a man into thinking he had made the right decision on his own.

Useful? They were two play manuscripts. Both, apparently, the text of *Hamlet, Prince of Denmark*, but in two different hands. Neither bore even a passing resemblance to the hand of Bacon, or of Andrewes. Gresham's interest had waned.

'No. Not useful,' he had confided. 'Confusing. Yet Marlowe kept these papers alongside those that damn the King of all England and Scotland as a lusting sodomite. They must have some value I don't know of. I need to meet Shakespeare. In some way I don't understand, he's a key to the sub-plot of this whole business.'

'He's renting rooms in the old Dominican Priory, at Blackfriars.' It was Mannion. 'And he's back there. I heard, yesterday. Just after you'd gone into your feast. There's talk he's trying to buy them. Quite the little property magnate, our Master Shakespeare. You know he's been buying up half of Stratford?'

Gresham didn't know.

'There's too much we don't know.' Jane and Mannion noted the use of the conciliatory 'we'. Perhaps the storm was over. 'What I do know is that I want to meet Master William Shakespeare again.'

14

September, 1612
The Dominican Priory, Blackfriars, London

'For now we see through a glass, darkly . . . now I know in
part; but then shall I know even as also I am known.'

THE KING JAMES BIBLE

The Priory was a warren of a building. Shakespeare was renting
rooms over the east gate. They had left The House by a back
entrance, disguised as masons in rough jerkins and with hammer,
mallet and chisel carried around their belts. It was a good disguise.
A hammer was a handy weapon. Strapped across his back, hidden
under the jerkin in a special harness made of the finest Spanish
leather, Gresham had strapped a sword, with a dagger positioned
just above each ankle. He had not bothered to ask what weapons
Mannion deemed suitable for the outing.

Jane was dressed as a housewife. It was always a worry how to disguise her. Even the worst clothes did little to hide the bloom and
leanness of her figure, and the high cheekbones, sparkling eyes and
lift to the chin made her a beauty however much soot was rubbed
into her face.

Gresham and Mannion followed immediately behind Jane. Two
of their men were stationed in front, two at either side and two to
the rear. It was easier to train men to kill than to train them to

accompany and guard their master and mistress without seeming to do so. It required intense concentration, as well as the ability to appear nonchalant when every nerve was straining.

Blackfriars was down The Strand and along Fleet Street, then over the stench of human and animal sludge that had once been the Fleet river. There was not one London, but several. A man who fitted into the hectic bustle of Fleet Street would be out of place among the weavers and cobblers of St Giles in Cripplegate, or the whores of Cheapside. Masons, however, went everywhere there was stone to chip, carve and repair.

The noise and bustle was immense. Everywhere the dust rose and clogged nostrils, put little icicles into eyes and caused the well-bred to walk with a handkerchief across their faces. Everywhere there were people trying to sell things, shouting out the value of their wares. Everywhere was the incessant building that seemed to be going on across all of London. The wooden scaffolding jutted out into the streets, where wagons, coaches and horses vied for what little space there was. Its own people filled its medieval walkways to overflowing, yet there was always more. London's teeming thousands needed feeding, and with every month that went by the city seemed to suck in more and more farm carts.

Mannion went to check with his look-out, who had alerted him that Shakespeare had been seen entering his rooms an hour earlier. 'He's still there,' said Mannion.

The gatekeeper was an old man, half asleep after his dinner. He woke to full consciousness with a start as Mannion banged on the half open door to his tiny lodge.

'We're 'ere to see Master Shakespeare. Master William Shakespeare. Some'at about some stone work he needs doin' up.'

'What you got that there with you for?' enquired the gateman, leering at Jane. She had rubbed her eyes hard and placed fresh spring water in them a few moments ago, blinking it out and over her cheeks. She looked as if she had been crying hard.

'Why, that hussy!' said Mannion, with feeling. 'If you'd a' seen where I had to drag 'er out from, you'd know why she ain't getting out my sight 'til I get her home! It's a trial in times like these, bein' a father and with no mother alive to keep her in order, I tell you!'

'Goin' to spank her, are you, when you gets 'er 'ome?' said the gateman, licking his lips and grinning like an aged satyr at Jane. 'Thrash her, are you? With a belt, an' all?'

Mannion was nearly knocked off his stride. His glance caught Gresham, who was frantically trying to contain the laughter threatening to explode inside him.

'Oh, sir, he will, an' that!' Jane's accent was an excellent imitation of Middlesex, "'e's so cruel to me, he is, so cruel . . . he beats me, he does, somethin' rotten.' She let her voice drain off into a pathetic snivel.

Good God, thought Gresham. Who needs to pay to go to the theatre? Let's just hope she doesn't start to strip off and show him her bruises . . .

'Ay, right then, up you go. Good luck to you. No time for these actors, me. Satan's chapel, that's what these theatres are. Satan's chapel.' The old man subsided into grumbling, though not without his gaze lingering lovingly on Jane's rear as they walked up the stairs.

They knocked on the heavy panelled door that Mannion had already established was Shakespeare's. There was silence. They knocked again, louder. A faint scrabbling could be heard from within. Gresham and Mannion exchanged a brief look, stepped back and in perfect unison drove with their feet at the place on the door that held the lock. It sprung open with a mighty crash.

When Gresham had first met him, Shakespeare, or William Hall, had been nondescript – medium height, medium build, medium everything. It was no bad thing for a spy to pass unnoticed. Even now, kneeling on the floor, hands raised in supplication, he was entirely forgettable. A bald pate with brown hair straggling on the side, a middle-aged paunch, the archetypal ageing prosperous merchant. How could the mind that wrote his plays be housed in a body of such drab normality?

Shakespeare had almost finished opening a hidden door in the heavy panels of the far wall as they burst in, an expression of sheer panic across his face. 'There's nothing I can do!' he shrieked now. 'I can't please you all! I don't have the papers!'

The gateman would be here any moment, calling out the watch. Jane stepped forward, knelt down beside the distraught man.

'Please,' she said quietly, 'we're here to help you. Not to harm you. Believe me. And send the gateman away when he comes.'

Gresham's heart went out to her. Most of the men he had worked with would not have recognised the danger the gateman posed without being told. Hardly any of them would have had the initiative to do something about it. Surely enough, clumping, urgent footsteps could be heard on the stairs outside.

Shakespeare looked into the most startling pair of dark eyes he had ever seen, housed in a face of such handsome proportions that it was guaranteed to take any man's breath away. 'No harm?' he asked pathetically. 'No threats?'

'No harm,' said Jane calmly. 'No threats.'

Shakespeare got up. 'It's all right, Ben,' he called out as the wheezing figure of the old man rounded the stairhead. 'Just a misunderstanding. These are . . . friends of mine.'

Ben looked suspiciously at the group.

'Well, I 'ope as 'ow they're better "friends" than some of those others you've 'ad comin' round 'ere these times. You sure? You don't need no 'elp?'

'I'm sure. Thank you. I'm sure.'

Ben left the way he had come, grumbling. Interesting, Gresham thought. The old man cared for Shakespeare, in his way. Servants – and particularly grizzled, perverted, cantankerous and liver-frazzled servants like Ben – cared for a very few people. Shakespeare must have something to command a residue of affection.

Shakespeare forced himself to look at Mannion. He is frightened he has made the wrong call, thought Gresham. This is a very scared man. Mannion saw the scrutiny coming. He stepped back, raised his arms, palms outwards. No weapons. No threat. It was a universal language.

The beating pulse in Shakespeare's neck began to subside. His doublet was of rich satin and velvet, copiously slashed. 'Do you close doors, as well as smash them to pieces?' he asked Mannion. Good, thought Gresham. There's wit there, at least, and a quick recovery. Gresham looked at the man's eyes. They were hooded, dark, as if a shutter was permanently closed over them. Normally Gresham gained a feeling for a person within minutes of their first meeting. Was there some strange smell, some ghostly aura invisible to the eye that passed between people? With Shakespeare he felt nothing. No sense of personality, no feel at all for what lay behind the exterior.

It was time for Shakespeare to know to whom he should talk.

'He does what I tell him,' said Gresham, 'usually. But he's no good unless he can smash something, sleep with it, eat it or drink it.'

'Then all he can do with me is the first. I doubt I'm his type in bed, and about the only thing no one's threatened to do to me recently is eat or drink me. God knows, they've tried everything else.' That wit again, with more than a note of tired resignation in Shakespeare's voice. He got up with Jane's assistance, and allowed her to help him to a chair. It was an expensive item, Gresham noted. Seasoned oak, with a high back and arms. A chair Robert Cecil would have been proud of. A rich man's chair. Even better, thought Gresham. The more a man had to lose, the more pressure could be brought to bear on him.

Shakespeare's beard and moustache were reasonably full, without being luxuriant. He wore a fashionably starched yellow collar, with two laces hanging down from it. Thickish nose, eyes quite wide-set. A drinker, Gresham thought – what actor wasn't? – with the veins just starting to go in the nose and cheeks. And those hands, with long, bony fingers. Why on earth did someone his age wear the earring in his left ear? It was the mark of a young dandy, not an ageing actor.

'So would you mind explaining why two . . . masons . . . need to smash down my door to see me?' Shakespeare reached for the goblet on the paper-strewn table. Jane, long practised with Ben Jonson, had the jug pouring the wine before he realised what was happening. He took a huge swig of the fluid.

He is outwardly quite relaxed, thought Gresham, but there was the faintest, most distant something in the air. Mannion looked at Gresham. Yes, they had both sensed as much as smelled it. Human fear. The smell both of them knew so well.

'May we sit down?' asked Gresham politely. There was another beautiful high-backed chair to match the one Shakespeare was seated on, and four or five stools.

'Be my guest,' said their host, his eyes not managing to stay on Gresham but flickering between him, Mannion and Jane.

'My name is Henry Gresham.'

'Sir Henry Gresham. I know your name,' said Shakespeare. 'I remember you from a past it seems I'm not going to be allowed to forget. My name is William Shakespeare now. Not William Hall. And how is Sir Walter?'

'Imprisoned, having lost most of his estates. Locked up on a false charge laid by a scum of a man with no morals except his own best interest. And he's still very angry. As indeed am I.' The menace in Gresham's voice was palpable. Shakespeare had begun to relax, but Gresham's speech caused him to bolt upright.

'You promised no violence!'

'Nor will I deliver any. Not yet,' replied an icy Gresham. Shakespeare blinked, and spoke again.

'You come to the theatre. You're the one they attacked in the riot at The Globe. All the company have done since is talk about you. You work for the King, don't you? Has the King ordered you to kill me?' The tension crackled out in Shakespeare's voice. It was nondescript, a slight trace of Stratford, country-boy burr, not un-attractive. The accent of rural England.

Now why on earth would a playmaker think the King of all England and Scotland would be bothered enough to have him killed?

'No one's ordered me to kill you,' said Gresham.

'Then what do you want?' asked Shakespeare. His voice was like footsteps treading on ice, fearful that it might give way at any moment.

'To talk to you,' said Gresham. 'And, please, if you could manage to spare some of that wine for my body servant here, it would stop his gaze boring into the back of my head like someone turning a screw.'

'Would you mind, Lady Gresham?' said Shakespeare, inviting her to fill a tankard for Mannion. He slurped away at it, happily.

A ladies' man, Master Shakespeare, thought Gresham, noting the brilliance of the artificial smile he flung at Jane. Full of contrasts. The wild smile of the actor, the drinker, the philanderer, the man with every mask at his disposal but no mask to call his own. The signs of dissipated living, the veins about to burst out. Yet at the same time the prosperity, the room with its fine chair, the fine hangings on the wall, the expensive goblet, all signs of worldly, rather than artistic, success. And hardly any books, just one chest with two or three volumes and some desultory papers! No pen, no paper! And no stains of ink on those long, bony fingers.

There was silence. Shakespeare looked away under the scrutiny of Gresham's gaze. 'What is it you want to talk about?' he finally asked.

'I was invited to investigate the loss of certain papers by Lord Cecil of unlamented memory, Sir Edward Coke and, I suppose, Sir Thomas Overbury.' At which name had Shakespeare started? He was trembling so much it was difficult to see. 'I now know much more than I did. I know, for example, that Kit Marlowe is back here in England and hell-bent on a killing spree.'

164

Shakespeare's hand gave a spasmodic jerk. His goblet flew off the table and rolled across the floor. There! That had made a crack in the wall! Shakespeare was not fat, at least not grossly so, but there were too many layers of softness over the bones that smoothed out his features. His gut wobbled as he jerked. A good few evenings in the tavern were stored there, thought Gresham.

'What I don't know is where a set of manuscripts relating to the work of Master William Shakespeare fit into this very complicated figure. And I would very much like you to tell me.'

'Will you kill me? Torture me?' Shakespeare's voice was plaintive now, almost as if he had been through this conversation before. Was it acting? Was it real? Or had this man lost the ability to distinguish between fiction and reality?

'If it appears you've betrayed me, or placed myself and my family at risk, I'll have no compunction in doing both. If you tell me the truth, then I'll do neither.' There was a certainty in Gresham's voice that was unanswerable. Jane remembered the spy of Cecil's infiltrated into their household years ago, held over a stinking pit that led to a deep, stone-walled chamber full of water, a chamber from which there was no escape. He had told the truth, eventually. They had then carefully broken his legs, as a reminder. No one betrays Henry Gresham. Jane shuddered at the memory. How was it possible to know so much and yet so little about a man?

'How simple life must seem as a spy!' barked Shakespeare. Another part, another role for the actor to play. The superior, angry man. Yet not played well, Gresham noted. He stopped short of making a true impact, like a punch pulled at the last minute. Shakespeare looked fully at Gresham now, into his eyes. 'You'll not torture and kill me if I tell you the truth, or so you say. Yet there are others who'll most certainly do both if I tell you what I know.'

This man, thought Gresham, is about to break up. He flings different personalities at me, each one less convincing, each one more fragile, each one less revealing of the man within. Whatever is happening to him, it has gone too far for him to be able to cope. Any moment now his heart will stop, or something will crack inside that bald pate. He is caught between a rock and a hard place.

'Is it Marlowe who's threatening you?' asked Gresham gently.

'Threatening me? He's tried to kill me once – and on stage! Good God! Some people really do take the theatre too seriously! If only it were that simple!' Shakespeare had slumped back in his chair and started to cry, a wailing, keening noise, racking sobs near lifting his plump body off the seat, his head held in his hands.

Gresham made a decision. 'Jane,' he said to his mistress. 'Would you please be nice to Master Shakespeare for a while, and talk about how bad you think some of Ben Jonson's writing is? You, Mannion, take Master Shakespeare's wine into a corner, after you've given him some of his own drink, and if he tries to run, kill him.' Gresham smiled at Shakespeare. 'I can't stand the smell of that bread through the window any more. We could all do with a bite to eat. I'll be back in a while.'

Gresham remembered the moment of communication with Andrewes, the single, fleeting meeting of minds in a strange communion. There would be no such meeting with this man. Every signal skittered off the face of his personality, tumbling, falling, never hooking in to anything permanent.

Gresham went down the stairs and greeted his men, who drew themselves up as he made his exit. He took four of them with him, leaving the others to guard the gatehouse. First stop was the bakery, where the soft, pungent aroma of freshly baking bread was taunting passers-by with its promise. Then rough-cut country cheese and butter from a farm wagon, and fresh smoked meats from a stall. Then to the tavern, a respectable-enough looking place, to explore the wine on offer. They haggled and, whistling, Gresham took his wine, picked up his men and went back to the gatehouse.

166

Jane was seated by Shakespeare on a stool, prattling away as if she had known him all her life. A storm of light flashed from her eyes as he entered, warning him off.

'And while I thought *Volpone* and *The Alchemist* were brilliant – and I told him so – I thought *Sejanus* was awful. Told him that, too, and he threw a chair out of the window. Fortunately, it was open . . .'

Underneath it all, her heart is bursting with worry – for me, for herself, for her children, thought Gresham. She hates the world I live in, and lives in it simply for me. Not so long ago she was fighting for her life and manning a boat like an Amazon. Now she's sitting here, chattering away as if she is a stage-struck girl hardly out of swaddling clothes. In a minute she'll tell me something I was too stupid to spot, and, God willing, by the time the night's over she'll have been a bed-mate for me and a true mother to her children. How many minds did God give this girl?

'I didn't think *Sejanus* was that bad . . .' said Shakespeare generously. Then he stopped. His eye had been caught by Gresham laying out a simple supper, two bottles of wine still under his arm. He was humming a tune to himself as he did so, Tom Campion's 'My Sweetest Lesbia'. The change from avenging fiend to table servant had startled Shakespeare. It had been meant to.

'But tell me about your plays, Master Shakespeare,' said Jane. 'I mean, I know he wants me to calm you down and soften you up so that you'll let out more information than you want to . . .' Shakespeare's eyes opened even wider. Well, thought Gresham, there's nothing like a dose of the truth to make things work. He had tried the tough way and lost. Let Jane do her worst. 'But I really, really do like your plays. And so, by the way, does he. More than that, in fact. He loves what you write almost as much as he hates the man who writes them.'

Why was this line of conversation seeming to make the man panic again? Gresham thought.

'I think you must be an amazing person, to write those comedies and then move on to histories and tragedies. If it was anyone else, they'd have stayed with one style, like Jonson has, and made it their speciality. Your plays – you seem to do each style better than anyone else and then move on! It's extraordinary.'

'Yes, isn't it?' said Shakespeare distractedly, as if he was trying to pass a large and sharp stone from his bottom. 'Actually, I prefer to talk about my poems, you know. The plays are how I earn my keep. The poems are where I feel I can write . . .' He wanted to talk about his *Rape of Lucrece*.

He babbled on, genuinely happier now he was off the subject of plays.

Gresham moved around the table. Shakespeare had only been renting these rooms for a month or so, Mannion had said. An old Dominican Priory, with more bolt holes and secret passages than a Catholic household, Gresham guessed. The water was only a few paces away, down St Andrew's Hill to Puddle Wharf. Had he moved here so he could run when danger threatened? If you looked carefully you could see where the door in the panelling opened up, but the carpentry was superb and it could only be seen as a door if one knew where to examine. There were no bookcases, Gresham saw with surprise, no sign of a library. Not even copies of his own plays, those that had been published. Only three books. *Venus and Adonis*. *The Rape of Lucrece*. His poems. And there were his sonnets, of course. Brilliant. Gresham, who had published his own sonnets under a false name, had felt the sharp sting of envy when he had read Shakespeare's work, always the sign of real power in another writer. It was a pirate edition, with the famous acknowledgement to 'Mr W.H.' as the 'only begetter' of the sonnets. In any event, the book was there, stuffed carelessly along with the others, in a chest with its lid open, a chest stuffed otherwise with printed pamphlets and broadsheets. One of them caught Gresham's eye. It had been torn out of something. *To our English Terence, Mr Will. Shakes-speare*.

Terence. The classical author.

Light exploded in Gresham's head. *Of course! The explanation! It had to be! What a fool he had been!*

'I'm sorry, Master Shakespeare,' Gresham said charmingly. None of the revelation in his mind showed. Shakespeare had paused in his explanation of *Venus and Adonis* to Gresham's own Venus. 'I really should have asked if you wanted to eat before I set your table. May I ask you to sit and sup of this very humble fare?'

Humble it might have been, but the way Shakespeare attacked the food after his initial hesitation confirmed what Gresham had thought. Master Shakespeare, who looked as if he had the capacity to be a good trencherman, had been feeding as well as drinking out of the bottle in recent weeks.

The wine was good. Not excellent, but good. Gresham treated himself to two glasses. Shakespeare had adapted with some ease to his attackers becoming his dinner guests. Actors, thought Gresham, do not live by any known codes. They are outsiders, perhaps even outcasts. They make their own rules. Shakespeare had insisted on moving to the next room – Mannion had moved casually to the door to make sure another priest's escape route was not being utilised – and bringing back four exquisite glasses, clearly Venetian. In Mannion's paw the vessel looked like a new-born babe in the hands of a devil. Just pray he doesn't smash it, thought Gresham. And that Shakespeare doesn't drop one, as he had dropped the goblet, when I tell him what I now know.

There are moments when humanity thinks history is made, when a great battle is fought or a mighty coronation observed. Yet there are other moments, hidden in the warp and weave of everyday conversation, masquerading as normality, that change lives and sometimes even the world. Moments which expose or hide a truth for ever more, that write a new version of human history. Moments based on the chance of a particular pamphlet lying at the top of a pile, and the chance of a particular man seeing it there at a particular moment when two glasses of wine had been drunk just ever so slightly too fast.

Gresham let Shakespeare finish his meal. He would need all the strength he could muster. He waited until the man, garrulous by now, was telling Jane about his plans for a new sonnet sequence. It was as if the room shivered before him. It was an extraordinary sensation, one he had never experienced. He had dealt with kings and queens! He had held their fate in his hands! He had kept secrets the world would have shuddered for! So why now, with the plump and drunk figure of a nobody in front of him, did he feel that something inexplicably important for the future was taking place in this room? He shook his head to rid it of this nonsense. He must have drunk more wine than he had thought. Then, in a pause while the actor reached for yet another glass, Gresham spoke.

'You didn't write your plays, did you, Master Shakespeare? You wrote your poems, I'm sure, but your plays – the work you've become famous for – *you didn't write them, did you?*'

Shakespeare looked at Gresham with an expression of such appalled horror that for a moment Gresham felt the most intense and cutting pity for the wreck of a man in front of him. Was he going to throw up the first food he had eaten in days? Or would he make it to speech first?

'I . . . how could you? Are you some devil incarnate?' There, it was out. And it was the truth, Gresham noted. If it were otherwise, the man would have denied it in his shock.

'No, no devil, as far as I know,' said Gresham. 'But I observe, and I listen. Manuscripts of plays are stolen, manuscripts presumably in the handwriting of their author. There's panic in the corridors of power. With the Catholics banished to hell for ever more after the gunpowder plot, there's a new power in the land. The Puritans. They get their Bible. They rail against the corruption of King and Court. And they hate the theatre above all else! They call it Satan's chapel, and the actors the spawn of Lucifer.'

'So?' said Shakespeare violently, rallying. 'We've endured their vilification for years. And not just them. We're vilified by the people who use us most, just like a whore! What of it?' There was a pathetic *braggadocio* to the man. Or perhaps a trace of real courage. Would Gresham have been happy to fight alongside this man? he wondered. Strangely, against all reason, perhaps he might have been. Providing, of course, he had been able to pour a bottle of wine down him first. Dismissing the thought, he bored in to Shakespeare.

'What if the very powers of the land, the Establishment, its aristocracy and nobility, have succumbed to the new power of the theatre? What if, instead of wanting their thoughts and dreams and the wild imaginings read out in private to a closed group of adoring Court ladies and fawning men, they want them played before thousands, night after night? What if they have found themselves lured into writing plays? Plays they cannot own up to, of course. Heaven forbid that the ruling classes should stoop so low as to write a play! Yet suppose their idle brains have found amusement in so doing? What easier than to find a cipher, a nameless man of the theatre, to give his name to their offerings? What if they chose a feeble poet, a man who had proved his ability for deceit in his life as a spy, and an actor of at best limited ability, to put his name to their work?'

'What if they have?' mumbled Shakespeare, seeming to see the end of the world in the bottom of an empty wine glass.

'Well then,' said Gresham, 'what if some mischief-maker decides to expose these idle aristocrats? Expose them to the Puritans. Expose them to the people as too cowardly to own up to their own words. Expose them as liars. Expose them as deceivers. *Expose them to ridicule!*'

'And what if they do?' Shakespeare had looked up from his glass now. He gazed into Gresham's eyes, but did not see them. He was looking into a void, an abyss of hopelessness that not even Gresham's greatest depression had plunged him in to.

'What if they do?' continued Gresham remorselessly. 'Well, we know our rulers are liars. Machiavelli told us why they have to be. Yet look at the response when Machiavelli dared to tell people the truth. He was consigned to hell. *We must not know that our rulers tell lies!* But if they do want to expose the truth,' Gresham carried on remorselessly, 'then two separate forces will work on the source of the lie. On you, Master William Shakespeare. The supposed author of these plays. The man who in reality takes the manuscripts, tidies them up a bit for theatre and puts them out as his work – all for a healthy fee, of course! There'll be the force of those who desperately want their foray into the theatre kept a secret. Then there's the other party, the ones who want their genius acknowledged, who want to take the glory of their writing for themselves.'

Shakespeare's head jerked up at that. So at least one person wanted their anonymity removed, wanted to claim the credit for the play they had laundered through Shakespeare's name.

'What a mess you're in, Master William Shakespeare! One party will try to keep your secret by having you killed. The other party will try everything to keep you alive and pressure you into telling the truth. And the manuscripts, the original manuscripts of the many and varied plays by William Shakespeare, will be in the handwriting of the original authors, for all that one or two may have trusted the writing to a treasured clerk.'

Shakespeare's head shot up. A hit! Which of Shakespeare's wealthy clients had sent his manuscript in by a clerk's hand, and not his own?

'No wonder you're being torn apart,' said Jane. 'You poor, poor man. You just can't win, can you?'

'How did you guess?' asked Shakespeare, looking bleakly at Gresham.

'The pamphlet. There, in the chest. "*To our English Terence, Mr Will. Shakes-speare*." Terence. Wasn't he the impoverished Roman writer who agreed to publish under his own name works that Roman noblemen had written but for one reason or another didn't care to acknowledge? Congratulations. Ben Jonson would be proud of you. For all your lack of classical learning, you've acted in a true classical tradition.'

'You think you know it all, don't you?' Shakespeare had gone beyond despair, into a region Gresham did not recognise.

'No,' said Gresham truthfully. 'I never think I know it all. I like to find out enough to survive.'

An agony of thought passed over Shakespeare's raddled face. Finally, he came to a decision. 'I was a nobody! I was struggling in the company. I can't act, you know. I'm hopeless! They were going to get rid of me, a poor country boy with no talent except a way with poems. Poems never filled a house. Then this manuscript arrived. A complete play! Addressed to me, with a covering letter and a promise of money if I did what I was told. I knew it was Marlowe, from the writing, the words, the way he used language . . . so I took it. And I gave it my name. I told Hemminge and Condell. My friends, no one else. They thought it was a gold mine. The others in the company, the ones who wanted to get rid of me, looked at me with new respect. "It's good, Will," they said, patronising me, when I produced the first script under my name. "We'll put it on, for a trial, you understand. See how it goes down. See if it works." And it meant I could stop working for Cecil. Say goodbye to William Hall. Be William Shakespeare only.'

'Poor old Marlowe, not wanting to be dead at all,' said Gresham. 'And most of all not wanting to be a dead dramatist.' He stopped for a moment. 'So what went wrong with the system?'

'I don't know!' said Shakespeare. His hands were running over his bald pate, as if the hair was still there. 'Marlowe's plays stopped, ten, maybe twelve years ago. They just stopped. Until now. When he came back. Mad. Diseased. Barking.'

'Any others know?'

'All the bloody world and their grandma for all I care!' exploded Shakespeare. 'Lots of people have suspicions. Jonson does, I know.

As for anyone else who knows for certain, well, you're the spy. You tell me!'

'But it didn't end with Marlowe, did it?' said Gresham, relentless. Shakespeare rocked back, hit hard. 'I knew Marlowe. I know the works he wrote under his own name. I know the plays you've written. My favourites?' Gresham was pacing around the room. '*Hamlet*. *King Leir*. Marlowe could never have written those! Marlowe's heroes never pause to worry about what other people think. Hamlet's crippled because he can think of nothing else. Leir's damned because he never listens until it's too late! *Who else writes plays with your name on them?*'

'Oxford,' whispered Shakespeare, seeming to draw into himself as a penis will shrink and shrivel with intense cold.

'WHO?' said Gresham with intense rudeness.

'EDWARD DE VERE!' Shakespeare shouted back. 'The fucking Earl of fucking Oxford! There were lots of people who wanted to write plays back then. People who didn't dare to have it known.'

'The one who couldn't forget the fart?' said Mannion, who had been listening, engrossed, to the developing conversation.

'What?' said Gresham.

'Oxford. De Vere. The one who couldn't forget the fart.' Mannion gave a guffaw of laughter. Edward de Vere, the Earl of Oxford, had been a fierce patron of the players. He had equipped and served on-board a ship for the Armada. Then he had farted. Before his Queen. In full assembly. He had run from the Court before a word could be said and exiled himself to Europe for years. There he had developed a fondness for the most extravagant Italian style of dress. On his return, he had presented himself before his Queen in all his finery. Whatever else she may have possessed, Queen Elizabeth had a raucous sense of humour. Faced with this extraordinary vision of Italian fashion, she had received his supplications of loyalty with regal splendour. Then she had reduced the Court to fits of suppressed laughter by her next statement.

'My lord, I had forgot the fart.'

De Vere could not now forget it. He had fled the Court a second time, permanently humiliated. He had died of the plague in 1604.

'*So who were these others?*' asked Gresham in a sibilant hiss.

If Shakespeare had made himself any smaller he would have vanished. 'Don't ask me any more!' he pleaded. 'You've a horde of men to protect you, against Marlowe and the rest of them! I've no one!'

'*Who else?*'

'Rutland.' It was said in a very, very small voice.

'*Who?*'

'Rutland. Roger. Roger Manners. Fifth Earl of Rutland. He died, in May. Just after your lord and master Robert Cecil! There! You've got it now, haven't you? Marlowe. Oxford. Rutland.'

'Marlowe. Oxford. Rutland,' said Gresham thoughtfully. 'What do they want of you?'

'Marlowe wants it shouted from the rooftops that he wrote my plays. All of them. Not just the handful he sent in a manuscript for. And he wants me to get The King's Men to perform his play, *The Fall of Lucifer*. He's tried to kill me once. Oxford and Rutland's heirs, they demand I keep silent. They don't want their illustrious parents damned by association with the theatre, don't want them seen as cheap conspirators. They've threatened me. Serious threats. Men with knives. I'm dead if I tell the truth, as Marlowe demands. I'm dead if I hide the truth, as the others want me to do.'

There were tears in Shakespeare's eyes, Gresham noted. There would have to be. He was an actor, after all.

'Marlowe. Oxford. Rutland. Are they the only ones whose plays you put your name to?'

'Isn't that enough?' Shakespeare shot back. 'How many more do you want?'

'One of the people you name is as mad as a hatter and likely to drop down dead of the pox at any moment. I can hardly be in

175

ignorance of him. One tends to remember anyone who's tried to skewer your wife on a crossbow bolt. The other two are dead.'

'So?'

'So I think you're only telling me the names of the people I can't talk to.'

Stalemate. Whatever Shakespeare was hiding, even his very visible fear of Gresham was not bringing it out.

'And you remained a spy, didn't you? Long enough to infiltrate the Bye Plot and place Sir Walter Raleigh in the dock?'

Shakespeare flushed. Yet he also fought back. 'I was seduced into the whole wretched business when I was too young to know better – as perhaps were you! It was exciting, wasn't it, when we were young? You were working for the greatest in the land, there was money in your pocket and you travelled as a king's messenger. And you, and Sir Walter Raleigh, greatly overestimate my part in his downfall. Sir Walter's always been his own worst enemy. Challenge him to be silent and you've a guarantee that he'll shout out loud.'

The problem was, Gresham thought, he was not far off the mark. Raleigh, one of the very few people Gresham had ever considered a hero, was too large for life. 'Your reward for Raleigh, and for acting as a front to other authors, was to have your company made The King's Men?' asked Gresham.

'Much more due to the latter than the former. My lord Cecil was amused to have a spy in the camp of a company of actors.'

Yes, I can see that, thought Gresham. The actors, the common players, despised of the Church, anarchic, a potential hot-bed of sedition and revolution and riot – and all the time, one of Cecil's men in a pivotal position in their midst. It would have amused Cecil, all the more so for the fact that no one would know.

'And if he was to have a spy in a company of actors, then of course it had to be the greatest, the best company of actors. Which meant we had to cease to be The Lord Chamberlain's Men and become The King's Men. And yes, Hemminge, Condell and

Burbage, they knew I was the reason. I told them. Though I didn't tell them why.'

'So William Shakespeare's plays aren't William Shakespeare's plays at all.' It was Jane, breaking a long silence. She was too old for there to be tears in her eyes. Yet the tears were there in her voice. 'Those plays that seemed so magical to me, they were nothing more than the playthings of noblemen too cowardly to admit their art, noblemen playing at writing plays, posturing beneath an adopted disguise. Well, my thanks to you, Master William Shakespeare. I used to think there was artistry and beauty and magic in the world of the theatre, even when it was stripped away from the world I actually lived in. Now I find it's just the same as everywhere else, just a little more dressed over. Thank you for educating me. Now I know there's no art. No magic. Only self-interest. How silly of me to need a reminder.'

She stood up and left the room, passing through the door to Shakespeare's sitting room, there presumably to commune with her own ghosts.

There were tears in Shakespeare's eyes, Gresham saw. One actually dribbled over his eyelid and fell down his cheek. It was a truism Gresham had heard countless times that a man could not counterfeit tears. His age respected emotion, not as something womanly in a man, but as a sign of genuine feeling. How good an actor was William Shakespeare? Gresham thought. Were his tears the burning mark of truth? Whatever the answer to that, Shakespeare was clearly a man who was down and out. Which, of course, was exactly the time for someone more ruthless to hit him twice as hard.

'How many plays did Sir Francis Bacon and Bishop Lancelot Andrewes write under your name?'

It had to be that! To hell with love letters! It wasn't those that Andrewes had asked him to destroy if he found them! It was plays! Bacon was too clever ever to put down in writing his love for another man. Andrewes would sooner burn his balls off with an altar candle than succumb to carnal temptation, if Gresham was any judge. But both men were prime candidates for the play-writing urge. They had fearsome intellects, the willingness to dare to be wise and the desire to try their hand at this new art form while knowing that their station and ambitions forbade them from so doing.

Gresham had never seen a man reduce in size before his eyes. Shakespeare seemed to wilt and shrink as he spoke his words. 'How much do you know?'

Gresham could have driven home then, taken all the advantage possible from his inspirational guesswork. Instead, remarkably, he decided to be merciful. Was it because the infinite compassion of Lancelot Andrewes had touched him to his soul? Or because he had seen his wife bid farewell to magic? Or was it because, all of a sudden, he was tired of the world, its double and treble deceptions?

'Far less than you might imagine,' he confided to Shakespeare. 'Yet I'd be willing to bet that Bacon and Andrewes were two of the men who submitted to your play-writing factory. Bacon wishes to be Attorney General. Andrewes wishes to be Archbishop of Canterbury. Neither would be helped in their ambitions by the realisation among the general public that they'd also wished to be stars at The Globe. Yet they're both writers of some brilliance. Both have minds that are incredibly active. Catch them at the right time and I doubt either could resist the chance to try their hand at this whole new world of plays. Like lambs to the slaughter, I imagine they were.'

'I . . .' Gresham had a sense that something had slipped in Shakespeare's mind, that at long last the truth was going to emerge. He waited, hardly daring to breathe.

There was a ferocious clatter of hooves outside and shouted orders. Jane came in almost immediately. Soldiers rushed up the stairs – the King's soldiers. Gresham's men would have been power-less. Their leader was Sir William Wade, the gruff Keeper of The Tower.

'Sir Henry. I am bidden by the King to bring you to his presence.'

'To Whitehall?' enquired Gresham mildly.

'No,' said Wade. 'To the Tower of London.'

Gresham would have expected a look of exultation on Shakespeare's face as they were led out. His victors vanquished. Instead, all he caught was a look of infinite sadness. William Shakespeare and Henry Gresham had stared into the same abyss, and were doing so even now.

15

September, 1612
The Tower of London

'Come, let's away to prison;
We two alone will sing like birds i' the cage'

SHAKESPEARE, *King Lear*

Damnation. This was bad.

'And is my wife also to be blessed with the privilege of meeting His Royal Highness?' asked Gresham.

'My instructions are that if she is with you, then yes, she also must . . . she also is invited.'

Jane had retained most of her colour. The eyes were at their darkest. He alone could read the tension in her body.

'My lady, we have the honour of an audience with the King. Shall we proceed?'

They left the house and entered the carriage Wade had brought along with him, watched by a small and silent crowd. Why were two masons and a housewife being whisked off to king's arrest?

The Tower was a royal residence right enough, but no king or queen had lived there for years. It was bleak, forbidding and not infrequently stinking, and its main use was as a royal prison. It had a dreadful reputation, a building erected to symbolise raw power where hundreds more had died within its walls than had been

180

executed on its green, and even more than that had screamed under its torture. The summons to The Tower was a signal. A signal of extreme disfavour.

God knew how Mannion had managed to be allowed to ride in the coach along with his master and mistress.

'He's trying to frighten us.' Gresham spoke tersely to Jane.

'It's worked,' said Jane, shivering inside her cloak. 'And there's me,' she said with a wry smile, 'with not a thing to wear.'

'Stay calm. Let me think.'

There was no point feeling fear at moments such as these. It was simply a diversion and a distraction. Nor was there time for tears or for talk. Focus. *Focus.* Become as hard as the stone of The Tower, as slippery as the eels in the river. On his ability to handle this situation rested his own fate, and that of Jane, his children and Mannion.

The bulk of The Tower and its grim curtain walls squatted over the Thames. First was the drawbridge leading over the moat, which was coated with scum and full of noisome lumps that did not bear close examination. The heavy wheels rattled over the wooden planking; they heard shouted instructions. A sharp left turn, the carriage groaning, under the Lion Tower, across the moat again and over the second drawbridge. The two round, squat forms of the Middle Tower stood in their way. More shouted instructions, a rattling as of chains, and the coach lurched forward again. Yet another drawbridge, and then the taller, round form of the Byward Tower. Under its rusting portcullis. Into the prison, with three vast towers and their gates blocking the route to freedom. At least they had not stopped even earlier and been put in a boat to be taken to The Tower through Traitors' Gate. Gresham's heart sank as it always did when he entered this desperate place, even on the weekly visits he made to see Raleigh. This time his wife was alongside him. Stop it! Don't divert! Don't weaken!

They were not to be sent pell-mell into some dripping, foul dungeon. James had hurriedly made a room in the White Tower available. It smelled of damp and decay, and there were bruised lumps on the wall where plaster had fallen off. The marks of the servant's brush were still on the floor. There was a vast fireplace in the echoing room, unlit, and one large window high in the wall. An ancient oaken table had obviously been retrieved from somewhere, behind which James had ranged seats. In front of the table were two poor stools. The judge facing the accused.

'The wisest fool in Christendom' an ambassador had called James. Son of Mary, Queen of Scots, he had been in his mother's womb when a group of Scottish nobles had murdered her lover, Rizzio, with cold steel in front of her. It was said he had a horror of naked blades from birth. Of no great natural beauty or form, his tongue was too large for his mouth and he was prone to slobbering as a result. He rarely washed, and seemed not to notice the filth that accumulated on the fine clothes he wore. Addicted to fresh fruit, his bouts of diarrhoea were legendary among those who had to clean his linen. Sweet wines were his other addiction. Few had seen him really drunk; even fewer had ever met him cold sober. Increasingly driving the late Robert Cecil, his Chief Secretary, to despair, James had spent more and more money as his reign progressed, perhaps a reaction to the poor, cold country of his birth and its famous poverty. And then there was his obvious lack of interest in women, and his attachment to young men.

Yet he must never be underestimated, Gresham reminded himself now. The King could order his and Jane's death immediately. This man had survived as King of Scotland, a country that ate its monarchs like others ate meat. While James was increasingly handing power to Parliament and the Puritans by his indolence and inaction, there was no hint of rebellion in the country. James was a writer and an intellect of no small merit. Like any king, he only enjoyed debates he was guaranteed to win, but the sharpness of his mind – when he cared to use it – had always been clear. King James I had an instinct for survival.

But so did Henry Gresham. And he had no doubt that it was his survival that formed the agenda for today's meeting.

James did not stand as Gresham and Jane were ushered in through the creaking door, and Mannion forced to stand by the back wall by the armed guards. Deliberate rudeness? Indolence? Or simply the Scottish informality James was renowned for, when it suited him? He had the pair of them at an immediate disadvantage, of course. Gresham was dressed as a mason, Jane as a housewife. The guards had taken the weapons from both men. Their disguise, and the weight of their personal armoury, made it clear they were up to some dissembling, devious purpose. It was extraordinary also how poor clothes stripped away a man's – and a woman's – self-respect. Well, Gresham had the power to imagine himself dressed in a king's ransom of clothing if he so wished. *He must not let it affect him!* It was also crucial to know how drunk James was. Gresham blotted all else out for the moment, even the other figures seated by the King.

The glass of wine was there, of course, easily to hand. Yet the hand was not quivering, and the eyes – small, hard – seemed steady enough. Oiled, then, but thinking. Well in control.

Gresham let his eyes move to the others at the table. Dear God. On one side was the popinjay Robert Carr, Viscount Rochester. On the other was Sir Edward Coke. Was this to be his tribunal? Was his vision of hell, to be in a court chaired by Sir Edward, now a reality? If so, he and Jane were dead. But give nothing away.

Gresham walked to a position just in front of the two stools. He bowed deeply to the King. The other two he ignored. He sensed the curtsey from Jane by his side. He was so proud of her. No tears, no wailing. She felt the fear, of course. Yet she had the mark of real courage. Feel the fear and conquer it.

'Sir Henry . . . and Lady Gresham . . .' The accent was already quite thick. Under pressure, or when the drink was truly in him, James retreated to a thick Scottish burr. The 'Sir' had almost been 'Sair'. *Pressure or drink?*

James waved a hand, carelessly. 'Or *is* it Sir Henry and Lady Gresham? Or two stonemasons and a housewife?'

There were titters from Coke and Carr. *Sycophantic idiots!* Gresham calmed himself.

'I believe we follow in a tradition set by Your Majesty's illustrious forbears,' said Gresham, bowing to the King. 'Previous monarchs of this country have changed their garb and wandered unannounced through their realm as though they were mere subjects . . .' *Or they had in folklore, at least. Most of them in reality wouldn't have lasted two seconds in a real bar room brawl.* 'It is sometimes good for those of lesser worth, such as my wife and myself, to emulate the actions of our superiors, and by doing so learn from them.'

You clever bastard, thought Gresham. *And, no doubt, thought King James. Yet it was good at this stage to not show too much fear.*

James paused for thought. Carr, Gresham had time to note, was gazing vacantly out of the window. There was a long pause.

'Would you care to take a seat?'

'We thank Your Majesty for his courtesy,' said Gresham. A seat in front of a monarch was a privilege. Courtiers spent most of their time standing. Yet the delay in asking them to sit had made it clear just what a privilege was being offered. Neutral. Neutral. Nothing yet on which to base a ploy. Listen. Look. Learn. Personally Gresham would have preferred to stand. He sat.

'Perhaps ye may be wondering why I summoned you here, rather to your surprise I should not wonder? I do apologise, of course, for any disruption to your plans.' The 'of course' rendered the apology meaningless. The threat was clear, unequivocal. It breathed out from the evil stone and brick that surrounded them. No one was brought to The Tower for their pleasure. 'I'm sure I may have dragged ye away from more important things.' The accent again. 'Ye' rather than 'you'. Had it been 'more', or was it 'mair'?

'There can be no more important things than Your Majesty's pleasure,' replied Gresham. *God, why do I hate this sycophancy so much?* 'We are more than pleased to serve Your Majesty, and count it a privilege to be in Your Majesty's presence at any time.'

'Aye,' said the King, 'you do that well, Sir Henry, well indeed.' Was there the slightest hint of a smile beneath the bearded face? If so, it vanished almost immediately. 'Yet the reason for my ordering this meeting is a good deal more important than the exchange of Court pleasantries, however weel ye may do them. There's shite on the velvet of your reputation, Sir Henry. I fear you may be working against me, sir!' James's coarseness was legendary. In the popular eye it was one reason why he had felt uneasy at appointing the clean-mouthed Andrewes as Archbishop of Canterbury.

Time for a hard stab.

'I am mortified to hear so, Your Majesty. Yet I will say to you now, sire, with your permission, that I have never in my life knowingly stood against any crowned monarch, or sought to dispute the right of any monarch to govern and to rule. I believe the health of the nation lies in the health of the monarch. I have been willing in times past to put my own life down as my bargaining counter to support that belief.'

Well, thought Gresham, that's almost the truth. I actually believe better the devil you know, and better any devil than the devil of rebellion. I've seen where that leads.

There was a dignity and power to Gresham's simple statement that carried its own weight of meaning. There was a prolonged silence. James reached out and took a lingering sip of his wine. Then he looked, pointedly, at Sir Edward Coke.

Coke was the accuser! That look told Gresham his true enemy!

Coke also knew that he was on trial. Yet there was the flush of achievement in his face. He had manoeuvred Gresham onto his own choice of battleground. This was a court hearing. Coke was the prosecutor. Gresham and his impossibly beautiful wife the accused. But there was no jury here to call the prosecutor to order. Merely a half-sodden monarch, whose single word could mean that this man and his wife never left The Tower.

'Yet you would not deny, Sir Henry,' asked Coke in his most silky voice, 'that you were instructed by the late Lord Salisbury to find and return certain . . . papers. Papers that were of importance to His Majesty? And that you were instructed by the same good lord to work with myself in pursuit of that aim?'

Carr was gazing, his mouth half-open, at Coke. The distaste he felt for the wrinkled lawyer was clear. Did Carr have any brain at all?

It was an old lawyer's trick. Start reasonable. Ask questions to which there was only one, positive answer. Establish thereby one's desire as a prosecutor to be fair to the witness. And then screw him. Therefore, it was necessary for Sir Henry Gresham to stop the process somehow.

First of all, he looked to the King, his eyebrow slightly raised. Do I have your authority to answer this man? the eyebrow said. After all, in a room where the King of England (and Scotland, in this case) sits there is only one authority. Before speaking to a lesser authority, one should obtain the permission of the higher authority.

There was an almost imperceptible nod from James. Yet he would have noted the courtesy.

'I fear I would deny that, Sir Edward.'

Coke looked as if he had swallowed a prune stone. This was not according to the plan.

'It is possible that for you a summons from Robert Cecil was a new occurrence. I regret that for me, and indeed latterly for my wife, it was no such thing.' Gresham turned to James, speaking as if in confidence. 'Cecil used me as an agent in Your Majesty's interests on numerous occasions. Such summonses usually came late at night, latterly in the form of one Nicholas Heaton.' The air froze for a moment. 'These calls were peremptory and always involved me risking my life. For some reason, it always seemed to be my life and never Cecil's. I grew accustomed to accepting the challenges, but not without noting with whom lay the danger.'

It was there! Something that was unequivocally a smile, albeit briefly, had passed over James's face.

'But you cannot deny that you were summoned, and that you were given instructions?' Coke bored in, only half-realising that he had given away most of his game plan. He was harsh, aggressive. This should have come later. Somehow Gresham had managed to jump the hearing forward.

'But of course.' Gresham was now all sweet reason. Yet he should have been nervous, on edge, and Coke the voice of calm. 'Of course I was summoned, as in countless times past. And, as in countless times past, I went. I went, Your Majesty,' and as Gresham spoke he turned again to the King, 'to meet Robert Cecil, your Chief Secretary. To my surprise, I found the meeting was with Robert Cecil and with Sir Edward Coke. And later, after he had beaten up a servant and tried to attack me, with Sir Thomas Overbury.'

'Ye met Overbury? And he was violent?' James had let his head sink into his vast ruff, but now he straightened up. Had Coke been stupid enough not to tell the King of Overbury's presence? Yes, by the look on his face! Before Coke could interject, Carr jumped in.

'Your Majesty,' he said, 'this slander against Sir Thomas is unfair, without Sir Thomas here to prove it false. Might I ask to summon him . . .'

'No, sir, you may not.' The King cut off his favourite with a sharpness Gresham had never seen before. That tightening across James's brow – James tolerated Overbury because he loved Carr, and Overbury made it so that the one had to come with the other. Yet even James was not insensitive to the awfulness of the man. 'And did it surprise you, Sir Henry? To find Sir Edward there?' It was the King who spoke, to Coke's obvious annoyance. Coke had raised his hand to respond as well.

'Yes, Your Majesty,' replied Gresham candidly. 'And horrified me.'

Was he prepared to take the greatest gamble of his life? A gamble that would risk not only his own life, but the lives of those he loved? One throw of the dice to decide it all?

He threw the dice.

'You see, Your Majesty,' he explained carefully, 'I despise Sir Edward.'

Robert Carr sucked in his breath so hard as to make it ricochet in the half-empty chamber.

'I do so,' Gresham flung into the silence that followed his bomb blast, 'because I believe he helped betray the man I see both as my early patron and hero, Sir Walter Raleigh.'

There was a gasp from Carr. Walter Raleigh, locked up for years now on the King's orders after a show trial led by Coke. Walter Raleigh, his estate at Sherborne ripped from him and given to Carr. To protest his case before the King and to claim an allegiance to Raleigh was to appear before God and declare a pact with Satan. Double jeopardy. Was Gresham intent on suicide? An expression of glee crossed Coke's face. An expression of distaste flickered on James's brow. Before it could take seat, Gresham spoke on.

'I beg your forgiveness, Your Majesty, for my feelings towards that man. I know that in speaking of my belief in him I risk forfeiting my own life, and that of my wife and children. I know you believe he has done you grievous wrong.'

King James loathed Raleigh, saw him as the last of the great Elizabethans and one of the greatest threats to the monarch who had succeeded Elizabeth. Gresham's friendship with Raleigh was widely known. Coke had hoped to introduce it perhaps two-thirds of the way through the interrogation, and use it to damn Gresham. However, it seemed Gresham was going to use it to damn himself.

'And do you challenge that he is a threat to me? Do you challenge that he has sought to do me grievous wrong?' King James leaned forward as he spoke, aggressive, almost violent in his tone.

'I know you believe him to be so. I know you have the power to make that belief a lasting judgement. I would plead with you, as others have pleaded with you, to review that judgement, though at a different time and hopefully in a different place. Yet I give you my word that at no time have I or will I ever conspire against Your Majesty, or use my friendship with Sir Walter to do so.'

'Words are fine things,' said the King after a pause. It was impossible to judge his feelings from his face. 'Sir Edward here for one deals with them very finely. But words are not always the truth, are they, Sir Henry?'

'That certainly is true,' replied Gresham, feeling his way, 'but I would ask Your Majesty to consider one thing.'

'Which is?'

'Sir Walter Raleigh saved my life. I am indebted to him. It would have been easy for me to cut off from him when Your Majesty's disfavour became clear, to dissemble, to lie about my feelings in order to worm my way into Your Majesty's favour. To become a fawning courtier. As so many have sought to do.' He turned pointedly to Coke, who had the decency to flush. 'My loyalties are worn on the outside of my body, for all to see. They are to Your Majesty, to my friend and to my wife and children.' Though in reverse order, as it happens, thought Gresham, bearing in mind that it would not be tactful to tell that particular truth at this particular moment. 'I suppose I am asking Your Majesty to see my declared love for Sir Walter as proof of something else. I am no dissembler. I am no liar. I am no threat. It may well be that I am a devil of sorts. At least I am the devil that is known.'

'Well, you have my eldest son and my heir on your side, Sir Henry, that much is true . . .' Prince Henry visited Raleigh, talked to him. Some said he viewed Raleigh as more of a father than James, admired him far more. It would not necessarily be of any help to Gresham. Indeed, it was rumoured that Prince Henry's affection for Raleigh increased his father's wrath against him.

'But yet . . .' King James's face lit up. Gresham had seen it do so once before, when he had paraded bishops and clergymen before him for a debate, and for a few brief moments the matter had gone beyond its tedious script and a real dialogue had taken place. It had been between James and Andrewes, Gresham now remembered.

'. . . this is the issue Sir Edward brings to me! He does believe you are a threat, Sir Henry. A most serious threat.'

Gresham felt the dryness in his throat, the tension rising in his neck.

'How might that be so, sire?'

Sir Edward leaned forward, eager to state his authority and his case. James waved him into silence, to an apoplectic response all the more fearsome for the fact that Coke could not vocalise it. Was he going to blow up? thought Gresham. It seemed Coke's fate to be told to shut up in Gresham's presence, either by the late Robert Cecil or by the King.

'I have a man called Marlowe in my care, Sir Henry. A dead man already, who from the wound in his arm is lucky not to have been killed twice over.'

Damn! How had Marlowe of all people gained sanctuary from the King?

'I understand that you were instrumental in "arranging" the death of this man many years ago. Testimony that despite your words, Sir Henry, there is much that you do and have done that is not worn on the outside, and about which the truth is not known.'

'Certainly, sire, I helped arrange for his escape. The fake death was Marlowe's idea. He never could distinguish between high drama and reality.'

'More importantly, I understand that this man had papers of mine that I wished to regain possession of. Sir Edward acted as my agent in this matter. You may speak now, Sir Edward.'

Coke needed no second bidding. Gresham could see he was straining to stand up, desperate to pace the courtroom. 'This man Marlowe approached me after you, Sir Henry, failed in your attempts to track him down.'

So that was how Marlowe had broken through into the King's hearing. He had gone directly to Coke this time, as he had gone to Overbury before.

'With His Majesty's permission, we arranged for the return of the papers. I even sent one of His Majesty's servants with Marlowe to supervise the collection of this material, hidden, I believe, in a strange place . . .'

Gresham could sense what was coming.

'Nicholas Heaton was the servant. He seemed suitable for these . . . underhand dealings, as he had gained experience under his former master. And lo and behold, what is the outcome?'

Coke was now well in his stride, declaiming, almost roaring. Gresham had seen the mood and the delivery once before, at Raleigh's trial. Its presence now, triumphalist as it was, did not bode well.

'We find that after weeks of apparent ignorance about this man Marlowe, the man whose false death you orchestrated all those years ago, all of a sudden you are there at the very time and in the very place these papers are being retrieved! An extraordinary co-incidence, is it not? We find these papers are taken off Marlowe – stolen from him – *by you*. Marlowe is grievously injured – *by you*. His servant is crippled – *by you*. And Nicholas Heaton ends up a bloodied lump at the foot of King's College Chapel – murdered, we must assume, *by you!*'

Put like that, thought Gresham, it did not sound as if he had a terribly strong case for the defence.

Coke was in his element. 'Do you view it as your right to murder the King's servants? And why, when you are so contrite about posing no threat to His Majesty, do you continue to hold papers that you know could be damaging to him?'

'Your Majesty,' said Gresham. 'I do not believe it is my right to murder your servants.'

Though I would like to ask why it is that they seem to consider they have a right to murder me.

A few precious seconds to think. Some things at least were clearer now. Marlowe had some other hold over James. He had used it to strike a bargain – money? His life? Even a performance of his play? Heaton had been sent along as his minder. With the

King's backing it became clear why the route into King's College Chapel that night had been so effortless, why so many doors that should have been locked had been opened. Gresham wondered whether the intended finale for the evening would not have been the death of Marlowe anyway.

'The story is a simple one,' Gresham said. Well, probably it was. The problem was that he had not yet written it. Gresham looked again to the King.

'Your Majesty, Sir Edward is correct in that I had failed to trace Marlowe. He despises me, by the way. I was instrumental in getting him over to France, but for whatever reason things went wrong for him after that and I became an object of his hatred. He attempted to murder me and my wife at The Globe theatre. By means of several vagabonds and a crossbow bolt. I'd even greater desire than Sir Edward to find Marlowe. He was a personal threat to me and my dearest, as well as to my ruler.'

James was clearly interested now. He had not sipped at the wine for minutes, was leaning forward with his head cupped in his hands, his eyes fixed on Gresham. James had enjoyed interrogating witches in the past, Gresham remembered, and had seen himself as a skilled cross-examiner. Unfortunately the witches had ended up being burned alive.

'Your Majesty, on the night in question I was visited by a drunken sot who is one of my Cambridge informers. LongLankin by name. He'd seen Marlowe in a house. LongLankin, and the college porter who saw me eject him after midnight, will confirm what happened. They're both simple men, not able to deceive. I set off to see if Marlowe was still there.'

'*Alone,* Sir Henry? Set off alone at night when by your own admission you knew you faced attempts on your life? Can we believe—?' Coke's tone expressed total disbelief.

So, to Gresham's intense surprise at her interruption, did Jane's. 'Yes, Your Majesty, we can believe! Hard though I found it to believe, and hard though I sought to make my husband's life when

I heard of his crass idiocy!' Jane, silent until now, had risen to her feet, her head still bowed in deference to her King, her every muscle tense, her eyes flashing. 'A *lawyer*' – what a world of scorn there was in her voice – 'would have waited for other people to act, would have considered his position, hidden behind someone else, sat back, weighed the odds. A normal, sensible man would have waited for help, called out to servants! A normal, sensible man would have stopped to think! Yet my husband is neither normal nor sensible. He is a fool, Your Majesty, a fool who cannot resist the excitement of action and who throws caution to the wind if by haste he can speed up the resolution of an incident. I sometimes think he is in a hurry to meet his own death, and has been since the day he was born.'

'And you still love him?' James's voice was flat, without emotion.

'Your Majesty, I have no option,' she said simply. James looked at her for a moment, with the dark, dead eyes of a fish. He nodded to her, not without courtesy. She bowed her head and retreated to her seat.

'Carry on, Sir Henry.'

'Your Majesty, I followed Marlowe and his servant to the chapel. Followed them in. Saw the servant take a satchel out from behind the beams in the space between the vaulting and the roof. I knocked out the servant and took the satchel from him. Marlowe threw a knife at me. I threw that same knife back, hit him in the arm. I had partly tied them both up, intending to remove them to a place of safe-keeping, when I heard a noise from the roof. I went up. Whoever it was tried to knock me off the ridge. I killed him, after he had tried to kill me. Only then did I realise it was Heaton.'

'Why did you hurl him off the roof?' It was Coke, trying to wind himself up again.

'He still had breath and some blood in him after I pierced his neck with my sword. I hung him over the parapet to try and extract information from him. Why was he there? Who'd sent him? Why had he tried to kill me? He was the King's servant. It seemed wise to know . . .' Gresham turned and gave a low bow to the King '. . . if I was indeed to have my murder sanctioned by Your Royal Highness. He died before he could speak, and slipped off the parapet. When I got back to the vaults, Marlowe had gone.'

'And if your actions were so innocent to the King's interests, why have you not returned these letters to me or to His Majesty?' Coke was almost screaming.

'Because the satchel was empty.'

There was a horrified pause.

'*Empty?*' It was Coke.

'And wad you be guid enough . . .' the accent was as thick as sour cream now '. . . to tell your King why you think it might have been so?'

'There is only one explanation,' Gresham replied. He said no more. The tension mounted with the silence.

'Go on!' said Coke.

'Nicholas Heaton. I guess he removed the actual papers some time beforehand.'

'Preposterous!' exploded Coke. 'Your evidence?'

'It is reasonable to suppose that Marlowe had told Heaton roughly where the papers were hidden. He would have to have done so, for Heaton to arrange for the relevant doors to be left unlocked. Yet there are very many bays behind the beams, any one of which might have held the papers. You have to reach over a top layer of bricks to feel inside the bays. There is years of dust and bird droppings on top. Do you still have Heaton's clothes? If you do, you will notice that the bottom half of the sleeves on his tunic are soiled with just such dirt, and part torn. I noticed it immediately. I think Heaton had searched several of the bays before he found the one with the papers in it. He took them out before Marlowe arrived.'

'Why would one of the King's servants do such a thing?' asked Coke, floundering.

'You are innocent in the ways of espionage, Sir Edward, for all your skill in a court of law!' Gresham was scathing. 'The charitable reason was that Heaton did not trust Marlowe, was expecting some surprise or other. Far more likely is that Heaton intended to use the papers for his own advantage. It is my guess that he would have killed Marlowe and his servant, perhaps coming back to you and saying the papers were not there. More likely, you'd never have seen him again. He would've sold the papers to the highest bidder and vanished overseas with the proceeds.'

'Is this not disloyalty beyond belief?' Coke spluttered.

'Think, Sir Edward.' Gresham was lecturing now. 'For years the man had bullied and chased for Robert Cecil, dealing with the lowest of low life and, no doubt, taking bribes as a matter of course. Important and loyal enough to be granted a new job, surely, but with none of the access to that master that guaranteed him so much favour with his first employer. A servant's wages, Sir Edward? Compared with the value of those papers, and a life in the sun where he would never have to call another man master?

'Your Majesty, I do not have those papers,' continued Gresham, his eyes meeting those of King James directly and without flinching. 'I never did. I do have the satchel in which they were contained. No doubt you are searching my homes now. You'll find nothing, except the satchel. My people in Cambridge will confirm what I have said. And if you send a messenger up into the vault of King's College Chapel, ask him to check how many of the bays behind the roof beams have had their layer of dirt and dust recently disturbed. See if Heaton's tunic has been kept, and examine it. Or ask of those who stripped him before his burial.'

'So you did nothing, Sir Henry,' mused the King, 'because you thought it might be myself who wished to dispose of you? Are you willing to call a king a murderer then?' The silkiness of James's tone did nothing to diminish its menace.

'I would be most loath to do so, Your Majesty. Yet Your Majesty will understand me if I say that where there are plots, a wise man considers that all things might be true until they are proved false.'

195

James had survived the Bye and the Gunpowder plots to kill him, as well as an attempt to blow him up in Scotland. 'I will suggest, with the greatest respect, that despite Sir Edward's attempt to have me beheaded, you've more need of my services than ever. Sir Edward is a great lawyer. He's a babe in swaddling clothes when it comes to darker matters. Those letters are still around. I will find them. I will return them to their author. If I am so permitted by Your Majesty.'

James sat back in his chair, reached for his wine and took a long, appreciative slurp. 'Well, well,' he said with a sigh. 'Who would have thought such a day could provide such entertainment.' He looked at Gresham. 'I am inclined to take you at your word. In every respect. As you have guessed, your houses are being searched at this very time. I will indeed send to Cambridge. I will send a trusted man into these vaults of which you speak. I will see if Master Heaton's clothing has been retained. In the meantime, I think a chamber can be found here for you, your wife and your man there. One with a real fire, perhaps.'

'I am thankful to Your Gracious Majesty for his hospitality,' bowed Gresham.

'One more thing,' said James, rising to leave. 'There will be guards posted at your door. For your own protection, of course. And to ensure that your close proximity to your good friend Sir Walter does not encourage you to visit him, or he to visit you.'

Gresham, Jane and Mannion bowed deeply as the King left the dank chamber. Coke waited behind.

'You—' Gresham rounded on him, cutting him short with the sheer compressed ferocity of his voice. 'You have tried to lose me my life, Sir Edward. You were unwise to make even more of an enemy of me.'

Guards came, politely enough, to march them off. Jane turned to Gresham, her eyes close to desperation. 'How could you . . .' she began. He knew what she wanted to say. How could you give all those hostages to fortune – the torn tunic, the scruffed brickwork, denying you have the letters when they will turn our houses over and find even your most secret of hiding places . . .

He placed a finger to his lips and tried to force a world of words into his gaze. The guards would have been told to listen out for just such a conversation, and one misplaced word could cost them their lives. In their new rooms there would most likely be a hole in the wall or roof with a man or two listening for the duration of their imprisonment.

All this he tried to tell her, and more, silently. To tell her that, before pushing the body to the ground, he had rubbed the tunic arms of the dead Nicholas Heaton across the stonework and the bird shit on the roof until they were stained and one arm torn. That, for good measure, he had torn off a tiny strip from one of the letters, with a single, harmless word on it in the King's hand, and stuffed it into the pocket of the dead man's tunic. To tell her that he had descended from the roof and back into the vaults, his every nerve straining for sounds of more visitors, and carefully reached over and disturbed the dirt in every single bay in the vaults, filling his nose with dust and making his throat like sandpaper. To tell her that the secret hiding places in The Merchant's House and The House were now covered with a thick layer of sand, as if they had tried to soundproof the floors of both buildings, and that the mechanism that swung up the plank had been removed, the plank nailed to the joist just like any other. There were two other hiding places in both houses, full of trifles, designed to be found in just such a search. To find the truly secret places they would have to rip up every floorboard in both houses, and dig deep into the sand. He wanted to tell her, without words, that even if they did, both gun-metal boxes were empty. The papers were where King James could never find them. All this, he wanted to tell her, he had done just in case. That he was above all a professional, and it was because he did such things that he had lived longer than any other. To tell her that he had taken extra care to prepare his alibi this time, because he knew it was her life he was playing with as well as his own. To tell her that they were secure. To tell her that he had mentioned none of the precautions he had taken because if she did not know she could not tell others of them, even by accident.

She looked, and she looked, and she looked into his eyes. And then, the guards noticed, something almost like a smile came over her face. She held out her hand. Sir Henry Gresham, Lady Gresham and his manservant walked together into captivity in the Tower of London, smiling.

16

7th November, 1612
The Tower of London

'And the king was much moved, and went up to the chamber over the gate, and wept: and as he went, thus he said, "O my son Absalom, my son, my son Absalom! Would God I had died for thee, O Absalom, my son, my son!"'

KING JAMES BIBLE

However much they built up the fires, the chill of The Tower entered into their bones. Winter had come to London late but with a vengeance; a cold, dripping winter rather than a fierce, freezing winter.

'How much longer?' Even though they were outside, in a brief respite from the cheerless rain, Jane half-whispered the question to Gresham. Sir William Wade, increasingly out of love with his job and his employer, had allowed them full use of his private garden. 'What a world for our children,' Jane spoke in her low voice. 'No mother, no father, a sense of dread hanging over them every bit as real as the sentence hanging over us.'

Gresham's own spies – James's court leaked information and gossip like a boat on the rocks – told him that the alibis had been proven. Heaton's tunic, too expensive to throw away, had been kept. The scrap of letter had been found, and taken as proof that

Heaton had in fact had the documents in his pocket. The searches of The House and The Merchant's House had been savage, and had led in the case of The House to a pitched battle between the soldiers undertaking the search and the servants. The servants had won, Gresham had been privately delighted to note, but someone had had the sense to call on Gresham to declare peace. He had been taken with Jane in a closed carriage to The House, where they had calmed their men down and told them to co-operate completely. They had shuddered at the ripped-up panelling and floorboards, but Jane had been stalwart in the face of Gresham's rising anger.

'Money can mend wood. Be thankful it's not more important things they've damaged.'

They had not found the gunmetal cabinet, Gresham noted, though they had found and ransacked one of the false hiding places behind a fireplace.

'How long?' Gresham answered. 'Who knows? There's no case to answer against us. I suspect the King no longer sees us as a threat. Yet he'll have Carr acting as a mouthpiece for Overbury, and arguing for us to be kept here for ever. And Coke will hardly want me on the loose.'

'Are you saying we're here for ever?' asked Jane, a plaintive note creeping into her voice. It cut to Gresham's heart, but he did no more than squeeze the warm hand that held his.

'No. I don't think so. I really don't think so, as distinct from simply telling you what you want to hear. James is indolent, above all. He takes the easy route. With Carr and Coke biting at his heels, it's easier to keep me here than to release me. It does no harm to James, and it makes a point to anyone who cares to listen that no one is above the King's law. He'll release me eventually. What a pity there isn't a crisis to provoke him into needing me.' He turned to Jane, eyes laughing despite the pallor of incarceration. 'Perhaps I ought to threaten him with those letters!'

'Sssh!' she exclaimed, horrified. The fact that her husband still held damning letters from the King to his lover, and had flatly denied doing so to the King, was the stuff of her nightmares.

She did not have to be in The Tower at all, of course. Queen Anna was a featherbrained barmaid who was as far away from Jane in appearance and personality as two human beings could ever be. Yet, from a distance, the two had struck up a perfectly servicable relationship in which both women actually seemed to quite like each other. Gresham had questioned the relationship.

'Imagine being married to a wet frog!' was all Jane had said. There was a language that passed between women that Gresham did not understand.

Queen Anna had interceded with the King, on one of the rare times they actually met, and spoke to each other nowadays. She had swept into Gresham's rooms in The Tower, nodded dismissively to Gresham and removed Jane to an adjoining room. Half an hour later they had returned.

'You are very blessed,' Queen Anna had announced regally, 'with your wife.'

'As indeed is the King,' Gresham had bowed low, 'with his consort and mother of his children.'

The two women had looked at each other and shrugged. Queen Anna swept out again.

The results of the meeting were immediately clear. Jane no longer had to remain in The Tower and was free to return to either of her homes. Equally, it was decreed, should she wish to move her children in with herself and her husband, accommodation would be found. She had compromised, staying in The House from Monday evening to Fridays, joining Gresham for the weekends. She had drawn the line at introducing her children to The Tower. Its air was frequently foul and always dank, the rooms cheerless and damp, and the atmosphere of the place was one of pain, suffering and terror.

'They're too young for this,' she had declared. 'When we have to, we'll cope, as Raleigh's family have coped. Until we have to, let the children have their freedom. Even without their parents.' Yet she missed her babes on her Saturdays and Sundays with Gresham, missed them desperately. Gresham heard her sobbing in the small hours when she thought he was asleep.

'How reassuring,' Gresham had said, 'that you assume periodic sojourns in The Tower are doomed to be our lot.'

'I know who I married,' she replied dryly. There had been a near disagreement over the children's nurse on the Saturdays and Sundays when Jane was ministering to her master.

'Mannion?' Gresham had exclaimed. 'Mannion! My young children lose their mother two days out of seven to Mannion? If fish drank like him there'd be no water left in the oceans. His manners make a pig look respectable. Given half a chance, he spends every evening in the stews. He's a threat to anything on two legs, and for all I know anything on four! Whilst I'm languishing in The Tower, my children are being brought up by an ageing lecher with a drink problem and no education.'

'Who brought you up?' Jane asked simply.

Gresham rocked back on his heels, thought for a moment, and grinned. 'Mannion,' he replied, remembering his loveless childhood and the rough affection that Mannion had lavished on him.

'Well,' said Jane, 'don't deny your children the same opportunities.'

There were times when this woman really annoyed him.

For all that, he wished she were there when a bedraggled King James of all England and Scotland walked unannounced into his chambers that evening.

Gresham had heard the news. Setting up a decent information system had been almost his first priority when he had been consigned to The Tower. Sixth November, 1612. Prince Henry, the eldest son of King James I, heir to the thrones of England and Scotland, had died. The most brilliant, the most perfect and the most promising heir England had had in many a year. Handsome, intelligent and with a charismatic flair that lingered long after he had left a room and its inhabitants. A young man with a sense of occasion, but also with a sense of justice. A man in love with martial arts. A prude, some said, blessed with too great a sense of his own righteousness. A boy obsessed with warfare said others. A king for all seasons said the majority. A real king at last. For many of James's subjects, surveying the decadence and expense of his Court, it was easy enough to tolerate King James when the prospect of King Henry lay on the horizon.

And now Henry was dead. Dead of a flux and a fever, despite the best efforts of every London doctor.

Gresham had heard of the illness, and of the death, and his heart had sank. Prince Henry was a future king for whom spies would be willing to die. Now all that was left was Charles. Weak, vacillating, desirous to please Charles. What would the future hold for England under King Charles I?

King James stumbled into his rooms long after the bell signalling the closing up of The Tower. There was a clattering outside, muttered words, scurrying feet. Then James walked in through the door, unannounced. He did not knock, Gresham noted.

There was more than the usual filth on the extravagant clothing of England's king. The jewels around his neck and sewn into his garments would have fed a city for months. More extraordinary were the marks of tears down his cheeks. His doublet was unlaced. He sat down in Jane's chair. Gresham had spent a lifetime training his mouth not to drop – had he not done so, it would have dented the floor. And, by the by, his eyebrows would have become permanently entangled in his hairline.

'Drink!' the King of England roared to someone outside the room. There was a hurried scuffling and a terrified footman brought in a wooden tray with five bottles on it. Wine of the most tremendous value. With two extraordinarily beautiful goblets of pure gold.

'Open!' said the drunken King. 'No! Not for us both. That bottle' – he pointed firmly to one pillar of dark glass – 'for me. The other bottle, that one *there*, for Sir Henry. For him alone.'

The King turned to Gresham. '*In vino veritas*, Sir Henry

Gresham. You'll drink that bottle there as fast as you can. And when you've drunk your fill, we'll talk. Man to man. Drunken man to drunken man. Drunken father to drunken father.' It was then the tears started to fall. Huge globules of water forming in the King's eyes and dropping from them down his cheeks, as if every liquid he had ever drunk was turned to tears.

And so it was that the strangest drinking session in English or Scottish history began and ended, in a set of rooms in the Tower of London in the late evening, with the King of England present and a prisoner his drinking companion.

Gresham took the bottle his monarch had gestured to and poured himself a full measure. He brought it to his lips. The wine was Rhenish – powerful, potent, intoxicating. He drank it in one single gasp. The King looked on, nodded approvingly and motioned to continue.

In the space of a few minutes, Gresham sank a bottle of wine from the King's cellar.

He had always had an extraordinarily good head for wine. Would it hold up tonight? The excitement, the unexpectedness, the sheer maniac improbability of the evening began to take hold of him.

'And now we'll bide our time awhile,' the King stated, sipping at his own goblet, the tears still flowing. He wanted Gresham drunk before they talked. As drunk as he was. Or even drunker. 'You!' the King yelled to the servant again. 'That other bottle! There! Open it for my guest. You'll keep drinking, Sir Henry, if you please. Not whole bottles. But keep drinking.'

James and his son had been in frequent disagreement, Gresham reminded himself. Prince Henry had been polite, prurient and careful with money. The young man, only recently named Prince of Wales, had made no secret of the extent to which he disagreed with his father's lifestyle. Perhaps for this reason, Queen Anna had preferred her next son, Charles.

Yet the drinking contest had to be entered in to. James had not asked him to drink a whole bottle of wine, he had commanded it.

First the lancing of thirst, then the tremors of excitement. Then the power of alcohol, the growing self-belief. Then the vainglory, the assumption that anything was possible. Then the tiredness, the overwhelming urge to sleep. Then the loss of consciousness. And then the payment, in pain and sickness, for the days to follow. Gresham knew all these. James thought he was the first person to have ensured truth with drink. Well he would, wouldn't he? Roman spies had used the trick as a matter of course. Roman spies, and spies for King James I of England and Scotland, had learned ways to cope. There was no point in denying the physical power of the alcohol. The trick was in learning to keep a part of the mind separate from it all.

'D'ye think they murdered my son, Sir Henry?' asked the King when there had been enough time for the bottle of wine to sink in.

The room was spinning slightly, and Gresham's brain seemed to have become so divorced from his speech centres and muscles. A chasm opened up in his mind, a dread, dark abyss that had nothing to do with the drink. Suppose the search for the papers had been nothing but a diversion to put me off the scent? To stop the country's best agent discovering or acting on a plot to murder the heir to the throne?

What had Cecil said? That on no account could the country be allowed to displace one king for another, however promising the heir? Could Cecil have masterminded the whole thing from the grave, removing from the scene the only rightful alternative to King James I? He had tried to sidetrack Gresham once before, attempted to send him off on a wild goose chase to take his mind away from more important things.

Gresham had to answer. He started to put his brain back in gear by clearing his throat, pushing through the vapours of alcohol to re-engage, and then halted. He had to sound as if he was part-drunk. It was his guarantee of honesty to the King.

'Your Majesshty,' slurred Gresham, 'it's . . . it's a terrible thing.' The tears formed in his eyes then. He had let the image of young

205

Walter and Anna come into his head, or the drink had forced it there. 'But . . . but . . . yes, it may be possible.'

The King gave a cry like none Gresham had ever heard. It was a call of pure agony, of a man into whose brain a white-hot knife-blade had entered, a knife-blade of recrimination and blame. Yet James, with his morbid fear of death, had fled to the countryside to avoid comforting his son on his deathbed. Queen Anna had locked herself up in Denmark House. *How much had he loved his son?*

'But sire . . .' Gresham spoke quickly. 'We learn in our trade that what *might* be is not always the same as what *is*. I shay . . . I say that a king's son may always be murdered, in Scotland as well as in England. But yet it need not be so. God knows, life is cheap enough.' Seven out of ten babies might die within months of being born, and even if a boy or girl made it to maturity, childbirth, the plague and a host of other illnesses still carried on taking their dreadful toll.

James was sitting back in his chair, eyes glazed, clutching his wine as a baby might clutch a bottle. 'I took scant care of him, my brave lad, scant care . . .' It was as if he was talking to himself. The accent was broad, pronounced. 'Too much love isnae any help to a future king. I had none of it, none of it, when I was a wean. It made me careful, it made me canny. He didna' need me.'

'Perhaps not,' dared Gresham, 'but I've no doubt he loved you.' The room had started to swirl now. He focused, hard. The room was *not* moving. It *was* still. It was only the drink. It slowed down, and the sickness that had started in his stomach abated. Why let it? He forced himself to go to the side of the room, picked up the chamber pot and vomited into it. The liquid burned his throat and tongue.

'Well, Sir Henry, the problem is this.' James's eyes were hard, bright. He had ignored Gresham's retching into the pot. The drunken man who had screamed in mental agony a few seconds ago was gone. 'I can no longer help Prince Henry.' The tears were still there. 'And all of a sudden I am short of people to whom I can turn.

You see, if they have killed my son ... then the next step is for them to kill me.'

Was that it? Was James's cry of agony for his son? Or was it for fear of his own life?

'Why so, sire?'

'To get the weakling Charles on the throne, so they can manipulate and dominate with all the more ease.'

'They?' Gresham left out any formal mode of address, always dangerous with a king or a queen. James appeared not to notice.

'All those who seek to deny a king his pleasures in hunting, or his few close friendships.' A maudlin, self-pitying tone was creeping in now. 'Or perhaps those who are friends of my few close acquaintances, and fear the loss of their influence if a man starts to listen to his son.'

There! That was it! James had more or less said what he feared. That Overbury might have acted to remove Prince Henry, fearful that the young Prince might one day find his semi-estranged father in a receptive mood and could damn Carr and Overbury as a package that could not be split. Was there real agony in James at the loss of his son? Possibly. But, as always with this complex man, there was the overriding sense of survival. Of self-interest.

Would Sir Thomas Overbury have so much evil in him as to murder the heir to the throne of England?

'Now tell me, Sir Henry, am I right in my fears? And do take a drink. You'll find it guid wine.'

The room was quite stable now, Gresham noted appreciatively, giving only the occasional lurch. 'I think Sir Robert Cecil would have appreciated your fears. As for the friend of a friend, he is capable of almost anything. Almost anything. But of this? I simply do not know. Yet, sire, if this man had done this terrible thing ... it would pose no threat to your security.'

'How do you mean, man?'

Gresham was thinking himself now, his brain working on the problem, his own fear that he had been duped cutting through the

207

alcoholic fog. 'The only reason for taking the life of the Prince would be to keep you on the throne, secure in your friendships. If there were those who wished harm to your son then, the damage done, there is every reason for them to keep you alive and well. You become the key to their continued success.'

How could this man maintain his relationship with Robert Carr while knowing that Carr's friend might have killed his son? How could Henry Gresham be playing with his own life, talking thus freely to the King?

'I think you speak with the voice of Machiavelli, Sir Henry. That Machiavelli of whom you have some knowledge,' said James in a low voice. Again, it was impossible to gauge his mood.

'Machiavelli spoke in the true voice of courts and those who seek power,' said Gresham. And in the true voice of kings and rulers, but perhaps I'd better not say that.

'And your friend, Sir Edward Coke? Would he do this to me? Take away my son and heir?' James was not looking at Gresham but into the ashes of the fire, untended now since his arrival.

Humans plan and plot and train for their future, yet forever delude themselves into thinking that they have control over their destiny. The moments that define our lives, the moment that can affect the future of millions of people, are often hidden from sight, tiny triggers that are pulled without a noise or a sign that a threshold has been crossed, a decision taken and the future changed, for better or for worse. Gresham responded instinctively and without hesitation to the King's question. It took him only a moment to respond.

'No, he would not. If the death of your son was through anything other than natural causes then Sir Edward would have no part in it.'

'Yet he is the man who is responsible for your stay in these surroundings, the hurt to your beautiful wife, the fear in the hearts of your two children that they may never see their father again. He is the man you hold responsible for locking away your greatest friend, your saviour, your hero.'

'He is all those things, Your Majesty. Yet if I am any judge of men, he is not a murderer of the heir to the throne. For one, he is too scared. For another, though he has sold out to ambition long ago, he has lived with himself by believing that he works for and within the law. For a third, he has no advantage to gain from such a death.'

'And could the man you call Robert Cecil have planned this action, from his grave, and be reaching out to punish me even now?'

This man was no fool! Again, Gresham responded instantly.

'I had thought, for a brief moment, that it might be so. He talked about it once, indirectly. At our last meeting. He said that however great the heir to the throne, he must never be allowed to replace the King in case the people came to believe they had the power to choose a monarch. I cannot tell you what happened in Cecil's mind. My instinct, despite an appalled moment when you first spoke and I wondered if I had been misled, is no. This would be too unsubtle for Cecil.'

'Did you feel the axe brush across your neck just now?' asked the King. A cold breath ran through the drink-heated fires of Gresham's brain.

'I have felt the axe resting on my neck for most of my life, Your Majesty. The answer to your question, since you have come here in search of honesty, is no, I did not.'

'Then you should have done, Sir Henry. You are not the expert reader of men that you think you are!' There was almost an air of triumphalism in James's manner and tone. 'You see, had you sought to damn Sir Edward or my dead Chief Secretary, and to exact your private revenge on the back of my grief and loss, I would have despised you and believed that not only do you read Machiavelli but that you are him. And you would have died, by axe or by poison. But died, beyond doubt.'

And do you think you could sneak poison past my defences, even in this, your holding-house for the damned? thought

Gresham. Kill me you might well have done. Yet you would have had to have done it by the axe and in the open air, where a man could at least breathe a deep breath at his final moment and not face a dingy reckoning in a darkened room.

The two men sat in silence. Gresham had no idea how long it lasted. Finally, James spoke. 'You tell me the truth, I believe, Sir Henry Gresham.' There was moodiness, self-pity in his tone. 'And there are few such men around me. You will work for me now. Not Sir Edward Coke, nor for . . . others. You are a free man, Sir Henry. You may leave. There are two conditions to your freedom. You will accept my commission to ascertain the truth of my son's death. You will tell me that truth. And should that truth need action, you will act on my behalf to make that action take place.'

Gresham jumped up and bowed deeply. James too stood up, unsteadily. He looked at the gold goblet in his hand and raised it to drain the dregs.

'You might care to know that a certain man in my care and custody . . . a man with a sore knife wound in his arm . . . escaped that custody three days ago. He had agreed to make certain other papers available to me. Not the letters you know of, Sir Henry. Other papers.'

'Would these "other papers" be connected to the theatre, Your Majesty?' That flicker again in his eyes, of amusement or pain, it was difficult to say. James looked at the door. It was firmly shut, the servants out of earshot.

'Aye, that they would.' He poured another dollop of wine into the golden goblet and drank it back in one huge swig. 'The second condition is this. You will meet, tomorrow night, in my Palace of Whitehall with two men who must needs speak with you. They will tell you of the second task I have set you. 'Tis better it come from them. Six o'clock, Sir Henry. Ye'll have had good time by then to take your wife in your arms, aye, and do more than hold her, I'll be bound.'

The King's lewdness, his fascination for other people's sexuality, was notorious. He gazed lugubriously at the pure gold in his hand, empty now, and weighted it. Then, unexpectedly, he tossed it to Gresham. Calling in a servant, he nodded at the man, who bowed deeply to Gresham and gave him a folded warrant.

'There, a present to your fine wife. The pair of them, this goblet and the one you are holding. Though I do not doubt it is the paper she will value more than the gold.'

With that, James stumbled out of the room, calling for his servants. Back, no doubt, to Whitehall, and a confused Court and a wailing wife and current beyond current of intrigue, suspicion and gossip. The environment, in fact, in which kings live all their lives.

As well as a pre-written warrant for his release, Gresham wondered, had James also brought along a warrant for his death?

17

11th November, 1612
The House, London

'Fortune is merry,
And in this mood will give us anything.'

SHAKESPEARE, *Julius Caesar*

Gresham went straight from The Tower, taking King James at his word. It was locked for the night, but the King's warrant was sufficient, with much grumbling, to have three huge doors squeakily unbolted and raspingly drawn back. Horses were summoned, hooves clattering on the greasy cobbles, and with two of the servants the King had allowed him Gresham rode through the gateway. He tensed as the final shadow of the Lion Tower fell over him, waiting for the call back, the clash of arms. Nothing came.

He was free.

He had already banished Mannion, worried about Jane and her safety at The House and feeling infinitely more relaxed knowing that Mannion was guarding her. He sent no messenger ahead, and it was in the pitch dark that he raced past the darkened bulk of St Paul's and up the length of The Strand. He pulled up the poor, panting beast that was all The Tower had been able to provide, hurled its reins to a startled doorkeeper and rushed into The House.

Jane was sitting in her parlour, the private room Gresham hardly ever entered. Even now he did not cross its threshold, but simply flung open the door. She turned, startled, towards him. She had been crying, he saw. She would do that – cry at night, when the children and the servants would neither see nor hear. Except Mannion, whose bed was positioned by the outside of the door. It was a campaign mattress, Gresham noted: rough canvas stuffed with straw.

He noted the expression of alarm and terror in her eyes and cursed himself for not putting himself into her mind.

'No,' he said, cutting in to her worst thoughts and disarming them. 'I've not broken out of The Tower, nor started a rebellion, nor come here three horse-lengths ahead of the executioner. Which would you like first? Two fine gold goblets that the King has gifted you – or his warrant freeing his good and noble servant Sir Henry Gresham from any taint of treachery?' He held the goblets out in one hand, the warrant in the other.

She looked for a brief moment, and then crashed into him with such force that goblets and warrant went flying and he, caught unawares, was cannoned into the back wall, pinned there.

'Are you really, truly free?' she said, stepping back to look at him, hardly able to breathe, her colour up in her face.

'As free as we've ever been. Which means, free until some monarch decides to lock us up, or a syphilitic maniac tries to kill us, or—'

'Do shut up,' she said, taking his face and holding it, looking into his eyes as though they were a marvellous, undiscovered country, 'and talk sense, for once.'

Mannion had stepped smartly aside as his master and mistress had rocketed from doorway to back wall. Ever practical, he had managed to catch both gold goblets as they went flying, and looked at them appreciatively before setting them down carefully on the floor on the tiny ante-room. Casually, he picked up the warrant from the King and read it, assuming that the pair of them would be cooing and doving for hours and not need him there at all. In fact, he was already making to leave the room when his eye was caught by some wording on the paper.

Mannion could read, very fluently. He just preferred people to think he was illiterate, believing reading to be rather foppish and unmanly. This time, whatever it was that had caught his eye made his face light up with a grin that was almost evil.

'Forgive me for interrupting, Your Lordship,' he said loudly, doing just that. 'But I thought I'd better check with His Lordship if His Lordship required my poor and humble services any more before I leave His Lordship and Her Ladyship—'

'What on earth are you prattling on about?' Gresham asked, confused. Jane addressed Gresham as 'my lord', a familiar title between women and men, but one the House of Lords had no trace of.

'You should read what the King writes for you,' said Mannion, grinning even more widely. 'Read it through to the end, I mean. According to this, you're not only a free man, you're also very shortly to be Henry Gresham, First Baron Granville. Congratulations, my lord.'

Gresham looked nonplussed. 'But two hours ago I was locked up in The Tower . . . I don't understand . . .'

'I think,' said Jane, the light dancing in her eyes, 'that the King has decided to trust you at last.'

18

13th November, 1612
Whitehall Palace, London

'All the world's a stage,
And all the men and women merely players.'

SHAKESPEARE, *As You Like It*

If there was insanity in the world, it all met and focused on the Palace of Whitehall. With so many candles, lamps and lanterns blazing fruitlessly into the cold November night, it was as if the Palace was on fire, lit from within, a funeral pyre to the finances of the monarch. So many were fed each day and night at the King's expense that a scurrilous broadsheet had christened it the Hospital of Whitehall. Even the servants seemed to have servants at Whitehall, yet it took ten minutes to find one servile enough to take their horses.

Gresham and Mannion were ushered through endless corridors. The two younger servants that had accompanied Sir Henry gazed open-eyed at the bacchanalia around them. What stories they would tell on their return! Even at that time, just before six in the evening, they passed two or three men clearly drunk, slumped in corners. A woman, clearly gentry, ran out of a door, giggling uncontrollably. One breast was out of her gown, the other bursting against its rich material, one gasp away from freedom. She ran into Mannion. Rebounding, she arched eyebrows at him, giggled again and ran off.

Interesting, thought Gresham. The King had made available to them the private dining room Robert Cecil had long employed at Whitehall, with the huge length of table and finely carved oak chairs that Cecil had used to intimidate his guests. But it would not be Cecil who revealed himself as the door swung open – it was Bacon, and Andrewes.

Both men rose as Gresham and Mannion entered, and both extended their hands. 'Congratulations on your release, my lord,' said Sir Francis Bacon, with what appeared to be a genuine smile on his face.

'Congratulations on your honour,' said Bishop Lancelot Andrewes. He appeared genuinely pleased that Sir Henry Gresham was now First Baron Granville.

Andrewes and Bacon were seated on either side of the head of the table. Bacon, seemingly more at ease in the royal palace, pointed to Gresham's place. At the head of the table. It was the seat Cecil had squatted in, radiating malevolence on so many evenings. Bacon had arguably the best brain in the kingdom. Andrewes was the only bishop Gresham had ever respected.

'I think not, Sir Francis,' Gresham said, 'with your permission. The seat at the head of this particular table is tainted for me. This evening is one where I'd hope to be treated as a third – an exact third – among equals.

With that, he sat alongside Andrewes. It allowed him the better view of Bacon's face. Of the two, Bacon would reveal his real thoughts and feelings far more vibrantly than Andrewes. Bacon smiled, and called out. His own servant was there, Gresham noticed, the grumpy, complaining old man Gresham had always associated with Bacon. Andrewes had no servant with him.

Those who ushered in the food were strangers to both hosts, looking around with interest as they brought in steaming dishes.

Expecting to be asked to wait on the three men, they were surprised, and rather offended, when they were waved away.

'I suggest we dine and talk at the same time,' said Bacon, ever courteous. 'There's much to cover. Will your man agree with mine to serve us?'

Gresham looked at Mannion, who nodded.

'I would like the truth,' said Gresham. 'I've been shot at with a crossbow, been subject to a mass assault, nearly died in two separate parts of holy ground and been locked up in The Tower. Normal enough, you understand,' he reached out to put some fish on his plate. 'But it's always nice to know why it is you're being assaulted, killed or locked up. What are these "theatrical papers" about which there's been so much fuss?'

'There are three sets of them, to be precise,' said Bacon, sipping appreciatively at his wine. His servant fussed over him, offering him dish after dish. They were all cold, Gresham noted. After his master, the old man took the dishes with a show of deference and offered them to Andrewes. Following that, he looked with scorn on Gresham, and dumped the dishes within his arms' reach.

I hope to God Bacon doesn't ask me to sink a whole bottle before he will talk to me, thought Gresham. His prayer was answered.

'The first of these "theatrical papers" is a complete script of a play. A rather bad play, to tell the truth. Well, actually, if we are telling the truth, an execrable play. Publicly deemed to have been written, among others, by one William Shakespeare. *All Is True*, or *Henry VIII* as it is sometimes known. Written, as it happens, by King James I. Incidentally, Shakespeare had even less of a hand in it than normal. It was so dire that when he got it he had a fair copy made and sent it off to Fletcher, to see if he could make anything of it. He couldn't.'

Well now, thought Gresham. The King had tried his hand at a play for the common players. That would be news. Very powerful news.

'Also in this batch of papers are two plays, again both thought to have been written by Shakespeare: *A Midsummer Night's Dream*, as I believe the older one has come to be called, and *The Tempest*. Both about magic. Both actually written by my lord the Bishop of Ely, Lancelot Andrewes.'

Bacon nodded to his companion, who waved a tired, sad hand back at him.

'Finally, these "theatrical papers" also include manuscripts of *Love's Labours Lost* and *The Merry Wives of Windsor*. Written, in part at least, by myself. With a little help from my friends.'

Bacon sat back and transferred some meat into his mouth, before turning to Gresham again. 'It wouldn't be good for the author and prime mover of King James's fine new Bible to be seen as combining that part of his career with writing for actors and the public theatre, my lord.'

Something of a shock went through Gresham's system at the still-unfamiliar mode of address.

'Nor would it be a good thing for it to be shown that such an eminent member of the clergy wrote a play dealing with a man whose ruling power is based on magic. Any more than it would be good for the country's leading lawyer to be known as a play-maker, an associate of theatrical scum.'

Bacon and Andrewes gazed at Gresham.

'As for the King,' continued Bacon, 'God knows what laughter would be provoked were it known he had secretly penned a work for the theatre. Particularly work as bad as his play appears to be.'

It was revenge, Gresham thought. Divine revenge for his asking Shakespeare to cope with so much new information in so little time. Picking one single item of debris from the maelstrom hurling around his brain, he asked one question.

'I can understand easily enough why you, Sir Francis, would try your hand at a play. A new medium. One with immense power to inflame the heart, the mind and the imagination. But why would the King write a play? And, my lord Bishop, aren't there sermons enough without your feeling the urge to write words for actors to make a meal of?"

'There are three answers for three different authors. I won't presume to speak for the second. As for the third, he's here and able to explain for himself. I can speak a little for the first.'

Bacon was picking at his food. A log fell in the hearth, and a cloud of fiery, red sparks shot up the vast chimney, for a moment giving Bacon's face a hellish tinge.

'Cecil started it. He saw how the theatre could inflame the popular heart and mind. Yet, as was always his way, instead of seeking to destroy it, he sought instead to control it. He was young then, in his father's shadow, a part cripple. He found out – God knows how – what few others knew, that this man Shakespeare was simply a front for Marlowe. Set up by Marlowe on his own, in the first instance. A country bumpkin who was a poet of sorts – a man with enough of a way with words not to be wholly unconvincing, but poor enough to be bought and to stay malleable. *Richard II* was Marlowe's. Along with *Julius Caesar*, and most of the plays that had a reigning monarch killed on stage. Marlowe liked to see monarchs die.'

'And you, Sir Francis? Your mind unable to resist the urge to write in this new manner, this writing that could reach three thousand souls at a sitting—'

'Ha! What power was there! It was shortly after Marlowe's supposed first death. A performance of *Richard III*, I believe, one of Marlowe's first offerings from the grave. It was a private showing. We entertained the actors afterwards. I fell to talking with this man Shakespeare. The wine flowed. We both had too much, I suspect. Did I ask him if a man such as myself might try his hand at a play? Or did he suggest to me that for a consideration – hefty consideration – such an opportunity might present itself? To be frank, I simply can't remember. And in any event, it matters little. A group of us emerged – myself, Rutland, Oxford, Derby. And did we have fun!' An expression of almost boyish enthusiasm filled Bacon's face.

'They were heady days, weren't they?' said Gresham, remembering the wild, mad and bad 1590s when everything had seemed possible.

'Heady indeed. We all thought we were destined to be the Queen's chief minister. We were all conspirators, vowed to secrecy in case our various political ambitions were threatened by involvement with the theatre. Yet in our heart of hearts, I believe we all looked forward to a moment when we would reveal our authorship, when we could bask in the notoriety and fame like adolescents allowed to walk up the aisle at their own funeral.'

'And Cecil spoiled it?' asked Gresham.

'How did you guess?' answered Bacon. 'He found out about the group, as he'd found out about Marlowe. Very gently, he started to blackmail us.'

'How so?' asked Gresham, intrigued. 'He'd no need of money, and while those you mention had power and wealth enough – you, Oxford and the rest – you weren't the prime shakers and movers of your day, with respect.'

'No, but we were all public figures, and Cecil loved to have hold over anyone in public life, or anyone who might become important.'

How true, Gresham thought. He had battled for years against the secret knowledge Cecil held on him.

'But it was more than that, if I may speak?' replied Andrewes. 'I was one of those early recruits, though only for one play initially, before good sense took hold of me again, and before I succumbed once more in dotage. In the last three years or so of the old century, Cecil began to build his true power base. There was no direct heir to Elizabeth, no issue from her loins. A king from Scotland, from our own nobility, from Spain or even from France – all these had huge potential for civil unrest, for disobedience, for civil war.

So Cecil began to force members of the group to write plays that would reinforce the absolute authority of kings.'

'Which created one or two rather lovely problems in its own right,' said Bacon. '*Henry IV* was meant to show the triumph of monarchy over the Lord of Misrule. But the great unwashed decided they preferred the Lord of Misrule in the form of Falstaff! Cecil was livid!'

Gresham thought briefly. 'I can see why you, my lord Bishop, a bright, intelligent man with a skill in and love of words, and a need to speak to an audience as you do so well in your sermons – I can see why you were tempted to experiment. But why in God's name would the King of England want to write a play?'

Bacon answered. 'Because he believes himself a writer and an intellectual, and because he cannot bear to think that he's not more skilful than others. And because Robert Carr suggested it to him, before the King or Carr knew about the convenient service Shakespeare provided for others. Andrewes here picked up wind of it and panicked, inasmuch as my lord Bishop knows the meaning of the word. He persuaded James out of publishing a play under his own name and told him of the service Shakespeare offered.'

'In doing so, I had to reveal my own involvement in the whole business.'

'James's reaction?'

'Initially amusement, rising to apoplectic anger. He is more proud of his Bible, believing that it will be his spiritual monument to future generations, than of anything else except his hunting skills. He persuaded himself that if it were known I had written for the actors it would devalue the whole work. Indeed, the King took steps to reduce my involvement dramatically as far as the public awareness went. I was – I am – the final editor of the King James Bible. The credit will go to another, for all history in probability.'

'And it lost you the Archbishopric of Canterbury?' asked Gresham.

'Indeed,' said Andrewes. 'A fair reward for youthful vanity. The King made it clear that he viewed the existence of this play as a sword of Damocles hanging over me were I to gain Canterbury. Or was he told so by Carr and Overbury? I don't know which.'

'And Marlowe?'

'He came to the King – via Coke – wounded. He said he knew the whereabouts of the manuscripts in the King's hand and in mine. In exchange for money and a free passage back to Europe, he guaranteed to provide them. James threatened to torture him. Marlowe laughed in his face. Asked if the King knew what pain he was in already. Laughed and said how much he would welcome death. Threatened, I believe, that if he, Marlowe, were to die then the manuscripts would be released anyway.' It was Andrewes speaking. Interesting to note, thought Gresham, that it was Andrewes who still had the ear of the King, not Bacon.

'And the King agreed?'

'Yes,' said Andrewes, 'but for the wrong reasons. He has a morbid fear of death, as you know. He fled to the countryside when Prince Henry was dying. It's likely he won't be at the funeral. In some way Marlowe made himself a symbol of death for James. A symbol of his own death.'

'So where do we stand now?' said Gresham.

'Marlowe's gone off, God knows where,' said Bacon. 'The man may be mad, but his capacity to vanish at will is exceptionally sane. Shakespeare hasn't been seen since Wade grabbed you and your wife from his apartments. The letters between James and Carr still haven't been found . . .' The eyes of both Bacon and Andrewes swivelled round to focus on Gresham. He met their combined gaze, unflinching, that infuriating half-smile on his lips. 'A group of people could be exposed at any minute as having written plays claimed by someone else. Some of those who wrote Shakespeare's plays want it kept secret, and will be seriously damaged if the truth comes out. There are others who want nothing more than for their genius to be recognised. It is, to be frank, a total mess . . .'

'And,' said Gresham, 'the rumours are already starting that Prince Henry was poisoned, a point to which I have to make an answer to the King.'

That brought silence.

'Was he poisoned?' Gresham looked straight at Bacon.

'I don't know,' he replied simply, after a few moments. 'But I doubt it. The only possible reason would be if Overbury felt Henry was threatening Carr's position, and hence Overbury's power. Yet there was no sign of it. James didn't listen to Henry. He thought his son was a prig, and Henry considered his father decadent.'

'So who are the *coterie* who wrote Shakespeare's plays for him?' asked Gresham.

Bacon and Andrewes exchanged glances.

'Do you really want to know?' said Bacon. 'You may find yourself hurt by the knowledge, mentally as well as physically.'

With a sinking feeling in his stomach, Gresham felt he could guess what was coming. 'Tell me,' he said. 'I need the truth.'

'Well,' said Bacon, 'myself and Andrewes here, obviously. The King. The Earls of Oxford, Rutland and Derby, in differing measures – and remember that sometimes two or even three of us worked on the same idea. Marlowe. And the Dowager Countess of Pembroke, who, by the way, is ruffling the most feathers by insisting that her authorship of two plays – *As You Like It* and *Twelfth Night* – is acknowledged.'

'Her son, the present Pembroke, knows the actors. Correction. He's besotted by them. He knows the truth and he hates his mother. He's keeping her silent by threatening to take all her money away from her. He tells Shakespeare it's to help him, but it isn't. It's because he can't bear the thought of his mother being seen as good at anything,' said Andrewes, with feeling. Pembrokeiana, as she was known, had made a favourite of

Andrewes, a situation from which few men emerged alive.

'And there is one more,' said Bacon.

Gresham knew what was coming. He had felt it in his bones. 'Sir Walter Raleigh,' he said flatly.

'Yes,' said Bacon.

His saviour and his hero. The man Gresham had named his eldest son after. The man he had visited, supported and sustained all these years past while he was imprisoned in that very same Tower Gresham had so recently left. The man who had seen fit to keep this a secret from his younger friend. The man who had chosen to do so despite knowing that Gresham's life was at risk from the moment he became entangled in the thorns and briars of these damned plays and their authorship.

As they road back to The House, their escort all around them, Mannion was clearly troubled. He spat down on to the roadside and turned his head to Gresham.

'He didn't give you your freedom, those goblets or a baronetcy for nothing. He's going to want results. And sooner rather than later.'

'I know,' said Gresham. 'I work it out as seven separate issues.'

'Well', said Mannion, 'I can see most of them. First, decide what to do with those letters. I agree with Her Ladyship.' He used the word without irony. 'Pretend you've found them. Get rid of them, and tell the King. Or, better, give them back to him. Then, second, sort out whether Prince popped 'is clogs from God or from that bastard Overbury. Third, give Marlowe his third and final departure from this earth.'

'Four, five and six are just as easy,' said Gresham. 'Find Shakespeare, neutralise Overbury and locate these manuscripts.'

'Fair enough,' said Mannion. 'What's number seven?'

'See Raleigh, and ask why he never told me this conspiracy with Shakespeare was going on.'

'I can help you on the first six,' said Mannion. 'I can't help you with the seventh.'

No, thought Gresham, no one else can do that. The anger started to rise within him.

'And you've left out Poke,' said Mannion. 'Not like you to let someone get away with it, especially when they've had you locked up for weeks.'

'Oh,' said Gresham, a sudden, fierce grin on his face, 'I've got plans for Sir Edward.'

19

21st November, 1612
Dr Simon Forman's House, Lambeth, London

'If you poison us, do we not die?'
SHAKESPEARE, *The Merchant of Venice*

It was a lovely house that Dr Simon Forman had rented in Lambeth, close to the river and with an orchard so luxuriant as to be able to supply a shop. On this cold, crisp morning the frost hung on every branch and twig and the breath steamed out of men's mouths. The orchard was a white hanging garden, a fantasy world of stillness and frozen beauty. Gresham would miss Simon Forman, self-proclaimed doctor, astrologer and dealer in secrets. For most of his life he had been courted by rich and poor alike for his medical skills, while being hounded near to death by the Establishment who considered him both a quack and an evil magician. Gresham had never made use of Forman's skills as an astrologer. On countless occasions he had needed his services as a doctor, and adviser on poisons.

Poor old Forman had died in September, taken by a fit while rowing alone across the Thames. According to his widow, Anne, Forman had predicted his own death a week beforehand. Well, if it pleased her to believe it, it did no harm, Gresham thought.

The days after Forman's death had seen a flurry of coaches and servingmen queuing at the widow's door, asking for papers and any letters their distinguished mistresses had sent to Forman. The rush had now subsided, and today's visitor was a quiet, bearded, thoughtful figure. Dr Napier was from Buckinghamshire and had been a close friend and an apprentice of Forman's for years. He was at the Lambeth house now to collect his inheritance – all of Forman's medical books and manuscripts and the details of his famous cures. It had taken Dr Napier a week already to see what he wished to remove back to Linford and what he felt could be destroyed. He was not a man accustomed to moving quickly. He was a man whose medical judgement Gresham trusted implicitly and, knowing that the heir to his old friend was in the Lambeth house, he had asked to meet him.

'Congratulations, my lord, on your recent honour,' Napier said ponderously, but genuinely enough. The King's proclamation had been almost instant, unusually so for such an indolent man. The formalities would wait.

'I think it more a payment in advance than payment for services rendered, Dr Napier,' replied Gresham with a grin, 'and in order to earn my fine title I need a medical opinion.'

'You may have it, such as my skills are,' replied Napier, privately flattered and not enough of a deceiver to hide it nearly as well as he thought.

'I will not dance around the edge, Dr Napier,' said Gresham. Enough secrets had passed before Napier's eyes, and not one of them leaked, for Gresham to be sure in him. 'I need to know if Prince Henry's death was from natural causes, or from poison.'

Napier's face blanched a little, but he maintained professional composure. 'I know only what the gossip says about His Highness's illness.'

'I have detailed the course of the illness here in this paper,' said Gresham, handing the document over to Napier. 'In summary, it is this. The Prince first became ill in the spring. Low spirits, weight loss and what he called a giddiness and a lumpishness in his forehead. He tried to drive out the illness by hard exercise and a spartan diet, to no effect. Increasing tiredness, headache, and by autumn severe bouts of fever and diarrhoea. His stool light yellow, like pea soup. Bleeding from the nose. He collapsed. Eyes couldn't endure light, lips started to turn black, complained of incredible dryness in his mouth. Convulsions, fits, serious pain. The rest you know.'

Napier made a noise that sounded something like 'Hmmph!' and sat down to read the papers, which included all the treatments given to the Prince. 'Idiots!' he exclaimed a short while later. 'Complete idiots!'

'Why so?' enquired Gresham. 'It's said they asked every leading doctor in the land for advice.'

'It's a great pity that the only one who could have helped them died in September,' responded Napier gruffly. 'The idiots shaved his head and put the warm bodies of pigeons to it, as if that ever did anything except give a poor servant a good dinner of pigeon pie shortly afterwards. Oh, and look here at this . . .' Napier flicked the paper he was reading with disgust. 'A unicorn's horn with stag bone and pearl . . .'

'Sounds impressive to me,' said Gresham.

'*Sounds* impressive is correct,' snapped Napier, 'but that's all it is. The unicorn is a mythical beast. Even if it weren't – and it is! – the chance of grinding up some chalk and selling it at a king's ransom to the King's idiot doctors is a business proposition very few of London's apothecaries could resist. Pah! Unicorn horn? You might as well prescribe the devil's pizzle!'

Gresham nearly asked if the good doctor had a store of that, but decided that for all his evident qualities, a sense of humour was not Napier's strong point.

It took the doctor over an hour to read through the papers. Seated by a blazing fire, a companionable cup of warmed ale in his hand, Gresham felt more relaxed than he had done in months. Mannion sat with him, while the four servants he had brought as bodyguards rested in the kitchen, where the noise suggested they were getting on well with two of the maids.

The pressures on Gresham were huge and the stakes high. But at least now he had direction, certainty and clear targets. The game was on, and he had an idea of the rules as well as the desired outcome.

Napier rose three times to consult books that were part packed away, and once to peer closely at a sheet of papers in Forman's cramped hand. Finally he came back to the fireside and sat down.

'My conclusion,' said Napier ponderously and with great assumed dignity, 'is this.' He paused to gain greater effect. 'You should understand that I did not have the chance to examine the patient myself, and that therefore at least an element of my conclusion must be conjecture.' He paused.

'And that conclusion is?' asked Gresham, hiding his impatience. All men have their hour, and need it.

'The symptoms are those of a specific fever. Even if that were not the case, the manner of the illness's growth and maturation argues against poison. The majority of poisons affect the digestion and stomach. Few of the known ones first affect the head, and indeed that is reported as being one of the hardest areas for a poison to reach. The illness developed over a long period when, according to these records, the Prince underwent several changes of diet, and periods of hardly eating at all. It would have been nigh-impossible for a poisoner to sustain an effective dosage over such a period of time.'

'So you believe the Prince was not poisoned?'

'No. On the contrary. I believe he was poisoned.'

Gresham felt a bolt pass through his body. 'How so?'

'I suspect the Prince was poisoned by drinking water. This fever of which I speak is often linked to foul water. The Prince was an abstemious man. I have no doubt he would order liquid drawn only from the finest well. Yet all it needs is for a servant to confuse two pails, or indeed for the servant who draws the water to be ill

229

himself, or for the servant to save time by going to the nearest rather than the purest source. Or perhaps the servant left his master's water by a privy. Dr Forman was most insistent that on no occasion should water be drunk. Small ale is the least that should be permitted.'

'Well,' said Gresham, 'at least the Prince's father is safe from this fever.'

'How so?' enquired Napier. Gresham had forgotten the absence of a sense of humour.

'His Royal Highness is not renowned for drinking water,' said Gresham.

He endured the lecture on the problems created by excessive consumption of wines, thanked Dr Napier profusely and left Lambeth.

Gresham and Mannion sat in the rear of the boat as they were rowed home across the river.

'It costs a fortune, you know, every time you do this,' grumbled Mannion.

'It's a fortune I have. And we have to find Marlowe and Shakespeare.'

Gresham had ordered every contact, agent and informer they knew in London to locate them.

'They're both of them good at disappearing, that's all I can say,' said Mannion. It was a difficult time to trace someone; the winter weather was making travel difficult. In addition, it was as near certain as could be that neither Marlowe nor Shakespeare were in London, where wagging tongues were far more numerous, and there was no sign of Shakespeare in Stratford, the only other easy possibility for his whereabouts.

'What do you reckon Marlowe's game is? And Shakespeare's?' asked Mannion.

'Shakespeare's easier,' said Gresham, resisting the temptation to drag his finger in the water as they rowed smoothly in mid-stream. 'He's got himself into a mess he can't get out of, so he's just bolted, like a frightened rabbit. Marlowe may have had an idea where these manuscripts – the one's in the writers' original hand, the ones that prove authorship – were, but Shakespeare must have moved them by now. He's the only one who knows their hiding place, unless Marlowe, or the King, or you and I torture it out of him. He's terrified that one of us will get to him.'

'Why doesn't he just burn the lot?'

'Who'd believe him? The risk then is that we'd all torture him to death, believing he knew where they were, and he'd have nothing to buy us off with.'

'And Marlowe?'

'He's harder. He wants the truth about the plays he wrote under Shakespeare's name acknowledged. He wants his new play performed. And he wants revenge. All before he dies of the pox. Most of all he needs those manuscripts to prove his authorship. His problem is that the minute he raises his head he's a dead man. He's not just got me on his tail, he's on the run from the King. I think he's probably hunting Shakespeare as hard as we are. *We need those manuscripts.* And Shakespeare's the only one who knows where they are.'

'Be a laugh, wouldn't it,' said Mannion, picking his teeth again, 'if he had gone and destroyed them? If we're all charging around for something that don't exist?'

'Hilarious,' said Gresham. 'Positively side-splitting.' Yet the thought had occurred to him. Life was fond of such great jokes as that.

20

November–15th December, 1612
Cambridge

'Thou unnecessary letter!'

SHAKESPEARE, *King Lear*

The King would not return to London, not for his son's funeral, nor for his new Baron. He hated London anyway, and now it was tainted with the death of his son. So it was that twenty-four chaplains, Prince Henry's pages, his gentlemen, his solicitor, his counsel-at-law, his groom porter, the grooms of the privy chamber and the bed chamber, his sewers, carvers, cup-bearers, his secretary, his treasurers and the Comptroller of his Household, his Master of Horse, distinguished nobles, friends, ambassadors from all Europe, four thousand mourners, servants, gentry and noblemen, took four hours to wind their way from St James's Palace to Westminster Abbey for the most ornate funeral service anyone could remember. Prince Charles, now heir to the throne, was chief mourner. Of his mother and father there was no sign.

Nonetheless, it was vital for Gresham's plan to have Coke, Bacon and Andrewes there with him when he met the King. Gresham's messengers took on new horses. The final agreed meeting ground was ironic. Granville College, Cambridge. Near to

James's favoured hunting grounds at Royston and Newmarket. Fitted out with rooms built for a king.

They held another feast, of course, but it was a strange, subdued affair, the students hardly daring to speak in the presence of the black-garbed and black-faced King of England. Even the Fellows were quiet, respectful. James drank heavily, but remained taciturn, the wine failing to lift his mood. It was, the announcement had said, a 'private visit'. As if the King of England, with his hundreds of retainers and the noise and bustle of a whole household, could ever go anywhere privately.

They met after the meal in the Combination Room, the five of them. King James, Gresham, Bacon, Coke and Andrewes. And Mannion, of course, slipping in behind them all. It was the same room Gresham had had built for the Fellows of the college. The fire was blazing to impossible proportions. The fine, oaken table, designed to hold the whole Fellowship with space to spare, had a high-backed chair made into a throne by the adornment on its back of the royal arms. The other chairs along that side had been removed. On the opposite side were four lesser chairs. A beautifully decorated silver jug sat by the King's throne, full of the King's favourite sweet wine. By it sat a golden goblet. One of the goblets James had given to Gresham in The Tower. Gresham had thought about the symbolism. The servants to their King are as silver to gold. What the King has given he can just as quickly take away.

Gresham bowed James to his seat, and motioned the others to go to their allocated places opposite him. Coke was fuming, angry and uncertain.

Gresham retreated to the opposite side of the table from James and motioned Mannion forward. He handed Gresham a bound package, which he opened. Inside it, written on fine paper, were two letters. Gresham brought the letters out and showed them to James. The letters from the King to his lover. The explicit, detailed letters.

'Your Majesty,' said Gresham, 'three days ago my servant here' – he nodded in the direction of Mannion, who bowed his head to the

233

King – 'heard that these letters had been, so to speak, placed on the open market. I assume that Nicholas Heaton released them, expecting to profit from his treachery. The new owner saw no reason in Heaton's death to postpone a sale. I sent my servant to purchase these letters.'

'And did he pay good coin for them?' asked James, staring at his own handwriting in the flickering light from the great fire and the candles.

'He paid in a different way, Your Majesty,' said Gresham. 'The owner paid with his life. Your Majesty, these are the letters, are they not? The letters Your Highness wrote? It is only Your Majesty who can confirm them for what they are!'

Gresham thrust the letters towards James. He let his eyes run down them but made no offer to take them. It was as if he felt distaste at touching them.

'They are the letters,' said the King, his lip lifting. 'I thank you for doing at least what others seem unable to do.' He did not look at Coke, but Coke squirmed. 'You may leave them on the table.'

Gresham threw the letters on to the wooden surface. 'Might I make a suggestion, Your Majesty?' Gresham asked.

James did not agree, but neither did he deny the request.

'Some time ago now, the Bishop of Ely asked if he could be given these letters. Were they to be found.'

James looked up at that, with a sharp snap of his head.

'The letters are dangerous. The Bishop asked that he be given them, I do believe, so that he might destroy them. Because if such a man as he stated he had destroyed them, then he would be believed. While, I regret to say, a man such as myself might not be so believed. These letters are a threat, Your Majesty.' Something approaching a pleading tone was there in Gresham's voice. 'As their finder, might I ask in all humility that the Bishop be allowed his request? To burn these letters? Here, in the fire in this hearth.'

James had still not touched the letters. He looked at Gresham, and then to Andrewes, who gazed levelly back at him. He nodded. No words. Just a nod.

234

Andrewes bowed his head, stood up and took the letters. He did not look at the writing. He walked slowly over to the great hearth. He held each page near the fire until it caught alight, let it burn almost through and only then cast it into the fire. No unburnt scraps would float up through the chimney to land on Cambridge's streets.

'It is finished,' said the Bishop. 'Thanks be to God.'

'You set me another task, Your Majesty,' said Gresham, standing beside his still unoccupied chair. There was a pause. 'It is my belief that your son died of natural causes.' James's mouth dropped open at that, and he took the golden goblet and emptied it. It was Mannion who came up and refilled it, as silent as night. 'I have written for you here the opinion of several leading doctors.' He drew more papers out of his pocket. 'One of the opinions is from the apprentice to Simon Forman. No man knew more about poison than Forman, who died recently. His apprentice believes there is no poison suitable to these symptoms. The fever of which Prince Henry died has a known progress. Moreover, events in the Prince's life prior to his tragic loss would have made it nigh on impossible for a poisoner to do his work. There is no one who might have contemplated such a deed who would reap benefit from it sufficient to justify the appalling risk. It is my belief that no human caused your son's death. Rather, it was God who called him.'

'I thank you, Baron Granville,' said James. 'You have resolved yet another problem. And do these three wise men here' – the King motioned to Bacon, Andrewes and Coke – 'agree with your conclusion?'

Bacon glanced at all three, and made to speak, but it was Coke who got in first. 'I agree with Gresham on nothing.'

James raised an eyebrow. Bacon started and Andrewes remained still. 'Except, Your Majesty, on this.'

Four bodies relaxed, three of them noticeably.

'My third task from Your Majesty remains to be achieved,' continued Gresham. 'The play scripts relating to yourself. Marlowe is still at loose, Shakespeare also gone to ground. They will be found. When they are, so will any other papers in Your Majesty's hand. They will also be destroyed, Your Highness. I give you my word.'

'Why were ye so insistent on these three others being gathered here tonight?' enquired the King, eyes resting on the ashes of the letters to his lover. He rose and went over to the fire. Taking the iron poker that sat by its side, he poked at the ashes until they were dust, caught by the heat and sent swimming madly up the chimney.

As the King had risen, so had Andrewes, Bacon and Coke. They stood by the table like naughty schoolboys told to stand in class.

'There has been much bad advice, Your Majesty, in these matters in which I have become involved,' said Gresham, standing by the other three and turning towards the King. James was backed by the fire now, the hellish red flames silhouetting him. 'Much bad advice, deceit, intrigue and lobbying for position.' Neither Bacon nor Coke shifted. 'It is better for me, and for Your Majesty, if any resolution I might bring to your dealings is done if not in public, then at least in front of a sworn audience. So there is no misunderstanding.' He paused to let the meaning of his words sink in. 'I was put on to these letters by Sir Edward. I resolve the issue in front of Sir Edward. I was put on to this play by Bishop Andrewes and Sir Francis. I hope to resolve the issue in front of them. If such can be allowed, as my fancy if nothing more, then I believe there will be no room for deceit, intrigue or jockeying for position.'

'Ha!' said the King. 'You would have done well in Scotland, I think. You have a mind for it. Would you take a peerage from me now from the land of my birth, on condition that you reside there and be my agent in sorting out that troubled country's deceits and intrigues?'

'Your Majesty,' replied Gresham, 'allow me first to sort out the deceits and intrigues of which I know here in England.'

'Yet you ask for these issues to be resolved in front of those who set you on to them in the first instance,' said the King. There was a small stool by the side of the fire, left in the hurried clearing of the room. James took himself to it, sat down. Half his face and body were lit by the flickering flames, half in darkness. An emblem for this man, thought Gresham. James motioned impatiently for the others to sit. They did so, turning their chairs towards the King. Gresham remained standing. 'There was another person present when you were first "set on" to these issues by Sir Edward. Sir Thomas Overbury. You did not call for him to be here tonight . . .'

'Your Majesty,' said Gresham, 'you have a rare jury here tonight.' He pointed to Andrewes, Bacon and Coke. 'A saint, a sinner and a solicitor. And myself.'

'Come, come,' said James, chuckling. He flicked his hand and as if by magic the golden goblet full of wine appeared in his hand. Mannion had been waiting for the signal and was the only one to understand it. '"Myself" is hardly enough to describe you. "A saint, a sinner and a solicitor", eh? Well, what word do you use of yourself, Baron Granville?'

'A dangerous word to use in front of a king who has shown his power so recently to the person in question. But if commanded, as I have been, I would add a fourth word. A saint, a sinner, a solicitor and a survivor. Which, Your Majesty, might perhaps make two of that latter kind present here tonight.'

The fire crackled in the grate and a log collapsed down, throwing up a series of sparks.

'Be warned, Henry Gresham.' The King spoke in level tones, looking directly at Gresham. 'You push things to their limit. And sometimes the survivor survives only at terrible cost to himself.'

'I know,' said Gresham simply. He let the silence work, then spoke again. 'I despise Sir Edward as much as he despises me. He was wrong when he said he agreed with me on nothing except one thing. There are two things on which we, as sworn enemies, agree.'

'And what is the second?' asked the King.

'It relates to the subject of your first question. Sir Thomas Overbury. You have a Privy Council, Your Majesty. On it sit the highest in the land.' And Robert Carr, thought Gresham scathingly. 'Yet will you accept the advice of this, your extraordinary private council, tonight?'

'I will hear it,' said the King. 'For this once.'

'We are united in one thing, other than loyalty to Your Highness,' said Gresham. 'We think it a wonderful thing for those in Your Majesty's court to have experience of serving Your Majesty abroad. Thus does a man prove himself. Sir Thomas Overbury is ripe for advancement. Yet he lacks something in the skills of diplomacy.' Something like a snort escaped from Coke. Bacon merely smiled, as if at a huge joke. 'A wise king might well seek to school such a man in these skills, as well as bind him even further in loyalty to His Majesty. What better answer than to appoint him as ambassador for His Majesty. Ambassador to a foreign country. A very far distant foreign country.'

There was silence from the fireplace. It was followed by another deep chuckle. 'You have another work in my hand that you must find, do you not, Baron Granville?'

'I do, Your Majesty.'

'Then find it,' said the King, with a sharpness that stung the air. 'Reward my largesse, as so few seem to do. And be my hawk, Baron Granville, as Cecil was my beagle.' The King had often referred familiarly to Cecil as his 'little beagle'. 'As for the rest, I have heard. I am a king, beset by more quandaries than ever a mere mortal conceived of. Yet still I listen.'

He stood, and the others stood with him.

'My saint.' His gaze lingered on Andrewes. 'The problem with sainthood is the trials those who receive it have to endure in order to earn it. They become too good, too divorced from the politics of power. My sinner? Well, all of those here are that.' He gazed at Bacon. 'Sin can be forgiven, if the quality of service merits the forgiveness. My solicitor? Well, there are two of those, are there not?' His gaze flicked between Bacon and Coke. 'And my survivor?' He looked directly at Gresham. 'There is a bond between those whose gospel it is to survive. And a special bond between those who believe that mere survival is not enough, and that to survive with honour is all that matters. Do you wish that bond to be cemented, Henry Gresham, First Baron Granville? I doubt it. Your survival has always been linked to your independence. Yet if my hawk is to return to my gloved hand, it needs to know I am its master. Perhaps the best way is to ensure that our survival is linked.' He paused for a moment. 'Thank you,' he said. His eyes were on Gresham. 'We will reconvene, I hope. My private council. When the business is concluded.'

He swept out of the room. The fears of those present were represented by the depth of the bows they offered to the departing monarch.

Later that night, Gresham lay with Jane. The house was silent, the flames dying in the hearth, the light that of one single candle.

'So the letters are destroyed . . .' She breathed, feeling easy in her mind for the first time in months. She lay with her head on his chest, arm flung over him, unconsciously seeming both to clutch and protect. She was naked. He could feel her breast pressing against his side, and the first signs of arousal.

'Well . . . sort of,' replied Gresham, shifting his body.

'Sort of? Sort of? What do you mean "sort of?"' The alarm was clear in her voice and the stiffening of her body.

'Well, the King and two of the country's leading lawyers saw them burned by one of its most respected bishops,' said Gresham meekly, fearing the storm to come.

'But?' said Jane.

'That's why the meeting took so long. I needed to slow the timing for the work to be done properly. It was so important for James not to hold the letters close, which is why we needed to meet in the Combination Room after nightfall. The light in there is always bad.'

'Why did you need bad light?' asked Jane darkly.

'The letters that were burned were forgeries. Brilliant forgeries, I might add. I doubt the King would have seen them for what they were even in broad daylight, but I wanted to lessen the risk.'

'But why burn forged letters?' asked Jane, confused now beyond all belief.

'So that I can retain the originals, merely as a bargaining counter, should the King decide to set his hounds upon his hawk. One never knows when such things might become useful.'

Was there no end to the lengths this man would go? Exasperated, Jane rolled on to her stomach and hit her pillow. Unwittingly it revealed more of the length of her body to her husband.

'Are they safe?'

You are not, he thought, looking at the sweep of her back and the tantalising hint of what lay beneath. Out loud, he said, 'They're safe. Where they can never be found, and where they'll be destroyed instantly if any hand other than my own turns the key.'

'Isn't this betraying the King? The King who's ennobled you, given you his trust?'

'I'll serve the King better than any,' said Gresham, 'and I'll give him my total loyalty. I'll risk my life in his affairs, if needs be. But what one must never do with kings or queens is give them your trust. Never. Not to them or to anyone, as it happens, if you wish to live. The only person to hold complete trust is oneself. His Majesty knows that of me, as I know it of him.'

'And do I have your complete trust? Am I the breaking of the golden rule? Or is there a part of you that's withheld from me?'

He swung round to face her, eyes taking in the glorious curve of her body. 'I intend to prove conclusively in a moment that I withhold no part of me from you,' he said, grinning. 'And the answer to your question, damn you, is yes. I've weakened myself in the way I swore I would never do. By allowing you into my heart. Now, enough of this prattling! Will you allow me to weaken myself a little more?'

She shivered as his hands began to move. 'Well,' she said, gazing at him with the innocence of a child and her eyes half closed, 'I don't suppose it'll do me very great harm.'

21

December 1612–13th February, 1613
The River Thames

'the story of my life,
From year to year, the battles, sieges, fortunes,
. . . moving accident by flood and field,
hair-breadth 'scapes . . .'

SHAKESPEARE, *Othello*

As Gresham had long ago ceased to believe in Christ, the feast of his birth meant precious little to him. Yet he enjoyed the entertainments laid on for his two households, seeing them not merely as a duty but as a way of thanking his servants. The excitement in the faces of Walter and Anna was something new for him. Unconsciously, he began to enjoy the twelve days of Christmas through the eyes, ears and stomachs of his children.

Destroy the King's letters. Done, to all intents and purposes. *Determine the manner of Prince Henry's death.* Done. *Neutralise Overbury.* Not quite done, but well on the way, Gresham thought. The King's response to his idea regarding Overbury suggested the ambassadorship would flower and flourish in its own good time.

Find Marlowe. Not done, and the man still a very real threat to Gresham and his family. *Find Shakespeare.* Not done, and a key to the manuscripts. *Destroy the manuscripts*. Not done. There was too much left undone, Gresham raged inwardly. Including his plucking up the courage to meet Sir Walter, he added to himself.

Yet there was something else troubling him. Beneath all this was the feeling that somehow and in some way that he did not understand, he was missing a vital clue, failing to see a piece of the puzzle that was yet there, waiting to be stared in the face. The nagging fear grew like a headache. However much he shook his head, he could not stop the growing pain.

The King seemed unperturbed, delighted that the Court could come out of mourning in time for the Christmas celebrations. One of them included a performance of *The Tempest* by William Shakespeare. Or, more accurately, by Bishop Lancelot Andrewes of Ely. Gresham hoped it might flush out either Marlowe or Shakespeare. He was disappointed. Gresham attended as few of the other celebrations as he could decently manage, but Jane still needed two new gowns to meet the minimum obligations placed upon them.

'Is that a dress or merely a pelmet?' asked Gresham puritanically, noting how low the neckline on Jane's fabulous gown had plunged.

'My lord,' said Jane, 'it is a positive curtain wall in comparison with most of those you'll see tonight.' It was true. Daring though it was to Gresham, his wife's neckline still covered her breasts, more than could be said for many of the flimsily dressed women giggling and shrieking their increasingly drunken way through the evening.

The festivities at Court were even more extravagant than usual. The Elector Palatine had come over to England to be betrothed to the Princess Elizabeth in November, but the death of Prince Henry had forced a postponement. Elaborate entertainments were laid on for his extended stay, which it now seemed would last until the wedding in February.

December passed and January crawled on. There was increasing excitement at Court about the impending wedding, and an increasing dread in Gresham's heart as silence greeted his every enquiry as to the whereabouts of Marlowe and Shakespeare. The strain was greater on Jane, he knew, never knowing as she walked in the garden of The Merchant's House whether or not a madman with a crossbow was hiding in the overshadowing woods, for all the extra men they had hired to police them.

'Perhaps he's dead, after all,' said Jane one morning, as the rain poured down and blotted out the view from her window. 'Perhaps he killed Shakespeare, and then died of the pox himself . . .'

Gresham desperately wanted to reassure her, to agree with her. Yet he knew that to do so might allow her to relax her guard.

'It's possible, but we daren't assume it's so,' said Gresham, hating himself.

'I'm only guessin' as to how far gone he is with the pox,' said Mannion. 'But I've seen worse than him live a year or more.'

Jane could not conceal her excitement at the festivities laid on for the royal wedding. Outwardly she scorned Court and its ladies, inwardly becoming as excited as a maid-in-waiting when a great event beckoned. The climax, the evening before the wedding, was to build a replica of the fort and town of Algiers on the south bank of the Thames at Lambeth, and stage a mock sea battle and storming of the town. Well over five hundred watermen and a thousand musketeers from the local militia had been pressed into providing this spectacle, and Rochester and Chatham stripped of every long-boat, pinnace and barge that could have mock masts strapped to it and bear at least one cannon.

There was the usual chaos at the Palace the day before the wedding. The old efficiency of Elizabeth's Court was a long-gone memory; James's household was run on excess and confusion. The Chapel Royal at Whitehall was relatively small, which to Gresham's common sense argued for moving the wedding to somewhere larger. Instead, attendance at the ceremony had been limited to barons and above, but in order for others to see the couple they would be sent on a circuitous route to the chapel prior to the wedding. To his intense chagrin, Gresham had been summoned to a rehearsal.

'You can guarantee the bloody King and his wife won't be at any bloody rehearsal!' he muttered, climbing into Court clothes. He had decided that Mannion could act Jane's part, to the immense amusement of the household, and spare her the need to kick her heels for hours in the shambles he knew they would find at the Palace of Whitehall. He would see her that evening, at the great naval battle, with the children. Their excitement had filled The House for days at the news they were allowed to watch.

So it was that Jane was left to her own devices on February thirteenth. Managing a household as vast as that of The House was second nature to her. She had become involved in its running as a young girl, when as a ward of Henry Gresham she had first entered its gloomy, almost derelict walls. It had been sadly neglected then, its servants corrupt, its fabric wasting. Gresham had had no wife, and The House to him had been no more than the extravagance of the father he had hardly known. Jane realised that in gifting to the man who was now her husband the best and most efficiently run household in London, she was in some way trying to pay back the man who had rescued her from rural squalor and given her his heart and mind as well as his body.

It was long after noon. Jane was humming happily to herself, checking the preserves in the vast larder, reassured that they would see The House well through into spring, when the messenger came. Young Tom was the grandson of Old Tom, who had for years been Gresham's Master of Horse. Increasingly, the servants in Gresham's household had a family lineage less illustrious in heraldic terms than those of nobles but nearly as long. Young Tom, as he would probably be known even if he lived to his sixties, had served only a year, and was at the gangling stage between boy and man. He was panting with exertion.

'Please, mistress. Master says as 'ow you're needed at the Palace as they've had to change all the plans, and please would you bring the little master and mistress along as well. Use the coach, he says, as it's safer, and for reason that all the landings at the Palace are clogged with boats for the fight tonight, and please you . . .' He said all this in one breath, having had little enough left to work with after his run home. Jane laughed, thanked him and felt only a mild twinge of annoyance. It was typical of the Palace to change plans at the last minute, or to have none at all. It was also increasingly the fashion to show off one's children at high-born weddings, using them almost as accessories, dressing them like little puppets in the high fashion of the day. Well, thought Jane, they could have her children if they wanted them, but young Walter would turn out in a very plain doublet and little breeches and Anna in a simple dress with no farthingales, and not a jewel in sight on either of them.

Jane felt a slight stir of unease when she bustled the children into the courtyard to enter the great coach and saw not John, who usually drove them, but his underling Nicholas. Nicholas too came from long-standing stock, men who had served the Greshams for years, but she had never been driven by him before, and the cargo, with her children on board, was precious. It would not have helped her unease had she heard that John had failed to return from the tavern last night, unprecedented in his long service. It would have been reported to Mannion that morning, had he not rode off so early with his master. No one had thought to report it to Jane.

'Can you manage us all in safety now, young Nicholas?' she called up to him, part in jest, as she clambered into the coach. He was white-faced, she saw, but put it down to nerves at his first full outing with his mistress and her children. He made no reply except to wave his whip reassuringly in her direction.

They assembled in the yard, as Gresham had instructed. Two riders in front, two riders each side and two at the rear, and a man with a charged pistol sitting beside Nicholas. The great gates were opened, and the whole magnificent *entourage* swept out into The Strand. The two lead horsemen, knowing they were heading to Whitehall, turned their mounts to the left.

With a cry, Nicholas cracked his whip and turned the lumbering coach right. Pedestrians turned in horror to see the huge vehicle with its fine horses bearing down upon them, gathering speed with every minute, and leaped to safety.

Jane felt a massive lurch and knew instinctively that they had turned the wrong way. Oh God! she thought. Nicholas has seen an enemy and driven the coach away from him.

The two lead horsemen failed to realise that the coach had not followed them. By the time they reined in, it had vanished from sight. Looking hopelessly at each other, and cursing themselves for their certainty that things would go as they had planned and expected, they yanked on the reins and reversed their path. Mannion's advice was ringing in their ears. *Always expect the unexpected!* They had been strutting ahead of the coach, clearing the way, full of their glory at serving the First Baron Granville. They knew the depth of their mistake, and in their stomachs hung the awful fear that tomorrow they would be dismissed in ignominy with no reference. Their panic lost them even more of their judgement. They drove their horses not back down The Strand but to the gates of The House.

'There! There!' shouted Nicholas meanwhile to the armed man by his side on the careering coach, his arm outstretched. The man gaped at him, looked in the direction indicated. The next thing he knew a tremendous kick landed in his side, and he was flung from the vehicle. He fell directly under the hooves of one of the escorting horsemen on the left-hand side. Reducing him to a bloody lump, the horse stumbled and fell, one leg at least broken, its rider hurled from his mount into a crunching, bloody collision with the earth. The horse lay there, twitching. Its rider lay still.

The five remaining escorts were confused beyond belief. Had a devil taken hold of Nicholas? Had the horses bolted on him? Had he seen an enemy they had missed?

Their confusion was not to last much longer. Heading into the

City and its warren of streets, Nicholas hauled the coach by sheer brute force to the right, down a noisome alley leading to the river. He knew the odds, had known them all along. He could commit the horses, now in panic and frothing, to the hole that formed the alley. After that, it was their instinct for survival that decided life or death. The horses chose life. They drove themselves neatly between the poor houses on either side, as neatly as a cork in a bottle.

The escorting horsemen were caught unawares by the coach's sharp turn to the right. The two on the inside reined back savagely as the coach threatened to squash them between its great bulk and the wall. Their horses stumbled, catching the sense of panic. The one remaining escort on the outside overshot completely. The two behind had time to rein in. Their mounts ground to a halt and reared in panic, but the riders controlled them and dug their spurs hard into their sides, driving them after the form of the coach. It was then that the men hidden in the alley dragged up the two ropes they had firmly stationed on either side. One at the height of a horse's head. The other at the height of its rider's head. Both horses caught sight of the first rope, instinctively dropped their heads and, at their speed, stumbled on their forelegs into a tumbling fall. Their riders were flung forward, still holding the reins. One caught the second rope full in his rib cage, the other on his Adam's apple.

Instantly the two men had fallen, a farm cart trundled across the alleyway. Its driver cut the traces, the horse bolting away. From nowhere four men appeared, cudgels in their hands.

The three remaining horsemen of the escort regrouped. None lacked courage. All felt a bitter sense of recrimination. They had failed their master and his mistress, delivered her and her children up to God knew what evil. Without a word being exchanged, they drew back on the reins and flung their horses forward at the barrier, trying to leap it in one bound and follow their mistress. The sickening thud of the crossbow bolts hit man and horse alike, the screams of the dying horses easily drowning the rattle and gurgle of the dead men.

One horse tumbled so hard that it careered into the farm cart, breaking a wheel and skewing it aside. The gap through to the alley had been opened at last. Yet there were none of Gresham's men to take advantage of it.

Except one.

Young Tom had delivered his message, then taken time to regain his breath. He was used to the comments of the maids and other girls, but he knew what he would get if he appeared among them breathless and sweating. He had caused a stir, right enough, by his message. He could see the coach being made ready. He considered going to the kitchen to claim his bread and cheese for lunch. He'd done his bit, hadn't he? And then a thought struck him, fiercer even than the pangs of his hunger. What about the horses? The man who had come from his master had said he would find a boy to look after the horses. But he'd been a rough sort of fellow, and what if he'd simply not bothered to find someone? Those horses had been his charge.

Tom ran out then, thoughts of bread and cheese banished, to see if he could beg his mistress to let him ride on top of the grand coach, so as to get back to the horses. But it was too late, the great coach was rolling out of the yard as he got there. What was there to do?

Be damned to bread and cheese! he thought. What matters is those horses. He ran after the coach. It was going the wrong way! Heart pumping, sweat pouring again, he chased after it.

He saw Nicholas, one of his heroes, point wildly with his arm, saw him kick his armed escort off the coach. He saw the carnage wreaked by the fallen body among the escort. From even further away, his limbs at full stretch, his breath threatening to tear his lungs apart, he saw the sharp, manic turn of the coach into the alleyway. And then, his ribs rising and falling as if there was no oxygen left in the world, he saw and heard the sickening noise of the crossbow bolts thudding into flesh. Saw and heard the death of men who had chafed him, helped him, guided him, men he had looked up to as the bastion of all knowledge in this world.

There was a gap. Between the farm cart and the entry to the alley. A gap rammed home by a horse still in spasms and a rider who lay totally still. Had the men with crossbows melted away like the men with cudgels? Or were they still there?

Well, the still very young but soon to be much older Young Tom thought – if thought is what happens in a man's brain at these moments – good men have died today. I will be in fine company if I join them. He ran for the gap.

No sudden blow in his side. No yells and cries. He was through.

He ran on, the narrow houses blotting out the sun. Despair. No sign of his mistress. How long could this winding alley run? Hope. The coach. Halted.

They were edging on the river. There were four, five men dragging his mistress from the coach. She fell out, drew herself up, seemed to be speaking. Seemed to be reaching to raise her skirt. One of the men flung out at her, knocked her back to the ground. She lay there, in the dust, motionless. The little girl was screaming. The boy just stood there, looking at the man who had struck his mother. There was a hurried conversation between the men, orders issued. Two of them picked up the body of his mistress, the others threatening the children to move in the same direction.

There was a boat by the rough jetty that abutted the alley. A longshoreman's boat, a cumbersome, single-masted thing designed to carry small cargo but needing four men to row it. The meat and drink of London's river traffic. They bundled the captives on board. The boat was unnamed, or, if it ever had been named, its emblem had fallen off through neglect. The men hauled oars out, prepared to row, the fitful wind giving them no help. As they did so, a figure flitted out from one of the poor lodgings that fronted the river. He was a small, dwarfed man with a strange, prancing high-step and a ludicrous wig. He stopped for a moment to give instructions to one of the men. That same man nodded, touched his forelock and hurried off back up the alley. Young Tom shrank into the wall as he passed by. He need not have bothered. The man had more important things on his mind than a young servingman.

An agony of indecision hit Young Tom. *What was he to do?* He had coin enough in his pocket to hail a waterman and follow the boat on her course through the Thames. Yet even if he knew where she landed, what use could he be, a mere apprentice? Far better, surely, to take what he knew and run with it to his master at Whitehall.

Young Tom was growing up by the minute. Let God decide, he thought. I will stand by this derelict jetty and raise my hand and cry '*Westward Ho!*' If a boat takes me to follow, so be it. If I am ignored, then will I rush to my master.

The first boat he hailed answered, and drew in to the jetty. He showed his coin first, as one did if one was of his status. 'Follow that boat ahead,' he ordered with far more conviction than he felt.

Would God or his master decide if he had made the right decision?

Ahead of him, Tom could see the men on the boat arguing. They gagged the little ones – the boy had been shouting, to try and attract attention Tom noted with approval – and bundled the two of them and their mother down into the forward hold. She was gagged too, his mistress, Tom's sharp eyes saw. Pray God they didn't suffocate her . . .

An overwhelming, burning sense of excitement came over Marlowe. Patience was hard for a dying man but he had grasped it as his only path to success. Vengeance, he thought, was a dish best savoured red-hot. He was about to enjoy the taste.

The boat was rocking up and down in a river that was frantically busy with the preparations for tonight's mock battle. This vessel was decked, with hatches cut into the planking to access the hold. The focs'le, at the bow and where the anchor chain was kept, was unusually large. A single lantern swung there, showing crude, straw-filled mattresses that had been nailed to the floor and halfway up the rough-timbered side of the hull. Set into the planking were three iron ring bolts, each with a short chain through them. At the end of each chain was an iron neck collar. Splinters of wood, lighter than the surrounding areas, showed where the ring bolts had only recently been screwed home.

Lady Gresham had been flung on the rough straw mattress, half-soaked through with river water. Her mouth was gagged, her hands tied behind her back with twine, her feet similarly imprisoned. The great, clumsy and half-rusted neck chain clasped her, rough against the smooth length of her skin. She was conscious now, eyes flickering wildly about the dim room. Her children had been similarly secured to the great ring bolts. The girl was crying quietly; the boy too, but trying desperately not to.

'Welcome to my royal barge, Lady Gresham,' said Marlowe. 'It is a pleasure to meet you, at long last.'

Jane shook her head back and forth, trying to speak through the filthy cloth rammed into her mouth.

'Take off the gag, Your Ladyship? I think not, really I do.' He was enjoying this more than he could ever have imagined, the old sense of power flowing through him. He felt the swelling in his groin. 'You see, you might shriek and draw attention to this poor and humble boat. I hope these precautions –' he motioned to the canvas sacking – 'will make this little patch of heaven almost soundproof, but why take an extra risk? You might cry out now, Lady Jane. You will certainly want to cry out, I hope, in a moment or so. *I want you to feel everything –*' he leaned his loathsome face close to Jane's. The teeth had almost all gone, and what were left were blackened and decayed – 'but the noise I make will be sufficient.'

Those huge dark eyes pleaded with him. There was a shout from on deck and the boat lurched. The rowers muttered curses and one shouted abuse at another craft that had come too close.

'What am I going to do?' asked Marlowe. 'Is that the question you would ask, were you free to do so?' The hold stank of fish and tar, and creaked with every sharp movement of the boat. 'Take my revenge. My revenge for your husband, who pretended that he wanted to help me, and who all the time intended to sell me into slavery as a spy for Cecil!'

He ignored the frantic shaking of Jane's head. Her hands were heaving on the twine so hard that blood was flowing from her wrists; a sharp, bright red against the pure white linen tracery on the dark of her gown.

Marlowe noted her breasts, their proud swell under her gown; the sculptured, chiselled perfection of her face. Very carefully, he leaned forward and delicately lifted the hem of her dress, strewn around her ankles, until it rested just over her knees. The slim, stockinged legs, pressed sideways down on the rough deck, were smooth yet muscled like an athlete. They were trembling, Marlowe noted with pleasure. He yanked the dress upwards, hearing it tear. Those delicious legs were now revealed in all their length, tapering into her hips.

'Yes, Lady Jane, proud Lady Jane, beautiful Lady Jane. I intend to rape you. There is a long history, you know, of conquerors expressing their power over the conquered by using their women.' Even through the cruel gagging some sound managed to emerge, a strangled cry of . . . hopelessness? Of anger? She was bucking and writhing against her bonds. Good, thought Marlowe. It would make it better when he had her. 'Your children? Oh, I would not rape them. But I think it will be good for them to watch their mother meeting her real master, don't you? And, oh, just one more thing. I have the pox. A dreadful shame. Yet in my temporary distressed state, the best gift I can find to give to you and your dear husband.'

She kicked then, as hard as she could with both legs tied together. Marlowe was expecting it, had moved to her side, forcing her to twist even more of her body. Yet still she caught a glancing blow to his wrist. It was bandaged, seeping a yellow and green puss. He screamed, and bent double, holding his wrist to his side. When he finally gazed up, it was with a look of pure and sustained evil that Jane nor no other human had expected to see this side of hell. It was to haunt her for the rest of her life.

He stumbled towards her, grabbed her with surprising strength, and flipped her over on to her stomach. The neck collar caught and held her cruelly. Half strangled, she was kicking with her legs, flailing, but there was a great weight on her back. He cut the bonds tying her legs together and hit the back of her legs hard, forcing them apart. Using a knife, he slit her undergarments. She was exposed, defenceless. Marlowe was gasping now, sweat on his face, lips drawn back, hands tearing at his own breeches.

There was a crash so great as to topple him over, and a series of yells, footfalls on the deck. The boat lurched and lurched again. High, imperious voices were speaking to the rowers.

'By the King's command!' a voice was roaring. 'We're ten boats short from Chatham and the King has need of this vessel! Shut your mouth! You'll get paid for your pains!'

There was a thud, more yells, feet hitting the deck. His ruffians had decided to make a fight of it. With an obscenity, Marlowe bound himself up, grabbed Jane's legs and tied them again, and went to the hatch.

The fight was taking place at the rear of the boat. Marlowe slipped out on to the deck and snapped the padlock shut over the hatch before he was seen. His men were losing the fight, outnumbered. The leader of the King's men was a serjeant-at-arms. The Palace must be desperate indeed if a man of such standing was sent out to scour the river for extra craft. Then, to his horror, the serjeant-at-arms called out, 'Hey! You there! Ain't you that Cornelius Wagner?'

In the hope that Marlowe might be lured into attending *The Tempest*, a full description of him, under the name he had chosen, had been circulated to all the Court.

Marlowe took one look around him and leaped into the river. Other boats had gathered as the King's boat had smashed up alongside. There were catcalls, whistles, shouts of support for the defenders. No one believed the owner of a boat so commandeered would ever see a penny this side of Armageddon. There was no love lost between the King's men and those who worked the river. Rough hands hauled Marlowe out of the water almost as soon as he landed in it.

The serjeant-at-arms wasted no time. Who cared about a man who had jumped overboard and been rescued? They were desperately short of craft for the King's display and desperately short of time to prepare the craft they had. As if in answer to his prayers, a sudden wind got up after the fitful spasms they had had all day. He roared at his men to unfold the primitive sail, put four of his best rowers on the oars and set off to find more vessels. The river had emptied around him as word spread.

In the forward hold Jane and her two children lay half-crippled with the chains around them, eyes staring, the cloth cutting terribly into their mouths. An agonised grunt was the only noise they could manage. Jane had wriggled and squirmed so that her dress had fallen over the triangle between her legs, covering her shame from her children.

Young Tom had seen the encounter and his heart had lifted. He had yelled and screamed at the men in the distance but to no avail. He was too far away. Frantic, Young Tom saw the sail drop, bellow and fill with wind, and the boat holding his mistress turn upstream to join the gathering masses at Lambeth. With the wind in its favour, it picked up speed and was soon lost in the mess of traffic on the river.

It was late afternoon and nothing of any significance had been achieved at the Palace of Whitehall except further chaos. Gresham had resigned himself and was reading a book, seated on the stone wall of a colonnade, when he sensed a bad smell.

It was Sir Thomas Overbury. There was a flushed look on his face, one of almost eager excitement.

'Good day, Gresham,' he said, halting before him, chin out.

Gresham said nothing, did not move from his stone seat, and gazed coolly back at Overbury. Overbury flushed. He seemed intent on walking away, but changed his mind.

'Look to your wife, Gresham!' he snarled.

A chill struck Gresham's heart.

He stood up and Overbury sneered at him, turning away. He walked straight into the bulk of Mannion, who had appeared silently from nowhere. Again Overbury appeared to be about to say something, but without warning he leaped from between Gresham and Mannion on to the balustrade of the stone archway, vaulted it and sped off across the grass. There had been something in his eyes. Triumphalist. Vindictive. Vicious.

Both men ran to the gatehouse without a word, to where their horses were. As they reached the place they heard a young man's voice, screaming. 'Let me in! Let me in! I must see my master!'

It was Young Tom, exhausted, frantic with fear and worry. Gresham reached for him, took him from between the two guards, nodding to them.

Betrayal! Tom poured out his story. *Never place your complete trust in anyone!* The coach driver had served Gresham's family for over ten years, and his father before him.

Jane and his children were locked in the bow of a boat commandeered for this evening's mock battle. The boat could be one of hundreds on the river, hurriedly rigged now to look like galleasses, galleons, carricks and argosies, their appearance changed even further.

'Send to The House,' Gresham ordered. 'I want every boat and every man on the river. Tell them to break through the booms if they have to.' The battle area was protected by booms upstream and downstream. 'Stop at every boat, check if the forehatch is open and its contents known. Explain there's been a kidnap.'

What if Marlowe had followed the boat, re-boarded it? What had he done to Jane before he had been forced to leave?

Men were flocking past them now to take their seats in the specially rigged stands from which the battle would be watched. Night was beginning to settle and torches were being lit.

'Master,' said Mannion. 'They're using real cannon, some of them live-shotted. Some of the boats are being blown up.'

'You, Young Tom, any other of our men – go down to the shore, grab a vessel each, somehow, anyhow. Start to check the boats. We know the size, roughly. We know it had only one real mast. It must shorten the odds. Go!'

It took a lifetime for Gresham to find Sir Robert Mansell, the Treasurer of the Admiralty and the man in charge of the evening. He was sweating profusely, despite the cold. He was flustered, angry.

'No, damn you, no!' he was roaring at a group of men. 'We must have more Venetians! More Venetians, I tell you! The men will just have to change sides, whatever they've rehearsed!' The river was in chaos. Several of the watermen were drunk, a payment in advance having been given to many to draw them out in the first place. There was powder everywhere. Some of the barrels were open-topped and perilously near to torches. Brass cannons had been hurriedly lashed to the decks of the vessels, many of which were dangerously overloaded with guns, extra masts, mock rigging and armed militia men.

Mansell's plan was for the invading forces to set forth from the Whitehall bank to be met in mid-stream by the vessels of the defenders. After a battle at sea, the attacking vessels, with the majority of the militia on board, would land on the Lambeth side and storm the fort. At the climax a whole section of the fort would explode, and defenders would put out from the breach for a last pitched battle before the attackers won home.

'My lord! You must cancel the battle!' cried Gresham. 'My wife and children are on board one of these vessels! Kidnapped by an enemy of the King!'

Wild-eyed, Mansell looked at Gresham. 'Stop it? Stop it? My lord, it's already started – can't you see?' There was a flare of smoke and a thin rumble crossed the river. The first cannon had been fired. Speckles of light began to flower from the walls of the mock fortress opposite. Muskets – though what idiot would fire a musket when no men had yet landed on the shore was beyond Gresham.

'There must be some way you can call back the boats!' insisted Gresham, shouting to make himself heard above the increasing noise.

'My lord, I tell you – I can do nothing to control this . . . this . . . chaos!' Mansell flung out his arms, embracing the anarchy around him. There was a crash and a scream and a newly rigged spar on one of the largest boats tore from its temporary mast, burying two men beneath it in a tangle of rope and canvas. The sail caught fire from the tub kept for lighting the cannon fuse and the crackle of flames was added to the noise as men rushed with canvas buckets to douse it. Gresham had to hold on to Mansell's arm as he went to turn away. 'If it is as you say, my lord, then there is every chance those who commandeered the boat will have found her,' Mansell continued, eyes already looking beyond Gresham. 'Half the boats commandeered never made it to Whitehall. Even if she is in one of the boats, the ones to be blown up have been in preparation for weeks. There's barriers round them. And the live shot, God help us! Only in a few guns, and those aimed at the lower section of the fort!'

He rushed off and was soon lost in the mêlée.

Gresham was ice cold. The time for recrimination would come later. All he could do now was focus his terror on action. Splitting his forces had been the only way. They had to achieve maximum cover of the Thames. He ran down to the river bank. He would seize a boat. If needs be, he would search every vessel before the night was out.

The battle was not going well. The wind had sunk again to virtually nothing, and what little there was was in the face of the boats on the north bank, driving them back to shore when they sought to set out. The overloaded boats were setting out and, with no wind to aid them, being swept downstream too fast. The smaller boats on the far side were milling around with no enemy to fight. When a boat did make it to halfway across the river, five or ten of the defenders surrounded it. Embarrassed at what in a military battle would have been a sinking, the attacking boats then retreated. There was much popping of muskets and the increasing blast of badly loaded cannons. To the spectators in the stands, including the King and Queen, it was increasingly boring.

For those on the river it was hell on earth. A sailor ran across a deck as one of his companions set off the vessel's only cannon. With no ball to stopper and focus its force, the burning powder sprayed the sailor's face and sides. The skin was ripped off him like a chef boning a fish, and with a scream he was hurled, his tunic burning, over the bow and into the river. Elsewhere, an excited boy ran to place another charge of powder into the smoking mouth of a ship's gun, forgetting to sponge out the barrel first. A fragment of still-burning powder caught the new supply as the boy spooned it down. The boy watched in disbelief as the exploding roar shot the ramrod out of the barrel, taking his hand with it. The gun captain was also unprepared for the involuntary ignition. He was standing behind the gun, which snapped back at him with the recoil, crushing his legs and pinning him against the mast. His scream drew the other crewmen to him. With no man at the helm, the boat veered out of its path, following the current. It crashed into another vessel, the splintering shock sending men overboard. Very few sailors could swim.

Jane felt as if she would never breathe properly again. She had bitten down on the rough gag in her mouth so many times and dampened it with her saliva that it had at least thinned. Yet it made no difference – she could not cry out. The boat had clearly caught a good wind, had turned, leaned over and beat up the

Thames to wherever it was heading, the thuck! thuck! thuck! of its bow driving into the waves. Jane eased herself over on to her back, her mind remembering the feel of the diseased hands spreading her legs. Pushing upright with all her might, she leaned against the side planking. Damn! Her head, as hard as she could push upwards, still rested half against the straw-filled canvas nailed to the wall. She had wondered if bloodying her body against the wood would have attracted the attention of those sailing the boat. She looked at her children. Their terrified eyes looked back at her. She winked at them, denying the despair in her own heart. It's all right. Mother is here with you. The man has gone. Someone will come and rescue us.

They did not believe her.

There were yells from the deck, and a lurching, forward motion as the sail was dropped and the boat brought round.

Jane struggled with all her might to get noise out of her mouth. The children, seeing her, tried the same. All that emerged were strangled, gurgled noises, easily absorbed by the straw, the timbers and the oiled canvas.

Footfalls on deck. Silence. The men had left. A lurching yaw to the right. Someone had hooked a rope on to their vessel. Movement, far less forceful than when they had been under sail. Silence on their own deck. Towed. They were being towed.

More shouts. As from afar. Cessation of motion. Footfalls on deck, brief. They were being moored to something, somewhere. Quick jerking movements of the boat. They were in quiet water, but water disturbed by other vessels. Heavy, heavy thuds on the deck aft of them. Strange noises, distorted, as of voices far away.

Jane knew what celebrations had been planned for that night, the celebrations she and her children should have witnessed from the stands at Whitehall. They had been commandeered for the great mock naval battle. Some man hired by the King had saved her from rape, saved her from being spoilt evermore for the man she loved. Perhaps a crew would come on board, find them, release them. Her heart soared. Yet she prayed to God the thumps she had heard on the deck had not been gunpowder.

And then, the lantern hung on the swinging hook so long ago began to flicker and die. Oh God, she thought. Within seconds the cabin was in total darkness. No sight now. No feeling in her numbed hands and legs. Only the sharp rocking motion of the clumsy boat on the short waves.

Above her, on the deck, the five squat barrels sat. From each a fuse led, joining together at deck level and running as a strand through a scupper on the side, hanging a foot and a half on the outside below deck level. A rough nail secured the fuse to the planking. An easy height for a man in a small boat to drive alongside, stand up and light the fuse, and get away before the powder exploded.

Gresham pushed through the increasing chaos to the waterline. More and more of the attacking boats were trying to set out. Many were simply swung downstream. A number, their rowers reduced to frantic exertion, were crawling towards the opposite bank. Every now and again a crew gave up and the boat shot off with the current.

A young man was roundly cursing five others. It looked as if they had set out, been swept downstream, rowed all the way up to Whitehall once more, and now he wanted them to start again. Gresham went up to him.

'I need to beg the greatest favour of my life from you,' Gresham said simply. 'Can I at least know the name of the person I'm asking?'

The young man gazed at the figure in front of him. Tall. Dressed in black, every fold breathing money. The most unsettling eyes the young man had ever seen. Soft leather shoes muddied to destruction. A courtier, all right. But something else.

'I'm called Walter,' the young man stated, equally simply.

'I'm called Henry Gresham,' he said, every particle in his body shrieking out for him to speed this up.

I bet you're not, thought Walter. I bet you're an earl of something like that, dressed as you are. But the man had given him his name.

'Pleased to meet you, Henry Gresham,' he said, offering his hand. Now he'd done it. Call an earl by his real name and it was your head bobbing along in the river the next morning. 'My full name is Walter Andrews.'

The first name of his son, thought Gresham. The second name – spelling apart – the only Bishop he had met and respected. Was it an omen? Henry Gresham did not believe in superstition. Yet his heart lifted. 'Pleased to meet you, Walter Andrews,' said Gresham as they shook hands solemnly. To business. 'My wife and my children have been kidnapped. Two of them. A boy and a girl. They're on one of the boats out there in this . . . mess.' As if to echo his words, there was a blast and a column of flame, followed by screams. 'Will you take me out on to the river and check all the boats . . .?'

Gresham had learned his self-control early. Learned to bear the taunt of 'bastard!', to bear the scorn of others, learned that to show what you feel is the ultimate weakness. Yet he had based that philosophy on a lonely, appalling selfishness. He had never allowed for the fact that one reasonably large person in his life, and two rather smaller people, would breach the route to his heart. So, for only the second time in his life, his emotion overrode his control. Disgusted and hating himself, he felt the hot tears burst up uncontrollably in his eyes and fall, burning, down his cheeks. 'Will you help me find my wife?'

Walter turned to his men. They were gawping at the scene in front of them. They had heard it all.

'Well,' said Walter, 'as for me, it's the first time someone's asked me to do anything useful all evening. As for these bastards –' he turned to his men – 'they're in revolt. Played out. Knackered. I don't suppose for a minute they'll agree to give up their sweat . . .' He turned to look at them.

'Bastards!' they called out in unison, with a strange happiness.

'We won't do it for fuckin' you, Walter Andrews!' said the oldest of them, rising to his feet.

Gresham's heart sank.

'But we'll do it for fuckin' 'im!' he shouted. 'Show us the way to your wife, master! We're the men for it!' There was raucous cheering, a rush to put the oars in the water.

'They're not exactly easy,' explained Walter. 'In fact, they're fuckin' impossible. But they're good when they do get it together.'

Gresham grinned at him, the fire of war in his blood. He grabbed Walter's hand. 'One-masted, biggish, a hatch for'ard and a much bigger one aft. Taken late in the day, so presumably with minimal decoration, fake masts and the like.'

'We'll find 'er,' said Walter Andrews, 'if she's there to be found.' His eyes were looking for a way through the crowded waterway. His hand was raised, waiting to drop and signal for his oarsmen to bite the oars into the water. Suddenly he saw the opening, dropped his hand. They careered through three boats, rigged as galliasses, whose rigging had become inextricably entangled.

'Where d'you want to start?' asked Walter Andrews.

'Where the danger is,' answered Gresham flatly.

It was clear even to Sir Robert Mansell that the promised battle was not going to happen. It was rumoured that the King and Queen were about to leave the stands, bored by a few small boats firing cannon and muskets with blank shot. James would be more than bored, thought Sir Robert, if he knew what this failed extravaganza had cost him. He had one ace up his sleeve. Half of the fortress of Algiers was primed to explode at the climax of the battle, its wood and plaster walls impregnated with barrels of powder set to ignite with the lighting of one fuse. Just before the walls collapsed, three of the attacking boats were meant to explode as if hit by shore batteries. The powder set in the 'walls' and that in the three boats was not normal gunpowder. Those responsible for the fireworks had been allowed at it. The boats would go up with a fiery blue flame, sending rockets into the sky. The explosion of the fortress would be predominantly red and yellow.

'Well, the mock battle was over, with all that did for his standing and his reputation. Current, wind and tide had meant that the two opposing fleets had never been properly able to meet. Not to mention the shamefully drunken crew, and the gross incompetence of the Court. Yet all was not quite lost . . .

To hell with it, he decided. They would only dismantle the fortress the next day were it not blown up. What had he to lose? His reputation was gone already, yet might be restored by this last throw. *If only he could manage the fortress to be blown up before His Majesty left the stands!* He hurried to give his orders. One of his lieutenants, the most trusty, was there. Six fresh oarsmen were in his boat. The twisted rope that would ignite the fuses was smouldering happily in its barrel. He sent them off to the three boats moored on the Lambeth side.

'There's three boats on the Lambeth side – primed with powder! Set to be blown up before the walls of the fortress fall apart!' Walter yelled to Gresham above the sounds of musketry, cannon and men being maimed.

'What of it?' yelled Gresham back.

'One of them ran into a stone jetty. Holed itself badly. My men tell me they were desperate. Word spreads on the waterfront. They set out to commandeer another boat. With one of the King's men on board.'

'So?' yelled Gresham.

'Look over there.' Walter pointed to the Lambeth shore. The Algerian fort was lit by what seemed hundreds, thousands of torches. In front of it, darkened and anchored, lay three other boats. Two of them were rigged as Venetian galliasses, double-anchored, a rude disguise over their plain origin as London riverboats. The third had no such disguise. Bobbing on only one anchor, it was single-masted. The barrels of powder, bound together by strong rope, were silhouetted against the light.

Hope flared in Gresham's heart. He nodded. Walter turned the tiller sharp over and yelled at his men. Already working hard, they redoubled their efforts.

Another boat shot ahead of them, for all their efforts. There was someone who looked like an official in its prow. As it crossed the halfway mark in the river, Turkish boats swarmed towards it, the fitful wind at their backs. The liveried official stood in the prow, shouting at them.

'Back off! Back off! Make way! Make way! On the King's business! Make way!'

Walter stood at the prow of his boat, hurling a gesture to Gresham to stand by him. 'Back off! Back off! Make way! Make way! On the King's business! Make way!' he echoed, pointing to the man dressed so clearly as a nobleman standing beside him.

The Turkish boats hesitated, backed off. Let them both through.

The King's boat shot towards the first mock galliass moored upstream. It made sense, work down the stream. The furthermost would have the longest fuse.

With a nod, Gresham directed Walter towards that furthermost boat downstream, the darkened vessel with no extra mast to hide its humdrum origins and only the five barrels of powder on its deck to show its purpose.

The current had eased now, wind and tide turning far too late to be of any real use. Walter still felt the need to heave a grapnel over on to the other boat, its claws digging deep into its wood. His boat slewed round, smashed against the hull of the other with a jarring crash.

There was a guard too on the middle galliass. He jumped up from his perch on deck, yelling at them, misunderstanding, warning them off the boat packed with powder.

Gresham leaped on board regardless, the ceremonial sword he had worn all day in his hand. There! A hatch for the main hold, beneath his feet almost. A smaller hatch forward.

The King's boat, on the orders of Sir Robert Mansell, reached the first of the ornately rigged galliasses. There was one man on board, keeping guard. Curtly, the steward ordered him into his own boat. He took the corded twine, smouldering redly at its edge, and applied it to the fuse, which was hanging over the side of the boat, at a convenient height for a standing man to ignite it. Thank God something had gone right tonight, as his own red-ended yarn ignited the spluttering fuse. On, he ordered, on to the second boat. Before they were blown to hell and beyond by this one. The men needed no encouragement.

There was a padlock over the forward hold, Gresham saw. All he had was his sword. He punched it through the hasp of the lock, wrenched it upwards. With a sharp 'Snap!' the blade broke off. With a despairing glance he turned behind him. Walter was there with something between an iron hammer and a chisel. He wasted no time going for the padlock. Instead he chopped, savagely, at the wood securing the hasps. One side sprang free.

Darkness. A stink of fish, tar and lamp oil hit Gresham from out of the hold. And something else. The smell of people breathing.

'A light!' Gresham yelled, beside himself. 'Give me a light!' Walter looked nonplussed for a moment, then yelled to his men. Something spluttered, and a thin, poor lantern was handed to Gresham, its flame already guttering. He half jumped down the ladder into the hold. In the dim light he saw his wife and his two children. Gagged. Eyes open wide. Necks held in cruel iron collars. Hands and feet bound.

He felt for the knot to Jane's gag, lost patience and grasped the dagger at his belt, ramming it into the stiff cloth behind her smooth neck. The gag came away and she fell forward, heaving, sucking in breath. Her hands cut into his body, holding him so hard that it was as if she was drowning. She turned her head, vomiting into the corner. He cut through the bonds around her wrists and legs, seeing the blood that stained the lace on the arms of her dress. The collar, the cruel iron collar, was still around her neck. He yelled to Walter, who smashed at the wood around the ring bolt. Gresham pushed

Jane away with all the gentleness his enraged body could muster, moved to the children, ripped the cruel binding off Anna and then Walter.

The thud of the explosion hit them before the vast, eyeball-scarring intensity of its flame. The first boat had exploded, those who had fired it unaware that the King had left his seat in the stands. A sheet of fire vented its way to the stars, a moment of blue and white brilliance turning night into day. Yet the King's boat, shielded from the blast by its next target, had already made its way to the second moored galliass. The guard on its deck was screaming at them. The captain of the boat ignored him. His vessel crashed into the side of the second galliass, the fuse directly opposite. He lit it, and it spluttered into life. Then he heard for the first time what the guard was screaming.

'She's shifted! She's shifted! The anchor's gone!'

Christ Almighty! Instead of the two anchors, fore and aft, that had meant to secure the boat, there was only one, and that had clearly lost its footing in the bed of the Thames and was dragging. Only a few ropes kept the vessel from careering down the Thames to explode in the midst of God knew what collection of other boats and people. Cursing, the captain turned to hack the fuse off, but as he did so three or four short sharp waves flung his boat upwards. He fell forward, into the gap that had suddenly opened up between the two craft. The next wave pushed his boat back in again. His head exploded like a squeezed orange as it was pressed between the two hulls. The men on the boat saw the fuse well alight and backed off, the guard hurling himself into their boat, threatening to capsize it. With a final, bucking scrape the second galliass lifted over the ropes holding it against the current and swept downstream.

The ring bolt came away from the hacked woodwork. Jane was free now, yet it would need a locksmith to take the collar off her neck, and she had to stumble to her feet holding the chain and heavy ring bolt in her hand. Gresham hacked at the bolt securing

Walter and, with a final, tearing sense of relief, saw it come out of the planking. He picked up little Anna, already free, silent and shivering now, in his arms, his hand under the harsh collar, the chains wrapped around his arm. Jane tried to pick up Walter, but Walter the boatman stepped into the crowded area and took him off her. They made their way on deck. Walter's men were waiting in their craft, arms open to draw the children and the woman into their boat.

From out of the dark a wildly rigged shape bore down on them as if from nowhere – the second galliass, out of control. Its bow swept Walter's boat aside, pushed it away as if it were paper. The stout timbers held, but the boat was pushed upwards, first hurling its men into the water and then capsizing. It floated forlornly for a few seconds, its crew hanging grimly on to it, and then began to move downstream.

The second galliass was crashing down the side of Gresham's boat when suddenly it snapped to a halt, dead in the water, bucking and yawling. Its dragging anchor chain had snagged on the ropes. Horrified, Gresham saw the fuse on the second galliass now hard by his side, fizzling to only a few yards away from the powder barrels.

There was a high-pitched yell from the other side of the boat. Gresham ran and looked out. In the darkness, lit by the strange flames of the mock battle, was a tiny rowing boat, a grizzled waterman at the oars, Young Tom in its bow.

'The other boat's about to blow! Here – take the children!' Gresham cried.

Tom grabbed a spare oar, dug it into the water and his boat careered to the side of Gresham's vessel. Walter the boatman was desperate to see if his men were still alive and his craft afloat, but he handed the boy Walter down to Tom as Gresham handed over Anna. Gresham turned to yell to Walter that there was a lit fuse on the second galliass, but the man had gone, a clean dive into the dark river to swim towards his capsized boat, still just visible in the murk, and the shouts of his men.

Gresham looked down into Young Tom's boat. It was dangerously low in the water. It might take one more, if they were lucky. Two and it would sink. 'Go!' he said to Jane, shrieking at her. She looked at him. Did he feel a squeeze on his hand or was it imagination? The little boat sank deeper, took water in over the side but righted itself as Jane tumbled more or less on top her children. Gresham took one glance back at the fuse. It was almost at the powder. He could just make it, perhaps . . .

There was a cry from the boat. Anna's chain had snagged on something. Young Tom and Jane were hanging on to it, taking the whole weight of the boat, or else Anna would have been dragged overboard, her neck broken with the impact.

Damn! Gresham followed the line of the chain in the darkness, saw it snagged on a rusty nail. With a superhuman heave he released it. The rowing boat swept away, off into the darkness. He turned. The fuse was two, three inches out of the powder. Time for him to do a deep, clean dive, hopefully be underwater when the explosion went off.

He turned to the water and did not see the line of fire jump two inches and bury itself in the heart of the powder. He felt an almighty blow in his back, something tearing at his arm, and the breath was punched out of him as if he had been hit by God's hand. His body, not under his control now, was hurled forward out over the face of the Thames, his arms outflung as if in a mock crucifixion. In the extended, terrible moment before his body hit the water, Gresham knew that he was losing consciousness; knew that something had hit and hurt him badly, though as yet there was no pain; knew finally that this was his time to die. As the waters closed over his head, his last vision was of Mannion screaming at him. Strange, he thought, in that moment of strange near-clarity that comes to dying men. I thought it would have been Jane. Then it was over.

The rest was silence.

22

Late February to March, 1613
The House, The Strand, London

'Tired with all these, for restful death I cry'
SHAKESPEARE, 'Sonnet 66'

He was in hell, he knew. The agonising, burning, searing pain was as anticipated and more, the perpetual agony of the incessant heat to be expected. But why was it so dark? Surely Lucifer would want his prisoners to see the flames as well as feel them? And why were there sometimes these voices, flittering in and out of his brain, never so close as to be understood? And the tiny, fragmentary moments of great peace, when a cooling balm seemed to come over him? It was strange. Well, he had eternity to understand it . . .

There had been two explosions, though Gresham had felt only one. The first as the powder on the second galliass was ignited by the fuse, the second as Gresham's boat blew up in sympathy. The blast had mostly been directed upwards – the engineers had secured iron panels around the barrels so that the explosion made a fiery plume up into the sky. It had still nearly swamped Jane's tiny boat, and for a few seconds she could see herself and her children being dragged down to the bottom of the Thames by the weight of the chains and the neck collars. Then there had been a thump alongside, willing hands reaching down to help them. The House. A boat from The House. The largest boat, sturdy, able to survive almost anything, full of men, angry men, their men.

Mannion had been in the second boat. For a brief moment he saw his master silhouetted, arms outflung, against the impossible light of the powder. He had ducked as the surprisingly weak blast passed over them, wrenching the boat around and leaving them deaf but otherwise unharmed. He had seen the body, face down in the water, the cloth ripped off its back, blood across the white of the flesh. As he came to within yards of it, urging the men on and on, it sank. Mannion dived cleanly into the water, into the pitch black, down and down and down. His hand flailing in front of him caught hold of something. Hair. His master's hair. He kicked upwards with huge force, arms now around Gresham's chest.

They thought he was dead. A huge, jagged splinter of wood had struck him in the arm, just above the elbow, and hung there. A leg was broken. *He was not breathing!* Mannion flung himself on Gresham's chest and pushed down with all his might three times. He turned his master over, hung his head from the edge of the decking, thumping at his back. One minute. Two minutes. Nothing. An awful, hacking retching suddenly came from Gresham's throat and his body convulsed, arching upwards in a spasm so powerful that it threatened to tip him over the side. Mannion waited for the vomit and foul water to dribble from Gresham's mouth, pushed down on his rib cage, waited, and then placed his mouth firmly over Gresham's. He removed his lips from the cold flesh of his master, repeated it. With another shuddering, heaving spasm, Gresham sucked in his own breath. Mannion cradled him until they reached the shore.

They sat by his bedside. His breathing was slight, feathery, threatening to stop at any moment. He was in a deep coma, showing no sign of consciousness. The first doctors shook their heads, retreated into a corner and muttered, and then suggested intensive bleeding.

He had been covered in blood when they had brought him back

home. A part of Jane rebelled, not least against the thought of the cruel little knives piercing her husband's flesh. God had put as much blood in him as he needed, and he had lost pints of it. Why did he need to lose more? Mannion took her aside.

'Look, mistress,' he said. 'I ain't no surgeon. But your master and me, we seen a lot of injuries on campaign, never mind the ones he's 'ad. He never did like bleedings, I can tell you for sure. He refused when he had a fever once, wouldn't be doing with it. We saw lots of people bled on campaign. Bled on purpose, that is. Didn't see any of 'em get any better for it, and saw a lot get worse.'

Dare she take the risk? No, she muttered firmly to the doctors, you will not bleed him. You will let him be.

It took an age for Dr Napier to come to them, for all that Jane knew he had come as quickly as he could. Gresham was weaker now, his face hollow. The gaping wound where they had taken out the huge splinter was angry and red, seeming not to heal, threatening at any time to break out into the gangrene that they knew would lose him his arm or more likely kill him.

Napier spent an hour by Gresham's bedside. He demanded the fire be built up to chimney-threatening proportions, then closed all the windows and doors, increasing the heat. Only then did he take the clothes off the bed and strip Gresham down to his bare flesh.

'Have him washed, while we're at it,' said Napier, 'from top to toe. Warm water, and soap.'

He came back to Jane and Mannion. 'There is one thing you must understand. I believe you are a strong woman, from what you endured on the river. Sometimes when a man is in water and does not breathe for a period of time, strange things happen in the brain. The life of the person, his character, his individuality, seems to leave him, the brain carrying on only the basic functions of the body. I cannot guarantee this is not the case with your husband. It may not be so. Yet you must prepare.'

'Is that all?' asked Jane bleakly.

'No, far from it. First, there is this.' He produced two boxes, each containing a paste, one white and one brown. 'Exactly *this* much of each paste must be placed on his tongue every night at nine. He must be watched to see he does not spit it out or the material drop from his mouth. In time it will dissolve. It is essential that the dosage is regular and that it is taken without a single exception.'

'Unicorn's horn?' asked Mannion hopefully, who liked his medicines exotic.

'No,' said Napier scathingly. 'The first is made of a mould that grows in very wet conditions on the bark of a certain tree. The other is a compound of roots and herbs.'

'Mandrake root?' asked Mannion, unrelenting. The mandrake was said to grow where a man had spilled his seed on the ground, and it was also said that it screamed when it was picked. Napier did not deign to answer. Instead he gave other instructions. Gresham must be kept warm, but given a cooling bath every hour. At all times someone must try and force beef broth through his lips. 'Most of it he will reject, some will stay. Place a small amount of fine wheat bread in his mouth. Watch him in case he chokes, but keep it there and let it dissolve. Also honey and sweetmeats. Any wholesome food that will dissolve in his mouth, anything, will help.'

Napier turned again, ponderous, slow. 'I believe he thought himself dead. Death has not called him yet, but it will do so if he waits long enough at its door. His mind has withdrawn. It is at a level we mere mortals cannot reach, somewhere near to Hades. Smell is a potent sense, a most potent sense. And sound. What smells does he respond to?'

'My perfume,' said Jane, looking down, flushing.

'Fresh bread, and bacon well done on the spit,' said Mannion instantly. 'A really good wine . . .'

'Music,' said Jane. 'He loves music.'

'Then sprinkle your perfume on his pillow at all times,' said Napier, 'and have music in the room – some half hour of playing, and then some half hour of silence. Bring your fresh bread in here, fry your bacon. And pray.'

'He does not believe in God,' said Jane, a terrible admission that could have brought a terrible punishment. Yet she trusted this cumbersome, pedantic man.

'No, but God might believe in him,' smiled Napier. He took a deep breath. 'I will stay, if I may, Your Ladyship, for the duration of his illness.'

And so the vigil commenced, Jane at Gresham's bedside until her head was dropping on the counterpane with fatigue, then a few hours of blessed sleep while Mannion took over, then the bedside again. They brought the children to see him, on Napier's advice.

'Children are more robust than anyone imagines,' he said. 'This is a world they do not understand, and from that lack of understanding comes fear. The more they are shown, within reason, the less they fear. The less they fear, the stronger they become.'

Had they been asked to understand too much? wondered Jane, the horror of that closed hold coming on her again. 'Was that man a bastard?' Walter had asked, remembering their father's outburst by the river side. 'What is rape?' queried a thoughtful Anna. Neither child seemed outwardly much hurt by what had happened, though neither wished to talk about it. Jane asked the servants to enquire gently, but they said nothing. And then Anna woke up screaming one night after such questioning, and Jane ordered it to cease. Scars can be covered up on the flesh, and covered up on the mind, but they never go away, she thought sadly. On her or her children's minds.

The vigil went on. The paste provided by Napier seemed to do something to lessen the angry redness of the wound. The broken leg was mending, a clean break. Yet still he lay there, breathing lightly, eyes closed, expressionless.

The chief beneficiary was Mannion. He had assembled nothing less than a small kitchen in front of Gresham's bed, cheerfully bringing the bacon to sizzle on the hearth and the newly baked bread to fill the room, and the wine for Gresham to smell which had, after all, to be drunk once it had been opened. Gigantuan snores were emanating from the corner where he had fallen asleep. Jane, for whom his company had become as natural as that of the sky or the walls around her, did not wake and move him.

'It is the small hours of the morning that are the danger time,' Napier had said to her. 'You must, if you can, be by his bedside at these times. You must talk to him. It will be hard, but you must talk.'

It was a half hour past two. London and The House were silent. The candles gave enough light to see by, softened the room. The servant would come any minute now with fresh coal to build up the fire. Mannion would wake with a huge grunt in an hour or so, see he had fallen asleep in the room and apologise. She would brush it aside, perhaps go and throw cold water over her face, see if sleep would come for a few hours. Then The House would slowly come to life as its people stirred and started their lives again, yet for Gresham that daily rebirth would have no meaning, and for it he would have no ears or eyes. Just lie there, breathing ever so gently.

And so she talked to Gresham. She talked of the doings of The House: the silly servant who had poured sugar instead of salt into the beef pie and the anger of the chef; that Young Tom's father and mother were both taken by an ague that looked to see them off this world and Young Tom was torn between going to see them and staying to wait out his master's vigil. And talked of how there seemed to be a dearth of good, fresh meat in the city, and the milk had come in sour yesterday, the farmer swearing it had come straight from the cow and an old woman had given the bad eye to his beasts, so she had.

And when she ran out of tittle-tattle, she told him of their children. How little Anna had asked her what rape was, and how she had tried to answer without spoiling the innocence of her little girl, and how Anna had known, as Anna always did, that she was not being told the truth but had said nothing more, choosing instead to spare her mother on an instinct that ran deeper than anything else.

She talked then of her love for him. How, as a beaten and starved little girl, this man had ridden into her village, thin and emaciated, with the trappings of a lord on his back and horse and that strange man-mountain riding beside him. How could a man so rich be so thin, and look so unhappy? she had thought. How could a man be more glamorous? He had talked to her, by the pond, and then her stepfather had come out and whipped her and he . . . he had broken his arm. And there had been a massive row and she, Jane, had found herself riding out of the village she hated with all her heart, seated on the saddle of the man-mountain's horse. And she had screamed and screamed and screamed until even these great men had listened, screamed that *he* had saved her and she was going to ride on *his* horse and no one else's, and so with an expression of disdain Gresham had plonked her on his saddle and they had ridden in triumph to London. How from the moment she had first seen him, her knight in grubby armour, she had decided that there would be only one man in her life. She had spurned the endless advances of other men, and even the servant boys, her contempt withering their pathetic desire even as it blossomed. She was not for them, nor for any other man. She had organised his house for him, put it straight, become his housekeeper without his knowing. And then, one evening, she had forced him to look at her as a woman.

And because she was lonely, appallingly lonely, and more terrified than she had ever been in her life of losing the man who gave meaning to her existence, she talked of that terror, the lurching, rattling moments in the coach when she had clasped the children desperately to herself, being flung from side to side and terrified that she would be hurled out on to the road. The awful silence as the coach had ground to a halt and she had been hauled roughly out, reaching down in a paroxysm of anger and fear for the knife she carried strapped to her inside leg and feeling the blow to the side of her head. She talked of the utter horrors of waking, devils beating at the side of her face, to find herself trussed and chained by the neck like a slave girl. The appalling feeling of helplessness in the face of this bloated monstrosity. The anger and the bitter recrimination . . . why had she not spotted something was wrong? Gresham would have seen something was wrong! She was just a weak, stupid woman, in her element checking the supply of preserves and feeble as a child when real business was in hand. And then the sickening, stomach- and brain-churning realisation that this foul, evil thing intended to have her, in front of her children, and there was nothing she could do! Without realising it, her hand tightened on Gresham's as she gazed into the fire and recreated her own hell. Could she have been born to be penetrated by this satyr? Well, many a woman had endured worse and stayed silent – *but her children would know and have seen her so violated!* The syphilis! The pox! To live on for a few more years in the face of her husband, diseased? And then the answer had come to her. *She could bite off her tongue!* And her mouth had been open at its widest, ready to clamp down hard and without hesitation, when the other boat had hit.

She was panting now, breathing heavily, her hand still clutching Gresham's.

His hand tugged at hers.

She looked down, disbelieving. His hand, gently, was squeezing hers.

She leaned over him. His eyes were closed still. Two, three huge tears dropped from her eyes and fell on his lids.

'Warm,' he said. 'Warm.'

An eye opened, blinked in her tears, and shut again. Hurriedly, she brought the cloth by her side to his eyes and wiped them. He was speaking, croaking, a half-whisper. She leaned forward, her ears nearly pressing his lips.

'I should . . . have been there,' he was trying to say. 'I should have

276

been there.' Then, something else, stronger this time. Both his eyes were open. 'You must never die on me. Never . . .'

She screamed her happiness, screamed it out for the whole house to hear, screamed it so that Mannion leaped up as if the whole Spanish army was in his tent and The House under attack.

'If he comes back, you must hold on to him. Do not let him slip back into oblivion . . .' Dr Napier had said.

Her grip threatened to kill him all over again. Crying, babbling, calling out, she made him keep those eyes open, made him speak, made him live.

It was easier being dead, thought Gresham. Much calmer. Much quieter. Yet perhaps, after all, this was better. He smiled into the eyes of his wife.

23

Late March–27th June, 1613
London

'I am as true as truth's simplicity,
And simpler than the infancy of truth.'

SHAKESPEARE, *Troilus and Cressida*

There was so much to do. Yet it would be months before Gresham was physically able to do it. He lay there, fretting, in his bed, knowing that the leg must be kept still at all costs in its wooden splint, knowing that on his calm depended his ability to walk again without a limp. He ordered weights, used them until his breath tore at his throat, building his upper body strength.

The arm had healed beyond his belief. There was an angry scar there, for sure, to join the others on his body, but he felt no lessening in his control, no weakening.

They had lost five men in all from the coach, and one disabled for life. John, the coachman, found in a back alley with his head broken open, a blow that should have killed him and was probably designed to do so. Two of the men had been on the river and at The Globe when they had beaten off the attackers. Gresham felt their loss like brothers. Scars mend, but never quite heal. People die, and are never quite replaced. Young Tom he promoted to deputy coach driver. No conquering general surveyed his army with more pride

278

than Young Tom surveyed the coach on the first morning he drove it out in all its glory. It was an ugly, cumbersome thing, but for Young Tom there was nothing more beautiful in the world. There were pistols, loaded and ready, on the coach whenever it set out, and four blunderbusses loaded with nails. Walter the boatman and three of his crew were working for Gresham now.

They had found Nicholas. With something approaching despair, Gresham and Mannion had known that Marlowe would slip again into anonymity. Walsingham's spies had received a training in the field that was second to none. Yet Nicholas was easier meat, a bought servant.

He told them everything, without torture. The thin face and bloated body of the man who had come up to him in the tavern. The bag of gold, more money than he could have hoped to earn in a lifetime. The moment when he had decided to betray a lifetime of service.

Weeks ago, there would have been no argument. An implacable Gresham would have killed Nicholas himself without thought. Instead, stuffed in his bed, he looked to his wife as Nicholas sobbed and screamed before them. She gazed at the face of the man who had betrayed her and her children, driven them to what would have been more than her death, her eternal shame, but for a chance holing of a boat and a random meeting on the river.

'Let him go,' she said quietly, 'and never let him come within a mile of my family again.'

Too much death, too much suffering. It would have been easy to have him killed.

Mannion dragged him to the gateway of The House. He looked at the traitor in front of him, itching to do justice. Nicholas jibbered and shrieked, convinced he was going to die. I would like to take the gold you were paid, thought Mannion, and heat it until the coins melt all into one. And then pour it into your mouth. Instead, he looked at the pathetic thing in front of him.

'If you're seen or heard of in London, in Cambridge, or within a hundred miles of my master and my mistress, you'll die,' he said flatly. 'And if I catch sight or sound of you ever again you're dead, as you deserve to be now.' He paused. 'Well,' he said, 'you came into this world with nothing. That's how you'll leave.' He turned to the men he had stationed by the gatehouse. Laughing, jeering, they came over and none too gently stripped Nicholas of all his clothes.

'She said I shouldn't kill you,' said Mannion, 'so I won't.' He smashed his huge fist straight into Nicholas's mouth and nose. There was an explosion of bone, teeth and flesh and Nicholas was flung to the ground in the dirt of the yard. Staggeringly, he was still conscious, more the pity for him. The branding iron, in the shape of a straight 'T' for traitor, was ready. Mannion plunged it down on to Nicholas's forehead. He screamed and bucked under the pain.

'Now, Master Nicholas,' said Mannion, 'go out and face the world as you've made it for yourself.'

Four men grabbed an arm and a leg each and like a sack of flour the naked and branded Nicholas was hurled into The Strand, the gate closed on him.

They contemplated kidnapping Overbury, in the long discussions Mannion held with Gresham by his bedside when Jane was not there. Kidnapping and killing him. In one sense it would have been easy enough. He was no great noble, no great lord surrounded by guards and walls and stout, locked gates. Yet this was no vanishing of a simple man, another body face down in the Thames, another unexplained disappearance. Robert Carr would scream, the country would scream and the King, for all they knew, might scream in sympathy with his bed-mate.

In the event, it was made easier for them. Overbury's closest servant, the chamberlain to his household, proved willing enough to talk. A man had come, he said, demanding to see his master, late at night. He had seen him before, had let him in several times for drinking sessions with his master. A strange figure, with a small head and a bloated body and a high-prancing step. He had papers his master would pay a king's ransom for, the man had said imperiously. Almost against his better judgement, knowing the violence of his master, the chamberlain had let him in. Overbury had drawn his sword at the sight of the man, buffeted him and pinned him against the wall. 'Thief!' he had screamed. 'Betrayer of my trust!' 'No,' the man had replied, calm despite the sword pinned to his throat, 'perpetrator of your sweet revenge!' There was a moment when he thought his master would have pierced the man's neck. Then Overbury dropped the sword. Ordered the chamberlain to leave, peremptory. Scuttling to the embrasure that should have been bricked in when the new building was made but somehow had never been done, the chamberlain sat and listened. Revenge. That was the theme. Overbury had been beaten, humiliated by this man Gresham, had he not? He, the speaker, had the most foolproof plan for revenge, a revenge that Gresham could never scrub from his body or his brain had he access to all the waters of Lethe. All it needed was gold to bribe servants and to hire men and boats. And in return, as well as the most beautiful spoiling revenge, there were papers! Papers that could be most damaging to the King, to his bishops and his ministers! Papers Overbury could use. Papers in exchange for the letters the man had stolen. And then, as the details of the plan to despoil this Gresham's wife had emerged in the strange, high-pitched voice of the man, a mixture of terror and fascination had overwhelmed the chamberlain, huddled behind the embrasure. He was primed to tell, hating his master, fearing the man who had visited him, out of his depth.

Revenge was enacted in another place. In April, a grinning Mannion came to tell Gresham that Sir Thomas Overbury had been required to undertake an embassy to Russia. Refusing the offer, the King had consigned him to The Tower, and was showing no signs of intending to release him. The two men's laughter shook the house.

Gresham had thought it fit to tell the King of the night on the river. At first, buttressed up in his bed and with the quill feeling strange in his hand, he had been tempted to get a secretary to write the note. Then he had rebelled against his own weakness and persisted. Four lines into his carefully penned manuscript he had crumpled the paper into a ball and hurled it from him. Then he had settled again, taken new paper, recharged the quill. He told the story simply; his wife's kidnap, Marlowe's plan, the frantic evening when His Majesty had been dismissing the evening's events as a damp squib and men had been dying on the river beneath him. He made no mention of Overbury.

He had thought there would be no response, had written simply to explain his own inaction, pinned to a bed with a leg in timber. The King's messenger caught him by surprise, arriving in a blare of trumpets. The messenger was obsequious, emphasised the gift was to Lady Jane Gresham. They opened it together. A jewel, a ruby of immense size and beauty. Set in a simple gold ring, the more to show off its extravagance.

'It's worth a thousand . . . two thousand pounds!' Jane gasped. The note with it was on the finest possible paper. 'For your pains', it read, with a simple 'J' scrawled at the bottom.

'Wet frog?' asked Gresham dryly.

'*Rich* wet frog!' said Jane in delight, pushing the jewel on to her finger.

Then came the morning that he walked for the first time. They took the wood off his pale, shrunken leg. It was strange to feel the air breathing against the flesh after so long. He sat up and tried to swing his leg off the bed. It did not move. He ordered it, more firmly this time. It obeyed.

Jane looked at him. Mannion looked at him. Dr Napier, the long-suffering, pedantic, marvellous Dr Napier, looked at him.

He stood up. Carefully, it was true; painfully, even. Yet he stood, on both his legs, and remained standing.

They clapped him, and he grinned back at them.

But still no sign of Shakespeare, and Marlowe lurking out there in the shadows. Jane felt a sickness to the pit of her stomach at the thought of him. The security measures they were now forced to take were more and more burdensome, the toll of so many seemingly endless nights and days sitting by Gresham's bedside mounting up. At times she felt like screaming with frustration.

Perhaps it was this frustration, the pent-up energy of a mind without enough to do, that turned the final key and made clear what had been muddied for so long.

Gresham needed to sleep less and less during the day, but in payment for the strenuous exercise he insisted on undertaking to rebuild the strength in his leg Dr Napier made him rest for an hour at noon. Jane sat by the window. She had gone for her copy of Shakespeare's *Venus and Adonis*.

'It's beautiful,' she said. 'What a pity they never really let him write his own plays.'

It was as if she was gazing into a full-length mirror when all of a sudden the whole length of it shattered, as at one single blow, and the world dissolved. And she was left staring at the truth.

'Quick! Quick!' She rushed to her feet, so urgent as to grab Gresham by the arm. 'The papers you took from Marlowe! The writings that were with the King's letters! Where are they? I must have them, now!'

'Are you mad?' he asked, grumbling, his thoughts disturbed. 'Bits of a play in two different hands, two hands we cannot recognise. That's all they are!'

'But don't you see? They were important enough for Marlowe to put them in the pouch! Get them for me, please! Now!'

He swung his feet off the bed, noting with satisfaction the strength in his legs and through his whole body. When he came back, minutes later, she had been to the library and was clutching a dusty volume.

'You're lucky,' he said. 'Most of my papers are still hidden elsewhere from when it seemed we were going to be searched. I've only brought back a few papers, and those the ones that seemed likely to do the least damage. Here they are, for all they're worth.'

He handed her the sheets of paper, watched as she sat back in her chair, eyes devouring the handwritten manuscripts. She delved into the book she had brought, scrambled through the pages until she found the passage she wanted.

'Yes!' she breathed, 'yes! Can't you see it?'

'See what?' asked Gresham, now totally confused.

'Do you remember *Hamlet*?' she said. 'We've seen it several times, here and in Cambridge. Do you remember?'

'You know I remember it. We've talked often enough.' Lines from Hamlet had stuck and resonated in Gresham's mind. '*The readiness is all. The rest is silence.*'

'Do you remember that speech about death?'

'Of course I do. "*The undiscovered country from whose bourn no traveller returns*".'

'Then look at this.' Her excitement was so great she nearly dropped the book as she thrust it into Gresham's hand. It was titled *Hamlet*, and claimed the play had been shown at Oxford and at Cambridge.

'There!' she said, her finger pointing. 'Read!'

He read.

> *To be or not to be. I, there's the point,*
> *To Die, or sleep, is that all? I, all.*
> *No, to sleep, to dream, I marry there it goes . . .*

He looked up at her, laughing. '"Ay, marry, there it goes!" This is gibberish. It's comic! This isn't the speech we heard . . .'

'Read on!' she said. Reluctantly, he let his eyes return to the page.

> *For in that dream of death, when we awake,*
> *And borne before an everlasting Judge,*
> *From whence no passenger ever returned,*
> *The undiscovered country, at whose sight*
> *The happy smile, and the accursed damn'd.*

284

> *But for this the joyful hope of this,*
> *Who's bear the scorns and flattery of the world,*
> *Scorned by the right rich, the rich cursed of the poor?*

'What is this book?' he asked, looking at it distastefully.

'Published in 1603,' said Jane. 'Now look at this . . .' She thrust one of Marlowe's papers into his hands. The speech, that same speech, commenced just over halfway down, in a florid hand.

'It's the same,' said Gresham. 'Word for word. I still don't understand . . .'

'Now read this.' Jane thrust the second of Marlowe's papers into his hands. 'There! Read it!'

> *To be, or not to be – that is the question;*
> *Whether 'tis nobler in the mind to suffer*
> *The slings and arrows of outrageous fortune,*
> *Or to take arms against a sea of troubles,*
> *And by opposing end them? To die, to sleep –*
> *No more; and by a sleep to say we end*
> *The heart-ache and the thousand natural shocks*
> *That flesh is heir to. 'Tis a consummation*
> *Devoutly to be wished. To die, to sleep;*
> *To sleep, perchance to dream. Ay, there's the rub;*
> *For in that sleep of death what dreams might come . . .*

'Magnificent,' he breathed. The words reverberating in his head were even more powerful now than they had been from the mouth of Burbage. He looked down the page for the lines he needed:

> *Who would these fardels bear,*
> *To grunt and sweat under a weary life,*
> *But that the dread of something after death –*
> *The undiscovered country, from whose bourn*
> *No traveller returns – puzzles the will . . .*

Had the man who had written this been where Gresham had been? Had he also so nearly crossed the divide between life and death? Whoever had written these lines had been everywhere men go, and to places men could only dream of, thought Gresham.

'*Don't you see it!*' asked Jane. 'We've assumed that Bacon and Marlowe and Oxford and all those others sent plays to Shakespeare and he just fiddled around with them for a bit – got them dressed up for the stage and stuck his name on them. But what if the scripts they sent in were rubbish? What if they were awful? What if Shakespeare has this . . . talent, this . . . knack of taking other people's work and making something beautiful out of it?'

Gresham was thunderstruck.

'*What if Shakespeare was the real genius behind the plays all along?*'

Something massively simple fell into place inside Gresham's mind. 'So there's this bumpkin from Stratford, this front man for half the nobles in England, this man who can't write anything worthwhile from scratch but has this skill when other people seed his brain . . . the skill to create amazing, incredible language, probably something he never realised he had until other people's manuscripts landed on his desk . . . and he starts adding bits and improving on the original, small bits at first, almost despite himself, and then the bits he writes get the crowd cheering so he does it more and more . . .'

'And the nobles can't do anything about it without breaking cover, or revealing that what they write is rubbish. Or they pretend to each other that it's what they wrote in the first place because they love to bask in the glory . . .'

'What a truly wonderful, god-awful, inspirational, appalling mess!' said Gresham, unsure as to whether to laugh or cry. 'So what are these papers?'

'I bet the one with the real speech on it is Shakespeare's writing. And if you want me to guess, I'll lay odds on the dire version being in the Earl of Oxford's hand.'

'Why him?' asked Gresham.

'You remember when you went out to get the food when we were in Shakespeare's rooms? I was pumping him about the plays all the time, and he was giving nothing away. But I asked him about *Hamlet*, because it was your favourite play, and all he would say was that the Earl of Oxford hated the way it was performed. Then he looked shifty and backed off, and I didn't think anything about it because he was looking so shifty all the time. I bet the other paper is Oxford's writing. And I bet something else too – that Oxford published that book on the bed!'

'Why so?'

'He died in 1604, remember? Been ill for long before that. Everyone says he was a strange man at the end, half mad. Mad enough to think his version was the real one, the better one. Mad enough to publish it too, particularly when he felt he was dying.'

'The Earl of Oxford's last will and testament, you mean?' said Gresham. 'If he wanted to be remembered by that he must have been mad!'

'Perhaps it helped kill him, poor man,' mused Jane. 'The book was a disaster. That's why I could pick it up so cheaply at St Paul's. I wonder if Oxford waited for it to be hailed as a masterpiece, and then died when it was laughed off the bookstalls?'

'He died of the plague,' said Gresham. 'In Hackney. Don't you remember? There was a scandal about it. Apparently he left no will, and his son forgot to put up a memorial to him.'

'So if there was a will, bequeathing his manuscripts . . .'

'It's gone now,' said Gresham. 'Buried by the heir who wanted nothing to do with it all. It's a brilliant theory. But we need a copy of something in Shakespeare's handwriting to prove it.'

But they found something better than that.

There was a crash on the door and Mannion appeared, throwing something in front of him. It was a drenched Shakespeare, shivering to his bones, dripping foul water all over the floor. He was dressed as a housewife, his beard and moustache gone but the stubble on his lips ludicrously at odds with the lace around his neck and the full-flowing gown.

'Look what I found crawling out of the woodwork!' said Mannion proudly. 'Thought I'd just go and check up on our man outside The Globe, the one keepin' an eye on things. Lo and behold, this woman comes out of the play. 'Cept no woman I've ever met walks like that. So I goes up to him or her, curious, and the rest's history. Very fetching, he was, in his little bonnet. Got swept away, that did, in the river.'

'*You great fat fool! You total idiot!*' This was another new Shakespeare, standing eye to eye with Mannion, his rage seeming to run through his every fibre. For the first time in his life, Gresham saw someone actually physically shaking with rage. '*I was coming to see your master!*'

Even Mannion was stunned by the intensity of the stupidly dressed man in front of him. What an extraordinary figure Shakespeare was, thought Gresham. He must have kept this rage in check for the boat journey over to The House and then unleashed it just now as he was thrust into the room. Could this man store moods, like others stored food, and bring them out of his emotional pantry on demand?

Shakespeare turned to Gresham. '*It's all over!*' He was calming down, but like a boulder that has tumbled down a huge scarp and is now on more level ground, his range still had momentum and power.

'*What* is all over?' asked Gresham, beginning to feel his own anger rise within him. If this damned man had had the decency to be either an artist or a fraud then perhaps lives would have been saved, the sum total of human terror reduced if only by a little. Yet he had to be both a supreme artist and a fraud, complicating things beyond belief.

'Marlowe. Your friend Marlowe.'

Gresham felt rather than saw the tide of revulsion, the gasp of fear from Jane at the mention of the dread name.

'He went to Burbage, Hemminge and Condell. My friends! My friends who at the clink of coin and sight of a manuscript were willing to betray me!'

The tears were of anger, not self-pity. Gresham motioned Shakespeare to sit down, Mannion to bring wine. Shakespeare looked for a moment, then sat, suddenly deflating like a stuck bladder.

'How to betray you?' asked Gresham quietly.

'They told him where the manuscripts were kept. The original manuscripts. In the handwriting of the King, Andrewes, Bacon, Oxford, Derby, Rutland, Raleigh –' there was the tiniest of flickers across Gresham's face – 'the Countess of Pembroke, you name it . . . and, of course, Christopher Marlowe. They knew, the three of them. Always have known. Encouraged me in the fraud . . .'

'And did they know that most of the original manuscripts were hugely enhanced when you put your hand to them? Did they know that the ideas came from others but that the real genius came from you, Master William Shakespeare? Did they know that most of these plays would be just another afternoon's entertainment if it weren't for the poetry you have in your soul?' Gresham's voice cut like a saw.

Shakespeare had wine in his hand now. It was forgotten. Two, three huge tears formed in his eyes, rolled down his muddy cheeks, carving a little wobbling path of white in the brown. 'They knew. And they were prepared to sell me out. My friends. My lifetime friends. That was the deal, you see. Marlowe would get all the manuscripts, after giving Burbage, Hemminge and Condell a great lump of money. There'd be a performance, a big one. And then Marlowe would appear. It's what he's always wanted, don't you understand? The biggest dramatic moment of his, of anyone's, life. Christopher Marlowe, the great Christopher Marlowe, the founder of the Elizabethan stage, the master of the blank verse line . . . and not dead after all! Here, alive, on stage. His great enemy Cecil vanquished by death.'

Something cold and still had entered Gresham's mind, speeding his thoughts as a sledge with razor-sharp edges cuts through snow, silent, powerful and vicious.

'And after he appears like a Jack-in-the-Box, and the audience is gasping with wonder and amazement,' said Gresham, 'then he makes his second announcement. That while they, his loyal public, thought he was dead, he was dead only in name. His writing continued, almost to the present day. They know the plays of William Shakespeare? Did they really think that such plays could be written by a poor country boy from Stratford with no education? No! He, Christopher Marlowe, in the long, long years of his exile, had used Shakespeare as other noble minds had used Terence thousands of years ago.' Gresham had risen to his feet now. He stood in the centre of the room and flung his arms wide in the manner of the great Burbage in a great tragic lead. 'I AM MARLOWE AND I AM ALIVE! I AM SHAKESPEARE, AND HAVE LIVED ALONGSIDE YOU IN THIS THEATRE AS HIM FOR TWENTY YEARS PAST! MY ENEMIES ARE DEAD! THE MASTER HAS RETURNED!'

There was silence in the room.

'My God,' said Mannion, 'wouldn't the little bastard love that? Wouldn't he really, really love that?'

Jane was struggling to overcome her revulsion, desperately seeking to prove to herself that she could think logically about Marlowe. 'But wouldn't the other authors complain? Claim the credit?'

'Don't you see?' said Shakespeare, almost in desperation now. 'He's cleverer than all of us. Many of the authors don't want to be revealed. They'll stay silent. Someone like the Countess of Pembroke will be laughed out of Court if she claims authorship – a woman, for heaven's sake, able to write like that? What a joke! Either that, or it will herald a very different attitude to women, for life. And without the manuscripts, and with half the original authors dead, where's the proof? If Hemminge, Condell and

Burbage are prepared to betray me – and they are – then he claims my plays as easily as a hawk cuts out of the sky and catches a newly born rabbit.'

'Are you sure they will betray you?' asked Gresham. This time he got up and poured a new measure of wine into the goblet of his old enemy.

'Yes. They've been different, strange with me recently, but that's not how I know. They did the deal with Marlowe in The Globe, over a meal they had brought in. They forgot the servant who served them the meal. Said enough to make him suspicious. He came to me. "Sorry, Master Shakespeare," he said. "Very sorry to intrude. But it sounds to me as if Masters Burbage and Condell and Hemminge are going to let someone else take the credit for all those plays what you wrote. And that ain't right . . ." Pathetic little man,' said Shakespeare with a sad and bitter laugh. 'His sense of justice was outraged by what he heard so he listened at the door. Didn't know it was Marlowe, of course.'

'Do servants often talk to you?' asked Gresham, remembering the grumpy old man at the Dominican Priory.

'All the time, actually,' said Shakespeare, rather wistfully. 'Don't know why. They always have. Remember that speech in *King Leir*? About poor wretches who bide the pelting of the pitiless storm?'

Gresham nodded his head.

'That came from the same man who warned me about Burbage and the rest of them. He came in drenched one day. Said as how wretches like him had no defence against the rain. Pitiless it was, he said.'

'And from that you wrote what you did?'

Shakespeare looked surprised, his grief forgotten. He also looked confused. 'Why . . . of course I did. I mean, he virtually wrote it for me, didn't he?'

'No, he didn't actually,' said Gresham, looking at Shakespeare with new eyes. 'He gave you the raw material. Very raw material. God – if he exists, which I very much doubt – gave you the poetry.'

There was a long silence.

'Well, that's it, isn't it?' Shakespeare had changed again. He was now the Stratford grain merchant, rather plump, needing to go about his business because time waits for no man. 'I suppose he'll leave me alone at last once he's made his grand declaration and claimed my work as his own. No one will listen to plain old William Shakespeare, uneducated old William Shakespeare.' He turned to Jane. 'Do you know, I shouldn't wonder if he claims my sonnets. And my *Venus and Adonis*. And *The Rape of Lucrece*. Why shouldn't he? He's got all the rest . . .'

And then he broke down into uncontrollable tears, the sobs racking his body as if each one was an arrow sinking into his flesh. Gresham did not stop Jane from going to him, putting her arms around him. She was holding him like a baby, rocking him back and forth. She was someone who knew what it was to have the products of one's imagination for ever claimed by someone else. She liked Ben Jonson, loved him in her own way. Yet what did it cost her to know that so much of his *Volpone* was her own work?

Gresham's voice came like a sudden cloudburst damping summer fire. 'I think if anyone has the credit for your writing, Master Shakespeare, it should be you. I will see it is so.'

Shakespeare looked up. He wanted to laugh out loud, yet something stopped him from doing so. Something implacable, quite fearsome in nature.

'Where are the manuscripts stored?' asked Gresham very quietly.

Stunned, Shakespeare told him. 'They're all in the thatch of the Lord's Gallery. I hid them there after Marlowe raided the book-keeper's room. I gambled he'd never think of my taking them back to The Globe.'

'Do you have a separate copy of all the plays? A fair copy? Kept somewhere else? Not in The Globe, I mean.'

'Yes, for almost all of them,' said Shakespeare.

'And when is the performance they're putting on to allow Marlowe to reveal himself?'

'Two days from now. *All Is True*,' said Shakespeare. 'The actors call it *Henry VIII*. It doesn't matter what you call it. It's the play written by the King. It's dreadful. But it's got lots of spectacle, lots of show. They decided it's the one that would drag the most people in.'

'Do you trust me to restore to you what Marlowe and the others are threatening to rob you of? The right to your work?' asked Gresham.

Shakespeare looked at the man who had been his sworn enemy, his tormentor, and had now offered to be his friend. 'Quite frankly, I don't,' said Master William Shakespeare. 'I doubt the devil himself could do it.'

Sir Thomas Overbury sat slumped on his bed in the Tower of London. The other prisoner sat opposite, on a chair Overbury had arranged to be carried over from his apartments. He was a poor figure, his fellow prisoner. Someone Overbury would not have paused to spit at only a few weeks before.

'I was right to refuse the King!' Overbury said bitterly. The other prisoner nodded, taking a gulp of the putrid wine that was all Overbury had managed to get into The Tower. 'Me! To go as ambassador to some godforsaken frozen hole! Oh, I know what they all wanted. The plan's clear as day. Get me posted overseas and then, with my brains gone from the scene, get rid of Robert Carr.' Overbury lurched to his feet, taking a swig of his own wine. 'My friend Carr wouldn't last weeks in the . . . cess-pit of the Court once I was safely posted overseas!'

'You were offered an ambassadorship? By the King?' asked Overbury's companion, who had damned the King without ever actually seeing him, and might well die without seeing him too. He was not sure whether to laugh at Overbury or bow before him.

'I refused it! Of course! Who is the King to tell me what to do?'

The other prisoner blanched at that. He knew who the King was. The person in whose name he had been arrested. The person in whose name he would most likely be tortured, executed or left rotting in this place. A trace of fear swept into his mind. Was this person, this Sir Thomas Overbury, a wise man to drink with?

'This imprisonment won't last! It was necessary. The King has to do it, for the form's sake! Carr will weedle and charm James into releasing me soon enough.' Overbury was pacing the narrow room now. 'And then there'll be revenge for those who put me in this stinking pile of stone. Carr needs me. *The King needs me!*'

This man *is* mad, the other prisoner thought. He put his cheap cup down and started to edge towards the door.

'Damn this imprisonment!' Overbury raged, hardly noticing the other man. The Court was a whirlpool of intrigue, current and cross-current, and here he was with his vessel swept into a back-water, land-locked with no oars and no sail. *The inaction was intolerable!*

A few miles away, Henry Gresham felt a quiet satisfaction at the way Overbury had been neutralised. Yet even he did not realise that when one man causes a prey to stop alive in its tracks, he opens up a route for others to give it the death blow.

24

29th June, 1613
The Globe Theatre

'the great globe itself,
Yea, all which it inherit, shall dissolve
And, like this insubstantial pageant faded,
Leave not a rack behind.'

SHAKESPEARE, *The Tempest*

'Ready for the big day?' John Hemminge grinned at Henry Condell.

'Are you sure this is . . . the right thing?' Condell answered.

'Look,' said Hemminge patiently, as if explaining to a child, 'we're actors, aren't we? We deal in *drama*. Kit Marlowe was a legend in his lifetime – for what he wrote, what he did and for who he was. There's been God knows what rumours about his death ever since it was meant to have happened. This revelation that the great Kit Marlowe didn't die in 1593, that we've been watching his work for twenty years – this is going to be the greatest defeat of death since Jesus! It's the most dramatic moment of our lives. Of anyone who's alive now! Remember poor old Will's speech in *Henry V*? About all those who would rue the day they weren't there at Agincourt? What will people give to have been there on the day when Kit Marlowe revealed himself at The Globe? In front of The King's Men, with The King's Men putting on his cursed play a day later! Henry . . .' Hemminge moved over to Condell, put his arm around his shoulders. 'Sometimes history asks you a question, and you have to say yes.'

Condell thought for a moment. 'But it's not the truth!' he said. 'You know what those scripts Marlowe sent in were like – *Richard II*, *Richard III*, *Julius Caesar*. Oh, I know they had good bits – but most of them were raving, ranting gibberish! We know it was Will who turned them into plays that the likes of us could perform. Is it right to ditch Will in favour of a man who was nothing but trouble in his first incarnation, and who seems to have brought nothing but trouble in his second? We're denying our friend his inheritance, John. We're taking Will's art away from him.'

'Art!' Hemminge snorted. 'Sod art! What are we players to do with *art*? We're to do with whatever gets them flocking over the river to see us perform. I know we fancy ourselves. *We* don't put on bear-baiting or cock-fighting after a play,' and he started a mincing walk, affecting a high-pitched voice, 'not like some of those other *low-brow* theatres. But we would, if it meant the difference between living like gentlemen or starving, wouldn't we? Would you starve for art? Would you?'

'Probably not,' said Condell with a long sigh, 'but if I was a king negotiating a treaty, I'd rather do it with Will Shakespeare than Kit Marlowe.'

'Forget it!' said Hemminge. 'We'll make it worth Will's while in money, and it's not as if he doesn't have enough of it already.'

'But I still worry—'

'Don't! He's claimed the credit all his life for stuff other people sent him. Now someone else wants a share. It's poetic justice. He's got his property and his business in Stratford. Not bad for a terrible actor. Don't worry about it! We'll be drinking with him and having a laugh about it in six months' time!'

Condell doubted that but did not show it. He had a part to play in the performance that was even now limbering up. His mind would not be on the show, he knew. It would be on the revelation that would follow it, at the point where the audience might have been expecting a jig. Christopher Marlowe. Killed in a bar-room brawl twenty years ago at the peak of his dramatic powers. Yet not dead. Alive, here in The Globe. And managing to talk to his audience these twenty years past as if from the grave. Dammit, they had to make Marlowe do a sequel to *Doctor Faustus*, before he really did die. Only a matter of time, and short time at that, given the look of him. It had to be a sell out.

Thank God Marlowe had come to them! Hemminge thought exultantly. What if he had gone to The Rose, or even The Red Bull? The mere thought made him grind his teeth. The Globe it was. As it should be. As it had always been.

'When's he turning up?' Condell asked aloud. He and Burbage had left the negotiations to Hemminge.

'He didn't – wouldn't – say,' answered Hemminge, rather distractedly. 'All I know is that he's going to make his appearance from the Lord's Gallery when we've finished the show. He's written ten lines for Burbage to say. Then he'll appear.'

The stage area was covered by a thrusting thatched roof, the underside of which had a painted canopy. Just above it was the turret, from which the cannons were fired for special effects and the flag hoisted and the trumpets blown to mark the start of a show. Sheltered by the roof, immediately under its protection, was the Lord's Gallery. Highly privileged members of the audience, who were willing to pay an extremely privileged price, could watch the play from there, on occasion having to share it with the musicians. For tonight's performance the musicians had been banished to the side of the stage, and no tickets sold to the Lord's Gallery. That would be Marlowe's platform, the podium from which he would return to life and reinvent it.

Hemminge and Condell disengaged, returned to the throng of actors ready and excited to present *All Is True* to a nearly full house.

For how many years had Christopher Marlowe been invisible? All those years of hiding, twenty in all, from the fact of which he was most proud: *he was Christopher Marlowe*. Twenty years of fearing above all to be recognised, of cultivating invisibility. And now this truly poetic opportunity to come back to life once and for all.

He would not enter for the start of the play. That would be too obvious, there could be too many people looking for him. One great moment, his liaison with Lady Jane Gresham and her children, had been spoiled by his being recognised. This time he would wait until the play had commenced, wait for its first great ceremonial moment and then slip in up the deserted stairs to the Lord's Gallery, hooded and cloaked. The knife he had with him was razor sharp. It would cut as a hot knife through butter into the hardened canvas that upheld the thatch in the Lord's Gallery. From out of the incision would tumble the manuscripts of that charlatan Shakespeare's plays, like a surgeon cutting out babies from a woman's flesh. The original manuscripts. He would pick up one or two. His *Richard III* for sure, his *Richard II* by choice, written so long ago in a faraway land, his version so greatly preferable to the one the upstart Shakespeare had chosen to write, with all his 'changes' and his 'improvements'. He would wait then for the end of *All Is True*. The great Burbage would make his announcement – instead of an epilogue for *All Is True* he would read the ten lines that Marlowe had penned and changed and corrected over twenty years of dreaming of this moment. Then he, Christopher Marlowe, would reveal himself. And when the double shock was over, he would announce that The Globe would be presenting tomorrow the first ever performance of his new masterpiece: *The Fall of Lucifer*.

It was a desert outside of The Globe ten minutes after *All Is True* had started. The hawkers had gone their way and only a few hopefuls guarding horses stood outside the whitewashed walls. He slipped in through the back gate, the attendant forewarned and granting him a brief nod. The stairs challenged him. How to climb such stairs when feet did not feel the bite of wood on flesh? The ferocious determination of his anger took him over. Ludicrously, stupidly, he raised each foot high and plotted with his eyes its course as it landed on firm surface.

He was in the Lord's Gallery. The bulge of the thatch was restrained by canvas strung underneath it. He put his own manuscript down, his *Fall of Lucifer*, took out the knife, slashed at the canvas. It hung, sliced, then spewed out two, three rolled papers, each tied with an innocuous ribbon. It was a truly Caesarian birth, except there was no blood on the papers.

On the main stage, Prologue came on, gloriously overdressed, to wolf-whistles from the Pit. There was a curtain drawn across the façade of the Lord's Gallery, blunting and dimming the words spoken beneath.

'*I come no more to make you laugh . . .*' Prologue pronounced.

'More's the pity!' came the cry from a wag in the Pit, and the audience roared.

> *. . . things now*
> *That bear a mighty and a serious brow,*
> *Sad, high, and working, full of state and woe,*
> *Such noble scenes as draw the eye to flow,*
> *We now present . . .*

More and more manuscripts came tumbling from the thatch where they had been hidden. Marlowe crouched on the floor, fumbling, opening, reading.

They were due a great moment on stage. The cue came. The boy playing Anne Boleyn said pipingly, '*You cannot show me . . .*' and Lord Sandys replied, '*I told your grace they would talk anon . . .*' On cue, the trumpets sounded, the drums rolled and there were two cracks of thunder from above, shaking the building. Two brass cannon had been placed in the turret, loaded with blank shot, making a terrifying noise.

'Christ Almighty!' said the armourer in charge of the cannon. He had loaded the weak charge of powder that morning, in preparation, and had then gone off for his beer and cheese in the tavern. He knew from the sound of the discharge that something was wrong. Somehow the cannon had been double-shotted. From the mouth of both cannons flew a flaming wadge of powder, still half-burned, followed by two or three sheets of burning wadding that the armourer knew he had never placed in the barrels. It all landed on the thatch on either side of the roof, smouldering. The armourer turned for the buckets of water and sand they kept up there if ever a chamber was to be fired. Damn and blast! They were gone. Where the hell were they?

The thatch took light almost immediately. In the first moments there was more heat than smoke, the only sign of the fire the shimmering heat haze immediately above it. Then, when the fire penetrated the surface layer to the slightly less sun-drained straw, there was a tell-tale, deceptively gentle wisp of smoke.

The audience ignored it, their attention drawn by the noise of powder, drums and trumpets, oblivious to the fact that a fire had been set in the roof that already no man could put out. Or rather, two separate fires, one on either side of the stage, racing through the thatch to meet in the area above the Lord's Gallery.

A part of Marlowe's mind heard the growing panic as both word and sight of the fire spread among the crowd. Yet it was not that which stopped his hungry examination of the manuscripts he had torn from the roof. It was a noise. There was someone here in the room with him. Hemminge? Condell? He turned with an ingratiating smile on his face. It froze where it lay.

'Good afternoon,' said Henry Gresham casually. 'We've met before, haven't we? And, of course, you know my wife.'

Henry Condell pushed a disconsolate toe into a small pile of the still-smouldering ashes that were all that was left of The Globe. His Globe. They had hoped that 29th June would go down in history: the day that Christopher Marlowe returned from the grave. Well, his wish had been granted. It would go down in history, that was for sure: the day that The Globe burned down. God knew where Marlowe had got to. No one had seen him enter the theatre. Well, he could whistle for Will's precious manuscripts. They had gone up in smoke together with the theatre. Will would be relieved, at least. Marlowe would want his money back, of course, that ludicrous amount of money, and his bloody play performed.

Condell felt a slight lightening of his spirit. They could still fulfil that part of the bargain, couldn't they? They still had Blackfriars. All right, it was smaller, indoors, but it was a theatre, wasn't it? And they were still the best company of actors in the country, weren't they? All they needed was the script. Marlowe – and he was half beginning to doubt he had been who he said he was – had been due to bring it yesterday. Still, if he'd lived twenty years after his death, a couple of days probably didn't mean too much to him. When he turned up with the manuscript, they'd do a deal. He could have his comeback at Blackfriars, couldn't he?

Condell's eye caught a lump, something blackish, sticking out of the ashes. His nose curled as he advanced and caught an overripe stench. There must have been birds nesting in the thatch to produce that smell of burned flesh. Thank God no one had died in the fire, only birds. It had caught in the roof and the Lord's Gallery had gone first, but the actors had known to evacuate and Marlowe's gold had paid for the gallery to be empty. One man's clothes had caught fire as he ran from the theatre, but another customer had had the wit to put the fire out with bottled ale.

Condell took the stick he had with him and poked at the lump. Half of it had melted with the fierce heat of the fire but the rest was clear enough. An iron neck collar, with a section of chain leading off it. Where on earth had they used that as a prop? *Tamburlaine*, with all its prisoners? Strange he couldn't remember. It must have dropped from the turret or from the Lord's Gallery. A pity The Globe hadn't been built of iron, he thought. If it had, more of it might have survived.

Well, he consoled himself, at least it was an accident. No one, not even Marlowe and certainly not Will Shakespeare, was mad enough to burn down The Globe to make a point.

EPILOGUE

**The Cambridge University Library
Cambridge, England
12th August, 2013**

'Our revels now are ended.'

SHAKESPEARE, *The Tempest*

They closed the library at 7.00 p.m. in the long summer vacation. It was irritating because he could only come in August, and the extra two or three hours it remained open in term time would have been a godsend. His old college helped with accommodation, of course, but it could do little about food. It was still an expensive luxury, his three weeks intensive research in Cambridge, taken at the expense of his new young wife and even newer children.

The library still had half an hour to go before its official closing time, but the thought police started the campaign to get rid of readers long before that. The litany of announcements stating that books could no longer be borrowed seemed to start at 5.30 p.m. and rise to a positive crescendo by 6.00 p.m. After 6.30, all the library staff, usually so helpful, seemed to start coughing in unison while making busier and busier packing-up noises.

All in all, a strong feeling that his presence was no longer welcome. One box to go of the eight boxes he had ordered that morning of papers pertaining to the life and works of Lancelot Andrewes, sometime Bishop of Ely and Winchester. He wondered if he would ever get this thesis written, with the demands of a parish that seemed to occupy most of Lancashire now being matched by the demands of two young children, and the crucifying worries about money. He was skimping the material, glossing over papers that in the first flush of academic youth he would have pored over for a whole morning.

He had actually started to stand up, on his way to taking the box back to the desk, when something made him stop.

Its catalogue designation stated that it contained unpublished papers relating to sermons planned by the late bishop. Unpromising material, essentially. Lancelot Andrewes had written clearly, fluently and with a commendable sense of discipline. Papers he had discarded as being worth little were likely to be just that, minor memorabilia of no use to someone trying to research the features of a great life. But the new preservation techniques they had applied to these papers were quite extraordinary. The injection process – or was it more properly a process of osmosis? – protected the manuscripts from heat and light depradation, but also meant they could lie on top of each other and be handled by greasy fingers, all the while with an invisible barrier between them and the handler. It also preserved their natural colour. Which was why his attention was drawn to the box. A corner of paper protruded from it. Its colour was different to all the others he had been looking at. More eighteenth-century than seventeenth. He sat back down again, heavily, more tired and dispirited than he cared to admit. Why not untie the box? If at the end of the day he could tell the library they had misfiled a bit of paper, at least he would have achieved something.

It was a folder, he saw, the clumsy eighteenth-century version of a modern wallet file. It had been catalogued with the GRESH prefix. Any historian from the late sixteenth-century onwards knew that was the code for the Gresham family. This was obviously something dating from the first serious attempt to catalogue the vast

Gresham papers, started around the 1780s but which sadly showed huge goodwill but little academic rigour. This particular folder had clearly been part of the Gresham collection, but at some stage had been transferred to the Andrewes papers. Interesting, he thought, his brain starting to engage again. A librarian walked heavily past him, sighing. He decided to ignore it. He opened the wallet.

There! The familiar look and feel of the paper Andrewes liked to use, flowing writing in the hand he had now come to see after three years of research as almost the same as his own. Then one final clutch of papers in a different hand, different paper. That could wait. He turned over the first document in Andrewes's hand.

The code! Andrewes had used a simple code for some of his letters, normally when in correspondence with his friend Francis Bacon and he had the need to say something vaguely scurrilous about a clergyman or courtier of their mutual acquaintance. A clever eighteenth-century librarian had spotted the code and who it belonged to, without having the key to translate it. With the marvellous freedom they had had in those days, the librarian had transferred the papers from GRESH to ANDREWE in the hope that someone else would make sense of them.

Despite this effort, it was probably nothing; just more gossip. Yet something made him take the table from his own file and convert the code to English. There was a heading, first of all. A librarian stopped by his work station and noisily began to gather up books, papers and boxes. He ignored him.

To My Lord Henry Gresham, First Baron Granville and Friend to My Heart
    I am dying, my friend, and will shortly find if the Maker in whom I believe with all my heart and soul will pass good judgement on my life . . . .

He could hardly believe what he was reading! The undiscovered last will and testament of the great man himself. Written to one of the most notorious figures of the age. A librarian could have exploded by his side and he would not have noticed. His eyes flickered from the original to the key, his hand starting to shake uncontrollably as it grasped the cheap biro and transcribed the code on to the thin, cheap-ruled A4 paper, far, far too slowly for the pressure of his mind.

. . . you preserved my reputation, and perhaps even my soul, when by your action you took my plays from me and gave them instead to William Shakespeare. I now concede what I found it hard to concede before. They were always his, for all that my vanity sought to persuade me that they were mine . . .

William Shakespeare? He ran the code again. Shakespeare. William Shakespeare. *Plays?* Plays written by the man credited with a great part of the King James Bible? He was set to move on, translate more, but his eye was caught by the bottom paper in the box. Different, cheaper paper. A closer hand. Paper was expensive in those days. All except bishops and the mightiest of lords wrote close and hard together on such a valuable commodity.

Most Gracious and Honoured Lord,
The honour done to me by the trust of your most recent package knows no bounds, as my admiration of the skill you bring to this most noble art knows no bounds. For this humble spinner of words to offer more than thanks is in itself an insult. It is therefore in a spirit of submission, regard and humility that I seek to question as I do, in the belief that even the noblest of buildings needs the humble mason to see to its design. It is in this spirit that I ask first of all if to call this work The Magic of Man *is sufficient testimony to its true brilliance and worth, where a proper description of its power is that it unleashes a tempest of thought and a tempest of wonders into the mind of its audience . . .*

The letter was *five* pages long. As he moved to continue the translation, his hand skewed the other sheets up, revealing the last page. The signature.

William Shakespeare.

For a moment, the world stopped. Then, slowly, colour, light and sound returned to it, though it was as if the pounding of his heart would never cease.

A librarian was standing by his side. 'I'm sorry, sir, but we're closing now. If I could ask you . . .'

He looked up at the man and pointed to the end sheet. He gathered up the five sheets as if they were the souls of his two children, held them up as an offering to the librarian.

'A letter,' he said simply. 'A five-page letter *by William Shakespeare*. Hitherto Unknown,' he added.

The librarian looked at him. Something in the moment had caught him, caught them both. Suddenly the librarian felt, knew even, that this was a moment that would be replayed time after time after time, replayed for as long as there were humans who cared about art.

'Not a will, or a legal document, or something about his second-best bed,' he said to the librarian. 'A five-page letter. A letter which seems to go into intimate detail about the authorship of Shakespeare's plays. A letter,' he added for good measure, 'which was found in the archive material of The Cambridge University Library.'

'A letter by . . . Shakespeare?' said the librarian in a reverential tone.

'Do you think,' he said, plucking up his courage, 'that just this once you could ask someone if the library could stay open a little longer?'

He saw little of what the future held for him as he proffered the five pages that had lain unseen for so long up to the lowly library employee. The fame, the notoriety, the divorce, the resentment of his children, the abuse and, finally, in his old age, the post as

Chaplain of Granville College, where he spent most of the day and night in his rooms, followed by the whispers of the tourists on the rare days when he faced the college quad.

Yet even then his heart told him something. Every book written about Shakespeare, or with even a passing reference to him, redundant now. Every film, every play and every parody – redundant now. The huge, vast and magnificent edifice of Shakespearian scholarship, its pontificating secular bishops, demolished, empty and meaningless. A hundred thousand voices who had sneered at their opponents over four hundred years that of course Shakespeare was, had to be, the only author of his plays, redundant now. A hundred thousand voices who had joined together in societies, campaigned, lobbied and sometimes sneered that of course Shakespeare could not have been the author of the plays credited to him, that they were written by Oxford, Marlowe, Rutland, Derby, all redundant now.

The huge, vast, multi-million dollar industry of Shakespeare, that world-wide industry, all redundant now.

My God, he thought, even then, before more than a tiny portion of the truth settled in his brain. The God in whom he believed every bit as much as Bishop Lancelot Andrewes. What have I done?

HISTORICAL NOTES

The first complete edition of Shakespeare's plays was published in 1623, edited by Shakespeare's old friends John Hemminge and Henry Condell. Both men commented in what is now known as the First Folio on the speed and ease with which Shakespeare wrote, evidenced by the fact that the copies on which they had based their text had so few corrections or blots on them. Debate over whether or not the man we know as William Shakespeare could have written the world's greatest plays has raged ever since. In this book, I have quoted from the Alexander edition of Shakespeare's *Complete Works*, Collins, London, 1975.

Lancelot Andrewes (1555–1626) had been made Bishop of Ely in 1609. He was a leading figure in the writing of the King James Bible and widely recognised for his wit, his command of English and his mastery of numerous other languages. Widely expected to become the Archbishop of Canterbury, he missed his chance and was appointed Bishop of Winchester in 1619. Throughout his career he refused to comment on political issues of the day.

Francis Bacon, First Baron Verulam and Viscount St Alban (1561–1626) supported King James in his view as to the absolute power of the monarchy. He was appointed Attorney-General in 1613 and Lord Chancellor in 1618. He flattered the then-favourite Buckingham, but was impeached partly because of his link with Buckingham in 1621, sent to The Tower and fined £40,000.

Released after a few days, he retired in disgrace and devoted the remainder of his life to writing. He was the first great scientific philosopher in England, and reported to be the most intelligent man of his age.

Robert Carr, Earl of Somerset (1586–1645) lost favour to the new favourite, George Villiers, later Duke of Buckingham, around 1615. He and his wife (he married the infamous Frances Howard, Countess of Essex, in December 1613) stood trial for the murder of Sir Thomas Overbury (see *The Overbury Murder: Henry Gresham and the Scarlet Woman*) and were convicted and imprisoned in The Tower until 1621. Carr lived in retirement in the country until his death in 1645.

Sir Edward Coke (1552–1634) was moved sideways in 1613 and Sir Francis Bacon appointed Attorney-General. Contemporary rumour related that one reason for his falling into disfavour concerned certain letters between King James I and Robert Carr. Though coming back into favour at later times in James's reign, Coke became something of a thorn in the side of royalty, seeking to limit in law the power of the king. Aligning himself more and more with the Parliamentary cause, he was instrumental in drafting the Petition of Rights in 1628.

King James I (b. 1566) lived until 1625, and was succeeded by his second son, Charles.

Sir Thomas Overbury (1581–1613) died of poison in The Tower of London in September, 1613, while being there on the orders of the King. The event and its aftermath are the subject of *The Overbury Murder: Henry Gresham and the Scarlet Woman*.

William Shakespeare (l554–1616) died in April 1616 in Stratford, where he seems to have been remembered as a grain dealer. His death took place shortly after Sir Walter Raleigh was released from The Tower of London in March 1616. For information regarding the controversy over the authorship of Shakespeare's plays, and his possible role as a spy, see the Author's Note on page ix of this book.

If you enjoyed *The Conscience of the King*, don't miss
The Desperate Remedy, the first Henry Gresham novel.

Will Shadwell may not be the most moral of men, but to Henry
Gresham – gentleman, scholar, courtier, spy – he is invaluable. For
in the dark days of the reign of King James I, a man must know his
enemies to survive; Shadwell, by hook or more often by crook, is
one of Gresham's best sources. Then Shadwell is brutally murdered
and Gresham is summoned to London by the man he fears most:
Robert Cecil, the King's Chief Secretary and Machiavellian master
of a sinister network of spies. As Gresham follows Cecil's orders
with ever increasing trepidation, his enquiries into Shadwell's death
uncover a plot so audacious it is scarcely believable: a Catholic
uprising, a violent insurrection, and a trail of gunpowder underneath the Houses of Parliament . . .

Chapter One of *The Desperate Remedy* follows . . .

The Desperate Remedy

Chapter One

Will Shadwell froze in terror. There was the noise again. Behind him, somewhere in the enveloping and impenetrable dark. He had heard it once before, a tiny crack like a twig breaking and the briefest rustling. Imagination? A cow, a sheep? Some idiot peasant's hog stirring in the field? Or men with knives destined for Will Shadwell's back, creeping up on him through the black silence?

He had trudged on, as the sun had hung like a raw orange ball over the horizon's razor edge, taking an age to set. The sense of danger, the fear, were ever present, tingling his bones. Something was wrong. He knew it.

Hot tears of self-pity welled up in him, burnt his eyes against the cold of the night. He was crouched low in a dry ditch, the dust in his nose and mouth, the debris of a country track already working its way inside his doublet and scratching against his skin. He had never felt more alone or more in terror of the nameless things hidden in the vast sweep of the flat countryside. He was holding back his breath, despite the red-hot iron bars in his chest, the impossible urge to scream and run. He had never meant to be on the road in the middle of the night. It was the horse's fault, that damned animal. He knew nothing of horses, could hardly ride. It had looked as good as any other in the dim light of the early morning, rolled its mad eyes at him like any other horse. He had thrashed it into action, hurling it towards Cambridge and the only man to whom he could turn, the panic driving him on and communicating itself to the animal beneath him. He had to see Henry Gresham. Gresham. The only man he could turn to, the only man who would know what to do with the terrible secret Will Shadwell had stumbled on, the secret he carried only in his head. The only man who might stop this terrible pursuit, take the wolves off his back.

The night spread round him, silent, still. There had been nothing now, no noise, for five minutes or more. Hope flared up in him. He knew every noise in London's mean streets, could interpret every sound. Here in the country the night spoke a different language, every sound of it in his heightened state of terror a possible death threat. Had it been some animal, treading lightly over the ground? Surely no men could be so silent. His breath was starting to come to him normally now, his heart thudding less against his eyes.

The horse had foundered outside Royston. He knew they would come after him, expected someone to notice his sudden run from London. With the horse under him he could at least match pursuit. With its useless carcass dead on the road he had had to branch off to avoid pursuit, on to the side roads and tracks. It had been a mistake, dull-faced peasants eyeing him as the only thing of interest to have passed that way in years, noting his progress and all too willing to tell it to whoever came behind. If only he could have hidden the horse, instead of leaving its lathered hide as a sign to any pursuer.

Dare he move? If there were pursuers still out there they might walk past him in his ditch. They were showing no lantern, lighting no flares, if even they existed. He knew he stank, but if they were there they had no dogs, that much he was certain of. He was lost, of course. The tracks he had taken weaved their way through the Flatlands, but the stars stayed where they had always been. He reckoned he was upstream of Cambridge, knew if he kept on he would meet the slow, flat river. Gresham would be in bed now in his College rooms, simple and book-furnished for all the man's impossible wealth, a world apart from the magnificence of the house on the Strand and the whore who kept it for him. He would know what to do. Gresham always knew.

He was feeling drowsy, despite the cold that was starting to penetrate the thin, ragged cloak that was all he had time to grab when he fled London. Perhaps he would sleep here in the ditch, wait until morning . . .

He did not hear or even sense the man. He felt his hot breath against his cheek, heard the words cut through the night in his ear, had time to note the almost caressing husky tone.

'Will Shadwell . . . a fine dance you've led us.'

He screamed then, a spasm tearing through his body and hurling him up out of the ditch. He dimly saw three, perhaps four vague shapes where the night was blacker. He twisted away, felt a thorn tear at his boot and into the soft flesh above his ankle. He felt a thud in his back, was knocked forward, and looked down startled at the blade that had appeared through his flesh, just beneath his ribcage. He opened his mouth, and the warm, salty taste of his blood hit him at the same time as the tearing agony of the pain. He felt himself falling, heard rather than felt himself thud into the soft ground. Gagging, gasping, drowning in his own blood, he felt a boot kick him over. The last thing Will Shadwell saw on God's earth was the thin blade driving down towards his eye socket.

'You'll pay me the usual?' sniffed the miller, who seemed to have a permanent cold.

Henry Gresham prodded the dead face with his boot.

'I've told no-one else . . .' the miller added morosely, wiping his nose.

Gresham cut a fine figure by the riverside. Tall, strongly built, there was an inner fire in his eyes and a slight smile that suggested he found the world both ludicrous and amusing.

The body bobbed gently up and down in the tiny ripples that lapped the edge of the millpond.

'I turned 'im over for you,' the miller said, half bowing and putting his head between Gresham and the corpse, demanding attention yet being sycophantic at the same time. The drowned always lay face down, as if turning their heads from the sun for the last time. The body was swollen, white with corruption, but still recognisable.

It was Will Shadwell. A murdered Will Shadwell.

Spy, informer, double-dealer, whoremonger, pimp, thief, gambler, sodomite, drunkard, occasional follower of Satan when the money was good – and one of Gresham's best men. He had possessed no morals, and so could not be suborned by a good cause. He was utterly selfish and ruthless, and therefore a thoroughly known commodity. He was greedy beyond belief, and hence utterly reliable, provided Gresham paid him more than anyone else.

Once, in a Southwark stew, Shadwell had falsely claimed that someone else was paying him more. Gresham had nailed his hand to the table, sinking his dagger through the soft flesh of the palm he was holding out for more money.

'I've given you a good dagger as well as your gold, Master Shadwell,' Gresham had commented mildly, leaving the room with the screaming and impaled man gaping at the blood seeping into the timber. 'Come back to me when it's spent up.'

And because Shadwell was all these things and yet a coward, he had come crawling back to Gresham three weeks later. He did not lie again about how much others were paying him. He appeared to bear no grudge. Violence was nothing in his world. Mastery and power had to be proven. If proven, they were acknowledged, as much a fact of life as lechery or drunkenness. The mark of the dagger was still visible now on the puffy flesh of his right hand. It waved liked a dead weed in the water.

Now he was dead, hunted down, a town creature flushed out of its habitat and hounded to death in the broad sweep of the countryside. Even the water damage could not disguise the tears the brambles and thorn had made in what looked like a pell-mell chase.

Something or someone had torn off a boot. He had been skewered from behind, enough to kill him in time. The actual killing blow, the knife thrust, had gone in through the eye socket and upwards, with so much power that it had broken through the top of the skull. It was a classic thrust, requiring pinpoint accuracy.

Gresham nodded distantly to the miller, and again to Mannion, his servant, who was behind them both. He heard the clink of money as Mannion drew a purse from his belt and started carefully to count out coins. The miller slavered over the sight, his eyes fixed on the money and his greed only thinly cloaked by a ragged air of servility.

'Thanks, master,' said the miller, who would have tugged his forelock had there been any hair left on his greasy pate. He gave a curt order to his lad, who started to drag the body out of the water. The miller was turning away to go back to the screaming wife and screaming brood who were warming up for the day in the stone-built mill when suddenly he paused. A thought must have struck him, Gresham realised, an event so rare as to stop him in his tracks. 'Why is it you're the only genl'man who pays to see corpses?' the miller asked, daringly. He sneezed, and a globule of something white shot from his nose and lay on an uncomplaining reed. Gresham turned to look at him.

'Why, a man must keep his finger on the pulse,' he replied, straight-faced, gazing down at an entirely pulse-free corpse. The miller, not surprisingly, failed to get the joke. As a trade millers were universally corrupt and oafish. All within a ten-mile radius of the city were bribed by Gresham to report any bodies in the water to him. Except babies. Gresham did not require to be shown the babies, unless, that was, they were finely dressed. The bodies always ended up in the millstream. At least Shadwell's had not been pounded to a pulp by the great paddle of the millwheel. It was no consolation to Shadwell, who was past caring.

As he went to mount the fine grey mare for the short ride back to Cambridge, Gresham halted, and went back to the corpse.

Something had caught the light, glinting fitfully inside a tear in Shadwell's tattered doublet. He motioned to the miller's lad to halt his labours, and bent down to feel inside the sodden, stinking material.

A bead. A single rosary bead, from a string of such beads that sold in their thousands in Europe. A dangerous item for a man or woman to wear openly in Protestant England, where to be a Catholic was all too easily seen as being an enemy of the state. The tear in the doublet looked new enough. Had Shadwell's flailing hand caught at the rosary as he fell to the ground? Well, one thing was sure. Gresham would never find out the truth from Will Shadwell.

A thick mist still clung to the river and its banks, reaching head height in the lower meadows. The dew clung to the ground and the heady smell of wet grass was everywhere. The towers of the great King's Chapel towered above Cambridge in the distance, and the pall of smoke was already beginning to cling to the town from the early-morning fires.

Henry Gresham saw none of it. He was preoccupied with his thoughts.

Why kill Will Shadwell? He and his kind lived in a raw, violent and a brutal world, yet even there the game was usually played by certain rules. Who among the vagabonds and thieves, the beggars and the rogues, the cutpurses and the pimps he called his friends would kill him? An argument over an unpaid bill? Some story of treachery? A whore who had caught the French welcome from him, paying him back as he sweated inside her spread legs? Or some noble Lord who had attended one too many Masses or plotted once too often to restore the true faith to England? Yet for someone as base as Shadwell there was no need for high treachery to explain his death, no need even for low drama. His death could be about nothing more than a debt that had gone on too long, or simply an opportunist robbery in a dark country lane.

It was possible, simple robbery, yet it stuck in Gresham's gullet.

Shadwell's killing was a professional's work. Someone had wanted Will Shadwell dead, and had been willing to follow him to Cambridge to see it done. Will had never worked in Cambridge, and had never been there long enough to make an enemy want him dead. That argued for a bigger secret than a debt or the wrong woman bedded. Had he sluiced a rich man's wife or daughter? Or had he latched on to something that the new government in London had decided should remain secret? Or was it the Catholics he had offended, the same Catholics who still carried huge power and influence for all that their faith was unfashionable?

The time was when a self-respecting assassin would never have travelled beyond Deptford. Yet these were troubled times, so early in the reign of King James I. How could they be otherwise? It was Scotland's King who now ruled England, and Scotland was England's oldest enemy. To add spice to the novel situation, the mother of the new King, Mary Queen of Scots, had been put to death on the order of the previous holder of the English crown, Queen Elizabeth, only a few years earlier. Men still alive had signed the death warrant of King James's mother. Henry Gresham had been in that business up to his neck and, in the final count, her neck as well. It was best to hope that King James had not been told of *that* side of his mother's death, for all that there had been no love lost between them.

A bird flew up from under the horse's hooves, with a sudden clatter of wings. Well trained, the mare took stock for a second of the irritating thing, decided it posed no threat and went calmly on its way. Gresham's hand, which had instinctively moved to his sword, relaxed halfway along its travel and returned to his side, his left hand continuing to take loose hold of the reins.

There had been a strange optimism two years ago when the new King had ascended the throne. It was already fraying at the edges, with mutterings in the streets and at Court. His Royal Highness's retinue of Scots Lords were as willing to take any money on offer as they were unwilling to wash, and their rapaciousness was becoming as legendary as their stench. James had offended the Puritans by having a Popish wife, and offended the Papists by declaring them excommunicate and appearing to go against his early promises of tolerance. The majority of the country, who wished nothing more than to be left in peace to procreate and earn a decent living, increasingly went in fear of a Catholic uprising, or a rebellion from the English establishment against the Scottish upstart.

Gresham almost found himself yearning for a return to the days of Good Queen Bess, the arch-bitch. Gresham had learnt the art of survival in part from her. She was an actress of unequalled power, and a ruthless whore who would have murdered her own mother without even a momentary qualm if need dictated it. She was also a Queen who would have wept bitter tears in public afterwards, whipped herself with barbs that, strange to say, seemed to leave no mark and provoked numerous plays as a result, as well as more sonnets than there was paper on which to print them. Queen Elizabeth I may have been so corrupt as to make Beelzebub turn in his grave, but somehow that corruption had never broken through the façade of the Virgin Queen, the pure preserver of the State. It had been true of her chief minister as well. Old Lord Burghley had made enough money to buy the Armada whilst producing an English fleet so decrepit that it might as well have farted as fired at the Spanish. With the Devil's own luck, the wind had farted instead, bringing Burghley the victory his ships could never have done. As one of Gresham's old informers had cheerfully stated, old Burghley may have knifed you in the back, but somehow you always felt it was being done by a gentleman. Burghley's son and successor, the wizened Robert Cecil, had a corrupted body that told all too well the tale of his corrupted soul. The double-dealing, the murders and the struggle for power might still be the same. The sense of style had gone, and there was a rawness to the brutal world of 1605 that had not been seen since Good Queen Bess had herself ascended the throne half a century ago.

Gresham's scalp itched, under his hat. He had a full head of hair, as yet not ravaged by the pox, and it was well washed. It always itched when there was trouble around. He had endured a lifetime of trouble. He neither feared nor welcomed it. It was simply a part of life, like the footpad on the road, the poison in the wine or the first spot that signified the plague. The particularly virulent itching suggested significant trouble. Well, trouble was a normal part of Gresham's life, and had been so for as long as he could remember. What was unusual was his inability to explain his chronic sense of foreboding, his inability to trace the sense of danger to its source.

It was all most irksome, and most inconvenient. Gresham flicked at his reins. The horse picked up a little speed, then deciding its rider's heart was not in it slowed down again to an easy amble. Gresham had lost a good worker in Will Shadwell. Will Shadwell had been Henry Gresham's creature. An attack on Will Shadwell was an attack on Henry Gresham, yet the reason was a mystery. Gresham did not like mysteries. They disturbed him. They cried out in the night to be explained. They threatened his survival. Survival, Henry Gresham had decided long ago, was all one had. Ruthlessness was required to survive. That, and a sense of humour, a dash of loyalty and a measure of courage.

The mystery was still crying out in his brain as he rode into the inner courtyard of Granville College. He had time still to go to his room, change from his riding clothes into suitably sombre doublet and hose and don the long gown of the MA or Master of Arts.

They gathered in the Combination Room, Gresham and the fifteen other Fellows, before going in to High Table. It was panelled, as was the Hall they were about to enter, very much in the new fashion. Gresham loved the depth of the wood, the changing pattern of its rich colour, but a part of him yearned for the ancient stone that lay behind it. The contrast of rough stone with rich hangings draped over it, hard against soft, wild colour against sombre grey, warmth against cold seemed an emblem for life. Contrast, change, the clash of ideas, these were what made Cambridge breathe and live.

'Well met, Sir Henry,' said Alan Sidesmith, the President Gresham had placed in nominal charge of the unruly crowd that went to make up Granville College. 'Was your ride restorative?' Gresham had never seen Alan Sidesmith drunk, nor ever seen him without glass or even tankard in his hand. Alan knew more of Gresham's other business than Gresham had ever told him, but Sidesmith was one of the few men in whom Gresham had complete trust.

'I've a good horse, good health and will soon have a full stomach. And it's summer in Cambridge . . . how could I not be restored?' Gresham replied lightly.

'That would depend, I suppose,' said Sidesmith equally lightly, 'whether a certain miller who sent you a message this morning was wishing to display to you his corn, or whether he had something else in mind.'

Gresham knew better than to be drawn.

'Yes,' he said, as if debating a matter of great significance, 'that would depend, wouldn't it?' He grinned at Sidesmith, who grinned back.

'Now, Sir Henry,' announced Sidesmith in a businesslike tone. 'Those newly knighted such as yourself are best placed to advise me on a tricky question of etiquette. Over *there* . . .' he pointed to a large and prosperous man whose desire to show off expensive clothes had overcome his reluctance to boil alive in the summer heat, '. . . we have a rich London merchant, a Trinity man, who wishes to transfer allegiance for his son to Granville. However, over *there*, we have a new Scottish Lord from Court who claims to have a degree from Europe. Who shall have the seat of honour on my right-hand side – Mr Money In The Bank and a good degree, or My Lord Influence At Court and probably not much else?'

'There is no choice, old friend,' announced Gresham. 'The Scottish Lord already smells to high heaven, whilst the merchant will take a good hour or so to do so despite all he sweats now.'

'Thank you, Sir Henry,' said Sidesmith. 'So helpful, as ever. Perhaps you would care to tell the noble Lord that he has been relegated because he stinks?' He moved off with a smile. The merchant gained the seat of honour on the President's right-hand side, the given reason being that he had his degree from Cambridge.

The great gong struck, and they processed into the Hall. Gresham's money had refounded Granville College, one of the most ancient and derelict in the University, yet he took his place on the High Table in strict order of seniority and the timing of his Fellowship, making him one of the most junior. The students in their gowns shuffled to their feet, benches scraping on the cold floor, as the President and Fellows entered. A student, a thin-faced boy with a face pockmarked from smallpox, came nervously forward, bowed to the President, and recited the long Latin grace. There was a subtle chorus of shuffling and, from somewhere among the depths of the student body, a hurriedly suppressed squeal as an arm was pinched. More bowing, and the business of the meal was allowed to continue.

Gresham's companion sniffed as he sat down.

'Out of sorts, Hugo?' asked Gresham, taking his own linen napkin from his sleeve.

The Fellow in question was a huge man, slobbering rolls of fat hanging over his neck and bulging out his thick arms into rotund sausages of flesh.

'I approve of tradition,' the man replied, grabbing at the warm bread that had already been placed on the platters in front of the Fellows. 'If three tables was good enough for this College in all its history, it's good enough for me.' He was already looking hungrily for the servant to bring in the first trenchers of food, and a glass of wine had already gone into the cavern he called his stomach.

'Ah,' said Gresham, 'but you didn't have the task of telling the eminent citizen of this town that he was good enough only for the second table, or telling that same to a man with an excellent degree

323

who sees some jumped-up favourite of Court dining here on high.'
It was an old argument, and Gresham did not offer it to convert,
but merely to annoy. It worked. Hugo spluttered and sent dangerously large lumps of bread firing from his mouth across the table.

'It is a *nonsense*! A *nonsense*! I firmly believe . . .' Dinner at High
Table was started, and would proceed along its normal path.
Gresham had insisted that Granville College have a High Table for
Fellows, guests and those with BAs and above, and the remaining
tables for those studying for their first degree or those with no
degree. He had proposed the abolition of the second, intermediate
table to the President.

Alan Sidesmith had smiled.

'It'll cause a rumpus, you know,' he had said, with no sign that it
concerned him at all. 'The young men of pleasure we seem to be
receiving at this University in such large numbers will dislike a
College where they can't buy their way into higher fare, and out of
the company of the poor students.' Under the old system, the third
table had been reserved for 'people of low condition'.

'What a great pity,' Gresham had replied. 'We'll just have to
make do with taking students who wish to learn, instead of those
who simply wish to play tennis, get drunk and swagger that they've
done their study in Cambridge.'

'Now that would be something new,' Alan had responded, a mischievous twinkle in his eye. 'But I do hope it won't restrain you
personally in pursuing those noble aims.'

In fact the young and the rich had flocked to Granville in its
new foundation. Its High Table was frequently extended to several
tables as it was besieged by the rich and the famous, its simple rule
that no man without his Bachelor of Arts could sit there giving it
an unexpected prestige. The fact that the rule had been waived
only once, for Her Majesty Queen Elizabeth I, had added to rather
than taken away from the distinction.

The heady smell of fresh-baked bread and roast meat mingled
with the sharper tang of the wine on High Table and the ale and

beer cheerily being consumed by the students. Granville College ate a good dinner, the platters loaded with meat and fish and the game pies being offered first to High Table, and then taken down to vanish into the gaping mouths of the students. A senior student was reading aloud from the Bible, one of many monastic traditions the Colleges had absorbed. The difference was that whilst total silence would have greeted the reading in the monastery, here a burble of conversation was allowed to accompany it.

Hugo was denouncing the decline of logic in favour of rhetoric to his other neighbour at table. Gresham turned to the man on his left. A man after Gresham's own heart, he had been fighting for a greater musical element in the Cambridge course.

'How goes the new material?'

Edward smiled at Gresham.

'Slowly, but surely. Master Byrd presents challenges to those who try to do justice to his music.'

'Musical challenges, or other challenges?' Gresham asked innocently. William Byrd was widely believed to be a committed Papist. He had published a book of sacred songs in 1575 which had circulated among Papists and found their way into Gresham's hands, and from thence to the man who ruled over the choir of Granville College.

'Challenges of all types,' answered Edward, with no sign that he wished to relinquish any of them. 'Firstly, it's a matter of debate whether or not the songs should be performed in a chapel at all. Secondly, singing them seems tantamount to declaring an allegiance to Rome. Thirdly, it's the Devil's own job deciding if they need an organ alongside them.'

'So in summary,' Gresham answered, 'their forthcoming presence in our order of service will result in the musical director being excommunicated for singing secular work in God's chamber, burnt alive for being a Papist and beaten by the Chapel organist for doing him out of a job?'

'Sir Henry,' answered Edward with a mock bow of his head, 'how can I challenge the wit and judgement of one so distinguished?'

'Not at all, if you know what's good for you,' said Gresham cheerfully, draining his glass. He was looking forward to the performance. 'But I wonder you bother with that music. There must be easier pieces.'

'When I meet music in which I hear God's hand,' said Edward sombrely, 'I'll risk the judgement of God's emissaries on earth to hear it played.'

There would be another stir when Edward believed he had the music to his standard, and allowed it to be sung. Accusations would fly back and forth, perhaps even the odd pate would be broken. Gresham ran his eye over the Fellowship of Granville College. One Fellow was a sodomite, making a play at every pretty boy who joined the College. Two others were bedding every serving girl who offered herself. Times being hard, there was no shortage of offers of either kind. Another had the pox, and had been seeing a local quack to little effect. Dipping the genitals in a mess of white vinegar was one of the least painful remedies, and the Fellow in question had been coming to dine for weeks smelling like a barrel of wine that had been allowed to go off in the sun. The newest Fellow was involved in a ruinous lawsuit, chasing an inheritance that an older brother would grab, at dreadful cost to the younger sibling. Two of them were Catholics to the core, two of them fierce Puritans. They sat at opposite ends of the table, and a pair of them had nearly come to blows in a recent public debate.

Opposites attract, thought Henry Gresham, and from the clash of opposites comes new ideas. He gazed contentedly, as much as his restless spirit could ever be content, over his High Table and the college he had refounded. He had no children that he knew of. He seemed destined to be barren. In the meantime, the 135 students and Fellows made a contented burbling noise in the Hall Gresham had built. It could hold two hundred with ease, and would do so before too long. His children? Possibly. His Foundation? Certainly.

The meal over, he had two reasons to retire to his rooms. The first was a letter written in his best handwriting, a letter which had been returned to him a few days previously by a man called Tom Barnes. Its style was faultless, and Gresham could only marvel at the sharp logic and intelligence that shone through the written words. There were only two problems with the letter. Firstly, Gresham had never written it, despite what seemed to be his handwriting and signature, and secondly, its content was sufficient to have him hung, drawn and quartered were it ever to reach any member of the Government. There could be many reasons for the existence of such a forgery, and Gresham needed time at least to eliminate from his mind some of the least likely. When that reading was over, he had his copy of the English translation of Machiavelli's *The Prince*, obtained from St Paul's for a King's ransom on his last visit to London. He had read it in the original Italian, of course. He was fascinated to compare the original with the translation. It was not to be.

The knock on the door was loud, insistent. Gresham slipped the letter through the gap in the floorboards beneath his feet, and shouted for the visitor to enter.

The courier stank of horse piss and sweat. He had arrived long after supper, his leathers stained with mud up to his armpits. Cambridge was at its most dank and dark, the Fenland mist swirling round the gates of the Colleges like a miasma of plague, waiting to strike. The feeble flicker of candle from the latticed and barred windows in the inner court hardly dented the blackness. The courier had arrived after nightfall. Every tongue would wag in the morning. Gresham called away 'On His Majesty's business', again. Some would snigger, nod knowingly, and gaze down in their tankards as he strode past to his place at table in the morning.

The Porter ushered the courier into Gresham's rooms. They were on the first stairway, built in the fourteenth century. He was Cecil's man, of course, and exuded a sense of menace. Silently he handed a package to Gresham. The Porter hovered over his shoulder, drunk, inquisitive.

'Time you kept your watch, old Walter,' said Gresham to the grizzled old man. 'Who knows how many fresh young virgins are queuing by your gate to test if men are like wine, better when they're old?'

Old Walter grinned, and clumped down the stairs. Gresham could just as easily have kicked him down the stairs, or snarled at him to mind his own damned business. As it was, Gresham saw nothing but an accident of birth in their different station in life. He treated Walter as he treated all people. God persistently refused to treat all people as equal until they proved otherwise, but that was no reason for Gresham to follow suit. As a by-product, old Walter would continue to tell Gresham everything that went on in the College. As far as most of the Fellows and the students were concerned, old Walter, the drunken sot, was invisible. Gresham had been using his sharp eyes and ears for years.

Gresham did not need to ask who the letter was from. There were only a small number of men in England who had couriers willing to ride through the night. The seal on the letter was far more ornate than the content. Come to London. Immediately. No formal greeting, no 'To that most beloved servant, Sir Henry Gresham . . .' Merely a blunt message. Come. Come now.

Gresham sighed. He sighed again as he turned to his purse, took out a small coin, remembered the courier, and chose a larger one. It was accepted. Without thanks, but with the merest nod of the head.

'Tell him yes. Soon.'

The courier nodded again. It was all that was necessary.

Cambridge was a haven. Its conflicts were explicable, its double- and triple-dealing following a strange local logic. True, its towns-people were low and squat, hating the University that gave them their living. A riot was never far away, which was why the Colleges were built like domestic castles, facing inwards into their courts and quadrangles and with a towered Lodge as their entrance. Yet the sense of power those buildings gave was illusory. The power in London was the power of life and, more frequently, death. The power in England was very simple, for all the puffed-out vainglory of the Cambridge Fellows. England's power was the power of the Court, nowadays the Court of King James I of England, erstwhile King James VI of Scotland.

So now Henry Gresham would have to drag himself out of the parochial world of Cambridge, back to the dark, brutal and blasphemous underworld of London, a world only recently rid of yet another outbreak of the plague.

He was rather looking forward to it.

Jack Wright sat in the darkest corner of the room, pushing the remnants of his meal idly around the edge of the wooden platter. The air in the room was greasy, stale. There were eight of them in all, in a room that would have more easily coped with four or five. The Catherine Wheel in Oxford had been chosen for recruiting the newest conspirators. It was safer than London, and Oxford was less full of Government spies than Cambridge. It was as safe as anywhere for a group of men for whom life would never be safe again. Jack could not stop himself looking nervously at the door every minute or so. He saw in his mind the soldiers bursting through it, the yelled commands, the kiss of iron round his wrists as he was led away. He shook his head, as if to clear it of the image. His nervous glance returned to the door. Part of him was trying to listen to his friend, but he had learnt at times to let the impassioned words of Robert Catesby flow over him, as unmarked as a stone in the river with the clear water washing over it.

John Wright, or Jack as he had been known since his early childhood, had taken his usual seat at the back of the room. He was a stocky figure, his apparent heaviness deceptive. His sword arm was lightning fast, his agility with a blade in his hand legendary. It was a skill he had tried to use much less since God had called to him and he had answered. Would that his mouth had the same skill as his arm. It was not that he lacked thoughts or ideas, but somehow the link between brain and mouth had eluded him all his life. For years he had felt the frustration of hearing the nonsense others talked, seen the strike of wit that won the applause and the adulation, felt the ideas seething in his head but stumbled at the final hurdle of their expression. As a child he had been laughed at and mocked when the few words he could muster had tumbled out and dried up, like an empty barrel with a hole knocked in it. That was where he had learnt his agility, turning to his fists in those days to make sure that his school fellows paid his body the respect they would not give his words.

He had known Catesby casually for years, in the way that all the sons of the oppressed Catholic families banded together and knew each other. They had attended a Mass together, in the small hours of the night when the fewest servants would see and hear and the risk was reduced. The priest had been impassioned, the liturgy powerful beyond faith. Afterwards, Jack Wright had been moved to tears, and Catesby had turned to meet him.

'It's a thing to die for, isn't it, as Our Saviour was willing to die?' he had said, a fierce light in his eyes.

'It is . . .' Jack Wright had started to say, wanted to say that it was more than life, that it was the source of life, a faith and a beauty so poignant yet so tragic . . . but the words had dried up, as they always did, and the red flush of embarrassment crept up on his face as his eyes dropped.

He felt Catesby's hand on his shoulder.

'We don't need words, do we? The words have been written for us. But we know the beauty. We of all people know the terrible beauty. To feel is enough, isn't it?'

Jack Wright looked up. Was it his imagination that a light pulsed from Robert Catesby's eyes? As if a tide of lovingly warm water had been released to sluice through his mind, the tears came to Jack's own eyes. Here was a man who knew, who understood. Here was a man who needed no words. From that moment in a cold chapel was the bond struck between Robert Catesby and Jack Wright.

Catesby's personality shone like a second sun, filling every corner of the tavern's room.

'Men have a *right*, a *right* given by God and by nature to defend their own lives and freedom, a right that no earthly power can take away,' he was arguing passionately, the light of martyrdom in his eyes, thumping the table for effect. 'We Catholics in England are mere *slaves*.' He dwelt on the word, drawing it out in all its shame. '*Lower even than slaves*. We're free men, yet we allow our lives and our freedoms to be removed without law, without reason and without authority. Our very life, our vigour, is being sapped by this passive resistance, this feebleness, this palsy of fear and cowardice that's all we seem able to muster in the face of persecution. We're the laughing stock of Europe: despaired of by our friends, and despised by our enemies as God's lunatics!'

Despite the familiarity, the power of Catesby's personality tugged at Jack Wright's soul. When Catesby talked to you, you felt that you were, for him, the most important person in the world. Catesby could reach into men's souls. His audience stared in rapt silence, almost adoration, as he reviled the King, whipping them up into a frenzy of self-justifying anger against the monarch and Robert Cecil, his Chief Minister. It was a brilliant performance. Jack had seen it many times, yet still it held a measure of magic even for his cynical eyes and ears. For a moment, for all of them, the fear retreated, the gnawing, bitter fear that governed their every step, their every breath.

'And is there hope? *No!*' Catesby spat out the negative, as if it were a red-hot pip from a sour cherry he had just eaten. 'With Robert Cecil pouring poison into the ear of the monarch, turning his eagerness into hate? *There is no hope unless we ourselves create that hope!*'

King James had seemed well-intentioned to the Catholic cause before his accession, and his wife was known to be Catholic. Cecil, the King's Chief Secretary, was widely credited with turning the mind of the King against English papists whilst at the same time toadying up to the Spaniards.

They needed some of Catesby's magic. At the mere thought of the tunnel Wright's flesh began to crawl and a spasm ran through his muscles. It had seemed easy enough. Hire the house, dig through until they were under the House of Lords, plant the powder. Yet before they were six feet into the tunnel they were gagging for air, their sweat turning the loose earth beneath them into greasy, salty mud. There was hardly room to move, the candle guttered and died in the rancid air and terror closed in with the darkness. The arm with the pick or shovel could only move back so far, the picking at the tunnel face tearing the same muscles time after time, reducing them to red-hot strings of pain. Their beards, hair and mouths became encrusted, unwashable, the dirt pitted into the skin. They felt the dust coat the inside of their lungs, their breath foul for hours afterwards, their racking coughs depositing a scummy yellow layer like vomit. They had reached the foundations after a lifetime of effort, half mad with the pain of their bodies, half mad with the thought of the soft, suffocating fall of earth and a hidden, slow and secret death. The ancient stone had seemed to bounce their feeble blows off its surface. They were tired, all of them. In time they would need money, horses, weapons, armour. Now their greatest need was for more brute strength and muscle. The two new conspirators would give them that at least.

Catesby finished his oration with a final flourish, and sat down, draining the tankard to its dregs in one huge gulp. Catesby did everything, from talking to drinking, as if he had half an hour of life left to him, and had to cram a lifetime's experience into a few minutes. He was a meteor in a dark sky. Jack could not help wonder how long that meteor would sustain its light, before it crashed to earth.

'Well spoken, Robin,' Jack said, going up to Catesby and taking his hand. Catesby had slumped down on a stool, as he sometimes did after one of his orations, as if his job was now done and the effort of speaking had drained him of his life force.

332

Catesby glanced up at his old friend, and smiled. It was a smile of total warmth that lit up Jack Wright's soul.

'I hope it was well spoken. But it's more than words we need now, Jack, much more than words.'

'We have a plan, don't we?'

'We do indeed,' replied Catesby. 'And there'll be those who'll seek to stop that plan before its rightful conclusion. They must be stopped, Jack. Stamped out like vermin . . .'

It was easy in talk to make a death seem nothing more than stamping on an insect. It was different when you forced the steel into the soft flesh, heard the shriek of pain, felt a man's dying breath on your face, saw the light fade from his eyes.

Wright shook the new recruits, Wintour and Grant, by the hand, and made his apologies. Both men were well-dressed, obviously prosperous, but both looked dour, old before their time. Jack hoped their muscles were more vigorous than their manner. The presence of the priest, with all the makings of a Mass, made him nervous. They were hunted men, these priests, hiding from one house to another, facing the rack and their innards ripped out if they were discovered, and bringing the same threat to those who hid them.

He slunk out into the late afternoon, feeling the bite of the wind on his flesh through the loose cloak, hand comforted by resting on the hilt of his sword. It would be more than the bite of wind he would feel if they all played the wrong hand in this particular game of cards.